THE

OLD

BLOOD

by

Edgar Mittelholzer

DOUBLEDAY & COMPANY, INC., GARDEN CITY, NEW YORK

1958

GRAHAM AND DIRK

Book One

THE OLD BLOOD

by Edgar Mittelholzer

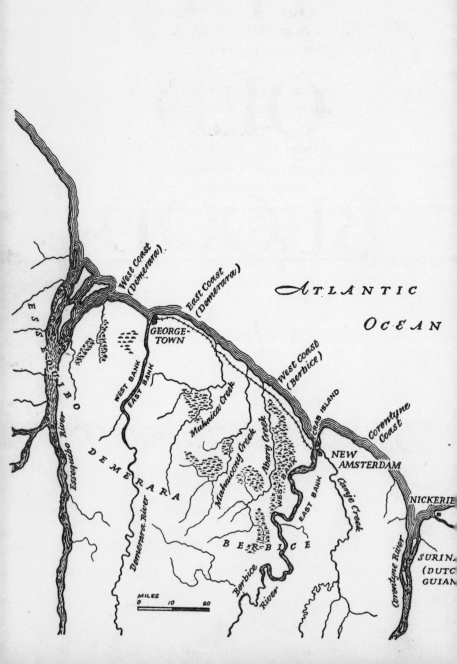

Library of Congress Catalog Card Number 58–8104
Copyright © 1958 by Edgar Mittelholzer
All Rights Reserved
Printed in the United States of America
First Edition

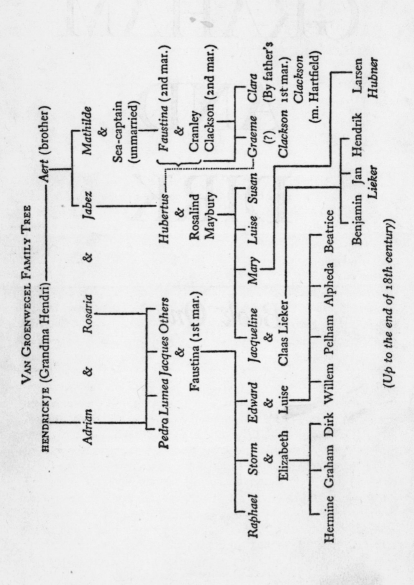

VAN GROENWEGEL FAMILY TREE

HENDRICKJE (Grandma Hendri) —— Aert (brother)

(Up to the end of 18th century)

1

T H E morning in 1795 when Mr. Fletcher brought the canister to New Signal Plantation, on the lower Canje, was an ordinary April morning in Guiana. Far away, over the coffee trees and the cane fields and the jungle beyond these, a mist could be seen like blue muslin floating on cobweb, and the fragrance of dew-wet shrubs and fruit-tree foliage hung refreshingly in the damp, cool air. There had been no rain for several days.

No one, at the time, marked this day as important, for no one attached any vital importance to the contents of the canister. Indeed, only a person gifted with the power to see into the future would have been able to recognise this day as a notable one in the destiny of the van Groenwegels.

The slaves went about their tasks as usual, and at the usual time—half past seven—Storm and Elizabeth appeared on the portico for coffee. Most of the Dutch planters had morning coffee on the portico, attired in slippers and morning gown. Storm and Elizabeth, however, were fully dressed, for in the van Groenwegel household things were not done strictly according to the prevailing custom. Elizabeth was of an English family, and though Storm was Dutch, the van Groenwegels had always been noted for their unusual habits. For instance, Storm never lingered until ten o'clock on the portico over morning coffee, smoking a pipe and taking nips of gin, as many another Dutch planter did as a matter of ritual. After his coffee and a pipe, Storm went off on a tour of the plantation, and he seldom left the house later than half past eight.

This morning, before he went off, he had a mild tiff with Elizabeth, who refused to change her mind about attending the ball that was to be held that evening at Colony House.

"You're in no condition to go," he told her, speaking in Dutch, as he generally did when annoyed (he could speak English with equal fluency, having been brought up from boyhood in close intimacy with English planting families). "What right has a woman four months pregnant at a ball? It's not proper—and it may be dangerous to your health."

"I've known myself to dance when I was six months pregnant," said Elizabeth, speaking in Dutch, too, which language she spoke as fluently as Storm spoke English. She was a tall girl with auburn hair, and at twenty-seven not much older-looking than she appeared in the large family portrait in the dining-room over the sideboard—a portrait painted by Edward van Groenwegel in 1789, when she was twenty-one and unmarried, and when the Mayburys were in Demerary. "You worry over such trifles, Storm, my dear. Have you forgotten the ball I attended before Hermine was born? No one thought me improper, and my health didn't suffer."

Storm made no reply. He was not a domineering husband, and detested conflict of any sort, yet he had views of his own, and was not afraid to express them. He had his father's droll green eyes, but, unlike his father, was not a ladies' man. Thirty-two and tall, rather handsome with his light brown hair and slightly freckled cheeks, he was known as the quiet, unremarkable one. Edward, his twin brother, was the remarkable one.

When his father-in-law came out onto the portico Storm looked up from his cup and said in English: "Elizabeth is insisting on going to the ball this evening, sir."

Eight times out of ten old Wilfred backed up Storm in an argument, but this time Wilfred supported Elizabeth.

"Let her go," he said with a loud, breezy guffaw, blinking. He sank down into the large cane chair, his white hair untidy as though he had not attempted to groom it after getting out of bed, his thin, loose limbs making an almost audible bony clatter under the red morning gown. "What harm c-c-can it do her, my boy? T-t-take her and enjoy yourselves. That's my advice to you."

"But she's pregnant, sir—have you forgotten?"

Wilfred waved his hand airily, and uttered another bark of laughter. "And what if she's pregnant! We Mayburys are a tough breed. Hee, hee! When everyone was dying around us like flies in '63 and '64, Father survived the Sickness, didn't he? And so did I—and so did Rosalind. No epidemic could kill us off. You t-t-take her along, my slaves recognised it, too. They said, indeed, that it was very likely this canister might have belonged to your son-in-law's family who once lived high up the Canje. Is this correct? Did the van Groenwegels ever own a plantation up the Canje?"

"Most certainly they did. Grandma Hendrickje and her grand-children owned and ran it. We've always heard lurid t-t-tales of their doings. Hee, hee! Was it anywhere near Horstenland or Magdalenen-burg where you came upon these ruins?"

"That is correct. Abandoned plantations, I was informed. The names were frequently mentioned by people we met at homesteads. As I can calculate, it must have been seven miles downstream from Horstenland where I came upon this ruined building."

"That is roughly where the van Groenwegel plantation would have been," said Wilfred excitedly. He nearly danced. "Damme, sir! This may be a highly interesting discovery. Interesting for the family, I mean. Old Hubert would be delighted to hear I'd come into p-p-pos-session of a canister of old papers belonging to Grandma Hendrickje. I must give them my attention without delay."

"If I'm not being presumptuous, who may old Hubert be?"

"Hubertus van Groenwegel. Of the Demerary branch of my son-in-law's family. Hubert married my sister Rosalind."

"Oh, yes, yes. I think you did mention to me that your sister had married a Dutchman."

"Four lovely d-d-daughters Hubert and Rosalind brought into the world, Fletcher. Luise is married to Storm's twin brother, Edward. They're all in Demerary. We're from there ourselves. It's only six years since we've been settled here in Berbice."

That day Wilfred did not retire, as customary after breakfast, for his siesta. He installed himself on a stool in a corner of the dining-room, and attacked the papers in the canister.

There were a lot of them, some in very good condition, some that flaked and crumbled at the touch, some on which the writing was too faded to be read, some that were clearly legible. None was moth-eaten nor mildewed, and it was evident that the canister must have been very carefully shut and sealed before it was stored away in the cellar where it was found. That the letters concerned the van Groen-wegel family was obvious from the outset. The very first letter Wilfred picked up was dated April 17, 1738, and was addressed to Hendrickje from her brother Aert in the Essequibo. The next was from Hubertus boy. Van Batenburg would be sorely disappointed if she didn't put in an appearance. He admires her tremendously."

"You have no need to mention that, sir. I can't think of a pretty woman in this colony the governor doesn't admire."

"Ha-ha! I detect the devil of jealousy there! Because he p-p-pecked her on the cheek at the last ball. Hee, hee! His favourite trick. He p-p-pecks all the ladies on the cheek, that van Batenburg!"

"If that were all he did it wouldn't be so bad," laughed Elizabeth.

"Eh? Eh? What's that?" Wilfred went red as the slave in attendance helped him to coffee. "What are you trying to hint at, my girl? I hope you're not suggesting you p-p-permit him to go further with you? Eh? Hee, hee! Keep an eye on her, Storm, my boy! This needs looking into, damme!"

Storm smiled. "I don't think I need to, sir. I have complete trust in her. It isn't the governor's charms I'm concerned over. It's her health."

"Then dismiss the matter. Her health is perfect—and will remain so."

"Since you feel that way, I won't oppose her going," said Storm quietly. Storm never resisted for long, especially when Wilfred uttered an opinion against him. He was very fond of his father-in-law, and respected his ruling in practically everything.

The next few minutes were spent in discussing the latest news received concerning the war in Europe. Wilfred had decided views, and, as usual, expressed them with fervour. Storm agreed—quietly, casually, intelligently, even venturing a view of his own occasionally. Now and then, his gaze—very casually, very unconcernedly—would move out into the compound upon Nibia, the children's nurse, who was watching her two charges at play under an orange tree.

Mr. Roger Fletcher, the English naturalist, had been a guest at New Signal for several days before his departure for the upper reaches of the Canje Creek two months previously. A complete stranger, he had been taken in as a free guest for as long as he wished to stay. Storm had met him at one of the two taverns in New Amsterdam, on the day of his arrival, and learning of his proposed expedition up the Canje, had offered to accommodate him at New Signal.

"We're on the west bank of the Canje," Storm had told him. "The most convenient point for you to set out from, I should say."

"But may I say, sir, that my means are somewhat limited? I can afford little in the way of remuneration for board and lodging."

Storm had given him a shocked stare. And a moment later Mr. Fletcher seemed equally as shocked when Storm explained that no Dutch planter ever expected remuneration from a guest in his home, whether that guest be a stranger or otherwise.

Mr. Fletcher was a round, short man with red hair and grey eyes that blinked rapidly whenever he smiled or stared at anyone. He was like Wilfred in this respect. On this morning of his arrival back from the jungle, his eyes blinked rapidly as he smiled at Wilfred on the back veranda.

"There it is, Maybury!" he announced, gesturing with a pudgy hand towards the old, rusty, metal canister a slave had lifted into the house a moment before. "Found it in the cellar of an old ruined building."

"I can well believe it must have been a ruined b-b-building," stuttered Wilfred. "Hee, hee! Looks fairly b-b-battered by time, doesn't it?"

"Yes. I should say it does have a timeworn appearance. I was after an owl's nest, and stumbled on it in a corner among odd bits of bones and pieces of metal and other rubbish." The naturalist uttered a gusty bellow of laughter. "For an instant I was inclined to think it might have been hidden treasure. Guilders and joes and doubloons and what not, eh? But I was only too soon disillusioned. When I eventually succeeded in getting it open—no mean task, too, I can assure you, sir —I discovered that it contained nothing but a stack of old papers— letters written in Dutch."

"Quite understandable. They would be written in D-D-Dutch. This colony has been D-D-Dutch for more than a century."

"Precisely, precisely! Well, the truth of the matter is, I know not a word of Dutch myself, but I recalled that you're very familiar with the language, and you told me you have a mania for keeping old records, so I thought it would be extremely fitting for me to bring this thing along for your inspection."

"Good of you, Fletcher. You were right. Old records do fascinate me, as anyone who knows me well will vouchsafe. And we never can t-t-tell what this may yield, can we?" Wilfred bent and squinted at the canister. At sixty-four, he could see perfectly. The squint he gave was only a mannerism. He had many mannerisms.

"What's this? What's this?" he bubbled over. "The letter K embossed on the cover! Well, I never! The van Groenwegel insignia. It's on the t-t-tent-boat pennant, have you ever noticed?"

"Exactly," nodded Mr. Fletcher. "I remembered that. And the

to Jacques, and dated July 10, 1740 (Jacques had been Storm's father; he had been killed with Grandma Hendrickje and the other grandchildren during the slave insurrection of 1763).

As he read, Wilfred nodded and grunted and muttered. Now and then he even uttered whinnying sounds of satisfaction and excitement. Once or twice he would frown and exclaim in horror, and then would follow a period of tut-tutting and clucking and sighing.

"Now I'm beginning to understand Hubert much better," he said aloud—just as Storm, who had a moment before, got out of his hammock on the back veranda, entered the room.

"What's that you're muttering about Cousin Hubertus, sir?"

"Eh? Eh? Oh, is that you, my boy?" Wilfred started round, reddening. "I was thinking aloud, I fear. It's these p-p-papers, Storm. Remarkable, some of them. M-m-most absorbing. Did you know that you had uncles called Pedro and David and Laurens on the Canje? And an aunt called Lumea?"

"Never knew their names, but I've certainly heard of their existence."

"Hee, hee! We all have. Hubert never let us forget them. The bad blood of the van Groenwegels. There's a letter here, though, that looks at the m-m-matter in quite a different spirit. Where is it? Ah, here! It's from some m-m-member of the family called Jabez in the Essequibo——"

"Cousin Hubertus's father."

"Was Hubert's father called Jabez? Tch, tch, tch! But of course! My memory is getting bad. Perfectly correct." Wilfred seemed quite upset. He sighed. "Anyway, the letter is from Jabez to some other m-m-member of the family called Adrian, and it says in one place: 'I cannot imagine how you can tolerate Aunt Hendrickje's strange moods, though I think she is right in being proud of the Old Blood. Father, too, is proud of our blood. He has often told us the Tales of Old —about Kaywana and how she fought the Indians when they attacked the house, and of how Willem and Aert, her sons, fired upon the attackers with muskets until help came, and of the brave defence of our Mazaruni house in 1666 against Major John Scott and his Caribs.' See what I mean! The Essequibo van Groenwegels weren't ashamed of the 'Old Blood.' Hee, hee! I wish Hubert could read some of these things."

"I think," said Storm, rather bored, "you should send the whole canister of papers to Cousin Hubertus. He's the oldest member of the family alive, and it's only right he should have them."

"Certainly, certainly, my boy. I'd already decided to let him have them." Wilfred nodded violently—then as violently started and shook his head. "No! Oh no, no! This morning, my boy, when I first set eyes on this canister I said to myself: 'This is for my dear friend Hubert. What ecstasies he would go into over old family papers from the Canje!' But now that I have read these letters, Storm, I see it would be wise for me to p-p-pause and reconsider my decision. Oh no, no! My feeling now is that never, never should we let d-d-dear Hubert see these papers. He would worry himself into the grave. He would never have a single moment's p-p-peace after he had assimilated the contents of these letters."

Storm frowned—then nodded slowly. "Perhaps you're right, sir. Thoughtless of me."

"You agree, don't you?"

"Certainly, sir. I do. Cousin Hubertus has always been inclined to harrow himself over trifles."

"We shall keep it here," said Wilfred. "I shall have the canister painted with creosote to keep away insects. And we must have it carefully stored away. Graham and perhaps other of your children may, in years to come, be interested to peruse the letters in it."

Storm smiled, smothering a yawn. "Yes, it's not unlikely that one of them may inherit your inordinate love for records and old documents. Will you come out on the veranda for your coffee, sir? The overseers will soon be arriving with their reports on the day's work. I should like to be on the veranda to receive them."

A few minutes later, when they were on the veranda, Wilfred sprang up with a dramatic cry, and dashed into the dining-room, bawling: "The children! The children! I've left the canister open!"

He was just in time, too, for Nibia, their nurse, seemed as curious as Graham and Hermine. Wilfred found them crowded round the open canister.

"Get away from there, my little pets! Get away! Shoo-shoo! Shoo-shoo! You mustn't t-t-touch those! Time enough when you can read and write, but decidedly not now!"

"What else is in the canister besides paper, Grandfather?" asked Graham, a fair boy of four and a half. "Didn't Mr. Fletcher bring any snakes?"

"Hee, hee," tittered Wilfred, patting his head. "Yes, my boy. A number of them. But I made sure they weren't brought into the house. You'll see them in their cages tomorrow morning. Nibia, take them up to their room. Don't let them m-m-monkey around in here, do you understand? These papers are far too p-p-precious."

"What papers are they, Grandfather?"

"Old letters, my boy. One day you'll read them with interest, I trust." He bent and snatched up Hermine with her dark hair and brown eyes which were staring up at him in smiling indifference, and seated her on his shoulder. "You, too, my pet. How old are you? Two and a half, eh? Another t-t-ten or twelve years and you'll be reading all about Grandma Hendri and your terrible great-uncles and great-aunt. Meantime, we must keep the letters safely for you." He gave her a squeeze and put her down, then carefully shut the canister, and shoo-ed them all out of the room. "Upstairs! Upstairs! Take them upstairs, Nibia, my girl!"

On the way upstairs, Graham asked Nibia: "Who is Grandma Hendri, Nibia?"

Nibia grunted. "She bad old lady. Your grandfather's grandmother. Live high up the Creek, long time back."

"How long ago?"

"Plenty time back. My father tell me about her. He know plenty people who say she was a bad, cruel old lady. Make slaves suffer bad."

"Where is she now? Still high up the Creek?"

"No. She get kill off. Long, long time back. My father say the slaves beat her to death in the old house up the Canje. She and her grand-children."

"Why did they beat her to death, Nibia?"

"Because she bad and cruel. Make slaves suffer plenty bad."

"She wasn't good, then? I mustn't ask God to bless her, must I?"

"No. She too bad and cruel. God curse her soul."

Nibia was only eighteen, shapely in body and of a pleasing face. Men found her extremely attractive—white as well as black men.

Mr. Fletcher surprised them that evening. He proved to be an excellent dancer, and was extremely popular, despite his unhandsome looks, with the wives of all the planters. Mevrouw van Batenburg, the governor's wife herself, the most attractive woman present, held him in conversation for nearly half an hour, and listened with interest to the stories he told about his adventures with wild creatures up the Canje.

Wilfred remained at home, but the fat Primrose, his wife, who never missed any social function, accompanied the others. Her excuse was that it would be the last occasion, for many years, on which John would be attending a ball, and she had to be there with him.

John Maybury, at twenty, was the only son Wilfred and Primrose had ever produced, and he had been born seven years after Elizabeth, when his parents had despaired of having any other children. He was Primrose's treasure—a treasure that she would be unable to set eyes upon for the next six or seven years, for John was going to England to study medicine; he was sailing on the same ship that would take Mr. Fletcher in less than a week's time.

Colony House, the governor's residence, was admittedly the most handsome building in the three colonies of Berbice, Demerary and Essequibo. It was built of brick near the edge of the wide Berbice, and commanded a view of the whole harbour. A curved flight of steps led up to the spacious hall where balls were held. From the western windows, however, the view was marred by a boatbuilder's yard, and every now and then a whiff of pitch and oakum would assail the nostrils. Whenever van Batenburg wished to go aboard his tent-boat, he and his party would be compelled to tread their way through this untidy area.

Elizabeth did not fail to gain the attentions of the governor. He danced with her several times. Like his wife and his sister—his sister lived at Colony House, too—Abraham van Imbyze van Batenburg was a charming and highly cultivated man, and never tried to conceal his weakness for the opposite sex (it was rumoured that his illegitimate children numbered over eighty, most of them dusky-skinned).

Almost as attentive to Elizabeth was Lieutenant Dirk Teuffel from the garrison at Fort St. Andries, two miles north of Colony House, and near the point where the Canje Creek branches off from the mother river, the Berbice. As young as Elizabeth, Dirk Teuffel was as bristlingly alive and gay as Storm was subdued and retiring.

Storm could often be seen dutifully dancing with his two-hundred-pound mother-in-law when Primrose was not dancing with John.

Like Storm, John was very quiet-mannered and unenterprising with the ladies. He had inherited none of the bubbling, agitated high spirits of his parents. For Primrose was even more garrulous than Wilfred, and always giggling or shrieking with laughter. Her bulk did not hinder her in any way; she was as active as Elizabeth, and at least two youngish planters, Rolf de Groot from across the river (his plantation was not far from York Redoubt, the fort on the western bank) and Heinrich Brandt, the German from upcreek, kept pestering her for dances.

It was on one of the rare occasions when Storm happened to be Elizabeth's partner in a dance that the first drunken incident of the evening occurred. Such incidents were common at balls, and had almost come to be regarded as the accepted thing.

When the gay Mr. Renfrey, a planter not long arrived in the colony from Barbados, suddenly uttered a yell of laughter and collapsed on to the floor, taking with him his partner, a sallow lady of colour who had once been the governor's mistress, the dancing became temporarily disorganised, but none of the dancers took offence. Elizabeth herself laughed and remarked: "Poor Mr. Renfrey. The rum has begun to take effect on him."

Storm, however, sniffed, and she saw a scowl of disdain pass over his face. "He should be thrown out," said Storm. "It is gross impoliteness."

Elizabeth gave him a look in which there was reproof as well as affection. "Trust you to say that. Why must you always be so correct, Storm?"

Storm smiled faintly. "Blame it on my training, my dear. The van Groenwegels are noted for doing the correct thing at the correct time. Correct, of course, according to the measure of correctness *we* have established."

"You almost sound like Cousin Hubertus when you say that."

"My brother Edward's idol." Storm nodded in the half-bored way that was his on nearly every occasion. "I don't mind sounding like Cousin Hubertus. He's a solid gentleman. It will be a long time before we have another van Groenwegel like Cousin Hubertus."

"We never know. Perhaps such another is in me at this minute." And then impulsively: "Storm, we must call him Dirk if it's a boy. I like that name."

Storm grunted. "And the possessor of the name, too, if we may judge by the number of times I've seen you partnering him."

"Would you mind if we called him Dirk?"

He shook his head. "If it pleases you—and does not displease your father—name him Dirk by all means, my dear."

"Poor Father! He does love his grandchildren. But he's getting quite absent-minded. Yesterday I heard him telling Mother to get the cradle ready and inform the midwife to be prepared. He was certain that I was already nine months with child and could be taken to bed at any instant."

"Yes, he's losing his sense of time. I doubt whether he remembers his own age. Ironical, when we think of how good a memory he used to have for dates and figures. Remember the time when he could prattle off statistical details from any of the big pile of documents and records he collected in his room?"

"It was most tiresome for people who weren't interested."

"I can't say I found it tiresome. I learnt a lot from him concerning the affairs of these colonies. He's a sound old fellow. I wish I could have a son like him."

"In a way, you've made him as much your idol as Edward has made Cousin Hubertus. It must be a van Groenwegel trait, dear."

"I believe it is. Father and the Canje uncles idolised Grandma Hendri."

A waft of cool breeze came in upon them from the eastern windows near which they were dancing at the moment. In it was the sourish smell of drying coffee berries from the neighbouring plantations. And also the dank scent of Creek water, laden with the vegetable particles of centuries. In it, too, could be detected the mud of the swamplands that extended as far as the Corentyne River, far beyond Fort St. Andries and the signal station three miles beyond at the mouth of the Berbice.

Elizabeth gave a slight shiver, and it was as though some wraithlike tentacle of premonition moved in her. As though the child in her had quickened in this instant and was trying to communicate to her some urgent message related to the events of the future. A disturbing message.

2

NIBIA, the children's nurse, slept in a hammock, or on a
mattress on the floor, in the large northeastern room allotted
to the children. She ought to have slept, like the other
slaves, in one of the troolie-roofed logies which stood some distance
from the house, on the southern side, but Graham was a nervous, imaginative boy who had, for some time, been in the habit of lying awake at
night and listening to the sounds outside. The coughing cries of raccoons and the laughing of the screech owls terrified him. Even the
sound of the wind humming through the darkness of the spacious
room troubled him. He would whimper and shriek in fear at fanciful
dangers reaching out at him from the dank forests of the Canje, and
Storm and Elizabeth had had to order Nibia to sleep in the room with
him and his sister. It was some months now since the girl had been
spending her nights in the house, and Graham nowadays fell asleep
without any trouble.

"I feel safe when you sleep in here," he told her.

Nibia loved him, and never settled down to bed until he was asleep.
Hermine, untroubled by fears of any kind, usually slept the instant
she was put into her cot, and the voices of her brother and Nibia did
not disturb her.

Nibia's routine was to undress and then sit by the boy's cot and
talk to him. He asked innumerable questions, and she was either sol-
emnly patient or affectionately teasing in response. Sometimes she
laughed softly and tickled him under the chin, nuzzled him in the
chest, and told him not to be so curious about things. She was a warm,
vivacious girl.

On the night of the ball, with Storm and Elizabeth and Primrose
out of the way, Nibia felt in an exceptionally free, gay mood. When

she was undressing she looked at the boy sitting in his cot staring at her, and laughed, saying: "You can't stop watch me when I undress, na, boy? What mek you like naked-skin woman so much?"

"I like to see you wearing nothing," Graham admitted.

This conversation was a bedtime ritual.

"I know so. Wicked boy." She pulled on her nighttime smock and came and sat on the chair beside his cot. The cool, damp wind droned in upon them through the high window, bringing with it the reek of coffee berries and the vegetable scent of black Creek water, whiffs of mud and fish from Crab Island, the islet in the estuary that, year after year, was growing in size, built up by the silt the river washed down around it. From not too far off—perhaps among the orange trees—came the "Hoo-yoo!" of a goatsucker, a pink jumbie noise stamped upon the mystery of the jet-black darkness outside the house where all was unsafe and uncertain.

"Why is it wicked to see you wearing nothing, Nibia?"

"You will know when you grow up big."

"When I grow up big like Father?"

"Yes."

"Is Father wicked?"

She stretched out and tweaked his ear, and he watched her dark brown face, pleasant and shiny in the candlelight, and felt weak with affection deep inside and very safe. "Is Father wicked?" he asked again.

"More wicked than he make anybody know." Automatically she glanced towards the closed door as she said this, then broke into fresh giggling mirth.

"Why is Father wicked, Nibia?"

Nibia looked sly. "You want to know too much, little boy."

"You must tell me. Our secret. Is he bad-wicked? Or nice-wicked as you said I was one night, remember?"

"He nice-wicked."

"Why is he nice-wicked?"

"Ow, boy! You like ask question, na? He like see me with nothing on same as you like. And he like touch me skin same as you like. That's why he nice-wicked."

Another ritual now had to be gone through. He tugged at the top of her smock, and she pulled it down so that he could admire her breasts and fondle them.

"You so young, boy," she giggled, vain and pleased, as always, even at his childish attentions. "If you want hold bubbies now, what will happen when you grow up into big man?"

"I like touching them. They're so smooth and nice."

"All right. Enough. Time for sleep now," she said, adjusting her smock. "Plenty, plenty years left before you to do that."

Obediently he lay back, smiling and contented. "You're good, Nibia. I like you. I'm glad Father touches your bubbies, too."

"Ssssh! Our lil' secret. Mama won't like to hear you say that."

"Why? She has nice bubbies, too. I see them when she undresses."

"Ssssh! All right. Enough talk. Sleep like a good boy."

"When does Father touch your bubbies?"

"When everybody gone to sleep he come in quiet and I get out the hammock and go and lie 'pon the mattress with him."

"Every night?"

"Ssssh! Time for sleep."

"Yes, I must sleep now." He smiled, and his eyelids began to droop drowsily. "The owls won't trouble me, Nibia?"

"No, you safe in here with me. No owls can trouble you in here."

"And the raccoons won't come in?"

"No. No raccoons can't trouble you. Me here with you."

He fell asleep, and she sat for a minute or two and smiled at him, then uttered a crooning grunt of affection and rose. She tucked in his mosquito net of fine muslin, and, blowing out the candle on the little bedside table, moved towards her hammock, which was already slung up diagonally across a corner of the room.

Two days after John Maybury and Mr. Fletcher sailed, news came from Demerary that Rosalind, Wilfred's sister—Cousin Hubertus's wife—was dead.

It was no shock, for they had known for some months that Rosalind was ill and not expected to recover. Nevertheless, the news cast a gloom upon them, and Wilfred fell into a reminiscent mood, and, for a long spell, could talk about nothing but the old days in Demerary.

"She was a good wife to Hubert. Very understanding."

"That was necessary," murmured Storm. They were at dinner (served at five in the afternoon), and Primrose gave Storm a swift, warning glance, which Storm, however, pretended not to notice. "Sometimes," Storm added, "it must have been even a strain upon poor Aunt Rosalind, trying to understand Cousin Hubertus."

Wilfred grunted, getting red. "I won't hear a word against Hubert,

my boy. His c-c-conduct with Cousin Faustina might have been ques-
tionable, but it was a fine relationship, for all that, and Rosalind would
have been the last p-p-person to censure them, I'm sure." He changed
the subject abruptly by announcing: "I've sent a message to Mrs.
Clarke, telling her to be p-p-prepared at any moment to be called."

"What for, Father?" asked Elizabeth.

Mrs. Clarke was a free coloured lady, a midwife of great repute,
and both Storm and Elizabeth looked at Wilfred in surprise. Primrose
began to shake with giggles.

"What is the matter, my dear?" asked Wilfred, blinking at his wife.

"Oh, my poor Wilfred! That memory of yours! I keep telling you
our new grandchild will not be with us for several months still, and
yet you will keep forgetting."

"Months! Good heavens!" Wilfred made tut-tutting sounds. Broke
into a titter. "I could have sworn on my head he was expected at any
moment. I even mentioned in my letter to dear Hubert that he might
arrive before my letter reached him."

"You're convinced it will be a boy, I see, sir," smiled Storm.

"Eh? Eh? Of course, of course! Most decidedly it will be," nodded
Wilfred. "I have no doubt whatever. Tch, tch! We must revoke that
message. We must send to Mrs. Clarke at once. She is a busy woman."

"She already knows when I expect the child," said Elizabeth. "She
was here a few days ago to consult with me."

"Somehow," said Wilfred, sighing, "I feel in my b-b-bones he will
be a remarkable boy. I've been dreaming about him of late."

Later that evening, Elizabeth said to Storm: "Poor Father. He has
taken to soothsaying now. I'd never have foreseen the day when he
would express a belief in dreams."

Before the new child was born, a number of notable events occurred.

In the following month, May, came the exciting news that the
French had overrun the Netherlands and that the Batavian Republic
had been created. Wilfred did not hesitate to declare himself pro-
Orange in sympathies. He even took an active part in many of the
public demonstrations that were held in New Amsterdam; he aired
his views in the taverns and at street-corner meetings. But Storm and
the others were indifferent.

"Why should we trouble?" said Storm, shrugging. "Let the political
gentlemen take care of the situation."

Wilfred snorted. "A typical planter attitude! You must wake up, my boy. We planters cannot afford to be indifferent about p-p-politics. These colonies could have been far more advanced than they are if we had been less c-c-concerned with our easy plantation living and more prepared to c-c-contest the issues of government imposed upon us from Europe. We're too complacent a group, we planters. Too indolent and luxury-loving."

"But I've heard," said Elizabeth, "that the Governor himself is indifferent in the matter. He doesn't care who is in power, so long as he is allowed to dine and wine well at Government House."

"Wrong!" yapped Wilfred, nearly dancing. They were on the portico at morning coffee. Wilfred rose and glared at them, his hand with the coffee cup shaking with emotion. "Don't you credit such t-t-tales, my girl! I've heard it on good authority that van Batenburg is d-d-definitely on the side of the Prince of Orange. Van Batenburg loves the English. That is no secret."

The discussion, as all discussions of this nature did, fizzled out very quickly. But on retiring that night, Elizabeth remarked to her husband: "I think Father was right this morning. This complacency among the planters in respect to politics is a bad thing. We're so defenceless here. No proper forts or military establishments. Fort St. Andries and York Redoubt could not stand up to half a dozen determined enemy soldiers well equipped."

"True. Very true, my love. But forts and military personnel and equipment are costly to maintain."

"It would be money well spent. Who knows but one day the French may again capture us—as they did in '82. I should hate to be under the French again."

Storm, seated in a chair beside the big four-poster, grunted, put down his pipe. He sighed and said: "The French were, at least, very constructive, you must grant, Elizabeth. They laid out the town in Demerary—Longchamps, which we now call Stabroek—and they introduced many new useful institutions. They had their annoying habits, I concede—that ridiculous census, for instance—but which government is not annoying at times? Shall I blow out the candle?"

"Please. And fan away the smoke from around the bed. These days I cannot bear to go to sleep smelling tobacco smoke."

"I understand." He stretched out a hand under the net, and patted her stomach affectionately. "Perhaps it is a portent that our son will not be a smoker."

"Then he won't be your son—and certainly no Dutchman."

After he had dispersed the smoke by waving a cushion around the
bed—the smell still lingered after this operation, however—he blew
out the candle and settled down beside her in the bed, carefully tucking in the muslin mosquito net. Yawning, he remarked: "I think I
shall have a bath after you have fallen asleep. It is unusually hot tonight."

"Not to me. But then I am pregnant. Every night seems damp and
chilly to me." She chuckled suddenly. "Why do you wait until so late
at night to have your bath, Storm? Only yesterday Mother was commenting on this recent eccentricity of yours."

"Was she? I don't consider it an eccentricity. It is very logical. If I
fall asleep without trouble, then I sleep on until morning and have
my bath, as I do every day. But if the heat prevents me from sleeping,
then I rise from bed and have my bath—and nothing induces sounder
sleep in me than a bath."

"Very well. I suppose it is logical. Though I feel it is unkind to poor
Nibia to rouse her from her sleep to attend upon you."

"She enjoys attending upon me. She considers it an honour, my
dear. In any case, she is a slave—and the only available one in the
house at night. Wouldn't it be more unkind of me to send out to the
logies and rouse up Marta? She is an older woman, and can less afford
to lose her sleep than Nibia."

Elizabeth sighed sleepily, and said that he was right, she supposed.
"Kiss me good night." And after he had kissed her: "You're so kind
and patient with me. I shall make up for it a thousand times after this
new child is born."

"There is no need to fret yourself, my love," he murmured. "Absti-
nence, on these occasions, is good for me. I have told you that already."

"Yes, but, still, it must prove annoying for you some nights, I'm
sure."

He laughed softly, and patted her cheek. "I have my baths, bear in
mind!—when the heat troubles me."

They both went into a quake of laughter over this sally, and the bed
creaked, and the muslin net billowed in gently in a gust of damp
warm breeze that came in through the louvred windows. Far away,
over the orange and sapodilla trees that grew around the house right
down to the creek's edge, a screech owl uttered harsh chatterings.
Elizabeth snuggled under the light blanket and was soon asleep. But
Storm, uncovered, lay on his back staring into the gloom of the tester.
When he was certain that she was asleep, he got out of bed and tip-

toed noiselessly out of the room and into the children's room at the eastern end of the corridor. He paused a moment just within the doorway, then moved with sureness towards where the hammock was slung up across the northwestern corner of the room.

Nibia was asleep, but she woke the instant he rubbed his hand over her breasts. Without a word, she rose and went out of the room and downstairs while Storm moved over to where he knew the mattress lay on the floor in the southwestern corner.

He settled himself on it, and listened to the sounds of the night. Nibia was drawing water at the storage vat just outside the kitchen. Then a moment later he heard the thump of her footsteps, followed almost at once by the spattering of water in the bathroom on the western side of the house.

In theory, Storm was, at this very moment, having his bath—and having it in the manner customary among all respectable planters and gentlemen in the colony. Which is to say, he was being showered from a watering can by a female household slave.

The situation in the colony continued to be tense, and at times disturbed—there were clashes between the two new groups, the pro-Oranges and the pro-Batavians. The news that Berbice, as a result of the upset in Holland, was to be regarded henceforth as state-controlled did not help to improve conditions.

Wilfred crowed. "What did I predict? Didn't I hint m-m-months ago that such a change would come about? It was inevitable. The Berbice Association has long been an abject failure. The insurrection of '63 left this colony too depleted for any company to make a success of our affairs. State control is the wisest course—and it had to come. The States General have been shrewd in dissolving the company at this particular time, I grant them that."

Storm made no comment. They were at dinner, and the late-afternoon sunshine made patterns on the wall under the portrait of the Mayburys. Storm's silence, however, did not derive from indifference. He was worried. That morning, as he was returning from his tour of inspection round the plantation, he had found Nibia waiting for him beyond the large storage vat. She had called to him—they could not be seen from the house—and when he had dismounted from his mule she had said: "Massa, I wake up this morning sick. I very sick."

He stared at her, arresting himself even as he was on the point of blurting out: "Why haven't you seen the surgeon for some medicine, then?" For understanding came upon him. He said instead: "You are with child, you mean?"

She nodded. She did not seem scared. It was as though she knew he would not be severe with her. She sensed the kindness in him.

"Didn't you use ochra and gully root?"

"Yes, massa. Every time you wake me I go outside and get ochra and gully root. While the water drawing I go to my logie and get it. But it no use. I making child inside me."

"Very well." She saw him squeezing his hands together hard. "I shall have to think on the matter. Meantime, you will say nothing. You have not told the mistress, have you?"

"Only that I feel lil' sick, massa."

"Very well. Go to the surgeon for some medicine. Ask for physic of some kind. Complain of bellyache—anything you care to complain of. But say nothing of the child until I decide what is to be done. I shall probably come to you tonight and speak to you on the matter."

That night he made love to her for the last time, and when he told her it was to be the last time, she said: "I not feel sick at night, massa. You can come again." She sounded dismayed and distressed. "I want you to come to me."

He grunted, and patted her cheek. "I understand, and I thank you. But it must not continue, Nibia. I am not naturally a deceitful man. This is the first occasion on which I have been unfaithful to your mistress, and it has worried me. You're a very attractive creature, and the circumstance of your sleeping in the house here tempted me beyond endurance. But now I must take myself in hand."

"What about the child I got in me, massa? You say this morning you will speak to me about it."

"I intend to. In a moment." He fell silent, and she waited. She heard his quiet breathing beside her in the darkness, and wondered at the oddness of his manner. He was a soft, kind man, but many of his moods she did not understand. Sometimes, in making love to her, he would chuckle and seem amused at some secret joke. Ofttimes he would lie still and say nothing, and when she asked him if anything were the matter he would murmur: "No. I am hearkening to the sounds of the night, Nibia."

After a long silence, he began to fondle her neck. Very gently. When his hand reached down to her breasts he said: "Today I did a great deal of thinking, Nibia. And here is the substance of what I thought: You are a slave, and it is in my discretion, as your master, to dispose of you as I deem fit. To avoid my wife and parents-in-law knowing that you are pregnant with my child I could have you undergo a painful ordeal of bush medicines which would probably rid your system of the foetus. As you probably know, many of the older slave women are adept at this manner of child disposal, if we may so call it." He chuckled, and she took the opportunity of saying: "Yes, massa. I think that, too. Marta and Janie know good how to boil bush for getting rid of child in belly. I hear them say that plenty time."

"Just so, Nibia. And as a van Groenwegel, I should be callous in the matter. Our family is reputed to be a cruel one. However, let me not digress on to that subject. The substance of the matter is that I have decided to let you have the child. I have spoken to Massa Frick, the second overseer. He has often admired you, hasn't he? Well, I had a long talk with him, and he has agreed to confess that he is the father of your child. I shall announce to my wife and my parents-in-law that this is so, and if you are questioned you will admit that it was Massa Frick who got you with child. Is that clear?"

"Yes, massa. But for me, I will always feel good inside me that it is your child. I like you. You good and kind to me, and you make love to me good."

"Again let me express my gratitude, Nibia. I'm flattered. But I must warn you never to permit sentiment to get the better of you. Never, never must your mistress nor the Massa Wilfred nor the Missy Primrose learn that this child you are having is mine. If you like me, then this is the way you can prove it. Will you do as I say?"

"Yes, massa."

"You will always remain in this household, and I shall see that you are well treated. But you must keep your promise in this matter of the child."

"You will treat my child good, too, massa?"

"Yes. I shall have him freed."

"Him!" She uttered a soft chortle. "And if it is a girl, massa?"

He patted her cheek, chuckling, too. "She shall be freed."

3

IN September, Elizabeth gave birth to a son, and he was called
Dirk Wilfred. His grandfather rubbed his hands together and
crowed: "Ha! you laughed at me, but didn't I predict it! I
dreamt of him on many a night. There is m-m-much in dreams that
we do not suspect, my children! Ha! He will be a great man in this
colony! Look at those ears! Look at that brow!"

The christening was a merry affair, and the Governor and Mme.
van Batenburg were among the guests at the reception held in the late
afternoon.

The children were not allowed downstairs, but were left in the care
of Nibia in their room. Marta, an elderly household slave, brought up
their food, and while they were eating Marta remained in the room
to gossip with Nibia.

"Your time come soon, me girl," said Marta. "How you feel?"

"Me feel good, good," said Nibia. "Me not feel afraid."

"The white man's God better help you. It's your first."

Graham, always on the alert, asked: "Why should God help you,
Nibia? Is something the matter?"

Nibia stretched out and rumpled his hair. "No, me baby. Nothing
matter. Marta talking stupidness. Don't listen to Marta."

Marta, a stout, gloomy creature, uttered a moan, shaking her head.
"That Massa Frick like too much women. You not the first he put
child into."

Nibia said nothing, and Marta gave her a suspicious glance. "Nibia,
tell me something—true-true. Is Massa Frick give you this child?"

Nibia started, her eyes glittering angrily. "Why you talk so, Marta?
I not tell you plenty time it's Massa Frick' child? You doubt me
word?"

Marta grunted, lowering her gaze. "Awright. Awright. Don't fret yourself, me girl. I only ask you."

"Why you ask me?"

Marta smiled slyly. "Because you talk, talk so much say it's Massa Frick' child. Every day you talk, talk, talk say how Massa Frick give you this child. It almost look as if it might be somebody else."

"You're a stupid woman!" flared Nibia.

"You mustn't say that, child. I'm old. I can be your mother. You must got more respect for me, Nibia."

Nibia hung her head, ashamed of her outburst. She muttered: "I don't like that kind of talk from you. You know it's Massa Frick' child."

Marta grunted, and rebutted: "But Janie tell me something else. That's what I trying to tell you, me child. Don't get vex' with me. I want to help you."

"What Janie tell you?"

"Janie tell me say Massa Frick had her plenty nights in his cottage, but that he never had you once. She say she woulda know if he had you."

"She lie! How she could know when he had me? He come to the house and have me. Plenty nights he come here to the house and had me."

Marta smiled. "I telling you what Janie say, Nibia. Don't get vex' with me. Janie say she see you come to your logie plenty nights to get ochra and gully root. She hear you draw water at the tank, and she see you go back into the house here. But you never go near Massa Frick' cottage, and he never go near the house here, because the same nights when she see you getting ochra and gully root and drawing water Massa Frick sleep with her."

"She is a lying girl. Don't listen to her, Marta." Nibia rose and began to pace up and down, and the children stared at her. Graham stirred in his chair, a worried look coming to his face. He could sense that Nibia was troubled, and it troubled him, too. She seemed so fat these days, though he did not mind that. What he minded was her strange, thoughtful moods when she sat by him at night. She did not laugh as gaily nowadays, and she always turned her back on him when she changed into her nighttime smock, though she still let him fondle her breasts before he settled down to sleep.

"Nibia, I'm sure something is the matter," he said, pausing again in his eating. "Has Mynheer Frick done something you didn't like?"

Nibia, ignoring him, turned upon Marta. "What Massa Frick say? Janie not ask him? He not tell her the child in me his own?"

Marta nodded. "Yes, he tell her so. He say it's his child."

"And she think he lying what he talk?"

"Don't fret yourself, me girl. Janie stupid." Her manner was conciliatory now. "I only tell you what she tell me."

"But you not believe it's Massa Frick' child, Marta? Who else it could be? You don't believe it, too?" Nibia was almost trembling.

Marta nodded, smiling in a motherly manner. She rose, "Me believe you, Nibia. Don't fret yourself. Janie stupid, and she can lie bad. You na got to tell me, me baby. Don't fret yourself. If you say it's Massa Frick' child you getting, and Massa Frick say it's his child, then it must be his child."

And Marta left the room, fully convinced now that it was Storm's child.

Nibia's child was a boy, too. He was born on the thirtieth of January of the following year, 1796, and both Wilfred and Primrose were certain that they could discern in him a marked resemblance to Albertus Frick, the second overseer.

"The same eyes!" Primrose gushed. "The same pale blue eyes. And the very same limbs."

"The identical brow!" Wilfred exclaimed. "There can be no m-m-mistake here, I warrant! What are you going to call him, my girl?" he asked of Nibia, who, self-conscious, sat on the steps of her logie, cradling the infant in her lap.

"Marta say Jacob, massa," she murmured.

"Excellent! Excellent!" cried Wilfred. He uttered ecstatic sounds, regarding the baby, with quickly blinking eyes, and rubbing his hands together. "Tch, tch, tch! What a remarkable resemblance, indeed!"

Elizabeth, who had also come to see the child, laughed. "To me, Father, I can see no resemblance whatever to either Frick or Nibia."

Nibia glanced up at her sharply, but Elizabeth reassured her at once by hurrying on: "He's too young, Nibia—that's what I mean. When he grows we shall begin to see whom he really resembles. You must take good care of him. And Massa Storm has asked me to tell you that your child will be freed and taught a trade when he grows up."

"Yes, missy. Thank you, missy. Massa very good man," Nibia murmured, hanging her head.

Elizabeth told her that for the next few days she could remain in her logie. Marta would take charge of the children for the time being.

In the weeks and months that followed, Nibia and Marta took it by turns to see after the infant. Marta had taken a great liking to the boy, and was always eager to go to Nibia's logie to relieve Nibia. Indeed, as Elizabeth remarked to Storm, Nibia seemed more eager to be in the house with her charges than with her own son. To a stranger, it would have appeared that Marta was the mother of the child.

The novelty of Nibia's child soon waned as political events of great note intervened to produce subject matter for conversation at breakfast and dinner. After April, in fact, Nibia and her son Jacob were forgotten. For on the twentieth of that month the British arrived in Demerary with ten ships of war, and demanded the surrender of the colonies. On the twenty-second Demerary surrendered.

"It is the best thing that could have happened," sighed Elizabeth. "I was so afraid the French might have come."

Storm laughed. "You and your fear of the French, my dear! However, I am pleased myself. In a few days, no doubt, we, too, shall have surrendered—and I rather have a feeling that van Batenburg is deeply relieved at the turn events have taken."

"M-m-most certainly he is!" spluttered Wilfred, nearly choking over his cup of coffee. "Damme, the man is entirely on the side of the British. I have m-m-more than once told you that, haven't I? He must be delighted. Simply delighted!"

Major General Whyte sent a frigate to Berbice, and a few days later the announcement came that van Batenburg had surrendered. This was on the third of May, but, to the surprise of Wilfred, the surrender was not along the lines of the one in Demerary. Van Batenburg, though undoubtedly a lover of the English, haggled quite a great deal, and the upshot was that while he agreed to the same terms as those offered to Demerary and Essequibo, he stipulated that he was giving up "the sovereignty of the colony alone, with the posts, forts, and military magazines." He made it clear that the plantations, slaves and other assets of the recently discredited company, the Berbice Association, were to be regarded as "private property" because they had not yet been officially handed over to the States General. The British officer accepted this condition, and van Batenburg held a ball at Colony House to entertain the newcomers.

Wilfred was so overcome with delight and excitement that he broke his rule about not attending balls, and accompanied Storm and Elizabeth and Primrose.

"On such an historic occasion," he said, "I could not p-p-possibly envisage myself remaining at home."

The English planters were not the only ones pleased at the new state of things. The Dutch were almost as enthusiastic, for the many improvements that had resulted from the first British capture of the three colonies in 1781 were still fresh in the memories of most people. Also, the genial Kingston, the British commander at the time, had endeared himself to everyone.

An indication of how pleasant were the relations between British and Dutch was the fact that it seemed in no way extraordinary when, on the departure of Major General Whyte, it was announced that Beaujon, the Dutchman who had governed Demerary before the advent of the British, would continue in rule. Nor did anyone think it odd that van Batenburg also carried on as before in Berbice.

Nor was anyone disappointed. During the next few years prosperity increased. Slaves were imported in large numbers, and, indeed, within a year or two, the slave population had doubled. Exports burgeoned.

When the nineteenth century opened, there were three hundred plantations in a flourishing state in Berbice alone. In Demerary and Essequibo four hundred. Not to mention others well on the way up. The British established a post office, and a newspaper, *The Royal Essequibo and Demerary Gazette*, came into being, every issue of which was automatically sent to Wilfred by Hubertus.

"I could not permit your records to be so gravely incomplete, my dear Wilfred," wrote Cousin Hubertus when he sent the first copy, "so be assured that in future I shall send them to you as a matter of course."

"Dear Hubert! Dear Hubert!" sighed Wilfred—and there were tears in his eyes. "Always generous, always thoughtful of others. Why is it that the years and the miles should separate us in this way!"

"Which reminds me," Storm murmured—they were on the portico in the late afternoon, after dinner—"Edward and Luise are thinking of paying us a visit. He hinted as much in his last letter, did I mention, sir?"

"Eh? Eh?" Wilfred started, as though just emerging from a reverie. "Who did you say? What did you say, my boy?"

Storm repeated what he had said, and Wilfred rose agitatedly. "No, no. You did not mention this to me. Edward and Luise! My sweet little p-p-pet, Luise. It is extremely remiss of you not to have mentioned this, Storm. When are they coming? Did they state a definite date? I must have all the details, my boy. This is startlingly splendid news."

Storm smiled and told him: "I purposely did not mention it before, sir, because I didn't want to raise your hopes in vain. Edward merely hinted that he would like to come with Luise and spend a week or two with us. He had in mind painting a few pictures—another family group and perhaps a landscape study. But he has only *hinted* so far. He has said nothing definite about it."

"And didn't you reply pressing the point, Storm? You should have replied without d-d-delay and insisted that he come, and bring Luise." Wilfred began to pace about agitatedly—and Elizabeth and Storm exchanged glances.

"My spirit lives on in Demerary, my children," sighed Wilfred. "Tch, tch, tch! I shall never forget those days." He started. Clapped his hands.

Juma, his personal slave, immediately appeared from inside.

"My writing things, Juma. I wish to write a letter. This instant. Dear Hubert. Dear Luise. I must write them both. Hurry, Juma! Hurry!"

Edward and Luise came to New Signal in July of that same year, 1798, two months after receiving Wilfred's letter. It was a rainy July, though the day on which they arrived was stiflingly hot, with sunshine that shone out of a sky grey-blue and cloudless.

Wilfred quivered and blinked in nervous spasms of pleasure. "Tch, tch, tch! My dear Luise! My dear Edward! What a moment! Oh, I'm overcome." Tears ran from his eyes, and his bony body almost rattled as laughter quaked out of him. He hugged them both, retreated, then clasped his hands together.

Luise, too, grew tearful as she regarded him with her bright-green eyes. At forty-five she looked about thirty, even younger than Edward at thirty-five, whose sensitive, frowning face—a replica of Storm's—made him seem older than he really was. Edward's smile was very faint as he stretched out both his hands to grasp his uncle-in-law's arms, but you could see that emotion went deep; he was as much moved as Wilfred, perhaps even more moved, thought Storm. A strange fellow. I've never understood him. I can't think of him as my twin brother.

"And look at her! Elizabeth! Primrose, my love! Look at Luise! She has not aged one whit! The same p-p-perfect complexion! The identical shapely young miss I knew at Good Heart. Hee, hee! Tch, tch, tch! This is too much for me!" Wilfred turned away, dabbing hastily at his eyes, while Luise laughed and said to Elizabeth: "He hasn't changed, either. The same excitable old Uncle Wilfred. Oh, I'm so glad to be here, Elizabeth. Uncle dear, sit down. You're trembling." She took a step toward him and wiped his eyes with her fingers. "There! You must contain yourself, or I shall take myself off again. How would you like that?"

Wilfred, trembling and chuckling and blinking, allowed her to press him down into a chair, and Edward remarked: "Don't scold Uncle Wilfred, my dear. You are hardly less emotional yourself."

"Is she? Is she, Edward?" asked Wilfred, giving him a tearful glance.

Edward nodded gloomily. "In private, sir—strictly in private—for which we must be thankful."

Luise turned, stretched out and pinched Edward's arm. Edward winced, and immediately retaliated, and Luise uttered an "Ouch!" She turned to her uncle and said: "Did you know he used to pinch me when he was a boy, Uncle? Of late I've begun to do it to him, too, for I have sworn to be revenged for all I suffered at his hands."

"A robust, vicious young woman of twenty imposing her libidinous will upon a sensitive boy of ten. You deserved to suffer, my love."

"It was delicious suffering, nevertheless, I admit," laughed Luise, and Storm thought: In spirit she has not grown up. She is the same passionate Luise.

At five o'clock when they were at dinner, it was raining steadily and heavily outside from a sky grey all over, but the weather did not blight their mood. It was an evening of gay reminiscence, and much irresponsible banter.

"Tell me—tell me all about Hubert," Wilfred demanded several times, even after Edward and Luise had told him quite a great deal. "I must know everything about him that has happened since I left D-D-Demerary. Is he still so pensive in his manner? Does he still wag his head and moan over the Old Blood?"

"He'll never cease to do that, Uncle," smiled Luise, her clear, deep-set green eyes fixed affectionately upon him. "Just as you are incurably excitable, Father is incurably despondent. He will torture himself about our blood to the day of his death."

"He is a conscientious man, sir," put in Edward seriously, scowling in his old way, as though intolerant of humour of any sort—an impression which was quite false, for he had a quick humour and a deep sense of irony. "He thinks deeply on every question, and anyone who does that, as I am tired of telling Luise, must of necessity give the appearance of being morbidly inclined. Is there a philosopher who does not leave the impression of despondency?"

"See!" cried Luise. "I have told you, Uncle Wilfred! No one must dare criticise Father in Edward's hearing."

"That is nothing to marvel at, my dear Luise," said Storm. "We here also have need to exercise care when uttering any remark of an adverse nature directed at Cousin Hubertus." He gave a significant glance at his father-in-law, and Wilfred fidgeted and tittered, reddening.

"Hubert is my friend, Luise," said Wilfred. "I have the utmost confidence in him. I must c-c-concur with Edward's view. Hubert has been much misunderstood."

Luise flashed: "No fear! I understand him, Uncle Wilfred! I even understand why, at seventy, he still visits the logies of his female slaves!"

Edward started back, and his scowl this time was fierce. "Luise!"

Luise, undaunted, cried: "The truth! Isn't it the truth? Father has always impressed upon me the necessity to face the truth, no matter how ugly. I think it was supposed to be old Hendrickje's dictum. Why shouldn't I mention that he is still virile enough to cohabit with his female slaves!"

Edward winced. "Polite society, my dear, demands that some things be left unsaid at the dinner-table."

Luise shrieked, pinkening and throwing her head back in abandon. "Oh, dear! That is why I love Edward so much. Do you see the conventional airs he can give himself? And he sleeps at night without a stitch of clothing, and sometimes even strays into the corridor as naked as Nature made him!"

Edward gave a sulky grin, and stretched out with the intention of pinching her. But she avoided him adroitly, shielding herself with Storm's help. Storm sat between herself and Edward.

Elizabeth and Wilfred laughed themselves into tears, and even Storm could not prevent himself from chuckling continuously.

Edward took a great liking to Graham, and Graham returned the feeling.

"I believe he is an artist," said Edward. "I can sense it in him. We must watch him as he develops," he told Storm and Elizabeth.

"By the way, aren't you going to paint a picture of us all, Edward?"

Edward frowned. "I have brought my painting equipment, but this rain has destroyed my mood for painting anything. If the weather becomes fine, perhaps I shall make a start, for I should certainly like to do another portrait of you people."

Graham, who was sitting on the arm of his chair, alert and even more precociously curious about adult affairs than he had been three years before, said to Edward: "I don't like the rain myself, Uncle, but I should like to paint a picture of trees with rain falling on them."

"One day I'm fairly certain you will, my boy," smiled Edward. He glanced at Storm: "What are you doing about his education, Storm? Is there a proper tutor in this colony?"

"Yes, we have Hiemens. He is excellent. He comes three times a week. And on two days a week—the other two when Hiemens doesn't come here; I'm excepting Saturday and Sunday, of course—Graham and Hermine go to the Laffertys' place downstream, where a fellow called Harvey—he's from Antigua—teaches a number of children English and German. Hiemens is not an English-speaking fellow. He hardly knows any English at all, except one or two words he's picked up."

"Just as well to keep them versed in their Dutch. I think every member of our family, as a matter of course, should learn Dutch, whether this colony remains British or not."

Luise laughed. "You see that! Edward has a strong sense of family pride behind his casual airs. It's no one but Father who has infected him with that!"

Edward sighed, and was on the point of retorting when Graham intervened by remarking: "I like Mynheer Hiemens, but Mr. Harvey spits when he speaks, Uncle Edward. You have to be careful not to sit right in front of him."

Elizabeth frowned at him and said: "You should not remark on such things, Graham. It is not polite."

"The truth," murmured Edward, patting his head affectionately. "One day you must send him to spend time with us in Demerary, Elizabeth. I should like to see what talent he has with the brush. I'm very, very certain he is artistic."

"By all means." Elizabeth smiled. "The change should be good for him."

"I'll miss Nibia, though," said Graham. "I love Nibia, and she loves me."

"Who is Nibia?" asked Luise, her eyes growing wide with surprise.

"His nurse," said Elizabeth. "He's very fond of her—since he was a tiny boy. Nibia sleeps with them all in their room. She has a child of her own, and I let her sleep with him in the room, too."

"Marta likes Dirk," said Graham. "She prefers Dirk and Jacob to all the rest of us. Jacob is Nibia's son. Nibia doesn't love Jacob as much as Marta. She loves me better than Jacob."

Storm growled: "Stop being conceited, young man."

"It's true, Father," Graham protested. "I know it's true."

Both Edward and Luise stared at the boy, as though fascinated by his intensity, as though remarking his almost adult-like keenness. Edward looked at Luise, and she returned his look. They both smiled —and it was a smile of understanding, a smile almost of collusion.

Later, in their room, Edward and Luise discussed the children. Edward said: "There's something in that boy Graham that reminds me of myself. I cannot define it precisely, but it is there." He paced up and down, running his fingers through his hair and scowling. "Something of myself at ten. He's too alert to what goes on around him. He is mentally older than what his years dictate he should be." He paused and looked at his wife. "Don't you agree, my love?"

Luise shook her head. She was undressing. "I do not, Edward—not entirely, at any rate. He possesses the alertness you speak of—but he is not like you as you were at ten. He is much softer, gentler. You were aggressive, cold, hard."

He winced, but nodded. "Yes, you are right there. Yet I can sense something that was me in the boy's general air. He's the questing kind, Luise. Ah, that is it!" He clasped his hands together and smiled. "Yes, that is it. He must have the answers to every riddle and problem that life holds. I was like that. There is the similarity."

"Yes, I think you have assessed him correctly in that respect." She laughed, approached him, and patted his neck. "It is time for bed, dear. On a rainy night like this you know what your duties toward me are."

He grinned—like a fiend. In a way he had sometimes done as a boy when he wanted to tease her beyond endurance. He looked at her and grinned, rubbing his hands together as if to warm them in the damp, rainy air. "You will never change, Luise. Nor will I, I suppose. People do not change, it is my firm belief. We remain what we were as infants." He nodded. "Yes, even as infants we reveal what we are, and what we shall always be to the end of our days."

Pressing herself against him, she agreed. "Yes, I agree. Edward, have you noticed Dirk? He is only three—not yet three, in fact; his birthday is in September—but there is a light in his eyes that startles me. If I were superstitious I would say that the soul of Grandma Hendrickje has been reborn in Dirk. He frightens me a little, tiny as he is."

He began to shake with laughter. He fondled her and said: "There can be no doubt that you are superstitious, love. Let me hasten to perform my duties."

4

T H E last few days of July and the first two weeks in August were fine and dry, with hot, brilliant sunshine that parched the earth and drew the sweetish, rank, dry-weather scent from the grass. It was during this period that Edward painted his portrait of the family. He painted rapidly, and never asked for more than one brief sitting every day. It was a large portrait—larger than the one over the sideboard in the dining-room—and Wilfred said that it would have to occupy a space on the southern wall of the sitting-room.

"That is where your earlier picture should have been hung, my boy," he told Edward, "but Primrose was most p-p-positive in her request that it should be hung over the sideboard. She said that p-p-people are more appreciative of portraits that can be seen when a meal is in progress. Hee, hee! I don't know if you will agree with such a theory, but I d-d-decided that she deserved to be humoured in the matter. Women must always be humoured in matters of domestic arrangements, mustn't they?"

Some weeks after Edward and Luise had departed, Graham and Hermine, with Nibia in attendance, paused one morning in the sitting-room to gaze upon the newly framed and hung portrait. Graham hugged himself, and stared open-mouthed. Hermine smiled a slight, half-indifferent smile. Nibia, with an awed expression, kept exclaiming: "Oh, massa! Look at this!"

Abruptly Graham turned to Nibia and said: "But do you see something, Nibia? Look at Dirk."

"Eh? What about Massa Dirk?"

"In the picture, I mean," said Graham, pointing.

"He's sitting in Mother's lap," said Hermine. "We can see him."

"Yes, we can see him," nodded Nibia. "What wrong with him, Massa Graham?"

Graham winced. "I've told you not to call me Massa Graham like that, Nibia. I don't like it. It makes me feel you don't love me."

Hermine laughed. She began to do a jig. "Silly, silly Graham! Always saying silly, silly things!"

"It's not silly. It's not silly!" Tears appeared in his eyes, and Nibia held him and hugged him, saying: "Never mind, me baby. I know good what you mean. But you growing up into big man. I must call you massa. Slave got to be respectful, you see, me baby?" She stroked his hair, and patted his cheek.

That put matters right, and he began to smile and return her endearments. He held her hand and said: "I was telling you about the picture, Nibia. Look at Dirk. And don't call him Massa Dirk, please. He's only three. Tell me what you see in the picture about Dirk, Nibia."

Nibia, in a voice of indulgence and affection, said: "I see him sitting in his mother's lap. The Missy got her hand around his chest. That what you mean?"

"No, no," said Graham patiently. "I mean his eyes, Nibia."

"What wrong with his eyes?"

"Don't you see?" asked Graham, puzzled. "They look so wild—like an animal's in the jungle. A raccoon's eyes. Why did Uncle Edward paint them like that, I wonder?"

"But Dirk's eyes do look like that," said Hermine. "They're not wild eyes. Silly, silly Graham!" She began to do a jig again, her manner teasing.

"I'm not being silly. I don't like Dirk's eyes in the picture. They make me a little frightened. Don't they frighten you, Nibia?"

Nibia pressed him close to her, and uttered a crooning sound. "No, me baby. It's only a picture. Nothing to get frighten over. It's Massa —it's Dirk, your brother. Massa Edward paint him like he is. Nothing wrong."

Graham was silent for an instant, clutching at her leg, then he nodded and said: "Yes, you're right, I suppose. It's only a picture, and Uncle Edward only painted his eyes like that because—because he's a painter. They're Dirk's eyes—only . . . only so wild-looking. Let's go and walk under the orange trees, Nibia. I'm tired of looking at the picture."

It was not only Graham, however, who thought there was something odd in Edward's portrayal of Dirk's eyes. One day, when friends were being entertained—friends from the neighbouring plantations and from the West Bank of the Berbice—a girl of about seventeen, a daughter of Mevrouw Swiffermann, the widow from Plantation Lambden, stared at the picture and remarked on Dirk.

"I don't like his eyes," she said.

Elizabeth overheard her and nodded. "Yes, Janetje, I agree. I told someone the same thing, but it was a trick of the light, I was informed."

"It is not," said Janetje, her voice positive, her manner a trifle puzzled. "They were painted that way by the artist. Mynheer van Groenwegel must have had a reason for doing it, I'm certain. Perhaps he meant it as a joke."

"Now, now, Janetje!" scolded Mevrouw Swiffermann. "It is not in your place to criticise Mynheer van Groenwegel. He is a gifted man, and you must not be presumptuous."

Elizabeth laughed. "Oh, but perhaps she is right, Rachel. Edward often indulges in strange, whimsical actions, and it is quite possible that he decided to have a joke at Dirk's expense—though why he should have selected Dirk in particular I cannot hazard a guess."

Primrose intervened here with a decided: "You are imagining what is not there, Elizabeth. I've told you before I can see nothing the matter with dear little Dirk's eyes in the picture. Edward has painted them in a very lifelike manner, I am sure. Everyone has said so."

Elizabeth flushed slightly, for there was a note of unusual sharpness in her mother's voice. Elizabeth retorted: "Janetje here has just noticed what I did. Surely she cannot be imagining it too."

Primrose, with Mevrouw's gaze upon her, flushed in her turn. She giggled and gushed: "Has dear little Janetje, too, seen something strange in Dirk's eyes in the picture? What is it that impresses you, my child? Tell me."

Janetje, however, fearful of being scolded again by her mother, smiled self-consciously and said: "I must be mistaken, Mevrouw Maybury, I'm certain. It's probably—it's probably the light, as Mevrouw van Groenwegel says."

"I didn't say so, my girl," said Elizabeth. "It was the person to whom I remarked, as you have done, about Dirk's eyes who said it must be the light. However, let us drop the subject. It is quite trivial, I'm sure."

After the guests had departed, Elizabeth stood for a long while before the picture. There could be no doubt that Edward's was a great talent. Vaguely she recalled some story about a van Groenwegel of the last century who had also been a painter. He had been a very unhappy man, from all accounts.

Storm joined her and asked: "What's the matter, my dear? Has my brother's picture trapped you in some spell?"

"I'm admiring it," she laughed. She told him of Janetje Swiffermann's remark, and he nodded. "Imagination, of course. There is nothing odd in the eyes Edward has given Dirk in this picture. They're Dirk's eyes."

She caught at his arm, and he felt her tremble slightly. She frowned and said quietly: "Yes, you're right. They *are* Dirk's eyes."

Nibia and Marta sometimes had quarrels over the children, and many bitter things were said. Graham had been right in his assessment of the situation. Nibia was indifferent about her son, Jacob, and Marta inordinately fond of the little fellow with his dark curly hair and olive complexion. Moreover, Dirk, among the other children, was Marta's special favourite, whereas Nibia showered her affection on Graham. Whenever a quarrel occurred over the children, it was either because Nibia had done something that seemed unfair to Dirk or Jacob, or because Marta had wounded the feelings of Graham in some way.

One morning, when they were strolling under the orange trees, Marta remarked: "It look as if the Missy stop having children. Missy Hermine shoulda got a sister to keep her company."

Nibia said: "Missy Hermine don't want no company. She always prefer to play with herself. She's a selfish child."

Dirk, now over five, his eyes a cold, clear grey-green, abruptly glanced at Nibia and said: "She's my sister."

Nibia looked at him in surprise, and laughed. "Who say she not your sister, boy?"

Dirk's eyes glittered—and Graham frowned, remembering the picture in the sitting-room. Raccoon's eyes. Dirk said coldly to Nibia: "She's my sister, and you're a slave. You must not say anything against her."

Nibia uttered a shriek of laughter, amused at the boy's adult manner. "But look at this lil' boy! Massa Dirk, you is a big massa already, na? Dat what you think? Want to scold me. Well, look at this thing!"

Marta, as much amused as Nibia, concealed her amusement out of a sense of loyalty to the boy. She frowned at Nibia and said: "Massa

Dirk right. You should remember you is a slave, and learn to speak respectfully of your betters."

Nibia sucked her teeth and tossed her head. "You can't teach me to be respectful, old lady. I know what to talk and what not to talk."

"You think you know. You young yet in years, I always telling you dat."

And thus another quarrel began. Graham, always disturbed when the two women went for each other like this, intervened eventually and asked Nibia not to let Marta upset her. He clutched Nibia's arm and said: "It's so silly to say such things about each other. You know you don't mean them."

Nibia would have desisted at this point, but Marta fired a broadside that was too much for the younger woman. "Look at the way you turning Massa Graham into a softy-softy young man. Nearly ten years old, and clinging to you day and night. Don't want to go and play with his friends after lessons."

Nibia stiffened. Her eyes spewed fury and resentment as she hurled back at Marta: "Me making Massa Graham softy-softy! And you! You old devil turning Massa Dirk into a wild animal. Cruel and no love in the boy. Always killing the poor insects he catch—and lizards and butterflies. Who encourage him to do that but you?"

"He's a boy. All boys like killing insects and lizards. Why he shouldn't do it? Yes, I let him do it. And I let him swim in the pool aback the provision plots. He's a boy. He and Jacob can swim already —but what Massa Graham can do? He sit down with his lesson books and read, and when he not reading he writing, and when he not writing he sitting in your lap like a big baby-child. He'll never be a man like Massa Dirk and Jacob."

Graham clutched Nibia's arm harder, and pleaded: "Don't quarrel, Nibia. I beg of you. I can't stand it."

Dirk had a faint, sneering smile on his five-year-old face. Jacob and Hermine had run ahead to search for a salempenter which had scampered across the footpath a few minutes before.

Storm and Elizabeth, at the instigation of Edward, who wrote fairly frequently, tried to encourage Graham to draw and paint, but the boy showed no aptitude in this respect. He was fond of music, however, and asked permission to take lessons in violin playing with Jim Lafferty. Mr. Lafferty, on the neighbouring plantation, Rye, downstream, had secured a man fairly good at the violin, and young Jim was taking lessons from him.

Storm and Elizabeth agreed, and soon Graham was outstripping even the tutor himself. Jim Lafferty remarked one morning when he came over: "By God, you should hear that boy of yours play, Storm! *He* should be the tutor—not Bryan. You've got a born musician, believe me! If he were in Europe he'd get far."

Graham, however, did not enthuse over his violin. He played well, but took his playing casually. There was no fire in his manner, no *élan*. He told Elizabeth one afternoon after dinner: "I like playing my violin, but I want to be a rich planter like Father. I like reading big books, but I think I'd much prefer to see after the plantation. Ride around on a mule and watch the cane fields, and see that everything is going as it should on the place."

Storm, who overheard, sighed and said: "A remarkable mixture. I've never yet heard of a planter who was at the same time literary and musical. Perhaps you will start a new fashion, my boy."

"We need a few cultivated people in this colony," said Elizabeth.

"The van Groenwegels have always been cultivated, my dear," he said—a trifle stiffly. "We have always had our tutors. Even the Canje lot knew their Greek and Latin, from what I can gather from those old letters."

"What old letters?"

"Have you forgotten the canister Mr. Fletcher, the naturalist, brought here some years ago?"

"Oh yes, of course. Have you been delving into it?"

"By way of curiosity—purely," nodded Storm. "Very interesting."

Graham exclaimed: "I remember the morning when it came!"

Storm clicked his tongue. "Don't be absurd. You were only four at the time. You couldn't possibly remember."

"But I do remember, Father," Graham insisted. "Grandpa came in and told us not to trouble the letters. He'd left the canister open, I think. I even asked him about the snakes Mr. Fletcher had brought back from the jungle."

Wilfred, who had been dozing, started awake. "What? What's that? What did Grandpa do, my boy?"

Graham repeated what he had said, and Wilfred nodded. "Of course, of course. Something of the sort did happen. Even my rusty memory seems to endorse that account. The little fellow did p-p-put some such question to me, I recall. Hee, hee! This boy's a genius. Mar-

vellous memory. We must watch him, Elizabeth, my girl. And speaking
of that, I think it's time he was allowed to see those papers. He can
read now, can't he? Those p-p-papers concern him, as a member of the
great van Groenwegel clan. Eh? What? Damme, but I am right!"

"Of course you are, sir," Storm smiled. "I mean to let him see them,
too. The canister is in the storeroom upstairs. This afternoon I put the
key in the drawer of the writing table in your mother's and my
room, Graham. You can always find it there. But I want the canister
locked whenever you complete your perusal of the papers. And the key
must be put back in the writing-table drawer. Is that clear?"

"Very clear, Father. I shall be very careful with the papers."

From the very next day, Graham began to make trips to the storeroom to read the old letters in the canister. He handled the documents
with great reverence, awed by their age and the knowledge that they
had been written by his forebears. Most of them bored him; they
seemed extremely dull. But here and there he came upon one that
caused him to stiffen and bend forward.

Soon he began to tell the others about the letters. "Can you believe
it, Nibia?" he said one day, when Nibia and Marta and the other children were sitting on the back veranda and he had just appeared after
a bout of reading in the storeroom. "I've just been reading how
Grandma Hendri had a slave buried alive. Think of it! He was old
and sick, poor fellow, and she had him buried while he was still living."

"Ha! That not nothing, Massa Graham!" said Nibia. "She do worse,
worse things than that. My father tell me about her. She was a wicked,
cruel old lady."

Dirk, now six and a half, turned his head sharply. He was standing
at the veranda rail, watching the progress of ants down a baluster. "You
must not speak like that of Grandma Hendri, Nibia. You are a slave.
Grandma is our grandmother. She lives on the Canje, and she is a
van Groenwegel like Father."

Nibia laughed. "She live on the Canje! Not now, me boy. She dead
years and years long past."

Dirk glanced at Graham. "Is that true, Graham? Is Grandma Hendri dead?"

"Long, long ago," smiled Graham indulgently.

Dirk frowned. "But she was our grandmother. Nibia has no right
to speak of her as if she was bad. Nibia is only a slave."

Marta laughed. "Good boy! Good boy! Tell her."

Nibia grunted. "It's you, Marta, who putting all these things in the lil' child's head. You should be 'shame of yourself. He only six. He not got right to speak such things to me."

5

S TORM and Elizabeth and the two older people also often discussed the precocious temperaments of Graham and Dirk, though Wilfred and Primrose were inclined to treat the matter in a jesting spirit. Wilfred once told Dirk he was a true van Groenwegel. "Hee, hee! Hubert would admire you, my lad—and despise you, b-b-both at the same time." Dirk stared at him, baffled but intent in manner. Elizabeth, on another occasion, said in a voice of concern: "I feel that Dirk doesn't like us, Storm. Even when I go out of my way to be affectionate toward him he seems to resent my attentions." Storm nodded, and said that he had noticed it. "He possesses a strange detachment, that little fellow—but I wouldn't say he's cold in temperament. There is fire in him—but it is of the latent kind. It appears to need a spark, if I express myself clearly, to set it free." And his wife nodded and murmured: "I understand what you mean. And I should wish fervently that such a spark will never touch him. It would be a terrible fire, Storm. My instincts tell me so." Storm laughed and, fondling her, said: "Is it a boy of seven we're discussing, my dear! Pardon! Six and a half. He won't be seven until September."

Hardly a week after this conversation, however, the children and their oddness were forgotten. News came that the Peace of Amiens had been signed and that it was the intention of Britain to return the three colonies to the Dutch.

Wilfred fumed up and down the house, and he was not the only planter who was upset. English and Dutch, alike, were perturbed, for there was no great love among the colonists for the Batavian republic.

Events, nevertheless, went forward, and the change of governments was effected. And, as had been feared, the government in Holland sent out recalling Beaujon, the governor of Demerary, and van Batenburg, for these gentlemen were to be asked to explain their flagrantly pro-British attitude and the reason for their ready surrender of the colonies.

"I won't be surprised if they are both thrown into dungeons," said Graham, "and left there to languish for the rest of their lives."

Storm smiled. "I don't think such a sensational fate awaits them, my boy. Nevertheless, it isn't pleasant to contemplate the departure of two such men."

"This colony will never be the same without van Batenburg," sighed his wife.

"I believe," chuckled Storm, "you are half in love with him."

"It's possible," she smiled. "He's a delightful man."

It was not only Elizabeth who thought van Batenburg delightful. This feeling was expressed among all the planters and their wives—and among the soldiers. Indeed, with van Batenburg's departure, the situation in the colony declined rapidly. Under the British the troops had been well treated, but the Batavian government had other ideas on the matter, and the soldiers—Dutch soldiers—at Fort St. Andries began to complain of the neglected state of their barracks, poor pay, poor food, and bad medical attendance.

One morning in May of the following year, 1803, Cornelius Heffer, a Berbice River planter and a good friend of the family, arrived in his tent-boat and came up to the house to give Storm and Elizabeth the news. The soldiers at the fort had mutinied. "They have occupied Colony House," Heffer told Elizabeth and Wilfred. Storm was on his tour of inspection in the fields. "They took those two figureheads prisoner—the fellows who were acting for van Batenburg. But the greatest joke is this, my friends. If you take a trip to Fort St. Andries you'll see what they've done to their flagpole. They've hoisted the English flag, and tied a piece of beef above it. You see the significance? Under the English they were well fed—now they're starving."

"They have a sound case!" cried Wilfred. "My sympathy is entirely with them. Those p-p-poor fellows have been suffering immensely since this new government has taken over, Heffer. You know it! You know it! No c-c-competence! That is what it amounts to, damme! You can't treat men like that. They must—they are b-b-bound to resent it and take action."

"I agree," Heffer nodded, "and they know we are on their side, too, Maybury. They aren't interfering with the plantations. In fact, they are going out of their way to be pleasant to us planters. That's what I came to tell you, as a matter of fact. There's no need for alarm. I met a group of them near the mouth of the Creek, on my way here, and they assured me I had nothing to fear."

When Storm arrived at the house, he told them that Jim Lafferty had already given him the news. He had met him aback, at the canal bridge. "He says one of their officers is leading them. Poor fellows. They can't hold out forever, so what is the use? Troops from Demerary will soon be here to deal with them."

Wilfred uttered a hooting sound. "Demerary! I've heard on excellent authority, my boy, that c-c-conditions in Demerary are no better than they are here. P-p-perchance, for all we know, at this very m-m-moment the troops in Demerary have mutinied, too. Hoo, hoo! Wouldn't that be a fine state of things! Eh? Eh? What? I ask you! Hoo, hoo, hoo!"

The troops in Demerary, however, had not mutinied, though themselves gravely dissatisfied with their lot, and before many days had elapsed the mutiny was put down. The mutineers put up a good fight, all the same, and at one time, after they had had to evacuate Colony House and retreat back to Fort St. Andries, they bombarded the Governor's residence, assuming it to be in the hands of the troops from Demerary. Many of the shots fell wide and went into the town. In fact, the artillery on both sides proved useless, for when a duel had taken place between the mutineers and York Redoubt, on the West Bank, the previous day, the shots fell short of their targets. It was a wild, and, in some ways, comic event, especially as, at the very end, a body of Indians, equipped with clubs and bows and poisoned arrows, arrived to reinforce the troops from Demerary and Surinam. These troops never went into action, but their presence in New Amsterdam certainly added to the general colour and excitement of the situation.

Once a group of them passed in canoes on the Creek, and the children saw them. Graham was fascinated, staring at their half-naked forms, decorated with strings of beads, and their long black hair and shy-looking faces, but Dirk and Hermine were not moved by the sight.

"We've seen Indians before, haven't we?" said Dirk.

"But these are warriors," said Graham. "Fighting men. Look at their bows and arrows—and those strange-looking clubs."

"But they're not fighting now, are they?" said Dirk. "What's the use of warriors if they don't fight?"

On this occasion, the children were on their own; Nibia and Marta were gradually relinquishing their roles as nannies and confined themselves mostly now to attending to the wants of their charges in the house.

At night the two women slept in their own logies, for Graham had lost his fear of the darkness and of the night sounds outside the house. Jacob slept with Marta in Marta's logie, an arrangement to which Nibia did not object, for Nibia had her men friends who visited her in her logie at night.

Jacob did odd jobs about the house, but most of the time he was allowed to play with the children. He and Dirk were close in spirit, and swam together in the pond aback of the provision patches. They went off on jaunts by themselves, trailed imaginary tigers and wolves, and fought battles against mythical French soldiers near the sugar mill and in the cane fields. Dirk did not regard Jacob as a slave as he did Nibia and Marta; in his eyes, Jacob was a play companion, a partner in adventures, a fellow soldier and a fellow tiger hunter. He even perferred Jacob to Graham, for he looked upon Graham as silly and soft and bookish. Graham was always fawning upon Nibia, or playing his violin or reading some heavy book. He never went swimming, nor hunting tigers, nor doing battle against the French. Hermine, though a girl, was far more ready to accompany Dirk and Jacob on their hunting and warring expeditions, and Dirk respected her more than he did Graham.

"Fighting is not good," frowned Graham as they watched the canoes go out of sight round the bend in the stream. "Only barbarians fight each other."

Dirk nudged Jacob, and Jacob whispered: "He's soft. Let's go and surround that French regiment near the canal. We'll burn all the officers at the stake, and imprison the men in the big barn. What do you say?"

"Off we go, by God!" snapped Dirk, and he and Jacob ran off and left Graham and his sister by the bank of the Creek.

"Silly little goats," smiled Graham. "I can't imagine what they find in all their fanciful tiger hunts and battles."

"I like tiger hunts," said Hermine, who, at ten, was almost as tall as Graham. "It's good fun chasing a tiger through the cane fields."

"You mean making believe you're chasing a tiger."

"Isn't it the same thing?"

"How could fanciful things be the same as real things?"

Hermine shrugged. "Anyway, I like it. And I like swimming in the pond. Why don't you learn to swim?"

"Such things don't interest me," said her brother, wincing sensitively. "I like reading and playing the violin, and talking to Mynheer Hiemens."

"And something else, too," sniggered Hermine.

"What do you mean? What something else?"

"Naked girls," said Hermine. "You think I haven't seen you watching the slave girls washing themselves by the Creek here?"

Graham blushed, and growled: "You've been spying on me, you mean."

"And you were spying on them, weren't you?"

Graham walked off and left her, making his way towards the house. Hermine laughed, and ran off to look for Dirk and Jacob.

A few days after Dirk's eighth birthday—on the eighteenth of September of that same year, 1803—Demerary surrendered to the British, for Holland and Britain were at war, and the state of things in the colonies was again tense.

Not long before the arrival of the British ships of war, news had been received that van Batenburg was in the hands of the British. The ship which had been taking him to Holland had been captured in the English Channel. But according to all reports, van Batenburg had been received by his captors as a guest rather than a prisoner, and the rumour was that he was to be sent back by the British to take charge of Berbice again.

"Let us hope this will be the last time we shall suffer a change of governments," said Primrose. "It must be so upsetting for my poor John. He should have sailed from England last month, but I'm sure his arrangements have been thrown into confusion as a result of this terrible war."

"I'm sure John is in no way p-p-perturbed," said Wilfred. He and Storm were in the big bedroom on the southern side of the house, sitting by Primrose, who was in bed. Primrose, for the past few weeks, had been ill with a kidney complaint. "Now that he is qualified, he must be very much sought after by the ladies, eh? What? Hee, hee! Don't you c-c-concur with that view, Storm, my boy?"

"Quite so, sir," said Storm quietly, with a glance at Primrose, who looked troubled. Storm knew that the remark would have troubled her, for Storm knew that Primrose could not bear the idea of John being attached to any other woman but herself. Storm added: "Yet

I feel that John is not the susceptible kind. It is doubtful whether he will return to us in the company of a wife."

Primrose looked cheerful again, and said: "I keep telling Wilfred that John is a quiet boy. I'm certain he won't hasten into an unwise marriage."

Wilfred, about to argue this point, felt Storm's hand on his knee and caught himself. He coughed, fidgeted, and suddenly glanced out of the window at the glaring day, and remarked instead: "I believe we're going to have some thunder this evening." He fanned himself. "This heat is p-p-positively unbearable."

John did not arrive until January of the following year, and before his arrival two deaths had occurred in the family.

In November news came that Cousin Hubertus had died at Huis Kaywana on Plantation Kaywana in Demerary. The letter containing the news was sent by Edward. "Luise and I were both present," wrote Edward, "and his end was very peaceful. He died as I have imagined him many a time dying. He was in a reflective mood, and inclined to be philosophic in his observations, but he smiled frequently, and did not seem harrowed."

For days Wilfred wandered over the house, silent, his face drawn with grief. His lips moved, but no sound came from them. He was absent-minded, and missed meals, and neither Storm nor Elizabeth could succeed in rousing him from the coma of sorrow that had descended upon him. He even forgot to visit Primrose on her sickbed, and when he did, by accident, enter the room would merely stare at her and then turn abruptly about and hurry out, as though guilty of having committed an indelicacy. Once he asked Storm, in a whisper, to apologise to Primrose for him. "Tell her I would depress her if I sat by her, my boy." He squeezed Storm's arm, sighed heavily, and moved on along the corridor, wagging his head.

Wilfred had hardly recovered from the news of Cousin Hubertus' death, and regained some of his usual high spirits, when, a week before Christmas, Primrose died. Wilfred, however, seemed inured to the situation, so that Primrose's death did not have the same effect upon him that Hubertus' had done. He was more resigned in his manner now, especially as the surgeon had assured them all weeks before that it was unlikely Primrose would recover.

"My one regret," said Wilfred, "is that she did not live to see John come back. It would have been a great c-c-consolation to her, I'm sure."

Some two or three weeks later, however, when the ship arrived with John, Wilfred had to admit that perhaps it was as well that Primrose had died before John's return, for John was accompanied by a wife— a tall, slim girl with blue eyes and light-brown hair. She was at least two inches taller than John, but she was as quiet and unassuming as John, and with the same shyish manner.

"I thought I would spring Mary on you as a surprise," said John. "I'm sure Mother would have liked her." He seemed stunned to hear of his mother's death, but only for an hour or so. He was very much in love with his wife, and this factor, it was obvious, would have compensated for the most disastrous piece of news that could have been communicated to him.

Wilfred took an immediate liking to his daughter-in-law. "You remind me so much of my sister," he told her. "Poor dear Rosalind. The same height. And the same eyes. The same sweet, k-k-kindly manner."

Mary seemed very happy to be among them, and fitted herself into their way of life without any difficulty. She became a favourite of the children—at least, of Graham and Hermine. Dirk looked upon her with suspicion. He avoided her whenever possible, and she noticed it. One morning after breakfast she met Dirk in the compound near the orange trees and smiled and said: "Dirk, where are you off to? Come and take a walk with me as far as the river."

"It is called the Creek—not the river. The Canje Creek."

She laughed. "Thanks for correcting me. Will you come with me?"

"Mynheer Hiemens will be here at any instant. I'm sorry."

"Are you so fond of your lessons? I wouldn't have thought so."

"I'm not—but I must learn to read and write, mustn't I?"

She hesitated, staring at him. He returned her stare—defiantly, coldly.

"You don't like me, Dirk, do you?"

Dirk stiffened. He shrugged, and turned off. "You're not a van Groenwegel," he said. "Why should I like you?"

John became very popular with the families on the Creek and the Berbice River. His practice was assured from the outset, for doctors were extremely few; most people depended upon the incompetent surgeons, as they were called, for medical attendance. These surgeons were not qualified men; their knowledge was purely empirical. Virtually all of them treated their patients by guess.

John had a high opinion of the midwives, however. "Their knowledge may be based on experience," he said, "but in their case experience has been an excellent teacher. That Mrs. Clarke, the widow, for instance. She is excellent. I would trust her with any accouchement."

"You have no need to inform us of that, my boy," said Wilfred. "We know Mrs. Clarke. She has delivered all my p-p-precious little grands. A fine woman! She has character, I warrant."

John and Mary accompanied Storm and Elizabeth to the ball at Colony House in June that year, for it was in June that van Batenburg arrived to resume his post as Governor under the British. Though their old gay selves, both van Batenburg and his wife showed signs of the strain of the past year. They looked thinner and pale, and van Batenburg was inclined to lose his temper over trifles.

It was shortly after this ball that an important letter arrived from Edward. In it Edward said that Cousin Hubertus had bequeathed Plantation Kaywana to himself and Luise, and that out of sentiment he intended to keep the estate in the family, though it would be difficult to manage his own plantation on the East Coast as well as Plantation Kaywana on the East Bank. . . . "However, I have secured a fairly dependable manager, and I feel that there is little to fear for at least the next two or three years.

"And now, my dear Storm and Elizabeth, I come to a delicate but most important subject. As you may perhaps have conjectured—from rumour and so forth—Cousin Hubertus was an extremely virile man, and it is not for any of us to look back in a spirit of censure upon his relations with certain of his female slaves. Sufficient for me to say that it has come to my knowledge, through Overgaar and Groud, his old overseers, who, during the latter years of his life, became his close companions, that a child resulted from one of these encounters. Cousin Hubertus himself spoke to me in a somewhat indirect manner of a child by some woman called Sarah, and this was some years before his death. Also, on his deathbed, he reminded me about the matter. I could not remember precisely who Sarah was, but, nevertheless, promised him that I would do what I could for both the woman and her child, a daughter by the name of Rose.

"Some weeks after the death of our beloved relative, Overgaar and Groud came to me and intimated that the woman Sarah, very naturally, was anxious to learn what their fate was to be. Cousin Hubertus applied for manumission papers immediately on the birth of the child in 1800, and both mother and child are now free people, but, though free, they have been dependent upon Cousin Hubertus for a livelihood. The mother is now concerned to know whether this support will be withdrawn; she pleads that Cousin Hubertus promised faithfully that she and her daughter would be taken care of after his death, and in this she is telling nothing but the truth. However, as I have said, the matter is an extremely delicate one. What am I to do for the child, especially? The mother, I have decided, can be given a gratuity, and I intend to find proper quarters for her in Stabroek, and set her up as a peddler of provisions, a proposal that meets her approval entirely, for she is eager to make her own way in the world.

"The child, however, is a different proposition. I have seen her, Storm and Elizabeth, and she is a lovely little creature, more white than black—of a pale olive complexion, and with features of European mould. Moreover, she may be tainted, it is true, with black blood, but she is Cousin Hubertus's flesh and blood, and for this reason I think we should do something better for her than leave her to be brought up as the daughter of a peddler.

"Here in Demerary, it would be awkward to adopt her into the family, but in Berbice, where virtually nothing is known of Cousin Hubertus, could it not be arranged by you that this child be adopted by some respectable coloured family somewhat above the degree of the peddler class? A seamstress, for instance, should be most suitable —or perchance one of these good ladies upon whom Governor van Batenburg has bestowed his bounty as well as his offspring. I wish you would consider this matter carefully, and write to me intimating what can be done for this little lady who carries our blood in her veins and who, if only for that reason alone, deserves to be given a proper upbringing. . . ."

Elizabeth had no sooner read this letter when she offered the solution.

"Mrs. Clarke, Storm. She is a widow, and childless. She has more than once expressed a regret that she does not possess a child of her own. I'm sure she would be overjoyed at the idea of adopting this little girl."

The very next day Mrs. Clarke was called to New Signal. She was a well-built lady of sallow complexion and greying, frizzy hair of a reddish tint. Her grey-brown eyes were steady and full of character; her whole mien inspired immediate confidence, and her deportment was that of a lady. She had been brought up in the home of her father, an Irish planter from Barbados, who had settled in the Essequibo some twenty years previously and had eventually found his way to Berbice. Unmarried and childless, except for the daughter borne him by a slave, he had freed the child, who had been named Kathleen, and had her brought up by his housekeeper in the plantation house. She had married a shoemaker, also a free person, but he had died within a year of the marriage, and it was at this stage that Kathleen Clarke had decided to take up midwifery as a livelihood.

Mrs. Clarke expressed her delight in very definite manner. "Nothing would please me better, Mynheer van Groenwegel. As I've told you many a time, I have always regretted not having a child. I can promise to take very good care of this little girl. You won't have cause to be disappointed, I'm sure."

"I am fairly sure of that, too, Mrs. Clarke," smiled Storm. "But tell me, would you object to permitting her to bear your name?"

"Certainly not, mynheer. It would be an honour."

Storm wrote Edward without delay: "Provided you approve of this lady—and, I can assure you, we here know her well and can recommend her highly—and also provided the child's own mother does not find the wrench too great, I see no reason why we should not proceed immediately to arrange for her coming. And be sure, Edward," Storm went on, "that both Elizabeth and myself shall keep an eye on the child and satisfy ourselves that her education is not neglected nor her welfare in other respects."

Edward replied saying that Storm had taken a great weight of anxiety off his shoulders. "Yes, Storm, I was anxious—more than anxious over this little mortal, and when you see her you will understand why. She seems a born lady. I have spoken to her mother, Sarah, also a surprisingly fine woman, and, though black, also one of Nature's ladies. I suspect that Cousin Hubertus must have spent some time training her in the graces of behaviour and deportment, and she, in turn, has tried to train her daughter in the same manner. As I say, I spoke to Sarah, and she is in complete agreement with the plan we have formulated on the child's behalf. She, also, is anxious that Rose should be given a proper upbringing, and she is resigned to being separated from her. I have told her that whenever she desires to see her I can make arrangements for her to travel to Berbice, or for Rose to travel to Demerary, whichever would be the more convenient, for I think it would be most inhumane if she were not to be permitted to see her daughter at intervals. . . . I am sure you will agree with me in this. . . ."

Two evenings later Graham went to his parents' room to get the key for the canister. For two or three weeks he had done nothing about reading the documents in the canister, but today he decided to devote an hour at least to some serious study of the papers. Every two or three months he would develop the craze to delve into the canister, then the urge would die down, and he would leave the storeroom to itself. A fortnight ago he had found a letter written by his grandfather Jacques to his grandmother Faustina, who had been in the Essequibo (Jacques had courted her by post). It was a letter that had evidently never been sent off, and Graham could understand why. It was a highly erotic thing, and Jacques must have thought it wise to keep it to himself.

Graham had just taken the key from the drawer of the writing table in his parents' room when the sight of two letters on the table attracted his attention. He recognised the handwriting at once. The letters were from his Uncle Edward in Demerary.

Without hesitation Graham read the letters.

6

R O S E was sent to Berbice by ship, in the care of one of
Edward's female slaves. Storm went to New Amsterdam to
receive her. He brought her back to New Signal, despite
his own misgivings about this procedure. He had suggested to Elizabeth that it would have created less gossip if he had taken the child
immediately to Mrs. Clarke, but Elizabeth had disagreed.

"That would only cause more speculation, dear," said Elizabeth.
"Bring her here first, and we'll announce that she is from Demerary,
and is intended for adoption by Mrs. Clarke. Then Mrs. Clarke can
come here and take her away. The straightforward way is often the
best sometimes, Storm."

When the yatch, as a tent-boat was also called, drew in by the little
stelling, Elizabeth and the children were awaiting it. Elizabeth had
informed the children that Rose was an orphan from their uncle's
plantation. "Like Jacob, she needs protection. Her father was probably an overseer, just as Jacob's father is."

"Are we going to keep her here?" asked Dirk, with a frown.

"No, my boy. Mrs. Clarke will come for her, but occasionally she
will be allowed to come here and play with you all and Jacob."

Graham said nothing. He was feeling guilty, because he knew what
the other children did not know, and he felt that he had obtained the
knowledge by underhand means. He had had no right to read the
letters Uncle Edward had written to his father and mother. Yet, in a
way, he was not sorry that he knew the truth. He had decided that he
would keep what he knew a secret from the other children. Only to
Nibia had he confided what he had learnt. To keep a secret from
Nibia was unthinkable. He was tense and fidgety as he watched the
yatch draw alongside the *stelling*, for his curiosity was unbearable.

What sort of creature was this Rose? Would he be disappointed in her, or would she live up to Uncle Edward's description of her?

The instant he saw her he knew that his uncle had not exaggerated. She was pretty, and she had the air of a little lady. Storm himself lifted her out on to the *stelling*, and Elizabeth moved forward to receive her.

Rose looked up and smiled shyly. She had blue-green eyes, and was of a pale olive complexion. Her hair was dark brown and wavy, but not frizzy in the negroid manner. And as Edward had said in his letter, her features were of European mould, though the wide nostrils betrayed the black blood.

Elizabeth made the children shake hands with her, and told them: "I want you to be very nice to Rose when she comes to play with you sometimes, children."

"Why?" asked Dirk. "Is she related to us?"

Both Storm and Elizabeth started and exchanged glances, as Graham did not fail to notice. Storm looked angry, and Elizabeth flushed. "Must she be related to you before you can be nice to her, Dirk?" said Elizabeth, her tone very sharp—and Dirk, in turn, flushed, and growled: "I didn't say that. Jacob is not related to me and I'm nice to him. I only asked."

"For a boy of nine," said his father, "your manner is most unbecoming."

Dirk made no reply, but he flashed Rose a glance of resentment—almost of hatred. Graham, also angry, glared at him, then turned to Rose and smiled. "You needn't be afraid, Rose," he said. "We'll be nice to you. Dirk is a pig."

Rose, more shy than ever, merely hung her head, saying nothing.

Two days later, when Storm told them that it had been decided to allow Rose to join them at lessons under Mr. Hiemens, Dirk said: "Father, what of Jacob? Isn't he to be educated, too? He wants to learn to read and write."

"Jacob will be taught a trade," said Storm. "I'm arranging to have him put in the care of a carpenter in New Amsterdam some time next year."

"That's unjust," Dirk retorted, his voice impassioned. "Mynheer Frick is his father, and Mynheer Frick is an overseer. Why can't he be given the same treatment as Rose if Rose's father is also an overseer?"

Storm gave him an icy look. "Since when have you decided to instruct me in the ways of justice, Dirk?"

Dirk said nothing more. He turned off, his eyes as icy as his father's. Raccoon's eyes, thought Graham. The eyes Uncle Edward had portrayed in the picture in the sitting-room.

It rained heavily that day, and Dirk and Jacob went swimming in the late afternoon. They swam in the punt canal aback, and when they emerged, sat on the bank in the steady, coarse drizzle. Across the canal, on the other bank where the jungle began, bullfrogs were croaking, and crickets beginning to churr, for night was well on the way. The air smelt fresh and clean and filled with the rank vegetable smell of wild plants and rain-wet trees. The rain did not bother the two boys, for they were accustomed to expeditions of this kind.

Dirk said, hugging his legs: "I spoke to Father about you, but he doesn't feel you ought to learn to read and write. He says you're to be sent to some carpenter in New Amsterdam to be taught a trade. Carpentering, I suppose."

Jacob nodded. He was not a very emotional boy. He had Storm's green eyes, though Frick, the overseer, also had green eyes, and no one was any the wiser. His hair was very curly, and in complexion he was a rather deep olive. "Marta told me long time ago that I got to take up a trade."

"It isn't just," said Dirk, frowning. "You said you'd like to learn to read and write, didn't you? If Rose can take lessons with us, why can't you? Isn't she half black as you are? Isn't her father an overseer, too?"

"One day I will try and learn by myself," said Jacob.

"I know what, Jacob. I'll teach you."

"You? How you can do that?"

"I can read and write already, can't I? I'll teach you. Every afternoon I'll come to your logie and teach you some Dutch and English. You must know both. And I'll get a quill for you, and paper, and show you how to write."

"You're good, Dirk. I always know you're good. Marta say that plenty time. But how we'll go swimming and hunting if I got to learn lessons in the afternoon in the logie?"

"We'll do it, no fear. We needn't spend *all* the afternoon doing lessons, you goat. Let's take another plunge. I'll race you to the tamarind tree."

Storm and Elizabeth eventually came to hear of this resolve of Dirk's to educate Jacob, and Elizabeth remarked that she doubted whether Dirk would keep to his word. "He is far too selfish a boy."

Storm uttered a grunt, and replied: "He's got subtle depths, that boy. I wouldn't be sure about anything where he is concerned."

And Storm, as it happened, was justified in his doubts, for Dirk did keep to his word. Every afternoon, after dinner, he went to Marta's logie to instruct Jacob in reading and writing. The two boys would spend an hour on lessons, then rush off aback to the canal to swim or frolic about in the bush. Sometimes they laid traps for tapirs or for birds, and sometimes they remained outdoors until it was dark so that they could watch the goatsuckers appear and utter their musical "Hoo-yoo!" cries as they swooped down and alighted on the ground, like mysterious feathery ghosts in the deep dusk.

Graham, at fourteen, began to take an interest in the conversations of his parents and grandfather on political matters. Now and then he would even ask questions and venture opinions of his own.

There was much scope for his interest within the next year or two, for the political situation in Berbice became more chaotic than it had ever been known to be in former years. Since his return as Governor, van Batenburg seemed to have soured. From the gay, liberal, easy-living individual he had been before his departure for Holland in 1803, he had now become irritable and inclined to pry into affairs too closely and with too much bureaucratic zeal. His popularity waned, and soon he began to acquire the reputation of a tyrant.

One day he quarrelled with the members of the Court of Policy, the governing body in Berbice, and dismissed two members outright, appointing two others to take their place without even consulting the populace. Next he made new port laws on his own, refusing to be advised by the members of the Court of Policy, as was customary; these new laws prevented the merchants and planters from sending their produce to Demerary for shipment to England or for barter with Demerary contractors. The result was that plantation stores and supplies generally obtained in Stabroek could not be had, and the planters began to complain of grave shortages and much inconvenience.

Wilfred expressed his disappointment in the Governor, and attended several of the meetings called by Lambert Blair, the planter who was most violent in his attacks on the Governor. These meetings were

held in a tavern in New Amsterdam, and one afternoon Wilfred returned home with the news that van Batenburg had sent soldiers to
the tavern to stop the discussion.

"This is an unheard-of infringement of our rights!" cried Wilfred.
"Think of it! The m-m-military! Interrupting a meeting, and declaring
that the tavern will, in future, be closed!"

Storm could not believe it. "How could he close the tavern! Such an
act is unheard of. He's going too far now."

"He's a tyrant," said Graham, who was on the portico with the
rest of them. "We should have him sent away."

"Blair won't leave the matter like this, you may be sure," said
Wilfred. "Van Batenburg has met his m-m-match in Blair, damme!
Blair says he will send a petition to England, p-p-protesting the in-
justices being practised on us."

"I heard Mr. Lafferty saying he'd heard about a new tax," said
Graham.

"That's correct, my boy," Wilfred confirmed. "Acre gelt, he calls it.
It's nothing but sheer spitefulness. And to act without the authority of
the Council is m-most unconstitutional. I shall refuse to pay any such
tax."

"No fear," murmured Storm. "He'll wait in vain for me to pay."

"Who is the owner of our plantation, Father?" asked Graham. "Is
it you or Grandpa?" And Storm told him: "Your grandfather and I
own it jointly."

Elizabeth, silent up to now, said: "I believe it is his health. He is
not well. Madame van Batenburg hinted to me at the last ball that
he was ailing."

"Naturally," smiled Storm, "you would find some such excuse for
him."

Elizabeth's theory, however, might not have been very far off the
mark, for when van Batenburg was called to England to answer the
charges made against him, it was known that he was in poor health.
He sailed for Barbados with the intention of recuperating before going
on to England, but died in that island on the tenth of November of
that same year, 1806.

The women of Berbice were the ones who mourned his passing;
the feelings of the men were mixed, especially as at this time a far
more serious cause for worry than van Batenburg's tyranny had loomed
up.

Governor Bentinck of Demerary had announced at a meeting of the Council in that colony that the British Parliament was shortly to pass a measure abolishing the slave trade. The Anti-Slavery Party in England were, at last, to have their way.

At first, the idea was laughed at. It was too absurd to be considered, felt most of the planters. Why, it would mean the end of all colonisation. As Jim Lafferty remarked to Storm: "Such a measure could never be passed. England depends upon her West Indian colonies for the bulk of her wealth. What would happen to the merchants in Bristol if the slave trade were abandoned? Parliament would never be so idiotic as to let a thing like this go through."

Of late, however, a cloud of fear had begun to gather, and there were many who thought that the Anti-Slavery Party was stronger than rumour had assessed it to be. Cornelius Heffer, one Sunday when he and his family were having breakfast at New Signal, said gloomily: "They are a fanatical group, Storm. I have spoken to several reliable people in the tavern, and they agree that Parliament won't be able to balk this measure. And these fellows I spoke to should know. They had just arrived from Bristol and are very conversant with the situation."

Elizabeth noticed that both Dirk and Graham—the children were now considered old enough to be allowed to eat at table with the grownups—listened very intently to all that was said on the new crisis. Within recent months Dirk, like Graham, had begun to take a serious interest in the affairs of the plantation, and once Elizabeth had overheard Dirk saying to Jacob: "One day when I'm master here I shall make you an overseer—my head overseer."

When the meal was over, Dirk and Graham went on to the back veranda, where Jacob was awaiting them. Dirk asked anxiously: "Did they give you a good meal in the kitchen, Jacob?" And when Jacob nodded and said: "Yes. Janki always feed me well," Dirk grunted ominously, his eleven-year-old face assuming a grim expression, and growled: "She had better, if she doesn't want a thrashing from me. She can be very impertinent sometimes."

Hermine, who had appeared just in time to overhear him, said: "You'd better be careful how you treat her, Dirk. Yesterday she complained that you kicked her because she was slow in bringing up water to the bathroom."

"So I did," snapped Dirk. "And she deserved it. These slaves need a kick or thump now and then to keep them active. They are too lazy."

"They are human," frowned Graham. "They can feel as you and I can. I disagree with being cruel to them."

Dirk sniffed. "You're repeating just what the Anti-Slavery Party in England keeps whining about. Human! They're slaves. Animals. They were made to be subservient, and it would be a mistake to treat them like human beings."

"You are an evil boy," said Hermine. "Satan is in you."

Dirk laughed. "I'm tired of hearing that nonsense. Who is Satan? A figment of the predicant's fancy. Do you believe in Satan, Jacob?"

Jacob smiled, trying to be neutral because of the presence of Graham and Hermine, but, secretly, definitely on the side of Dirk. His loyalty to Dirk was absolute. To go against any opinion of Dirk's was, for Jacob, unthinkable. "That is jumbie talk," said Jacob. "Satan is only a jumbie, and what is a jumbie? Only slaves believe in jumbie."

"One day," said Graham, "slaves as well as white men will be taught about God and Satan and the Bible. They are black, but they are human. They have a right to be instructed in religion and to partake in religious services like Christians."

Dirk hooted. "Those black boboons! What can they want to know anything for about Christ and God! They came from the jungle of Africa. They're heathens, and they must be made to remain heathens. It's bad enough the English want to abolish the slave trade, but what will happen if we begin to teach these slaves about Christ? They'll soon feel they're our equals, by God. Eh, Jacob?"

"Quite right," nodded Jacob. "Better to leave them just as they are."

"You're half slave, don't you forget, Jacob," frowned Hermine.

"But he's free!" snapped Dirk instantly, his eyes like glittering pebbles. "Father secured his manumission papers years ago, and you know that!"

"Let's go and do lessons, Dirk," said Jacob uncomfortably. But Dirk said: "No. We'll look at those letters in the canister, Jacob. Father has promised me the key for the canister. I spoke to him about it this morning, and he said I could have it this evening. Let's go and get it, Jacob, and leave these two slave lovers to themselves."

"You'll find the key," said Graham coldly, "in the left-hand drawer of the writing table in Father's room. And I should advise you to handle those papers carefully. Some of them are very flimsy."

It was a Sunday in December in that year 1806, the Sunday before Christmas, and it was after noon, and the sky outside the house a dull sheet of grey-white cloud from which an uncertain, sparse drizzle fell, though the sun shone through palely, and the air was steamy and damp and warm. It was not an unusual December day, this first day on which Dirk opened the canister to go through the letters of his forebears.

The first letter he took up, as it happened, was dated December 11, 1709, and began: "Dear Jabez, Christmas will soon be here, but I am not looking forward to this day with much joy. I shall tell you why I am not . . ."

Jacob sniggered as he leant over Dirk's shoulder to read the letter. "Who is he now? Jabez? You know who is Jabez?"

"One of my ancestors," said Dirk. He turned the sheet of paper over, and after frowning at it for a second or two, announced: "It is signed by somebody called Adrian. See if you can make it out. Isn't that Adrian?"

Jacob began to frown, too, but, at length, nodded and said: "Yes, it look like Adrian. Must be another of your old people."

"Yes. Sit down, Jacob. Open that other window. We must have some more light. This is important. I want to read about my ancestors. We're a great family, don't forget." His head jerked round. "Do you hear me, Jacob? Don't you ever forget that."

7

ONE afternoon, not quite two years later—in August 1808—
Graham and Hermine and Rose were sitting on the portico
watching the sky darken over the sapodilla trees in the east.
The compound was dry and dusty, for rain had not fallen for several
days, and this was the dry season when the sun was always at its hottest,
and when unexpected thunderstorms came roaring up from the Corentyne Coast, sometimes lasting the whole night.

Perhaps it was one of the long-lasting ones that was approaching
now, thought Graham. He hugged himself, not afraid so much as
excited. Thunderstorms frightened him, yet created in him a feeling
of heroism. He would think of himself defying the thunder and lightning and the rain and rushing out of the house to go and rescue some
girl in danger. A slave girl, or Susan Lafferty, Jim Lafferty's elder
sister, who was nineteen, only two years older than himself. A *camoudie*
was chasing her through the *mucca-mucca* shrubs on the bank of the
creek, and she was unaware of her danger as she hurried home. But
Graham, in some miraculous manner, had divined her plight, and so
he rushed out of the house to go to her rescue. As he dashed through
the storm he told himself that it was Susan he was going to help,
then would change his mind and decide that it was Melia, the girl
who lived in the logie near the large water tank. He had seen her
undressed, and had shivered with desire for her. Anything could
happen after he had rescued her.

Hermine and Rose were talking about the orange preserves Mrs.
Clarke, Rose's adopted mother, was good at making. Rose, at eight,
was a talkative little thing, and more pretty than Hermine could ever
hope to be, thought Graham. One day he could see her like Melia,
shapely and desirable. . . . He stirred and rose.

"Where is Dirk, do you know, Hermine?" he asked.

"He and Jacob went off towards the Creek a little while ago," said Hermine. At sixteen, Hermine was tall, but not too developed in figure, and though she had lovely hair like their mother's, she was not pretty in face. Her nose was too short, and her jaw too square. She had very kindly eyes, though, thought Graham, and he was fond of her. She was good to Rose—and to the slaves.

Graham loved the slaves, and regarded with favour any white person who treated slaves well. He smiled to himself and thought: I think I know why I'm so passionately fond of the slaves. It's because of Nibia. I'll never be able to forget those nights when I was a small fellow and she used to let me fondle her breasts before I settled down to sleep. And she has been so kind to me in other ways. But for her, I would have suffered terribly from a multitude of fears. For me, there is nothing but love and kindness associated with a dark skin.

Thunder rumbled in the distance, and Rose squealed and said: "Hermine, I should go home, don't you think? It's going to rain, and Mother will be anxious."

"It doesn't matter," smiled Hermine. "You could sleep with me."

"I like sleeping with you. I hope it rains, then."

Graham, biting his thumb, ignored them and continued to stare introspectively out at the darkening scene. . . . That sky reminds me of everything that has been happening to us in this colony, he mused. A dark cloud seems to have appeared over the whole colony during the past few months. All the planters are worried about this new edict concerning the abolition of the slave trade. The price of slaves has gone up tremendously, and their numbers have already begun to dwindle. I heard Grandpa saying that the sales of our produce are virtually at a standstill. And the bond warehouses in British ports are getting filled up with unsaleable consignments. He says Parliament is about to appoint a committee to look into the matter. There is talk of securing labourers from the Eastern countries—India or China and Japan. No, not Japan. It was some other country Grandpa mentioned. Perhaps Malta, or some name like that. . . . Anyway, it seems as if we are faced with ruin. What a pity. Because I feel the British Parliament was right in stopping the slave trade. It is horrible to think of those poor fellows stacked down in the holds of ships and dying on the way from Africa, and then being treated so badly by the crew when they did manage to survive. Only Dirk cannot see the evil in such a system. He is a strange fellow. And now that he has taken up so hotly with this canister of letters he is stranger than ever. Always talking about the Old Blood, and the family. The family. The family. He cannot utter a word nowadays without mentioning the van Groenwegels and their greatness as a family.

I myself, thought Graham, am proud of being a van Groenwegel, but I cannot agree about the greatness. Those letters show that our forebears were cruel. Is it a virtue to be cruel? Does cruelty make one great?

Thunder again. Nearer and louder. Graham hugged himself again. The rain would soon be down, and the compound would lose its dustiness and become slushy, and the lightning would crackle and dart its fiery fingers amidst the foliage of the trees. The whole house would vibrate in the clatter of thunder. Where could Dirk and Jacob have gone to, he wondered?

At this same instant, Dirk and Jacob were squatting before the logie of an old slave, Cushy, and listening to stories of the old days. Cushy was nearly seventy, and he had been a young man in his twenties when the Berbice insurrection occurred. He was Nibia's father, and Jacob had persuaded him to talk, for Cushy was not fond of talking about the old days. Jacob had traded on the fact that Cushy was proud of his half-white grandson, and Jacob, egged on by Dirk, who was determined to get as much information out of Cushy as possible, had, at last, succeeded. This was the first time they had been able to hear Cushy's account of what had happened during the insurrection.

". . . I was with Atta's men, and we had our camp near Magdalenenburg. Not good thing to talk about, Massa Dirk. Ow! Not good. Hear? Thunder roll. Rain coming. You better go back to the house, Massa. Jacob, go back, boy."

Dirk clicked his tongue and said: "Continue. What is a little thunder! It won't hurt us. We can sit inside your logie if it rains. The stink will be annoying, but I can tolerate it for a short while, I suppose. Go on. Tell us about Atta. He was one of the leaders of the rebels, wasn't he?"

"Yes, Massa Dirk. Atta and Cuffy and Akkara, they was the big leaders. I never like them. They force me to join with them. I was on the Teuffer plantation high up the Berbice. The Teuffers was related to your family, massa. One of the Essequibo people marry a Teuffer, and I remember a Missy Juliana——"

"Did you know her? Did you see her?" Dirk lent forward eagerly, his thirteen-year-old face flushed, his grey-green eyes flashing a light-ning of fervour that caused Cushy to cringe back instinctively.

Cushy, uncertain, almost a little afraid, nodded and murmured: "Yes, massa. I know Missy Juliana. I see her plenty time. I see when her baby get drown, and I see when they capture her——"

"Did they capture her? By God! The brutes! I always wondered about her. Those letters, Jacob! Do you remember? In two of them there was mention of Juliana. She was Father's aunt—a sweet person, by all accounts. But she didn't live on the Canje. She went to the Berbice, but it wasn't clear whether she married somebody there, or what happened to her eventually."

"She married a Teuffer, massa. Brave woman. Ow. Brave woman, Missy Juliana. I don't like talk about it, massa." Cushy groaned, and they saw his eyes grow watery. "Spare me, Massa Dirk. It hurt me heart to talk about those days."

"Oh, don't be soft. Talk away," snapped Dirk. "This is important. What happened to Missy Juliana? You say she was captured by those black brutes?"

"Yes, Massa. She get captured. Ow! The suffering that poor missy see. And she so brave. They never break her spirit. She brave to the end."

"In what way was she brave? Talk on. Tell me everything you remember."

"You won't like it, massa. Better go home. Rain coming."

Dirk uttered a snarling sound. "Jacob, speak to him. I'm going to strike him if he makes me lose my patience. I *must* hear what he has to say."

Jacob spoke to his grandfather in a pleading voice. "Talk, Grandpa. No matter how bad it is. Tell Massa Dirk all you remember. He want to hear."

So Cushy began to talk—but now there was apparent in his manner just a trace of spite. It was as though, finally piqued by Dirk's arrogant manner, he had decided to tell all, and tell it so that Dirk would feel the full impact of the horror about which he had been warned.

Dirk felt it. Once he sprang up with a cry. "What! Spat in her bowl of food! A van Groenwegel!" He trembled, his hands clenched. "I wish I were there! Oh, I only wish I were there!"

A moment later he interrupted Cushy with a shriek. "You're lying! You're lying! That could never have happened! A black pig like Atta! In bed with—with my great-aunt! Where was everybody else? Why didn't the other white men do something about it? How could they let such a thing happen?"

Rain began to come down in large, sparse drops.

Cushy stumbled to his feet and retreated into his logie. Jacob followed him, but Dirk, though he stood up, did not move in after them. Dirk glared at the old man and barked: "Did I give you permission to go in, Cushy? Come out here at once and continue to talk!"

"Massa Dirk, de rain falling. Come in out the rain, me massa."

Dirk's hands clenched. "I order you to come back out of that logie, Cushy!"

Jacob growled: "Don't be foolish, Dirk. You getting wet. Come in."

"He's a slave, isn't he? Is it in his place to disobey me?"

Cushy tittered uncomfortably, shaking his head. "Boy, you young yet. You mustn't talk that way. Ow! The misery I see in this world before you born."

Dirk advanced a pace. "I shall strike you, Cushy! Do you hear me? Obey me this instant and come back out here. I won't enter your stinking logie."

Jacob laughed. "Stop all that talk, Dirk. It's my grandpa."

Dirk, the rain beginning to soak his clothes, for it was now a steady, heavy downpour, breathed hard and swallowed. He looked shamefaced and said: "You are right, I suppose. I'm being a fool. This is most undignified. Come and let's get back to the house, Jacob."

Jacob obeyed at once, and they began to run towards the house. Abruptly, however, Dirk stopped and said: "Let's not go in right now, Jacob. Let's imagine we're after a party of rebels in 1763. We're tracking them to their headquarters at Magdalenenburg through the pouring rain. We're defying the elements because we're two brave van Groenwegels who won't be scared by God, man, or dirty slaves. What do you say?"

Jacob, who understood this kind of talk, agreed without hesitation. He grinned and replied: "Good. Off we go! After the dirty rebels! We'll burn them at the stake when we catch them."

"And we'll torture Atta before we burn him," said Dirk. Lightning clicked and forked amidst the trees in the near distance, and thunder prattled like the sound of a million muskets through the savage hissing of the rain. Dirk and Jacob laughed their defiance and set out at a trot towards the *mucca-mucca* shrubs that could be seen hazily in the darkening afternoon beyond the orange and sapodilla trees. They bent low as they went, imaginary muskets in their grasp.

From the portico of the house Graham saw them and cried: "There they are! Dirk and Jacob! Where could they be off to in this storm!"

"Why trouble about Dirk?" laughed Hermine. "Dirk is mad."

Graham said nothing, but as he frowned out at the two retreating figures he was disturbed. Why he should be disturbed he could not explain. Could it be that he was really envious of Dirk? Of late, everyone was calling Dirk mad, but mixed with their amusement was admiration. Only yesterday Grandpa had tittered and said: "That boy —he's quite off his head, but he has spirit, damme!" And Susan Lafferty and Lumea van Niffens had said openly that they liked him. Dirk was a brutal, arrogant boy. Did Susan and Lumea admire brutality and arrogance?

A ball of fire burst over the trees and thunder crashed down after it like a hundred cannon going off all at the same time.

Graham winced, and turning, hurried inside.

About two weeks later Storm made an announcement. Jacob was to be sent to New Amsterdam to begin his apprenticeship as a carpenter's assistant. All arrangements had been made, and Jacob must be ready to leave on the following day.

Contrary to expectations, Dirk indulged in no wild outburst of rage. He went pale, but he was calm. He said: "It had to come about. We knew it, and we've planned for it. We've made a pact between us—a pact of loyalty. I shall never betray him—and he will never betray me. We shall be friends until we die."

Elizabeth and Storm stared at him, struck by the intensity of his manner. His eyes were cold and hard as he spoke, and his hands tightly clenched.

Storm chuckled and said: "Considering that you have taught him to read and write, he, at least, should have reason to be perpetually grateful to you."

Dirk said nothing. They were all in the sitting-room having morning coffee, for it was raining and the portico was wet and uninviting. Wilfred, in a new scarlet morning gown, uttered old-man titterings, watching Dirk with affectionate indulgence over his cup. Then Hermine, seated with Graham on a couch under the big family portrait, asked: "What name is Jacob going to take, Father?"

Storm glanced at her sharply—so sharply that Graham noted it—and said: "His father's name, of course. Frick. Jacob Frick. Why do you ask?"

"Only because once I did hear Marta and Nibia arguing over something. Marta seemed to feel that Frick was not Jacob's father."

Storm stirred in his chair and clicked his tongue. "You should be more careful how you pay attention to talk among the slaves, Hermine."

"Marta and Nibia are always quarrelling over some nonsense," said Hermine. "I never pay heed to what they say."

"Jacob doesn't resemble Frick," said Graham.

"I don't like the name Frick," Dirk put in. "I've told Jacob it would be much better if he adopted a name that sounded grander. I suggested Greenfield."

Elizabeth and Hermine laughed. "Why Greenfield?" asked Elizabeth. And Dirk told her: "Because it seems an elegant sort of name in an English way, and it's not far from Groenwegel in sound."

Elizabeth glanced at Storm. "Perhaps he could adopt the name of Greenfield, Storm dear. Why not ask him what is his preference in the matter?"

Storm, however, shook his head. "The name Frick is good enough. Let him keep that." He frowned at Dirk and added: "Stop putting foolish, romantic ideas into the boy's head, Dirk. You'll soon have him feeling above his station."

Dirk stiffened. "Father, is that the real reason why you want him to go to New Amsterdam to become a carpenter—because he must be made to feel he is beneath us in station?"

Storm flushed. "What do you mean by such a question? Is there any doubt that he is beneath us in station?"

"I didn't say so. Jacob knows his place. He's not white, and he's not a van Groenwegel. But he's a fine fellow. He can beat me in a race from the *koker* to the big tamarind tree when we go swimming in the canal. I don't think he should be treated as if he's a menial—or somebody inferior."

Storm sighed. "This discussion will get us nowhere, I fear. When you're older you'll understand how society functions, my boy. Let us leave it at that."

"There is nothing I don't understand about the society in this colony," snapped Dirk. "What's hard to understand about it? There are white planters and merchants and white overseers, and there are free coloured people who are carpenters and masons and hucksters and seamstresses and suchlike, and whom we white people treat with patronage because of the white blood we've put into them. And then we have the black slaves who must serve us because they were born to that kind of life, and we've paid big sums for them. What's difficult to understand about that?"

Wilfred shook with laughter. "Hee, hee! Damme, Storm, this boy —this young lad will soon be writing some kind of m-m-monograph on social conditions. Eh? What? He's a p-p-professor, by gad! Hee, hee."

"He's too precocious," growled Storm. "I don't particularly admire that kind of learnedness in a boy of his age. It is not becoming."

"Every van Groenwegel worth his salt has been precocious, Father," said Dirk. "Haven't you read the letters in the canister? We're no ordinary family."

"I'm tired of hearing that from you," said Storm. "This family pride of yours is becoming an obsession."

"Which van Groenwegel can read those letters without feeling a deep pride, sir! Have you read about Kaywana and her fight with the Indians who attacked the house, and of how old Willem and Aert fired upon them. And what about the defence of the house on the Mazaruni in 1666? That wasn't anything foolish or small. It was a magnificent event." Dirk's fingers kept tapping against each other rapidly as he spoke, his eyes darting from one to the other of them in a trembling, shifty agitation. "Grandma Hendri was right. We should be proud of our past. We should tell the Tales of Old to our children, and see that our name goes down with honour and glory."

"And should we also be as ruthless and cruel as Grandma Hendri?" asked Graham.

"All life is cruel," snapped Dirk. "And sometimes you have to be ruthless to achieve some big thing. Look at the time when Jacob and I wanted to capture an alligator in the little creek aback. We had to kill a puppy and tie it to a pole as bait. It was a puppy we both liked, but it had to die. The capture of an alligator was more important than the life of a mere puppy."

"I cannot agree with that, Dirk," said his mother.

"Nor can I," said Graham and Hermine in chorus.

"That's because you're soft," said Dirk. "There are two kinds of van Groenwegels—the hard, practical ones, and the soft, sentimental ones. Grandfather Jacques said so in a letter he wrote to Grandma

Faustina. He admitted he was one of the soft ones. Grandma Hendri and Uncle Pedro and Uncle David and the others, they were the hard, practical ones. The fighters."

"And I suppose," said his father, "you are aware what sort of end they suffered?"

"I know. Cushy has told me about it. They were shot down by Atta's men when they were trying to escape from the house. Atta's men lay in ambush for them, the cowardly dogs. Months before, Uncle Pedro and Uncle David and the others stayed in their house and defended it against Cuffy and all his men. They were the only family that didn't run away. They stood up and fought. Isn't that something to be proud about?"

Dirk was on his feet. His head trembled, and his fingers kept curling into the palms of his hands as he glanced at each of them in turn.

Wilfred kept tittering. Storm smoked with an air of bored tolerance, the long pipe stretched out before him, the smoke coiling upward from its bowl in leisurely wisps. Graham frowned at the floor with a troubled air. Hermine smiled faintly in a contemptuous manner. Elizabeth, her hands clasped lightly together in her lap, gazed at the picture of the family, a slightly strained expression on her face. Her gaze seemed centred on the three-year-old infant seated in its mother's lap.

In the silence, they heard the rain outside. A steady, not too heavy downpour. August rain. Dry-weather rain that might fizzle out before noon and give way to fierce, ruthless sunshine. Sunshine that would glitter within the arum-like leaves of the *mucca-mucca*. Sunshine that would be merciless on the black-sage shrubs and the pasture grass on the savannah lands. Sunshine that would set the eddo and cassava leaves into fertile activity so that the roots in the ground would bulge bigger and bigger with their store of starch.

8

THE loss of Jacob as a play-companion affected Dirk's way of life quite considerably, for, unlike Graham and Hermine, who were friendly with several of the children on neighbouring plantations, Dirk had never been a good mixer. He was known as a selfish boy—selfish, proud and standoffish. Other boys did not like him, though their sisters found him attractive and on social occasions indulged in many wiles of coquetry in order to gain his attention; indeed, they employed such bold tactics that sometimes their parents would be compelled to take them to task. Dirk himself reacted with amusement and mild contempt, but this, if anything, only spurred them on to greater efforts.

After Jacob's departure Dirk took to roaming alone in the bush in the late afternoon, though often he would visit the storeroom and spend an hour or more with the canister of letters before sallying out of the house to go off on his lonely expeditions. Occasionally, he stopped at Marta's logie, and sat down with the old woman to question her about the family. Marta, like Cushy, was so old that only very light tasks were allotted to her, and most of her time was spent in her logie—or just outside it—and at almost any time of the afternoon she could be seen sitting on the two steps of the logie, smoking a clay pipe.

Jacob came to New Signal on Sundays, and this was Dirk's happiest day of the week. He and Dirk went swimming and bird hunting, and the routine of the old days seemed never to have been interrupted. Jacob said that he liked his work with Benjamin Green, the carpenter, though Green could be ill-tempered sometimes. He was not bad, though, said Jacob, and the food was ample—and there were two nice daughters who seemed to want to make friends with Jacob, though

Green and his wife were very strict with them and never permitted any familiarity.

"They were surprised to hear I could read and write," grinned Jacob. "I told them that if they like I could teach Millicent and Joanna, but even that didn't make them less strict with the girls. They watch them like cats."

"Be careful with girls, Jacob," frowned Dirk. "They're soft, and they can upset a man's plans. I like them myself, but I never give in to them."

"I don't give in to them, either," said Jacob. "But I like to watch them and hear them laugh." He grinned. "You can get plenty fun with them."

Marta, too, took it upon herself to broach the question of girls with Dirk. "You too lonely, boy," she told him one afternoon as he sat with her on the steps of her logie. "You must seek out friends like your brother and sister. And what about girls? You must make girl friends. Not good to move round with Jacob and nobody else. You will turn woman-hater like your Uncle Raphael."

Dirk started. "Yes, yes. I meant to ask you about him. He's on some plantation on the west bank of the Demerary, isn't he?"

"Yes, he's a good manager, Massa Raphael, but he don't like girls. Dress up and powder up himself, and always want to got boys round him. Not good, that."

"You mean he isn't married? He has no children?"

"No, he won't get married. He never have nothing to do with women."

"You knew him well, I suppose, in Demerary?"

"I come from Demerary with your grandfather and your father and mother, boy. I must know Massa Raphael. I know all your family —Massa Hubertus and Missy Rosalind, Missy Faustina, Massa Cranley, Massa Graeme. And all your cousins, Massa Edward and Missy Luise and Missy Mary."

Dirk began to rub his hands together, then frowned and began to tap his fingers against each other in an agitated manner he had sometimes. "No fear," he told Marta. "I shall marry and have children. The family name must be carried on. And I shall train all my children to be careful to respect our traditions."

"Your what, Massa Dirk?"

"Our traditions. The Old Blood, Marta. Those letters in the canister have shown me what an exciting lot of things have happened to my ancestors, and how some of them were soft and some hard. I want my children to be hard. Hard people will do things and get somewhere, bring power and glory to the name of the family. But soft people will bring us only disgrace and—and a fading out of our name. Graham is soft, and he'll probably train his children to be silly fools. But my children must be daring, brave van Groenwegels."

Marta watched him with affection, shaking with old-lady laughter. She relighted her clay pipe and said: "Boy, you young yet. You will forget all that talk when you turn a man."

"Never. Those letters have taught me what I want to know, and I shall never cease to want to live up to the glory of the past, Marta." He shook his head, his eyes shifty with fervour. "Oh, what a pity Jacob isn't white and a van Groenwegel! The two of us would have worked together in the cause of the family."

Marta grunted, and giving him a sly look, said: "You sure Jacob not a van Groenwegel?" And Dirk snapped: "What do you mean?"

"Ssssh! Awright, Massa Dirk. Only fun old Marta making."

Dirk stared at her suspiciously. "What sort of fun is that? You can't say things like that in fun, Marta. You know something about Jacob. Wasn't Frick really his father? I've heard it said more than once that there was some doubt about his father—and Nibia has never spoken about Frick as if he once had something to do with her, and she talks about all her men friends."

"Ssssh! Boy, you on a dangerous matter. Hold your tongue."

"I won't. You must tell me, Marta. Who is Jacob's father?"

Marta was silent for a moment, then she said quietly: "You not a stupid boy, Massa Dirk. I believe I can trust you, but you got to swear you will never tell a soul what I tell you this afternoon. Not a soul. Not even Jacob."

"You needn't have any fear about that. I talk to no one. Well, that isn't true. Jacob and I have no secrets. He is the only one I talk to freely. We have a pact of loyalty between us, you see. We shall never betray each other."

"But even to he you mustn't say nothing about this, Massa Dirk. Promise?"

"Very well. Since it's the only way I can get you to tell me, I promise."

And so Marta told him: "Massa Storm, your father—it's he who is Jacob's father, boy. You and Jacob is half brothers."

Dirk went very white, and his fingers grew still, intertwined to form a sort of basket resting in his lap. Abruptly the basket disintegrated as his hands flew apart. "How do you know that?" he rapped at Marta, sitting forward.

Marta told him, and he listened, gulping now and then, nodding, frowning. Suddenly he said: "We must make sure by asking her. I'm going to call her."

"No, Massa Dirk. Don't do that. You will get me in trouble. Ow! She will want to kill me if she know I tell you such a thing."

"But it's important. It's a family matter. I must know the truth."

"Massa Dirk, what I tell you is the truth. Massa Frick never had nothing to do with her. It's your own father. She used to sleep in the house every night because your brother, Massa Graham, was afraid to sleep alone. It was before you born. She used to sleep in a hammock in the room you and Massa Graham and Missy Hermine had as children, and she had a mattress on the floor, too. I sure it was on that mattress Massa Storm used to lie with her."

"You're speculating, Marta. I must have the truth—and only she can give it to me. But don't be afraid. You won't be mixed up in it. I'll speak to her, but I won't tell her it was you who told me——"

"She will know. She will know, me baby."

Dirk grunted—and grinned. He stretched out and patted Marta's wrinkled cheek—a brief, affectionate gesture. "Leave it to me, old lady. I have a plan. I'll get it from her, and she'll never guess it was you. I can be wily when I want to be. Old Adriansen was a wily fellow. You should read about him in the letters. Grandma Hendri used to lecture Grandfather Jacques about old Adriansen's wily ways. I've read all about it, and I believe I'm like him. Very wily."

That very night—it was February, during the short dry season of 1809—Nibia heard a knock on her logie door. She was expecting Franky, her latest man friend; he was a boatman on the family yatch. Without hesitation, she opened the door—then gasped. For standing in the pale moonlight on the two steps outside the door was not Franky, but Dirk.

"Eh-eh! Massa Dirk! What you doing here, boy! You not in bed?"

"I'm supposed to be, but I didn't feel like sleeping, so I went out."

She could detect a certain tension in his manner despite his attempt to appear calm and nonchalant. She laughed softly and said: "You is such a strange boy. Eh-eh! At this time of night. What you want to come to me for?"

"I've come in Franky's place."

"What! What you mean you come in Franky' place?"

"Isn't Franky your man friend of the moment? Why are you pretending?"

"I am not pretending. I know Franky is me man friend." She giggled, her manner still amused and indulgent. To her, he was only still a boy of four with whom she must be patient. "But what you mean you come in Franky' place, Massa Dirk?"

"Just what I say. I have had a little chat with Franky. I gave him some tobacco and some salted beef, and told him I was coming to see you tonight and that he must keep away. He agreed, so you needn't be afraid. He won't disturb us."

Nibia uttered an "Eh-eh!" of astonishment, staring at him. Dirk stood on the steps, wrapped about in a black cape, like some comic demon in the moonlight. His hands were not in view, and Nibia seemed to wonder at this, for she suddenly asked: "What you hiding under that cloak?"

Dirk smiled. The frowsy smell of the logie disgusted him, but he did not show his disgust. "Perchance a little present I've brought for you, too," he said. "I gave Franky tobacco and beef, didn't I? Why shouldn't I give you something, too, Nibia? Especially if you let me stay with you for a little while."

"Stay with me? In here? A lil' boy like you? You not fourteen yet!" She adjusted the blanket about her still luscious body—for she was quite naked under it—and shook with giggles, bending in two. "Eh-eh! But look my trouble this good night! Massa Dirk looking for woman already. This lil' baby boy who Marta and me used to put to bed at night. Boy, go back to your bed before I tell your father and mother. Go on. Back to the house!"

"I'm not going," said Dirk—his voice calm, cold, not at all baby-like.

Nibia stopped giggling. She felt the sternness of him, and began to change her attitude. "What you really want, Massa Dirk? What happen of a sudden make you come here to me like this, boy? Tell me."

Dirk took a deep breath and told her: "Graham and Hermine have been teasing me. They say I don't like girls. They say I'm an aunty-man and will never marry and have children. They say I'll be like Uncle Raphael, a woman-hater. I want to prove to them this is not so. That's why I've come to you, Nibia."

Nibia smiled, feeling that she now had the situation in focus. "You mustn' mind when Massa Graham and Missy Hermine tease you. If you want to mix with boys, what wrong with that? You still young. Plenty time for girls."

"Very well. But I want to prove the matter in a practical manner now."

Nibia laughed. "You talking too much big words for me. What you mean?"

Dirk brought out from under his cape a bundle of cloth. He shook it out, and in the moonlight Nibia saw the glimmer of silk. It was a woman's dress. "I'm sure you'll understand what this means," he said. "I've brought it for you."

Nibia gasped. "What this, Massa Dirk? It's the missy' own. She wear it to the ball at Colony House more than once. What you doing with it here?"

"I asked her for it. She doesn't need it any longer. I told her I'd like to have it to give to an old slave on the Lafferty plantation. She was puzzled, of course, but I explained that the Lafferty woman had done me a favour—helped me kill an alligator in the little creek aback. The alligator attacked me, and I might have been badly injured if the old creature hadn't come and helped me. A mere tale I invented, but sometimes one must tell lies."

Nibia stared from the boy's face to the dress, and exclaimed "Eh-eh!" for the third time. "But you is a queer boy, Massa Dirk. And what you will tell your mother when she see me with this?"

Dirk chuckled. "I changed my mind and decided it would look better on you than on that old crock on the Lafferty plantation, so I gave it to you, and gave some tobacco to the imaginary old crock on the Lafferty place."

Nibia sighed. "Well, look at this thing! Lil' boy like you and you got such clever brain to make up story like that. What you will do when you is a big man, Massa Dirk!"

"Do you want this dress or not?"

"It nice." Nibia, unable now to restrain her pleasure, let the blanket fall from her, and took the dress from him, examining it by the light of the moon. She turned into the logie, saying: "Come in, boy. Come in. I'll light a candle." And Dirk followed her, shutting the door after him.

He wrinkled his nostrils at the frowsy odour, and looked round the tiny room as she lit a stump of candle on the floor in a corner. There were a mattress and two blankets and a pile of odds and ends against one wall—pieces of linen of various colours, smocks, and other clothing of a feminine nature. And nothing more. Slaves did not need furniture.

"Sit down on the mattress," said Nibia as she stood there naked in the candlelight, turning the dress over in her hands, a look of ecstasy on her face.

Dirk lowered himself on to the mattress, his nose still wrinkled. The sight of Nibia's nakedness did not move him. For one thing, she was too familiar a person—his old nanny—and for another she was a slave. He could not bring himself to touch a slave. It amazed him that his father had been able to cohabit with her—yet he felt no reproach, for the thought loomed in him that had his father not done what he had with Nibia, Jacob would not have come into the world.

Dirk's feeling for Jacob went deep. . . . But was Jacob really his half brother?

"I suppose this was the same mattress you had in the house when we were children and you used to sleep in our room?"

"Yes, Massa Dirk. Same one, but new covering. Ow! But this dress nice! Massa, you sure the missy say you can give it away?"

"Don't be foolish. How would I have been able to get it if she hadn't given it to me to give away? Doesn't she keep all her clothes locked up in the big wardrobe?"

Nibia, who had already known that this must be so, but had, nevertheless, asked just to be certain, laughed and said: "When I wear this all the women will eye me with envy. Hey, hey!" She suddenly sank down on the mattress beside him and gave him a hug, brief and affectionate. "Boy, you puzzle me. I don't know what to say when I look at you. You so force-ripe."

The sight of her breasts so close to him disturbed him, and he frowned and stirred. "I'm tired of hearing how precocious I am. I'm a van Groenwegel. We're not an ordinary family, that's why. Look here, let's talk."

Nibia giggled. "Oh, only talk. You don't want to do nothing more!" She regarded him with amusement, but behind her amusement was perplexity. "I thought you say you come to take Franky' place." He grinned and said: "I have, no fear!"

After some more badinage like this, he suddenly told her: "I had an interesting little chat with Overseer Frick this morning aback. I met him near the canal. He told me something that astounded me, Nibia."

"What that?" Nibia looked alert at once. "What he tell you?"

"It's something I shall never repeat to a single mortal. But I thought I ought to come and discuss it with you."

Nibia's hands came together nervously. "What you saying, Massa Dirk?"

"How old are you, Nibia? Thirty-two, aren't you?" Dirk was smiling in a chilly, ominous way. "You must have been eighteen when you had Jacob."

"Yes, that right. I thirty-two years old now."

Outside, they could hear the "Hoo-yoo!" of the goatsuckers in the night silence. The candle burned steadily in the draughtless little room. Dirk gazed idly at the large black areolae of her breasts, thinking: Jacob must have sucked them when they were smaller and not so black, and I remember Graham saying once she used to let him fondle her breasts before going to sleep at night. They are lovely breasts still, but I despise them because they are slave breasts. Only white breasts are good enough for me.

"Massa Dirk, what you trying to tell me, boy?"

"I was giving you a moment to think, Nibia," said Dirk. "Well, it's this. I happened to ask Frick if he minded that Jacob had taken his name, and Frick said that he was indifferent in the matter because he was not Jacob's father."

Nibia stiffened. "He say that! What a lying man!"

"No, he wasn't lying, Nibia. He told me who is the real father of Jacob. He said it's Father. Father spoke to him and asked him to claim that he, Frick, was the father of Jacob." This was a blind shot, but Dirk saw at once that it had got home, for Nibia gasped: "Frick tell you that! And he promise the master never to talk—ow! That man! How he could tell you such a thing." She added quickly: "He lying, Massa Dirk. He not know what he saying."

"Look here, don't be a fool. I know he was telling the truth. I only came to say to you that I shall never repeat it to anyone, and I want you, too, to go on keeping it a secret, Nibia. Will you?"

Nibia was silent an instant, then she sighed. "Ow. Frick shouldn'ta talk tell you such a thing. When you meet him? This morning, you say?"

"That's right," lied Dirk. "Near the canal aback. Anyway, don't upset yourself, Nibia. I won't say a word to a soul—not even to Jacob himself."

"Yes, don't tell him, Massa Dirk. He mustn't know. I promise your father solemn I wouldn't tell nobody, and all these years I keep my word."

"You can trust me, Nibia." Dirk rose. He grinned. "Now you see what it is I really came for. You're not puzzled any longer, are you?"

She wagged her head, not rising. Only staring up at him. "Massa Dirk, you frighten me sometimes, me baby. Yes, true. You frighten me. You not natural."

"Good night, Nibia. Sleep well." He bent and patted her shoulder, opened the door and went out.

On the Sunday following, Dirk's mood was so serious and taciturn that Jacob was compelled to comment on it. "Who been troubling you, boy?" he asked.

Dirk frowned and returned: "No one. I've been plotting."

"Plotting what?"

Dirk shook his head and began to tap his fingers together. They were sitting on the ground under the big tamarind tree near the canal.

"Something happen. Somebody trouble you. You can't fool me," said Jacob.

Dirk frowned again and said: "Your speech is suffering, Jacob. That man Green and his family speak badly, I suppose. Like black slaves. You should try to speak well. If you want to get on in the world good speech is important."

Jacob grinned, flushing under his olive complexion. "I can speak well when I want to, no fear. What happened since I last saw you, Dirk? Tell me."

So Dirk told him. Jacob listened with an incredulous expression, exclaiming every now and then. He began to bite his lip in an embarrassed manner when Dirk told him about the incident in Nibia's logie.

"It was the only way to confirm Marta's story," said Dirk. "I had to find out from Nibia herself before I was satisfied."

Jacob was silent, squeezing his hands together and staring at the black water of the canal. Dirk watched him for a moment, and then grinned. "I know how you feel," he said, and struck him a playful blow on the shoulder. "You simply can't believe that all the time we were half brothers. Anyway, it's a fact, and I've been plotting many things. When you grew up I'd intended to have you on this plantation as head overseer, but now it's different. Now that I've discovered that you have the Old Blood in you it would be improper to have you here as a mere overseer. Something better must be done for you, Jacob. You're not white, and therefore it would be impossible for you to carry the name of our family. Our family must be kept pure-blooded. That's important. But, all the same, you have the Old Blood in you, and that can't be overlooked. I'm going to see to it that you prosper. You must be one of the leading free coloured men in the colony. Do you like being a carpenter, Jacob?"

Jacob nodded. "Yes. I like it. But I'd prefer building a house to just hammering in nails and planing wood. I tell Mr. Green that— I told Mr. Green that, and he gave me a bad look and said: 'You must be humble, boy. Don't get big notions in your head before your time.' He's a very strict man."

Dirk grinned. "All these free coloured fellows are. Anyway, I'm glad you like building houses, because when we grow up I'm going to see you do a lot of building. You'll be the most important builder in New Amsterdam. And another thing, Jacob! I've been plotting, as I've told you, and I thought of something. You mustn't go and marry any silly, ignorant coloured girl. She'd only spoil your life. Now, I've thought of this. Rose Clarke is getting a good education. She can write very well already, and she can read simple sentences. And she speaks like one of us—I mean like Hermine and Graham and me, and like you when you're not being careless. And she's pretty. She's going to be a lovely woman. Well, what about your marrying her? She'd make you the perfect wife—well-educated and cultivated. She'd help you to rise in the world."

Jacob flushed once again, stirring uncomfortably. "But Rose is only nine. I'm thirteen. Millicent Green is twelve—just my age except for a few months."

Dirk gave him a pitying look. "Don't be foolish. You haven't got to marry a girl your own age. Why, look at Father! He's six years older than Mother. When Rose is seventeen you'll be twenty-one. She'll be right for marrying at seventeen, and so will you. You must think about it, Jacob. We can scheme like two good friends and see that she doesn't marry anybody else. Get friendly with her, and show her from early that you like her and mean to marry her."

Jacob nodded mechanically.

Dirk, in the silence that followed, kept tapping his fingers together, his grey-green eyes staring coldly at the water. He might have been a soothsayer, watching in the dark-brown depths the events of the future take shape.

9

IT was two Sundays later that a tragic incident occurred. Wilfred, on his way back from New Amsterdam on muleback, fell and broke his hip. It was raining heavily, and the tracks were muddy and slippery. A slave from the van Niffens' plantation came upon him lying in the slush, his clothes soaking wet.

On the Tuesday following, Wilfred died of pneumonia, despite all the efforts of John to save him.

Because of the tropical heat, the funeral had to take place within twenty-four hours of his death, and so it was not possible for any of the Demerary relatives to be present. Four days after the funeral, however, Edward and Luise arrived and spent three weeks at New Signal. They were both very grieved over the death of Wilfred, especially Luise, for Luise had been his favourite niece. "When every hand was against me because I wished to marry Edward, Uncle Wilfred supported me," she told Storm, who nodded mechanically.

"He was the most big-hearted man I've ever known," murmured Storm. And to himself he said: "Thank heaven he died without learning about Jacob. I should never have recovered from the shame of his knowing that I'd been unfaithful to Elizabeth." He stirred in his chair, his gaze moving up to the large portrait above the sideboard, for they were in the dining-room. "If he hadn't fallen from that mule I believe he would have lived to a hundred. Look at him in the picture there. When he died he hardly looked a year older than he did in 1789."

Edward nodded. "Like the van Groenwegels, the Mayburys are a tough breed."

Towards the end of their stay Edward and Luise went into conference with Storm and Elizabeth, and as a result of their deliberations,

Graham was asked whether he would like to go and spend time on Plantation Kaywana in Demerary.

"Wouldn't you like to learn something of planting, my boy?" asked Edward. And Graham replied: "I've always wanted to, Uncle Edward, but will I be alone at Huis Kaywana? I don't think I'd like that."

Edward smiled. "I hear you used to be afraid of the dark as a child. I'm sure there are many ghosts in Huis Kaywana, my boy. But they won't bother you. Cousin Hubertus must rule them all with an iron hand."

"It's not the ghosts I'm afraid of," grinned Graham. He frowned and flushed, fidgeting. "It's being alone—I mean, without anyone to talk to."

"No fear, young man. You'll have as much company as you wish. Stabroek is very near at hand, and you'll meet more friends and relatives than is wholesome for you, I warrant. I only hope they don't lead you into evil paths."

"Have you noticed what a prig my Edward is becoming in his old age?" laughed Luise. "I dread to think what he will be like when he's fifty-five and decrepit like my poor self."

"I should lose less sleep if you would behave your age in bed, my dear," sighed Edward. "I have developed into a prig as a means of self-defence."

"What conversation for Graham's ears!" said Storm, and Elizabeth laughed and said to Luise: "It's Storm who is the prig, my dear. You wouldn't guess how proper Storm can be. By contrast, I'm a loose woman."

Before he left for Demerary, Graham told Dirk: "I'm going to write every week, and I'd be glad if you would write me and keep me informed on everything that is happening." To which Dirk replied: "Have no fear about that. I'm all in favour of us corresponding. I shall put your letters in the old canister with the others, so that future van Groenwegels will be able to read what you said about the family in Demerary. I'd advise you to look for a wife while you're about it. There must be a lot of fine girls in Demerary who would be suitable to mate with a van Groenwegel. Be careful how you choose. Avoid the soft, sentimental ones."

Graham laughed. "You speak as if you're eighteen and I am thirteen. Anyway, don't let that bother you. I don't know that I'll marry at all."

"But you must. You've got to carry on the name!"

"I'm not obsessed with family pride as you are," said Graham lightly. Suddenly he caught Dirk's arm and led him on to the back veranda, saying: "There's something I think I should confide in you before I go to Demerary, Dirk."

"What's that?"

"You must promise to keep it to yourself. Do you promise?"

"Of course," said Dirk. "I promise. Tell me what it is."

"It's about Rose. Would you have guessed that she has our blood in her?"

Dirk started. "What! What are you saying? Rose Clarke?"

Graham told him about the letters from Edward that he had read some years ago. "I read them myself. Rose is Cousin Hubertus's daughter by a slave called Sarah. Didn't you wonder why she was sent to Berbice here and adopted by Mrs. Clarke? Didn't it strike you as strange that she takes lessons with you and Hermine as if she is one of the family? Uncle Edward asked that she be given a good education and be brought up like a lady."

"I see," said Dirk quietly. "Yes, I never thought of it. Stupid of me."

"Dirk, I'd like you to be nice to her. You're so sharp and abrupt. You make her feel so uncomfortable sometimes. She deserves better treatment."

"Of course she does—if she has the Old Blood in her veins." Dirk's hands clenched. "By God! To think of it! Rose Clarke a daughter of Cousin Hubertus! Very well, don't be afraid, Graham. I shall be nice to her in future. What you've told me makes all the difference."

"And be good to Nibia, too—for my sake. I'm very fond of Nibia."

"I shall keep an eye on everybody for you," smiled Dirk. "You can depend upon me. I shall write and tell you about everybody, slaves included."

The change in Dirk's attitude was noticeable to everyone, and for some weeks after Graham's departure was the subject of discussion between Storm and Elizabeth. Storm was of the opinion that Graham's absence had given Dirk a sense of responsibility. "He probably feels that he is the man of the younger generation now, in the home here, and must therefore be careful to be gallant towards his sister and Rose." Elizabeth did not agree. Elizabeth felt that there was something else behind it. "I can't fathom that boy, Storm dear. He is so calculating that I wouldn't be surprised if his new attitude is deliberate and derives from some notion of his about family pride."

Storm smiled. "A little fool, but I cannot help admiring him. I have complete trust in him so far as the future of this plantation is concerned."

"That is because, secretly, you are pleased that he is obsessed with family pride. You don't admire Graham to the same extent, do you, Storm?"

Storm stirred uncomfortably. It always discomfited him to be challenged on any issue of an intimately personal nature. "Oh, I wouldn't go so far as to say that," he hedged. "Graham has many very admirable traits, but if I may so express it, he—well, he lacks a certain fire. Wouldn't you say so?"

Elizabeth nodded. "A fire that Dirk does not lack." She sighed and went on: "I can be at ease with Graham, but never with Dirk—and I don't know whether that is a good thing or not, Storm."

"However," said Storm, a note of optimism entering his voice, "he seems to be undergoing a change for the better. He is treating his sister and Rose with a courtesy I'd never thought he could be capable of. It may be a sign that he has decided to grow up and discard his unbecoming pretence of being an adult, if that does not sound paradoxical."

Elizabeth smiled and said that perhaps he was right—though, to herself, her opinion remained unchanged that behind Dirk's new front there was some plan known only to the boy. Try as she would, she could never feel tender about Dirk. Rooted deep in her was a fear of him, and it was this fear that always put out any fire of tenderness that attempted to glow alive in her when she thought of him.

On Sundays, Dirk would invite Hermine and Rose to accompany Jacob and himself on their rambles in the bush, and it was Dirk, too, who insisted that Rose should be taught to swim in the canal. Hermine, already a good swimmer, fell in with this plan, and soon they all four would go swimming on Sundays, and would picnic by the bank of the canal. Some Sundays, Hermine invited the Lafferty children, John and Patrick and Maureen; Jim, who was about Graham's age, had left for England to study engineering, and Susan considered herself too old to mix with Hermine and Dirk and the others. Susan had her young men.

Hermine, seventeen to Dirk's fourteen, tried to dominate these outings, but without avail. It was always Dirk whose word carried in the long run. The Lafferty children respected him more than they did Hermine, and, indeed, Maureen, who was fifteen, was definitely infatuated with him.

As a rule, Rose was taken home on Sunday evenings by Paul Hart, a boatman who plied up and down the Creek and who, a free coloured man himself, was well known by Mrs. Clarke; he was a reliable man, and had a good reputation both as a boatman and as a man of moderate habits in his personal life. Jacob returned to town either by boat or by pathway along the bank of the Creek. But Dirk changed this routine, and arranged that Jacob should accompany Rose always on Paul Hart's boat. "One evening some snake might take a liking to your ankle," said Dirk. "I don't like the idea of your going back by the pathway. And I'm sure Rose wouldn't object to your company on the boat. Would you, Rose?"

"Let him come if he wants," said Rose indifferently. "I don't think Mother would say anything. She knows Mr. Green very well." Rose, at nine, was under the impression that Jacob was the adopted son of Green, the carpenter.

Jacob raised no objections to this new arrangement, especially as Dirk never failed to supply the money to pay Paul Hart for the fare he asked on the boat. Jacob, however, could not be persuaded to look upon Rose as other than a little girl and well beyond the pale of sentimental relations. For, secretly, Jacob was attracted to Millicent Green, his employer's elder daughter. Millicent often smiled at him, and he knew that she reciprocated his feelings, and whenever he indulged in romantic dreams he made Millicent the heroine—never Rose. He took care not to tell Dirk this, though, for Dirk would have felt that he was trying to upset his plans for the future. Of late Jacob was acquiring a sense of independence. He was still loyal to Dirk as a friend, but more and more he found that he was inclined to treat Dirk's pronouncements with indulgence and sly amusement. A certain shrewdness began to manifest itself in him, and he would tell himself that he must be careful never to offend Dirk, that Dirk was really serious about this family pride of his, and was in earnest in his intention to assist him to become a prosperous builder.

Openly, Jacob tried to please Dirk by showing a fondness for Rose. That Rose accepted his attentions in a spirit of indifference did not discourage Dirk, for as Dirk confided to Jacob: "She's still a child, of course. We can't expect her to respond until she gets much older."

10

GRAHAM fell in love with Huis Kaywana at first sight. To his fancy, the large old house with its latticed portico-veranda and spreading bulk seemed like a castle—the kind of castle he had read of in books but never seen in actuality. He went over it with Edward and Luise, his eyes continually widening in wonder as they wandered from room to room in the various wings. The dining-room was about four times the size of the dining-room at New Signal, and there were portraits all around it—portraits done by Edward many years ago. One large landscape scene caught Graham's attention, and he asked: "Where is that? Is it an old mill, Uncle Edward?"

He noticed that his uncle winced as he nodded and said: "Yes, the old sugar mill at Good Heart."

"Good Heart?"

Edward nodded, and it was Luise who explained: "It was the first plantation Father owned. The one he started out with—high up the river here, not far from Borsselen Island. I was born there, and grew up there."

"And why isn't it—what happened to it?"

"The land deteriorated, my boy," said Luise, "and your Cousin Hubertus had to sell it and come here lower down-river where the land is more fertile. It is a subject your uncle and I don't care to dwell on. We loved Good Heart." He saw that her eyes were moist. "We have treasured memories of there."

In the drawing-room Graham saw a portrait on the southern wall, and almost instinctively he knew that it was of Cousin Hubertus. He exclaimed: "So that is Cousin Hubertus!" And when his uncle and aunt assented, he declared: "I knew it at once. I've never seen a portrait of him before, but from what I've heard of him I knew that could only be he."

All three of them stood, as though by mutual consent, for several minutes in silence, staring at the portrait of the massive man with his high cheekbones and well-trimmed beard, his grey-green eyes that looked both pious and worldly, that seemed to twinkle with a sly mockery at Graham as the boy stared into them.

It was Edward who eventually broke the silence by murmuring something which Graham barely caught. "Perhaps the greatest of them all," Edward murmured, his face twitching in that scowl characteristic of him when he was moved or when he wanted to conceal some emotion he deemed reprehensible. Graham noticed the swift, tender glance Luise gave her husband, and wondered what memories could be moving in them. They seemed to understand each other so perfectly, thought Graham. I envy them. I envy anyone who can be at perfect accord with another. . . . He felt himself swept by a sense of great isolation; a fear gripped him that he would never be able to get close to anyone, male or female. . . . Dirk, cold and mad as he is, has Jacob. . . .

Suddenly he remembered something, and asked his uncle: "I meant to ask you this, Uncle Edward. In the picture you've painted of us at New Signal, you gave Dirk very fierce eyes. Was this intentional?"

Edward smiled, and his face took on a demoniac expression. "You've noticed those eyes, have you? Yes, it was intentional, Graham. And it was not a jest. Your Aunt Luise commented on Dirk's eyes before I painted the picture, and I laughed at her—but when I was doing the picture, when you were all sitting for it, I saw what she meant about Dirk. There is a devil in that boy."

Graham winced, and Luise laughed and said lightly: "Grandma Hendri, that's who it is. She's come to life again in Dirk."

"That would be hateful if it were true," murmured Graham, shuddering.

"Take no notice of your aunt, my boy," said his uncle, gripping his arm. "She'll never outgrow her capacity for girlishly irresponsible flights of fancy."

Luise's shriek of laughter seemed almost irreverent to Graham; standing as near as they were to Cousin Hubertus' portrait, they ought to be of a serious mien, felt Graham, casting a furtive glance at the massive figure within the dark frame. Self-conscious and discomfited, he murmured hastily: "Cousin Hubertus had grey-green eyes, too, I notice."

Later, when they were in the yatch on their way back to Stabroek —they had spent the previous day at Edward's town house—Edward said to the boy: "I'm pleased that you have taken a fancy to Huis Kaywana, Graham. Pleased and relieved. Because I may tell you this now—I've already discussed it with your parents—I intend to let you have Plantation Kaywana."

Graham showed no surprise. He smiled and replied: "I had suspected that, sir. It is very kind of you, and I shall try to be worthy of the gift."

"Fine speeches seem to come naturally to you," chuckled his uncle, hunching his shoulders, that demoniac look coming to his face again. "However, let me explain the position. In Dutch law—and though this colony is British, the Dutch laws, according to the terms of surrender, are still in operation—in Dutch law you won't be considered of age until you are twenty-five. This means that you cannot take possession legally until you are twenty-five. Nevertheless, no one can prevent you from being in this house and running the place as though you were the master of it. And so far as I am concerned, you are already in possession. It is only left for you to prove yourself capable of running the plantation, and that is why I want you to take charge without delay. Rattray is a good manager, but he has bought a small place of his own in Essequibo and is itching to be off to see after it himself, and of late I don't think his heart is in his work here. Your Uncle Raphael, on the West Coast, was very kind to him some years ago, and he has never forgotten, and has a soft spot for our family— that is why he has not deserted his post so far. Now, tell me, does the prospect of your being in sole charge here at some early date terrify you?"

"Not at all, Uncle Edward. I'm very desirous of making the attempt. I have always had a strong wish to be in charge of a plantation, like Father."

"That doesn't mean," said Luise, "that you must give up the violin. I hear you are an excellent musician."

"And a great reader of books." Edward laughed. "No, we're not making fun of you, my boy. Your aunt and I are great readers, too. We admire people who are cultivated—which, of course, is a rare thing in this colony. But Luise and I are a rare couple. Aren't we, my love of the green eyes?"

Graham, now more at ease, said: "I've heard a great deal about your painting and building, Uncle Edward. Only yesterday morning, just before the ship came alongside, someone pointed out the buildings in Stabroek which you had designed. They say your buildings never sink in the mud as many others do."

"That is because thoroughness is my vice, youngster."

It was a hot, sunny day, but as they left the *stelling* and began to move along the road in the horse-drawn carriage that was waiting for them, Graham kept listening to the wheels squelching in and out of the muddy ruts, for rain had fallen the night before, and the road was not one of those built up with bricks. They soon turned off it, however, and came to the Brickdam, which was firm and hard and the most respectable of the main thoroughfares that ran from west to east from the bank of the river. There were lamp standards on either side, and the houses were all two-storeyed and in good condition.

The smell of mud and muddy water saturated the humid air, for parallel to the main thoroughfares were two canals known as South Canal and North Canal. These acted as a means of drainage and sewage disposal; at certain times of the day, when the tide permitted, the *kokers* were opened to allow the filthy water in the canals to run out into the river. The smells still lingered, however, and both in and outdoors in Stabroek one had to accustom oneself to them.

Graham asked many questions about the place, and Edward and Luise answered them eagerly. Edward laughed softly and said: "I am anxious for you to become acquainted with conditions here, my boy, so don't be afraid to ask questions."

"Very well, sir. I shall take you at your word. By the way, do you know what is the population of Stabroek?"

"Fifteen hundred white people," said Edward. "I know that for certain, for I was speaking to a fellow the other day whose business it is to take a census of the population in Demerary. He said there are about two thousand free people of colour, and five thousand Negro slaves."

On either side of the road, the houses loomed up, stiff and boxlike —all wooden buildings, and all built on low brick foundations. Many of them had colonnaded porticoes and balconies with awnings. They were most of them painted green or white or yellow, and the roofs were shingled, though one or two here and there were slated. The windows were of the louvred, shuttered type.

One pink-painted house stood out prominently—not only because of its colour but because it was a shop and residence combined. The

sign outside the shop read: HARTFIELD & CLACKSON—GENERAL MER-
CHANTS. Something familiar about the name of Clackson caused Gra-
ham to frown and ask: "Aren't we related to some family called
Clackson, Uncle Edward?"

"Your grandmother—Faustina—married Cranley Clackson. Graeme
their son, is a partner in the firm of Hartfield & Clackson. He's your
half uncle. You'll be meeting everyone in a matter of minutes. I've
invited them to breakfast with us. A family gathering specially for
your benefit, my boy."

"Quite a fine building there. Does it happen to be one of yours,
Uncle?"

"I must confess so, my boy," murmured Edward, and Graham
thought it must be sheer fancy on his part that made him feel that
his uncle's manner seemed not quite at ease. Yet the sensitive frown
on his uncle's face, and the worried glint in his eyes, did not strike
the boy as natural.

Edward House stood about two hundred yards east of the Hartfield & Clackson building. It was an older building of the conventional
boxlike design—Edward had had to build it that way for reasons of
economy; in 1782 he had not been as prosperous as he was now. He
did not acquire the plantation on the East Coast until 1790.

Much smaller than Huis Kaywana, it was a solid building. The
lower storey was entirely of brick, and there was a latticed gallery-
veranda, and a small portico darkened by many flowering vines. It
was Hubertus who had insisted that it should be called Edward House.

The dining-room was spacious, and the dining table held them all
with ease. Edward's children were all there: Willem, the eldest, who
was twenty-seven, and Pelham, who was Graham's age, and Beatrice
and Alpheda, two lovely young women in their early twenties. Beatrice was married to a Scots merchant attached to the firm of MacInroy, Sandbach. Jim Menzies was his name, and he reminded Graham
of Jim Lafferty; he had the same reddish colouring.

Graeme Clackson, thickset and rather sad-faced, for some reason
reminded Graham of Cousin Hubertus. Was it the cheekbones, or
the eyes? His wife, a gay, small, slim little woman, seemed not the
kind of wife for him, yet Graham could see that she was devoted to
him.

The woman who fascinated Graham most was Clara Hartfield. She
was a well-shaped, voluptuous creature with a ringing laugh.

"As usual," Graham heard her telling Edward and Luise, just before they were seated, "John is too busy to come. I've given up all hope for John, Edward. As I tell him, when something terrible happens one day and no ships are able to come here with goods for his shop, he'll die from sheer dismay."

Edward nodded and smiled—Graham noticed once again the sensitive frown, and the worried glint in his uncle's eyes—and replied: "Yes, I really can't understand John's obsession with the shop. Now that the business has expanded to such an extent, we should have thought he would be able to leave most of the heavy work to his underlings."

As it happened, Graham was put to sit between Clara Hartfield and Willem. The two of them vied with each other to claim Graham's attention. Clara told him he was the most handsome of the van Groenwegels. "Even more handsome than your uncle," she laughed, darting a glance across the table at Edward, who averted his gaze at once. Graham, flushing, replied: "And I think you are the most beautiful woman I have ever met." She threw her head back and shrieked, her laughter like a streamer of yellow silk shimmering across the room. "My dear boy! From a boy of eighteen to a woman of forty-nine, such a compliment is like a celestial elixir!" And Graham started and exclaimed in genuine astonishment: "No, I won't believe that! Forty-nine! You couldn't be forty-nine! I took you for about thirty at the most. I mean it, Mrs. Hartfield!"

"She'll never get old," said Willem. He was short and thickset, like Graeme, but was far from sad-faced. His was a mobile face like his mother's. He had Luise's green eyes, too, and mischievous smile. "When I'm seventy and grey Clara will still be ogling the young men."

"Willem! I won't have you lose respect for me!"

"It would be your gain if I did, for I should straightway make plans to lay siege to your heart. You would have won another lover, Clara." And as Clara shrieked again, Willem said to Graham: "Tell me something about the situation in Berbice, old fellow. How is the slave shortage affecting you there?"

"Pretty badly, but we're struggling along. Father is a little worried."

"A little worried! I wish we here were only a little worried. I can see disaster before us if something is not done very soon. And these confounded missionaries and their damned religion are only helping to aggravate the situation."

"Oh yes, I did hear about that. You mean Mr. John Wray. He arrived from England some time last year, didn't he?"

"Yes," scowled Willem. "Sent out by the London Missionary Society to teach the slaves about God and Christ and educate them in reading and writing." Willem snarled and stamped under the table. "Have you heard of anything more absurd? Why should these black heathens be taught Christianity and be instructed in book learning? They're slaves. They're intended for labouring in the fields and about the house. It's only going to give them grandiose notions when they're made to sing and pray and read the Bible. It should be forbidden."

Graham stiffened and returned: "I cannot agree with that. I feel Mr. Wray and his assistants are doing a very good work. They should be encouraged."

"I'm on your side, Graham," Clara put in. "I, too, feel the poor black wretches should be given a chance to be Christians. They are people, aren't they, Willem? It is only we who have made them slaves."

Graham, pleased that he had an ally in Clara, gained more confidence. "My brother Dirk speaks as you do, Willem," he said, "but I feel it is a wrong attitude to adopt. It is not humane to treat the slaves as we do now."

Willem's green eyes seemed to get greener as he flashed Graham a look and said in an ominous voice: "I'd advise you to keep your views to yourself, my dear fellow. You won't be popular in this community if you let it be known that you're on the side of the missionaries."

"Don't let him intimidate you, my boy," said Clara. "Be a man and hold what views you please—and speak them out. We need courageous men in this colony. I keep telling John that every day."

"By the way, Mrs. Hartfield," asked Graham in a puzzled voice, "please don't think me uncouth, but could you tell me how you're related to our family?"

"Me? My relation to your family is slim, Graham, though, if I may say so, very close and binding." Her eyes twinkled roguishly, and she glanced swiftly across the table, Graham noticed, at his uncle. "I'm a Clackson—Cranley Clackson's daughter by his first wife. Cranley Clackson married your grandmother, as you perhaps know. I grew up with your father and uncle, my stepbrothers, and the others up the river."

"Heaven knows how their morals survived with you amongst them," said Willem.

"Willem, I shall throw a spoon at you!"

"Very well—but not a knife!"

"Your cousin is a disreputable young man, Graham," sighed Clara. "I can see I shall have to protect you from him while you're amongst us here."

"That means she's planning to seduce you, my dear fellow. Keep her away from Huis Kaywana if you value your virtue."

Despite their bantering tones, Graham felt intuitively that there was a background of seriousness to their chatter. Something seemed to tell him that he would see more of Clara during the weeks and months that were ahead of him. She awoke in him the same excitement that Nibia had done when he was a small boy.

He spent a week at Edward House while his quarters at Huis Kaywana were being prepared for him. His uncle and aunt kept him company. "We won't let you languish in loneliness from the very outset, my boy," Edward smiled.

"And you'll be having visitors at Huis Kaywana," said Luise. "Clara Hartfield and Graeme will see to that. They've taken a great liking to you."

"I like Mrs. Hartfield," said Graham. "She's very friendly and easy to talk to. I'm sure I shall get on well with her."

Graham saw the swift glances his uncle and aunt exchanged. Edward scowled, but Luise smiled and said: "She will see that you get on well with her. She's a very determined woman, my boy. Nothing stops her when she wants anything."

It was not until he was settled in Huis Kaywana a few days and had got friendly with Harvey Rattray, the manager, who occupied a room in the north wing, that Graham learnt what was the true position in respect to Clara Hartfield.

Rattray, a soft-mannered fellow, with blue eyes and light brown hair, and rather slightly built, nodded in a knowing manner when Graham told him that he had received a message that Mrs. Hartfield would be calling the following afternoon. "I knew she wouldn't be long in coming," he said. "She never waits when she sets out to get her man."

Graham frowned and said: "Come, tell me, what is all this about? Why does everyone keep hinting that Mrs. Hartfield is a loose woman?"

Rattray uttered a soft sigh. He was an effeminate man, and Graham suspected that he must be somewhat like Uncle Raphael on the West Coast. The two of them were on muleback on a tour of inspection round the plantation on a hot, sunny morning. The air was filled with the buzz of bees and the fragrance of flowers, for they were passing one of the many plots of land which Edward and Luise, when they had been resident at Huis Kaywana, years ago, had had cultivated with flowering vines and bougainvillaea. The arbours were falling to pieces, but the vines still flourished in savage disorder.

"I'm afraid you'll discover that she *is* a loose woman, my friend," said Rattray. "She is notorious in Stabroek and makes no attempt to conceal her sins. Her husband is resigned to the situation. He keeps a mistress, so that evens up matters, you see. Nevertheless, she is a fine woman. Oh yes, you will like her, even if she does succeed in seducing you, as seems to be her intention. She is very intelligent, and her conversation is excellent."

"She upsets Uncle Edward, I've noticed."

"She would," smiled Rattray. "It is now open knowledge that he had an affair of the heart with her some years ago."

"What! Is that true?"

"Yes, it is true. I've heard it on good authority. Indeed, her son, who is my namesake—Harvey—is whispered to be your Uncle Edward's child."

"Good heavens! And where is he? I haven't seen anything of him——"

"He is in England at a good school. Mr. Hartfield has very influential relatives in England. I think they succeeded in sending Harvey to Eton College. Or it might be Harrow. I won't be certain on the point." Suddenly he pointed and added: "Look! There is the barn I was telling you about. The one I was suggesting we should have dismantled."

Graham looked ahead and saw an old-looking but very sturdy structure. They had gone past the garden patches, and were passing through an orange orchard.

"You say it is not in use any longer?"

"No," said Rattray. "Our output has dropped considerably due to lack of labour. This slave question is getting more serious every day."

Graham, not sorry that the subject had been changed, plunged readily into a discussion of plantation business, though in the background of his mood lurked the image of Clara Hartfield clouded over by the smudge of gossip Rattray had imparted to him.

The following afternoon he received a surprise, for Clara Hartfield did not come alone. She came in the company of a quiet-mannered, middle-aged man whose blue eyes held a light of benevolence and character; he was not the kind of man Graham expected to be in the company of a loose woman. Clara introduced him as Mr. John Wray. "Mr. Wray is the missionary who is doing so much good work among the slaves, Graham. I told him that you were kindly disposed towards the slaves, and he expressed a wish to meet you."

"It is a great pleasure, sir," smiled Graham, who, nearly six feet, was like a tall palm in contrast to the missionary's smallish figure.

As they settled down in wicker chairs on the portico, Mr. Wray said: "I cannot afford to miss the opportunity of becoming acquainted with anyone who is well disposed to the slaves, Mr. van Groenwegel. Such people are so few, alas!"

"I've told Mr. Wray that you will soon be in complete charge of this plantation," smiled Clara, who looked as attractive as she had done at breakfast a week or two before. She was very fashionably dressed, and half her bosom was exposed. "He will need your permission to operate amongst the slaves here."

"There will be no difficulty on that score, sir," said Graham, suddenly uncomfortable at the realisation that so much power was to be in his hands. He fidgeted, gauche and self-conscious, especially as he felt Clara's admiring eyes upon him. "But—but haven't you already begun to take our slaves in hand?"

Mr. Wray shook his head with an air of sadness. He smiled and said: "No, I'm afraid not, my boy. Your manager here is not in favour of the slaves being instructed in the Scriptures. He forbade me to come here."

"What! Rattray forbade you! I can't believe it. I shall have to speak to him about it." In his anger his self-consciousness began to dissolve.

"Yes, speak to him, Graham," urged Clara. "I have done so more than once, but he will not listen to reason. He's an inhuman cur."

"Please," said Mr. Wray, putting up his hand. "I have no wish to create any dissension between you and your manager, Mr. van Groenwegel. I pray that you will be gentle in approaching Mr. Rattray on the matter——"

"But I'm astounded, Mr. Wray, that my uncle did not speak to him. Surely Uncle Edward permits your work on his plantation on the East Coast!"

Clara laughed harshly and flashed: "He would—but your Aunt

Luise and Willem are against it, and he has yielded to them and refuses."

Again Mr. Wray put up his hand. "Please, Mrs. Hartfield! May I explain the position in respect to your uncle, Mr. van Groenwegel? It is not that Mr. Edward van Groenwegel has yielded to the wishes of his wife and son so much as that he feels that the time has not yet come to teach the black people about God and our Saviour Jesus Christ. He was willing that I should instruct them in reading and writing, but he stipulated that my energies should be limited to this sphere of activity. In reply, I said that I could consider no such thing. Religion must go hand in hand with education. God's word must be imparted to these unfortunate souls in bondage. That comes before everything else——"

"Excuse me interrupting you, sir, but tell me. Do all the planters in Demerary feel as Uncle Edward does? Do they all prevent you from instructing their slaves in religious matters?"

"No, no. There are one or two who are very co-operative, my boy. But, as I have already said, these are so few—so very few. Since my arrival here nearly a year ago I have been treated by the majority of white people as an outcast, an interloper, even a danger to the community. My position is extremely precarious, indeed, but I am not discouraged. God will give me the strength to withstand every degree of opposition that is shown towards me, and, in the long run, all will be well."

"You may count on me as one of your chief supporters, sir," said Graham—and he was trembling with emotion. "I shall issue orders that the slaves must gather on any night you name so that you may come and talk to them."

It was only after Clara and Mr. Wray had left that Graham realised, with a shock, how arrogant he must have sounded. Why, I spoke almost exactly as Dirk might have done if he had been in my place and had felt as I do, he told himself. In his fancy he heard Dirk chuckling and saying: "How can you help it? Soft as you are, you must show spirit and arrogance when the occasion demands. It's the Old Blood. The fighter blood. It must show up in you."

The following morning he tackled Rattray about the slaves, and he found himself trembling again with emotion. "Why should you have prevented Mr. Wray from instructing our people in the Scriptures, Rattray? Don't you think they deserve to be treated like human beings?"

Rattray looked at him in surprise, but did not lose his composure. "When you gain some experience, my young friend, you will know why it is unwise to let these missionaries preach to the slaves. Mr. Wray and his assistants can do only harm in this colony by attempting to turn heathens into Christians. The instant our black people feel that they have God on their side, the instant they feel that they are human like the rest of us, in that instant, I say, they will want to rise up and drive us whites out of our homes——"

"That's nonsense. I can't agree with you. If they're kindly treated and told about Christ and Christ's teaching, why should they want to rebel? On the contrary, they should become better men and women. They should feel better disposed towards us. Christianity cannot turn them into brutes, can it?"

"Human nature is a strange thing, van Groenwegel. I am not trying to appear superior because I have the advantage over you in years and experience, but I am stating what I know to be the truth about people, and especially these black people. I have seen many instances of managers who tried to be soft and kind in their manner towards their people —and what was the result? Less work, more grumbling, more discontent, then ill feeling, then anger and rebelliousness. I have seen it happen on two or three plantations, and I thought it wise that no missionaries should be allowed to spoil our people on this plantation; that is why I have refused Mr. Wray permission to operate here. And I think it is for the same reason that your uncle has refused permission, too. He knows, too."

Graham, despite a feeling of having been justly chided, did not weaken in his resolve. He said: "I don't deny your experience or your wisdom, but I still hold to my opinion that it is a fine and humane thing to treat the slaves as fellow humans and give them the benefit of Christian instruction, and I have already told Mr. Wray that he has my permission to operate on this plantation."

"In that case, you cannot go back on your word, so let him proceed," smiled Rattray. He seemed in no way put out, and Graham gave him a puzzled stare.

"You don't object, then? I mean—you won't make a quarrel?"

Rattray shook his head and patted him on the shoulder. "I never quarrel, my friend. Quarrels do more harm than good, and lead to no useful results whatever, so I take care always to eschew them."

Four days later Graham, in a letter to Dirk, wrote: "Last night we had our first service on the plantation here for the slaves. Mr. Wray himself came, and the slaves gathered in the compound behind the house. There were many torches and the setting was most delightful to watch. Our people listened with great attentiveness to what Mr. Wray had to tell them, and I feel that soon they will be able to sing hymns and join in the prayers that Mr. Wray wishes to teach them. I have offered to play my violin as an accompaniment to the hymns, and Mr. Wray expressed his deep gratitude. It makes me very happy to be in a position to bring such a benefit to our people, and I shall never agree with Rattray, nor with you, in feeling that these meetings can harm them. Tomorrow Uncle Edward and Willem are coming here to discuss matters with me, for, naturally, word has already reached them of my friendship with Mr. Wray and of the meetings on the plantation which I have sanctioned. . . ."

11

IT was in June, and the long rain season had set in in earnest, but the morning broke with brilliant sunshine and a sky specked with tiny white clouds. The sun was still shining, though clouds were banking in the southwest, and then a distant rumble of thunder sounded, when Edward and Luise and Willem arrived. Graham was on the little *stelling* to meet them, and he was tense, his finger tips cold, for he was expecting to do battle. To his surprise, however, they were all three smiling and cordial. Willem's smile was ironic and sophisticated, Edward's was demoniac, and Luise's kindly if a trifle flighty.

"We haven't come to skin you alive, my boy," chuckled Edward, patting him on the back. "You probably received that impression when my letter reached you. I ought to have put it differently. It occurred to me after I had sent it off. When I said that you were young and green in many matters I didn't mean it as reproof, but merely as a statement of fact. We were all young and green at some time in our lives. When I was your age I was a complete imbecile, as your Aunt Luise can affirm. Anyway, we'll postpone our 'discussion' until after breakfast."

And so it was not until the meal in the vast dining-room was at an end, about an hour later, that Edward reopened the subject.

"First of all, Graham, my boy, I may say this. We're pleased with you, even though we don't think you're being wise in permitting these meetings on the place. You've proved that you have a will of your own—and this is a valuable asset."

"It's probably Grandpa's portrait," said Willem. "Who could live with a portrait like that and not acquire a strong will!"

Luise threw out an arm dramatically, and cried: "No stronger will than that, my boy! I resisted him, but I respected him." Her cheeks were flushed, and Graham was sure she had had too much wine. He himself had had more than he usually did, and his tension had departed. He felt far more confident now than when he had been standing on the *stelling* waiting for the yatch to come alongside.

"Nevertheless, what I want to say particularly," Edward told him, "is that now you have committed yourself to this project, if I may so term it, you must take care not to weaken. The slave mind is a strange one, Graham. You can mould it as you please, but you must have a firm, sure hand. The instant you show signs of hesitation, of weakness in your policy, you create an adverse impression, and the result is instability, mistrust, and a general falling off in discipline. They are human, but they are really only animals in their reactions to the training imposed on them. You're new here, and they must feel it natural that you should adopt new methods in handling them. But keep strictly to the new methods you introduce. If you intend to be harsh from the outset, then you will always have to be harsh. The instant you soften you are in for trouble. They will turn upon you like a pack of peccaries in the bush. On the other hand, if you intend to be kindly and considerate with them, then you will have to sustain that policy for all time. They will love you for being kindly, and they will be loyal to you—but there is a danger. If they feel at any time you have been unjust to one of them they are going to grumble and be dissatisfied, and this discontentment will spread unless you can, by some act, nullify the supposed injustice——"

"And if I may interrupt, sir," put in Willem, "there will be a number of occasions when you will be accused of injustice, Graham. It is for you to see that they are convinced that no wrong has been done to them."

"True. Very true," agreed Edward—then abruptly broke into chuckles, a look of fiendish delight coming to his face. "How I enjoyed that little lecture, Graham, my boy. I remember giving it to Willem when Willem was your age, and Luise chided me for my pomposity. Didn't you, my love?" Edward squeezed his hands together. "I like being pompous on occasion. It is a reminder of the days when Cousin Hubertus and myself indulged in serious, philosophic conversations."

Thunder sounded distantly, and Willem rose. "I think we should be going, Father. We must be back home before the overseers come in from the fields."

"Yes. And it seems like rain." As he rose Edward said: "I have purposely left for the very last what is perchance the most important item, my boy." He gave Graham a slightly mocking stare and added: "From the beginning of next week you will be entirely on your own. Rattray handed in his resignation to me yesterday. He says he can no longer delay his departure for the Essequibo to take over that plantation of his."

"But he never even hinted this to me," said Graham in dismay.

"A very noncommittal fellow," smiled Edward. "Not easy to fathom. But that is neither here nor there. How do you feel, my boy? Can you face it alone here?"

"Certainly, sir. I'm already quite familiar with the running of the plantation. It is really nothing new, for in Berbice I used to observe how everything was done. Father taught me a great deal."

"And you're a van Groenwegel," said Luise, her manner again histrionic. "It is in your blood, Graham." She threw out her arm. "The Old Blood!"

Graham gave an uncertain smile, reminded unpleasantly of Dirk, and replied: "Yes, of course, we do have planting in our blood. I'm sorry you have to go now," he hurried on. "I thought it might have been possible for you to remain on and spend the night. Mr. Wray is coming to hold a service in the compound this evening. It would have been a good opportunity for you to see how my people are responding to his teaching."

"I wish it were possible," said his uncle, "but Willem and I have much to attend to on the East Coast—and your Aunt Luise is too devoted to me to consider spending even one night away from me. Since our marriage we literally have never spent a single night apart."

Clara Hartfield came with Mr. Wray that evening. She brought him in the Hartfield tent-boat—"an act of great kindness and consideration," as Mr. Wray told Graham. "Mr. Wilkins, my assistant, has had to use the mission boat to go to a service up the river. But for Mrs. Hartfield's offer, I should have had to plod my way here along the muddy paths."

"It is always a pleasure being of assistance to you, Mr. Wray," smiled Clara. "My husband is only a merchant and doesn't possess many slaves, but we're both very sympathetic to your cause."

"That has been patent from the moment of my arrival," said Mr. Wray. He smiled at Graham and told him: "Mr. Hartfield offered me the use of a shed of his in Stabroek in which to hold services for the black people. That was within a week of my arrival in Stabroek. And both he and Mrs. Hartfield have co-operated most splendidly in every way. Much of my success in Stabroek is due to their kind help."

Graham flushed, and said: "From the instant I met her, sir, I knew she was a generous person. And—and I've only met Mr. Hartfield once," he stammered on, "but I'm sure that he, too, is equally as generous."

"Oh dear, what compliments," laughed Clara, her breasts on the verge of leaping out of her low-necked bodice. "I'm sure John and I don't deserve them, either. What we've done is what any normally decent Christian ought to have done."

"Ah, but that is the whole question, madam. The normally decent Christians in our community here can be numbered on the fingers of one hand."

Clara sat on the back veranda with Graham, and together they watched the service in progress in the compound. The black faces stared up intently at the missionary as he spoke to them, and the torches flickered in their holders—three heavy jars. Behind him, Mr. Wray's shadow was long and distorted on the muddy ground, and under the sapodilla trees tree frogs kept up a chorus of chirrupings. And farther off, amidst the slaves' provision plots, a bullfrog uttered hoarse, quarking sounds at long intervals. The night was close and damp, and a thunderstorm, threatening all afternoon, seemed to be approaching in earnest now. Lightning flashed frequently in the east, and thunder boomed nearer and nearer.

Rain began to fall, and the service had to be abandoned.

"You must both spend the night," Graham said. "There are enough rooms in this house, and I've had them all cleaned and prepared to receive guests."

"That is very kind of you, my boy," smiled Mr. Wray, "but I must go. Early in the morning I set out for the Abary. All arrangements have been made, and I must be in Stabroek tonight to complete one or two little matters."

"But what a night to be out in!" exclaimed Clara. "This lightning is terrible. You really should spend the night here, Mr. Wray."

"Thunder and lightning must not hinder me in my kind of work, Mrs. Hartfield. The elements are of God's making, it is true, but God intended us to overcome the inconvenience of rain and lightning when engaged on His work."

So Mr. Wray went back to Stabroek in the Hartfield yatch, but Clara decided to spend the night at Huis Kaywana.

"I won't require night clothes," she told Graham, after they had seen the missionary off on the portico—Graham lent him a cape and ordered a slave to accompany him to the *stelling*. "I sleep absolutely naked," she added, and as the boy flushed, she laughed her ringing laugh that triumphed even over the clatter of thunder that broke upon them at that instant. "Oh, my God! What weather! I don't mind the rain, but I am terribly frightened by thunder and lightning."

Later Graham stood at the window that looked out over the portico—his room was immediately above the portico—and watched the storm, remembering the Canje house and the many storms he had witnessed there. It seemed years since he had left Berbice, but, somehow, he did not regret having come to this house with its mellow air, with its legends of Cousin Hubertus, and its nearness to Stabroek. On the Canje he had felt ineffectual and purposeless, especially with Dirk always harping on the family-pride theme and reminding him that he was "soft." Yes, he was soft, he supposed. Dirk was hard, and so was Willem. Girls admired hard men. Lumea van Niffens and Susan Lafferty had always spoken well of Dirk. They liked his arrogant airs and his brusqueness, had even smiled and looked excited when Dirk had snubbed them. . . . Me they treated with indulgence and politeness. Their eyes never shone when I spoke to them.

Lightning crackled sharply, whitening the room, and he hugged himself, feeling the damp through his thin nightshirt. The house vibrated in the crashing weight of the thunder that descended upon it. The noise of the rain on the roof was deafening—deafening and spiteful and insistent. Almost threatening.

I'm too imaginative, he told himself. Dirk never has any silly fears and fancies. To him rain is rain, and thunder and lightning merely thunder and lightning. But me, I go putting things into the elements that aren't there in fact. Since I was very small I used to do that. The dark always seemed to be peopled with fearsome beings, waiting to reach out their ugly arms to enfold me. . . . Anyway, in this house I feel differently. I feel more a man here. I feel full of purpose, and very effectual. I can shape things as I want them shaped. I am the master. If I say Mr. Wray can hold services here, he can hold them, and I care nothing for the criticisms of other people. In November I am nineteen, and I am tall and well built. I look older than my age —and I *feel* older. I may be one of the soft van Groenwegels, but

I am going to distinguish myself. . . . Yes, I see it now. Now I see clearly what I must do. I must prove that soft people can also achieve great things. That must be my purpose in life—to show what kindness and gentleness and consideration for one's fellow humans can bring forth. I shall prove to Dirk that it isn't only hardness and brutality that can win power and glory for a family. Old Grandma Hendri taught her grandchildren to be loud, arrogant, cruel monsters, and they certainly fought well, from all reports, against the rebels in 1763 —but what did they achieve because of their aggressiveness? They died by violence, every one of them, even my own grandfather, poor fellow. Old Jacques was the soft one—his letters prove that he was a kindly, humane man—but he must have suffered with the others merely because he was a van Groenwegel. . . . I am soft like him, but I shall use my softness wisely. . . .

Another flash of lightning turned the room into a glowing fairy den, and out of the corner of his eye he could have sworn he saw some lovely nymph lurking by the huge wardrobe—a lovely creature with breasts like Nibia's; in a moment she would lure him out into the storm, and guide him to some secret bower, where he would make love to her. . . .

"Are you so fond of thunderstorms?"

He started round. "Who is that?" he gasped—though he knew. The voice was not one that he could mistake. He trembled. And the lightning flashed again, and he saw her. She was still standing near the wardrobe, and with nothing on.

"Mrs. Hartfield!"

"Everyone calls me Clara. I wish you would, too. You said yourself I didn't look as old as I really am." She laughed and came up to him, touched his arm.

"But—but you have nothing on."

"Didn't I tell you I never wear anything at night! John frowns on the notion of a wife who retires without a nightdress, but he excuses me on the grounds that the climate is a hot one—and it stimulates his own torridity, if I may so express it." She shrieked. "Am I not a naughty woman, Graham?"

"But—but what have you come in here for? This is my room."

"I know it is—but I wanted to come in—to talk to you—and to be naughty, perchance. To live up to my reputation. Are you surprised?"

He could say nothing. He hugged himself hard, trying not to tremble.

It was like one of the fantasies of his introspective adolescence come to life in actuality. How many times in Berbice had he not watched rain falling and imagined himself in the company of some luscious creature whom he had rescued from terrible dangers! When they were in bed and he was fondling her breasts it was of Nibia he thought; he might have been four years old and in the darkness of the northeastern room. Hermine was asleep, and in the corner where Nibia's hammock was slung up he could hear the creakings of the rope as Nibia settled down. For often he would still be awake when she blew out the candle and left him to go to her hammock. He would pretend that he had fallen asleep so as to make her feel she had succeeded in soothing him and quietening his fears about the dark. . . . He was almost sorry when the lightning flashed and revealed Clara's white body. . . .

She was very patient in initiating him into the act of love, and he felt grateful and tender. She gave him confidence in himself. The dim fear in him that females would always find him too soft, the fear that because he lacked Dirk's hardness and cruelty he would be rejected by girls, receded, and a sense of reassurance stirred in him.

Clara surprised him in another respect that night. After their love-making, she became quite serious, and he saw an entirely new side of her. She treated their love-making as though it were something to be taken for granted. "I have never been able to view love as something sinful," she said. "It seems to me so natural that one should use one's body to express one's deep feeling of attachment to a member of the other sex. And I took a liking to you—a very deep liking—from the instant I met you at breakfast that morning." And then she told him about the past, about her affair with his uncle. "He painted a portrait of me. You've seen it in the house in Stabroek. It was when I was sitting for that that we used to make love. I really loved Edward. Since we were very young—before I married John. I did everything I could to attract Edward, but without avail. Luise had already had him too firmly in her coils. I have nothing against her, of course. She is a fine person—but I have always been jealous of her."

"But what of Mr. Hartfield? What will he say if he hears that we have made love together like this? Won't he be jealous?"

She told him about a free coloured woman called Lizzie, with whom John had been intimate for years. "We have been very frank with each other," she said. "He likes to go to his Lizzie—or some other woman—some nights, and he has never hidden the fact from me. Nor do I conceal it from him that I sometimes indulge my affections for some man. John and I are on excellent terms, but there is one great sadness of which I should tell you. It is Harvey, our son. John now knows that Harvey could not be his son. We try to keep up a pretence that the boy is ours—that is, that he resulted from the union between John and myself, but it is sometimes a pitiable pretence. For some physical reason, John cannot have children. At first, we thought the fault lay in me, but then when I had that affair with your uncle I immediately proved pregnant, and Harvey came into the world. John believed that it was his child, and I did nothing to correct this belief. Though your Uncle Edward knew the truth, for he had seen Lizzie and discovered from her that she never used any preventatives when having relations with John, and it was years she had been John's mistress before this. So Edward knew that John was sterile and the child I bore must be his. And in all these years since Harvey has been born I never proved pregnant again, and John, I am sure, must realise what the true position is in respect to himself, for none of his mistresses —and he has tried out more than two or three, I am certain, within the past ten or twelve years—none of his mistresses has ever got pregnant by him. One day I shall have to tell him frankly who is Harvey's father. It will be kinder than this pretence we keep up at present."

The storm lasted most of the night, and they lay awake talking until well into the morning. Before they fell asleep, he asked her: "Will you come again often to make love like this with me?" And she replied: "Yes. I shall come again—not often, though, my darling boy. That would be bad for all of us. But off and on I shall come. It does me good to be with you like this—and I believe it will do you good. You are going to be an outstanding van Groenwegel—perhaps as outstanding as Cousin Hubertus."

12

IN Stabroek illicit relationships were taken for granted, and, contrary to Graham's fears, there was no sensation when it became known that Clara and himself were having an affair; there were no raised eyebrows and exclamations of horror. Even Edward and Luise and their children behaved as though it were something normal, something they had even expected to happen. Graeme had misgivings, and once said to Graham when he called one afternoon: "Such a relationship can prove harmful if you let it grow too serious. You're very young, my boy." As for Clara's husband, he seemed the least affected, and, indeed, remarked to Luise: "I'm glad to see Clara has taken that boy under her wing. Alone on that plantation, he needs a woman's presence sometimes."

In Berbice, Storm was amused, but Elizabeth disapproving. "Clara should be ashamed of herself. Why, she could be his mother! She's eight years older than I am." To which Storm, with a sly, half-bored smile, replied: "True, my dear. She might quite easily have been his mother. I could never get used to the fact that she was my stepsister, and often found myself regarding her with predatory eyes. It was only her obvious attachment to Edward that stopped me."

Dirk was disgusted. He wrote in a letter to his brother: "It is nothing but weakness. Why couldn't you have looked around for a young, strong, lusty girl, and married her? This woman is already married, isn't she? What is the sense of being intimate with her as you're doing? Why, if it was purely a matter of indulging yourself, you could have taken any of the slaves. You have no aversion to slave women, as I have."

Elizabeth also wrote in admonition, but Graham was too confident and happy in his new situation to be disturbed. Before a year had elapsed, Clara was not only his mistress, but his unofficial hostess when he entertained his relatives and friends to dinner. She was his mentor, and he took her advice in virtually everything, save plantation matters. "Where the plantation and the slaves are concerned, I must make my own decisions," he told her one day when she had expressed her disapproval of his acquiring new machinery for the mill. "As it is, I won't be legally in possession of this place until I'm twenty-five. That's the Dutch law. And before that time I want to prove to Uncle Edward what a legal infant can do on his own—and I'm determined it must be entirely on my own."

"You have a strange vanity," she smiled, "but I appreciate your attitude."

"Arrange the social side of my life and I shall not mind," he told her. "You're very capable in that sphere, and I want you to have a free hand there."

It was he himself who made the offer to Mr. Wray in respect to the disused barn near the orange orchards aback. "For some time I've been considering having it dismantled, sir, but it has just struck me that it may be of use to you in your work. Instead of trusting to the clemency of the weather, you could hold your services in there and be perfectly safe, rain or clear sky."

The missionary accepted gratefully, and within the next few weeks the rumour spread in Stabroek that a chapel had been founded on Plantation Kaywana. This time a definite bad mark was registered against Graham, for feelings among all the white members of the community had, of late, intensified against Mr. Wray and his assistants. It was claimed that the missionaries were causing unruliness among the slaves. A number of planters had had trouble with their people, and more than one overseer had reported overhearing talk of rebellion. On the East Coast and on the West Bank there had actually been minor uprisings, and most of the trouble had occurred after chapel meetings at night. Meetings were possible only at night, for all day the slaves were in the fields. On Sunday, the only day of the week on which they were free from their toil, the slaves were obliged to see after their own provision plots and had little time to spare for religious services.

Edward and Luise uttered no protest, but Willem spoke out. He told Graham: "You're going to be very unpopular, old fellow. This is something vital. It's bad enough you have been allowing Wray to come here and hold services in the compound, but it's another thing

when you go to the extent of permitting him to use one of the buildings on the place. Whoever heard of a chapel on a plantation! It's a
bad example. Other plantations will hear of it, and the black fools
will begin to feel they have a right to convert their masters' barns into
places of worship. You've made a bad blunder, Graham."

Graham, running his fingers through his tousled fair hair—he kept
it purposely tousled because Clara had a passion for seeing it so—
smiled and replied: "You mean by a blunder that I have lost the
approbation of my fellow planters—isn't that it? But suppose it is that
I am indifferent whether other planters think me unwise. Suppose it
is that I feel I have acted rightly, then where does the trouble lie? Can
you answer that, Willem?"

"It lies in the question of *esprit de corps*. If we planters, as a group,
do not hold together and act in uniformity, if we don't show the
black people that we are unanimous in our feelings and in our policies,
then the ruin of this colony is a certainty. It is bad enough that we
are being plagued by the Anti-Slavery Party in England, and that the
slave trade has been abolished, but what will there be for us if we
permit these missionaries to spoil our people and put mutinous notions
into their thick heads!"

"I shall tell you what there will be for us. There will be a body of
men and women willing to work for us with eagerness and love, instead of with hatred and reluctance as at the present. These black
people work for us because they must. We feed them and shelter
them as we do our cattle, and if they do not work as we wish them
to, we beat them and punish them in a variety of ways. You and my
brother will term that the hard way, and no doubt the material
benefits are not inconsiderable. This hard way has worked well in the
past; it has made our fathers and grandfathers rich in worldly goods.
But what has it done to the spirit? Has it benefited their hearts and
souls? Has it made them better Christians? No. It has coarsened them.
How many of these planters care for the finer things of life? For books
and music and pictures? Uncle Edward and perhaps two others are
the only ones I can think of who care for such things, and they are
the ones who show most kindliness and compassion towards the black
bondsmen who work for us."

"Father and Mynheer de Vriesmann and Mr. Bentley are certainly
compassionate towards their people—but they have not gone to the
extent of permitting religious services in the buildings on their plantations. They know better than to allow such practices to flourish."

Graham, however, was not disconcerted. He experienced a rock-like calm as he ran his fingers through his hair again and said: "Perhaps it is that they lack the courage to implement their convictions. Many fine people suffer from such a lack. Fortunately, however, I do not, and my intention is to show that it will pay us, in the long run, to treat these black serfs of ours like Christian fellows, and permit them the rights of Christians, despite their status and their complexions. That is why Mr. Wray and his assistants will always be welcome to use my barn for their services. I shall not stop them."

Several planters refused to visit Huis Kaywana when invited, but several came as of yore, being too indifferent to care whether Graham was siding with the missionaries or not. Indeed, after a few months, even the ones who had fallen into a huff began to forget that Graham was supposed to be in disgrace, and came to breakfast or dinner when asked—and Clara saw to it that invitations were sent out to all who were usually on the list. "Take no notice of their airs and graces, my darling," she told Graham. "They have their passions, but they are not vindictive towards their own kind. They soon forget old grievances, and they know what good breakfasts and dinners the van Groenwegels provide."

Within a year Graham and Clara had won back all the ostracisers —but the campaign against the missionaries did not cease. Indeed, it grew more violent. More and more instances of rebellious behaviour on the part of the slaves began to convince the planters that the work of the missionaries must be brought to a stop. Matters came to a head in 1811 when Governor Bentinck, forced to take notice of the planters' protests, issued a proclamation that henceforth it would be illegal for slaves to gather in any numbers at night for any purpose. And thus, at one stroke, all Mr. Wray's work was brought to a standstill.

"Have no fear, my boy," said the gentleman to Graham and Clara, who had invited him to dine at Huis Kaywana. "I shall protest to the Anti-Slavery Party in England. There will be an outcry when it is learnt what your governor here has done. The matter will not rest as it is now, you may be sure."

"It is tyrannical," said Graham. "I am ashamed of Mr. Bentinck. I had always considered him a just man."

"He is a just man," said Clara. "But he was forced to act by the planters." She uttered a sound of disgust. "And by the Dutch planters in particular. They are far more bitter and harsh than the English. They cannot forget their traditions of cruelty and supreme dominance over their slaves."

"But what strikes me as most unjust," said Graham, "is the nature of the arguments they adduce. When did Mr. Wray arrive here? Not three years ago—in 1808. Have disturbances amongst the slaves dated from only three years ago? Why, from the time I can remember hearing people talk of slaves, as a boy, I have heard it said that slaves were troublesome and perpetually causing anxiety. Were there any missionaries at work among the slaves in Berbice in 1763 when that terrible insurrection occurred? It is so unfair to lay the blame for these petty incidents on Mr. Wray and his assistants. There has been no widespread plot among the slaves to revolt, and even if there had been why should Mr. Wray's sermons and hymn singing be alleged to be at the root of the trouble?"

"My own arguments are very similar to yours," said Mr. Wray, "in the letter I have penned to send to England, and I am confident that action will be taken without delay to have Mr. Bentinck's proclamation annulled."

Mr. Wray's prophecy was correct. The Anti-Slavery Party was horrified when news was received of Bentinck's proclamation, and the Home Government gave instructions that the edict was to be rescinded. Bentinck, however, a great friend of the planters, took it upon himself to delay the matter, and kept the ban in force. Again Mr. Wray sent a protest to England, and this time—a year had in the meantime elapsed—the Home Government sent a message which could not be ignored. It was to the effect that Bentinck was to be relieved of his post as Governor. His successor, the Commandant of Troops, Major General Hugh Lyle Carmichael, immediately cancelled the ban imposed by Bentinck.

Graham, in his exuberance, planned to hold a fete for the slaves after the first religious service in the barn for more than a year. "And we must also invite Mr. Wray and his assistants to dinner the same evening," he told Clara. And she agreed that this was what she herself had had in mind.

Everything went as planned. The religious service was a triumphant success. Graham played a violin accompaniment to the hymns, and Mr. Wray preached an inspired sermon. The fete in the compound was a gay affair, the Negroes themselves contributing the music on various instruments, drums and fifes in predominance. And while the fete was in progress, Graham and the missionaries and Clara dined in the candlelit dining-room.

Yet something was wrong—a something that only Graham noted. Sensitive to every whim and mannerism of Clara's, Graham was certain that this evening she was not herself. Her laughter did not ring out as it should, and now and then he noticed that her face would twitch slightly as though she were in pain. She seemed tense in a way that was not usual, though she evidently was doing her best not to show it. Graham cast many anxious and affectionate glances at her, and when the festivities were over and the missionaries had departed —she had already announced that she was spending the night at Huis Kaywana—he lost no time in tackling her about her mood.

"You were not yourself this evening. What is the matter?"

She smiled quietly and gripped his arm. They were in the portico, and the night outside was rich with the peace of pale moonlight. The shadows of the sapodilla trees around the edge of the compound held a pleasant mystery, and the glittering leaves might have been reflections of all the flakes of laughter that had flashed within the precincts of the house during the past few hours now grown cool and subdued. Dimly, from the river, came the splash of oars as the yatch with the missionaries moved off from the *stelling* on its downstream journey to Stabroek. And from the other direction, from somewhere near the old arbours and their flowering vines, came the unfailing music of the goatsuckers . . . "Hoo-yoo . . . ! Hoo-yoo!" Music of the Canje that little boys of four in their beds listened to before falling asleep.

"You did notice that I was in a mood, then?"

"It was obvious—to me, at least," he said. He pressed her to him and kissed her. "You look younger than ever this evening. You will never age."

"Strange that you should say so, because this evening I feel my age."

He shook his head. "But you don't *look* it. Tell me what is the matter."

"Let us go upstairs."

"You're reluctant to tell me, I can see."

"Yes, I am," she said as they went up the curving stairway. He could feel her trembling against him. "But I shall. It is imperative that I should tell you." As they were nearing the balustered landing she paused and held his arm tight, and said: "Oh, Graham my dear!"

in a strangled voice, and he gave her an anxious glance. The slave girl who was lighting their way up paused on the landing and stared back at them with uncertain eyes, the brass candlestick in her hand tilting at an acute angle so that grease began to trickle down.

"You are giving me some alarm now, Clara. What is it? Tell me at once."

"In good time, Graham. You must make love to me first." She began to ascend again, in agitated steps. On the landing, the slave girl, startled by her sudden upward surge, dropped the candlestick and they were all cast into darkness. Both candles had gone out. The girl began to utter apologetic sounds as she stooped to retrieve the candlestick, and Graham stumbled into her, and caught her arm, laughing and exclaiming: "Poor Mabel! You are sleepy. You should have sent Janky to light us up." The moonlight came in at the tall window nearby, and the girl, in her smock, reminded him of Nibia. Often in Berbice, as a boy, he had seen the moonlight on Nibia as she crossed the dark room to get into her hammock.

"Don't trouble to relight the candles, Mabel," he told her. "There is enough moonlight for the missy and me to find our way unaided to my room. Go to bed and sleep deeply, there is a good girl."

As they went on toward the end of the landing, Clara murmured: "I shall remember these little incidents—your kindness to the slaves. Your many little gentle attentions to me and to everyone."

He tensed and said: "I'm beginning to suspect what it is you are going to tell me." But she gasped: "No, no. Please suspect nothing. Wait. Wait, Graham."

It was not until more than an hour later, when the muslin net that shielded them from the whining mosquitoes was looking like a goblin creation within the shaft of moonlight that had struck in upon it, that she told him anything. The moonlight did not quite reach her side of the bed. It shone upon him, on his forearm, as he lay on his stomach, his chin propped in his hands, watching her beside him. Her white skin was greenish with the reflected moonlight, and she seemed to him a being of fantasy that might melt into nothingness if he did not keep watching her.

Far away outside the open windows the "Hoo-yoo!" of the goat-suckers came in the stillness of the night, soothing and bringing back Canje memories.

"I knew it was that," he murmured. "You gave yourself away when we were on the landing. But why? Why must this be the last night?"

"Harvey came back this morning from England, Graham. Nearly as tall as you, and such a fine boy. He is about a year younger than you. Oh, my dear! My dear! You don't know what a torture of mind I've suffered."

"But what of John? He's asked you to give me up because of Harvey. I can understand that. It would be embarrassing for Harvey to have to face his friends with the knowledge that his mother was engaged in an illicit affair with someone his own age. I can see that clearly, Clara. But what of John, I repeat? Has he decided to give up Lizzie and the other women he keeps?"

She nodded, squeezing her hands together distractedly.

"He has? He's going to give up Lizzie?"

"Yes. The sacrifice won't be on my side only, beloved. We spoke seriously together today and discussed every aspect of the matter. John is a fine man, Graham. I've always admired him. He has strength, and he also has prudence when prudence is necessary in any situation. I'm fond of him, as I have told you on many an occasion. Graham, I'm fifty-two. Oh, my darling boy, you're not twenty-two yet. Not until November, isn't it? Your mother was right in what she wrote to you. I had no right to foster this relation between us——"

"You had every right, because I needed someone like you, Clara. You've brought more riches to my spirit than this whole plantation is worth. You—you—the past three years we've been friendly have made me a man. I should not have had the courage to do half the things I've done here but for the knowledge that you were there behind me, loving me and wishing me well, inspiring me. Oh, words are of no use to me tonight. I'm talking foolishly, idiotically——"

"No, you are not." She touched his cheek with her hand. "I'm glad to hear you say that I have been of some use to you. This is the first time in my life that I have been able to do something really useful for a man. It will soothe me in my old age when I reflect back on it."

Silence came upon them, and the moonlight began to shift over to her side. It touched her thigh—but the parallelogram was getting smaller as the moon sank into the west. The mosquitoes whined hungrily outside the net . . . "Hoo-yoo!" . . . Perhaps it was lying flat on its breast near the barn. . . . "Hoo-yoo!"

"Do you hear the goatsuckers?"

"Yes. I won't hear them in Stabroek. They never come near the town." She caught his hand and pressed it hard against her breasts. "Every second of this night will remain with me until I die, Graham."

After another silence, he asked her: "Have you told John about Harvey?"

She shook her head. "That is something that must remain for another day. Perhaps the day will never come. Perhaps it is better to leave the truth unspoken. There is Harvey's future to think of now, Graham. He is going into the firm with John. He will take John's place when John retires. Do you think it would be wise for me to destroy the illusion of family ties that link us together?"

He nodded. "Yes. I see that. Of course, I prefer the truth. But as you've often said, the truth can be destructive."

After another silence: "He's providing very generously for Lizzie. She already has a little shop on the other side of North Canal. He's going to restock it for her, and he is going to advise her to marry an elderly man—he's a boatbuilder—who, for years, has wanted to marry her." She stroked his wrist and said: "You should go and see her one day when you are on that side of the town. She's a weak character, but pleasant. She has been good to John. From all reports, she has never been unfaithful to him."

"I have always been curious to see her. I must wend my way there one day. How will I find her shop? Has it a distinguishing sign?"

"Yes, there is a crude sign outside it: LIZZIE GREAVES—PROVISION SHOP. I've seen it from the carriage in passing. I've even stopped now and then to go in and speak to her."

"You would do that. Such generous natures as yours must be born once every ninety years on this earth. But I'm tired of telling you that." He shook his head a little distractedly. "Does this mean I shall not even be permitted to see you at all—even on social occasions or—or—you know what I mean?"

"Most certainly it does not mean that. We shall still see each other. You will dine with us, and I shall dine here—but like respectable people under respectable conditions. It is only these nights that will be no more."

"And these nights have been the jewels in our friendship."

He watched the parallelogram of moonlight creep up her belly, then grow into a thin line and vanish. In the silence they could hear the sound of oars on the river. The sound faded as the craft went past. Then not very far off came the hacking cough of a raccoon, a softly predatory noise beyond the sapodilla trees.

13

GRAHAM recovered very quickly from the gloom that settled upon him during the next few days. He awoke one morning to discover that he had never really been in love with Clara as he had often tried to assure himself during the past three years. Physically she had satisfied him, and he had valued her advice in social matters; he had admired her tremendously. But she had not ignited any great flame of passion in him, nor had she ever been able to stir up in him an obsessive devotion. Now and then, indeed, in moments of depression, he had even assured himself that love was something he would never know. He lacked fire. Dirk would know great love. Dirk had fire.

What helped a great deal, too, in his rapid recovery was that change had come not only into his life, nor even only into the lives of Clara and John. At this particular time it was evident everywhere.

The new Governor, Carmichael, had hardly been in office a month when he announced, to the consternation of the whole colony, that henceforth the town was to be known as Georgetown and not Stabroek. The new name was in honour of the Prince Regent, for the new Governor was a man fanatic in his sycophantic allegiance to the throne. He would tolerate no bantering remarks directed against the Prince Regent, and he seemed determined to wipe out as many Dutch institutions as he possibly could, and in the shortest time. The colony was British, he argued; therefore he abolished the College of Kiesheers, the old Dutch political coterie which had always been responsible for selecting candidates for the Court of Policy. In future, ruled Carmichael, Financial Representatives, as they were now to be termed, should be elected in open franchise. The College of Kiesheers, he argued, was too pro-Dutch in its policy, and the nominations it submitted were always in favour of Dutchmen; Englishmen were kept out, and this was an absurd state of things when it was considered that the colony was under British rule. And, furthermore, he felt that the custom that members of the College should hold office for life was an abuse.

Then news arrived in the colony that America was at war with England. Merchant vessels were being attacked at sea. And Carmichael, forever itching to do battle with any and everyone, organised a fleet of ships and sent them out to harry the enemy craft, for the Americans had blockaded all the rivers of the three colonies.

Graham could not help admiring him, and was often glared at by Willem, who could not bear to hear Carmichael's name mentioned. "That strutting little peacock of an Englishman" was what Willem called him. Willem was now married—the event took place in July, and there was a grand reception at Flagstaff, the East Coast plantation; the whole family was present; Storm and Elizabeth came from Berbice, and Raphael, bewigged, powdered and perfumed, and smilingly elegant and affected, was among the guests. The bride was Christina van Banff, the daughter of an Essequibo planter turned merchant. She was thin and flat-chested, but had a delightful personality, and a very pretty face.

In February, the following year, 1813, a naval action took place off the coast of Demerary. It happened on the twenty-fourth of the month, between H.M.S. *Peacock* and the American frigate *Hornet*. The *Hornet* was the more heavily armed and manned, and the *Peacock* was sunk with virtually all her crew.

Poor Carmichael, ironically enough, was ill, and unable to attend the funeral service held to commemorate the loss of the *Peacock*.

It was when Graham was on his way back to Edward House from the service—he always stayed at Edward House when in Stabroek for any reason—that he happened to notice from the carriage a sign outside a small shop on the bank of North Canal that read: LIZZIE GREAVES—PROVISION SHOP. He told the coachman to stop by the shop. "I want to see someone in here, Harry. Wait a few moments."

Harry's dark brown face took on a look of dismay, for it was most unconventional for a gentleman to be seen going into a provision shop—especially on the North Canal, which was a poor district of shops and the shacks of free coloured people. "If you want anything Mr. Graham, massa, I can get it for you," Harry offered. But Graham waved playfully at Harry and smiled. "I know how you feel about the matter, Harry, but permit me to be indiscreet for once."

So Graham, to the even greater dismay of the slaves and free people who were in the shop, entered and said to the olive-complexioned woman behind the counter: "You are Lizzie Greaves, aren't you? I have always wanted to have a chat with you. I am Graham van Groenwegel from Plantation Kaywana."

Lizzie, plump, her curly hair greying at the temples, but her face still pretty, curtsied and replied in a voice of awe: "I thank you, Mr. van Groenwegel, for the honour you give me. How you come to know of me?"

"Various people have told me about you. My Uncle Edward knows you, and so does Mr. John Hartfield and Mrs. Hartfield." Graham abruptly began to regret his impulsiveness, realising that he had nothing to discuss with Lizzie. How could he tell her about Clara and himself and that Clara had asked him to drop in and see her here? How could he refer to the matter of her having once been John Hartfield's mistress? It would be discourteous, especially in the presence of her customers. He had just stammered a hasty: "Well, I—I—it's been good to see you in actuality after having heard so much of you," and was about to withdraw when a voice at his elbow said: "I'd be glad to be able to say a word to you, Mr. van Groenwegel, if you would care to listen to me."

Graham was surprised at the gentle, almost cultivated sound of this voice, and stared blankly at the middle-aged black woman, rather well-dressed in grey satin, who was smiling at him. "May I ask who you are?"

"My name is Sarah, sir," she said, curtseying. "I call myself Hubert. I am a free woman, and I know your family very well."

"Sarah? Sarah Hubert? But—I'm afraid you have me at a disadvantage. I don't recall anyone of that name. None the less, I'm very pleased to meet you, Sarah Hubert. What members of my family do you know?"

"I went to Berbice two months ago, sir, and your father and mother invited me to have a meal at their house. I am Rose Clarke's mother."

"Good heavens! Why, of course." Graham flushed. "That lovely little girl who came to us in—when was it?—1804, I think. She was a little thing of three or four. When last I saw her she was about eight or nine. I suppose she must be very tall now—and even more pretty?"

"Yes, sir," smiled Sarah. "She is getting more pretty every day, and your parents are very kind to her. Your sister, Miss Hermine, gives her books to read, and she is taking lessons with a seamstress."

"Yes, my brother Dirk did mention in a letter that she is taking sewing lessons. He gives me all the news about everybody there. What do you do for a living yourself, Sarah?"

"I have a shop, sir. It stands further along the road here. Mr. Edward and Miss Luise have helped me to make my way in the world, and I shall be grateful to them for ever, Mr. Graham."

"I'm glad to hear that. If at any time you happen to be near Kaywana don't fail to call and see me, Sarah. I don't know when I shall have the opportunity of going to see my parents in Berbice—it's years I have not been back—but whenever the opportunity does arise I shall make it a point of informing you so that I can take any little gift you may have for Rose."

Sarah curtsied, and Graham saw that her eyes were moist. "God will bless you, sir. God will bless your whole family. You are kind people."

As a result of this encounter with Sarah, his thoughts, on the way home, were all of Berbice. He tried to picture what Dirk must look like now—and Hermine. And Jacob and Rose. For some reason, he could never imagine his parents looking any different from what he had known them to look when he left the Canje place nearly four years before. Dirk must be taller, though—and Hermine. In a letter about a month ago, Dirk had hinted that Hermine and Jim Lafferty were attached to each other. . . . And Nibia. His dear Nibia. It was difficult to see her in his fancy as a mature woman. He could think of her only as the shapely creature she had been during his boyhood. Even when he had left, four years ago, she had still been good to look at—still young and fresh-faced, alive and laughing. Still eager for her lovers. . . .

Two days later, a letter from Dirk told him: "I have to report two deaths. Two deaths within a week. Old Mynheer Hiemens died in his sleep. There was the volume of Virgil in bed with him—the same one from which he used to give us our lessons. He was seventy-eight—quite time enough to die, I should say. The other death is that of Marta. Marta fell down with a stroke when she was sweeping the compound. She died within an hour. I was very grieved, for she was extremely good to me as a young fellow. I persuaded Father to have her buried in our private family cemetery behind the sugar mill, and

I planted two cabbage palms the day after she was buried. . . . More happy news I must now impart. Hermine and Jim are now officially betrothed, and Father and old Jim are very pleased about the match. Mother is not too fond of Jim; she thinks he is rather too fond of rum, and that later in life he may make Hermine unhappy. In a way, her fears have some justification, for I have seen Jim drinking, and for a fellow of his age I did not consider him as restrained as he ought to have been. However, we must hope for the best. . . . I trust you will not resume your friendship with that woman, Mrs. Hartfield, but will make every attempt to find yourself a wife. Remember you are the owner of a plantation that bears the name of one of our most venerated ancestors—Kaywana. It is essential that you have sons to take charge when you are too old, as Willem has virtually taken over from Uncle Edward. You are twenty-two. It is time you were married. . . ."

In reply, Graham wrote: "I am beginning to wonder whether I shall ever get married. I have seen no young woman here who appeals to me, either in a physical or spiritual sense. It will be no easy thing to replace Clara. I did not love her passionately, I now realise, but I was deeply fond of her; had she been of my age and unmarried, I think I could have taken her for wife. There is goodness and sweetness and generosity in her, and, for me, those are the qualities that seem most valuable. I care nothing about sons to carry on our name or take charge of the plantation. You will frown upon this attitude of mine, no doubt, as you have done before, but I cannot help how I am fashioned in temper. . . . I am sorry to hear of Marta's death, and I am pleased that you were so considerate in seeing that she was decently interred. Your loyalty to the people you love is, indeed, remarkable, and does not appear consistent with the other parts of your character, if I may be so critical as to mention such a matter. . . . Please give my love to Nibia, and tell her I think of her very often. . . . I was nearly forgetting to mention that I met by accident a woman called Sarah Hubert who claims she is Rose's mother and recently visited you there. No doubt she has named herself after Cousin Hubertus. She is a fine woman, and her speech is remarkably good. It is evident that Cousin Hubertus must have taken her very close under his wing. Though it is also evident that she is naturally a woman who desires to improve her lot and her cultivation of manner. I trust that Rose will follow closely upon her mother's example. I notice that you make no mention of how your efforts are proceeding to bring Jacob and Rose together. Must I assume that you are failing, dear brother, to shape the lives of these two in accordance with your principles of family cohesion? I am jesting, but, in truth, I should be pleased to see such a match, for, like yourself, I am fond of Jacob and consider him a fine fellow. . . ."

Nor did Dirk, in his reply, make any mention of his hopes for Rose and Jacob, nor did he even comment on Graham's jeering remarks, which, thought his elder brother, most unusual for Dirk. Dirk was never reluctant to take up a challenge. His only reference to Jacob was: "Mr. Green took Jacob to the Goole plantation on the West Bank, where a new residence is being erected for the manager. Jacob has suggested that it might be a profitable thing to develop a timber grant. Timber, he feels, will one day be as important as coffee and sugar. I am giving thought to his opinions. He may be right."

"He's a strange fellow," Graham told Pelham, his cousin, one evening when he was at Flagstaff; his gaze strayed out of a window of the sitting-room to the distant fringe of bush that bordered the seashore, and his grey-blue eyes had a slightly pained, tortured look. "There is not a day since I've left Berbice that I haven't been conscious of Dirk's presence in the world, if I may so express it. He has coloured my every thought. When I plan anything, I ask myself if this would have met with Dirk's approval. Or would he have frowned upon the notion? Or would he be indifferent? I can't say I have any deep love for him—but I know that I respect him, younger than I as he is." He clasped his hands together tight and shook his head in a baffled way. "Would you believe it if I told you that in all the four years I have been here in Demerary I have never once felt a passionate desire to return to my home on the Canje. And do you know why, Pelham? It's because of Dirk. Deep down inside me, I feel afraid of him. I'm a coward—that is what it amounts to, I suppose. But I cannot help it. I keep remembering those raccoon eyes—in the portrait Uncle Edward has done—and in the living state—and some instinct, or intuition, if you will, warns me to keep my distance from Dirk."

Pelham, tall like his father—and like Graham—but very fair, with eyes of a washed-out blue, and tiny reddish freckles on his forehead and cheeks and even on his neck, was a good listener. Unlike the brusque, ironic, and often forthright Willem, he knew how to be sympathetic to Graham's sensitive, feminine moods. "I haven't met him," said Pelham, "but from what you've told me of him, I can realise that he must be an unlikeable fellow—even a trifle mad, as you suggest. But that shouldn't surprise you," added Pelham, with a smile just a little reminiscent of his brother's. "We are noted for our unbalanced tempers, aren't we?"

Graham laughed. "Yes. I understand. Those letters do reveal much madness as well as cruelty, I warrant. But Dirk's madness is of a special kind, Pelham," he said seriously, wincing. He heard the booming of the sea, and the sound seemed laden with omen, and he cursed himself for his fancifulness. "There is too much sanity contained in its workings," he went on, after a pause during which Pelham watched his face with patience and interest. "He is obsessed, yet he does not act rashly or hysterically. For instance, this matter of Jacob and Rose. I made a jesting remark about his plan to have them married, but he was silent in his reply. That baffles me. It instils in me a feeling that he is furious because I have dared to make fun of him, so furious that he is compelled to ignore my remarks. And this gives me the further feeling that he is awaiting his opportunity to strike at me—and strike in a way that will be deadly."

"That," said Pelham, "is the height of fancifulness. And I'm sure you must see it is when you ponder calmly on the matter. You are permitting your mind to magnify Dirk's personality into what it could not possibly be. He may be obsessed and rather obnoxious in many ways, but he is not the ogre you imagine, I'm certain. What you want," added Pelham, "is a good torrid wife." He patted his cousin on the shoulder. "I mean it. Dirk is right there. You should look for a wife."

"Willem didn't marry until he was thirty," said Graham. "Why should I hurry? And what of you? You're about a month or two older than I am? Aren't you looking for a wife, too?"

"I have found her. Elfrida McLeod. The announcement is next week—and the marriage, we trust, in May."

Graham mumbled his congratulations, swept by a sudden feeling of ineffectuality and defeat. A chill of isolation began to close in around him, and he was aware of an inner trembling of panic. Willem was married, and now Pelham was betrothed. His cousins were fulfilling their duty as expected of them; they would have children and carry on the illustrious name of van Groenwegel. In his fancy, he could see Dirk smiling and nodding at Pelham.

It was at a reception at the Governor's residence, a few months later, that Graham was able to have a long chat with Clara. The occasion was one that could not be neglected by anyone who mattered in Georgetown society, for it was the first reception given by the new

Governor, Brigadier General John Murray, who had succeeded Carmichael. For Carmichael had never recovered from his illness. He died on the eleventh of May. Murray had come from Berbice, where he had been acting as Governor, and it was known that he was a great friend of the planters, Dutch as well as English. He felt as the planters felt about the missionaries, and the planters were determined to keep him feeling that way.

Clara was quiet in her manner, and not as daringly dressed as was her wont. It was obvious that her outlook on life had undergone a distinct change within the past year. She looked older. When she smiled, the crow's feet around her eyes were far more pronounced than of yore, thought Graham—but he did not mind. To him, she was the same sweet, fine person who had brought so much richness into his scheme of being. He still saw her as something infinitely precious, and he told her so, as they stood near an eastern window, engrossed in each other and oblivious of the milling, jabbering crowd of people in the large room.

"How devoted a worshipper you are," she returned. "But I feel it is time I took action on your behalf again, Graham. And this time it will be to find you someone who can replace me. No, no. It is no use protesting. I mean it. Pelham is married. Willem's wife is expecting a new member of the van Groenwegel clan. Harvey is a year younger than you, and we are soon to announce his betrothal to the Hampton girl—the elder one. She is two years older than Harvey, but a very pleasant girl, and very suitable. It must be your turn now, Graham. I am going to take the matter in hand without delay."

Graham smiled—but he knew that she meant what she said.

14

ON the Canje, in Berbice, Dirk, though not yet eighteen, was already actively on the hunt for a wife. He made no secret of the matter, and one day even told his mother: "The moment I see the right one I shall marry her, and I trust you and Father will raise no objections because I am not yet of age."

Elizabeth opened her eyes, smiled coldly, and replied: "We should certainly raise objections if you were to find her before you are twenty." And Storm, who overheard, remarked: "I am in complete agreement with you, my dear."

"You reckon," said Dirk, smiling as coldly as his mother, "without my wiles."

Elizabeth was silent, and Storm smoked on composedly, at the other end of the sitting-room, ostensibly engrossed in the book he was reading.

Dirk chuckled and left the room, a slim, wiry fellow of medium height with a narrow head, his eyes still like raccoon's eyes, bright, sharp, penetrating, cold. "I'm going upstairs to write Graham," he said as he was at the door. "Any messages for him, pray?"

"My love, as usual," murmured his mother. Storm said nothing.

Breakfast was behind them, and soon it would be siesta time. The day was hot and steamy, the sun shining through a hazy layer of grey-white cloud. Rain had fallen heavily during the morning, and the air smelt of mud and wet leaves.

After Dirk had written his letter, he left the house and went to the *stelling*, boarded the yatch and sat waiting. Presently, his father arrived, got on board, and the boatmen became active with their oars.

In the little cabin aft, Storm read his book while Dirk stared out at the monotonous vista of *mucca-mucca* plants that fringed the bank of the Creek. Storm had greyed considerably during the past few years, and he had grown stouter about the middle. He was a very avid reader, and indulged in less and less conversation as the years passed. "The secret of happiness," he had once said to Elizabeth with a faintly ironic smile, "is to be imperturbable." And after a pause, he had added with a twinkle: "And to be taciturn."

Once a week, however, he travelled to New Amsterdam for his visit to the tavern in the High Street which he had frequented almost from the first day of his arrival in Berbice twenty-three years before. Dirk always accompanied him on the yatch, for Dirk liked to take this opportunity of despatching his weekly letter to Graham and of calling on Jacob at his workshop.

Just before they parted on the *stelling* at New Amsterdam, Storm said: "Dirk, my boy, I'd be glad if you would call on your Aunt Mary and see whether she has recovered from her fever. Tell her I shall try to come in about five o'clock to see her, and trust Doctor John will be at home, too."

"Very well, Father. I'll deliver your message." As Dirk strode off along the muddy street that ran past Colony House, and led towards the Greens' cottage and workshop, Dirk smiled to himself, for he knew that there was no real necessity for him to call at the home of Doctor John to inquire after Aunt Mary's health. But his father had heard that Doctor John and Aunt Mary were concerned because Dirk treated them with such indifference. Since they had moved to this new home of their own in February last, Dirk had only once called upon them, and then only because Elizabeth had asked him to do so. In Dirk's estimation, his uncle was a nonentity. "Weak and soft," he had told Jacob once. "Even Mother has more guts than Uncle John. And Aunt Mary is always crooning and mewling over me. I can't stand her. They haven't even produced a child. What are they good for!"

Dirk decided that he would make the call before going to the Greens', and even before despatching his letter. "Get it over and be done with," he muttered, as he turned off into the High Street. Ahead of him, in a southerly direction, the carriage with his father was just coming to a stop outside the tavern. The High Street, as muddy as any other street in the town, was about a quarter of a mile in length, with shops and two-storeyed residences on both sides. His uncle's home was on the western side of the street, and going up the long stairway that was built, like its fellows on all the other houses, on the outside, Dirk could look across the open tract of land that lay between the High Street and the river. It was a splendid view, and the harbour, at the moment, looked particularly picturesque with the seven or eight ships that lay at anchor, their tall masts elegant against the watery-blue sky.

To his surprise, Dirk found that someone else was standing in the portico besides himself. He had been so captivated by the sight of the harbour that he had not noticed the figure waiting within the gloom of the dense vines that covered the latticework on one side of the portico. He started and exclaimed: "Who are you? What are you doing here?"

"I have been knocking for the past few minutes," said the girl. She was about his own age, he estimated, and very dark-haired and dark-eyebrowed. She was taller than he by at least an inch and a half, and her dark-blue eyes stared fearlessly at him from under the shelter of the dark eyebrows. She was slim and pleasingly shaped, and dressed like a lady, though not very fashionably.

"Why have you been knocking?" asked Dirk, unsmiling. He was impressed by this creature, but decided that he must be careful not to show it.

"For an obvious reason," said the girl coldly. "I want the doctor."

"I see. And have you received no reply?"

"None—not yet. It appears that everyone is out."

"There must be servants at home. Unless they are asleep at the back. I won't be surprised. Doctor John and my aunt are such weak fools, it would be nothing extraordinary to discover that they are slack and easy with their slaves."

"Who are you?" she asked, her voice as assured as his own.

He told her, and asked: "Who are you?"

"Cornelia Rueff," she answered. She suddenly bit her lower lip, and, with a shock, he received the impression that she was in pain. "I am from the house next door. My parents and the rest of us are staying there until we move to our plantation house on the Canje. I met with a slight accident, that is why I am here." She spoke beautifully, he thought, and wondered whether she knew English.

"An accident. I see. I'm sorry to hear that. Anything serious?"

In silence she raised her right hand and showed him the palm. A long splinter of wood had run deep into the flesh, and the wound was sticky with blood. After a pause, she sighed. "I was sliding down the banister of the stairs," she said, "when it happened."

"You? Sliding down the banisters of the stairs? Why were you doing such a thing?"

"Because I like to. Since I was a child I've liked sliding down banisters."

Dirk gave her an incredulous stare, then grunted: "You're odd."

"You're odd, too. And uncouth."

"Am I? I'm a van Groenwegel." His hands clenched slowly.

"Who are they?"

"You are living in this colony and don't know who are the van Groenwegels?"

"I'm just from Essequibo. My father has bought over a plantation, the owner of which has gone insolvent. I know no one in Berbice. And I still think you most brusque and uncouth, though a van Groenwegel."

Dirk smiled. "I like you. You have fire. By God! You're the first girl who has ever talked back at me like this." Suddenly he frowned. "But why didn't you get a reply when you knocked? This is gross slackness!" He strode to the door, and hammered thunderously on it. "Did you knock like that?" he asked her.

"I'm afraid not. Not as loud." She was wincing—evidently from the pain.

Almost at once the sound of bare feet came inside the gallery, and the door was opened. A short, red-eyed slave in a dirty smock stared at them. She was old and looked shaky on her feet. "Massa? Missy? You want Doctor John?"

"Where is he? Why didn't you answer the door when this lady knocked? I suppose you were sleeping."

"Ow! Yes, massa. I got fever, massa."

"Where are your master and mistress?"

"Massa Doctor John gone out visiting, massa. And Missy sleeping, and say nobody must disturb her until four o'clock."

Dirk clicked his tongue. "I could have thought so. Get inside. And next time put on something cleaner before you answer the door. It's disgraceful that a filthy hag like you should be allowed to receive callers." He gave her a push into the gallery and slammed the door shut. Turned to the girl and said: "Come. Your hand must be seen after. I have a plan. Follow me."

She made no move. Only stared at him, hostile, resistant.

He jerked his thumb towards the street. "Did you hear me? I want to have your hand seen after. Come with me. Follow me."

He began to descend the stairs—and, after an instant's hesitation, Cornelia Rueff followed. Without a word, they made their way, side by side, in a northerly direction along the High Street, both set of face, but not tense.

In a few minutes, as they turned off into a narrow street, even more muddy than the High Street—a mere dam it was, in reality, bordering the cane fields of Plantation Vryheid—he gave her face a swift glance and felt relieved to note that she showed no finicky distaste at having to plod through all this soft mud. He could not stand girls who were finicky about discomforts.

"You don't seem to mind the mud," he remarked—and she sniffed, gave him a contemptuous glance, and replied: "Is this mud? If you'd lived on the Essequibo then you would know what mud is like."

"I like you more and more," he said with a brief grin.

Abruptly he held her arm and said, "It's here we're bound for," and led her on to a bridge of two planks that spanned a deep trench. They crossed it without mishap, and he could see that she was accustomed to negotiating such improvised bridges. His heart beat rapidly. Here was the girl he was looking for, there could be no doubt about it.

The tiny cottage was of shingles, and the roof of palm-leaf trash. The tiny shed behind it was strong but very rudimentary, also with a palm-leaf roof.

Mr. Green stopped planing a board, and smiled a welcome to Dirk and the girl, and Jacob, thick-chested and burly, his curly black hair very untidy, his coarse hands dusty with chalk, grinned with his large, white teeth, and said: "Who is this young lady you've brought to see me, Dirk, boy?"

"You had better be respectful how you refer to her," warned Dirk, giving him a cuff in the chest. "I'm going to marry her. She is Cornelia Rueff, and she has been sliding down a banister and got her hand badly injured."

Both Mr. Green and Jacob examined the hand the girl held out, and Mr. Green said: "I have a pair of pincers that will get the splinter out, my young lady. Have no fear. Wait a moment and let me get it clean."

Dirk gave Cornelia an anxious look, but the girl was quite calm. "Please proceed with whatever you wish to do," she said. "I don't care what you use, so long as you get the splinter out."

"You're a brave girl," said Jacob as he went off to get a basin of water. "And you have to be brave," he added before he vanished round the tiny water tank, "if you're going to marry Dirk."

Dirk threw a block of wood at him, but Jacob was too agile.

A few minutes later, she merely bit her lower lip and uttered a gasped "Oooh!" as Mr. Green caught the end of the splinter and pulled it out. He held it up in the pincers for them to see, and it was about an inch and a half long. Mr. Green's lined olive face beamed with admiration. "Yes, you're a brave young miss. My commendations. And now we must put some salve on it for you." He wanted to bandage it, too, but the girl said he must not bother.

"I have had worse accidents than this happen to me," she smiled. "I'm known to be very wild. Wounds heal very quickly, and I never pamper them."

"Will you have a cup of coconut water, miss?" asked Mr. Green, and the girl nodded and thanked him. "I should be glad." She pulled herself up on to the workbench, and Dirk and Jacob seated themselves, one on each side of her.

"I like carpenter's work sheds," she said, looking round. "I used to help our carpenter on the Essequibo, and once I built a whole shed."

"Where is this new plantation your father has bought?" asked Dirk.

"It's on the Canje," she said. "Don Diego it is called."

Both Dirk and Jacob exclaimed in chorus: "The van Niffens' place!"

"That is right. Do you know it? Mynheer van Niffens is insolvent."

"I should think we know it," said Dirk. "Our place is next door. We've known the van Niffenses since we were all tiny children."

"I heard old van Niffens was in bad water," nodded Jacob, "but I didn't think it would have come to their having to sell out."

Later that afternoon, after Dirk had seen her home and despatched his letter, he returned to the Greens', and in the workshop, as the shed was called, he and Jacob had their usual talk on current affairs, though on this occasion Dirk kept straying back continually to the theme of Cornelia. "A fine creature, Jacob. She has fire, did you notice? I'm pretty certain she is the one for me. I can feel it inside me. She's no softy. Did you see how she behaved when Mr. Green pulled out that splinter? She's got guts. She would make a fitting wife for a hard van Groenwegel like me, and I mean to pursue her." Suddenly his raccoon's eyes fixed themselves upon Jacob, and he said: "When last have you seen Rose? I suppose you don't bother to call on her."

"She's a busy young lady," said Jacob. "Making dresses for high and low, rich and poor. No time for a rough-and-ready carpenter like me."

"She's budding out nicely, have you noticed?"

"I couldn't miss that," grinned Jacob. He winked. "But have you seen Millicent lately? She's got more than buds. Nice firm, fat mangoes."

Dirk gave a sly smile. "Jacob, you can say it plainly now. I've known for over a year how you feel about Millicent. It's she you want to marry, isn't it?"

"Sssh! Mr. Green got sharp ears, boy. He's in the kitchen."

"It's Millicent, isn't it?" persisted Dirk, lowering his voice. "Tell me."

Jacob fidgeted and shrugged. "I like her, I won't fool you, Dirk."

"I knew it. You think Rose pretty, but you still look upon her as a child."

"Something like that," nodded Jacob. "And more than that. I don't think I could ever like Rose. I simply don't take to her—and she doesn't like me."

Dirk nodded, his face serious. "That's one big plan of mine fallen to bits. Graham asked me in a letter, some months ago, whether I'd failed, but I never replied on the matter, because I'd begun to feel he was right, and it annoyed me to think he had guessed correctly."

"I'm sorry, Dirk—but I can't help how I feel about Millicent."

"Are she and her sister still going to that school the missionaries have set up in the Winkel?"

"Yes. She can read and write as well as me," said Jacob. "Joanna, too. Harry Logan, the shopkeeper's son, has his eyes on Joanna."

"Rose knows even Latin and Greek," said Dirk. "Old Mynheer Hiemens used to compliment her often. She's a cultivated person, and I'm sorry old Hiemens had to die off like that. Father hasn't thought it worth while to procure another tutor. Hermine and I have completed our education—at least, we have gone as far as is necessary for cultivated people in this colony. Father couldn't very well get a tutor for Rose's benefit only."

"Naturally not. And Hermine is getting married next month." Jacob winked. "And you're getting married next year to Cornelia Rueff."

"I'm serious about that, you goat!" snapped Dirk. "I like that girl. And if she's going to be next door to us on the van Niffens' place, be sure I'm not going to miss a chance to pursue her. I like her. I can feel my hands on her already."

"And your legs."

"Stop being obscene." His fingers began to tap together, and his eyes glittered and became shifty. "She's tough, rough, hard. She'll produce the kind of children I want. Forceful van Groenwegels brimming over with fighter blood."

"Who're they going to fight?"

"The world. All men. They must be masters in this colony. They must control the whole sugar industry, the whole timber industry, the whole cotton and coffee industry. A master family." He jerked round nervously, brittly. "Yes, Jacob, I believe you're right about timber. As soon as I get into my stride I shall see about securing a timber grant. How would you like to be my manager?"

"I'd like it very much. Timber has a big future, boy."

"Good. Well, at least I'll be able to know how to plan in that direction. Pity about Rose and yourself—but I suppose it's no use troubling. Heart matters are always so damned unstable and unpredictable. I shall never let my heart get the better of me. I shall see that my heart is kept on a rein, by God!"

Jacob grunted, and Dirk glanced at him sharply. "You don't feel that way, of course. You believe in drooling over your womenfolk."

"Millicent is worth drooling over," sighed Jacob. "I dream about her every night."

"And probably all day long." Dirk gave him a cuff. "Damned idiot!" He clenched his hands. "Sentiment must be kept in its place, Jacob, if you want to reach the heights. You should read some of the things old Hendri wrote to Grandfather Jacques. The letters are all there. Old Jacques must have brought them back to the Canje house when he returned from Berbice. Power. The pinnacles. We must aim to reach the pinnacles, old Hendrickje used to keep telling him. And that's my aim, too, for the van Groenwegels of the future. Power—and the pinnacles!"

15

I T was not long before the Rueffs had established themselves at their new plantation, Don Diego, a few miles upstream from New Signal. Mynheer Karl Rueff was half German and half Dutch, but in temperament and habits was Dutch through and through. He was a severe disciplinarian, and believed in doing things in the traditional way. He allowed Indians to hunt and fish on his land, because he felt that this was an excellent means of obtaining game for his table; the Indians always shared with the plantation owner whatever fish or game they won. Also, felt Mynheer Rueff, the presence of Indians on his plantation was salutary in that the black people regarded the Indians as policemen; no slave would attempt to run away, for it was a foregone conclusion that he would be tracked down and brought back within a matter of hours. Indians, for two centuries, had allied themselves with the white planters against the Negro slaves, so that an uprising was less likely when Indians were encamped in the neighbourhood.

At table, Mynheer Rueff insisted on his female slaves being clean and very respectful and formal in their manner of address. All household females were compelled to wear only a piece of linen about their loins. No smocks were tolerated. This again was traditional, for the Dutch planters of the past had frowned upon their young Negresses cohabiting with the males before such time as the master approved. A naked girl could not easily conceal her pregnancy, and should her breasts betray signs of her being in this condition, she was instantly banished from the house and sent to work in the fields as a punishment.

"Very sensible," Dirk agreed when Mynheer Rueff one Sunday, at breakfast, commented on his adherence to the old customs. Dirk was sitting next to Cornelia in the large but rather shabby dining-room at Don Diego. Cornelia's parents had heard of his attachment to the girl, and went out of their way to encourage it. "I believe in old customs myself. Progress in a practical sense, in the working of a plantation and so forth, I can understand—but one's personal life at home should be governed by strict rules and customs."

"I don't feel that way," said Cornelia. "I detest customs and rules of any kind. The English people do not let their female slaves appear in a nude state, and I think we ought to follow their custom."

"In our home we have always let them do as they please. Some bold wenches have preferred discarding their smocks; others have worn them as a matter of habit. Janie used to wear nothing when serving at table, years ago, but Nibia always wore her smock. When you're mistress of New Signal you can arrange matters to suit yourself. Nude female slaves affect me neither one way nor another."

"You seem to take a lot for granted," she said, tossing her head. "Are you so sure I shall be mistress of New Signal?"

He nodded. "Quite sure. When I am ready for you I shall come here and haul you off—and you'll like being hauled off. Won't you?"

She gave a reluctant smile, and said nothing for a long while after, despite his persistent baiting. She was a girl of very equable temperament. She seldom grew heated in her conversation, and often it was difficult to tell what she was thinking or feeling. She had a mystery about her, and Dirk preferred her this way. It stimulated his interest in her. She was a girl, he felt, who must be explored. She must be probed into, but with care, for she was strong. He could feel her strength. Yet he was not lacking in confidence. He had no doubt whatever that he would win her. He was not impatient, for he had no fear in the matter. And he could sense that she was responsive, despite her subtle airs of contempt.

Like himself, she was fond of the open air, and would often roam about in the bush or go swimming in the canal. Once she accompanied him and Jacob and a party of Indians on a *labba* hunt. She could handle a musket as well as himself or Jacob, and could throw a spear; the Indians on the Essequibo had taught her, she told them. She was an only child, and had had to adventure alone; there had been no children on the neighbouring plantations in Essequibo. Indians had always been her companions; she loved them, and could even speak their tongue.

One Sunday about six months later—in May of the following year,

1814—Dirk decided that the time had come to show her the canister and the letters which, nowadays, he kept in his own bedroom, under his bed. The Rueffs and three other families were having breakfast at New Signal, and when the meal was over, Dirk said to Cornelia: "I want you to come upstairs to my room. I have something important you must see."

She smiled and returned: "You need not make a mystery about it. I know what it is, and have been waiting for you to tell me you were ready to show me. It is the canister of old family letters."

"How did you guess?"

"I know you better than you think I do—and your canister is talked about far more than you probably imagine. Let us go upstairs."

He grunted, annoyed that she had destroyed the drama of the moment. "I had intended this to be a sacred occasion," he said, "and now you treat it as though it were nothing. I don't allow everyone to see that canister, you understand?" He gripped her arm as they reached the top of the stairs. "This is a privilege I'm conferring on you because I have chosen you to be the mother of my children—the van Groenwegels of the future."

He glared at her, and she stared back at him, unsmiling, but with a faint twinkle of amusement in her dark blue eyes. "I thank you for the honour," she said, after a pause, not attempting to conceal the irony in her voice.

"Come on," he growled abruptly, and almost dragged her into the northeastern room, which, since Hermine's marriage and departure nearly a year before, he had claimed for himself. The wind hummed in at the high windows, and they could smell Creek water and cane juice mingled with the sourness of coffee berries drying in the sun. It was a hot, sunny day outside, and the compound was dusty, and the orange and sapodilla trees rustled in a soft breeze coming from the Corentyne.

For a minute, as though hypnotised, they stood silent, in the middle of the room, staring through the window nearest at the glaring scene with its glitter of leaves. It was almost as though they were already man and wife and this room their own—the big double bed in the southeastern corner the one in which they would make love, and in which their children would be born.

She touched his arm and said quietly: "I'm sorry I spoiled your sacred moment, Dirk." And he started, scowled, and then grinned briefly and said: "No need to be sorry. I was making a fool of myself, as usual. They all say I'm obsessed with this family pride of mine.

But I can't help dreaming of the future—I can't help remembering the past as revealed by those letters."

"Let me see them."

They spent nearly two hours seated on the bed, with the canister on the floor before them, exuding its aroma of old parchment and creosote, for Dirk, like Wilfred, had taken care to see that the lid was regularly painted with creosote to keep away insects.

"I keep Graham's in a special box near the writing table over there," he told her. "At first, I put one or two of them into the canister here, but I had to take them out, for they began to get too numerous, and the canister would not have been able to hold them all and the others."

"Let me see some of his," she said, after they had read a number of the old ones. So he opened the box near the writing table—a large cedar affair with brass hasps and fittings—and showed her Graham's letters.

"He doesn't write as often nowadays," he frowned. "Especially since he has become betrothed to this girl from Barbados Clara Hartfield found for him. I think she's distantly related to Graeme Clackson."

"You have told me about this Clara Hartfield. She seems a forceful woman."

"Something like you, I agree. She manages Graham, because he's soft, but I can see now that she would have made a good wife for a strong van Groenwegel." He handed her Graham's last letter and said: "Read that. That will give you some idea of the state of things between her and Graham."

". . . I was somewhat doubtful about taking this step, for I am not deeply in love with Mary Beckles; I am merely fond of her, for she is a kindly, sweet-tempered girl. However, Clara convinced me that she would make me just the kind of wife I would be most happy with, and Clara is so wise in everything she decides for me that I yielded and asked Mary's parents for permission to become betrothed. They were pleased, and gave me their consent, and have even agreed that when they return to Barbados next week they will permit Mary to remain with Mr. Beckles's brother and his family at Sarabelle on the West Coast—not far from Uncle Raphael's place. So I shall still be able to see Mary. As for when the actual marriage is to take place, I shall not predict. It depends so much on what Clara feels on the matter. I have come to rely on her wisdom. . . ."

"Can you envisage me relying on the wisdom of a woman! Pah!"

Cornelia said nothing—merely smiled in her mysterious manner.

"A man must rely on his own judgments." He suddenly gripped her arm, fixing his gaze upon her with a fierce intensity. "I'm nineteen in September, and you're nineteen next month. Next year about this time would be ideal for our getting married. But things are too uncertain. In *my* way of seeing the matter—and I rely upon *my* wisdom—it would be imprudent for us to get married so soon. We must wait until this period of doubt in Europe and in the colonies has passed. Napoleon has just been defeated, and there is talk that we may be handed back to Holland. If that happens, the climate of our politics and economy will undergo a complete change. These Britishers and their sentimental attitudes towards the slaves are ruining the colonies. I can make no plans for the future until I am certain whether we are to remain British or go back to the Dutch. So we must wait, Cornelia. Do you hear? Do you mind waiting?"

She shook her head, then shrugged and smiled, and said: "I can wait, because, contrary to what you feel, I am not certain I have seen the man I want to marry."

He glared at her, then broke into a grin. "You think you are not. That's what you mean. I have no doubt about the woman I'm going to marry. It's you. And I'll have you when I'm ready for you." He gripped her arm again, and this time he hurt her, for she winced. He did not relax his grip. "I shall have you when I'm ready—if I have to abduct you and carry you into the bush."

"And what will happen when we're in the bush?" she laughed.

"I'll keep you there until I tame you, then lead you back here as my devoted wife." He laughed. "I'm hurting your arm. Never mind! Sometimes I shall have to hurt you—but it will be for your good, in the long run." He started round with a snarling exclamation, for footsteps had sounded in the corridor, and Rose and another mulatto girl appeared.

"I was looking everywhere for you, Dirk. What are you doing up here?"

"Oh, it's you," scowled Dirk. "I don't want to be disturbed. I'm showing Cornelia the letters." He shut the canister hastily. "Who is this girl?"

"She has come with me to help me measure your mother for her new dress. Her name is Priscilla David. She's Miss Henson's niece."

Miss Henson was the seamstress who had taught Rose to sew and for whom Rose now worked.

"You had no right to come in here to disturb me," frowned Dirk, but did not sound fierce. "Get out and go and attend to your business."

Rose, at fourteen, was as tall as Dirk. She was a light olive, with long, wavy hair. She was very pretty, and had features that revealed only a trace of the Negroid—and, if anything, these traces enhanced her loveliness. She had full lips—the full lips of the Negro—though they lacked the thickness of the Negro's. In body she was lissome and graceful in a way sometimes reminiscent of a bird and at other times of a cat. Dirk often teased her, calling her a cat-bird. "Sometimes I'm sure you're on the point of taking off, and then I can see what you want to do is to spring upon me. A cat, damme, and a bird in one!"

Her companion, shy and very awed by the big house and its white occupants, hung back in the corridor, but Rose, who had grown up with Dirk and Hermine and been tutored with them, experienced no shyness. She entered and told Dirk: "I'll get out when I've told you what I want to."

"And what's that?" asked Dirk, conscious of Cornelia's gaze upon him, for in Rose's presence he was always unsure of himself; deep within, he knew why, but it angered him to admit it openly to himself. Such an admission, he felt, would put him in a vulnerable position. Secretly he feared Rose.

"It's about Jacob. You've been putting ideas into his head, haven't you?"

Dirk grinned, and fidgeted. "Only ideas that I consider good," he growled, trying to look serious again. "Has he been talking to you recently?"

"Yes, he has. And I think you've been very foolish. I've always looked on Jacob as a kind of brother—and I'll always look on him as such. He says that since I was eight or nine you've been trying to make a match between us."

"Oh, get outside, Rose! Go and do your measuring for Mother."

Rose began to laugh. She stood there, her shrill fourteen-year-old voice filling the room. Her slim body trembled as though it were the fuel around which the flame of her laughter curled and flickered. Dirk rose from the bed and made a dart at her. She dodged, and she and Dirk began to play a game of grab-and-dodge around the room. Eventually Dirk lunged desperately forward and caught her, swept her off her feet into his arms and bore her out of the room into the corridor. He dumped her on to the floor, dashed back into the room and slammed and locked the door. Outside in the corridor, Rose's laughter continued for a moment, still shrill and vital, then faded away toward the western side of the house. Dirk, scowling and grumbling, returned to the bed where Cornelia still sat, quiet and impassive, as though entirely unaffected by all the recent commotion. She smiled slightly as Dirk seated himself beside her and took up Graham's letter. She said: "You're trembling."

"What! Trembling! What do you mean?" he snapped. The letter fell from his hand. He retrieved it hastily. But there could be no doubt. His hands did tremble. And there was a trembling in his limbs as well. He sprang up and said: "Mustn't I be trembling after all that horseplay? Stupid fool of a girl!"

"A very lovely little creature, isn't she?"

"I suppose so, I suppose so! But a mulatto!" He clenched his teeth hard, but his head was still inclined to tremble. "Let me get this canister locked up again. Shall we go for a swim in the canal?"

"The day is so hot. I think that would be a splendid way of cooling off."

As he locked the canister his self-assurance returned. He straightened up after he had shoved the canister under the bed, looked at her, and said: "I'm not trembling now. So stop laughing at me."

"Am I laughing at you, Dirk?"

"Yes. Under that calm face of yours you're laughing. I know you are. But you are wrong in what you think. I am master of myself, and when I'm ready I shall be master of you." He stretched out and gripped her shoulders, stared into her eyes, and saw her stare back at him, calmly, without fear.

"There isn't a physical weakness I cannot conquer. Understand that."

"You are hurting me, Dirk."

"You can stand pain. I knew it on the first day I met you. You're hard and stoical. You're the woman I want—and nothing will divert me from my course. I can tremble—but I can stop trembling when I will it. Let's go and swim."

On their way downstairs, they heard Rose's laughter again, and he tensed. His hands clenched. Then the tension passed, and he began to chuckle. Harshly, with a slight note of bravado.

16

GRAHAM'S marriage was fixed for the seventeenth of December of that same year, but it did not come off. About the middle of November, Lashley, one of his overseers, returned from Georgetown, where he had been sent by Graham to purchase plantation supplies, and handed Graham a note. "Mr. Hartfield says his wife asked him to have this sent to you, sir. It is urgent, I believe."

The note said: "I have such evil news to give you, my darling Graham, that I feel I cannot do it on paper. Will you please come to see me today?"

Graham asked Lashley, who was a Barbadian of Scottish-Irish extraction and one of his most trusted lieutenants: "Did you have any hint from anyone in Mr. Hartfield's shop that something untoward had happened?"

Lashley shook his head, his manner uncomfortable. "No, Mr. van Groenwegel—but on the *stelling* I heard some talk that disturbed me."

"What talk was that, Lashley? Tell me. I'm not afraid. Has there been an accident of some sort to one of my relatives? My Uncle Edward? Mr. Willem?"

"No, sir. It's not that. It has to do with your lady, sir."

"My lady? Miss Beckles?"

Lashley began to shift his feet about awkwardly. "Yes, sir. I won't like to say anything about it to you, if you won't object, sir."

Graham gave him a reassuring pat on the shoulder. "Don't be a fool, man. You know I'm not an ogre. I won't kill you. What has happened?"

After a pause, Lashley told him: "I have heard it talked, sir, that Miss Beckles sailed on the *Marion Logan* by the morning tide."

"Sailed? Sailed for where? I'm marrying her next month."

"She sailed on the *Marion Logan*, it is said, sir. I heard it from the mate of the *Amsterdam*. With her was Mr. Ralph Hartmansworth of Plantation Sarabelle, the brother-in-law of Mr. Beckles of that plantation."

"Ralph! Ralph was with her? Ralph was to have sailed for Jamaica."

"That is where the *Marion Logan* is going, sir."

"And she was with him, Lashley, did you say?"

"Yes, sir. So the mate of the *Amsterdam* told me."

An hour later, at the Hartfields' residence in Georgetown, Clara shook with rage as she said: "Graham, you are well rid of her. She's a heartless young hussy. And this young rogue, Ralph Hartmansworth, deserves to be shot. He's a ne'er-do-well, and a coward. He insulted Pelham on Sunday, and Pelham challenged him to a duel. The duel was to have taken place this morning near the fort. Pelham was there with his seconds—but Ralph never turned up. And then Willem came with the news that Ralph had persuaded Mary to go to Jamaica with him. He had been making overtures for some time, Willem said. He heard it from your Uncle Raphael, who one evening saw Mary and Ralph kissing on the pathway near your Uncle Raphael's place. Oh, my dear! I scolded Willem. I told him he ought to have spoken to you about it, ought to have warned you that Mary was being untrue to you——"

"There was no need," Graham interrupted. "I suspected it. Indeed, this is no surprise to me, Clara. I'm not even downcast, for I don't love Mary. I hinted to you I was marrying her merely because I felt it my duty to take a wife and produce sons to carry on our name——"

"Don't speak that way, Graham. I cannot bear it when you say such things. You are not passionate as I am, and as your Uncle Edward is, but you have it in you to cherish a woman. I must know, because I have been intimate with you. In time you would have come to love Mary—and even before your emotions had matured you would have been a devoted husband. That is what matters in a marriage, my darling. To be devoted even though passion may be lacking. It is so that John and I have lived. We always been devoted companions, though deficient in passionate love for each other. Oh, I am so depressed—depressed on your behalf."

He drew her to him. They were alone in the dining-room. He dabbed away the tears on her cheeks, and said: "So long as you are my devoted friend I can never be depressed, so you are wasting your energies in being concerned over my happiness. This should be a lesson to you, Clara. Stop attempting to arrange my matrimonial affairs. I am happy living as I am. Perchance some day when I am forty I shall meet an unattached woman who will move me as you have moved me, and I shall venture to marry her. Until then let us call quits!"

In the course of a letter he wrote to Dirk a week later, Graham said: "I experience at the moment a greater sense of independence. Secretly I had been looking forward with dread to this marriage; now I can devote my whole soul to the plantation, and already I can see the solution to many problems that had seemed beyond me. Shortage of labour has prevented me from developing the terrain aback of Canal Three, and now I am decided that I must leave this section in its present state and even abandon the adjoining section cultivated with coffee seedlings some two years previously. I have evolved a plan of concentration, so to speak, Dirk, lad, and though Willem scoffs at it, I believe it will prove beneficial. These are days when it would be a mistake to expand. We have no slave labour to boast of, remember, and though I am pleased for the poor black souls themselves, it is disappointing to my planter ambitions that the old days with their surfeit of slaves are no more. However, my plan is to concentrate my energies—and my labour—on certain restricted areas, and work these areas to their utmost, leaving the rest of the plantation to return to the jungle. In this way I hope to avoid unnecessary expenditure and eventual insolvency. There is hardly a plantation that is not threatened with insolvency. I have warned Willem and Uncle Edward, but they laugh at me. Uncle Edward hardly troubles about plantation matters these days. He gives virtually all his time to his painting and his building. Willem and Pelham make all the vital decisions. But I believe they are wrong. They have the traditional notion of grandeur, and feel that expansion must be achieved at any cost. We shall see whether they or I prove right. The issue should not long be delayed. . . . Here in Demerary everyone is in a state of doubt in respect to the fate of our colonies. If only we could be sure what the powers in Europe will decide. Shall we be Dutch or English next year? As the newspaper says, we are in a state of 'betweenity,' and know not what is to happen. Some even predict that we may have to learn Swedish, as Sweden may claim us for their own, and not the Dutch. For myself, I am composed in my attitude towards the whole affair, and wait patiently for what is to be. . . ."

Dirk replied: "Some instinct tells me that in this instance you are wise in adopting the policy you have about the plantation. I have spoken to Father, and advised him to concentrate as you are doing on certain selected areas. Father scoffs at me, as Willem and Pelham do at you, but I believe that, in time, he will come to understand that this shortage of slaves is more serious than he thinks. I curse that stupid, obtuse Anti-Slavery Party in England. They are at the bottom of all our troubles. Poor Mynheer van Niffens would not have gone insolvent if he had been able to procure some more slaves, and I know of a dozen others who have gone insolvent recently who would still have been flourishing had they been able to procure enough labour. More and more my ambitions begin to incline towards timber. The forests of this country are more valuable than we suspect. Jacob, I confess, first put the idea into my mind, and it keeps growing every day. Like you, however, I can make no progress with my plans until I know definitely whether we are to remain British or be handed over to the Dutch or the Swedish, and, of course, I am in no position as yet to manage affairs on this plantation. I superintend operations at the mill, and accompany Father on his morning tour of inspection, even discuss matters of planting with the overseers, and am quite fit to take charge, but Father will not relinquish his hold and retire to his books and his tobacco. I suspect that both he and Mother do not trust me. I sense always a hostility in their manner. They feel I am heartless and, perchance, even evil, and because of this they are withdrawn from me. Sometimes I feel baffled and isolated, and wish I had some understanding companion, and it is in such moments I go to Don Diego to see Cornelia. Yet even she with her mysterious airs does not give me true companionship. Like Father and Mother, she seems to suspect me of evil, and there is an element of hostility in her manner, though I am certain that she is attracted towards me. Only one female treats me with entire freedom and easy friendship, and does not show towards me any hostility, but her name must not be mentioned, for friendship with her on an intimate basis is out of the question. I had not intended to refer to this, so put it out of your mind and do not ask me questions concerning the matter. I will not discuss it. Regard it as an indiscretion, and fain would I cross it out at this moment but that would make my letter untidy, and I eschew untidiness of any sort. . . ."

It was Cornelia herself who, one afternoon early in July, of the

following year, 1815, invited Rose to join herself and Dirk in a picnic
on the bank of the canal back of New Signal. When she told Dirk
of it he frowned and said: "You know very well she is socially on a
different level from ours. I have told you that while I do not wish
to snub her, I cannot encourage her company. It will only cause her
pain later on. She will marry a coloured man like herself, won't she?
How could we have her in our home with her husband on a social
occasion?"

He kept twining his fingers together agitatedly as he spoke, his eyes
flashing from side to side, and she watched him calmly, a faint smile
on her face. They were on the portico of the Don Diego residence,
and the pale sunshine fell on his sandy hair, which made such a contrast with her near-jet tresses.

"Never mind, Dirk," she said. "She will understand when she gets
older. For the time present there is no harm if she joins us in an
outing on the canal." A low chuckle sounded within her, like some
tiny bell chiming within the gloom of an unexplored cave. "And you
won't find her presence too unbearable, I am certain, will you?"

He was on the point of snarling out an admonitory tirade, but
checked himself, for at that instant they heard a shrill call from the
pathway that led towards the stream. It was Rose.

Seated by the bank of the canal, they were relaxed and at ease, but
only Rose's manner was genuine. Under the surface, both Dirk and
Cornelia were somewhat tense. Despite her apparent calm, there was
something too erect in the way Cornelia sat, something too abrupt in
the glances she cast at Dirk. And Dirk laughed a little too loudly at
Rose's teasing remarks. Now and then his fingers would tap lightly
together.

They had brought food and wine, but Rose did most of the eating
and drinking. Dirk said he was not hungry, and Cornelia said: "I've
never had a big appetite," when Dirk challenged her about not eating
enough. "You know that very well. So stop scolding me."

The sky was overcast, and the sun shone down upon them weakly.
The air was warm and damp, and though it was daytime, crickets and
other insects kept clicking and cheeping amidst the bushes at intervals.

Then Jacob arrived, and Dirk seemed to breathe more easily.
"Thought you would never put in an appearance, you great big ba-
boon!"

"I'm a working man, you know," said Jacob. "And today isn't Sunday."

"You said you weren't busy just at present. Don't try to appear as if you are bound hand and foot to your workbench." Dirk laughed and jerked his thumb at the food. "Sit down and gobble up everything you see. Cornelia and I aren't hungry, but Rose is. Rose has been destroying it all for us."

"Dirk is sickening for a fever," said Rose, laughing. "He can't eat, poor boy. We shall have to send for Doctor John within the hour."

"I've brought news," said Jacob.

"What's that? Have they murdered someone in Colony House?"

"No. Napoleon. He's lost the war. The Duke of Wellington routed his armies at some place called Watertoo or Waterboo. A strange name. However, that is the news. A ship's captain told me an hour ago."

Dirk stiffened, and his hands clenched. "Napoleon defeated again! Are you sure, Jacob? Who was this ship's captain?"

"Klaart—he's Mr. Green's cousin, though he wouldn't like to hear it."

"Old Klaart! Then it must be true. The *Friesland* is in port, then?"

"Yes, she arrived by the morning tide."

Dirk's mood underwent a complete change. During the next hour he was thoughtful and taciturn. Even Rose's attempts to tease him and draw him into an argument did not succeed. He kept muttering: "I want to think. I have to plan." Once or twice he would rise suddenly and pace to the edge of the canal, and stand staring into the black water, and Rose would call out a jeering remark which he would ignore. . . . "He's thinking of the alligators now! I wonder what plans he's making for them!" Jacob would grin his indifferent grin, exchanging glances with Cornelia, who sat very still, her face calm, but something vaguely anxious about her eyes as they moved from Rose to Dirk and back to Rose.

Abruptly, after one of his canal-staring bouts, Dirk turned and said: "You people don't understand what this means. If Napoleon is finished, it means big decisions are going to be made within the next few weeks. I wager that within a month we shall know for certain whether we are to remain British or go back to the Dutch—or become Swedish property."

"What a sensation!" cried Rose. She looked dramatically at Cornelia. "This is something new! Did you know, Cornelia, that we were in any doubt as to which power would possess these colonies?"

"Shut up!" bawled Dirk, stamping. "I'm tired of your quips! Your sarcasm doesn't impress me. Damned mulatto idiot!"

Rose took a swift breath, flushing—but in an instant her self-assurance had returned. She rose, skipped up to Dirk, and wagging a finger in his face, said: "Don't you dare curse me for being a mulatto, Dirk. Don't you dare. And you know why you mustn't. Shall I tell you?"

"Oh, get away, get away," growled Dirk, moving away from her. He gave her a swift glance and said: "I lost my temper, that's all. I apologise. Jacob, come. Let's leave these two here and take a walk along the track. I want to talk to you about important things. Come."

Dirk and Jacob had hardly gone out of earshot when Cornelia looked at Rose and said: "You're not particularly tactful with him, are you?"

"I never am," said Rose. "I don't want to be. Not with Dirk." She gave Cornelia a challenging glance, and there was a slight sneer in her manner. "That is your mistake. You indulge his whims too much."

Cornelia smiled, in no way upset. "I can afford to, I think. He wants to marry me, don't you know that?"

"Because you are white. Only because you are white like him."

"That isn't quite true. He respects me, admires me, and is fond of me. He knew other white girls before he met me, didn't he? But did he choose any of them?" Cornelia laughed softly, a little contemplatively. Rose might not have been present, and Cornelia might have been musing aloud. "He's the oddest young man I have ever met—and I want him. I love him. He will probably make me unhappy when we are married, but it will be worth it. He likes the fire in me, he says. I like his fire, too. I'm prepared to be burnt. Sometimes it will hurt, but most times it will be a pleasant burning."

"You are very sure you will marry him, aren't you?" Rose was tense now, and her eyes had a furious, cornered look. Cornelia started, and glanced at her as though just becoming aware of her presence again. "What did you say?"

"I say you seem very sure you will marry him."

"I am. Perhaps that is what he has gone to discuss with Jacob now—that and the prospects for sugar and timber. This news of Napoleon's defeat stirs him because he is impatient to proceed with his plans.

He will do nothing until he is certain which European power will own us. An odd boy—but I want him. I like him because of his oddness and his hardness, and I love him because of his male strength and earnest resolve and his fiery spirit. He's my Napoleon—but he will never be defeated."

"You have never told him this, I'm sure."

"No—because I'm too tactful. With him I'm mysterious and feminine. It is the best way with Dirk. You don't understand that, Rose."

Rose sprang to her feet. She was breathing hard. "Why did you ask me to join you on this outing, Cornelia? Is it simply to taunt me?"

"No. It is because I wanted to see what effect you would have on him in a situation such as this—quiet, intimate, and each of us on socially equal terms. On most other occasions, you are at a disadvantage, Rose. In the house, you are on your guard, because you know you are not considered an equal——"

"I am never aware of any unequality when I'm in Dirk's home. His parents treat me as civilly as they do anyone else—and so does Dirk."

"But do you sit in the dining-room to table when there is company? Do you join the company in the sitting-room on social occasions?"

Rose flushed, and her eyes spewed hatred as well as fury. "You would point that out, wouldn't you? I know my limits. You don't need to tell me them. But you are wrong in some of your notions. I have known the family since I was four, and Dirk treats me in a familiar manner that you don't dream." She uttered a shrill, supercilious laugh. "When your back is turned and I happen to be at New Signal, Dirk and I have little chats that you know nothing of."

"You are wrong. He tells me about his little chats with you. There is nothing he keeps from me."

Rose stared at her for an instant, baffled, uncertain—then she said: "Very well. Do you know what I meant when I cautioned him not to curse me for being a mulatto? Do you know what I meant when I told him he mustn't?"

Cornelia, still quite composed, nodded and said: "Yes. Because your father was a van Groenwegel, Cousin Hubertus of Demerary."

"You know that!" Rose's hands clenched. "Did Dirk tell you that?"

Cornelia nodded again. "He tells me everything."

"The traitor! And he told me it was in strict confidence. He said he would tell no one, not even you. I knew nothing about my father's identity until Dirk told me three months ago. My mother in Demerary told me a lie. She said I was the daughter of an overseer named

McLeod. That time when she came on a visit I asked her—and somehow I felt she was lying. And my adopted mother has never discussed the matter with me. I've asked her, but she never gives me an answer. Then Dirk told me—and he took me into his room, and showed me the letter his Uncle Edward wrote to his father. I read it with my own eyes. He said I was never to mention it to a soul—nor would he mention it to anyone. It was to be our secret for life. He said he would always look upon me as different from other coloured girls because I have in me the Old Blood. And now he's told you. He's broken his word to me." She burst into tears, and sank down on to the grass.

Cornelia moved up to her, put her arm around her and comforted her. "That is Dirk, Rose. You should not be surprised. He's a strange mixture of good and bad. And he knew I would keep it to myself——"

"He had no right to tell you. No right! I love him—love him more than you can ever hope to. I would kill for him, I swear!"

"You're only fifteen. It's nothing but an infatuation. In a year or two you will have outgrown it."

"Never! I shall never outgrow it. I shall love him until I die." Rose shook off the older girl's arm. She was trembling—trembling and still sobbing. "And you—you will never hold him. He might marry you, but he will want me. He will want me all the time. I know it—and you know it. And he knows it." She raised her head. Rain began to fall in sparse, large drops. The sunshine, pale when they had set out, was entirely gone now. The sky had a blue-grey, thundery look. The air was still and oppressive. "You know he wants me, Cornelia, don't you?"

Cornelia nodded. "Yes, I know it," she murmured, and rose. "We must go. Help me to gather the things together."

17

DIRK was not disappointed. Within three weeks, in fact, news came that the issue had been decided. Demerary, Essequibo, and Berbice would be retained by the British, as well as the Cape of Good Hope, and Sweden was to be pacified with the sum of a million pounds sterling, in compensation for her claims on Holland. As the *Demerary Gazette* expressed it: "Thus, as last, they have condescended to inform us to whom we belong."

The news was received shortly before noon, when Dirk was with the head overseer on the dam bordering the canal aback. Storm had already returned home after his morning tour, and was settling down in the portico to enjoy a pipe when Hooper, the second overseer from the Lafferty plantation, appeared, came up respectfully and said that Mr. Lafferty had asked him to bring some news.

After the man had departed, Storm rose and went upstairs. Elizabeth was in their room, superintending the rearrangement of the furniture. Like her husband, she had gained in girth with the years, though, in face, she looked much younger than her forty-seven years. Between herself and Storm there was still a secure bond of love, and though Storm had grown taciturn with middle age, Elizabeth had retained her gaiety and garrulity, and her love of quiet teasing.

"You have come to scold me for not being ready for breakfast," she said. "Never mind, Storm dear, we shall neither of us suffer for starving today—you least of all with that rising paunch of yours."

"Just so," returned Storm with a twinkle, indulgent and bored. "But it is not food that has provided the incentive for my coming up here. I bring you tidings. We are to remain British. Jim sent a message."

"No, Haly, push it a little further to the right! Yes, that will do.

So Dirk was right, Storm. I didn't think it would have been decided so soon."

"Well, it's time enough, isn't it? They've kept us in suspense longer than was decent. Why are you having this room rearranged, my dear?"

"I got tired of seeing that wardrobe where it was, dear. Don't you like a change now and then?"

He nodded, uttering a noncommittal grunt. "What of breakfast?"

"Yes, I mustn't keep you waiting a minute longer."

At table, a few minutes later, their mood changed. A silence and a certain tenseness came upon them. It was Elizabeth who eventually glanced at him and asked: "Has he heard the news yet?" And Storm shook his head. "I doubt it. He is aback with Levi inspecting the newly planted fields."

After another silence, she said: "He will want an answer from you."

Storm nodded. "I think I have already made up my mind."

Elizabeth stopped eating and stiffened, staring at him with alarm. "Are you going to give in to him, Storm?"

"I'm fifty-two, Elizabeth. I want peace."

She made no comment, but her face took on a troubled look.

"I think you rather exaggerate his evil leanings, my dear."

"I hope so," she sighed. "Every day I pray that I am wrong."

About five o'clock that afternoon, Dirk wrote to Graham: "It is settled. Father has agreed that I should plan matters in my way. We had a long discussion today after I had returned from aback and been told the news that we are to remain British. I must say he was very reasonable and gentle. He surprised me, for, as I mentioned in a letter before, he refused consistently to listen to my advice. Perhaps it is because of the news received today that he has decided in this sudden fashion to do as I have suggested. He must realise that there is no point in delaying the issue, and he must see the sound good sense in this scheme of mine. When I come to Demerary next week I hope to be able to convince Willem and Pelham, too. You, I know, will support me wholeheartedly, for you have already agreed with me that it is the best step we can take in these times when the slave problem is so desperate. Don't weaken, I pray you. Don't allow that woman, Mrs. Hartfield, to advise you against my scheme. Now I must close this letter. I shall despatch it tomorrow. In less than ten minutes I shall be on muleback on my way to Don Diego, for there is another matter I have to attend to before this day is ended—and it is an important one, too. I have no need to mention what it is. You can guess without much trouble, I am sure. . . ."

"I can guess, too."

"In the name of all that's . . . !" The quill flew out of his hand, and he barely avoided knocking over the inkwell as he started to his feet. "Rose! How did you——? What are you doing in here? I never heard you enter."

"I crept in very, very softly—that's why." She stared at him without the slightest diffidence. She smiled and said: "I've been peering over your shoulder for the past five minutes, at least. I watched you write nearly half a page."

He glared at her—then his fury abated. "Mother is not at home. Did you come to see her about something?"

"Not this time. I'm just from Don Diego. I went there to fit a dress for Cornelia. I'm on my way back to town now."

"And why have you stopped in here? Have you left the boatman waiting?"

"Yes, I told him to wait for half an hour—but no longer. I told him he must continue to town without me if I don't appear by then."

"What new scheme are you engaged in now?" He tried to make his voice sound stern, but he failed. His voice shook. He began to squeeze his wrist as he watched her wander about the room. It was a habit of hers. She was the restless kind. The cat-bird. The bird-cat. Slim, sleek, yet feathery. She paused in the middle of the room, her face half turned towards him. She was about to take to the air—or could she be preparing to spring lithely, lightly, upon his shoulder? Her dark, wavy hair hung loosely behind her back nearly to her waist, and her grey-brown eyes watched him teasingly, laughingly, fearlessly.

"Cornelia told me she was expecting you this afternoon. That's why I came, Dirk. I wanted to see you before you went to her. Because I know what you're going there for. Today is the day of the great news. And you never wait. You're such an impatient boy, aren't you?"

Clenching his hands, he said: "You'll never know your place, it seems."

"Never," she said. "When I'm with you I know no place—save the place you want me to be in. Near to you."

"Don't try to make witty speeches. You're no good at them."

She laughed, and her laughter spattered through him like a spectral shower. He felt himself on the verge of an ague.

"You are indiscreet in coming to the house here this afternoon, Rose. Father and Mother are dining at the Huislands. They left about an hour ago."

"So Cornelia mentioned. I wanted to be indiscreet." He saw the sparkle in her eyes, and turned away, his fingers beginning to intertwine rapidly.

She darted noiselessly across to him and pressed herself against him. "I came to you, Dirk. To you. I wanted to come to you. You're going to Cornelia to ask her to be your betrothed—to seal matters finally. Aren't you, Dirk? My love! My love! You have it all planned out, haven't you? Tell me, Dirk."

He stood still, neither repulsing her nor responding to her embrace. He stared past her out at the sapodilla trees, quietly glittering in the late-afternoon sunshine. A bell was ringing in the distance. The overseers were summoning the slaves to their evening repast. Rations would be shared out for the following day. Men who had been guilty of misdemeanours would be dealt with—not flogged as in the old days, but severely reprimanded, and threatened with short rations if the offences were repeated. From next month the overseers would be coming to him with their reports on the working of the plantation. He would be the master instead of his father. Events were moving on. In a few days he would be on his way to Georgetown to meet the rest of the family. To put to them his plan. . . .

"Don't go to her this afternoon, Dirk. Please. I want to be with you."

He was silent. The calm within him was like a crouching demon. While he kept his will fixed upon it it would remain crouching— his servant. But take away by a feather's breath the weight of his will, and it would spring up and become a thing of violence and passion; it would be the master and he its servant.

Calm. It was good to be calm—and to retain one's calm. Everyone could not do it. . . . But I can. I am Dirk van Groenwegel. I am Kaywana. I am Hendrickje. I am of the fighter blood.

He felt her glide behind him, but did not turn. He continued to stare out of the window at the trees of New Signal—the trees he had grown up with. My plantation, he thought. Mine to mould. And I must have sons to take over from me when I'm fifty or sixty. Worthy male van Groenwegels with iron in their hearts—with the steel to conquer. To carry them to the pinnacles. We must spread, old Hendri said in that letter to Grandpa Jacques, and we must be a powerful family. . . . Yes. No mulatto wench, however ravishingly lovely, must balk me. I must conquer this passion. I can hear old Hendri's voice. "Strike her out of your path!" He turned to glance toward the bed under which he still kept the canister with the letters. He always left a corner of it showing under the draped sheet. . . .

"Good God!"

Where the corner of the canister should have been visible there was a heap of clothes. Petticoats and feminine things, flung down haphazard on the floor.

"Rose! Have you gone mad?"

She shook her head, smiling at him, half sitting on the edge of the bed, the afternoon light, reddish and mild, on her olive body.

"This is—I can hardly—are you lost to all sense of modesty?"

She laughed, and her breasts—erect, fifteen-year-old breasts—quivered slightly, with a feathery, fluttering jolt. "Come to me, Dirk."

Calm. I must fight. I must not let my calm dissolve. Remember 1666. Remember 1763. The van Groenwegels never run. . . .

"You're only fifteen, Rose." His voice, to his surprise, did not shake. "Do you want to be ruined?"

She laughed again. He had to avert his gaze. "Yes, I want to be ruined—so long as you ruin me, Dirk. I won't mind, love. I won't mind."

He uttered a growl, hitting his clenched hands together. "Incomprehensible. Is there another mulatto girl who would flaunt herself before me like this?"

"Not another, I agree. But I'm different from the others—and you know why. You yourself have told me. The Old Blood, Dirk, my sweet. Am I not the daughter of Cousin Hubertus? How can I help being different?"

He pressed his hands to his eyes. "Rose, put on your clothes."

"I won't, Dirk dear." She was trembling a little. The laughter had left her. In a moment she would be sobbing. "I'll kill myself if you force me to dress. I won't live if you go to Don Diego this afternoon to ask for Cornelia's hand."

"It's long been understood that I'm to marry Cornelia."

"But not settled. You must never settle it, Dirk. You don't want her."

"Dress, I tell you. Dress."

"It's me you want. I've seen it so often in your eyes, in every gesture you've made when in my presence, Dirk. I'm no ordinary mulatto girl. We've grown up together. We've done our lessons together. We used to swim together in the canal long before Cornelia came to the Creek. You've treated me as an equal. You've treated me as a companion—as you've treated Jacob. Dirk, you can't let me drift away from you as if I didn't matter to you. You know I matter. Come. Take your hands from your eyes and look at me. Come and hold me."

He continued to stand there, however, not daring to remove his hands from his eyes. The breath in him felt like toasted grains of sand. He could hear the sapodilla trees rustling in a sudden gust of afternoon breeze. If only he could have been under them at this moment, sheltered from the heat of noon that lurked in this room. Wasn't it afternoon? Hadn't the bell rung for the slaves to gather for their evening repast? Why did noon persist in here . . . ? He began to grind his teeth together. Stop this fanciful stupidity, Dirk. Face the issue like old Hendri. How would Great-uncle Pedro have dealt with this situation? Or Great-uncle David . . . ? "Strike her out of your path, boy!"

He removed his hands from his eyes, and stared at her. There was a dark brown mole at the base of her left breast. A beauty spot matching the darker brown of the large areola around the nipple. A hot shiver swamped his limbs. His knees trembled. In a moment he would gibber.

But he did not gibber. He said: "You have black blood in you, Rose. I never touch anyone with black blood in them. I have never touched a slave girl. You are different, as you say. Not only because you have the blood of my family in you but because—because . . ."

He took a deep breath and mastered the trembling in him. "I'll say it. To me, you're different, also, because I want you. I could make an exception of you. I won't pretend otherwise. I want you from the very guts in me. But it must not be, Rose. I cannot afford to be weak. There is a soft streak in my family. I'm afraid of it. Graham has it. Women can twist him and mould him in their grasp. But I'm one of the hard ones. The future of our family may depend upon my being strong and hard. If I yield to you, my sweet, I may be lost for ever. I'm afraid of you, Rose. It's a compliment to you that I reject you."

He began to pace about, shaking his head and clenching his hands. "You're the one female who has treated me with easy friendship and with unreserved freedom. I told Graham that in a letter some months ago, though I did not mention your name. My own mother regards me as a monster. And Cornelia—Cornelia loves me, but she holds herself in, and she is tactful with me. She plays a game of cat and mouse with me. Almost every girl I know treats me with caution,

as though at the back of their desire to be close to me there is a deep
suspicion of something dangerous in me. Only you have not been
afraid of me, and I'm grateful to you for that, Rose. I've admired you
for it. But you must understand that there are some liberties you cannot take with me. You have black blood in you."

"If you loved me, you could ignore that."

"I do love you—and how deeply you'll never discover. But I shall
still not ignore the black blood in you. Put on your clothes, Rose."
He turned his back on her, his hands clasped together tight.

This time she obeyed. She put on her clothes while he stood with
his back to her, unmoving, a lean, rigid male figure. A hard van
Groenwegel.

"Are you still going to Cornelia, Dirk?"

"Have you finished dressing?"

"Yes."

He turned. "Yes, I'm going. I shall see you to the *stelling*, then go
to Don Diego by the pathway." They stood looking at each other
for an interval, each fearless, unflinching. Then he gripped her shoulders and said: "I still admire you. To challenge me in this manner!
To undress in here—it took guts to do that. There's iron in you, Rose."

"And black blood."

"And black blood. That hurts you, my sweet. But you'll survive.
From afar I'm going to watch you always. You'll be safe, because you
are strong. This world won't beat you down."

"It won't." She uttered a bitter laugh. "I don't know yet how I'll
do it, Dirk, but I'll show you what I can do—despite the black blood
in me. You're going to live to look upon me as a full equal. I swear
you will."

"Come and let us go, my love. The boatman will be getting impatient. Your half hour must be nearly up."

The dusk was deep when he arrived at the Don Diego residence.
Cornelia was in the portico, waiting for him. She rose from a wicker
chair as he ran up the steps, a tall, composed figure in sea-green muslin, smelling faintly of some perfume. Her skin seemed unusually pale
in the dusk, but her hair and eyebrows and her eyes themselves were
creatures allied to the night, in collusion with the spirit of the bush
with its insect sounds coming alive, with the flashing of the fireflies
and the secret "Hoo-yoo" calls of the goatsuckers, with the dank scent
of Creek water in the humid evening air.

He came to a halt and looked at her. "You look good. You look like the evening."

"I was expecting you, Dirk. I had to dress for the occasion."

He made no attempt to touch her. He stood rigid and said: "You know why I've come, don't you? You guess correctly everything I plan to do, long before I've made the decision myself."

She nodded, almost as rigid as he, though, somehow, inwardly relaxed—and impressive in her height. She was a clear two inches taller, and he had to look up slightly to meet her eyes, though this never gave him a feeling of inferiority. On the contrary, he always felt a particular satisfaction that, though shorter in stature, he was the master of this lovely, towering creature.

"Yes, you have come to ask me to marry you—to become officially your betrothed. As soon as we heard the news about the colony's fate I knew I would get a message from you telling me that you would be coming here today."

"Did your parents guess too?"

"They did, Dirk." She laughed softly. "They are not fools."

"By the way, are they at home?"

"No. They have gone to the Huislands' silver-wedding dinner."

He clicked his tongue. "I should have known that. Father and Mother have gone, too. And I particularly wanted to speak to them."

"There is no hurry, surely. Isn't it necessary for you to speak to me first and hear how I feel about the matter?"

He grinned. "Meaning, I take it, that there is the possibility you may refuse my suit. How many times haven't you threatened me with refusal!" He stretched out and gave her chin an affectionate pull. "Let us walk. Come. It's a dry, pleasant evening. The air smells good."

"It's late. Wouldn't you prefer to sit with me inside?"

"No. We must walk. We're open-air creatures. We've swum and hunted together, and roamed about in the bush, haven't we? This is our terrain."

Arm in arm, they made their way along the familiar pathway that ran parallel to the bank of the stream. As the dusk deepened, the half-moon directly overhead began to coat the scene with a blue-green unreality. The *mucca-mucca* shrubs, like thin skeletons with living, glittering heads, kept obscuring their view of the black water of the Creek, but it did not matter, for the *mucca-muccas* were old friends. As close in spirit to them as the odd gurglings and tinklings in the water made by some alligator or fish as it rose to watch the moon or retreated at the startling glow of a candle fly or firefly.

"Do you like my dress?"

"I do. It goes well with the dusk—and the moon and the bush."

"It was fitted and made by someone you know."

The stiffening in him was involuntary, but it was for only a fraction of a second. Very casually he said: "Yes. Rose is an excellent seamstress."

"She was here only an hour or two ago."

"Was she?"

"I mentioned that you were coming to see me."

"Did you?"

"And she said she might stop in at New Signal on her way to town."

"Did she?"

She laughed. "Poor Dirk. Why do I take a pleasure in teasing you! But tell me, did she stop in at New Signal?"

"I'm afraid she did. Shall we discuss something else?"

She gave him a swift look. "Your parents were not at home. Only you."

"That's right. And what of it?" He snapped the words at her, tensing.

"Aren't you going to tell me what happened?"

"What *could* have happened?"

"Remember your pledge to me. No secrets. Or is this to be the exception?"

He uttered a growling sound. "You're losing your tactfulness, Cornelia."

"For this evening I shall be different, Dirk."

Something rustled in the clump of shrubs ahead of them to the right. They came to a stop automatically. He began to toy with his riding crop in a casual but studied manner. They saw the dark blob of a beetle rise and go whirring off into the gloom.

"I wish it had been a *labaria*," he said as they moved on. "I'm in the mood to kill a snake."

"You were born too late, Dirk. You should have been a brother of those on the upper reaches in 1763. Then you would have had so many opportunities to kill and to be cruel."

He laughed. "I can see you mean to be different this evening. This is the first time you have had the temerity to tell me I'm cruel."

"I've never lacked the temerity. It was simply that I thought it wiser not to be too frank with you."

"I understand. The cat-and-mouse game. Why? Why?" His voice shook with fury. Then abruptly his composure returned. "My fault, no doubt. I inspire distrust in everyone—even in my parents. Even Jacob treats me with a certain caution. But what does it matter? I can stand alone. I can defy the whole lot of you. Let everyone distrust me. Let everyone treat me with caution——"

"Stop being conceited. I'm waiting for you to tell me what happened between yourself and Rose at New Signal."

"Are you so concerned about that?"

"I am—because I love you, Dirk. I've loved you from the moment I met you in the portico of Doctor John's house in New Amsterdam."

He came to a halt. "At last. At last, you have told me that in plain language. I thought I would never hear it from your lips."

They stood there staring at each other in the moonlight, the candle flies flaring silently in the shrubs, the Creek making its secretive bubblings amidst the *mucca-muccas*, insects ticking and churring in the humid spaces of the softly glittering bush. Far off upstream sounded the splash of oars, and farther away a night bird kept uttering lonely screeching cries. Time as well as the jungle seemed to observe them standing where they were measuring the depth of each other.

"Aren't you going to kiss me, Dirk?"

"Not until I have told you what happened this afternoon at New Signal."

He told her, slashing at the wild plants with his riding crop, and looking from side to side in nervous agitation. She stood with her hands clasped lightly together and listened, not once interrupting. When he stopped speaking, she said in a strangled voice: "So you actually told her you love her, Dirk."

He nodded, stiff as a soldier on parade. "I did. I'm not afraid to admit I did. And I do love her. But it is a physical thing in entirety. I love you, too, Cornelia—with a difference, but as powerfully. There is the physical and—and the spiritual commingled in what I feel for you."

She said nothing. She took a long breath and began to shake her head in a half-distracted manner. Her eyes were very dark and unblinking, her skin very pale. A tent-boat went past, and they listened to the splash of the oars, and did not move. Distantly the "Hoo-yoo" of a goatsucker, clear but questioning, broke the night silence. The old monotonous sounds went on as before, indifferent.

He came alive. "There is no cause for gloom, Cornelia. We know

where we stand, don't we? I shall never lay my finger upon Rose."
He gripped her arm. "Come. Let's do as we used to when you first
came to live here. The canal. A good swim will invigorate us and
knock the sentimentality out of us."

"At this time of the evening?"

"There is moonlight, isn't there? Are you afraid?"

She gave him a stare, and he stared back at her. She uttered a soft,
quavering sound of comprehension and nodded. "Very well. Let us
go."

On the way—they had to take another path—he told her about
Jacob. "This path always reminds me of Jacob. That day of the picnic,
a few weeks ago, it was along this path we walked. Remember when
I left you and Rose after Rose got me into such a rage? Before you
and your people came to Don Diego, Jacob and I used to come along
here at this very time of evening, even on dark nights. We killed a
raccoon about halfway between here and the canal. I shouldn't tell
you, because it's our secret. I have secrets with Jacob too. Fools! We
made all sorts of pledges."

He gave a groan. "These days I can see the idiocy of my boyish
enthusiasms in a clearer light. And I'll confide this in you. Jacob is
weak—soft. He will get nowhere in this life, Cornelia. I know it now.
It came to me that day three weeks ago when I walked along this path
and talked to him about my plans. In a flash it broke upon me.
Jacob is of the Soft Streak. He's indolent in mind and spirit, and not
really ambitious. He will be a carpenter and nothing but a carpenter.
I had such great schemes for his future. I saw him as the manager of a
big timber company. I envisaged him as my chief lieutenant—Frick by
name and a mulatto, but, unknown to all but us few, a van Groenwegel. One of the Fighter Family. I saw him in league with me in
everything I did. My old friend—my boyhood companion. I would
help him to reach the heights in his own sphere. Socially we would be
apart, but in spirit together. But now I know it is hopeless. He lacks
fire. He lacks iron in his soul. He will marry his Millicent Green and
be a nonentity. He will die a respected carpenter-contractor and be
given a very respectable funeral."

"But in the meantime he may be very happy with his Millicent
Green and their sons and daughters. Has that occurred to you?"

He sniffed. "Yes, happy. But what is happiness? Thousands may
know happiness, but only a half a dozen feel the cold thrill of power.
Power, my sweetheart. To be in a position to tread upon or lift up

your fellow men—that is the dream only a small *élite* among us ever realise. And I'm determined that the van Groenwegels shall be of that *élite*. Who cares about the rabble? The happiness of the rabble is, at the best, shoddy and contemptible. No, no. Grandma Hendri was right. We van Groenwegels must aim at the pinnacles."

"One day I shall drop that canister of letters into the Creek."

"I'll make you dive after it—and retrieve it." He laughed. "I feel good this evening. I feel events maturing about me. Next week this time I shall be in Demerary, facing the rest of the family—putting before them my master plan. I believe I shall win them over to my way. I'm confident."

"And if you fail?"

"I never contemplate such a thing. When it happens time enough for me to regroup my forces, so to express it, and plan new manœuvres. But I act always in the firm belief that I shall never fail."

They emerged on to the bank of the canal, which, now in the pale moonlight, looked deep and forbidding. But, to them, it was a friend, familiar and innocuous. It smiled in welcome. They undressed under the big tamarind tree without a thought to modesty, for this, too, was nothing new. They had done it before on several occasions, and in daylight, with Jacob in their company, or the two of them by themselves. Though never with Rose.

They plunged in and swam easily in a westerly direction, saying nothing to each other until they had got as far as the sugar mill, when he paused and suggested turning back. "Are you enjoying it?"

"Very much."

"The water is very warm."

"It's the hot weather we're having. No rain. By morning it will be cool."

And silence again until they were clambering out under the tamarind tree.

"I wonder if we shall do this after we are married, Cornelia."

She laughed—but it was a brackish sound.

He took up his riding crop and slashed the grass swiftly, briskly, for a minute or two. "No *labarias*. We can sit here in safety and dry off."

The moonlight sifted through the fine-leafed foliage of the tamarind tree and touched their wet bodies in tiny blue-white flecks.

"You look like something out of Greek mythology," he chuckled.

"You, too," she said—but did not chuckle. She sat still, her hands by her sides on the grass, her gaze on the canal.

"You've guessed, I suppose?"

"What?" She turned her head sharply.

"That this little swim of ours wouldn't end like the others we've had."

"Yes, I guessed you would try to be different, Dirk. I guessed you would try to view my body without innocence, and perhaps even try to make love to me."

"Your intuition is infallible." With a jerk he turned and pinioned her arms—stared into her eyes and said: "But I didn't plan it beforehand, Cornelia, my sweet. It came in a flash when we were on the Creek path a while ago. I wanted to make love to you there and at that instant—but I knew I mustn't. That mulatto cat-bird was too much in our thoughts. We had to wash her out first."

"Have we done so, do you think?"

"I have. Perhaps you haven't." He kissed her breasts. "Lovely. You have breasts like Nibia's—very full, and as white as Nibia's are black. I must be careful not to let Graham see you unclad. He might grow enamoured of you. Nibia used to let him fondle her breasts when he was a small fellow, and since then he cannot resist a pair of full breasts."

"Dirk."

"Yes, my true love?" He kissed her throat. "What is it you want to say?"

"I can't let you make love to me."

"You have no choice, my sweetheart. I am your master, and I have decided."

She stiffened, shook her head, her eyes shut. Across the canal a raccoon was on the prowl. They could hear its hacking cough. The vegetable smell of the water saturated their senses as they stared at each other for a brief spell. Then she shut her eyes again.

"I shall not yield, Dirk. I shall not be your wife. I shall never marry you. Release me. I must get dressed again."

"We shall have to fight, then." He buried his nose in her hair, snarling. "I like a fight. Come on, my hard warrior-woman. Let us struggle."

"I'm serious. Release my arms. I want to dress."

"I, too, am serious."

She was still for a second, then began to resist, and in silence they

struggled, the grass swishing under them, their breaths panting a subdued accompaniment to the clicking and hissing of the insects about
them.

The raccoon had stopped. Now it began to utter its deathly coughs
again—a little farther off.

"Do you hear the raccoon, Cornelia?" It was a whispered gasp
mingled with the tangle of her hair.

"I'll never yield. This is useless. Stop it, Dirk."

They struggled on. Once she nearly succeeded in tearing her left
arm out of his grip, but he countered her effort just in time.

"You're strong," he gasped. "I like your strength."

The raccoon hack-hacked in the bush across the canal, getting
nearer, now getting more distant, then getting nearer. On the prowl.

"Long legs. I like your legs. You're taller than I, but I'm your
master."

She would not give in. The smell of sweat began to mingle with
the vegetable reek of water they had brought with them from the
canal. The evening was very warm. A windless July evening on the
Canje. Humid. The canal made tiny bubbling noises at intervals, and
once something rustled sharply a few feet away from them, and they
both grew still, alert, his mouth on her throat, one arm curved around
her back, his left hand closed tight about her right wrist. They panted
softly as they waited for the rustle to repeat itself.

The moon shone now directly upon them. They were out of the
shadow of the tamarind tree.

"I don't think it's a snake," he said. "Are you ready to yield to me?"

"No." They heard the rustle again—farther off. "I shall not."

"It's an *agouti*. Come on, warrior-woman. Yield."

"Release me. This is absurd—and undignified. You are a madman."

"It's a fight to the end. The van Groenwegels never run. And I'm
Dirk—the hardest of them all. Let us fight on. I'm enjoying it."

"You're still a boy, after all. With your foolish family obsession."

"I'm twenty in September. A strong boy. Ah! There! Your legs are
weakening. They're coming apart, my love."

"You're hurting me, Dirk."

"You can stand pain. You're no ordinary girl. That's why I love
you. That's why I've chosen you. See! Strength. Your legs . . ."

She began to struggle again, but he pinioned her in a way that
caused her to wince and grunt. She stopped struggling. "You're hurting me, Dirk."

"You can bear it. Stop resisting. You're fighting in vain."

Her eyes were shut, her head thrown back amidst the tangle of her hair. On the edge of the Creek, half a mile away, a goatsucker called "Hoo-yoo!" Lying flat on its breast, perhaps, on the very spot where they had stood when he had told her about Rose—yes, perchance on the very spot, he thought, hearing it again, and feeling her legs slowly, steadily, parting under the pressure he exerted upon them. . . . "Hoo-yoo!" A candle fly made an arc of light out of some black-sage shrubs near the base of the thick trunk of the tamarind tree.

"Aren't you glad I'm too strong for you?"

"You're cruel. You're mad. You're a monster, Dirk. Your mother is right."

"But you still love me, don't you?"

She kept her eyes shut, and she was biting her lower lip. Abruptly her legs yielded.

"Tell me. Don't you? Don't you love me?"

She nodded.

"And you've given in, at last, do you observe? Are you glad to surrender to me, my sweet? I want to hear you say it."

She uttered a weak mumbled "Yes." Her eyes opened in a quick blink, then closed again.

"Lovely, lovely. Precisely as I'd dreamed you'd be, my love. Not another shall I ever touch. I pledge that to you—and let everything around us witness my pledge. The trees, the insects, the hidden snakes, the *agoutis* and the goatsuckers. Not another shall I ever touch. Lovely, lovely. I'm hurting you?"

She nodded.

"But you don't mind? You want me? Now? And on the other nights after we've been wed?"

Her head moved again in assent.

18

AS the hour of Dirk's arrival grew nearer, the tension of dread in Graham rose. It was the old irrational fear of his brother at work in him again, he realised, and tried to laugh it off, telling himself that it was absurd that he should feel this way about Dirk. Irrational or not, however, the fear persisted, the dread remained.

On the *stelling*, in Georgetown, after Dirk had disembarked from the sloop which had brought him from New Amsterdam, the two brothers stood for a moment and regarded each other in smiling silence before clasping hands in greeting.

The raccoon's eyes are no different, thought Graham. If anything, they seem colder and more rapacious.

The inclination to lower his own gaze was strong, but he fought it. It would not do to be outstared by Dirk at this first instant of their reunion.

"You're just about the height I'd imagined you were, Dirk."

"Yes, I'm resigned to the sad circumstance of my lack of height," grinned Dirk, extending his hand. Graham's fingers were cold from nervousness as he took it. "Even Cornelia is taller than I am."

"You've said so in your letters. By the way, is it official now—your betrothal?"

"Yes, the betrothal is official—but we have agreed not to be married for at least a year."

"Why the delay?"

Dirk frowned. "For certain reasons. I wish I could tell you all about it, but I cannot. It is very confidential. Even to her parents and Father and Mother we've thought it wise not to tell our reasons."

"I'm not curious," murmured Graham.

Dirk lost his frowning air abruptly and slapped him on the shoulder.

"It's good seeing you, Graham. You look tall and commanding as a van Groenwegel should."

Graham uttered a quavering chuckle, wincing. "Such a pity looks do not always constitute an accurate indication of character. Isn't that what you mean?"

"There's no need to speak in bitterness, old fellow. Come. Let's forget what I've said in my letters. Forget the Soft Streak. You're my brother and a van Groenwegel—that is what really matters. And we have important business to discuss."

Dirk was captivated by Huis Kaywana. He could not stop staring at the portrait of Hubertus. "There's a man, by God! Graham, you're lucky to live in a house with such a portrait. It is an inspiration. I shall have to bring my children here at frequent intervals to let them gaze upon that picture. Cousin Hubertus. There's a van Groenwegel to boast of!"

Graham smiled slyly. "He used to curse the Old Blood. He called it the blood of beasts."

"Only in his morbid moments," snapped Dirk, giving him a scathing look. "Intrinsically Cousin Hubertus was proud of our blood. He was one of the Hard Ones. Uncle Edward would be the first to tell you that, I am sure."

"Very well. Let us not argue on the matter."

"This is a plantation we must never relinquish, Graham. Uncle Edward was generous in passing it over to you. He could have given it to Willem and Pelham."

"If you wish to know, he did offer it to Willem and Pelham. But they told him they could never dream of living on a plantation that was not situated on the coast. They prefer Flagstaff to anywhere else. Pelham told me that himself."

"Never mind. You are in possession, and you must treasure this place. It must always remain van Groenwegel property. Plantation Kaywana. Kaywana was one of our greatest heroines. The wife of old Adriansen. She was half Indian—and she fought like a warrior when her home was attacked. Went down fighting. This must be the greatest plantation in Demerary. This house must never be allowed to fall to ruin. It would break my heart if it were neglected."

"Can I detect a little envy in your voice, Dirk?"

Dirk laughed. "Most assuredly you can. I do envy you. But never mind! You are my brother. We bear the same name. Plantation Kaywana is van Groenwegel property—that's what really matters."

Steeling himself, Graham said: "Don't think me a boor, Dirk, but I feel I must say this. If you wish to be popular with the gathering tomorrow it would be better if you did not indulge in this—this tiresome habit of yours of referring to the van Groenwegels. *They* won't like it."

Contrary to his expectations, there was no explosion. Dirk nodded —and laughed. "You are right. Ah, my dear fellow, by now I should be well accustomed to rebukes about my 'tiresome habit.' I get them from Father and Mother every day—and from Cornelia whenever I see her. Even Jacob scolds me. I realise that it must be annoying, and one day I trust I shall be able to control the habit. But tomorrow— well, I can't promise. It is necessary that I impress upon them the importance of my obsession. That is the basis of my whole plan, Graham. It is the family—the future greatness of our family—that is the impelling motive behind my presence here to speak to them and bring them to my way of planning our fortunes. However, I am glad you have cautioned me." He gave Graham a swift, keen glance. "You must never be afraid of hurting my feelings. I'm not easily hurt."

He was silent for a moment, his finger tips tapping lightly together as he stared musingly out upon the glaring white day.

Could he be insane? Graham asked himself. Truly mentally diseased? Perhaps I should be sorry for him instead of being afraid of his intense moods and fanatical declarations. I wonder what sort of husband he will make for that poor creature to whom he is betrothed. I should like to meet her in person and hear her private opinion of him. Could she really be in love with him? Is it possible that any woman can feel tender towards him?

Suddenly Dirk frowned and asked: "About the gathering tomorrow —are you certain they will all be here—every member of the family related to us by blood?"

"Everyone, with possibly the exception of Cousin Mary on the West Coast. She is over sixty and seldom travels. She is virtually bedridden, I believe."

"Aunt Luise's elder sister. A daughter of Cousin Hubertus. A great pity. I should have liked to meet her. However, you say Uncle Raphael runs the plantation for her. He makes all the decisions?"

"Yes. Larsen is content to be a glorified overseer. He has never been interested in planting. A moody fellow like his father."

Dirk frowned. "Larsen? Pray, who is he? I don't recall——"

"Larsen Hubner is Cousin Mary's son. The plantation was originally the property of Cousin Mary's husband, old Cornelius Hubner.
He was middle-aged when he married her, and she was quite young.
He died years and years ago, leaving everything to Cousin Mary. Then
Uncle Raphael went to Degries—that's the name of the place—to
manage it for Cousin Mary, and now he owns a third of it, and is as
good as complete manager and master. Larsen is lazy and never as-
serts himself."

"Despite his effeminacy, Uncle Raphael rules the roost, does he?"

"He does. But don't gain the impression that he is a tyrant. He is
not. A very kindhearted fellow—and extremely charming in manner."

It was not until they were on the point of rising from the breakfast
table that Graham was able to tell Dirk something that, for the past
few days, had been heavy on his mind. His finger tips were cold as he
took a deep breath and said: "Dirk, I have a confession to make. It is
about tomorrow."

"Yes?"

"The occasion is supposed to be a social one, pure and simple. Our
relatives are coming here for the pleasure of meeting you and to dine
with us."

"What do you mean? Don't they know that I have come here ex-
pressly to discuss with them the schemes I mentioned in my letter to
you?"

"They don't. I could not tell them that, Dirk." Graham uttered a
whining, impatient exclamation. "How could I? They would have
thought me mad. They would have laughed at me. You're not even
twenty yet. How could I inform them that you wanted them to gather
here for the sole purpose of your advising them how to run their
affairs!"

Dirk stared at him, nodding slowly, comprehendingly.

Graham felt sick. He could have melted into the floor from shame
and self-disgust. In his letter to Dirk he had promised faithfully to do
everything in his power to prepare the rest of the family for Dirk's
discussions.

"I'm sorry," he murmured. "I am not opposed to your schemes
myself, but I feel for a certainty that the others will laugh at you.
They won't listen."

"Why hadn't you the courage to tell me that in your letter?"

"I—well, I didn't care to discourage you."

Dirk began to hammer the table slowly with his clenched hand. Abruptly he desisted and said: "Very well. I can see what is before me. Leave it to me. I shall handle the matter myself."

"You will bring the matter up tomorrow?"

"Most decidedly I shall. That's what I've come here for, isn't it?"

Graham shrugged. He felt relieved—and also as though he had received a whipping. Fidgeting, he said: "By the way, I've asked Clara to be here, too. She is not a van Groenwegel by blood, but her connection with the family is of long standing, as I've mentioned before."

"I should be very glad to meet her," said Dirk. "What you've told me of her has awakened in me only admiration."

Graham gave him an uncertain glance, then cleared his throat and said: "I've also asked Sarah to come and help in the house. She was delighted."

"What is this now? What Sarah?"

"Rose Clarke's mother. She is a free woman. I've told you about her."

"Oh. Yes, yes." Dirk suddenly seemed unaccountably agitated, and Graham gave him a puzzled stare. "I hadn't thought of that Sarah."

"She knows this house from top to bottom. After Aunt Rosalind's death she was Cousin Hubertus's right hand here. She kept house for him and managed the other slaves. I've had some interesting chats with her. She comes to see me occasionally. She loves every corner and cranny of this house."

Dirk grunted. He had recovered his composure. "And she will be here tomorrow to help generally, you say?"

"Yes. We are rather shorthanded in the house at the moment."

Dirk was silent. He had a pensive air.

Graham asked him about Rose. "When is Rose going to visit Georgetown? I do think she ought to come and see her mother."

Dirk snapped: "Her adopted mother is Mrs. Clarke, the midwife. I don't think Father and Mother would care to have it known that this Sarah Hubert woman is her real mother. Nor would Uncle Edward and Aunt Luise, for that matter."

"Of course, of course. I was forgetting it was supposed to be an indiscreet topic." Graham asked hurriedly: "By the way, how is my dear Nibia?"

"As libidinous as ever," Dirk replied shortly, then frowned and added: "Why do black people interest you so much, Graham?"

"I love them," smiled his brother. "I should have been a missionary. I'd have liked working amongst them as Mr. Wray does."

Dirk regarded him for a moment, then grunted. "I noticed a big Bible on a table in the sitting-room. I suppose you read it every day. How Cousin Hubertus's ghost must sneer at you!"

Graham uttered a triumphant laugh. "That Bible belonged to Cousin Hubertus. Indeed, Dirk, so deeply religious was Cousin Hubertus that he held family prayers every morning without fail. To-morrow Cousin Jacqueline or Aunt Luise will confirm that if you care to ask either of them."

19

THEIR Uncle Raphael and Larsen Hubner were the first to arrive. Dirk and Graham stood on the portico and watched them approach along the driveway, accompanied by two slaves carrying their baggage. Raphael, tall, handsome, fair, and blue-eyed, made a striking contrast with Larsen's shortish, thickset figure. Larsen had a gloomy, old-man look, but Raphael kept glancing about him with a smiling good cheer, as though appreciative of the brilliant midmorning sunshine and the scent of jasmine and honeysuckle in the air. He was also a striking sartorial contrast. For while Larsen wore merely the conventional outdoor costume of any Demerary planter, Raphael's dark-blue velveteen breeches and crimson jacket compelled attention.

"He looks younger, not older, than Father," Dirk chuckled.

A few seconds later he almost gasped as his uncle embraced him, exclaiming: "My dear Dirk! Dirk the terrible, if report may be trusted! But you don't *appear* terrible, my boy. I'm simply delighted to meet you. Tch, tch! Fancy Storm producing two such sons! I shall have to write him and congratulate him."

"Thank you, sir," smiled Dirk, withdrawing as gently as he could out of his uncle's arms and trying not to wrinkle his nose at the perfume that exuded from Raphael's person. "I'm very delighted to meet you, too."

Larsen, like a raincloud hovering in the background, was swept forward hastily by Graham, who introduced him in a nervous voice. Thirty-seven, but looking over forty, Larsen had dark hair plastered neatly down on his large head. He broke into a dismal smile and nodded his head sombrely as he held out his hand, mumbling in Dutch: "Very happy to meet you, Dirk."

Raphael apologised for arriving so early. "I'm aware you invited us for dinner, my boy, but travel is a bit difficult on the West Coast, as you know, and I was compelled to take whatever conveyance I could get at whatever time, and as it happens, Sydney Bennett's carriage was coming to Vreed-en-Hoop, so we shared it with him at his invitation."

"It is a pleasure to have you for breakfast as well," smiled Graham. And, "Certainly, certainly," said Dirk—but Graham noticed the look of dismay on Dirk's face. Dirk added quickly: "But, Uncle Raphael, haven't you a carriage of your own for making long journeys?"

His uncle clasped his hands together dramatically and shuddered. "Had, my boy. Had. Now it is a one-horse gig for *short* journeys. Times are not as good as they used to be, Dirk, my lad. Slaves are expensive, so economy must be our watchword, mustn't it? Eh, Larsen?"

"Most decidedly, sir," agreed Larsen, speaking in English this time.

Dirk gave a brittle smile and said: "Quite so, Uncle Raphael, but surely there are certain appearances, if I may say so, which should by all means be kept up. With a name like ours in these colonies . . ."

Raphael started, uttered a hooting laugh, and hugged himself—this time, however, not dramatically, but naturally and with an almost boyish exhilaration. "Tch, tch, tch! But of course, of course! The family name! How thoughtless of me to have mentioned such a circumstance, my boy! You are very sensitive, I've been told about the 'honour and glory' of our name." Raphael patted Dirk's shoulder. "Never mind, my dear fellow. Never mind. It isn't sheer meanness —not mere parsimony. And I do think a damned lot of our name, I can assure you." He bent close to Dirk's ear and said in a stage whisper: "In confidence, we are planning to secure a new carriage to replace the one that has fallen into disrepair. It won't materialise this year. Perhaps next year—or the year after. But definitely we shall have a new carriage. Eh, Larsen?"

"Very true, sir," rumbled Larsen, nodding mechanically.

Graham threw Dirk a glance, and his eyes said: "Now you see for yourself what you are up against!" But Dirk's face remained grimly noncommittal, and Graham could sense that his brother was in no way discouraged. He must be a dolt as well as a madman, thought Graham, and within him there burnt an ugly fire of malice and frustration. This is wrong, he chided himself. I'm trying to hate him because I'm aware of his strength and my own shameful weakness. I wish he were gone already. I feel strangely unsafe when he is beside me.

It was a relief when, a few minutes later, Clara arrived. They were in the sitting-room, and were just settling themselves in chairs for coffee when she was shown in. Graham had asked her to come in time for breakfast.

"My good, dear Clara! You never fail me!" It was only by an effort of will that Graham prevented himself from embracing her before them all. But his relief was so great that he experienced no embarrassment as he turned to Dirk and said: "Well, here she is, Dirk. Mrs. Clara Hartfield, my sweet, faithful friend."

Dirk bowed formally, but Clara advanced towards him with outstretched hand, and Dirk flushed and took it, smiling in a boyishly awkward manner as he said: "Very delighted to meet you, I'm sure, Mrs. Hartfield. Graham has told me so much about you in his letters. I have a high opinion of you."

Raphael shuddered delicately and in his dramatic manner, and smiling at Clara, said: "Yet another conquest, Clara, my dear! How I envy you sometimes."

"You shouldn't, Raphael. Remember my reputation." She uttered her shrill, golden laugh, and gripping Dirk's arm, told him: "Your uncle is a hypocrite, my boy. I've known him since he was four years old—younger, in fact, but it was from four he began to impress me as a person. Never take him at face value."

"I find him extremely charming, I must admit," said Dirk. "And extremely young-looking, too. I mentioned that to Graham on the portico when we watched him coming towards the house."

Aha, thought Graham. So this is how he hopes to coax Uncle Raphael into compliance. By flattering him. It won't succeed, though. Not with Uncle Raphael.

Raphael smiled at Dirk and bowed deeply. "Thank you, Dirk, my lad. I can sense that you are in earnest. Flattery I can smell at a distance."

"I never flatter, sir," Dirk snapped, and Graham saw the green eyes come alight. "I mean every word I say. You are younger-looking than my father, though you're actually older. I wish I could have persuaded him to come here so that we could all have compared the two of you for ourselves."

"Why didn't he come, too, Dirk?" Clara asked. "And your mother? It would have been so good to see Elizabeth."

Dirk frowned, and Graham noticed the uneasiness in his brother's manner. "If I may be frank, Mrs. Hartfield, Father and Mother told me outright that they would not care to be present in this house at the same time as myself. You see, I have come here with a purpose other than that of a mere social visit."

"Have you? Oh." Clara was visibly embarrassed, for Graham had confided in her the real reason for Dirk's visit. She tried to smile and pass the matter off lightly by saying: "Well, never mind. We're still pleased to have you."

Raphael, not to be balked, however, asked: "Is it something of extremely confidential nature, my boy? Or am I permitted to enquire what it could be?"

Dirk, stiff, suddenly relaxed and chuckled. "It concerns us all, Uncle Raphael, but if you'll pardon me, I think I prefer to wait until after dinner this afternoon to broach the matter."

"I shall simmer patiently in anticipation," smiled his uncle. Watching him, Graham was sure that Raphael's air was one of kindliness and even admiration. Dirk might have complimented him instead of snubbing him. Graham experienced a sense of deep bafflement. I shall never understand people, he thought.

Dinner, as was customary, was at five o'clock. By four all the other guests had arrived, including the Liekers from the West Bank. Claas Lieker, nearly seventy and totally grey, was at least three inches shorter than Jacqueline, who, at sixty-five, was hardly grey at all. She had something of Luise's roguish sparkle. Though tall and thin, there was nothing about her, thought Dirk, that would have led anyone to think that she was the daughter of Cousin Hubertus. Seeing her beside her husband, Dirk told himself that this was how he and Cornelia would probably look when they were elderly. And with three sons! Benjamin Lieker, at forty-odd, or somewhere in the late thirties, was a massive fellow, brown-haired and green-eyed. Dirk could envisage himself having such a son. And Jan and Hendrik, Benjamin's younger brothers, were also well built, Jan fair and Hendrik dark, both robust fellows, sunburnt and hardy-looking, Jan tall like his mother, Hendrik shortish and thickset, not unlike his cousin Willem of Flagstaff.

Their wives came too. Hendrik had married an English girl, but Benjamin and Jan had chosen Dutch. What a pity, thought Dirk, their name is Lieker and not van Groenwegel. However, it was good to hear Pelham say that he was the father of a son. "And he's every-thing like Pelham," smiled Elfrida, Pelham's wife, who sat on Dirk's right at dinner. "Even to the little reddish freckles on his face."

She was a plumpish, very cheerful creature, though not particularly pretty. Dirk liked her. She put him at his ease, treated him without reserve—almost as Rose did. "I'm hoping I'll have all sons," Dirk told her. "Sons to carry on our name." And Clara, who sat on his left, interposed: "Ha! Be careful, Dirk! Men who wish fervently they'll have only sons generally end up by having only daughters. Aren't you fond of girls?"

Dirk frowned slightly, for he was not sure of Clara. He had gained the impression that she was going out of her way to be nice to him; it was almost as though Graham might have instructed her: "Keep him amused for me, please, Clara. Keep him from saying tiresome things about our family."

"Yes, I am, I am," he replied a trifle impatiently. "But sons are important. In more ways than one."

"Don't you know Dirk is simply insane on the subject of family pride, Clara?" smiled Elfrida, giving Dirk a teasing glance. "We're always discussing him at Flagstaff."

Clara winced, as though in preparation of an outburst from Dirk, and said hurriedly: "Oh, I feel certain he has other interests. Haven't you, Dirk?"

Dirk grinned. "Let's change the subject before I prove tiresome. Go on telling me about little Francis, Elfrida. By the way, why did you call him that?"

Elfrida laughed and turned to Pelham, sitting next to her. "Pelham, Dirk wants to know why you called our son Francis. Shall I tell him?"

Pelham broke off his conversation with the thin and flat-chested Christina, Willem's wife, to tell Dirk: "I had a mistress called Frances, a lovely mulatto girl. I promised her, just before we ceased to be friendly, that I'd name my first son after her. And, Elfrida, please don't call on me again to make that explanation. You know very well it troubles my conscience."

Dirk joined in the laughter, but, within, he felt a raw simmering of agony. The image of Rose's nude body sitting on the edge of his bed rose up to plague him, as it had done innumerable times during the past few days. "A lovely mulatto girl." Could Pelham's mistress have been more lovely than Rose?

His gaze wandered to the black woman in dark-blue satin who was superintending the servants attending upon the table. Sarah Hubert —Rose's mother. Graham had not been wrong in his letters. She was an impressive woman. She had character. She might be black, but she stood out among the others. Nothing subservient about those eyes. They were steady and fearless—like Rose's.

He caught himself with a jerk and barely heard what Elfrida said. "What? Oh yes, yes. Cousin Hubertus had four daughters and no sons. Of course. But I don't hope to repeat his performance. If anything, four sons and one daughter. And I believe Cornelia will not disappoint me. A fine creature. Sturdy, physically and mentally. You should see her! She towers over me." He found himself suddenly garrulous. Talking helped to lessen the agony.

"Have you heard recently from Hermine?" Pelham asked.

"Yes, she had a daughter earlier this year," Dirk told him. "She likes Jamaica, she says—but Jim is not very happy. He fears some earthquake will happen and ruin the bridges he has taken such a pride in constructing."

"Does he still drink so hard?" asked Elfrida. And Dirk nodded and replied: "Just as hard—but, somehow, it doesn't seem to affect his work. He has won a reputation for being able to hold his liquor to the last ditch—and never falling in. A remarkable fellow, Jim."

"We think of you as remarkable, too," said Elfrida. Clara caught her eye and shook her head, but Elfrida did not heed. "You're a regular legend in the family. Everyone was curious to meet you."

"Is that so?" Dirk felt himself swept by a sudden warmth of affection for this forthright creature whom Pelham had married. He could understand Pelham being attracted to her, despite her plainness. "And may I ask why?"

"Well, surely it is natural to be curious about anyone who is rumoured to be remarkable." Across the table, between Edward and Luise, Graham kept casting furtive, anxious glances at his brother. Perhaps it was a mistake putting him next to Elfrida, he thought. Elfrida can say the most indiscreet things. Yet I thought he would like her because of her candour, which is so similar to his own.

Dirk chuckled. "I grant that. But how did you come to hear of my remarkable qualities? Graham is the only person I've corresponded with."

"Through him—and through your parents and others in Berbice who know you. In these colonies nothing is secret, Dirk. From all sources have come tales of your fierce and fanatical family pride, of your cruelty and arrogance, and of how the ladies love you but fear you."

"You don't fear me, though, it's obvious," laughed Dirk, flushing.

"I confess I don't," smiled Elfrida. "Not that you don't *look* a monster. You have terrible eyes, Dirk. Oh. So penetrating and cold. But now that I've talked to you I see you're really quite harmless—and even likeable."

"Thank you. I'm grateful to you for saying that. More grateful than—— Oh! Sorry! Were you saying something, Mrs. Hartfield?"

"No, no, I didn't mean to interrupt you. But I was asking you how long you intend to stay in Demerary. I should like you to meet Harvey, my son."

It was less than an hour later—dusk was gathering and the slaves had lit candles; the meal was nearly at an end—when Dirk acted. He rose in an easy, casual manner, and said: "Ladies and gentlemen of the van Groenwegel family, may I ask you to give me your attention for a short while. There is something of great importance I wish to say to you."

At the head of the table sat Claas and Jacqueline Lieker. ("As the eldest daughter of Cousin Hubertus," Graham had told her, "I think you ought to sit at the head of the table, Cousin Jacqueline. I'm sure Dirk would like that, too.") Jim and Beatrice Menzies were opposite them at the other end. ("You're our prettiest female cousin, Beatrice. You and Jim must sit at the foot of the table. I don't think Dirk would disapprove.")

Raphael, on the same side of the table as Dirk, exchanged a glance with Jim Menzies, to whom he had been talking family affairs only a few minutes before, Jim a silent but sympathetic listener. Raphael's glance said: "I warned you!" and Jim's twinkling grey eyes replied: "You're a good prophet."

"What's this now?" Jacqueline murmured to Claas, and Claas, who had seemed half asleep, started slightly and asked "What's what?" in an old-man mumble.

Conversation rippled to a close all round the table. Graham had gone pale and tense at the sound of Dirk's voice. Edward, beside him, began to murmur: "Ah. Ah. A speech, it seems." And Luise chuckled: "Our beloved monster."

Graham stared across the table at the rigid figure of his brother, and thought: He's not human, but I can see why people admire him. At *this* moment I can see it. How I wish I had his courage!

In the silence that had come upon the table, and with every face turned towards him, Dirk began to speak again. "You'll probably deem me boorish for springing this little speech upon you in the final stages of our meal, but I thought it better to speak now than later when we are more disorganised a crowd in the sitting-room. I've been hearing that most of you have heard rumours about me, that I'm considered a monster even here in Demerary. In Berbice—and I state this not in bitterness, but as a simple fact—I *am* deemed a monster, and by my parents as well as by our acquaintances. I am very thick-skinned, and am never troubled by the opinions people hold about me. What would disturb me is if I were to hear unfavourable opinions about our family. Yes, our family!"

His voice rose slightly, and he turned his head from side to side to survey them all, his eyes more coldly green than Graham had ever known them to be.

"I am supposed to be obsessed with the notion that our family is a great one, obsessed with the idea that we must attain to greater things. That supposition is correct. For me, ladies and gentlemen of the van Groenwegel family, it does not seem unnatural that I should be so obsessed, but then you will tell me"—he grinned suddenly, and it was like the sun showing through a bank of slate-grey clouds at sunset, thought Graham—"you will tell me that a fanatic could not know that he is being fanatical. Madmen do not know that they are insane."

He paused, but there was no sound from anyone. Edward's brows were raised in a fixed, demoniac way. Raphael leaned back in his chair, a delighted smile on his face, his hands clasped together as though in static applause. Willem, between Larsen Hubner and Dahlia Lieker, Hendrik Lieker's wife, had a puzzled air. As Dirk paused he glanced across at his wife, Christina, as though appealing to her for an explanation.

Dirk continued with his speech. His manner was serious, earnest, yet tinged with something that suggested that, in the background, his sense of humour was very much alive. Even while he referred to the past, to Kaywana and her sons and Hendrickje, his lips would twist in a vague smile suggestive of irony or mockery. Yet he left no doubt about his sincerity. He spoke of the canister of letters—"One day I shall put that canister in a special family museum of our own, so that its contents may be available for our children and their children to peruse, so that they may have the opportunity of acquainting themselves with the Tales of Old, as Grandma Hendri termed them"—but he did not waste many more words on sentiment and heroics.

"Now, fellow kinsmen and kinswomen," he suddenly declaimed, "I have a plan! Yes, a plan! A plan for our future prosperity as a family! I have described it in some detail in a letter to Graham, and I had hoped he would have given you some idea of what it is about before I came here so that you would have been able to think it over and come here prepared to discuss it with me. Graham, however, says he was afraid to tell you about it lest you laugh at him and look upon me as an impertinent coxcomb. Very well. I shall have to spring it upon you now in complete freshness, and ask you to give me a patient hearing. But may it be understood that I wish you to interrupt me freely if you disagree with me on any point. Yes, I ask you. Do not hesitate to cut in and criticise with utter candour any statement I may make."

That swift, unexpected grin broke the seriousness of his face as he turned his head from side to side to survey them. Graham glanced from Clara to Elfrida, noting the fixed smile of admiration on Elfrida's face and the uncertain, rather dismayed, expression on Clara's. Both of them stared up at Dirk, creatures entranced.

Dirk, his face rigidly serious again, began to tell them about his plan. After a few preliminary comments on the present difficulties that faced the planter, he said: "There is nothing very complicated in the plan I have in mind. It may be called a plan of co-operation and of concentration—co-operation between us all and a concentrating of our assets into one central fund.

"Van Groenwegels, these are times when insolvency is rampant because of labour shortage. But if we get together as a family and bring our labour into one consolidated mass, and if we plan our cultivation in such a manner as to dispense with all unnecessary undertakings, we shall prosper because we shall act as a united whole and not as scattered units. If, for instance, we agree that in Demerary we should maintain only one sugar mill between all our estates then this will result in a saving, not only in labour, but in machinery."

He paused, as though expecting comment—and comment came.

Willem, in a chuckling, indulgent voice, asked: "Whose sugar mill are you suggesting we should dispense with, Dirk? Not the one at Flagstaff, I trust?"

"Nor mine at Degries, I should hope!" Raphael chimed in.

Dirk nodded and smiled. It was as though he were enjoying some private joke. Graham searched his face for any sign of annoyance, but had to admit to himself that he could find none. On the contrary, he had a look of aloof amusement. He is regarding us as though we were so many beetles!

"Any other comments?" asked Dirk, still smiling. "What of the Liekers?"

"We're coffee growers," said Jan.

"So you are. I had forgotten that for the moment. I shall say something about that in a short while. To continue, then. No, I hadn't your sugar mill in mind particularly, Willem—nor yours, Uncle Raphael. But here is the situation. You are on the West Coast, Uncle Raphael. You are on the East Coast, Willem. And Graham is on the East Bank, Now, suppose you sold up your estate, Uncle Raphel, and secured a place on the East Coast near to Flagstaff, or near to Graham's place here—no, no, just a moment before you interrupt. Let me finish. As you are situated now at Degries, you are separated from Graham and Willem by nearly two miles of river and more than ten of land. Co-operation between you and the others here won't be easy, will it? But if you were on the eastern side of the river, wouldn't it be much easier to amalgamate with Flagstaff and Kaywana? Now, assuming you did take such a step, this is what I suggest could happen. There could be *one* sugar mill on one of your three plantations to grind *all* the canes produced on all three. Wouldn't that constitute a sweeping economy both in respect to labour and machinery?"

"Good heavens! But, my dear boy, you couldn't be serious!" cried Raphael. "Are you expecting me at this time of life to sell out my lucrative property on the West Coast and speculate in some place on this side of the river that has gone to nothing through bad management and lack of labour?"

"A revolutionary step, I warrant, sir—but it would be profitable. Every day we hear of some plantation being sold out through a failure that has resulted from lack of slaves—purely from a lack of slaves, sir. The land is still fertile. It merely requires the labour to make it yield, and yield richly. There would be no risk involved in your selling your West-Coast place and investing in another place on this side of the river. You have the slaves. And, as I say, you would have no extra expenses to incur over new machinery if you had your canes sent by canal to Flagstaff. Our canal system is excellent, and I'm suggesting that it would be comparatively simple an undertaking to have the canes of the two plantations whose mills were dispensed with conveyed to the one whose mill was in operation. That is what I meant when I said that we should concentrate our assets. The canes we grow constitute our basic assets, so to express it. Let us co-operate by channelling them all into *one* mill—one family mill either here on Kaywana or on Flagstaff or on the place Uncle Raphael could buy if he were so disposed. And you, Liekers! You grow coffee. My advice to you is to give up coffee. I feel that in the years ahead sugar will be the dominant produce of these three colonies. Again it may seem a revolutionary step, but it will pay you, I think, if you sold out your coffee plantation and secured a sugar property somewhere on the East Bank here or on the East Coast."

Claas Leiker uttered such gasping, old-man sounds of dismay that the whole table exploded into laughter.

Dirk joined in the laughter. "Yes, I understand. I am not such a heady fool as may be imagined. I know full well that this sounds like impossible foolishness. But remember, kinsmen and kinswomen, I am not planning for today, but for the future. I don't expect you to rush and sell out your properties tomorrow. What I am doing is to plant a seed in your minds, in the hope that within the next few months, or even years, this seed will take root and perhaps grow into the plan I have sketched. Now, let me tell you this. I have predicted that sugar will be our dominant produce in the future, and I will predict yet something else—and pay heed to this above all. Not many years hence the situation will worsen tremendously in respect to labour. Anti-Slavery Party members in England are always active. Had we been handed back to Holland, I should not have had this fear, but we are now permanently British, and the British are clamouring for the emancipation of all slaves in their empire. Complacently we are telling ourselves that they have already done their worst. They have abolished the slave trade, and the matter ends there. But I feel in me that it does not end there. In five years, in ten years, perchance, slavery will be abolished in entirety in these colonies, and where shall we stand then?"

No one laughed now, for the slave question was too serious a matter for levity. Willem frowned and said: "What do you mean precisely by that, Dirk? Do you think the British would be so idiotic as to set free even the few slaves we now have in our possession to work our lands?"

"I mean precisely that, Willem. The Anti-Slavery Party in England is strong."

"That is absurd, Dirk," said Hendrik Lieker. "How could they set free the slaves we now possess? Why, the colonies would be immediately ruined."

"The British know better, my boy," smiled Raphael. "More than half their wealth is won from these colonies and the colonies of the West Indian islands. If they ruined us they would be ruining themselves."

"The British are sentimentalists, sir," Dirk snapped. "For any foolish, religious, idealistic notion they would be prepared to cut their own throats. I say that with all due deference to the Britishers amongst us now, but I must state the truth, and I am sure the Britishers themselves will not attempt to say me nay in this matter."

"You are only too right, Dirk," agreed Elfrida, clapping her hands.

"That is no untruth," said Jim Menzies. "But I don't believe it will be as bad as you say. They will never go so far as to free the slaves in these colonies."

Dirk shrugged. "I trust you will prove right, but, nevertheless, I still feel strongly that that is going to happen in the not too distant future, and that is why I advise that we take measures *now* to put ourselves in a strong position. Now within the next year or two, of course; not abruptly and rashly. Now that we are in a prosperous condition ourselves and can act without constraint. That is what I mean by now. Please don't misunderstand me. I don't expect you to exclaim in joy at what I have told you and agree on the instant to change your present way of existence. No. I want you to think it over and *plan* for the future in the way I have suggested. Amalgamate, co-operate, concentrate. Think on it with those three words in mind always. All I want from you today is an assurance that you will go away from this house and ponder on what I have said. . . ."

Later, when they were in the sitting-room, Elfrida said to Dirk: "Your oratory was not first class, but your sincerity was terrifying."

"But what do you think?" asked Dirk, smiling. "Do you feel I impressed them? Do you feel they will ponder on my words and perhaps be influenced into following my suggestions?"

She shook her head. "The chances are small of their ever adopting your suggestions. The planters of this colony—and, I think, of Berbice, too—are not fond of change, Dirk. Especially drastic change such as you advocate. Surely you must be aware to what depth their complacency goes."

He nodded slowly. They were standing near the window that looked down upon an arbour of honeysuckle on the southern side of the house. "I'm aware of it. But I had to make the attempt. And I shall still hope."

"You must come and see us at Flagstaff before you return to Berbice."

"I shall. I want to see young Francis."

"He has eyes like yours. Perhaps he will be remarkable, too."

Raphael approached and patted Dirk's shoulder. "An excellent speech, Dirk, my boy. But alas! I fear you were born before your time. Tch, tch! A pity."

"Why a pity, Uncle Raphael?" flashed Elfrida. "We need men like Dirk in our colonies. Men with daring ideas. New schemes. And the courage to undertake seemingly difficult enterprises. You would do well to think on what he said this afternoon at table."

Raphael shuddered in ecstasy, hugging himself. "How delightful to hear you championing my courageous nephew, Elfrida! And, believe me, I mean to ponder on what he told us at table. Oh, I mean to, my dear." He gripped Dirk's arm, and added in a husky whisper: "You impressed me more than I revealed, young man. But it was for reasons of policy—family policy—that I could not reveal this. Tch, tch! Remember, I am only part owner of Degries."

20

WHEN Dirk visited Flagstaff, he took care, Graham noticed, not to make the slightest reference to his speech the evening before. He probably realises, poor fellow, thought Graham, that it was all in vain, that he has wasted his time and his energy. It should be a good lesson to him for the future.

Dirk showed a great interest in his cousin Francis. "I agree," he nodded, as he stood with Elfrida beside the infant's cot. "He has my eyes. They're green like mine—but they are not raccoon's eyes."

"Raccoon's eyes?"

"Didn't you know that Graham thinks I have raccoon's eyes?"

They were alone in the room, and Elfrida sighed and said: "I can't say I consider them fierce. Poor Graham. I wish I could do something for him."

Dirk frowned. "What do you think is the matter with him? He doesn't seem alive, Elfrida. He has a cringing, shrivelled air, if I may so express it. He's not the same person I knew just before he left Berbice."

She gave him a twinkling look and smiled. "Haven't you in your letters to him called him the Soft Streak? He has taken that to heart, you know."

"Nonsense. Surely that isn't enough to have turned him into the retiring, over-cautious, self-effacing creature he is. I won't believe that my letters could have had such an effect on him."

"I don't say so. No, it is he himself, Dirk. He is naturally retiring, and that affair with Clara Hartfield did not help. When they ceased being intimate, he seemed to withdraw further within himself. Then there was the disappointment he suffered when his engagement to Mary Beckles ended as it did."

"He assured me in a letter that he was more relieved than hurt. He was not greatly attached to her. Indeed, from what he said, it was Mrs. Hartfield who had manœuvred the whole thing."

"That may be so, but I still feel that he underwent some mental suffering over the incident. He hardly mixes with people. More and more he is growing into a hermit. I wish you would speak to him about it, Dirk."

"He's very religious, too, I understand."

"Yes. He goes to chapel every Sunday without fail, and he is still very friendly with the missionaries, and gives them much help in their work."

"Isn't Mrs. Hartfield still his mentor and friend?"

"Very much so. He sees her at least once a week in Georgetown. I think he dines with them every Sunday evening, and then they all go to chapel."

That same evening Dirk tackled Graham on many things. Graham had accompanied him to Flagstaff, but Dirk waited until they had arrived back at Huis Kaywana before launching his attack. Seated on the portico after dinner, Dirk said: "Now we've got to discuss one or two matters of a personal nature, Graham."

Graham immediately began to fidget. "Yes, yes," he murmured with a nervous chuckle. "I knew you wouldn't let me off. You're going to scold me for your failure yesterday. I suppose."

"Nothing of the sort—and, in any event, I am not sure that I failed. The next year or two will prove whether I did or not. No, it's about yourself." He went on to tell him of the chat he had had with Elfrida, and Graham scowled and snapped: "Elfrida is too tactless for my liking. Really, I can't understand how Pelham came to marry such a person."

"She's a fine woman—not pretty, but with a magnificent soul. I like her immensely, and I feel she and I are going to be very friendly in the future. She treats me without caution and reserve, and that is so rare in my experience with women. But I've told you that before."

Graham gave a sly snigger. "Yes, of course. You have told me that. They have infallible instinct, it is said—women, I mean. They know the good from the bad, Dirk. And the strong from the weak."

Dirk laughed. "My dear fellow, do you realise that your manner is like that of an old and soured grandpa? What's the matter with you, Graham? Why don't you mix with your acquaintances more than you do? And with your relatives? Elfrida says you hardly visit Flagstaff once in six months, and you don't invite people to the house here. And what about marrying? Haven't you seen any girl here who takes your fancy?"

"No. And I don't think I ever shall. I shall remain a bachelor, Dirk."

"Absurd! It isn't healthy. Feminine company is essential."

Graham uttered a sound of mock astonishment. "Is that all?"

"What do you mean?"

"Aren't you going to mention that I am, by duty bound, compelled to marry so as to produce sons to carry on our illustrious name?"

Dirk smiled, and gave his brother a curious glance. "Sarcasm, eh? You sound embittered, old fellow. A pity. Look here, what about spending some time at the old place in Berbice? Father and Mother have asked you so often to come and see us. You have a reliable head overseer to keep things going for you in your absence, so you have no excuse."

"Not only have I a reliable head overseer," said his brother, his eyes shining in a self-satisfied manner, "but I treat my people kindly, Dirk. Of all the slaves in Demerary, none are more happy than mine on this plantation."

Dirk frowned, again giving him a curious glance. "I don't doubt that. We treat ours well, too. We don't flog them for misdemeanours any longer. We only use the whip in the fields."

"I've dispensed with the whip even in the fields."

"Have you?" To himself, Dirk said: "He's mentally sick, I'm sure of it now. It's this lonely life he's leading in this vast house."

"Anyway, that is beside the point, Graham. Won't you consider spending a month or two with us on the Canje? It will get you out of yourself. Think of it, you haven't even met Cornelia yet!"

"I'm certainly curious to meet her," smiled Graham, staring at the floor. He had not once met Dirk's gaze directly since they had come out on the portico. He uttered a little sigh which plainly was equivalent to: "Poor girl!"

Dirk chuckled. "I can see you're sorry for her. I think she'll like you. You'll probably like her too. You must come."

Graham shook his head. "I'll come for your wedding, I promise, but I'm not in the frame of mind to travel at the moment. Besides, I've business to transact. I took your advice about the timber grant up the river."

"Have you acted already?" asked Dirk in surprise.

"I can be a man of action when I want to be, no fear!"

"Well, I'm glad to hear that. Have you secured the concession?"

"I have. And arrangements are already afoot for work to commence."

"Excellent!" Dirk stared at him for a moment, baffled. Abruptly he said: "Why can't you show the same enterprise in your social relations?"

"Let us not discuss society, Dirk. Tell me of your plans. You say Father agreed to secure a timber grant up the river. When do you move to put the matter into effect? Have you a site in mind? And a good man to superintend operations?"

"I'm making a trip up the Berbice next month to look for a site. As for a good man to superintend operations, I've been disappointed. I had Jacob in mind. I spoke to him about it some weeks ago, and offered him the post, but he refused. He does not relish the idea of living so far away from the town. The truth is, he is in love. He wants to be near to his Millicent Green."

"He is not very ambitious, then? Is that it?"

Dirk nodded. "I'm sadly disappointed in Jacob."

"I could get you a good man, if you wish."

"Someone I could depend upon absolutely?"

"Yes. A man of the highest integrity—and a good Christian."

"I care nothing about his religious propensities. So long as he is honest and capable. What is his name?"

"Benjamin Hartman. He's a mulatto."

Dirk grinned. "I might have thought so. Is it because Nibia used to let you fondle her breasts when you were a boy that you have in you such a deep love for Negroes and coloured people?"

Graham shrugged. "That may be partly responsible. Who knows?" His eyes came alive. "I should give anything to see my dear Nibia again."

"Where's the difficulty? Come and spend a month or two with us and you'll see her every day."

Within three months of Dirk's return to Berbice he had found and secured a timber site on the upper reaches of the Berbice River. He made the trip in the company of a party of Indians from the Don Diego plantation, and was away from New Signal for a little over six weeks. When he returned his face and hands were covered with the bites of *kaburi* flies, but he made little of this circumstance.

The experience, he assured his parents and Cornelia, had been worth the discomfort and inconvenience he had suffered on the trip. He brought back the skin of a fourteen-foot *camoudie* which, he said, he had shot himself. The timber site he had selected was rich in greenheart and mora. It was more than a hundred miles upriver, but there would be no difficulty in bringing the rafts down to New Amsterdam. He had secured three Indians to begin felling operations at once, and would send up four Negro slaves with the manager Graham had promised him.

Storm and Elizabeth congratulated him, but he could sense that there was no real fervour in their manner. He told Cornelia: "Mother feels I coerced Father into agreeing to this scheme, and finds it hard to forgive me, especially as it has always been her belief that I lack a heart. On Father's part, he is still suffering from his planter's complacency. He has confidence in me, but, in his heart of hearts, he disapproves of new ventures. He does not trust progressive schemes. He is a Dutchman to the core."

"Yes, their attitude towards you is unfortunate—but understandable."

They were in a skiff, drifting upstream on the tide in the early afternoon sunshine: watery sunshine, for it had rained all the morning, and the sky was hazed with thin strips of cloud through which the sun shone weakly.

They sat opposite each other and he stared at her and said: "I think I recall you saying that before—in precisely those words. Tell me something, beloved. Deep in your heart, have you forgiven me for that evening on the canal?"

She smiled her old mysterious smile, and nodded. "I told you I wouldn't, but I have. Now that I look back on it, I'm glad that you did force me."

"Why?"

She shrugged. "Something tells me I wouldn't have agreed to marry you if you hadn't acted as you did. I can't explain it, but I know it is so. And I would have been unhappy for the rest of my life if I'd refused you."

He frowned past her at a clump of floating grass towards which the boat was heading. As he brought the oar into use to avoid colliding with the grass he winced and clicked his tongue, and growled "Mother may be right, after all."

"Right about what?"

"My lacking a heart."

She stretched out and touched one of the healed bites on his forehead. "I can tell her she is wrong. Your heart is very sound. But your head is terribly strong, sweet. Sometimes far too strong. Did you tell Graham our reasons for delaying our wedding for a year?"

"No. I could not, Cornelia. I lacked the courage. My God! Think of the irony! Confessing to Graham, that slave lover, that I was in love with a mulatto girl! Explaining to him that we had to wait a year to marry so that I could prove to you I was strong enough to keep my hands off Rose! He would have fidgeted and squirmed himself into a Gordian knot from sheer incredulity."

"Have you seen Rose since your return from Demerary?"

"Fleetingly in New Amsterdam. We passed in the street."

She stared at him for a long while, tenderly, searchingly, a trifle anxiously. He did not return her gaze, but kept watching the black water as it swirled past the side of the craft, flecked here and there with *mora* blossoms, fine and golden. Now and then the seed of an *aeta* palm, purple and polished, would roll past, bobbing up and down just beneath the surface of the water. It was very warm and humid, and today the Creek abounded with clumps of *Missouri* grass.

As he stretched out his oar to push aside a clump of grass, he glanced at her and growled: "It won't happen. Not in a year. Not in twenty years. I didn't make that pledge in vain."

By Christmas the timber grant, under its manager, Benjamin Hartman, the mulatto sent by Graham from Demerary, was well established. The first six rafts of greenheart arrived in New Amsterdam early in January, each log already hewn and shaped in readiness for shipping.

Jacob was with Dirk on the *stelling* to watch the loading of the logs on a schooner, and as the first log was manœuvred aboard, Jacob grinned and said: "Everything going according to plan, Dirk. Aren't you proud?"

"Of course I am," snapped Dirk. "Why shouldn't I be? Lazy fool! You could have shared my pride, too, if you'd wanted."

Jacob nodded, in no way put out. "I prefer not to share in it and go on watching Crab Island, boy. *Kaburi* flies and blackwater fever don't seem to me a good exchange for Millicent and carpenter work in New Amsterdam."

"You have no spirit, that's what's your trouble, Jacob. *Kaburi* flies didn't kill me, did they? I didn't like their bites, I admit, but I survived."

"You only spent a few weeks up there. I would be up there for months and then years—if I survived. No, old fellow, I haven't the guts for that life."

Dirk looked at him and grunted. "You aren't, at heart, any different from my father and the other Dutch planters, Jacob. You love security and safety and the humdrum inside of a home. I've noticed that you coloured people have imbibed the spirit of the Dutch planters wholesale. I can see you in future generations living like them, quietly, securely, plodding along from day to day, never venturing out on any daring schemes, never progressing beyond what you are today."

Jacob chuckled. "You may be right, boy. But you know what has just come to me, Dirk? If you're going to go in for this timber seriously, don't you think you should set up a sawmill in the town here?"

Dirk stiffened. "By God! A sawmill. Now, you know, I hadn't thought of that." He stared at Jacob, then broke out: "I shall have a sawmill erected. Yes. And, Jacob, here is an idea! What about *you* being the manager of it?"

"I wouldn't turn down *that* proposition."

Storm objected at first, as Dirk had expected, but, eventually, he gave in, and plans were made for the erection of a sawmill in New Amsterdam. In May it was a thing accomplished—at least, the building was up; the machinery would arrive during the following month from Demerary, where it was lying in a warehouse. Graeme Clackson had got it down from England, for Hartfield & Clackson, besides being general merchants for provisions and textiles, had always dealt in machine parts for the plantations. Their hardware department had been well known since the days before Graeme went into partnership with John Hartfield.

Dirk and Cornelia were to be married on the first Monday in August.

"We hope to have the mill started on the last Monday in July."

"Congratulations, Dirk," said Rose. And for several seconds they stood there in the portico at New Signal staring at each other. Outside the morning was steamy in the bright sunshine of May, for it had rained heavily during the night. This was the first time they had encountered each other since February, and in that month they had met only briefly in the dining-room at Don Diego.

It was she who broke the silence. "Tell me, Dirk, do you feel truly happy about the first Monday in August?"

"Why shouldn't I? Most certainly I do." His tone was sharp now, his eyes very green and hard. "Did you think I wasn't?"

She regarded him in a dazed way, shaking her head slightly, foolishly. "I don't know what I thought," she murmured. "I only asked to hear what you'd say."

He began to glance agitatedly from side to side. "What have you come here for? Are you making some—some gown for Mother?"

"I came to measure her for her dress. The dress she will wear—on the first Monday in August."

"Oh. I see." His face softened. "Look here, Rose. I don't mean to sound harsh, but—I'll admit it. The sight of you still harrows me."

"Does it? You're trembling, Dirk."

"Are you going now? Are you on your way to the *stelling*?

"Yes."

"I'll walk with you to the *stelling*."

They had just got past the first few sapodilla trees along the driveway when he caught her elbow to help her evade a puddle. His fingers were icy, and she laughed and said: "Your fingers, Dirk! My God! Why are they so cold?"

He made no reply, and she said: "I will tease you. I shall never stop. I'm going to do it whenever we happen to meet." She took deep breaths. "What a lovely morning! Smell the wet leaves! I wish I felt like the morning."

He still would say nothing. He kept looking straight ahead towards the Creek. They were passing the orange trees now. There was fruit on the trees, but they were young. Rose said: "These oranges will be nice and ripe—on the first Monday in August. I'm making the bride's dress. Did you know?"

"Yes. She mentioned it."

"Dirk, stop here!"

"No, we must not stop, Rose."

"Remember the last time you walked with me to the *stelling* here?"

"Yes, I remember."

"You've been so busy since then. You and your schemes. You've conspired to avoid me. But I've conspired to avoid you, too, so I can't scold you." She was breathing agitatedly. She caught his arm and said: "This may be the last time we shall talk together before—before August."

"It may be."

"Wouldn't you like to kiss me? One kiss, Dirk. Only one."

He said nothing. His eyelashes kept fluttering.

"It's such a lovely morning. I'd remember it for years and years if you could only stop for a moment and touch me. Only touch me, Dirk. My cheek with your finger. My chin. My forehead. Anywhere you like. Only touch me, Dirk, love."

He gave his head a faint shake. That was all.

"No one can see us. I won't tell her I met you this morning." She came to a stop, and he halted automatically, too, his face as anguished as hers.

"We've spoken about you, Dirk. Only two days ago when I was at Don Diego. She knows. She admitted she knows."

"Knows what?"

"That I'm your true love."

On one of the uppermost branches of the sapodilla tree on their left a kiskadee kept crying "Kee-ee-ee!" lugubriously. He could make out its yellow breast as he let his gaze rove upward.

"I like her. She is a frank, fearless person, and she loves you deeply. And she does not believe in deceiving herself." She uttered a gasp and caught at his sleeve. "Dirk! My darling! You have tears in your eyes! I've never once seen you with tears in your eyes."

"Shall we move on, Rose?"

"My poor, sweet love. You're not all iron. I've always known it."

"Let us move on."

She made no move. She stared at his twitching face. And he watched the kiskadee. "Kee-ee-ee!" it cried again—on a more sustained and mournful note.

She began to say something, but her voice broke. She blinked rapidly, and turned away. In silence they continued on their way to the *stelling*.

21

GRAHAM kept his promise and came for the wedding. He arrived on the Tuesday preceding, and Storm and Elizabeth were on the *stelling* to meet him, as were Dirk and Cornelia and Nibia.

It was Dirk's suggestion that Nibia should be there, and Storm and Elizabeth had raised no objections. "I'm sure he would be overjoyed to see her," said Elizabeth. "He has always been so attached to her."

Nibia could hardly contain herself, especially as the occasion gave her an excuse to wear her silk dress—the same silk dress Dirk had whisked from under his cape in her logie seven years before. She had taken great care of it, and not a single moth had succeeded in eating a hole in it. And though she had lost her youthful figure—she was now thirty-nine—and had put on weight, the dress fitted her passably well. She was the proudest slave on the *stelling* that day.

Her proudest moment, however, was one she had not anticipated. Graham had hardly kissed his mother and shaken hands with his father and brother and Cornelia when he turned off quickly and cried: "And Nibia! My dear, good Nibia!" Without thought to restraint or propriety, he took a pace up to Nibia and embraced her. Nibia shook and gurgled with pleasure—then began to sob in an excess of happiness and pride.

"Ow, me massa! Massa Graham! But look how tall you get!" she wailed.

"And look how fat you've got, Nibia! But your face hasn't changed. You're just as pretty, I warrant!"

The afternoon was inclined to be drizzly, and Graham insisted that

Nibia should drive in the carriage with them to Doctor John's house, but Dirk shook his head firmly. "No, she must walk," he said. "It would be a squeeze. The carriage cannot hold six of us comfortably."

"Most certainly it can," said Storm, giving Dirk a cold stare.

Dirk stared back at his father—as coldly. "Yes, it can hold six, sir— but not comfortably if the sixth is a slave." He turned to Nibia with a brief smile. "I'm sure you understand, Nibia, don't you?"

"Yes, Massa Dirk. I will walk, massa," said Nibia, her exuberance fading.

Graham paled, but he did not pursue the matter. He shrank back into himself. He lost his initial spontaneity, and his eyes grew furtive and shy. "Anyway, I shall see you again, Nibia," he said hastily. "Take care of your dress in the mud when you walk."

There was silence in the carriage on the way to Doctor John's house, where they were dining. Storm, like Graham, had shrunk into himself. Elizabeth looked cold and vaguely defiant, though she tried to smile pleasantly at Graham when her gaze encountered his. Dirk and Cornelia looked entirely composed. Dirk sat beside Cornelia, and kept his hand over hers, which he had taken into his lap, his manner both affectionate and possessive.

Doctor John and Mary greeted them in their quiet, cordial manner. They were still childless, but seemed resigned to it. "Yes, it is a very pleasant house to grow old in." Mary smiled when Graham commented on the view of the harbour. "John and I often watch the ships come in from our bedroom window."

"For me," said Dirk, "I shall never forget the portico."

"Ah yes," chuckled his uncle, "that is understandable." He glanced at Cornelia and nodded amiably. "I'm so sorry I was not at home that day, my girl, to attend to your hand, but I heard you were taken care of quite efficiently."

Dinner was a pleasant meal. The atmosphere was easy and cordial, and it was not until they were rising from the table that a certain tension threatened to engulf them. It was a remark of Graham's that did it.

"Rose must be a very pretty creature now. I've brought a hamper of fruit from her mother for her. I must go and see her tomorrow and take the hamper."

Dirk stiffened, and Cornelia glanced quickly at him.

Elizabeth said: "Yes, you did say in your letter Sarah was giving you something to bring for her. As it happens, she's coming to New Signal tomorrow to give me a final fitting for my dress."

"A renowned seamstress, I've heard," smiled Graham. He glanced at his brother. "Of late you've hardly mentioned a word about her, Dirk."

Dirk snapped: "I'm sure I had more important matters to discuss in my letters. I'm not interested in dressmaking and seamstresses." Then as though regretting his asperity, he added with a grin: "Mother's letters should have told you all you wanted to know about Rose."

Why, thought Graham, should he want to bite my head off because I've mentioned Rose? He said nervously: "Mother only writes me once in about three months, and most of her news treats of social events. Births and deaths and weddings and scandalous behaviour." He uttered an uncertain laugh and put an affectionate arm about his mother. "Most interesting, though, Mother dear. I enjoy your letters."

It was good to see the Canje again, to watch the fireflies in the dusk from the old bedroom window, and to recall the nights when he was a small boy terrified by the sounds outside. The room was different, of course. And it was Dirk's room. From Monday night next it would be Dirk's and Cornelia's.

He turned at the sound of footsteps. It was Dirk.

"Staring out at the twilight and remembering your dear Nibia?"

Graham uttered a quavering chuckle. "Yes, I was reminiscing a bit. This room holds so many memories—all of them very precious."

"I'm sorry I had to handle Nibia like that this afternoon, but a slave is a slave. We cannot have them driving with us in our carriage."

"You're probably right. I was inclined to be somewhat unrestrained."

"What do you think of Cornelia?"

"I like her. She is very quiet and sweet, but she doesn't seem weak."

"She isn't." Dirk began to pace slowly, hands clasped behind him. "I could not have found a better wife."

Graham watched him in silence, and thought: Something is the matter with him, but it is hard to say what. Some of the fierceness has gone from his eyes. Or could it be my imagination? I'm almost inclined to think that he is suffering secretly—but what could possibly be the cause?

"So you have made Jacob your manager at the new sawmill?"

Dirk halted. "Yes. Yes, I have. I'm glad he accepted. I want to see him get on in the world. I'm very fond of Jacob."

Silence again. Lightning flashed over the cane fields in the southeast.

Dirk paced. Graham stared out at the dusk. Abruptly he began to chuckle.

"What amuses you?" asked Dirk, halting.

"I was remembering something you said—years ago, before I went to Demerary. You said you and Jacob had made a pact between you —a pact of loyalty."

"Yes. True. I haven't forgotten."

"You were so earnest, so terribly serious. I remember, too, you suggested that he should adopt the name of Greenfield instead of Frick."

Dirk said nothing. He paced again.

"By the way, Dirk, is Mother still unaware of Jacob's paternity?"

Dirk grinned. "Don't sound so formal about it. Your speech has got damned stilted, Graham. No, so far as I know, she still doesn't know it was Father who used to come in here to tickle your dear, good Nibia."

"I think it would be better if we never told her."

"She'll never learn through me."

"Does anyone else know besides you and me and Nibia?"

"Well, Jacob does. And I've told Cornelia. We have no secrets."

"You've never mentioned it to Rose, have you?"

"Rose! No. Of course not. Why should I?"

"Dirk, what is the matter? Have you anything against Rose?"

"What could I have against her?"

"I don't know, but—well, your manner. This is the second time within a matter of hours you've snapped at me because I've mentioned her name."

Dirk laughed—but there was a cracked note in his laughter, which Graham did not fail to remark. "The older you get the more fuzzy your imagination seems to become. Let's go down to the sitting-room. Father and Mother are there. They must be wondering what's keeping us so long up here."

"Yes. Yes, we ought to be going down. Mother is not the same gay person. She has grown quieter—and sadder. And that is not my imagination."

"I'm the cause, didn't you know?"

They both stood staring out at the cane fields. Lightning flashed again. And after a moment they heard the thunder. Far away over the jungle.

Dirk broke the silence. "You did destroy that letter as I asked?"

"What letter?"

"The one in which I told you about Father and Nibia?"

"Yes, I did. I remember distinctly. Clara and I were very friendly at the time—I mean in an intimate way. But I wouldn't let even her see it. I tore it up at once and had the pieces burnt."

"Good. Good. Let's go downstairs now. Come on."

It was Dirk, these days, who left the house every morning at half past eight to make a tour of inspection round the plantation. Storm lazed on the portico until breakfast time, smoking and reading. Graham expressed his surprise that Dirk had to go off on his tour. "Hardly any planter bothers nowadays," he said, when they were at coffee on the portico. "I never do. I leave my overseers to do all the inspecting there is to be done."

"Dirk believes in tradition, my boy," murmured his father.

At that instant, as though to confirm Storm's statement, Dirk drew from the pocket of his dressing gown a small ivory whistle and blew a sharp blast on it. Two slaves emerged almost at once from the house. Benji and Sarabelle.

"More coffee," said Dirk. "And bring my pipe, Benji, and some of the Brazilian tobacco."

"Yes, massa."

When the two slaves had returned inside, Graham laughed and remarked: "Even to the whistle, I notice, Dirk. I use a bell at Kaywana. Most planters do now. The whistle is going out of fashion."

Dirk smiled. "I'm old-fashioned. I like the old customs. So does my father-in-law-to-be. His household girls are clad only to the waist."

"Do they observe that custom at Don Diego?"

"They do." Dirk looked suddenly grim. "There's wisdom behind it, but you won't agree, I know. In any case, this colony is British forever now. All the good old Dutch customs must eventually die out. And the language with them, too."

"In another ten years Dutch will hardly be heard at all," Graham agreed.

"What does it matter, after all?" sighed Elizabeth.

"I agree," murmured Graham. And Dirk flashed him a glance and said: "It shouldn't matter to you, Graham, considering you don't intend to marry and have children."

"Who said he doesn't intend to marry?" Elizabeth's voice was icy as she stared at Dirk. But Graham could see that this was nothing new. Dirk merely smiled and returned: "Ask him, Mother. He's said it more than once in his letters."

"It's going to rain again today," said Storm, clapping his hands to call the slaves. He had never used an ivory whistle. Elizabeth sighed again and agreed with him. Graham kept fidgeting and frowning out upon the morning. Blue-grey clouds were banking in the north and east.

Rain did not fall, however. The clouds continued to bank and look menacing. And the air was taut. The trees looked rigid and alert, as though listening for thunder that never came. Long after Dirk had gone off on his tour Graham and his parents reclined on the portico, Graham and his mother chatting at intervals, but Storm silent and engrossed in his book. He was reading a collection of tales in English, a volume lent to him by Jim Lafferty a few days before.

Once a sudden gust of wind came from the east, and the sapodilla and orange trees began to rustle softly. Then the wind as suddenly died away, and the waiting calm continued. Graham smiled and murmured: "I know this kind of weather. The more threatening the clouds look the less likelihood of a storm."

"I think you are right," Elizabeth smiled. "It won't rain."

They saw carrion crows circling high up, hundreds of them like black mourning dots against the blue-grey masses of cloud.

After a lull in their conversation, Elizabeth remarked: "I think I hear a boat coming. It must be Rose."

"Ah yes! The hamper is safe in the pantry, isn't it? I promised Sarah faithfully I wouldn't forget to give it to her."

"Yes, it is quite safe, my boy."

Another gust of wind. And again it died away abruptly.

"Those vultures circling up there—they look very ominous."

"Ominous?" Elizabeth raised her brows.

Graham stirred in his chair, frowned and said: "I'm very imaginative. You mustn't take me seriously." He uttered an uneasy chuckle.

Silence came upon them again.

She is still very beautiful, but the grey hairs have come. I can see several of them. Poor dear Mother.

"Would you say you're very disappointed in me, Mother?"

"Good heavens, no!" She smiled affectionately and stretched out and touched his neck. "Not in any way, my boy. Why do you ask?"

He grunted. "I was remembering Clara—what you said in that letter you wrote me. You didn't approve of Clara, remember!"

"That is over. I have forgotten it—and forgiven your youthful weakness."

"She gave me strength, Mother."

Elizabeth made no comment. They watched the clouds and listened to the distant twittering of sackies. The carrion crows formed two concentric circles now, almost like some cabalistic sign of ugly portent. So thought Graham, and began to squeeze his hands together. He gave a start when his mother murmured: "Yes, I was right. It's Rose. Here she is now."

Graham sat up and looked along the driveway. He grunted. "Is that Rose?"

The wind again. A very brief gust. It brought the scent of orange leaves—and another scent not easy to define. Could it have emanated from the girl in pale blue coming along the driveway? She is lovely. She has grown. She has developed. I wouldn't have recognised her. . . . Mighty God! She *is* lovely!

She ran up the steps, and her laughter burst upon them like pleasant rain from a sun-drenched sky. "Miss Elizabeth! Mr. Storm! You don't mean this is Graham! Yes, it is! Graham, I wouldn't have known you if I hadn't heard you were expected!"

The carrion crows kept circling.

"Yes. Yes, it is me, Rose." He heard his voice coming as though from high up amidst the lowering clouds. Above them. When he rose from the chair he felt he had left his body reclining. "You're lovely, Rose. Lovely."

"Thanks. And what a giant you are!"

Storm had looked up from his book.

"Lovely. My God!"

Elizabeth sat forward, clasping her hands.

Rose blushed slightly. She seemed about to retreat a pace in confusion—but she did not move. Her clothes rustled faintly, like the stirring of distant tissue. It was as though a shudder had been arrested halfway down her body.

For several seconds the four of them remained motionless. Some spell from the oppressive morning might have swept down upon them, compelling them to listen to each other breathing.

Each seemed to sense that a new ruthless force had shivered into being, and that this was a moment that might weigh heavily in their memories throughout the years, and even decades, to come.

22

THE southeastern bedroom had been prepared for Graham, the room his grandparents had occupied when they were alive. Its windows commanded a view of the slaves' logies, which stood some distance away from the house, beyond the orange and sapodilla trees. From its windows could also be seen the large water tank into which the rain that fell on the main roof of the house was channelled through a system of gutters.

Graham did not sleep that night. He paced his room in his night-shirt. Now and then he would pause by a window to look out at the water tank or at the slaves' logies showing through the foliage of the trees. It was a night of bright moonlight. Once he settled himself in a chair and tried to read by the light of two candles, but he could not concentrate on the printed words. Once he filled and lit his pipe and smoked, then abruptly put it down and began to pace again.

The moon had set and the sky in the east had begun to turn grey when, at length, he was overcome by a great tiredness and lay down on the bed. He slept at once, but tossed and moaned in his sleep. When a knock sounded on his door, he started up with a cry to find the sun shining in upon him.

Sarabelle came in and asked him if he was ready for his bath. He told her yes. Yes, could she prepare it for him immediately. He spoke in a stammer, and the girl gave him a curious stare before she said: "It ready now, massa."

So he went to the bathroom, and Sarabelle attended upon him. The water she sprayed upon him from the watering can felt icy, and he shivered, and Sarabelle asked solicitously: "You got fever, massa?"

"No. No, Sarabelle. No fever. But I did not sleep well."

On the portico he was silent and pensive, his eyes with a hunted glint, and his parents and Dirk remarked on it. "Are you unwell, Graham?" asked his mother anxiously. And he started and shook his head. Then as though catching himself, he stammered: "Perhaps. Yes, perhaps. I have a slight headache," and in his eyes a sudden cunning light gleamed. "I think it would be as well if I went to New Amsterdam and consulted Uncle John. I'll go this very morning."

"But if you're not feeling well you must go to bed, my boy. Your Uncle John can be sent for."

"No, no. Good heavens! For a mere headache. No, Mother. I'll drop in and see him. In any event, I want to go to New Amsterdam. I am anxious to see the new sawmill—and to have a word with Jacob." He glanced at Dirk, who was frowning at him in a puzzled manner. "Jacob will be at the mill this morning, won't he, Dirk?"

"It's very likely he will be, though I don't think we're doing any milling today. The rafts that arrived early this week have already been dealt with."

"I'm eager to see what he looks like." He clapped his hands, and Benji and Sarabelle appeared. "Benji, send a message to the boatmen to have the tent-boat ready within the hour. I want to go to New Amsterdam."

"Yes, massa," said Benji, and withdrew.

Storm, puffing at his pipe, frowned and said: "I'm going to town after breakfast. Wouldn't you care to wait and come with me, my boy?"

Graham gave a soft gasp. He had a cornered look. After a pause, he shook his head agitatedly and said: "Thanks, Father, but I think I should like to rest after breakfast. I didn't sleep very well last night. No, I must go within the hour, I'm afraid."

A silence came upon them. Storm and Elizabeth exchanged glances, and Dirk looked tense and baffled. Graham fidgeted uncomfortably. Suddenly he rose and said that he had better go up at once and get dressed.

He had hardly gone through the doorway when Dirk looked at his father and growled: "Something is the matter with his mind. I'm convinced of it now."

Elizabeth flashed: "There is nothing whatever the matter with his mind!"

"Would you say his behaviour is normal?"

Elizabeth made no reply. Storm frowned: "He's lonely, Dirk. Nothing else."

Dirk shrugged, sipping his coffee.

After a pause, Storm asked him: "Did he discuss anything with you before going to bed?" And Dirk shook his head. "No, Father. I haven't spoken to him alone since yesterday morning on the portico here."

"Are you going to town today?"

"Yes, sir—after breakfast, at the same time as you are. I want to see Jacob and post a letter. I wrote Elfrida last night."

"Who is Elfrida?"

"Pelham's wife. We've promised each other to correspond regularly."

Another silence. When Dirk happened to glance at his mother he noticed that there were tears in her eyes.

The stable where the van Groenwegel carriage, together with the carriages of several other Creek families, was housed stood hardly fifty yards from the *stelling*, and the head boatman offered to go and tell the coachman to bring the carriage, but Graham stopped him. "Don't bother, my man. I shall walk. It is not far, and the morning is pleasant." He added with a nervous but lighthearted laugh: "New Amsterdam is a small town, Isaac, and I know my way about."

"But the streets muddy from de rain, massa."

"I don't mind mud sometimes. Be waiting for me here, Isaac. I shall be back in about an hour's time."

Many stares were directed at him as he made his way south along the High Street, picking a precarious path among the puddles, but he did not care. Much of the tension had left his manner. There was purpose and resolve in his stride.

He turned into a side street even more muddy than the High Street. It was a mere track, narrow and grassy in spots and deeply rutted from carriage wheels. Water gurgled in the ditches as it hurried towards the river. The tide was low, and the *kokers* had probably been opened to drain the town of the rain that had filled the ditches during the night. He smiled, telling himself that it was the same old New Amsterdam. In Georgetown there were canals; in New Amsterdam ditches—and Crab Island in the estuary of the river. You could smell the nearness of the jungle in New Amsterdam—and hear the goatsuckers' cries at night.

He crossed over by a little wooden bridge into the front yard of a little shingled one-storeyed cottage on eight-foot pillars. He went up the steps and knocked on the door, and almost at once a pair of dark eyes were fixed upon him through one of the louvred windows of the small gallery.

He waited, and the door opened to reveal a half-scared black girl. She curtseyed and said in a bated voice: "Yes, massa?"

"Are you Mrs. Clarke's servant?"

"Yes, massa, she replied, curtseying again. "You want to see Missy?"

"I should be glad to—but I've come to see Miss Rose Clarke in particular. Is she at home?"

"No, massa. Nobody at home. Missy Clarke gone to deliver Mr. Gale' missy' baby, and Miss Rose at Missy Henson up de street."

"Oh. Who is Missy Henson?"

"Missy Henson mek dresses, massa. Miss Rose work wid her."

"Ah! Yes, yes. Where is Missy Henson's cottage?"

"You want me run wid a message, massa?"

"Would you? I'd be glad. Tell Miss Rose I'd like to see her at once. It is a matter of great importance, tell her."

"Yes, massa," breathed the girl, curtseying. "I go now. Not far. You tek a seat and wait, me massa?" She was about to go through the door when she stopped and looked at him. "What name Ah must tell she, massa?"

Graham laughed. "Good God! How thoughtless of me. Say Massa Graham van Groenwegel."

"You Massa van Groenwegel, massa?"

"Yes. I arrived yesterday from Demerary."

She gave a nervous little laugh and fled down the steps.

Graham looked round the gallery at the sparse furniture. There were only two chairs and a small bamboo table. No rugs or carpet. He moved to the door that gave into the tiny sitting-room and saw that this was, unlike the gallery, overcrowded with little tables and chairs. There were a sofa and a tall bookcase, and a dark-blue carpet covered the greater part of the floor. Brightly polished brass candlesticks stood on every table. It was a well-kept and cosy room, despite its over-crowded appearance.

He turned suddenly at the sound of footsteps on the stairway. He darted to the door and opened it, and Rose, a little breathless, nearly collided with him, a sinuous creature in a flowered calico dress, her hair in disarray about her shoulders—long, dark, wavy tresses that reached nearly to her waist.

"Graham! Heavens! I couldn't believe my ears when Marie came and told me that you were here. I wasn't expecting you."

"I know you were not. Where is Marie, by the way?"

"She has gone round by the back. What's the matter, Graham? Why have you come here? Did you want to see Mama about something?"

"No. I came to see you, Rose. I've taken you from your work, haven't I? You were busy, I suppose, with your dressmaking?"

"Yes, I am somewhat busy at the moment—but it doesn't matter. I can spare a few minutes. Miss Henson won't mind." She gave him a curious, anxious look. "Won't you sit down?"

He shook his head. "Mama Clarke might consider it improper for you to receive me here alone, Rose. Couldn't we take a walk? I want to talk to you."

"A walk? A walk where? At his hour of the morning?"

"I'm aware it is most unusual, Rose, but I must insist. It is important. Let us get out of this street on to the dam that borders the canal. We shall be alone there, and only the canes of Vrymen's Erven will overhear what I have to discuss with you."

She agreed, but she seemed disturbed and perplexed. As they moved east along the little street, she laughed and said: "I can hardly believe you are here. You are the last person I expected to see this morning."

"I didn't sleep last night, Rose."

"Why?"

"Let us get on to the dam before I tell you. I'm sure everyone is staring at us—and listening to us." He gave an agitated glance from right to left at the cottages they were passing. "You must think me mad—and probably I am. I feel mad, Rose. If I don't talk to you I shall be raving by evening."

When they emerged on to Vrymen's Erven's dam, a breeze came across the cane fields as though to greet them. It blew about the girl's hair, and Graham turned his gaze upon her and said: "Rose, haven't you guessed? Yesterday before you left New Signal weren't you aware what had happened to me?"

She frowned. "You did seem a little strange—but—but—Graham, what is it you're trying to tell me?"

"You know already. You must. Wasn't it apparent on my face, in my every gesture, yesterday when I met you in the portico at New Signal? I'm in love with you, Rose. My whole being is on fire. The very thought of you makes me dizzy and unhinged. My God! I couldn't believe my eyes when I saw you run up the steps into the portico. I—I knew you must have grown into a pretty creature—but such loveliness! And your voice, your laughter! Heavens! I would never have believed it if I had been told in Demerary that such a thing could have happened to me when I came to visit my parents." His head was trembling. There was a glazed look about his eyes. "I don't feel sane, Rose. It has happened too suddenly. It's the shock, the shock, my sweetheart. That—that you could have been in existence here in New Amsterdam and I not aware of you. Away in Demerary at Huis Kaywana, absorbed in plantation business, growing bitter and lonely and soured—and all the while you were here. I didn't sleep last night. I couldn't. This morning I had to come and see you to tell you, to speak to you, to gaze upon you, Rose. My God! How lovely you are! Cousin Hubertus's daughter. Sarah Hubert's daughter. You were only a mite of nine when I last saw you. You were pretty then, I know, but this! No, not this, Rose! Never in my most heated fantasies would I have envisaged you as captivating as this!"

Her grey-brown eyes looked wide and startled as she listened. More than once her lips moved as she made an attempt to interrupt him, but no words came. Now that she could take the opportunity of his pause to say something she discovered that she still could say nothing, and the pause lengthened, and the wind hissed amidst the canes, and the canal that ran in a north-south direction became gently rippled, the ripples glittering in the hot sunshine. A punt with canes was approaching in the distance from the south, hauled by slaves walking on the dam. The dam was muddy under their shoes, and added to the hissing of the wind amidst the canes was the squelch of their foot treads.

He began to look around him distractedly and murmur to himself. "A lovely morning. Every detail of this scene will remain scored on my memory. In the years and decades to come I shall remember the canes on Vrymen's Erven. And the ripples on the canal. It is like our canal at New Signal. The water is clean—not stinking like the water in those two canals that drain Georgetown, North and South Canal. They don't run parallel to the river like this one. They run from east to west into the Demerary, taking all the filth of the town into their depths." Abruptly he turned towards her. "Rose, you have never been to Georgetown. You have never once visited your mother."

"No. That's true," she murmured, the startled look still on her face.

"Wouldn't you like to go to Georgetown—to Demerary?"

"Certainly."

"Rose, would you like to be the mistress of Kaywana?"

She came to a halt, and he halted, too. "Graham, what is this? Are you—I think you are right. You are not yourself today."

"Rose, I want you to marry me."

"Marry you?" She laughed. "Please, Graham! Really, I'm sure you are not well. Let us turn back here, shall we? Miss Henson must be wondering what has happened to me."

"Yes, let us turn back. But answer me. I must have an answer."

"You don't expect me to take you seriously, Graham?"

"I do, Rose. It must seem strange, I'm aware, my sweet. But I mean every word I utter. I want you to marry me. I want you as the mistress of Kaywana. Will you please tell me if you are willing to consider my suit?"

"Oh, my God!" She uttered a little laugh and shook her head, gave him a glance of incredulity. "I must be dreaming this. I'm sure I'm going to wake up."

He laughed, too. "I understand. I feel like that, too. I've been living in a dream since yesterday morning, Rose. But tell me, my dear. Will you think over what I've asked you? Will you speak to your Mama Clarke and hear what she thinks? You're only sixteen, and she may frown on the notion of your marrying now. She has taken good care of you during these years past, and I should not like to offend her in any way. But you must assure me, Rose, that you yourself are willing to have me as a husband. Only then shall I approach Mrs. Clarke to ask her consent formally."

There was a long silence. Rose kept shaking her head and breathing audibly in her agitation. At length, she murmured: "I shall think it over, Graham." She spoke automatically, as though not fully aware what she was saying. She looked up at him abruptly with a stunned air, and her lips parted to say something, but no sound came.

"What is it? What do you want to tell me, Rose?"

"Nothing. Nothing, Graham."

The moment he arrived back at New Signal he went up to his room and sat down to write a letter. He wrote quickly and concentratedly for about half an hour, then lay down his quill and read over what he had written, and the tension in his manner began to lessen. It was as though the written words were ramparts he had erected in preparation for a coming battle. He was safe now, he assured himself, smiling. . . . "I know I can depend upon you, dearest Clara, to support me in this the hour of my greatest turmoil. You are the one human being I can appeal to without fear of being turned away. And so you must come. I need you, as I have never done before, to give me strength. . . ."

As he was taking his place at the breakfast table, there was no agitation in his voice when he said: "Mother, I have just written Clara. I have asked her to come and spend a week or two with us. You don't object, do you?"

There was an instant of silence while the stares of the others were turned upon him. Then his mother spoke. "Clara? Clara Hartfield? You have asked her to come here, Graham?"

"Yes, Mother. Have you any objections?"

A hesitation, then: "Well, I should not have thought of asking her myself, but if you have done so in your letter then let her come."

"But you think she will come?" asked Storm. "I doubt it."

"She will, Father. She is my dearest and most loyal friend, and I need her advice and support. She will not fail me."

Another silence while they stared at him. Then Dirk asked: "Why do you need her advice and support?"

Sitting erect in his chair, his gaze steady, he told them.

23

THE following morning Dirk instructed Frick, the head overseer, to take his place on the tour of inspection. "I have to go to town on urgent business, Frick. I may not be back until breakfast time."

A little more than an hour later Dirk was being admitted by Marie into Mrs. Clarke's cottage in New Amsterdam. "Is your mistress at home, Marie?"

"Yes, Massa Dirk. She at home," said Marie, curtseying. "Please sit down, massa, and I will call her for you."

"Tell her I must apologise for calling in this way. Is Miss Rose at home?"

"No, massa. Miss Rose at Missy Henson sewing." Marie curtseyed again. "Ah must go and call her for you, Massa Dirk?"

"No, Marie. My business is with Missy Clarke."

Dirk did not sit. He paced the gallery, and he was still pacing when Mrs. Clarke, fully dressed for going out, bustled out of the sitting-room. She had grown thinner rather than stouter with the years, and, if anything, more energetic. Her reddish frizzy hair was almost entirely grey now, and though the lines of her face had deepened, her sallowish complexion had not darkened in tint as was generally the case with most ageing people of mixed blood.

"It's inexcusable of me, Mrs. Clarke, intruding upon you like this," Dirk began—but she interrupted him: "Not at all, Mr. van Groenwegel. I was about to go out, but it is not very urgent—and I'm glad you have come."

"You know what I have come about, then?"

She nodded gravely and asked him to be seated. "Yes, I think I know—though I had been expecting to see your brother, Mr. Graham, rather than you."

"Quite natural, I suppose." Dirk took the chair she indicated, and she seated herself opposite him with a soft sigh. There was an instant of silence while each of them seemed waiting for the other to begin the discussion. Dirk had just parted his lips to speak when Mrs. Clarke said: "I've sent Marie to call Rose."

Dirk started. "Have you? You shouldn't have troubled. I didn't care——"

"Yes, I think she should be present, Mr. van Groenwegel." Her voice was firm and decisive. "After all, it does concern her, doesn't it?"

Dirk stiffened at the veiled rebuke, but he had a great respect for Mrs. Clark. Coloured though she might be, she never cringed before white people. She did not live in awe of any planter family. Perhaps it was because she was herself the daughter of a planter and had been brought up in a planter's home. Perhaps, too, it was because she had assisted in bringing so many of their sons and daughters, including himself, into the world, that she could assume her air of confidence in the presence of the whites.

He grinned briefly and nodded. "I agree it does, but I would have preferred talking to you alone, all the same. Rose unnerves me, if I may say so."

She smiled slightly, noncommittally, and asked: "Why have *you* come, though, Mr. van Groenwegel? Has Mr. Graham asked you to speak to me on his behalf?"

"He hasn't." Dirk's fingers began to tap together, and his eyes glanced quickly from side to side. "I came here without consulting him. He is not well."

There was the drumming of footsteps on the stairway, and the door opened abruptly. It was Rose. She had been running, for she was a little breathless.

Dirk rose, and the two of them stared at each other, Dirk flushing, but she rather pale and excited. She was in the same flowered calico dress that she had worn the previous morning when Graham had called, her hair in the same disarray behind her and about her shoulders. Sinuous, lithe, she shut the door and came in and stood beside her adopted mother's chair.

"Why have *you* come, Dirk?"

Dirk flinched as though the question were a tongue of fire that had flicked his cheek. Mrs. Clarke asked him to be seated, and he sank back down on to the chair, his face twitching a trifle.

"I thought it my duty to come, Rose. I was on the point of explaining to your Mama Clarke. Graham is not well. I have come to apologise for him."

"Apologise for his not being well? I don't understand, Dirk."

"Rose, I think you had better let me discuss this matter with Mr. van Groenwegel," said Mrs. Clarke. "Do I understand you to say, Mr. van Groenwegel, that your brother, Mr. Graham, is not well enough to come and see me?"

"No. I mean, Mrs. Clarke, that he was even yesterday in a state of mental disorder. He was not responsible for anything he said to Rose yesterday, and I want to apologise for the inconvenience both you and Rose might have been caused as a result of his visit to this cottage. And I should like you to ignore any proposal he may have made to you, Rose. He is not well, I repeat. We mean to have Uncle John come and put him through an examination."

"Well, I must thank you for explaining that, Mr. van Groenwegel," smiled Mrs. Clarke, "because I was certainly upset by the proposal he made to Rose yesterday morning. I knew he could not have had the approval of his parents when he came here unannounced to tell Rose what he did, and I can well believe that he could not have been in a calm state of mind to have acted in such a manner. I'd intended to call at New Signal during the course of the day to see your parents and inquire into the matter."

Dirk rose. "I'm glad I spared you the trouble, then, Mrs. Clarke," he smiled. "And may I add that my parents have asked me to convey to you their compliments, and their regrets that you were bothered yesterday. They were very upset, too, I can assure you." He added, beginning to move towards the door: "Well, I mustn't keep you any longer. I know you're a busy person——"

"Please wait a moment, Dirk!" Like another tongue of fire, Rose's voice flicked across the gallery.

He paused, frowning. "What is it?"

"Mama, could I be permitted to speak to Dirk for a few minutes—alone?"

"What could you have to say to Mr. van Groenwegel that I cannot hear, Rose?"

"I'm asking you, Mama. Do you give me permission?"

Mrs. Clarke glanced from Rose to Dirk, then back to Rose. "Very well," she said. "I shall leave you for a few minutes. I trust you will forgive the impropriety, Mr. van Groenwegel, but you have grown up together with Rose so I don't think you will be surprised at her unusual request." She smiled as she added this, and Dirk smiled back— a brittle, agitated smile—and said: "Of course, Mrs. Clarke. Yes, I'm quite accustomed to Rose and her ways."

The older woman had no sooner gone inside when Rose said: "On the stairs. Come on. We can't talk in here or she'll hear us." She spoke in a husky, urgent voice, and he followed her out on to the steps mechanically.

She glanced towards the waiting carriage, and remarked: "Graham walked to come here yesterday. You've come in the carriage. My sweet, formal Dirk!"

"What do you want to say to me, Rose?"

"Many, many things, Dirk, but there isn't time." She clutched his sleeve, and her hand trembled slightly. "I know how you feel—and I'm sorry."

He made no reply, only stood there squeezing his fingers together.

"Suppose I were to accept Graham, Dirk. Suppose I were to persuade Mama to give her consent, you would hate me for the rest of our lives, wouldn't you?"

"The supposition does not arise. Graham is unwell, I tell you. His mind is disturbed. He was not responsible for what he said to you yesterday."

She smiled. "No, my sweet. You say that because you are desperately anxious to keep him away from me, because you're alarmed he may persist in trying to make a marriage with me—me, a mulatto girl. Think of it, Dirk! A mulatto girl as the mistress of Plantation Kaywana! Wife of a van Groenwegel! Your sister-in-law!"

"Stop that, stop that, Rose!" His hands clenched, and his eyes became hard and icy. But she laughed and told him: "Graham is not unwell, Dirk. He knew what he was saying to me yesterday. I was shocked, I admit. I never thought he would have taken such a fancy to me—and so suddenly. At first sight of me! I still can't believe it. But it has happened before. I've heard of such happenings."

He gripped her wrist. "Rose, stop speaking in that manner. I shall kill you if you persist. You know what I feel about our family. Don't you dare to set your cap at Graham. Do you hear me, Rose? Keep away from New Signal until he has returned to Demerary. If I see you on our place I shall strangle you, as there is a sky above us this morning." He spoke in a low, grating voice, and his head trembled. His whole frame shook. He released her wrist and began to move down the steps. She caught his sleeve and stayed him.

"Dirk, wait. I'm not afraid of you. You know I'm not. And you know I never shall be. Your threats don't trouble me. I expected you to speak like this. If I have business at New Signal I shall go there. And I do have. There is your mother's dress for the wedding——"

"She will send for it, or come herself to Miss Henson's cottage——"

"I shall bring it myself, as arranged, tomorrow before breakfast."

"You will not!" He gripped her arm. "Do you hear me? You will not."

She laughed. "I'm still not intimidated, sweet. How delicious it is to feel your hand upon me, even though it's in anger. My poor Dirk. You're not what you make people think you are. You're not really a monster, as your mother thinks. I know you for what you are. At heart, you are soft. You *say* you are hard——"

"God damn you!" He released her arm, uttering a snarling sound. "Why were you ever born! Simply to upset me, harrow me, make me lose my temper——"

"And don't you love me more when I upset you, Dirk? I know you do. You detest girls who treat you with tact and caution——"

"Rose, shut up! I'm going. And remember what I've said. You're not to come to New Signal on any business whatever until Graham has returned to Demerary."

"I shall disobey you, sweet," she laughed. Then in a suddenly serious voice she asked: "Dirk, will you tell me something? I must know, my love. Speak and be honest. Why have you come here this morning? Is it because you are upset over what might be my answer to Graham, because you're jealous, or is it the family pride you have in mind only? Tell me, Dirk. That's what I wanted to ask you when I stopped you and asked Mama's permission to speak to you."

He did not answer for a moment, only standing there rigid in his old way, his hands clasped together tight. Then he grunted and looked at her, and said: "You may as well know, then. For both reasons." The rigidity left him. He seemed to sag with a sudden tiredness. He had a baffled look, too, as though he had, at length, been presented with a problem that was beyond his ability to master. He gave her an appealing glance and said quietly: "It's for my sake as well as the family's I ask you to keep away from our place, Rose. The sight of you maddens me more than it could ever madden Graham."

She did not try to stay him this time as he turned and went down the rest of the steps. She stood and watched him get into the carriage. Before it moved off she saw his hand wave briefly.

24

B EF O R E paying his call on Mrs. Clarke and Rose, Dirk had felt complete confidence in his ability to impose his will on Graham and deflect his brother in his avowed purpose of marrying Rose. That same afternoon, however, disillusion began to set in, for Graham surprised him by showing a complete indifference in the face of all the arguments Dirk put up. Dirk talked to him for more than an hour after breakfast in the northeastern room, but Graham merely smiled and shook his head. And what depressed Dirk more than ever was the lack of tension in his brother's manner. The agitation and fidgety uneasiness had disappeared. Graham's manner now was calm and filled with resolve. "I am a living being now," he murmured more than once, and there was no strange, glazed light in his eyes as he said this. He had thrown off his old-man air of gloom and introspection; he looked younger; there was a determined sparkle in his eyes.

"You have persistently scolded me for my weakness, Dirk. You were right. I know I am intrinsically weak—but there are times when I can be strong. When they were all against me because of my attitude towards the missionaries I stood up and defied them. Remember? It is true Clara gave me moral support, but, still, I knew that because the issue was an important one I must be strong. I prayed to God for strength, and He answered my prayer. Here again I am faced with an important issue—a vital issue—and again I have prayed for help, and God has not deserted me. I feel strong, Dirk. And with the vision of Rose in my soul, I gain in strength hour by hour."

What could one do against that kind of talk? At breakfast he had spoken in exactly the same fashion when their parents had tried to reason with him. Dirk had taken particular care to be silent on that occasion. He had left the elders to do the talking entirely, knowing that they would have resented interference from him. There had even been the chance that his mother, out of sheer perverseness, out of the sheer antipathy she bore him, might have sided with Graham. There had been a tricky moment when Storm had said: "My boy, no one loves these black people and coloured artisans more than I do, but there is a boundary of intimacy beyond which we must never step."

Dirk saw Graham start slightly, saw the sly smile that came to his face. Graham glanced at Dirk, and for one terrible instant Dirk thought his brother would have blurted out before their mother the whole story about their father and Nibia.

Graham merely grunted and lowered his gaze, however. After a pause, he said: "They are all equal with us in God's sight, Father. They are all human, and, for me, there is no boundary."

"But think of your cousins and your uncles and your brother and sister, Graham," Elizabeth said. "Do you think they will be comfortable entertaining in their home a mulatto girl? And do you think they and all your friends in Georgetown will want to be entertained in Huis Kaywana by a mulatto mistress?"

Graham raised a playful forefinger. "Not very long ago, Mother—I was eleven or twelve, I think—I heard you and Grandfather discussing Governor Meertens and his coloured wife. She was the first lady of Demerary, remember?"

"Meertens was most unpopular," said Storm.

"He was unpopular because of his anti-Orange views, and because he was appointed Governor by the Batavian government, which was itself highly unpopular. I have a good memory for those days, Father."

"He was also unpopular because of his mulatto wife, Graham," Elizabeth said. "And, in any event, he was not in office very long—hardly a year—so we can't tell how the white society of Stabroek would have accepted his wife. It was too short a test. You are not the Governor of Demerary, Graham. You're a planter, and no one can put you out of office. Rose would be your wife for the rest of your life, and your social position would suffer."

"Apart from that, think of the taint, my boy!" added Storm. "It's true Cousin Hubertus had Indian blood in him—I think he was a quarter Indian—but no one frowns upon Indian blood. In fact, many planters consider it a fortunate circumstance, for it gives them great influence with the Indians—and the Indians are not slaves. Rose's mother was a slave. Your children would have in them Negro slave blood. They would be branded for life. Never would your children nor grandchildren be regarded as white people. They would be on a par with the free coloured people. Quadroons, octoroons. Is that a pleasant prospect?"

"Your children would be discriminated against," Elizabeth told him. "Can't you visualise what it would be like, my boy? Pelham's and Willem's children, Dirk's children, would be known as the white van Groenwegels, and yours would be dismissed contemptuously as the coloured van Groenwegels. They would curse you for the humiliation you had bequeathed them."

It was another hot, close day, with thunderclouds in the southeast and south. Now and then they would hear the distant muttering of the thunder, and now and then wind would come in brief gusts from the northeast, causing the orange and sapodilla trees to hiss faintly.

From the windows of the northeastern room the Creek was visible between the trees, and as Dirk watched the dark brown streak of water, he saw a tent-boat glide past. He did not hear the splash of the oars until it had gone out of view. And now, far away towards the east, came the bell for the slaves. The overseers were calling them in for their midday meal. Before the clanging had died away the thought came into Dirk's mind. . . . That bell ringing reminded him of something. Yes, it was the day when Rose was in the room here. He had stood staring out of this very window, and he had heard the bell in the distance. Then it had been late afternoon, and the slaves were being summoned in for their evening repast. . . . Suddenly he had turned, and there she was, half sitting on the edge of the bed. . . .

"Graham."

"Yes, Dirk?"

"Mother and Father spoke to you at breakfast, and now I've spent more than an hour trying to make you see the impossibility of this step you're determined on taking. And still you are of the same mind."

"That is so. You are all against me, and yet God has granted me the strength to resist you. Next week Clara will be here—and she will support me. Dear, loyal Clara."

"I wonder why you bothered to ask her to come, since you don't seem to need more than God to help you."

"I shall feel doubly strong when she is here—and, in any event, I want her to meet Rose and see for herself what a fine, lovely wife I have chosen."

"Very well, Graham. I didn't want to do this—but you have forced my hand. You've driven me to the wall."

"Why the dramatics?" asked Graham, surprised. Some of his calm deserted him. The old fear of his brother began to uncoil in him again. The raccoon's eyes, in their chilly, unflinching stare, unnerved him.

"No dramatics," said Dirk. "I simply want to tell you something I think you ought to know before you proceed any further in this business. Rose is desperately in love with me. She has been in love with me for the past two or three years."

Graham had been sitting at the writing desk, toying with a quill. He put down the quill, and one of his hands pressed hard on the edge of the table while the other closed about the lapel of his coat.

"Furthermore," said Dirk, "she has been my mistress for the past year."

Graham rose. He had gone very white. Suddenly the blood returned to his face, and he laughed. "A clever ruse, Dirk. It nearly fooled me. You forget what you have always told me in your letters? You never touch slaves or coloured people. It is a strict rule of yours."

Within him, Dirk swore. It irked him to have to lie and dissemble. But there was no help for it. This sentimental fool must be dealt with by fair means or foul. He jerked his thumb towards the bed. "In that very bed, if you want to know. We've rolled together in there on many an afternoon when Mother and Father were away visiting. You fool! Do you think she's a saint? And do you think I'm not capable of making an exception of a luscious morsel like Rose? I've felt guilty about it, and I wouldn't have dared mention anything in my letters to you. But no fear! She's a hot little wench. Ask her if she didn't undress herself, despite my protests, in this very room on an afternoon in July of last year. I can tell you the exact day. It was the day on which we received the news that the colonies were to remain British. I was writing a letter to you at that desk, and Mother and Father were away at the Huislands' silver-wedding dinner, and Rose came in here to me. I ordered her out of the room, but she wouldn't go. She undressed herself and offered herself to me. Let her deny that. Ask her. That's the little wanton you're planning to make the mistress of Kaywana!"

"You're lying! You're lying!" cried Graham—but it was apparent that he believed. There was agony on his face.

"Why should I want to lie," growled Dirk, unperturbed, leaning against the window sill. "I admit it's not something I like talking about, and I never would have mentioned a single word to you if you hadn't driven me to."

Graham began to shake his head foolishly and mutter.

"No, no. Rose. Offering herself to you. I won't believe it. Oh, my God! No, I could not believe that. That sweet, lovely creature. Oh, my God!" He did not address this to Dirk, but to the desk. He sank back down into the chair and rested his head on the writing table, groaning.

"You should have guessed it," Dirk pressed on. "You asked me why I wanted to bite off your head on Tuesday when you mentioned Rose's name. It's because the thought of her upsets me—that's why. Cornelia is jealous of her. She knows that Rose and I have been intimate. I told her how Rose offered herself to me that afternoon. Cornelia and I have no secrets."

The singing of the slaves could be heard on the early-afternoon air. They generally sang when they came in from the fields for their meals. Free-hearted souls. It was only their bodies that were in bondage. By leaning out of the window, Dirk could see one or two of them between the trees beyond the compound. Black, shiny faces in the hot noonday sun. Frizzy black hair, in mops on their heads. To think of future van Groenwegels inheriting some of that pigment. And that coarse, rough, kinky hair! Never! Never!

25

ON Monday the wedding came off without a hitch, but Graham was not among the guests at the reception which was held at the Don Diego house, nor did he even accompany his parents and brother to New Amsterdam to the Lutheran church for the ceremony. It was announced that he was indisposed, which was hardly an untruth, for Graham had not left his room since Friday afternoon. His meals had to be taken up to him, though he would eat nothing even when the food was placed before him. Elizabeth tried to coax him, but without avail. Doctor John came and gave him a sedative, and on Saturday night he slept. But on Sunday he was still inconsolable. He lay in a hammock slung across the southeastern corner of the room, and stared at the rafters, and now and then he would mutter to himself. Once Elizabeth came into the room and found him on his knees by the bed, praying.

Cornelia, who was accustomed to the atmosphere of tension that existed between Dirk and his parents, thought nothing of the strained silences at the table when they were having a light supper on Monday evening at New Signal. Neither she nor Dirk felt hungry, for the wedding breakfast had been a lavish enough affair, but Storm and Elizabeth had insisted on a meal when they arrived home.

"A gesture of welcome, my girl," Elizabeth said. "Look upon it as that."

Both Storm and Elizabeth were very fond of Cornelia, and never failed to show it on every occasion when the girl was present.

"I'm so sorry Graham isn't well," smiled Cornelia. She glanced at Dirk. "If this weren't our wedding night, Dirk, I'd volunteer to sit up and be a sick nurse for the poor fellow."

"You may have to sit up for me, love—after all that wine they made

me guzzle today. And now this supper Father and Mother are insisting I eat!"

To their surprise, they found that when they began to eat they
were hungry, and it was not necessary to have to make a pretence
of disposing of the food simply to please Storm and Elizabeth. They
ate with relish, listening to the rain outside. It had been raining since
shortly after two o'clock—a steady, light drip-drip. The air was heavy
with moisture, and rain flies flitted everywhere, shedding their gauzy
wings on their clothes and on the tablecloth, and some of them falling
foul of the candle flames.

With and without wings, they crawled on the outside of the muslin
mosquito net draped around the large four-poster in the northeastern
room, and Dirk's first comment, as he and Cornelia entered the room,
was: "There'll be rain flies to help us make love, my sweet. Look at
them! Some are sure to get in with us."

She laughed. "We didn't grumble at snakes and *agoutis* that night
on the canal, did we? Are we going to let rain flies put us out?"

He held her and kissed her, and for a long moment they stood there
in the middle of the room, locked together and listening to the rain,
their gazes wandering around the candle-lit room alive with the leisurely rain flies.

It was he who broke the silence by murmuring: "This is good. I'm
happy."

She nodded and grunted. "I can see you are—and I'm happy you
are, Dirk."

He grinned and fondled her. "Any more mutual felicitations before we get undressed?" And abruptly she broke away from him, exclaiming: "Oh, but I was forgetting! I meant to ask you to let us go
to Graham's room before we undress. It's only considerate that we
should inquire after his health before we go to bed."

He frowned and said it might not be advisable. "He won't appreciate our intruding upon him, Cornelia. He wants to be left alone."

She gave him a puzzled look and asked: "What *is* the matter with
him, Dirk?"

Dirk avoided her gaze and shrugged. "His mind is disturbed," he
muttered. He began to pace about the room. "I'm very worried about
him—and so are Mother and Father. It's pitiable, pitiable."

After a pause, she said, with a keen stare: "Dirk, you look guilty
about something. What is it? What has disturbed Graham's mind?"

He clicked his tongue. "This is our wedding night, isn't it? Do you think we ought to stand here discussing Graham and his ills?"

"No, we oughtn't, my dear, I know. But I'm curious. It's just struck me that you haven't wanted to discuss Graham these past few days. You have avoided doing so every time I happened to mention him. I thought he was down with a fever. You never mentioned that his mind was in any way the centre of the trouble."

He nodded slowly, sighed, and said: "Very well. Now more than ever I must keep no secrets from you." And he told her of everything that had happened during the past few days. Standing there in the middle of the room in the candlelight, she in her long white dress that Rose had made, and the rain plip-plepping against the louvred windows and the two large glazed windows, and the rain flies drifting lazily and clumsily around the room, alighting on them and shedding their delicate gossamer wings. Once a gust of wind caused the windows to rattle faintly, and the scent of rain-soaked orange leaves oozed in upon them, refreshing even while creating the inclination to shiver at the reminder of the great burden of dampness in the dark outside the house.

She interrupted him only with gasped monosyllables—an astonished "What!" or an incredulous "No!" Once he had to grin and remark, tweaking her chin: "Ever the good listener! Anyway, that's how it is, my dear! To continue . . ."

Eventually she wagged her head and said: "That was despicable, Dirk. To have lied to him like that. It was unfair to him and to Rose."

He nodded, frowning heavily. "It hurt me to the guts to have to do that, Cornelia—but how could I let him go ahead with this mad, idiotic plan! Rose is intelligent and well bred, and she was educated as we were, but nothing can cancel the circumstance of her being what she is racially. How could I allow him to marry a mulatto? He talked about Governor Meertens. What have we to do with Governor Meertens and his mulatto wife!"

"Governor Meertens did not marry a mulatto woman. His wife was of white and Indian origin. She was a quarter Indian."

"Was she? Ha! So much the better! I hope you're right there, for that would be a good point in argument if he should ever want to dispute the matter again. Though I don't think he will persist after what I told him on Friday. His good friend, Clara Hartfield, is coming on Wednesday, and she should be able to cheer him up and persuade him to return to Demerary. He believes in her."

After a pause, she said, a pensive look on her face: "You are justified, in a manner—but I'm sorry for him. And for Rose."

They listened to the rain.

"And for us, too, Dirk, love."

"What?"

She shook her head, smiling, her old look of mystery suddenly on her face as she turned and gazed at the muslin-netted bed.

"What do you mean by that, Cornelia?"

She pressed herself against him and whispered: "I want to go to bed."

He responded at once, and they undressed and got into bed.

It was not until Wednesday night, during the exhaustion that succeeded the storm, that she explained to him what she meant.

26

CLARA had written to say that she would be arriving in New Amsterdam by sloop on Wednesday morning, but she arrived on Tuesday at noon, having travelled overland by coach along the coast, a journey that, in the rain season, could occupy as many as eight or nine days because of the muddy roads. It was Dirk who met her at the ferry *stelling*, and it was by sheer accident that he was there at all.

Several rafts arrived from upriver that morning, and Jacob had sent a message to New Signal asking Dirk to be in New Amsterdam to confer with him on the shipping of certain logs, for not all the timber received from the grant was milled; much of it was exported to the West Indies or sent to Demerary.

After they had superintended the distribution of the timber, Jacob suggested their going to Mr. Green's cottage for a glass of sangaree. "After all, I couldn't be at your wedding," said Jacob, "but the least you can do is to come and have a drink with me to celebrate the occasion."

"Let's be off," grinned Dirk. "I can do with a sangaree in this heat. Wish we'd had this weather yesterday afternoon."

"Don't try to fool me. I'm sure you must have liked the rain. Who doesn't like rain when they're in bed?"

"Oh, I enjoyed it at bedtime, I won't deny. When are you getting married, by the way?"

"Since you ask, in November. It's settled definitely now."

"Good man. And I mentioned what my wedding present would be, didn't I?"

"Did you really mean it, Dirk?"

"I always mean what I say. And I said I would give you a cottage as a wedding present. Now, you busy yourself looking for a site and we'll arrange about the lumber. I'll tell our bookkeeper to charge it up to me."

They had begun to move towards the path, Jacob's tough, muscular, thickset form swaying slightly in the way it always did when he walked. Millicent often told him that he walked like a sailor. Jacob's olive face was freckled, and when he smiled as he was smiling now —with a kind of languid, perplexed affection; it was the smile that only Dirk could bring to life on his face—his dimples became shiny and his freckles seemed to stand out more clearly, especially on the humps of his cheekbones. He turned his lazy, grey-brown eyes on Dirk and said: "To my dying day I'll never understand you, Dirk."

"I don't want you to," snapped Dirk—and suddenly grunted and exclaimed: "Look! That boat making for the *stelling* here! It's the military boat from York Redoubt—but there's a lady in it."

"Yes, that's right. Very strange. You don't usually see ladies in the military boat." They both came to a halt and watched the boat.

"I don't believe its making for here," Jacob murmured, after a pause. "It's going to the ferry *stelling*."

Then Dirk shaded his eyes with his hand and exclaimed: "Good God! I'm sure I know that woman. Even from this distance I can recognise her. It's Clara Hartfield—the lady we're expecting tomorrow."

"She must have come overland, then."

"Come, let's get into the carriage and hurry to the ferry *stelling*."

"We don't need the carriage. How far away is the ferry *stelling*?"

Dirk scowled but agreed with him. "Very well. Let's do a quick trot, then."

The ferry *stelling* was less than a hundred yards off along the riverbank, and the pathway was in fairly good condition despite the rain of the day before. Dirk told the coachman to follow them, and he and Jacob set out at a trot along the pathway. The carriage passed them and reached the ferry *stelling* well ahead of them, the coachman glancing back with distinct perplexity at the trotting figures of Dirk and Jacob. He was not accustomed to such unconventional behaviour on the part of Dirk. Nor were the hucksters and white planters who happened to be in the vicinity of the ferry *stelling*. Many stares were directed at the two young men.

Dirk flushed and growled: "You're always making me do something I know I oughtn't to do, God damn you!"

Jacob grinned: "All for the good of your soul, you stinking snob!"

The military boat was just drawing in, and Dirk was right. The lady was Clara Hartfield, and she was as surprised and delighted at seeing him as he was at seeing her. "How extremely fortunate you happened to be in town, Dirk!" she exclaimed. "It saves me the bother of arranging for the hire of a boat to take me to New Signal." She looked at Jacob and exclaimed: "Jacob Frick! Isn't this the Jacob Graham has told me so much of? Your boyhood friend and now the manager of the new sawmill!"

"Perfectly correct," smiled Dirk, then flushed, for Clara held out her hand to Jacob, her manner very unlike that of a white lady towards a coloured young man. It was an embarrassing moment, because people were staring at them, including the two soldiers in the military boat. Dirk hurried on to explain that he and Jacob had been at a *stelling* lower down the river, seeing after some timber.

"We were just about to leave when I caught sight of you in the boat."

"I'm sure you will be a successful manager," gushed Clara, regarding Jacob with admiring eyes, her hand still clasped in his. "You look sturdy and strong—in body and in mind. You're lucky to have him, Dirk."

"Yes, yes. I agree—but the carriage is waiting, Mrs. Hartfield. If you care, we can get in and go to the *stelling* where the tent-boat is moored." He glanced at Jacob and added: "I'll have that sangaree with you tomorrow, Jacob."

In the carriage Clara explained that a Major Langley, a good friend of her husband's, had offered, at the last moment, to bring her to Berbice by land route. He and two other officers were bound for York Redoubt on the West Bank, and as the weather had been exceptionally dry for several days—there had been no rain in Demerary the previous day—a pleasant and fast journey was anticipated. They had slept the night at the home of a planter at Mahaica Creek, after leaving Georgetown at four o'clock the day before. "Which reminds me, Dirk," she gushed on. "I told Graham to tell you to arrange to spend a fortnight with your wife at Mahaica. The Valerys would have been charmed to have you at their home. Mahaica is such a delightful place—so healthy. It is our most fashionable pleasure resort. Why didn't you write to the Valerys, my boy?"

"Neither Cornelia nor I felt much enthusiasm for the notion of spending a fortnight at Mahaica," frowned Dirk. We preferred to settle in without delay at New Signal. And, as you know, Graham is not well."

"Not well! No, I never knew that. What is the matter with him?"

Dirk stirred uncomfortably, scowling. "I'm sorry. I spoke without thinking. Naturally, you wouldn't have heard yet."

She clutched his arm anxiously. "What is the matter with him, Dirk? He merely mentioned in his letter that he had met his future wife—the loveliest girl he had ever set eyes upon—and he wished me to come posthaste to meet her and tell him that I supported him in his choice. That is all I know."

"Very well," sighed Dirk, "I'll tell you. But here we are at the *stelling*. Let's get aboard the tent-boat first."

When they were settled in the cabin of the tent-boat, he told her of the events of the past week. Unlike Cornelia, she kept interrupting him at frequent intervals, and indulging in dramatic lamentations. She irritated him, but he persisted, for he thought it would be as well to see how she would react to the situation. When he told her that the girl in question was Rose, she started and gasped: "Heavenly Father! No! Dirk! Rose Clarke, the child Edward sent here to be adopted! Cousin Hubertus's natural child! You're not serious, Dirk! Oh, no! My poor, dear Graham!"

"I am serious, Mrs. Hartfield. He wants to marry Rose—a mulatto. We tried to reason with him in every way possible, but he simply would not heed. He kept on talking a lot of nonsense about God seeing us all as equals, and referring to Governor Meertens' mulatto wife——"

"Oh no! Governor Meertens' wife was not a mulatto. She was of Indian and white admixture. There was some such rumour, I know—but it was untrue."

"Ah. Well, I'm glad you say that, too. So Cornelia mentioned. I do hope you will speak to him, Mrs. Hartfield, and make him see how stupid he has been."

"Most certainly, Dirk. I agree that such a marriage would be disastrous. My poor dear boy! But why is he *ill*, Dirk? You haven't told me yet."

Dirk took a deep breath and told her. He did not mention, however, that he had lied to his brother. "That's the creature he wants to marry, Mrs. Hartfield. A wanton who offered herself to me without a thought to morality."

"Heavens! You mean she has been your mistress, Dirk? Actually that?"

Dirk steeled himself and nodded. "Yes. Actually that," he growled.
"And you told him that?"

He nodded, staring at the *courida* bush of Crab Island as the boat
entered the mouth of the Canje. He heard her sigh.

"My poor boy. He is so sensitive, Dirk. Now I can understand why
he is ill. You should not have divulged that to him. That was wrong
of you."

Dirk nodded. He made no attempt to defend himself. Crab Island
went out of view behind them. The arum-shaped leaves of the *mucca-
muccas*, perched on their slim, bare stalks, began to peer at them from
the banks, glittering in the hot August sunshine. The water, from a
muddy amber, began to turn dark brown.

When they arrived at the *stelling* at New Signal, Dirk insisted that
she should wait until he had sent for a sedan chair. "The driveway is
very muddy from the rain we had yesterday. Your shoes would be
ruined," he told her.

"How thoughtful of you, my boy," she said, and there were tears
in her eyes. He tried not to wince. He could not stand extremely
emotional women. As they stood on the *stelling* waiting for the sedan
chair, she chattered about Georgetown and her journey, about Major
Langley and the Valerys of Mahaica, and, listening to her and watching
her animated face, he suddenly realised that she must have been an
exceptionally attractive creature when she was young. He had heard
some rumour of an affair she had had with his Uncle Edward, and he
could believe it. He could even understand how Graham had come to
be infatuated with her some years ago.

A little later when she was getting out of the sedan chair in the
portico of the house, Dirk saw his father's face lose its look of languor
and complacency and take on a youthful, alert mien. Storm rose from
his chair, dropped his book and almost ran forward to greet Clara.
And Clara received him with open arms.

"My wicked, mischievous Storm!" she sobbed. "Oh, Storm! Do you
remember Rylands! Do you remember Good Heart!" She suddenly
backed off and regarded him. "I can still see you as you were then,
Storm dear! Remember the day at Rylands when you and Raphael
and I sat barelegged on the *stelling* waiting for the yatch that was
bringing Luise and Cousin Hubertus from Good Heart? Remember
how Edward sat by himself a little way off, and we kept teasing him?"

Storm, ruddy with pleasure, shook. "Of course, my dear. One does not forget such things. How old were we then? Eighteen, nineteen. Ah, well! But you must want some breakfast, Clara. We weren't expecting you today. I must call Benji——"

"No, no, Storm dear. I had breakfast at York Redoubt with Major Langley and Susan, his wife. The weather has been so dry and delightful in Demerary that we thought we could do the journey by land. The roads were hard and dusty. We had an excellent journey. But where is Elizabeth? Having her siesta? And your new wife, Dirk? I'm burning to meet them both."

"Yes, they are both resting, Clara," said Storm, "but I'm sure they would be glad to see you. I'll send up and tell them——"

"No, no, Storm. Don't disturb them. Later will do. It is just as well, I'm sure. I must go up immediately to my darling boy. Dirk, take me up to Graham. Oh, Storm, I'm so distressed to hear of this terrible situation."

Storm nodded—and the brooding look returned to his face. "Elizabeth and I are, too, my dear. It is most unfortunate. And so entirely unexpected. He never seemed the kind of boy who could be struck down by such an infatuation all in a matter of hours. His behaviour has astounded us."

Dirk took her up to the southeastern room, where they found Graham, unshaven, untidy and hollow-cheeked, lying in the hammock. At sight of Clara he uttered an unnatural whimpering sound and bounded up. Dirk winced and withdrew hurriedly, closing the door carefully after him.

Within an hour Clara had had Graham washed and shaved and dressed, and had made him eat the meal Sarabelle brought up. He ate hungrily, and his spirits improved minute by minute. He could not take his eyes from Clara. He kept laughing at intervals—in a jerky, nervous manner. "I feel that if I stop looking at you for longer than a minute you'll vanish, Clara. Oh, it is so good to see you! I was dying. Yes, I was on the point of death. You have come just in time."

"My poor darling. I'm so glad you feel happy now."

He paused in his eating and shook his head. "Happy? No. No, not happy. I shall never be happy again, Clara. Never as long as I live."

"Many are the times we feel that way, Graham—but the weeks and the months and the years build up their healing scabs, and then we realise that the pain is gone. Both the sweet pains and the bitter pains vanish under the influence of time, my darling." She stroked his head.

"Yes, some pains are sweet, and we secretly wish they would never die, but time kills them just the same."

"This is a bitter one, Clara—and time won't eradicate it."

At the end of an hour, he was still in the same mood, and a look of concern had come to her face. She said quietly: "Even I seem to be failing to comfort you, my darling. Graham, is it as serious as all this? Do you honestly feel that this girl is the one soul you will ever love?"

He nodded, his gaze out on the slaves' logies. In the south the sky was blue-grey with thunderclouds, and now and then they would see a yellow fork of lightning slice the looming piles. And after an interval the thunder would sound, far away over the jungle. There was no wind. The trees had a rigid, carved look.

She sighed. "What a pity! What a pity! A mulatto. It would ruin you, my sweetheart. You would be cut off by every white person in the colony."

"That would not have troubled me, Clara, as I've said before."

"Then you mean it is simply because your vision of her has been destroyed by what Dirk has told you that you have lost your desire to marry her?"

"Yes. I conceived of her as pure, lovely, spotless, Clara—but now, with the knowledge that she has been Dirk's mistress! Dirk of all people! That hater of slaves and of all dusky people! The supreme irony of it, Clara. No, no. I shall love her to the end of my days, but I could not marry her with the knowledge that Dirk had soiled her virtue."

After a silence, she uttered a soft, musing sound, and murmured: "Virtue." And he looked at her in inquiry. She smiled and said: "I'm thinking of myself, my darling. In your way of viewing it, I am a very much soiled person."

He shook his head and gripped her arm. "No, no. You're the exception to every rule. There's nobility in you, Clara."

"How do you know there is no nobility in Rose? But we shall see." Her manner became suddenly decisive. "Tomorrow I shall go and visit her, and when I return I shall tell you what I think of her. Now you must rest."

27

WEDNESDAY was another scorching day. The long rain season was coming to an end, and the long dry season was setting in. From now until November showers would be few, and the dams between plantations would grow dry and hard, the roads in New Amsterdam thick with dust that would rise in clouds under carriage wheels.

"To the Blairs'!" Dirk told the coachman as he helped Clara into the carriage and stepped down back on to the dry, hard pathway that skirted the entranceway to the most northerly of the little *stellings* along the riverbank. "I shall be waiting for you here at noon," he told Clara, waving his hat as the carriage began to move off. And Clara replied: "I shall be in good time, never fear!"

Dirk watched the carriage go round the bend that took it into the High Street, then turned to make his way towards the building, about fifty yards south along the Water Path, or Water Street, as some called it, that was his sawmill. It was built right on the water's edge so that the rafts could be hauled up on to the mudbanks and so into the troughs where the saws operated. He could see Jacob's burly figure directing the slaves who were at work on the water-driven machinery, and remembered that he had promised to have a sangaree with him at Mr. Green's cottage. He must be sure to remind him, and be sure they found time during the morning to go and have the drink. Jacob put a great deal of value on such occasions, and Dirk liked humouring him. Of one thing he was certain. Never would the warmth of affection in him for Jacob lessen. And it was not because Jacob was his half brother, not because the Old Blood ran in his veins, that he felt as he did towards him. It was simply because he was Jacob, the good friend whom he had taught to read and write, with whom he had adventured in the Canje bush, and confided in from the time he could remember himself. The olive, curly-headed boy with whom he had made a pact of loyalty when they were both foolish, reckless, irresponsible young asses running about the plantation.

He grunted and kicked a dry *awara* seed that happened in his path at the moment. An *awara* seed sucked and scraped clean of the bright yellow pulp, sticky and stringy, that had once covered it. He grinned briefly, remembering the many *awara* and *cookerit* palms Jacob and himself had raided, and the many feasts they had had sitting on the bank of the canal aback. . . . But this is August 1816. I'm a married man, and Jacob is getting married in November. Time, by God! Time hacks away at the past, chops down all your green and cherished escapades. But it builds up, too. Yes, time builds up. There's the sawmill. There's the plantation I mean to turn into the most compact and most profitable sugar plantation in Berbice. There's the timber grant upriver. And there's, last but most vital and most cherished, my dear beloved. My tall, sturdy, mysterious wife. And soon there'll be our sons. The new van Groenwegels to take the Old Blood to the pinnacles!

The carriage with Clara had hardly turned into the High Street when Clara called up to the coachman: "Just a moment, my man! A word with you!"

"Yes, missy?"

"Do you know where Missy Clarke, the midwife, lives?"

"Yes, missy. Lil' street we call Essex Street. It lead out to the dam dat run near de canal bordering Vrymen's Erven plantation."

"Well, before we go to the Blairs', my man, I should like to call and see Mrs. Clarke on some business. Go there directly, please."

"Very well, missy."

Marie, once again in a flutter at seeing a white face at her mistress's door, curtseyed and said in a bated voice: "No, missy. Nobody at home, but Miss Rose only up de street at Missy Henson. I could call her for you if you like."

"Yes, please do, my girl. I shall wait."

A few minutes later, Rose appeared, in pale blue, for she was dressed to go up the river to a client. Her hair was not in disarray, but neatly plaited and coiled up on her head. It was only when she went to New Signal or to Don Diego that she allowed it to trail loosely behind her and about her shoulders, for on such occasions there was always the chance of meeting Dirk—and Dirk, she knew, liked to see her hair in loose disarray, unplaited and wind-blown.

Clara introduced herself, and Rose asked her to be seated.

"Thanks. So you are Rose. You are very lovely, indeed."

Puzzling and wondering, Rose seated herself opposite the elder woman. "You are from Demerary, did you say?"

"Yes. I arrived yesterday. Graham asked me to come."

Rose started. "Oh, you're the Mrs. Hartfield I've heard Dirk speak of!"

"Did he speak very unkindly of me?"

Rose pinkened. "I'm afraid he did, but now that I see you for myself I feel certain he must have been unjust in his findings."

Clara stared at her for a moment, then murmured: "Child, you speak beautifully, beautifully. Pardon me being so personal. I know it must embarrass you, but I cannot help remarking on it."

"I understand," said Rose quietly. "I was brought up and educated with Dirk and Graham and Hermine at New Signal, Mrs. Hartfield."

"Yes, yes. So you were," sighed Clara. She gave the girl another long stare. Then abruptly: "I like you, Rose. I have an intuition for people."

"Thanks."

"Are you in a hurry, or may I sit here and chat with you for a while?"

"I was preparing to go up the river on a short trip, but it can wait. It's not very urgent."

"I won't keep you longer than I can help, my child. I can see from your face that you are curious about my visit. Very well. Let us talk."

The moment Dirk helped her out of the carriage he knew that something was the matter. Her manner towards him had changed. When he remarked: "You're very punctual, Mrs. Hartfield. Didn't keep me waiting at all. It's hardly three minutes past twelve," she smiled and returned: "Yes. I'm very fond of punctuality." She spoke cordially rather than with that cheery spontaneity of hers, and her smile, somehow, thought Dirk, held a certain stiffness. It puzzled him.

As they were getting aboard the tent-boat, he asked: "Did you enjoy your visit? A good breakfast at the Blairs'?"

"Very good," she replied. "Have you breakfasted?"

"Yes. I generally eat at the tavern when I'm in town at this time of day."

Then silence for a long interval—and this convinced him that his first impression had been right. He gave her a look of surprise and said: "You're very quiet, Mrs. Hartfield. Did anything upset you at the Blairs'?"

She sighed softly and shook her head. "No, Dirk, not particularly." She hesitated, then added: "Of course, as you must know, old Mrs. Blair is very ill with a cancer. It was very sad to watch her sufferings."

"Yes, I heard of her illness. She has been laid up for some months, poor old lady." Perhaps, he told himself, it could be that. Old Mrs. Blair was in great pain, by all reports, and it must have been a harrowing experience for Clara to enter the old lady's room. From what Wilfred Blair had mentioned some weeks ago, there was an unpleasant smell, not only in the sickroom, but about the whole house. . . . As Clara's silence continued, however, he began to feel uncertain again.

"Are there any other families you know in New Amsterdam besides the Blairs, Mrs. Hartfield?" he asked—and watched her face keenly as he spoke.

She gave a slight start, and replied—a trifle too hastily, he thought: "No, no. I'm afraid I know no other people. Why do you ask?"

He shrugged. "Simply a matter of interest."

And after that he made no other attempts to probe her. He resigned himself to the uneasy silence that settled on them for the rest of the trip.

There was no need for a sedan chair to take her to the house, for the driveway had been dried hard by the sunshine of the morning and of the previous day. As they were walking towards the house, they heard distant thunder in the southwest, and he remarked: "I wonder why these thunderstorms always keep far off over the jungle. Every day for the past two or three weeks we've been hearing thunder, but it's always been distant and somewhere in the south."

He watched her face to see the reaction to this comment, and saw her smile in that stiff way again. She nodded and replied: "Yes. I've wondered myself. Just as well, I suppose. I'm not a lover of thunderstorms."

A few minutes later, he went into the northeastern room, to find Cornelia reclining in bed. It was siesta time, and the house was very quiet. Cornelia was not asleep, however. Nude above her waist, she sat up, fanning herself. Tiny streams of perspiration gleamed between her breasts and along her arms.

He rubbed his hand down her back and uttered deprecating sounds.

"What a sweaty wife I have!" Bent and kissed her throat as she rebutted: "And I seem to have a husband who doesn't mind fondling sweaty backs."

He grinned. "We must have a bath together—and no slaves in attendance!"

"Come into bed and keep me company sweating in this heat." She stretched up and began to help him undo his coat buttons. "We can have our bath later in the afternoon."

It was not until more than an hour later that he commented on Clara's odd silence in the boat. "Can't understand why a visit to the Blairs should have put her into such a mood. Even old Mrs. Blair's illness shouldn't have depressed her to the extent of curbing her garrulity."

Cornelia stopped rubbing her hand over the hairs of his chest and frowned. "Are you sure it was only the Blairs she visited?"

"What do you mean? She said she knows no one else in town."

"Perhaps she doesn't—but what of Rose?"

"Rose! She isn't acquainted with Rose, so far as I'm aware." He sat up and frowned at her. "Why do you think she might have visited Rose?"

"Lie down, love. Don't upset yourself."

He lay down again, but he was still frowning. She told him that she had spent some time with Graham in his room before breakfast. "He's fairly calm and normal now," she said. "That woman must have a real power over him."

"How did he seem? I mean, was he resigned to things? Did he say anything about returning to Demerary?"

"He seemed resigned—but he made no mention of Demerary."

A sharp, prattling noise disrupted the afternoon silence, ending in a deep rumble. They sat up, startled, then laughed as they realised that it was another peal of thunder in the south. "Sounded like concentrated musket fire," he said.

"More like a lot of kettle-drums to me."

They lay back again, damp and sticky with perspiration. Not the vaguest wisp of wind could be felt. The heat swirled in at the windows like invisible swathes of silk. The trees had a waxen look—a stiff, almost frightening, immobility. After a silence, she turned her head towards him, lifted her hand to his cheek and murmured: "Brooding on something." And he stirred and grunted. "I'm remembering what you said. About Mrs. H. Graham could have asked her to go and see Rose, now I come to think of it. Though for what reason I can't imagine."

She uttered one of her mysterious sounds, and when he asked her what was the matter she shook her head and said: "Nothing. Nothing at all." She raised herself and began to stroke his hair and kiss him. They heard thunder again, and then forgot the heat of the day and Rose and Clara Hartfield as a surge of passion engulfed them. Slave footsteps in the corridor did not register on their hearing.

When he stretched out and took up his heavy silver watch he saw that it was after three. "Our bath?" he asked. And she nodded, so he blew his ivory whistle, and when Sarabelle came in—it was of no importance if a slave saw them naked in bed together—he told her to prepare a bath for two. "And we won't need your help, Sarabelle."

"No, massa," smiled Sarabelle. "Me know dat good. It show you marry happy." Sarabelle was about thirty-two. She reminded him a little of Nibia when Nibia was her age. A very sensual creature. . . . Thunder again, but still distant.

It was nearly four o'clock when they had bathed and dressed. They had planned to drift on the tide in a skiff before dinner, and were both in a mood of great peace. They kept smiling at each other for no reason.

A slight breeze came from the northeast, bringing the sourish smell of coffee berries from the plantation on the opposite bank of the Creek. Cornelia, near the window, said that it was the first breath of wind she had felt for the day. She glanced out of the window as she spoke— and then grew still.

"Dirk."

"Yes, my pet?" He was at the writing table, glancing through an unfinished letter he had been writing to Elfrida that morning before going to town.

"Come. Come quickly."

He joined her at the window in two strides.

Coming up the driveway towards the house were two females— one Mrs. Clarke, the midwife, the other Rose.

Dirk went white, and his hands clenched. "What do they want here? I told Rose that she was not to set foot on this place until Graham had returned to Demerary."

At that instant they saw Graham emerge from the portico and move quickly along the driveway to meet the two women.

Dirk turned from the window, his eyes fierce. "I think I'm beginning to see what it is all about now. It's that woman, Cornelia!"

Cornelia nodded. "Yes. I believe I guessed right, Dirk. She must have gone to see Rose and her adopted mother. It's she who has asked them to come here."

"The interfering fool! What does she hope to gain by this? And she said she agreed with us that Graham should not be encouraged to see Rose."

"Ssssh! Wait!"

They fell silent, and heard Clara's voice in the portico welcoming Mrs. Clarke and Rose. Dirk swore and began to pace. "This is mischief. Sheer downright mischief. Mother and Father should ask her to leave this house at once."

"Be calm, Dirk, dear. Getting into a rage won't help matters."

"How can I be calm? I tell you, Mrs. Hartfield is a mischief-maker. What right had she to go to Rose! She said she was going to the Blairs', the deceptive meddler! Now I know why she was so cold towards me on the return trip."

They heard the footsteps of a slave in the corridor. Benji came in and said: "Massa Dirk, Missy Hartfield and Massa Graham ask if you can go down in de sitting-room. They would like talk wid you."

"Very well, Benji." And after Benji had left: "By God! I'm going to choke the whole pack of them. I'm going to kick Rose out of this house."

Cornelia gripped his arm. He was trembling. "Come, my dear. Control yourself. For my sake. Let us go down. I'll come with you."

They went down, her hand still on his arm.

Storm and Elizabeth sat opposite each other under the large family painting. Rose and Mrs. Clarke were on the sofa near the southern windows, and Graham stood behind the sofa like a protective sentinel. Clara sat on a small upright chair in the middle of the room. There was still the smell of lemons in the room, for that morning the slaves had mopped the floor, and lemons were always used as a cleaning and scenting agent. Clara rose after an instant's hesitation. She began to say something, but Dirk shouted at her to be silent.

"You damned interloper! What have you come in this house to do? Why did you bring these women here?"

The fury of Dirk's attack caused Clara to stumble against her chair.

It brought Storm to his feet. Graham moved round to the front of the sofa as though to forestall possible violence to Rose and Mrs. Clarke. His hands clenched.

"Are you addressing me, Dirk?" asked Clara, her voice shocked and incredulous. It was obvious that she had not anticipated anything like this.

Dirk's head trembled. "I *am* addressing you. I think you are a snake."

Storm said: "Dirk, are you aware that Mrs. Hartfield is our guest?"

"Very much aware of it, sir. A guest who has come to blight our family. I ask you again, Mrs. Hartfield, why have you brought Rose and Mrs. Clarke here?"

"Dirk, my dear." Cornelia clutched his arm, but he shook her hand off—jerked round and snapped: "Go and sit down, Cornelia!" And Cornelia desisted at once and left him alone, seeming to sense that she had no power over him now. A bare quarter of an hour ago he would have indulged her slightest whim. Hardly ten minutes ago they had been smiling at each other in fatuous tenderness. Now he was the quivering, obsessed monster his mother resented and detested, his father respected but shunned, and his brother admired but feared.

"I am waiting for an answer, Mrs. Hartfield."

Clara, pale and confused, glanced appealingly at Storm for the second time, then seemed to realise that no help would come from this quarter. She seemed to sense the weakness and ineffectuality in Storm. In a stammer, she said to Dirk: "I thought, at least, I could expect you to behave like a gentleman, Dirk. This is a painful surprise." Her voice broke, and her eyes grew tearful.

Dirk was unmoved. He snapped his gaze upon Rose. "Rose, I told you distinctly that you were not to set foot on the plantation while my brother was here. Why did you allow Mrs. Hartfield to persuade you to come here?"

Rose was on her feet at once. There was no fear or confusion in her manner. She, too, trembled, but only with the same rage that possessed Dirk. "She did not have to persuade me to come here, Dirk." Her voice, shrill but controlled, might have been the lightning flash that caused the distant rumble of thunder that sounded at that instant over the jungle. "When she told me of the cowardly lie you told about me I needed no persuasion. I would have come here to confront you, whether she had asked me or not."

"Rose, sit down," ordered Mrs. Clarke.

"I shall not sit down, Mama. I intend to tell Dirk what is in my mind."

Elizabeth stiffened and said: "You have forgotten yourself, Rose."

Dirk snarled: "I promised to choke you if you came here, Rose."

Graham took a threatening pace forward. "Try it, Dirk. Try it."

"As for you—you infatuated fool! I'm ashamed of you. Going into hysterics over every nigger and dusky person who comes your way. I always felt in my bones you'd let our family down."

Rose grasped Graham's arm and stepped in front of him. "Leave him to me, Graham. I know how to deal with him. I'm not afraid of him, and never shall be—and he knows it. Let him try to choke me."

Dirk and Rose now faced each other with hardly two feet between them, both taut, quivering figures. The glare of the afternoon struck in on them from the southern windows, showing up the tiny beads of perspiration on Dirk's pale forehead, putting a hint of copper into the long, dark hair that flowed down the girl's back. Benji and Sarabelle were at the door watching and listening, their black faces matching the gloom in the corridor.

"This is what comes of being too familiar with you mulatto people," Dirk snarled. "I knew it was a mistake having you educated with us, and giving you the freedom of this house. You should have been put in your place from the beginning."

"How well you've imbibed the snobbery preached by your Grandma Hendri in those musty letters you have in the canister upstairs!"

"Storm, I will not tolerate this!" It was Elizabeth. She was on her feet. "I won't have this slip of a coloured girl speaking like that in here."

Mrs. Clarke rose—but Graham made her resume her seat. "Mother, so you are going to side with this evil, despicable brother of mine! I'm amazed."

Now it began to be clear what Elizabeth felt towards Clara. Elizabeth said: "It is not a question of siding with anyone, Graham, but I do think Clara Hartfield and yourself have been most ill-advised in asking Mrs. Clarke and Rose to the house here. This is a disgraceful and vulgar scene, and I won't, I repeat, have Rose speak to any member of our family in the manner she is doing. It is disrespectful. This interview must end at once."

Clara, in a tearful voice, said that she alone was to be blamed. "I'm sorry, Elizabeth, but I thought it was only right that Dirk should be made to apologise to Rose for having told such a dastardly lie against the child. He averred that she had submitted to him as his mistress during the past year. He deliberately slandered the girl's good name so as to turn Graham against her. Was this a noble act? Wasn't it meet that he should face her and admit his wrong——?"

"Be silent, Mrs. Hartfield!" barked Dirk. "You speak that way because you don't know the kind of person you're up against in me. I have a reputation for being dastardly, didn't you know? Why be surprised at anything ignoble I do? And as for thinking you could get me to apologise to this impudent wench, whose conceit is incredible beyond bounds, you might as well expect the moon to drop into your lap. This is no time for me to be a gentleman, understand! The fate of our family is involved in this matter, and I don't care what you or a thousand noble, sickly fools like you may feel about the right and wrong of it. My intention is simply, at all costs, to discourage this idiot of a brother of mine from ruining himself and our family. But here it is, you had to turn up in our midst to upset our household with your simpering, gushing sentimentality."

"Dirk, I won't have you speak to Clara in that way," cried Graham, white, his hands tremulous at the lapels of his coat.

Again Elizabeth intervened. "Your brother is justified, Graham. I don't usually support him, but this time I feel he is right. This demeaning scene should never have been engineered. Clara should have known better."

Clara burst into tears and hurried from the room.

Graham, uneasy but defiant still, cried: "Dirk always wins. Since he was a child he's been allowed to have his way. But this time he won't balk me, Mother. I have asked Rose to marry me, and my proposal stands. She may be a mulatto, but she is worth a thousand of the worthless white degenerates I've met in Demerary. You won't balk me, nor will anyone else."

Mrs. Clarke was moving towards the door. "Rose, come!" she called over her shoulder. She was the only one who had retained her dignity intact.

Rose did not move. She was still glaring at Dirk.

Graham followed Mrs. Clarke to the door, pleading with her to wait.

"I'm sorry. Not a moment longer, Mr. van Groenwegel. Rose!"

But Rose was slashing out at Dirk again. "I never had the slightest intention of marrying your brother, but now that you have acted as you have, Dirk, I have changed my mind. Now, just to show you

how much I care for your contemptible family pride, I shall accept
Graham's suit. If he wants me to marry him I shall marry him. You
cur!" She stamped, her head shaking, her eyes like electrified beads.
"And I'd thought you were changing. Getting more human. You're
no different from the cruel, stupid, cold-blooded little reptile you
used to be in your earlier years. The family! A curse on your family!
I have your blood in me, too, haven't I? You've drummed that into
me yourself, have you forgotten? Cousin Hubertus—isn't he the one
you hold up as a god? Well, he was my father, wasn't he? I have as
much of the Old Blood in me as you have, so why should I feel so
infinitely inferior to you! Why should I cringe before you, and know
my place! Simply because my mother was black? I'm not ashamed of
the black blood in me. I don't remember it. If I marry Graham I
shall do so as an equal. He won't be doing me a favour. It won't be an
honour. Not in my eyes. I shall be as much at home in the house at
Kaywana as any white wife he may have chosen—perhaps more so.
Isn't it the house my father lived in? Isn't it the house my mother
ran for my father after his wife had died?" She uttered a cackling
laugh. "You made a grave mistake, Dirk, when you told me the
family secrets. Good-bye! Perhaps one day I *may* entertain you at
Huis Kaywana!"

She swept past him and out of the room.

Dinner was a farce, for hardly any of them had an appetite. They
sat round the table as a matter of habit, but the storm raged on.
Graham, in a hysterical voice, accused them of having grossly insulted
Clara, his dear, good friend—Clara had left for New Amsterdam abruptly and without saying good-bye to anyone but Graham; she intended to put up at a tavern until she could get passage back to
Georgetown; Graham had implored her in vain to stay on for a day
or two longer.

Elizabeth, in furious but controlled tones, told Graham that Clara
deserved to have been insulted. She was the kind of woman, said
Elizabeth, who went out of her way to invite insults. And Graham
retorted bitterly that he knew what was at the bottom of his mother's
attitude. "Because she befriended me when I went to Demerary—
that is it, Mother! I haven't forgotten your letters at the time. You
hated her because she won my love and friendship, and you have
never forgiven her for becoming intimate with me. Confess it!"

At this point Storm intervened to say that Graham was straying from the real issue. While it was unfortunate that Clara should have been hurt, he agreed with Elizabeth that Clara had had no right to invite Mrs. Clarke and Rose to the house, and especially to do so without first consulting Elizabeth or himself. It was highhanded, and most imprudent in view of what had occurred during the past week. It was bad enough that Graham had put ideas into Rose's head——

Here Graham interrupted with a hysterical shriek. "What do you mean, sir! What ideas have I put into Rose's head? I have asked her to marry me—that is all! Haven't I the right to choose my own wife?"

"From among your equals!" barked Dirk.

And so it went on until, at length, Graham, in a bitter but triumphant voice, shouted: "I am entirely indifferent what any of you feel in this matter. I am of age, and I have decided that Rose is to be my wife, and nothing that is said against it will stop me. Moreover, I leave this house within the hour. I shall take up residence at a tavern in New Amsterdam until I have settled my affairs and am ready to return to Demerary." And he went striding out of the room, calling Benji to get his baggage ready for departure.

Lightning continued to flicker in the south, and the air was warm. They could hear the murmur of the Creek amidst the *mucca-mucca* and the *Missouri* grass—now and then a gurgling sibilance as some fish or alligator emerged for an instant amidst the reeds in the water and swiftly dived again.

"I was sorry that you had balked them," said Cornelia, stroking his head, "and now I'm glad and relieved that he is still determined to marry her. For you, in one way, it is a disaster that he should insist on marrying a mulatto, but, in another way, it is a happy solution for us, Dirk, dear. Now we need fear nothing for our marriage. What is family pride, my sweet, in comparison with our lifelong happiness? Had she remained here in Berbice you would always have been a tortured being, Dirk. I don't doubt that you would have remained faithful to me, but you would have been bound to meet her occasionally, and you would have burned every time you set eyes on her. In Demerary as Graham's wife, she will be permanently away from you, and you will become resigned to forgetting her——"

"But I shall never forget that she has brought a taint into our family," he interrupted, sitting up. He clasped his hands and shook his head, staring out at the dusk. Lightning again. And the fireflies had begun to glow amid the dense gloom under the sapodilla and orange trees. "That won't ever cease to burn in me, Cornelia. My God! The mistress of Plantation Kaywana! Haven't I read some of those letters in the canister to you? Kaywana. She was one of our greatest heroines. And to think of Rose as the mistress of a plantation named Kaywana." He got out of the bed and began to pace. "That portrait of Cousin Hubertus that I'd hoped to take our children to see! How could I ever go near Huis Kaywana with Rose there as Graham's wife! My God! And can you bear the thought that there may soon be coloured van Groenwegels in the world! That isn't the future I'd planned for our family. That way isn't the way to the pinnacles."

She chuckled and pleaded with him to come back into bed. "Poor love! If only that canister of letters had never been brought to this house! But perhaps I shouldn't say that. But for those letters and the obsession they have generated in you, it may have been you instead of Graham who would be insisting on marrying Rose. Have you thought of that, Dirk, dear?"

He might not have heard her. He went on pacing. A goatsucker called. It sounded somewhere on the opposite bank. A mutter of thunder came, very remote, dying away almost in the same second that it had come into being.

"It isn't finished yet, though," he said, halting suddenly. "I shall still fight. Somehow, in some manner, I shall have to avert this great shame that Graham is threatening to bring upon our name."

DIRK
AND THE
FAMILY

Book Two

28

DIRK did not succeed in his main purpose, but he won an important concession. Graham agreed, on his brother's suggestion, to change his name, by deed poll, to Greenfield. Storm was present with Dirk for that final and painful interview in the tavern in New Amsterdam where both Graham and Clara were guests for nearly a fortnight. Clara was in no way repentant. Her argument in defence was that after meeting Rose in person she had been completely won over by the girl's charm and intelligence and good breeding; never could she have dreamt of discovering in a mulatto girl so many fine qualities, and on leaving the cottage that morning of her visit, she had made up her mind that Rose, despite her racial admixture, would be just the wife for Graham's sensitive, refined nature. She could understand fully why Graham had been instantly attracted to the girl, and it pained her to her heart to think that Dirk could have been so cowardly as to fabricate the disgusting slander that he had done. She felt no guilt whatever for having invited the girl and her adopted mother to New Signal, and she was determined to support Graham to the hilt in marrying Rose.

The wedding was a very inconspicuous affair, and Clara was the only white guest present at the church and at the reception held in Mrs. Clarke's cottage. Two days later, Graham and his bride and Clara sailed for Georgetown.

Not only the family, but the whole plantocracy of Demerary and Berbice groaned in reproof. A van Groenwegel married to a mulatto! Raphael, on the West Coast, called it "a deplorable mistake." Willem, at Flagstaff, blamed it on the influence of "those damned missionaries," and said he had always known that Graham would eventually have "coddled to his breast some infernal nigger." Pelham agreed.

"Too much religion, poor fellow. I warned him he was overdoing it."
Even Edward and Luise, the liberals, shook their heads. "A big disappointment," said Edward, and Luise added: "We must be thankful
that he has decided to change his name." Elfrida, Pelham's wife, was
the lone dissenter. Elfrida thought that it was perhaps the best thing
Graham could have done. "I doubt that he would ever have married
a white girl. Better a coloured girl than a soured bachelorhood."

John, Clara's husband, at first would not countenance the idea of
Graham and Rose as regular visitors in his home. But Clara insisted
that he should, at least, meet the girl before making any decisions in
the matter, and after Graham and Rose had dined one afternoon
with them, John discovered, like Clara, that he could see no reason
to be ashamed of entertaining Rose. The truth was that Rose's physical
beauty conjured up for John instant and delicious reminders of Lizzie,
his old-time mulatto mistress who still kept her little grocery shop on
the bank of North Canal. In his fancy he saw Rose as a Lizzie not
only rejuvenated, but imbued as well with the graces of literacy and
good breeding which the old Lizzie had so completely lacked. Many
times throughout the afternoon John subjected Rose to a mental
stripping, and found this pastime so entertaining that there and then
he decided that he would certainly not put up any social barriers
against the girl. The more often she came, he told himself, the better.
How he missed the old sensual life with Lizzie and his other mulatto
mistresses!

Rose, despite her precocity in most things, was still a girl at heart,
and for the first month or two the new life dazzled and awed her.
Huis Kaywana and its family portraits and large rooms and its slaves
delighted her, and she told Graham that it was a matter of indifference
to her if no one visited them. Merely to be privileged to live in this
house was enough to make anyone supremely happy.

By Christmas, however, the novelty had worn off, and more and
more she began to hark back to the Canje and Dirk. The old ache
returned, and regret and disillusionment set in. She grew restless and
irritable, and impatient with Graham when he was too fawning and
sentimental. From the very outset she had shown a reluctance to submit to him in bed, but he had put this down to her natural modesty,
and had been very patient and gentle. Now she told him frankly that
she detested being fussed over, and even suggested that they should
occupy separate rooms.

Puzzled, but in his blind devotion determined to indulge her every whim, he agreed to this arrangement, but his fawning manner did not alter, and one night, to his dismay, he discovered that she had locked him out of her room. Her excuse, the following morning, was that she had not been feeling well and had not wanted to be disturbed. Thereafter she locked her door every night against him, and it was only after his persistent knocking and pleading that she would open and permit him to get into bed with her. On these occasions she submitted with bad grace, not attempting to conceal her boredom.

This phase, however, did not last. In January she discovered that she was pregnant, and suddenly she became possessed of a great contriteness. The perverse irritability began to fade, and a spirit of resignation spread through her. She developed a docility, and was grateful for the fuss Graham made over her, especially as many days she was compelled to remain in bed.

Clara, who visited Huis Kaywana without fail every Wednesday afternoon and dined with them, saw to it that Rose had the best of medical attention. She herself arranged with a Dr. Hepburn of Kingston, a village about a mile to the northwest of the town, to visit Huis Kaywana once every fortnight.

In August, Rose gave birth to a daughter. For more than thirty-six hours her condition was critical, and it was feared that neither she nor the child would have survived. Graham sobbed himself into prostration one night, despite Clara's attempts to console him. When, eventually, Dr. Hepburn announced that all was well, Graham collapsed from sheer exhaustion and slept for eighteen hours without waking.

The child was christened Ernestine Clara.

In Berbice, neither Cornelia nor Millicent, Jacob's wife, experienced any difficulty when their time came. Cornelia was delivered of a daughter weighing seven and a half pounds. The child was christened Amelia Hendrickje, and was born in June, two months before Rose's. Millicent Frick's was a son, and came into the world in September. Dirk stood godfather, and the boy was called James Dirk.

"Damned lucky fellow," said Dirk, giving Jacob a cuff in the chest. "I wanted my eldest to be a son—and look what Cornelia has gone and given me!"

"Plenty more chances," grinned Jacob. "What are you worrying for?"

Dirk had kept his word, and Jacob and Millicent lived in the cottage which Jacob and his father-in-law had built at Dirk's expense. The land on which it stood, however, had been purchased by Jacob himself out of the savings of years. Dirk had been shocked when Jacob had announced that he had put by during the years of his apprenticeship the incredible sum of nine thousand guilders.

"You helped old Green to secure a lot of jobs," said Jacob. "He knew it was through me, and he was more generous with me than would have been the case under different circumstances."

Dirk heard of the birth of Rose's child through Elfrida, Pelham's wife, with whom he continued to correspond regularly. In reply to the letter containing the news, he told Elfrida: "I'm relieved to hear that she came through the ordeal successfully and that all is now well with both mother and child. Believe me, my dear Elfrida, I bear them both a deep affection—Graham and Rose, I mean—and despite the circumstances which resulted in their assuming a new name, I still within myself look upon them as van Groenwegels. How can I ever forget that they both carry in them that grand Old Blood!"

It was through Dirk's corresponding with Elfrida that Pelham and Elfrida and their two children, Francis and Matilde, spent Christmas of 1817 at New Signal. Among the presents they brought was a portrait of the three-year-old Francis by Edward. Elfrida said she had had it done specially for Dirk. "His grandfather dotes on him, and I didn't need to do much persuading to get him to paint it for me." Dirk was pleased, and gave Elfrida a hug, brief, self-conscious, but very expressive of the affection he bore her. He told her: "I'm afraid I am going to dote on him, too. He's a fine little fellow. I have great hopes for him."

"Which means," laughed Cornelia, "that Dirk is going to insist he peruses the letters in the canister the moment he learns to read."

Storm and Elizabeth got on very well with Pelham and Elfrida. The atmosphere at New Signal, since Dirk's marriage, had grown more and more relaxed and pleasant. Cornelia's presence in the house had contributed in great measure to the easing of the tension between Dirk and his parents, and the arrival of their grandchild so softened Storm and Elizabeth that the chilly resentment in their manner towards Dirk vanished within a matter of days. Storm became less torpid and indifferent; when the infant was present he forgot the book he was reading and showed a marked tendency to join in the fuss Elizabeth and Cornelia made over it. Much of Elizabeth's sadness and silence disappeared; her old gaiety began to come to the fore again.

Before Pelham and Elfrida returned to Flagstaff, Dirk had a quiet talk with them near the canal aback, in the course of which he said: "I'd be glad if you could do something for Graham and Rose. I know it will be awkward to have them to Flagstaff, or at your town house, but couldn't you steal away now and then and call on them? They must feel very cut off at Kaywana. For Graham, it won't matter so much. He's been accustomed to living like a hermit—but Rose is fond of mixing with people. She must feel a prisoner in that big house."

"Clara goes to see them every Wednesday. She dines with them," said Elfrida. "And on Sundays they dine at her place at Kingston before going to church. I understand John is quite taken with Rose—though he tries to hide it." Elfrida gripped his arm. "Never mind. I'm going to think about it and see what can be done. Pelham wouldn't mind meeting Rose, I'm sure. He has a weakness for mulatto girls himself. Eh, my darling?" she asked. And Pelham sighed and admitted that there was no point in trying to deny it. "Aren't you always reminding me that I named Francis after my last light-o'-love?" he said.

Back at Flagstaff, Elfrida immediately set about to sound out the rest of the family on the matter. Willem and Christina were emphatic in their refusal to go to Huis Kaywana, and Willem added that if Graham and Rose came to Flagstaff he would remain in his bedroom until they had departed. Edward and Luise, however, promptly decided that they would be delighted to call on the Kaywana couple. "I think we have been very uncharitable in our attitude," Edward frowned. "I'm not a little ashamed of myself." And Luise agreed. "The poor things. They've probably suffered enough because of the remarks we've all thrown at them. It's time we tried to behave towards them in a more humane manner."

Early in February, Edward and Luise and Pelham and Elfrida paid their first visit to Huis Kaywana since Graham's marriage. Graham welcomed them warmly, and Rose, who had been inclined to lapse back into her irritable phase, was her old vivacious self. She made a great impression on the Flagstaff quartet. Like Clara, on her first meeting with the girl, they were taken aback at such poise and ease and unaffected charm in a coloured person. "And her speech!" said Luise, when the four of them were on their way back to Georgetown. "She speaks like one of us. I've never heard a coloured girl speak in such an educated manner."

"She's a beauty," Pelham murmured, and there was so much fervour in his voice that Elfrida gave him a warning glance.

Edward said he would like to paint her. "We must have them to dinner at Flagstaff, and be damned to that stiff-necked son of mine!"

"I wager," said Pelham, "that if Willem sets eye upon her he'll forget all his prejudices, and promptly discover a thousand excuses to take him to Huis Kaywana at least twice a week. Especially," added Pelham with a touch of malice, "as it's so obvious that Christina, of late, has developed towards him a distinctly shrewish attitude."

"She seems to get thinner and drier every day," sighed Luise. "And that poor child of theirs is so sickly!"

In April, Graham and Rose dined at Flagstaff, and though Willem and his wife did not appear, the occasion was a very happy one. Edward asked Rose if she would care to sit for a portrait, and Rose said she would be honoured, so Edward and Luise arranged to spend a fortnight at Huis Kaywana. Edward made Rose pose against the arbour of honeysuckle on the southern side of the house. Luise chose a dress of dark red satin from among the girl's things, but Rose said that she simply could not see herself in such a colour for a picture. "I'd keep thinking too much of the Old Blood!" laughed Rose. Edward agreed with her. "It must be a cool colour. Something blue or green, my girl."

On the last day of the fortnight—the portrait had been completed two days before—Pelham and Elfrida came and dined, and Clara and John were present, too. When the meal was nearly at an end Graham made an announcement. "I have come to a decision about your portrait, Uncle Edward," he said. "I feel that it deserves to be placed in the most honoured position in this house. Accordingly, I am taking down the picture of Cousin Hubertus and putting your portrait of Rose in its place. And I feel that it would be most fitting if the portrait of Cousin Hubertus were given to someone who reveres it more than any of us here could. I shall have it carefully packed away in a crate and sent to New Signal as a present to Dirk."

Two months later, Dirk wrote to Graham: "I am deeply touched, and shall never forget this gesture of yours. This portrait means almost as much to me as the canister of letters. I need say no more. . . ."

Graham showed this letter to Rose, who read it with an expression-less face.

"There is nothing like prayer," sighed Graham, stroking her head. They were in the drawing-room, and outside, the June afternoon was grey with rain. It was nearly time for dinner. "I prayed that all would be happy and amicable amongst us, and God has answered my entreat-ies. Who would have guessed that Elfrida and Pelham would have come to see us of their own volition, and that they would have asked us to visit Flagstaff. God moves in a mysterious way, my love——"

"If you want to know, Graham," Rose interrupted impatiently, "it was Dirk who spoke to Elfrida and Pelham when they were in Berbice and asked them to come and see us. Elfrida confided that in me herself."

"Was it Dirk who spoke to them?" Graham smiled and clasped his hands together, sighing again. "Well, there, my sweetheart! That proves my point only more strongly. God touched Dirk's heart, don't you see? Of all people, can you imagine Dirk trying to persuade Elfrida and Pelham to come here! It is a miracle. Only our dear Father on high could have achieved such a feat. Prayer, my dear heart," he said, stroking her head again. "There is nothing like prayer."

Rose clicked her tongue and got up abruptly. She paced off to the window and stared out at the rain, then crossed the room and stood regarding idly the portrait of herself in its large black frame. Graham joined her, smiling and sighing softly, wagging his head sentimentally. "Lovely, isn't it? Uncle Edward undoubtedly is possessed of genius. Look at the dress—every fold depicted so realistically! I'm glad you wore green, and let down your hair. What lovely, long tresses you have, my sweet!" He put out his hand to stroke her hair again, but this time she avoided him. She snapped: "Leave me alone, can't you? My God!"

He did not show surprise. He smiled solicitously and murmured: "I'm sorry, my dear. I should have remembered that you are in a delicate way again. Oh, how happy I am, Rose! My cup is full, be-lieve me."

Rose stiffened, her hands clenching. She seemed to make an effort to control herself, then suddenly her will snapped. She said through clenched teeth: "Graham, haven't you yet realised what a disgusting bore you are!"

"Never mind, my dear! I understand. You must rest, Rose. You're not well. Come and recline here until it is time for dinner, my little pet. Come."

Rose, without moving, flashed: "And your hide is so thick—that is what amazes me. You're so insensitive and unperceptive. It's incredible."

He clasped his hands together, watching her with devoted eyes, indulgent, worshipping, unruffled. "It's because I love you, my sweetheart. Love must of necessity be blind. I have prayed to our Father above to give me strength to be kindly, tolerant, and insensitive to the whims and tempers of my fellow men. Why should I be angry with you, my dear—you of all people who are the jewel of my heart? Would you prefer me to be like Dirk—harsh, cruel, intolerant?"

Again she seemed to make an effort to control herself, but again something snapped in her. She said in a voice of scorn: "Don't you utter Dirk's name. If you were like Dirk's little finger I'd be in heaven instead of wanting to fly from you."

That wiped the smile from his face. It was the first time she had spoken with such frankness about Dirk. "What do you mean, Rose my dear? Surely, you didn't admire Dirk, did you? His behaviour before we were married——"

"He's a man—that's all I know. You're a toad. And one day you'll be squashed underfoot. Oh, God! How you sicken me!"

Graham paled. "But I'm devoted to you, Rose. I do my best to make you happy in every possible way, my sweetheart. I'm afraid I don't understand——"

"You wouldn't. Of course you wouldn't. There's too much religion on your brain. God, God, God! I'm tired of hearing you utter God's name."

"Would you prefer me to utter curses and evil blasphemies as Dirk does?"

"I would, I would!"

"So you really did admire Dirk, Rose?"

"Admire him? You blind idiot! I loved him. I adored him. And I still love him with my whole soul. Haven't you guessed?"

"Rose!"

"Yes, that shocks you, at last. Thank heaven something can shock you."

"Rose, are you speaking the truth?"

"Most certainly I am. He told you no lie when he said I offered myself to him. I did offer myself to him. I stripped myself naked in his room and offered myself to him. But he wouldn't have me. He refused me. I have black blood in me. The hard, stiff-necked villain! But I still love him. I'll love him until I die."

"You never mentioned this to me before we were married, Rose."

"Why should I have done? Would it have mattered? Would it have prevented you from marrying me?"

He stared at her for a moment, blankly, a little dazedly and incredulously, then shook his head and said quietly: "No. No, it would have made no difference. I should still have married you, my sweetheart."

She laughed. "Didn't I tell you? A toad! That's what you are. You were made to be walked on—and you'll always be walked on."

From the shock of this revelation Graham never recovered. The changes that took place in him during the years that followed would probably have occurred in any event, but the likelihood is that Rose's outburst on that evening of June 1818 accelerated matters considerably.

29

MORE and more, as the years went by, the shortage of
slave labour made itself felt on the plantations. Before
the abolition of the slave trade, a slave could be purchased for fifteen or twenty pounds; now the price had soared to four
or five times this amount, and even at this price it was difficult to
secure a good, able-bodied man. By 1820 the situation had reached the
point where plantations were being put up for sale virtually every day
of the week, and in almost every case no purchaser could be found for
the site and buildings, though the slaves were immediately and eagerly
snapped up. Insolvency was the vogue of that year.

Among the van Groenwegels, Dirk's speech at Huis Kaywana, in
1815, was often discussed, for Dirk's prophecy in respect to coffee and
its prospects seemed not quite as absurd now as it had done at that
time. Indeed, both coffee and cotton fell in price, especially cotton,
for the competition which the southern states of America had begun
to give was proving severe. Sugar, however, remained stable, and the
Liekers, on the West Bank, complained that their slaves were growing
restive and discontented and urging the cultivation of sugar instead
of coffee. Slaves had always been known to grumble at coffee picking,
and not much notice was taken of this aspect of the matter, but the
truth was that the Liekers themselves were beginning to consider selling out and switching to sugar.

Early in 1819, Mary Hubner died, and Raphael and Larsen, without
hesitation, sold Plantation Degries and purchased a larger sugar place
on the East Coast, not many miles east of Flagstaff; they paid a quarter
what they would have had to pay in normal times, and with the slaves
from Degries added to the slaves from the new place, there could be
no doubt that Raphael and Larsen had acted wisely. In a letter to

Dirk, Raphael said: "I for one, my dear boy, did not ponder in vain upon what you told us that day at Huis Kaywana. If all goes as I seem to envisage it, you may yet live to see us as a family 'amalgamate, co-operate and concentrate.' Bravo, dear nephew! I am also acquiring a carriage!"

Raphael not only acquired a carriage, but he built a house at Kingston Village, the fashionable district adjoining the fort and garrison, to the northwest of Georgetown. Raphael did not do it on the cheap, either. He erected a house as good as any of the others in Kingston. Houses in this district were built on brick foundations and painted white, as a rule, with roofs of wallaba shingles. Each house was surrounded by its spacious garden. Every planter and merchant who mattered in Georgetown and the East Coast prided himself on owning a house in Kingston. John and Clara had lived there since 1814, and Willem had bought a retired colonel's cottage—a one-storeyed bungalow affair, but very roomy and in extensive grounds—since his marriage seven years before in 1812. Edward and Luise had scoffed at the idea of building another town house (for Kingston was referred to by the East Coast planters as "town"). "An unnecessary extravagance," ruled Edward, "when Edward House is still standing in Newtown." Willem, however, had claimed, and rightly, that Edward House was no fit place for any gentleman to reside now that business places had sprung up on all sides.

Newtown, where Edward House stood, was the heart of the commercial district of Georgetown. Many Englishmen called it the Cheapside of Georgetown. It abounded with retail shops of every variety, as well as the establishments of goldsmiths and watchmakers, chemists and hatters, tobacconists and slop sellers. Along the river front there were mercantile wharves, the chief of which was the American *stelling* where vessels from America came alongside to discharge their cargoes of horses and cattle.

Many of the lesser merchants in Newtown lived in shabby houses erected in the village of Werk-en-Rust, to the southwest along the river. Werk-en-Rust had once been a plantation, and was not far distant from Kaywana. Nowadays Graham did not need to travel by tent-boat to Georgetown, for the road along the riverbank had been well made up, and carriages travelled on it in all weathers with a fair amount of comfort. There was also an excellent carriage road between Georgetown and Kingston, and when Graham and Rose paid the

Hartfields a visit it required no more than one continuous drive that took about three quarters of an hour.

The road along the East Coast was poor, and often in the rain season it was impossible to drive by carriage from Flagstaff to Georgetown. As a result, planters on the East Coast travelled to town during the rainy months only when compelled by sheer necessity.

In Berbice, New Amsterdam, though an active port, had the appearance more of a large village than of a capital town. There was no definite residential district. The best houses straggled along the High Street, with shops interspersed between them, and the town was divided into quarter-acre lots, each lot surrounded by a ditch. Each ditch drained into a large trench which emptied into the river. At low tide the main *koker* was opened to allow the dirty water collected in the ditches to drain off. The houses, unlike those in Georgetown, were low, long, and narrow, most of them with galleries—closed-in verandas—and a number of them thatched with *troolie* palm leaf instead of shingles, though the wealthy Dutch and British planters who had town houses always took care that their houses were built with shingled roofs, for the *troolie* roofs harboured centipedes and tarantulas and other vermin. In New Amsterdam the jungle loomed near. In the estuary, Crab Island, a low hump of soft mud and dense *courida* trees, infested by crabs and mosquitoes, two miles in circumference, kept growing in size as the years passed. Entirely uninhabitable, the island was frequented only by woodcutters and such gentlemen who were fond of shooting parrots. There were innumerable parrots on Crab Island.

In January 1819 Rose gave birth to a son—four months after Cornelia had presented Dirk with another daughter. There was great excitement at Huis Kaywana, and Graham, in a hysterical voice of triumph, cried: "Dirk won't like to hear this! His last was a girl, like his first! I've beaten him, Clara. Oh, I've beaten him in this, at least!"

Clara insisted that the boy must be named after her, but Rose objected to the name Clarence, which seemed the only name near enough to Clara for a boy. It was the first time Rose had opposed Clara openly, and Graham found himself in a quandary. He pleaded with Rose. Clara, he said, had been so good to them in all their tribulations. Wouldn't Rose accede to her wishes in this one respect? Rose, however, held out, and Graham was obliged to tell Clara how sorry he was—but could Clara think of some other name? Always understanding, Clara bowed to the situation, and the child was named Reginald—Rose's choice.

"We must be patient with her," Graham said to Clara in confidence, one evening when they were alone for a moment at Kingston. "She suffers from whims and tantrums." He winced sensitively and Clara smiled and said: "She's a self-willed girl, but good at heart." Then suddenly: "You have not been quite happy these past few months, my darling boy. Far in the background something has been troubling you. Am I not right?"

He denied it strenuously—too strenuously—and said with a laugh: "No doubt, I do give that impression sometimes, Clara dear—but actually it is merely that my mind is so occupied with plantation and timber matters. I'm doing very well with timber, too—but it keeps me busy, of course. I've just secured a new grant up a creek not far from Borsselen Island, and I'm having a sawmill built in Newtown. With all these things on my mind, naturally, I must give the impression of being worried, mustn't I?"

His garrulity, however, did not fool Clara. She knew that he was not happy as he should be, and she suspected that Rose was proving difficult to live with. Tactfully she changed the subject. She said: "I have spoken to John, and he has agreed to get in touch with his relatives in England. I'm sure there'll be no trouble about having young Reginald's name registered at Eton."

"Ah yes, yes, a splendid idea," he said, patting her arm. "How good of you to see about it for me, Clara! Eton is a distinguished college, from all I've heard——"

"A school. A public school, you ignorant boy!" she laughed. "Oxford is a college. And we must see that Reginald goes there when he is finished with Eton. You'll show them yet, Graham, that the Greenfields, though *mestees*, can be ladies and gentlemen as good as the van Groenwegels."

Graham frowned. "Are people already referring to my children as *mestees*?"

"How can we stop them, my boy? What does it matter? The child of a white man and a mulatto is always called a *mestee* in these colonies. A mere term." She gave him a keen glance. "Are you worried about the colour in your children?"

"No, no. Not in the slightest." He avoided her gaze, and began to fidget. "I have too much else to occupy my thoughts, my dear. Laver, my timber manager, is due tomorrow. A fine fellow, Clara. Trustworthy."

"So you've said before. And such a young man!"

"Yes, he's a year younger than I." His gaze became a trifle abstracted. He clasped his hands together lightly. "A good Christian fellow. I took to him the instant I met him some years ago. So handsome. Very handsome fellow."

He was staring through the window, and did not remark the sudden freezing of Clara's smile, nor did he observe the vague light of anguish that appeared for an instant in her eyes.

Dirk, too, was prospering in timber. His manager, Benjamin Hartman, the mulatto whom Graham had secured some years before, proved a very reliable and capable man. Of near middle age, he was an experienced timber man, and Dirk did not hesitate to take his advice when he suggested acquiring two new concessions a few miles higher up the river. Indians provided all the labour that was needed, and Dirk was even able to withdraw the few Negro slaves he had previously sent up and put them back on New Signal, where they were very much needed.

It was on Jacob's suggestion that Dirk built a new sawmill and storehouse at the southern end of New Amsterdam. Jacob, despite his air of indolence and apparent lack of ambition, was a man of ideas, and always on the alert for opportunities to improve the business. So much so that one day Dirk regarded him contemplatively in their little office at the old sawmill and said: "You once told me you'd never be able to understand me, Jacob—but sometimes I wonder if I really know you as you are. Thinking back on it, I seem to remember that it was you who, when we were still in our teens, mooted the idea of going in for timber. And it was you who suggested building our first sawmill. Now again it's due to your urging I've had this new mill and the storehouse erected." He nudged him in the ribs, and grinned. "The lazy, good-for-nothing scamp is turning out not to be such a fool, after all, eh?"

"I try my best," murmured Jacob, shrugging. "You aren't the only one I give advice to, boy. That old father-in-law of mine has just made up his mind to do as I've been telling him to for the past two years."

"You mean the hardware and dry-goods shop?"

Jacob nodded. Rain came down in a loud prattle on the shingled roof, and Jacob rose, saying: "Wait a minute. I've got to see about that wallaba." He hurried out, his tough, burly frame moving with a speed and agility that always amazed Dirk. In less than five minutes he was back, and almost as though there had been no break in their conversation he said: "Yes, the hardware and dry-goods shop. He's agreed to start on the venture. I'm going into partnership with him."

"Good man, good man. Safe proposition so long as you're behind it. We need a really good hardware and dry-goods shop in this town. What about money?"

"I think we have enough for a start. Old man Green is a thrifty fellow. He has saved up a tidy amount during the past ten or twelve years."

"Probably on your advice, too."

Jacob grinned. "The other way round would be better. I started saving on his advice." As suddenly as it had begun the rain stopped. The sun came out, hot and sharp, and the logs outside began to steam. Jacob said: "I'm busy now, Dirk. I'll give you the details about this new venture another time. Run off to your tavern and have your breakfast. I can promise, though, I don't mean to resign as your manager."

"I should hope not. You devil! One day you may be buying me out."

The latter part of that year, 1819, and the early part of the following year saw three deaths in the family. News came from Antigua that Susan Herd, the youngest of Cousin Hubertus' daughters—she had married a British Army surgeon in 1775 and lived most of her life in Antigua—had died after a long illness. This was in November. In February, Hermine wrote from Jamaica to say that her four-year-old son, Harold, had been killed in an accident in Port Royal when their carriage had overturned. She did not say so in actual words, but, reading between the lines, Storm and Elizabeth, to whom she addressed her letter, gathered that Jim's drunkenness was to be blamed for the accident.

In March, Jacqueline, just three months short of her seventieth birthday, died after a week's illness, casting a new gloom over the Lieker household, which, for the past few months, had been mourning the drop in coffee prices.

Returning from the funeral on the West Bank, Edward patted Luise's hand and said: "Well, we still have you, my love—the last of Cousin Hubertus's four delightful daughters. You'll go on to ninety, I'm sure."

"I feel I shall," smiled Luise, huddling closer to him, for even at sixty-seven she had not lost her romantic traits. "A hundred, more likely, Edward dear. Grandma Hendrickje lived to over ninety, didn't she?"

"True," nodded Edward. "The wicked always live longest. Wasn't poor Mary noted for being the most correct and upright of Cousin Hubertus's daughters? Yet January last year she was the first to go. Susan, another good soul, went in November, and now Jacqueline is off." He added in a whisper: "Remember that scandalous affair she had with Robert Guire at Good Heart. Like you, my sweet, she was by no means a saint."

On the Canje, just at this time, however, there was no cause for mourning. Two days after Jacqueline's funeral—on the seventeenth of March 1820—Cornelia gave birth to a son. The sky was getting pink and yellow over the sapodilla and orange trees, and another short dry-weather day of cloudless sky and bright sunshine seemed indicated, when this new male van Groenwegel uttered his first cry. Dirk, who had fallen asleep since three o'clock in the southeastern room, was awakened by Benji, who shook his shoulder and gasped: "Wake up, Massa Dirk! Wake up! He come, massa! He come!"

"Who the devil has come?" scowled Dirk, starting up.

Benji, superstitious, shook his head. "Aw! Na, massa. Na call de devil 'pon him. It's your own son I talking about, massa."

A few minutes later, however, in the northeastern room, as Dirk bent over the bed, he grimaced and exclaimed: "Damme! At last, eh? The little devil!" He kissed Cornelia. "Good work, my dear! Good work! I'd begun to despair of his ever coming along."

30

THE first meeting between Dirk and Rose, since her marriage to Graham, occurred in August 1823. And, as it happened, it was the time of a tragic event.

At Elfrida's invitation, Dirk and his family were spending the month at Flagstaff. The house was a large one, and there was no difficulty about accommodation, especially as Willem and Christina and their daughter, Lucy, had left Flagstaff about a year before to go and live permanently at Kingston. Willem could no longer tolerate the visits of Graham and Rose to Flagstaff, and, in any case, Elfrida and Christina had not been getting on well for some time.

For the past month or two rumours had been abroad about some new law that had been passed in England concerning the slaves. These rumours had culminated in a special meeting of the Court of Policy, when a despatch from the Secretary of State had been read announcing that three resolutions had been passed by the British Parliament. The first was that the general conditions of all slaves should be improved, and the second that slaves should be granted civil rights, and the third that these measures should come into operation as soon as possible.

Among the planters there was an immediate buzz of protest. Whoever heard of slaves being granted civil rights! It was unthinkable that a Negro should be permitted to give evidence against a white person in a court of law. And why should there be schools for educating these black baboons? It was this sort of pampering that would get the slaves feeling they were the equals of their masters. It would cause trouble. "I curse the day the British took over these colonies!" Willem exclaimed savagely one day at Kingston. And he was not the only Dutch planter who expressed himself in such terms. Even some of the British planters were inclined to be testy about these new resolutions.

At a meeting of the Court of Policy on the sixth of August—two days after Dirk and his family had arrived at Flagstaff—an ordinance was reluctantly proposed and carried on three points: to prohibit the flogging of female slaves, to discontinue the use of the whip in the fields, and to provide measures for the control of females.

Dirk laughed at Willem's rantings and said: "I see nothing to be alarmed about in these measures. Recently we stopped using the whip in the fields at New Signal, and it's a long time since we had cause to flog a female. Only a few of the old-fashioned planters will be affected——"

"Times *are* changing," barked Willem. "I remember you yourself remarking only a few years ago that you were all in favour of traditional customs. Is it marriage that has altered your outlook?"

Dirk flushed slightly—but grinned and returned: "I believe it has, my dear Willem, but not in very drastic fashion. I've altered my outlook only in those respects that I deem politic and prudent." Dirk's green eyes suddenly hardened. He leaned forward and stared at Willem across the table. They were dining at Willem's Kingston place. "What you should be alarmed about you aren't," said Dirk. "Remember my warning in 1815. This new law is merely a prelude, you blind fool! The Anti-Slavery Party is preparing us for the abolition of slavery. Yes. It's coming, Willem. Before we know it, it will be sprung upon us. So don't grow enraged over this innovation. This is a mere trifle we'll soon forget."

As usual, Willem and the others—Graeme Clackson and John Hartfield and Jim Menzies and their wives were present—scoffed at the idea. The British Government knew how far they could go. They valued their West Indian colonies too highly to want to ruin them, for what else could follow but ruin if slavery was abolished? No, Dirk was allowing his imagination to get the better of him. "You're a born pessimist, laddie," Jim Menzies rumbled in his deep Scots accent.

When they were alone in their room at Flagstaff that night Cornelia said with a laugh: "You should not make these terrible predictions before company, Dirk dearest. They only prove upsetting—and then you get upset, too."

"I can't stand crassness," frowned Dirk, pacing. "Why can't the fools see what's ahead of us? It seems so clear, so patently logical."

"Clear, perhaps, dearest, but not logical."

"The Anti-Slavery Party knows nothing about logical reasoning—that's why it's logical to conclude they would ruin us in the face of all good sense."

"Ssssh! That will do, my sweet. It's time for your bath. Here's Susie. I'll go and have a look at the children in the meantime. A bath is what you need in this hot weather—to cool both your skin and your rage."

When Susie was sprinkling water on him in the bathroom a few minutes later he detected in her manner a strange excitement, and asked her what was the matter. She was a stout, unattractive creature of about thirty or thirty-five, and uttered a kind of whinnying sound as she replied: "It's something Ah hear, me massa. Ow! All day Ah trembling and breathing hard, me massa. You must pardon me."

"Breathing hard? You keep panting and squeezing your hands together as if you were on the verge of seeing some heavenly vision. What is this something you heard today?"

"Ow, me massa. Everybody talk tell me how de English Guv'ment pass law dat all slave woman must go free from dis week. Is true, me massa?"

Dirk laughed. "I know nothing about that."

"Plenty people talk say dat, massa. It must be true. Ow, me massa! We got to dance and sing all night dis week. Slave woman free!" Susie squeezed her hands together and whinnied again.

Dirk clicked his tongue, irritated. He made no attempt to disillusion the woman. Let her continue in her false paradise, poor simpleton, he told himself. Not that she would have to wait so long before her paradise was realised.

He was still in an explosive mood when the bath was over and he had returned to his room. It took Cornelia nearly an hour to soothe him.

The following morning Dirk told the others, at coffee, what Susie had said, and Pelham nodded, his face rather grave. "I've been hearing that everywhere this morning over the house—and yesterday evening Greaves, our head overseer, told me he overheard the same thing. The field slaves are passing it round among themselves. Don't know where they could have got such a thing from—and it isn't wholesome."

"Is there any evidence of discontentment?" asked Dirk.

Pelham nodded. "A certain amount, yes." He passed his hand through his pale yellow hair, nodding slowly. "They're saying that the British Government has granted them their freedom, but the local government is trying to stifle the law. Some such idiocy. I've told Greaves to have a sharp eye out for trouble."

Elfrida laughed. "You're as much a pessimist as Dirk, Pelham."

They were on the back veranda, where coffee was generally served in the morning at Flagstaff, for it was very cool here, with the trade winds blowing in straight from the sea. The booming of the waves could be heard on the wide beach beyond the fringe of *courida* bushes about a hundred yards distant, and the air smelt of fish and iodine, and very refreshing.

Edward and Luise, also, agreed with Elfrida. "They are a fanciful lot of people, these slaves," was Edward's view. "They probably heard that female slaves are not henceforth to be flogged—and from that it became twisted into freedom for female slaves—then freedom for all of them, male and female. Nothing new, my children. Don't let it upset you."

"That's what I feel, too," nodded Luise, in her purple morning gown that gave her a look of some thin, eccentric royal personage who had strayed in upon them overnight. She gave Dirk a sly, old-lady glance and said: "I can see the battle light in Dirk's eyes, Edward love. The blood is stirring in him. Old Hendri hoping for an opportunity to use the muskets on the black brutes!"

"The van Groenwegels never run!" intoned Cornelia in a solemn voice.

"Poor dear!" said Elfrida, stretching out and patting Dirk's knee. "They will tease you. But that reminds me. When next I'm in Berbice, Dirk, I want to have a thorough look at the letters in that canister of yours."

"It will be a pleasure," grinned Dirk. "Time you acquainted yourself with the Tales of Old."

"I believe," said Cornelia, about an hour later, when she and Dirk were alone in their room, "the true reason for your mood this morning and yesterday evening lies in this evening's occasion." She gave him a long, keen look. "Am I not right, my darling?"

He stiffened at once and glared at her. "What do you mean, pray?"

Still very much desirable, despite her four children, Cornelia had lost none of her mystery and subtle feminine charms. She smiled and said quietly: "If I mistake not, dearest, today is Tuesday the twelfth of August."

He gave a reluctant smile and grunted. "So it is. Yes. I won't deny I am in somewhat of a nervous state about this sojourn of ours at Huis

Kaywana. I wish it were Saturday already and we were on our way back here."

She seated herself on the window sill and said out into the morning: "Ah, but within you, my dearest, you are throbbing excitedly, I'm sure, for the arrival of our carriage at Kaywana this evening."

He said nothing. He began to pace. She laughed and said: "When will you be cured of that habit of pacing when you are agitated, Dirk?"

He halted abruptly and growled: "It's all these rumours we've been hearing that have upset me, my love. Elfrida is not the sort of person to write and tell me anything that is not based on firm truth, and from what I know of Graham, I can well believe that he is neglecting Rose in favour of this missionary, Mr. Smith, and his wife. Again, there is this ugly tale concerning his attachment to his timber manager—that Laver fellow. Can it be really that he is losing his masculinity, Cornelia? Damme, but it would be a tragedy for Rose!"

Cornelia nodded but made no comment. She was watching the children with their nurse under the big sandbox tree to the east of the house. Amelia, at six, was a tiny, dark-haired creature. Sybil, not quite five, was as tall as Amelia, and had her father's green eyes and hair like Pelham's—a pale yellow. The three-year-old Hendrik Storm was also fair, but had his mother's dark blue eyes. Mary—known as Father's Pet, for Dirk certainly showed an inordinate fondness for her—had red-gold hair and blue-green eyes, and, at two, already had a personality of her own. She was a gay, coquettish little thing—"and she has inherited some of your mysterious airs," Dirk had once pronounced. "I can sense it."

Dirk began to pace again. "Religion—and now effeminacy! What a fortunate circumstance that he was persuaded to change his name!"

"Though everyone knows that he is a van Groenwegel, Dirk—and they know that he has probably only taken after his Uncle Raphael."

He grunted. "Blood, blood, blood. These things will come out, I suppose. A great pity. At least Uncle Raphael had the good sense not to marry. He and Larsen have remained bachelors, and no one can accuse them of open indecency. But think of Rose—a vital, feminine being like Rose—faced with such a situation!"

Cornelia smiled—and pretended to be interested again in the children.

A gust of breeze came in at the windows, humming through the room, and wisps of Cornelia's dark hair waved around her forehead.

She uttered a little gurgle of merriment at one of Sybil's pranks. Dirk gave her a swift glance, but sensed that it was something outside that had occasioned her merriment. He continued to pace. The boom of the sea sounded continuously, with a muffled ominousness, and Dirk suddenly paused, remembering the distant thunder of an afternoon in 1816. He grunted and remarked: "It was August then, too."

Cornelia asked: "What did you say, love?" She turned her head.

"Nothing," he murmured, rubbing his hands together slowly.

"Yes, I remember, dearest. It was August, and there was thunder in the south. Is it the sea that reminds you of then?"

He frowned and said: "I believe you're a witch, woman."

She laughed. "I've always been good at seeing into your thoughts, haven't I?" She rose from the window sill and approached him, kissed him, and said: "Let us go down and watch the children at play. It's no use allowing yourself to be troubled about what cannot be helped."

There were the usual August thunderclouds in the south when they arrived at Huis Kaywana at four that afternoon, but no thunder was heard.

Though only thirty-three, Graham had already acquired a few flecks of grey at his temples. Otherwise, he appeared at peace with himself. He was in no way nervous, nor fidgety, when he greeted them. He looked quietly satisfied—slyly satisfied, Cornelia remarked later to Dirk —and there was no malice in his manner when he glanced at Rose and asked Dirk: "Would you say she is the mother of two children, Dirk? Doesn't she appear as fresh and virginal as she did the day I saw her at New Signal for the first time after years?"

Dirk made no audible comment in reply to this, but as he gripped Rose's hand and returned her frank, unabashed gaze, he said to himself: "My God! I should think she looks as fresh and virginal!"—and it might have been the afternoon in July, 1815, when he was battling with the hot shiver threatening to swamp his limbs. The same old shiver attacked him now. And his knees trembled. He wanted to gibber, remembering the brown mole at the base of her left breast. Anger began to rise up in him at his weakness, and it was all he could do to smile and say: "It's good to see you again, Rose."

"It's good to be able to entertain you at Huis Kaywana, Dirk," she smiled—and he flushed furiously, recalling her last words to him before she swept out of the sitting-room at New Signal on that painful afternoon seven years before. He caught himself quickly, however, and grinned, thrusting back with: "Your wishes have certainly been fulfilled, Mrs. Greenfield."

Cornelia intervened here, saying quietly: "Will you postpone your duel for a little later, Dirk dearest? Rose, don't encourage him, please." And that put matters right and destroyed the tension. Graham laughed softly, remarking: "They're both fighters, aren't they, Cornelia, my dear? The one a raccoon—the other a tigress. Ah me! I don't regret being of the Soft Streak."

To their surprise, Dirk and Cornelia found that Graham had invited two people to dine with them that evening—a small, mousy man with a rather too humble and too benevolent manner, and a woman not unlike the man. They were the Reverend Mr. John Smith and his wife. "Mr. Smith has a little chapel not far from Uncle Raphael's place on the East Coast," Graham told them in effecting the introductions. "It's on Plantation Le Resouvenir. He's doing a magnificent work for the poor Negroes on the East Coast."

"So I have heard," said Dirk stiffly, boiling within. This was just the sort of thing Graham would deliberately plan in order to embarrass him, thought Dirk. He knows what I feel about these missionaries, and by God, on the very first evening I spend in his home he brings this simpering jackanapes and his wife to join us at dinner! I suppose this is how he intends to vent his spite on me for what has happened in the past.

Throughout the meal Dirk could see that Rose felt as he did about the missionary and his wife. Her manner towards them was stiff and cool. Graham, however, at complete ease, something almost callous in his nonchalance, seemed entirely unaware of anything strained in the atmosphere. He smiled and chatted to them all with the air of a good host, his manner impeccably cordial.

After dinner he sat in the sitting-room with Mr. Smith and his wife —whom he kept addressing as "my dear, good Jane"—while Dirk and Cornelia, accompanied by Rose, went upstairs to see the children.

"You have lovely children, Dirk," said Rose. Her voice had deepened with age; it was a rich, resonant contralto. As she moved on ahead of them up the stairs, Dirk watched her hips, which, he noted now, had thickened somewhat. She had lost the birdlike look. But the feline grace was still there. Her waist was small, and her breasts high, her movements still lithe and easy.

"Why haven't you had more than two?" he asked—and suddenly

realised that he had committed a *faux pas*. He saw her eyes flash with anger and pain—but knew that it was not at him her anger was directed. She paused at the top of the stairway and said: "By now you ought to have heard what my situation is like in this house—so you shouldn't ask me that, Dirk."

"I know. I'm sorry," he said hurriedly. He gave her an anguished glance and said: "I do mean that, too. I am sorry, Rose."

"Never mind," Cornelia put in. "You have two children—and I can return your compliment with all sincerity. They are lovely, Rose."

"I'm very fond of them. They are my only incentive to live."

When they were in the room with Rose's Ernestine and Reginald, they heard violin music downstairs, and Rose remarked: "Yes, he still plays his violin—but he plays only for the missionaries and for his Albert, when he is here."

"Laver, isn't that his name?" asked Dirk.

"Yes." Rose nodded—and gave him a glance bright with the same old passion. Cornelia was stooping beside Reginald, who was on the floor with a toy carriage, and did not see the twitching that attacked the faces of both Dirk and Rose in that instant. Dirk moved away quickly and began to bend over the cot in which Ernestine was sitting, already in her nightgown. The nurse was slapping the pillow. Dirk tweaked Ernestine's cheek and said: "You'll soon be too long for this cot. Tell me how old you are."

"Six. My birthday was Sunday last."

"Of course, of course! You were born in August. I'd forgotten that."

Except for a certain sallowness about their complexions, both children could have passed for white. Reginald even had Graham's fair hair. And Ernestine, though dark-haired like Rose, was green-eyed. Their features were entirely European. Yet Dirk was not sorry that their family name was Greenfield. Never, never would he be able to reconcile himself to the thought of coloured van Groenwegels. To be of the *élite* one must be pure white. He remembered Jacob and his family. Jacob's children were all a deep olive, with dark, curly hair. Delightful little creatures, and Dirk felt almost tearful with affection when he thought of them. In the years to come he would always be a godfather towards them, never fail to give them a helping hand when necessary. But he would have to see to it that his own children did not associate with them. Inhuman though it would be, he would have to drive it into his own children that intimate relations with people of colour must be eschewed.

In the years to come, Huis Kaywana would be out of bounds to his children.

At coffee the following morning Graham outlined some of his plans for entertaining them during the next two or three days. "So sorry you cannot remain longer," he smiled, "but I know how the Flagstaff people must be eager to have you back there."

"But you said," Dirk rebutted, "that you were leaving for your grant upriver on Monday morning. That's why I suggested staying until Saturday."

"Of course, of course," said his elder brother, in no way perturbed. "I am leaving for Ubaree on Monday morning. Albert is coming down tomorrow to get some things he needs in town, and I'm accompanying him back to see how everything is getting on up there. My usual visit of inspection. But there is no reason why you couldn't stay on here, Dirk, my dear fellow. Rose could entertain you and your family. I'm sure she would be delighted. Wouldn't you, Rose?"

"Very," Rose replied, sipping her coffee, her gaze out on the morning, her face expressionless.

"Thanks," said Dirk. "But we've already promised Uncle Raphael to spend a few days at his place from Monday, so there's nothing we can do now about it."

"Dear Uncle Raphael! Yes, you certainly couldn't disappoint him. Anyway, you are with us now, and we are happy to have you. Tomorrow, when Albert is here, I was thinking of taking you all for a trip to Barrasikki Creek, where I recently acquired another timber grant. It's merely a few hours by boat, and as the weather is so dry it should be a pleasant outing." Graham smiled from Dirk to Cornelia, his manner not unlike that of a generous uncle trying to be specially kind to them. "What do you think, my dears? Does the prospect meet with your favour?"

Dirk said he had no objections, and Cornelia thought it should be pleasant.

Graham gave Rose a tentative glance, and Dirk noticed that his smile grew a trifle mocking as he asked her: "May we look forward to the pleasure of your company, Rose?"

"What?" Rose snapped her gaze upon him, and frowned. "Most certainly not! You know I never accompany you on any of your trips anywhere."

Graham sighed, clasped his hands together delicately, and then smiled and shrugged. "So be it, then, my love." He took a sip of his coffee, and, as though to change the subject, remarked: "Never mind! You'll have delightful company this evening. Pelham and Elfrida are coming to dinner."

Dirk saw Rose stir uncomfortably. There was the suggestion of a blush in her cheeks, and Dirk glanced from her to Graham, puzzled. Graham was uttering soft, simpering sounds. He remarked with a sly glance at Cornelia: "We're the same age, did you know, my dear Cornelia?"

"Who is that?" asked Cornelia, taken by surprise.

"Pelham and I," said Graham. "We were both born in 1790. A matter of a month or two between us." He threw Rose another mocking glance, and tittered. "Splendid fellow, Pelham. You still correspond with Elfrida, don't you, Dirk?"

"Yes. Yes, I do," growled Dirk, more puzzled than ever.

Later, in their room, he said to Cornelia: "What the deuce was Graham insinuating when he referred to Pelham and Elfrida? Did you understand?"

Cornelia smiled her inscrutable smile, and returned: "Was he insinuating something?" And he clicked his tongue. "Don't attempt to be so ignorant now," he snapped. "You know as well as I do that he was."

Unruffled, she said: "If he was insinuating something, dearest, why should I be any wiser than you as to his meaning?" She patted his cheek, chuckled and added in a half-teasing voice: "Go and ask Rose, darling. I'm sure she would be able to enlighten you."

"There are so may things I want to ask her. . . . Oh, damme! I wish we'd never accepted his invitation to come here."

Cornelia gave him a long stare, then said: "Dirk, here's my suggestion to you. Stay back from the trip tomorrow, and have a long chat with her. I think it would do you both good."

He grunted. "I would like to have a chat with her alone—but Graham may be offended if I don't go. No, it's not practicable."

"Graham wouldn't mind, sweet. So long as dear Albert is with us, Graham would be quite indifferent to your absence."

They must have been halfway through dinner that afternoon when Dirk got the shock. Because of the excessive heat of the day, they dined at a small table placed on the northern veranda which Graham had had added to the building some years previously. It opened out from the sitting-room and corresponded with another veranda on the southern side which opened out from the dining-room.

Graham and Rose sat at opposite ends of the table, and on one side were Dirk and Elfrida, and on the other, facing them, Pelham and Cornelia.

The conversation had been of a general nature until Dirk asked Pelham about the rumour going round among the slaves. Pelham frowned and said the situation was still troubled. "It's the Government's fault," he said. "I don't know why they don't publish the details contained in these resolutions in the form of a proclamation, so that everyone may read it and the slaves learn exactly what it's all about. When they preserve this secrecy, they only make the damned fools guess and speculate and form false conclusions."

"But slaves can't read, can they?" Rose commented. "What would be the use of publishing the details in the form of a proclamation?"

"No fear. The missionaries would see to it that any proclamation is read and explained to them. And quite a number of coloured people can read and write. A proclamation would solve the matter and stop the rumours, I'm sure."

Rose did not pursue the argument—but Dirk noticed that she smiled to herself as though enjoying some joke that only she could appreciate. Elfrida and Graham had taken up the discussion, and it was when Graham was extolling the many activities of the Reverend Mr. Smith and his wife that Dirk got the shock.

Out of the corner of his eye, Dirk glanced at Rose, and saw that she was still smiling slightly—then he flicked his gaze at Pelham, and surprised Pelham in a smile almost identical to Rose's. In a flash Dirk knew that there was something conspiratorial afoot between Rose and Pelham—and then he saw Pelham look up from his plate, saw him stare at Rose, and saw Rose return the stare—and now there could be no doubt. There was stark lasciviousness on both their faces.

Dirk quivered through and through, but kept himself under control and pretended to be paying attention to what Graham was saying. Now he began to see what Graham's mocking insinuation at coffee, that morning, signified. It was this. He felt a dull burning at the top of his head, and his throat went dry. A hollow cave seemed to form within his chest. All inclination to eat left him.

He made a mere pretence of finishing the meal, and Elfrida once laughed and asked him what had happened to his appetite. He growled out an excuse about the heat. "When the weather is like this, my appetite has a habit of deserting me."

Though he kept a surreptitious watch, he failed to catch Rose and Pelham staring at each other again as he had seen them doing, and their faces looked so conventionally noncommittal whenever he happened to glance at them that he almost began to wonder whether he had not made a mistake. Could it have been his morbid imagination that had brought alive on their faces the expressions he thought he had seen? The next instant, however, he knew that he had not imagined anything; it had happened as he had witnessed it.

He kept the matter strictly to himself, and in going to bed said nothing even to Cornelia—but he decided that on the morrow he would not go on the trip to Barrasikki Creek.

31

IT was not until they were halfway back to the house from the *stelling*, after seeing the others off, that she as much as glanced at him. When she did, however, she smiled and put her arm through his, and said: "You've surprised me. I didn't think you'd have remained behind with me." He could sense the trembling in her, despite the calm manner in which she spoke.

He frowned and replied: "It was Cornelia who suggested I should remain behind and have a long talk with you alone. But I'll admit I wanted to myself—and especially after something I noticed at table yesterday afternoon."

She started. "At dinner? What did you notice then?"

He gave his head a slight shake, saying nothing. Staring ahead, troubled.

She did not press him for an explanation. She led him round the house, and they sat on the bench near the honeysuckle arbour on the southern side. The vines were not in bloom, but it was shady and cool here, and very pleasant now that the sun was still in the east. He remarked at once that this was the background of the portrait in the sitting-room, and she smiled and nodded. "Uncle Edward chose it himself," she said. "The vines were in bloom then."

"Did he choose the dress you were wearing, too?"

"No. I did. Aunt Luise chose a dark-red thing, but I refused to wear it. Uncle Edward agreed with me, and suggested something cool— blue or green. I chose green—because I remembered it was the colour you liked to see me in best."

He grunted, wincing. Tried to smile. "And your hair loosed out . . . ?"

"As *you* always liked to see it—yes. It has always been you, Dirk.

Everything I've thought and done has been inspired in some way by you."

They were silent, listening to the tick and click of ants in the grass and shrubs nearby. Dew still glistened on an odd leaf here and there, though it was nearly ten o'clock. Remotely they could hear the chug-chug of the sugar mill, which nowadays was steam-driven. Now and then the strong smell of cane juice came into their senses, mingled with the sourish odour of the trash and refuse. Once or twice the clank of chains would disturb the morning peace as the slaves manipulated a huge bundle of canes out of some punt just arrived from aback along the canal. But that was out of their sight, beyond the fruit trees and the sandboxes and the cabbage palms that grew everywhere in the grounds around the house. Here everything was domestic, indolent, intimate. Here and in this moment there was no need to be troubled about the price of sugar and slaves, of machinery and timber.

Abruptly he began to speak. He told her about what he had noticed at dinner, and she listened without interrupting, though her manner became tense. She smiled and nodded, and said that he had not imagined it.

"Then what must I understand? You're his mistress?"

Seven years ago she would have flared out at him, but at twenty-three, and as the mistress of Huis Kaywana, she had acquired greater control of herself. She shook her head and said quietly, staring at the grass: "No—not yet."

"Not yet. I see."

She uttered a soft sound that was tender as well as bitter, and in a calm, undramatic voice told him of what her situation had been like during the past two or three years. "In a way, I suppose I am to be blamed, for I treated him abominably from the outset. I rebuffed him and rejected him in shameless fashion, and indulged in whims and tantrums that would have taxed the patience of a saint. But something in his nature repelled me, Dirk—a mean, toady, ingratiating trait. He was never meant for me—but you know that. I married him out of spite against you and when I was in a pique. I was a foolish girl of sixteen then. But that is beside the point. What matters is that he has changed in his manner towards me. He has lost his ardour as a man, and we have not been intimate for more than two years. His interest has been turned upon members of his own sex. There was an overseer he tried to befriend, but he was rebuffed, for the man was not effeminate. Then he turned his attention to Albert Laver—

the man who manages one of the timber grants upriver—and it happened that here he found a kindred spirit. Since then I have become superfluous in his scheme of living. But within the past few months Pelham, who sensed what the position was, began to show a fondness for me, and, I admit, I have found myself inclined to respond, Dirk. I am human. I can't live indefinitely without a man. And before long I am going to yield. I shall try to avoid a scandal, but I know that it is inevitable that Pelham and I are going to become intimate." She turned her head and looked at him, her eyes bright with emotion. "Do you understand now why you surprised us yesterday afternoon looking at each other as we did?"

The bench was small, but roomy enough for them to sit without touching, and that was the way they had sat up to now. Suddenly he put his hand over hers, and their gazes met, and a great stillness came upon them both, as though some spirit from the idyllic morning had invaded them, linking their awareness and creating complete harmony. He said, after they had stared at each other like this for an interval: "Aunt Luise, I think, it was who said that Grandma Hendrickje was reborn in me. But I wonder if it couldn't be you, Rose, who possesses Grandma Hendri's soul. The cruelty is there, though subdued—but above all, there is the fire and the strength and the fearlessness." He began to tremble.

She smiled. "You haven't outgrown that yet, I see—the family-pride obsession." And he shook his head. "No. I haven't—and I never shall."

"Look yonder there, Dirk dear. Between those two cabbage palms, and near the rather small sandbox tree. Do you see a roof showing?"

He looked, and then nodded. "Yes. What of it?"

"It's an old barn that Graham, years ago, had converted into a chapel for meetings. Since Mr. Wray's time. Mr. Wray used to hold services in there for the slaves. Nowadays it isn't used by Mr. Smith. There is a much better place Graham has built near the roadway."

He gave her a puzzled look. "Why are you telling me this?"

"I sometimes go alone to that old barn when I'm very miserable. I sit in there in a hammock and read. It is very peaceful and secluded, and there are a lot of dry leaves on the floor. Wild vines have run up into the rafters, and only one window is free of them. That's where I have my hammock. The light strikes in through that window. No one ever goes near there."

She paused, her eyes wide and bright, and he knew before she said it what was coming next, so that when she uttered the words he was prepared and shook his head. "No, Rose. No," he told her. He felt her tremble. "The same old reason?" she asked, her voice with a break. "The black blood in me?" And he smiled and shook his head again. "No, not that. I've outgrown *that*, at least—where you are concerned, at any rate. It's only my children now I must teach to beware of black blood." He gave a groan, and held her face between his hands. "Rose, my sweet. My love. How you will keep tempting me! You'll never know the agony of regret I've suffered because of that July afternoon eight years ago when, like the ranting imbecile I was, I rejected you! Rose, my dearest, you've left your ghost in that northeastern room. It gives me no peace. I've relived that afternoon a thousand times. I've sometimes wept—yes, wept, my sweet—because it wasn't in my power to go back in time and alter the issue. I sometimes hate the strength in me which permitted me to turn from you and order you to dress. Remember how I shut my eyes? I pressed my hands to my eyes to shut out the sight of you. God! Why didn't you rush at me and drag my hands from my face? Oh, damme! But this is lunacy." He took his hands from her face and clasped them tight in his lap. "Pardon me, Rose. I lost control of myself."

"You still," she said, her voice barely audible, "haven't told me why we couldn't do as I've just asked you to, Dirk."

He raised his gaze and looked towards the roof of the barn. A thatched roof, it looked picturesque nestling amidst the trees. He could envisage the cool gloom contained within its shelter. Dry leaves on the floor.

"They won't be back before two o'clock, Dirk love. It's barely ten now."

He nodded. "Yes, I know. But I couldn't, Rose. It would mean the end of my marriage. It is too late. You gave me my opportunity eight years ago, and I threw it away."

"Why would it break up your marriage?"

"Because I know the extent of my own strength."

A very slight wind came from the northeast, and they could hear the trees rustling. Then the wind reached them and they smelt the cane juice strong in the air. The chug-chug of the sugar mill rose louder, then died down again to the old dull beat. The wind faded, and the trees were silent once more.

"Yours is a flexible strength, Rose. Mine, alas, is brittle. I must be strict in the guard I place over my integrity, over my code of stability, for damage done to it—and this would be serious damage—would be irreparable." He turned and held her face again between his hands. "Tell me that you understand, my sweet. Tell me that I shall live to regret another lost opportunity, but that the memory of us sitting here will be a lasting solace to your stiff-necked Dirk—a memory that will saturate his future reflections with more soothing tenderness than he deserves. My lovely Rose with her black blood. When all other ghosts have ceased to haunt me you'll still be there, plaguing me and consoling me, by turn."

He kissed her forehead, and her cheeks, and her chin, and her lips—very lightly—and then sprang up and said that they must take a walk in the grounds. It was such a pleasant, cool morning for August. "Later it will be sizzling. Let us make the best of it now, love—before the thunderclouds gather in the south. We'll walk about and talk."

"And take care not to go too close to the barn?"

He grinned—and held her and kissed her again. On her forehead, on her cheeks, on her chin, on her lips. Very lightly. Both of them trying not to tremble too much.

It was Cornelia, too, who suggested that Rose should spend the weekend at Flagstaff, and Rose went back to the East Coast with them on Saturday, for, as she told them, the Flagstaff people had given her carte blanche to come and spend time whenever she felt like it. Many of her weekends in fact, were spent at Flagstaff. "That is how," she whispered to Dirk, when they happened to be alone for a moment, on the Friday evening, in the portico, "Pelham and I have come to build up our secret friendship. We've been so discreet that I doubt if Elfrida suspects anything. If only I could have fled away somewhere with you, Dirk dear—into the bush—anywhere." On this occasion, Dirk noted, her breath smelt of rum, and he could see that her calm was the artificial calm induced by insobriety.

He turned away from her hurriedly, his vision getting blurred.

When they were going to bed at Flagstaff that Saturday night, Dirk and Cornelia were both in a pensive mood. Dirk said: "You should not have asked her to come here, my dear. The sight of her unhappiness weighs on me."

"But it makes her happy when you are near, Dirk dearest. I like her very much. I'm as depressed as you are to see her in this state."

He groaned. "Poor Elfrida. It will be a terrible blow to her when she learns what is happening. You must never whisper a hint to her, Cornelia."

"Why should I? Not that it will make much difference. She will discover it sooner or later. I believe Pelham, too, is drinking harder than he usually did."

He nodded. "I've noticed it."

"Dirk!"

"Yes?"

She was standing before the wardrobe mirror combing her hair, tall and straight-backed in her white nightgown, but no longer the slim girl of seventeen who had gazed coldly upon him in Doctor John's portico, no longer the shapely creature of nineteen in sea-green muslin who had risen from a wicker chair to greet him that July evening in 1815. Her hips and waist had thickened, and her breasts were overfull and low. Yet she was still desirable, and her face was still pretty. Even as he stared at her, in appraisement, he knew what she was going to tell him. It was as though he had just acquired the gift of second sight.

"Yes?" he prompted again—and now she stopped combing her hair, turned and said: "Why don't you give her what she wants? It might help."

"I knew you were going to say that. I read your thoughts. Are you mad?" He felt his finger tips growing cold, felt the breath receding within him.

"I'm not." She smiled, her gaze very steady. "It might help you, too."

He clicked his tongue, flushing. "Let us go to bed. I'm in no mood to listen to tomfoolery."

"I don't deem it tomfoolery. I'm serious. I give you my permission, sweet."

He gave her a frowning stare and shook his head, muttering: "To the day of my death I'll be baffled by you."

She chuckled, and turned back to the looking glass, continued to comb her hair, and the wind hummed through the room, and they could hear the sea roaring hoarsely beyond the *courida* bushes. They blew out the candles and got into bed without referring to the subject again.

After coffee, the following morning, they went for a drive in the carriage. Pelham did not accompany them, for he was still worried about the rumours going round among the slaves, and thought it prudent not to leave the plantation.

"I concur," Dirk told him. "In July 1762 Laurens Kunckler left his plantation to go to Fort Nassau, and in his absence his slaves burnt down his house and started a little rebellion. It took Hoogenheim and the burgher militia several days to put matters right. Two letters in the canister at home refer to the incident. It was like a prelude to the big insurrection in March the next year."

Pelham's pale blue eyes twinkled humorously as he regarded Dirk. His tiny, reddish freckles looked blurred together from sunburn. During the past few days he had been patrolling everywhere on the plantation, for hours on end. At thirty-three, he had lost the soft, refined air he had possessed up to the time of his marriage. These days he looked tough and wiry, a man of the open air. Over six feet, he was a handsome fellow, and Dirk could understand Rose being attracted to him physically.

"Those damned letters of yours!" he chuckled. "Why don't you publish them?"

Dirk grinned and shook his head. "They're only for van Groenwegel eyes."

Dirk and Cornelia and the others picnicked in the open savannah, in the shade of a *courida* tree. They spent a pleasant day, and in returning at sunset, they passed a carriage going in the opposite direction —a carriage containing Graham and the Reverend Mr. Smith and his wife, Jane. Graham waved and smiled, and they all waved back, except Rose.

"Where could he be going to now, I wonder," said Luise—and Rose replied: "No mystery, Aunt Luise. I heard him arranging with them to be at the service this evening at the Le Resouvenir chapel. He's going to play his violin."

"Is that a chapel for white people?" Cornelia asked—and Rose shook her head and said: "No—purely for niggers. Mr. Smith is their champion, didn't you know? If you lived in Demerary you wouldn't need to ask."

"The planters can't bear the best bone in him," sighed Elfrida. "He must be a good man, but he irritates me considerably. I can't appreciate that sort of humility and benevolence. It is somehow degrading. I can't explain it."

"I know precisely what you mean, my dear," Dirk nodded. "I've met him."

"He puts dangerous ideas into the heads of the slaves," rumbled Edward. "It is imprudent to teach these black people Christianity. They are heathens, and it only upsets them. I have no objection to their being taught to read and write—but that is as far as it should be allowed to go."

Rose sniffed and said: "If Graham had his way, we should soon be having Negro parsons in our midst." And Luise laughed and added: "Not only Graham, my child. His dear, good Clara is of the same mind."

"By the way, how do they get on together these days?" asked Dirk.

"Still as devoted to each other," said Rose. And Edward grunted and put in: "Ah, but with a difference, my dear Rose! Clara is a sad woman. She grieves in private over his new outlook. She has told me so herself."

"She is a loyal old soul," sighed Elfrida. "I don't care what her past might have been like—she's worth a thousand of the other feather-brained women in town. I wish Harvey had taken after her."

Edward fidgeted and growled: "Oh, he's a foppish fool. I hope you won't get it into your head, Elfrida, my dear, to send Francis to Eton. These English schools are noted for turning out the most unutterable idiots."

"I don't agree, Uncle Edward," said Rose. "Mr. Benlyonson went to Eton, and he's a charming and sensible man. He even greets me in the street, and is never ashamed to drop in at Kaywana when he is passing our way."

Edward shrugged. "You may be right, my girl. After all, I suppose it is a matter of what disposition one is born with."

Luise began to shake with laughter, and then Elfrida joined in—and Dirk saw Edward scowling and fidgeting. Puzzled, Dirk stared from his uncle to his aunt. It was only later that evening when he and Cornelia and Elfrida happened to be alone on the portico that Dirk learnt what had occasioned his uncle's embarrassment. Elfrida told Dirk and Cornelia: "Didn't you know it's rumoured that Harvey is his own son!" And Dirk started and gasped: "Good God! But of course! I think Graham did mention in a letter years ago that Uncle Edward had had an affair with Clara. What a moral crew you Demerary people are!"

"Are you any better in Berbice? Why is your husband such a strait-laced prude, Cornelia?" she laughed. And Cornelia murmured: "It's not that he is a prude, my dear. It's because he is one of the Hard Ones."

At that moment Rose came out and joined them. She had overheard Cornelia's last few words, softly as Cornelia had uttered them, for she uttered a shrill little laugh reminiscent of the Canje days, and said: "Of course, our Dirk is one of the Hard Ones. Poor boy! If only the core of his dear, hard self could have been as hard as the shell he wears, how much happier he would be!"

Dirk saw her eyes in the light from the large glass-shaded candles, and he detected the suffering in their depths. Leaning against the vine-clad latticework, he began to squeeze his hands together slowly. He turned his face away in a gradual way, as though to gaze out through the diamond-shaped window at the garden, but, in actuality, it was to avoid the fumes of the rum in her breath as she related to Cornelia and Elfrida a story she had overheard about Willem and Christina, one evening when she and Graham had been dining at Clara's.

They were having coffee on the back veranda, the following morning, when the alarming news reached Flagstaff.

Rose had just remarked that Graham and Albert must be well on their way up the river, and Luise had begun to say that Rose should spend the rest of the week at Flagstaff, when Edward interrupted her by exclaiming: "Look! Isn't that Larsen coming along the road there?"

They all looked towards the public road, and saw a figure on horseback. Elfrida was certain. "It is Larsen! Out at this hour! He's improving." But Pelham frowned and said: "No laughing matter, Elfrida. Something has happened."

He was right. A few minutes later, Larsen's shortish, thickset figure came lumbering out on to the back veranda. His gloomy face broke into a self-conscious smile as he said in a deep rumbling voice: "I'm sorry to disturb you at your coffee, cousins, but I bring grave news." The smile faded as he added: "The people on Le Resouvenir are preparing to riot, and disaffection is spreading. You should order your overseers to call in all your people from the fields, Pelham. We've got some big trouble on our hands today."

"Sit down, my dear fellow," said Pelham. "Have some coffee and let's hear some of the details. How did you hear of all this?"

Larsen said he wanted to go on to the next place to warn them, but he sat down, nevertheless, to have a cup of coffee. He told them: "Some time about six or half past, at Le Réduit, Simpson's mulatto house servant told Simpson he had overheard the field slaves plotting, at a meeting, to rise up and murder the overseers. Simpson took it for nonsense, but we've all been on the alert this past week, so he investigated as a matter of routine—and he discovered that several of his people have disappeared, and they stole some muskets he had in his tool shed. The shed was broken into last night. Simpson rounded up a few others who were trying to run off into the bush, and he questioned them and learnt that the rising is planned for this evening. After chapel meeting last night they hatched the whole business—and I believe that bounder, Smith, and his wife, knew about it. Yes, I'm firmly convinced they have had a hand in this, Pelham. Heard it on good authority that they were at the chapel with Quamina, who is the ringleader, until nearly eleven o'clock. These damned missionaries——"

"What of Graham?" Dirk interrupted. "Was he with them until eleven?"

"No, no. I heard Graham left at nine—as soon as the service was over. That Laver fellow came for him in a gig, and they went off together at once."

"Anyway," continued Larsen, breathing a little hard now, "that's the position, and Simpson acted swiftly. He sent around warning other places, and he despatched a messenger to Governor Murray. Simpson, as you know, is a burgher officer. You'll have to report, by the way, Pelham. There'll be a muster in Georgetown some time this morning. Meantime, I advise you to call all your people in from the fields. Keep them in their logies until the trouble is put down. Uncle Raphael has already ordered ours in. We've had no trouble with ours yet."

Pelham nodded, rising. "Perfectly correct, Larsen. We never can tell when some of them will try to bolt into the bush. Slaves are scarce enough as it is these days. Thanks for coming to tell us, Larsen. Have some gin before you go."

Pelham was off—and Larsen said he could not wait to have the gin. And, after breaking into another self-conscious smile, he went hurrying out, and they heard his horse galloping away on the other side of the house.

Dirk said: "These confounded politicians in England think they know everything about conditions in the colonies. They go passing their 'humane' laws, and this is the result. The ignorant fools get a hint of the matter, and construe it to mean complete freedom. And now they want to kill us all out of hand. By God! If only Fowell Buxton and Wilberforce and that whining fellow Canning could come here and try to run a plantation for a month or two. See how quickly they'd begin to understand that only the cat-o'-nine-tails can make these slaves work as they ought to." He rose and snapped: "I must get dressed, I'm reporting for duty in the militia."

His uncle laughed. "You are not a burgher of Demerary, my boy. You're from Berbice. The law doesn't require you to report for duty."

Dirk gave him an astounded look. "What does it matter what the law requires, Uncle Edward! Good heavens! I'm a white man and a van Groenwegel. Do you expect me to sit in the house here when trouble is brewing outside, and behave as though I'm a helpless invalid!"

"But you're on holiday, Dirk," said Luise. "And there are soldiers in Georgetown. The situation is not so serious that you need to volunteer for duty."

"Are you forgetting that the van Groenwegels are a fighter family, Aunt Luise?" Rose remarked, adding a little gin to her coffee.

"The van Groenwegels never run!" intoned Cornelia and Elfrida in chorus.

Dirk grunted—then grinned and said: "Very well. Mock me if you care. Nevertheless, I shall still go to Georgetown and volunteer."

As he was moving inside, Luise called after him: "Good luck to you, my boy! But Colonel Wray, the commandant of the militia, doesn't like us at Flagstaff. Your Uncle Edward refused to paint his portrait— and he's a nigger hater. He thinks we should be shot for entertaining Rose here!" Her laughter faded on a sigh. "Ah, my poor Dirk! Grandma Hendri again—I've always said it. Rose, my child, you will stay on for the rest of the week, won't you?"

"Yes, Aunt Luise, I think I will," said Rose. "I'll be less tempted to drink if I remain here. I do nothing but read and drink when I'm at Huis Kaywana."

"Poor child, poor child! I wish I knew what to do to help you."

32

O N the way to Georgetown, Dirk and Pelham passed a group of cavalry moving east, in the opposite direction, and following the cavalry was a carriage in which Pelham recognized Governor Murray and one or two other government officials.

"Murray has acted quickly," Pelham murmured. "A hopeful sign. Sight of the cavalry alone should be enough to frighten the fools back into their right senses."

"Are you certain all is safe on your place?" Dirk asked anxiously.

"Yes. Greaves and Parrott have the situation well in hand. They're armed—and every man, woman and child has been ordered not to stray farther than ten yards out of the logies. They're grumbling, but they've obeyed so far."

The roadway and parade ground at Kingston were cluttered with carriages, and the whole garrison was in a ferment of voices, foot treads and the clatter of arms. A crowd of youngish men stood about outside the militia headquarters—a long, two-storeyed building with a shingled roof that faced north—and several voices hailed Pelham as he and Dirk approached. Pelham introduced Dirk, and everyone began to gather round them, asking for news. "Did you see Murray on his way up, Pelham?" . . . "Is it true they've burnt down Simpson's house?" . . . "Where is that rascal, Smith, and his wife?" . . . "Are your people all right?" . . . Then Dirk felt a touch on his shoulder and turned to see Harvey Hartfield smiling at him. "How do you do, Dirk, old fellah?" Harvey's accent was as English as that of any of the high-ranking regimental officers. "Mother told me you were on holiday. I think you're dining with us some time next week, aren't you?"

Dirk was certain he could make out a distinct resemblance in Harvey's features to Uncle Edward. "Yes. Cornelia said you'd invited us to dinner. It will be a pleasure, I'm sure. You live in Kingston, too, don't you?"

"Oh, decidedly, my dear fellah. Goes without saying. We're next door to Uncle Graeme, as a matter of fact—and not very far from Mother and Father. You have met the pater, by the way, haven't you?"

"The who? Oh, your father! Yes, yes. I've met him," said Dirk, flushing. To his relief, a voice began to bawl: "Fall into line, burghers! Fall in!"

"Begad! Well, we must do our duty, old fellah," said Harvey, moving off. "We shall look forward to seeing you next week."

A number of middle-aged men began to come out of the building, accompanied by uniformed army officers. Dirk recognised Graeme Clackson and John Hartfield, Harvey's official father. Three ragged lines were formed, and a bombastic voice shouted: "Silence! Silence in the ranks!" And Dirk heard somebody mutter: "That perishing coxcomb of a Wray!" Dirk asked the man next to him, a pimply-faced fellow with red hair: "Where is this Colonel Wray?" And the man replied: "You cannot mistake him, friend. Black moustache fit to thatch a dozen logies."

"Silence!" barked the voice again. And this time Dirk saw that it was the officer with the huge, thick, black moustache, and knew this must be Lieutenant-Colonel Wray, the commandant. He was strutting importantly about, by his side a junior officer with a black notebook. His sword clattered rhythmically with every stride he took.

When all the murmurings and mutterings had died away, Colonel Wray came to a halt, surveyed them and began to speak. He told them that this was a preliminary muster. The older men would be excused for the present. The need was not urgent at the moment for every burgher to be under arms. Nevertheless, he was greatly pleased to see the splendid turnout. He offered the compliments of Lieutenant Colonel Goodman, his superior officer, who was at the moment on the East Coast with the Governor's party—and now Captain Fairweather would take the names of all those present, and issue arms to all who were immediately needed for duty.

Colonel Wray stood to attention while Captain Fairweather took down the names. As Dirk called out his name, Colonel Wray started, frowned, glared at Dirk, and interrupted: "Just a moment, Captain! What was that last name?"

The Captain stiffened and said: "Van Groenwegel, sir—Dirk Wilfred van Groenwegel."

Colonel Wray strutted along the line and halted opposite Dirk. "I know of no *Dirk* van Groenwegel in Demerary, sir. Are you from up the river?"

Dirk, crimson, glared at him and replied: "I am from Berbice, Colonel. I am not a burgher of Demerary. But I am volunteering to serve."

"Indeed you are! Huh-huh-ff! Very gallant of you, I'm sure, sir—but the situation is not yet of a gravity that merits the call upon burghers outside of this colony. I offer you my felicitations, but would ask you to fall out." He turned abruptly to Captain Fairweather. "Score out Mr. van Groenwegel's name, Captain."

Dirk's hands clenched, and his eyes blazed with fury and hatred—but he restrained himself. The realisation came to him that to dispute the matter would be more damaging to his dignity than to withdraw at once. He fell out of the line and began to make his way towards where the carriages were parked. Behind him he heard a murmuring along the three lines of men, and knew that the sympathy of them all was with him. He was a planter—and a van Groenwegel.

"Silence!" barked Colonel Wray. "Stop that muttering, damme!"

The heat rose in gauzy waves from the dusty surface of the East Coast road. There was hardly any wind from the sea, and the dust made clouds behind the carriage, heavy and sluggish. Other carriages went past, going towards the town. Every white man, according to law, was compelled to report for duty in the militia. Only the overseers superintending slaves on the plantations were exempt.

When they were passing through Plantation Sparendaam, Dirk saw a carriage stationary by the side of the road, and told the coachman to stop beside it. An elderly man and a lady were in the carriage, and along the driveway a youngish man was approaching. They were evidently waiting for him.

"Good day to you, sir!" greeted Dirk, addressing the man in the carriage. "What is the news from higher up? Have you heard anything fresh?"

"The Governor is still there, my boy. I hear a whole band of them is blocking the road, and armed with sticks and stones and a few muskets. Very ugly situation. Are you from town? What are they doing about it at the garrison?"

"The militia are mustering, sir."

Arrived at Flagstaff, Dirk found the house unusually quiet, and then remembered that the womenfolk had arranged to go to Uncle Raphael's place for the day. He called Susie and had her give him a bath. She breathed hard and wagged her head, and deplored the behaviour of the slaves at Le Resouvenir. "Ow! Why they must mek so much trouble! Guv'nor na tell dem what de law say! No freedom yet."

"Oh, has the Governor explained to them about the new laws? Did you hear that, Susie?" asked Dirk. And the woman nodded, breathed heavily and replied: "Yes, massa. Me hear it from plenty people who come from dat side. Guv'nor Murray mek long speech and explain about de new law. He say it only for us women. No more flogging. So English Parl'ment say. But no freedom for slaves yet."

"Well, I'm relieved to hear the Governor told them. Now there should be no doubts in their minds. They have no excuse for misbehaving themselves any longer."

After a light meal—it was long past breakfast time—he went to his room, fanning his face with his hand and whistling, for the heat was overpowering. In his dressing gown, he paced slowly about, undecided whether to settle down with a book or lie down and doze. The others would not be returning until evening, and his uncle had probably joined Pelham at the garrison. It was unlikely that Uncle Edward would be detained for duty. He would probably spend the rest of the day at Willem's or the Hartfields'.

He yawned and decided on having a siesta. There was no hammock in the room here. He preferred a hammock for a siesta. It was cooler, and he could swing himself until sleep came. There was nothing like swinging gently in a hammock on a hot day. He remembered that Rose had had a hammock slung up in her room, and decided to go in there. The whole house was his for the day, so it did not matter whether he trespassed in anybody else's room. God! What heat!

He left his room and moved along the corridor. Rose's room was two doors away. The door was slightly ajar. He pushed it open and entered —and then he came to a halt and the breath left him. The heat had hatched a mirage. A dream.

Rose was there. She was in the hammock, which was slung in the northeastern corner of the room, near a window. She was fast asleep and without a scrap of clothing. On the floor, under the hammock, the book she had been reading—Miss Austen's novel, *Mansfield Park*; he remembered her talking about it—lay in an untidy clump, as though it must have slipped from her hand when she fell off to sleep. It was much cooler in the room here. The wind made a sudden humming, soft and soothing, and then it died away. He heard the sea—booming far away. A dream.

Her lips were slightly parted. Her head rested on her left arm. Her right hand lay on her stomach. He watched the dark-brown mole at the base of her left breast, and remembered July, 1815. He must rush away quickly before the trembling began, before the inclination to gibber attacked him. He must wake up and weep.

He could not move. He watched the slow rise and fall of the olive breasts. Childbearing had not ruined them. They were still erect and lovely. Suddenly, however, he knew that it was not only desire that moved in him at this instant; his feelings went deeper. A warmth of tenderness and protectiveness spread through him, and a deep pity. He remembered Graham and what she had been suffering these past two or three years, her recent addiction to rum and gin. He remembered the morning not long before his wedding when he had walked with her to the *stelling* at New Signal. The kiskadee uttering its lugubrious cries in the sapodilla trees, and the agony in his spirit as he watched her face . . . Time to wake . . .

"We've spoken about you, Dirk. Only two days ago when I was at Don Diego. She knows. She admitted she knows."

"Knows what?"

"That I'm your true love."

So right. Cornelia knew. Even today she knew. She was too intelligent, too perceptive, not to know. . . . "But for those letters and the obsession they have generated in you, it may have been you instead of Graham who would be insisting on marrying Rose. . . ."

He nodded, smiling. Yes, who could tell? I might have married her. . . .

A musing chuckle escaped him—and he frowned, for he had chuckled aloud. He must be careful not to wake her. He turned to leave.

But it was too late. Her eyes opened. She uttered a soft gasp and sat up.

Neither of them spoke for a moment. His hands began to clench. Then the blood came to her cheeks. She smiled and said: "Dirk. Dirk, my sweet. You're back, then? I didn't expect you back until evening."

The trembling overtook him. "Yes. I—I wasn't accepted by the colonel. Susie told me you were all out—at Uncle Raphael's. I came in

to use your hammock. I . . ." He could say no more. He turned to go.
. . . Only a siesta dream . . .

"Don't go, Dirk. Please." No, it was real. It was her voice. No
mirage.

He halted, his gaze out in the corridor. "Why are you here, Rose?"

"Don't turn your back on me again, Dirk, love. Please."

Beyond the *courida* bushes the sea boomed monotonously, indifferently. Perhaps later in the afternoon there would be thunder in the
south. August thunder.

"I can't laugh as I did in July 1815, Dirk. I've lost the habit. You
used to like my laughter. It used to excite you. Don't turn your back
on me, my sweet."

He turned and was at the hammock in two paces. "My poor Rose!
My sweet true love! God! No, not this time. I won't turn my back on
you this time." The trembling in him now was like a cloud of fulfilment settling through his limbs—a thundercloud wreathing with
heat and murmurous with soothing noise.

They could hear the clock in the dining-room downstairs striking
the hours. It was shortly after three o'clock when she murmured: "I
heard thunder."

He nodded. "I heard it, too. In the south, as usual. August," he murmured.

"August," she murmured. "And it's real, love. We're not dreaming."

"August—seven years ago." He grinned and fondled her. The bed
creaked.

A quiver of mirth ran through her. "I could have killed you that
afternoon."

"Tigress. I could have killed you, too."

At four o'clock, he said: "My poor sweet. Will you promise me
something?"

"Anything. Anything, my love."

"Will you stop this drinking, Rose?" He gripped her shoulders
hard.

"For your sake?"

"For my sake. It hurts *me*, beloved, to see you in a drunken state."

He watched her face. She had a musing look, her eyes narrowed.
He kissed her forehead and her ears and her chin, touched with his
finger the brown mole on her left breast. "For my sake," he repeated.
"Promise." He shook her fiercely.

"It will be hard, Dirk. But after this—yes, I promise. After this I'll have something to console me for months and months to come. Oh, my darling!"

At five o'clock: "And, Rose, love, I'm jealous."

"Pelham?"

"Yes."

She shook her head. "No need. After this—no, dearest. I won't let him."

"I'm selfish. I have no right to be—where you're concerned."

"You have every right. I belong to you, sweet. Every inch of me."

Thunder in the south. The sunshine was red and mild. Five-o'clock sunshine. They could hear carriages going past on the road. And sackies twittering amidst the foliage of the trees. The sea kept on booming.

At six o'clock: "I wish I could have a child, Dirk."

"Are you mad?"

She rubbed her hand over the hairs on his chest. Some of her old laughter quivered through the room. "It's six o'clock. We've loved three times since I woke. Three chances of Dirk the Younger taking root in me."

"That must never happen. Fate won't be so unkind, I'm sure."

"Unkind? It would be heaven for me, sweet. Nothing would give me greater joy than to bear your child. Oh, dearest, don't frown. Say you would be pleased, too. Say you wouldn't mind the black blood in Dirk the Younger."

He grinned. "That wouldn't trouble me. It's the scandal—for you."

"A married woman having a third child? Where should the scandal lie in such an event?"

"What of Albert—dear, good Albert? People are not fools. They must know that you and Graham have ceased to be intimate."

She gave a groan of abandonment. "What do I care about people? What do I care?" She rubbed her cheek against his, pulled at the lobes of his ears, kissed his nose. "What do I care, Dirk, love?" She stroked his hair, glided the tips of her breasts against his chest, her face in an agonised wince of tenderness. "When I dream back on this afternoon, my darling, nothing will seem of any import. Nothing whatever. I *shall* have your child, dearest. I will it to happen. I will it. I feel it happening in me now, now. This instant. Oh, my sweet! How happy I am that I didn't go to Uncle Raphael, after all! Think of what I would have missed! Oh, God! There is Providence in this, Dirk. Why should I care what happens after? To hell with all the people! Love me, sweet. Love me again. It's after six, but we're still alone. Love me, love me!"

33

T H E others did not return until shortly after eight o'clock, by which time Dirk and Rose had bathed and dressed and had a meal. They were sitting in the portico like two respectable people when the sound of carriage wheels came in the driveway. They were relaxed and at great peace. Dirk told her that for the first time in his life he felt at harmony with the world. "Even the family," he grinned, "seems of little importance this evening." Rose nodded and smiled, making no comment. She shut her eyes, and in the candlelight they listened to the sea. Now and then an insect would make a buzzing round one of the glass-shaded candles. The fragrance of flowers moved continuously in the portico in the cool evening air, and now and then a whiff of cane juice intruded, pungent and emphatic. When they heard the carriage Rose opened her eyes and looked at him, and said: "Remember, sweet." He nodded—but a frown came to his face now. "But I don't agree," he murmured. "I think she should know." She shook her head. "No, Dirk. I'm a woman myself. Allow me to know better." He nodded again—but said: "She herself suggested it, my love. She's very fond of you. She said it might help. She said she gave me her permission." She laughed softly. "Never mind what she *said*, Dirk dearest. Allow me to know best. Don't tell her."

"Very well."

A few minutes later Elfrida said that she had heard about the incident at the garrison. Everyone was talking about it. "Graeme was furious. And so was Willem. He's a hateful man, that Colonel Wray."

Dirk scowled and said: "I can afford to ignore such trash."

Cornelia asked: "Did you come back here at once?"

"Yes. I decided it would be better to come back. I had no inclination to call on Willem or the Hartfields."

"I found him mooning about in the garden when I came down after my siesta," laughed Rose. "What a mood he was in!"

Luise laughed. "Never mind! It's just as well. You're on holiday, Dirk. Colonel Wray has done you a good turn."

"Is Pelham on duty tonight?" Rose asked, and Uncle Edward said "Yes, and so is Larsen. Raphael and I may be needed tomorrow, according to what I hear."

"What is the position like now, sir?" asked Dirk.

"Still very troubled," Edward told him. "The Governor may have to declare martial law tomorrow. Several other plantations have become infected with this stupid disease that has attacked the people on Le Resouvenir. Murray told them what the new law was about, but it made no difference."

When they were alone in their room, an hour or so later, Dirk and Cornelia discussed the events of the day. Cornelia stroked his head and said that she was sorry about what had happened at the garrison, and Dirk thanked her for her sympathy, adding with a grin: "And let's hear no more of it, my love. Elfrida has offered me her sympathy, and so has Aunt Luise, and so has Uncle Edward, and no doubt Pelham will when we see him again."

"Didn't Rose offer you hers when you told her of it on returning here?"

"What? Oh—well, of course." He flushed. "Of course she did." As he was hauling on his nightshirt, he added casually: "Why shouldn't she?"

"Why, indeed? By the way, wasn't it odd, dearest? She actually refused when Uncle Edward offered her a tot of rum this evening. Did you notice?"

He gulped, and said: "Yes, yes." And after a hesitation: "I had a long talk with her while you people were at Uncle Raphael's. She's promised me to give up this drinking habit she's cultivated."

She gave him a long stare, but her face was entirely noncommittal. Then she smiled and said quietly: "I told you what a good influence you are in her life, Dirk, dear heart." Could there be a mocking note in her voice? He tried to assure himself it was only his fancy. "How glad I am you were able to have another long talk with her alone."

He stiffened, suspicious. "Cornelia!"

"Yes?"

"Did you purposely persuade her to remain at home today because you thought—because you knew I might have been sent back . . . ?"

He could not finish his sentence. He felt the peace in him beginning to disintegrate.

"No. I swear it, my dearest. At the last moment, she herself decided to stay at home. She said she was not feeling in a sociable mood, and there was Miss Austen's novel she was eager to continue reading."

The tension left him, and relief spread through his spirit. He said quietly: "I believe she will keep her promise." He felt her gaze on him, but somehow he experienced no discomfiture. He was possessed of a lightheaded detachment, an almost ethereal dizziness, as though he might have been under the influence of some drug. There was no guilt in him. Only a low, singing contentment that in some way seemed related to the dull roar of the sea in the darkness beyond the *courida* bushes. He glanced through the window and saw a flash of lightning. Far away in the southeast.

"I believe she will. She's like you, Dirk, sweet. Strong. One of the Hard Ones." This time there could be no mistaking the mockery—but it was her kind of mockery. Good-natured, teasing, entirely lacking in malice.

In bed, he could be attentive towards her without constraint, and with the same old tender fondness—there had never been any wild passion between them—and no tension of fear built up in him concerning his ability to acquit himself in required conjugal fashion, for, fortunately, this was the time of the month when they could not make love. . . . Fortunately, providentially. . . . He found himself smiling in the dark before he fell asleep, remembering six o'clock. . . . "There is Providence in this, Dirk. Why should I care what happens after . . . ?"

Why, indeed? Why should *he* care . . . ? Nevertheless, he did care. And this secrecy. It troubled him. And yet Cornelia herself had suggested . . .

Sleep swept him into the lulling roar beyond the *courida* bushes.

34

T H E next day, Tuesday the nineteenth, the barricades went up. All along the coast spread the alarm that a large body of Negroes had massed in a cotton field near Plantation Ann's Grove, and was preparing to attack the homes of the planters. The rebels, it was rumoured, numbered over two thousand, and were armed with cutlasses and muskets and sticks and stones. "Another 1763!" was the general cry, for the Berbice insurrection had not been forgotten. Here in Demerary in this year 1833, however, there was a difference. The planters resolved that there would be no panic, no running away. They would stand and fight.

Dirk crowed: "They're taking a leaf out of our family's book, I see! Since Kaywana's day the van Groenwegels have stood their ground and fought."

No attack came, however, at Flagstaff nor at any other plantation house. The regular soldiers and the provisional battalion of militia were sent to Ann's Grove, and there was a brief clash, but no real battle. The rebels, from their positions in the cotton fields in the neighbourhood, shouted abuse at the military, demanding their "rights." Parliament in England, they said, had granted them their freedom, and they would not go home in peace until the local government proclaimed them free. A few stones were flung, and a few shots exchanged, with hardly any casualties on either side.

Throughout the night there was skirmishing on both sides of the public road, but no serious clash occurred. When the morning of the twentieth broke, Colonel Leahy, who had been put in command of the combined forces, decided to take decisive action. He advanced towards the main body of the rebels, massed now in the vicinity of Plantation Bachelor's Adventure. Within hailing distance, he warned them that unless they surrendered immediately, he would open fire. Shouts of defiance came in answer. Again the colonel attempted to caution them, but without avail. And now the rebels began to hurl stones and fire upon the military.

Colonel Leahy gave the order, and volley after volley thundered out across the cotton fields. The rebels broke ranks and ran. Leahy and his men pursued them, firing all the while. Within less than three hours the battle was over, with more than two hundred Negroes lying dead in the cotton fields.

The remnants of the rebel mass fled to the bush, and Leahy and his men pursued them, aided by the ever eager Indians. By the end of the week most of them had been caught and brought back. And the trials and public executions began.

Driving along the public road, on their way to Kingston for dinner at Clara's home, Dirk and Cornelia and Rose and Pelham and Elfrida were witnesses to several gruesome sights. The heads of decapitated slaves were stuck on poles and grinned at them as they went past, rigid and bloody. Black corpses dangled by the neck from temporary gibbets erected by the side of the road.

The women averted their faces hurriedly. Dirk said: "Drastic measures were necessary. These sights are disgusting, I admit, but it is as well that the survivors should see what happens to ignorant, rebellious imbeciles who think they can defy law and authority."

"What worries me," frowned Pelham, "is the loss of labour. Over two hundred dead, not including those executed! Do you know what that means in these days of labour scarcity!"

"And I hear," said Elfrida, "that Reverend Mr. Smith never reported for duty in the militia. He was the only man who failed to show his face at the garrison. I'm certain he knew a great deal about the plot the Negroes hatched."

"There is no shadow of doubt about that now," said Pelham. "He knew, and could have warned the Governor days in advance. But no fear! He'll have his just deserts. I heard on good authority that he will be arrested in a day or two."

Rose laughed. "What a shock it will be for Graham when he returns from Ubaree! His dear, good John Smith under lock and key!"

"Left to the Anti-Slavery Party and these missionaries," growled Dirk, "this colony would be destitute and denuded in a matter of weeks. When will they ever learn that you *must* be severe on savages! Halfway measures and milk-and-water talk about humanity and kindliness only unsettle these black baboons. The iron hand—that is what they need. They must be ruled. And ruled with firmness."

Dirk and Rose did not have another opportunity to be alone. Neither of them attempted to engineer such an opportunity. Together with the serenity of spirit they had both experienced since Monday, the eighteenth—the date they would always remember—there had settled in them a resignation to the circumstances of their situation. They both looked back on Monday as a gift from Providence, too good ever to be repeated—the kind of gift that, in any case, could never again be bestowed on them with the same agonising spontaneity and deliciousness.

Edward and Luise held a farewell dinner for Dirk and Cornelia at Edward House, and Rose and Graham were invited. Graham had returned from Ubaree three days before. Raphael and Larsen were among the guests, for they had both long since accepted Rose into the family circle. John and Clara Hartfield and Graeme and Cynthia Clackson were there, too; Graeme was fond of Rose, but Cynthia was still inclined to be distant in her manner.

Dirk had no doubt in his mind that Cornelia had had something to do with the seating arrangements at the dinner, for he found himself between Cynthia and Rose. Cornelia must have known that Cynthia would avoid speaking to him because of Rose's presence on his right, thus leaving him and Rose free to speak to each other without interruption. No one sat at Rose's right. Later, when he asked her, Cornelia confirmed his suspicions.

Neither Rose nor Dirk, however, was inclined to indulge in much conversation. They limited themselves to occasional murmurs. Once she said: "Is this the last time I shall be seeing you for another decade, Dirk?" And he smiled and murmured back: "It may be, my dear." And after a long silence: "I shall write you as well as Elfrida when I return to Berbice." She nodded and said: "I shall write you, too—very long letters." And suddenly, after another long pause: "Do you think Graham would accept an invitation to spend time with us at New Signal, Rose?" She shook her head: "I doubt it—but I would." She gave him a mischievous glance, and he grinned and said: "I think Father and Mother would be pleased to see your two children—and even you. I'm going to think it over." He saw the colour coming to her cheeks. She said: "Who knows, then? There may yet be another Monday the eighteenth, sweet." He frowned and returned: "There

mustn't be, my love. Remember, I live by a stern code. I broke it that
Monday, but it must not become a habit." She smiled and murmured:
"Dearest Dirk. You must never change. Even your stern code I love.
Even the side of you I detest I secretly love—simply because it is you."

In her first letter to him she said: "I still go to the barn to recline
in the hammock and read, all by myself, but now I am not lonely,
because I dream that you are with me. I dream that you are standing
outside the vine-clad windows and spying upon me, too stern and
restrained to enter and surprise me as you did that Monday at Flagstaff. I often take off my clothes and lie naked in the hammock, and
shut my eyes, and imagine you are about to lift me into your arms
and take me into a corner on the dry leaves. There is no need now
for me to drown my misery in rum or gin, for there is no misery to
drown. . . ."

In reply, he told her: "I try to feel guilty, but guilt will not take
shape in me, sweet, and this despite a strong feeling in me that Cornelia knows what happened on that Monday. I have whispered no
word to her, but she is a strange, intuitive soul, and equipped to per-
fection with the ability to conceal her thoughts. Half her charm lies in
her baffling airs and her intense kindliness. I wish I had her capacity for
pity and understanding, and the control she exerts over her emotions.
She has suggested that you and Graham come and spend two weeks
with us at Christmas, bringing the children with you. She has spoken
to Father and Mother, and they are all in favour of the project. Will
you speak to Graham and sound him out on the matter? Should he
decline, would you care to come alone and bring the children? Tell
me in your next letter. . . ."

This was in late September. There was a long delay before she wrote
again. Not, in fact, until towards the end of October did Dirk get a
letter from her, and the instant he began to read it a chilly shudder
of foreboding rippled its way through his spirit. Yet it started quite
innocently.

MY SWEETEST AND MOST PRECIOUS, You must be wondering why I
have been so long in writing to you, and I shall tell you the reason
in a moment, but first let me assure you that I am still happy and
still with you in spirit, and still abstinent from intoxicating spirits. I
have been trying to persuade Graham to come with me and the children to visit you people at Christmas, but he has kept putting me off

for an answer, and yesterday he informed me definitely that it is out of the question for him to travel at Christmas. Dear, good Albert will be coming to town at the merry season, and it goes without saying he will be spending some time at Huis Kaywana. Moreover, Graham says that he should not be happy to inflict the company of the Greenfields upon the illustrious van Groenwegels of New Signal. He said this, however, with great charm and delicate sarcasm. How I loathe his 'delicate' airs and graces! In addition, he is greatly upset, as you may well imagine, over the trial of the Reverend Mr. Smith. The trial, you may have heard, started on the thirteenth of the present month, and is still proceeding. The newspaper reports the matter in some detail regularly, and everyone talks about nothing else. I am sorry for the poor missionary, but I am rather of the mind that he is guilty. He must have known that the slaves were plotting against their masters that Sunday night and even a day or two previously. The evidence proves this beyond doubt. Everyone thinks he will be sentenced to death, and I am inclined to agree that this, indeed, will be the outcome of the trial.

"My sweet, I come now to my reason for delaying to write to you. I am fearful to put pen to paper at this stage, but within me I am seething with such joy as I have never experienced in my life before. Yes, my darling, I delayed on purpose, because I wanted to be sure when I imparted the news to you that Providence had granted me my wish. Dirk, my love, I willed it, and Providence heard me, and it smiled upon me. I am pregnant, Dirk, sweet. Heavens! Were I only there to see the expression on your dear face at this instant! Be it what it may, however, I am still happy beyond what my pen can express. Dear heart! I am blessed and punished at once, for now I shall not be able to come to New Signal at Christmas. Pregnancy is a difficult time for me always. Indeed, I am in bed as I write this, more faint and ill than the the words I write might indicate. . . "

After a sleepless night he decided that he could no longer preserve his secrecy. He handed the letter to Cornelia and asked her to read it.

She read it, and the colour gradually left her face. At one point he saw her eyes narrow in a slight wince, and nearing the end of it she began to bite her lip. Otherwise she expressed no perturbation. She looked at him when she lowered the paper, and her eyes were moist. She smiled faintly and said: "Of course, I knew what happened between you on that Monday in August. I didn't expect you to tell me, dearest. That was one secret you had every right to keep between you and her."

He looked out of the window. They were in the northeastern room, and it was late afternoon. The sunshine was not so fierce as it had been an hour ago. On the edge of the compound where the sapodilla and orange trees used to be, there were mango trees now. The sapodillas and oranges had died. It was Jacob's idea that he should have mangoes planted. He murmured: "You never gave a hint that you knew. Weren't you jealous?"

"Yes," she said quietly, sighing. "Very jealous, Dirk."

"You didn't chide me. Why didn't you sulk, or show in some way——?"

"Because I knew it would have been fatal," she interrupted quickly. Her voice was husky, and it was evident that she was having difficulty in controlling her feelings. "Had I chided you, had I sulked, I should have driven you from me. You would have gone closer to her. Men do not feel well disposed towards wives who chide them and assume sulky airs. I want to keep you, Dirk—not lose you. Before we were married I knew how you felt about Rose. Would it have helped my own cause if I had kept reminding you by scoldings and sulks where your true love lay? No, my dear. I knew better than that. I have made a study of human beings—and of you in particular. I knew what would happen in Demerary when you met Rose again—or, better, I knew what *could* happen. To have tried to prevent you from meeting her would have augmented in you the yearning to be with her. It would have sharpened your desire for her. So I even abetted your meetings with her. It was better so—for you both. I could put myself in her place, dear. Poor Rose! And yet lucky Rose! How happy you must both have been on that Monday afternoon! Why should I hate you, or chide you, for being happy!" She was regarding him, smiling and trying to blink away her tears which now were running down her cheeks. She shook her head. "I'll never do that. I'm glad you were happy. And don't you see how she writes, Dirk? She *wants* to have your child. This is the final joy. Now it will matter naught to her that Graham has lost interest in her."

He had no words to counter this, so held his peace.

They stood side by side, looking out at the afternoon. From somewhere on the other side of the house the children's shrieks came on the air. Now and then the voice of the nurse could be heard admonishing them.

A warm wind came suddenly from the northeast—from the direction of Don Diego. It held the sourish smell of drying coffee berries. They could hear the splash of oars on the Creek—and the flapping of wings. Probably a *hannaqua* winging its clumsy way from one clump of overhanging bush to another. A whiff of tobacco smoke drifted up from the portico beneath them. Storm was down there reading and smoking a cigar and awaiting the call to dinner. His before-dinner cigar was becoming a habit nowadays. Elizabeth sometimes teased him about it.

"Do you know if Elfrida suspects anything?"

"She knows how you and Rose feel about each other—but I don't think she suspects what happened on the Monday in August."

The gong was being rung for dinner.

"She will soon know—and I shall sink in her esteem."

"I don't think so." She touched his wrist. "She admires you for your strength—but she recognises that you are human. Let us go down for dinner."

35

I N all the seven years past, Sarah Hubert had never once attempted to take advantage of the fact that her daughter was married to the master of Huis Kaywana. She had kept in the background, running her shop as before, and only, occasionally, and when it was convenient for Rose, visiting the house. She never showed herself when company was present, and never entered the sitting-room. More than once Graham invited her to dine with Rose and himself, but she refused. She thanked him, and said: "It is very kind of you, Mr. Graham, but such is not the custom. I am black. I was once a slave. You must never let anyone black sit at your table to eat. It will lower you in the sight of your equals, and I wish to see you and Rose prosper in the society of this colony." Graham had stared at her blankly, incredulously, unable to say anything, and she had smiled and said: "I'm older than you, my young man. Allow me to know best. Mr. Hubertus would have understood. He and I understood many things that others could not."

During Rose's difficult pregnancies Sarah would often come and attend upon her in her room. She had been present at the birth of both children. She was on a visit at Huis Kaywana early in November when Rose told her that she was again pregnant. Rose was in bed in her room.

Sarah showed surprise at the news. Her fearless gaze—Rose had inherited this from her mother—became fixed on the girl, and after a pause, she said: "Have you started to have relations with Mr. Graham again?" And Rose, though in the throes of nausea, returned her stare, alert and arrogant, and replied: "That is a strange question to ask me, Mother."

Sarah was not abashed in the slightest degree. Her face, if anything, grew stern. "I think not, Rose. It is a natural question. The whole town and countryside knows that Mr. Graham has other friendships, and despises women."

Rose was in no condition to fight the issue. She nodded and said: "You may as well know, then. It is not his child."

Sarah remained very still, then she rose and said: "You have committed adultery, child. Have you told Mr. Graham that you are in this state?"

"No."

"You must tell him at once."

"I shall tell him when I choose, Mother."

"No, child. He is downstairs in the sitting-room. He must be told now—without a moment's delay."

"Are you going to handle my private affairs for me? Since when?"

Sarah smiled, in no way put out. She said: "It is because I wish you well, Rose, and desire to see you respected by the highest in this society that I speak like this. Mr. Hubertus always said that no matter how vile an act we commit we must face it with courage, and all will be well. It's a coward's way, Mr. Hubertus said, to conceal our knavery, and cowards perish in misery and shame."

"I'm not afraid to tell Graham, if that's what you mean."

"Then tell him now." She began to move towards the door. "I shall go down and call him up here. I shall say that you have something to tell him."

Rose shrugged. "Very well, Mother. I'm feeling far too ill to argue."

Two minutes later, when her mother returned with Graham, Rose put down her bottle of smelling salts and smiled weakly. "What were you doing, Graham? Writing a letter to dear, good Albert?"

Graham tittered. "As it happens, my dear, I was doing precisely that. I understand you are not feeling very well. And Sarah here tells me you want to speak to me about something. I am all attention."

"I'm pregnant. That's what I wanted to tell you."

He blinked, then frowned, and his hands came together in a light clasp. "I'm afraid—did I hear aright?"

Behind him, Sarah stood, like a solemn sentinel, her arms folded, her face noncommittal but exuding strength. It was almost as though she felt the presence of Hubertus' ghost beside her, mocking but approving.

"Yes, Graham. Your ears have not played you false. I'm pregnant."

He nodded slowly, paling a trifle. His smile now was unnatural.

"So! You are pregnant." He gave Sarah a quick, uneasy glance, then looked at Rose and said: "No doubt, I must presume that this is an addition to Pelham's family?"

She smiled—and her eyes glimmered with pure hatred, undisguised venom. "You are wrong, Graham," she said. "It's Dirk."

"Dirk!" The blood came to his face, then receded.

"Yes, Dirk."

He was quite still for a moment, then he uttered a low, hoarse sound and lunged forward, caught her by the throat. "You little scheming wanton! Dirk! Of all people, Dirk! That callous, cold-blooded reptile!"

"Mr. Graham!"

Graham released her and drew back. He gave Sarah a distracted glance, his head trembling. "Did you hear that, Sarah? My brother Dirk! I shall never forgive her for this. Had it been Pelham I should have overlooked it—but Dirk! Father in Heaven! What a victory for him! How he must be sneering at me, and congratulating himself on his cleverness!"

"Do you wish me to leave your house, Graham? I can go to Flagstaff."

"And create a scandal? No. You will remain here." He clenched his hands. The old haunted, mad light was in his eyes. He muttered: "Dirk, Dirk. Heavens!" seeming suddenly to have become unaware of other human presence in the room. He began to wag his head. "Dirk, Dirk. Heavens!", seeming suddenly to have become unaware wandered out of the room, muttering to himself all the while.

The shock soon wore off, however, and within a fortnight he was himself again—but he never came near her room, never inquired after her health. On the few occasions when she was able to leave her room she went to the old barn and reclined in her hammock, and read the books with which Clara always kept her supplied. John was also a great reader, and had a standing order with several book publishers in England. Every ship brought a selection of novels and other works. Clara came to dine at Huis Kaywana every other Wednesday, and invariably brought with her a parcel of books.

In a letter towards the end of that month, November, Dirk wrote saying that he had told Elfrida about her pregnancy. "I have told her that I am responsible, and have asked her to be kind to you. I have asked her to visit you at least once a week to keep you cheerful, and I know she will accede to my wishes."

The day after this letter came, Elfrida arrived, concerned and sympathetic, and sat with her in her room for half the morning. Graham was not at home. He had gone to Georgetown to see if he could obtain permission to visit Mr. Smith in prison. The day before, Mr. Smith had been sentenced to death. In fact, after Elfrida had discussed Dirk's letter and Rose's condition, their conversation, for a long while, became centred on the missionary's trial. It was the one theme of every conversation all over the colony. Both Rose and Elfrida agreed that he should not have been sentenced to death. "Poor man," sighed Elfrida. "I hear he is not in good health." And Rose nodded. "Yes. I've heard that, too. They have been too harsh on him. He should have been censured and released."

Before she left, Elfrida promised to come every week. Rose thanked her. "I shall look forward to seeing you. Sometimes I wonder if you haven't a soft place in your heart for Dirk, too, Elfrida dear." And Elfrida's round, dimpled face pinkened as she returned: "A very soft place, Rose. From the time I met him at that dinner in this house, years ago, I've felt tenderly for him." She chuckled and patted her huge thighs. "But, of course, I have never feared any indiscretions. Look at my size, dear. Can you imagine any man but my husband attempting to make overtures to me?" Her voice was entirely free of bitterness, and Rose smiled and said: "I can see why you are so happy. You never yearn for what you feel you cannot have. Kiss Francis for me when you get home."

At the door, Elfrida turned and said: "Only Francis, I know. Dirk's favourite—and, of course, yours. How alike you two are!"

In April, labour pains set in prematurely, and Dr. Hepburn gave as his opinion that there would be a breech presentation. Sarah had messages sent to Clara and Elfrida, at Rose's request, and Clara and Elfrida arrived within less than two hours. This was in the late afternoon. By seven o'clock Rose's condition was such that Elfrida decided to write Dirk.

The agony lasted all night. The doctor had proved right. It was a breech presentation. At shortly before six the following morning the child, a girl, was born. It died an hour later, and Rose's condition was critical.

At about eight o'clock, out of her coma of exhaustion, Rose smiled up at Elfrida and murmured: "Terrible—but I'm happy, Elfrida. It was worth the ordeal. My darling Dirk! Is it a girl—or a boy?"

Elfrida glanced in desperation at Clara on the other side of the bed, and Rose seemed to detect something was wrong. She tried to raise herself, but Clara and Elfrida both pressed her down. "You mustn't move, Rose dear," said Clara. "Dr. Hepburn says you must be very quiet if you wish to get well."

"But the baby—Dirk's and mine. What's the matter? Where is it?" She began to glance round in a panic. "Hasn't it been washed yet? Is it in the next room? What have you done with my child? I want to see it."

"Rose, don't upset yourself, dear," Elfrida pleaded.

At length, they had to tell her. She went grey. She shut her eyes, and moaned softly. It was several minutes before she spoke, and then all she said was: "Providence wasn't so kind, after all."

Clara rested her hand on her forehead in an attempt to console her, murmuring: "You mustn't worry over it, my dear. It's God's will."

Rose smiled. "Is it? Strange God. Like Dirk, I am a trifle doubtful about His authenticity. Dirk said once that God is the special property of the missionaries and the Anti-Slavery Party." There was a note of hysteria in her voice.

"Don't excite yourself by too much talking, Rose," said Elfrida.

"It doesn't matter, Elfrida," Rose replied. "All is over now. God's will, was it? Now it is *my* will to depart in peace. I shall enjoy dying."

Two days later, when Dirk arrived, she was very low. The delirium stage had passed. A lassitude had settled over her. Dr. Hepburn said she would not last out another night. "Yet," he told Elfrida, "I believe she could recover if she assumed a more positive attitude. I have done all I can for her, but she won't exert her will to rally. It is pitiable."

Colour came back to her cheeks when she saw Dirk. She smiled and said: "You have come in time, my beloved. I'm so glad."

Dirk scowled and told her: "I wish I could shake you, Rose. The doctor says you're deliberately languishing away. You're not fighting to live."

"Why should I, my darling? My child is dead. Yours and mine—my treasure that I'd dreamed of all through my miserable pregnancy. The one incentive for me to exist has been taken from me. I am happy to die."

He made a growling sound, held her hand and said: "God damn you, you're of the Old Blood! Do you forget? A daughter of Cousin Hubertus. Never mind the black blood in you—you're a van Groenwegel, just the same. And one of the Hard Ones—like me. Our sort don't give in, Rose. We're fighters. Like Kaywana. And old Willem in 1666. And Hendri and the others up the Canje. You *must* fight. You can't let a thing like this drive you to your death."

"You'd be disappointed in me?"

"Most certainly I would be. I'd feel desolated. Come along. Tell me you'll fight, my love. Fight death. Fight the world. Fight destiny. The van Groenwegels never run. You know our motto."

"What have I to exist for after this, my darling Dirk? I see only dismal emptiness ahead of me. Reading in the old barn. No husband. Dirk far away in Berbice. Perchance more rum and gin to drown my misery and loneliness. Is that what I should fight to live for?"

He gripped her hand hard and growled: "Don't be a fool. I'll still be there, won't I? You're always welcome at New Signal."

"After this? Would Cornelia have me there? And your parents?"

"Certainly they would. You know how fond Cornelia is of you. And Father and Mother would be only too pleased to see you and their two grands upon whom they have never set eyes. Come on. You must fight. You *must* live, Rose."

A sigh, like a miniature earthquake, quivered through the limp mass that was her body. She shut her eyes, and was silent for several minutes. Once she muttered: "You'll still be there," her voice dreamy and weak and ill. Then suddenly she opened her eyes again and smiled. "Very well, sweet. It may be too late, but I shall from this instant fight and fight—for your sake."

Two days later she was pronounced out of danger and on the way to complete recovery. And Graham heaved a great sigh, and said: "She has sinned, but I prayed for her, poor soul. There is nothing like prayer."

Throughout the crisis he had been simperingly cordial to everyone, even to Dirk. Indeed, he had welcomed Dirk to Huis Kaywana with a gushing affability. He had patted him on the shoulder and cried: "Welcome! Welcome, you old sinner! I have forgiven you. No ill feelings whatever!"

Dirk discovered that his contempt for his brother had turned into pity. How could one, thought Dirk, feel anything but pity for such

hopeless naïveté, such weak sentimentality and unreserved effeminacy!
At this time, especially, there was every reason to be sorry for him,
for, apart from Rose's trouble, he had undergone great emotional
strain as a result of Albert's illness. Albert had been brought down
from Ubaree only a fortnight before suffering from what seemed to
be blackwater fever; his life had been despaired of, but he had recovered. And not many months ago, there had been the other emotional
storm brought about by the death of the Reverend Mr. Smith in
prison. Sentence of death passed in November had not been carried
out, pending an appeal, but in the meantime the poor fellow, who
had been suffering from tuberculosis, died in February, several weeks
before the order granting him a reprieve had been received. Graham
had grieved for months.

On his way back to Berbice, Dirk was in a very chastened mood.
He travelled by sea, for the long rainy season had set in, and the coast
roads were in no condition for comfortable travel. As a rule, he prided
himself on his ability to foresee the future, to envisage the pattern of
events to come, in respect to his own family and relatives and even
of the colonies and their economic prospects. On this occasion, however, he admitted himself balked. No picture of the near future would
take shape. He was resolved to keep his family intact. Nothing must
cause a break between himself and Cornelia; there must be no repetition of the eighteenth of August. Yet he felt it his solemn duty to see
that Rose was made happy; he had encouraged her to go on living,
and had promised to give her the freedom of his home. There could be
no going back on that promise. And in any case, what he felt for her
was too big to be ignored. He would never be happy himself unless he
could succeed in making her happy. But there lay the snag. What
could he do to make her happy? She would be content with nothing
less than his physical union with her—and that he ruled as forbidden.
No, try as he might he could not visualise the future course of events.
    He welcomed the presence aboard the sloop of two fellow passen-
gers, both planter acquaintances. They took his mind off the problem
by involving him in a heated discussion on the present state of things
in the colonies. Only a few weeks before, Governor Murray had been
deprived of office—chiefly through the East Coast insurrection of the
year before, coupled with the handling of the trial of the Reverend
Mr. Smith, whom the Anti-Slavery Party in England now looked upon
as a martyr—and the new Governor, Major General Sir Benjamin

D'Urban, now hardly a week in Demerary, had dropped a bomb. The Home Government, he had informed the colonists, had instructed him to introduce into the Court of Policy a bill proposing that slaves should have the right to purchase their own freedom, with or without the consent of their masters. Protests were arriving in Georgetown from every corner of Demerary-Essequibo and Berbice.

Dirk snorted and said: "It's no surprise to me, Hesketh. I foresaw it all years and years ago. I warned my own relatives at Huis Kaywana since July 1815. They laughed at me, but I knew I was right. Take it from me, that Anti-Slavery Party will not be satisfied until every slave in these two colonies is set free to do as he pleases. It's coming. You say D'Urban is on their side, de Groot? I don't believe it. D'Urban is taking instructions from his Government as a soldier takes orders from his superiors in rank. Personally, I believe he is on our side, just as Murray was—but time will settle that issue. We shall see."

De Groot sniffed. "Little chance of his being able to side with us openly when we've got that spying, officious fool of a representative of the Anti-Slavery Party right in Demerary, always whining about the 'wrongs' and 'injustices' we're supposed to be inflicting on 'the poor souls'! Protector of Slaves! I wish some of these ultra-humane Englishmen would spend a few months on the spot to see what happens among the slaves. See how they would behave if they were in our places and had to cope with the problems we have to tackle!"

Dirk grunted. "That fellow who calls himself the Protector of Slaves needs protection himself, if you were to ask me. A more blind, sentimental, befuddled fool it would be difficult to imagine. The British may have done us a lot of practical good by taking over these colonies. We've made immeasurable progress under their rule, I won't deny, but by God! If only they could be sensible and stop showering us with their sentimentality and humane ideals!"

When Rose and her children arrived at New Signal about a month later, the furore in the colonies was at its height. The Court of Policy refused to pass the bill, and the newspaper called *The Colonist* launched such a savage attack on the Home Government that Governor D'Urban was compelled to suppress it. Rose told Dirk, however, that this act of D'Urban's was merely a stratagem. "He is trying to show the Protector of Slaves and the Anti-Slavery Party in England that he is a good administrator who wants to carry out the orders of the Home Government, but secretly he is on our side. His policy is evidently to tread a cautious path between the planters and the Anti-Slavery Party."

They were in the carriage on their way to New Amsterdam, for the pathway linking the Canje plantations with the town had now been so much improved that carriages could travel on it. Tent-boat journeys to and from town were less frequent. Because of the rains, however, the going was very muddy.

The two children were with them, for they were on their way to visit Rose's adopted mother, Mrs. Clarke. At the peak of good health again, Rose looked her old lovely, desirable self—and she was happy. Once she touched his hand, smiled and said: "You're pensive. Don't trouble, sweet. I'm not upsetting myself about the future. You sounded so pessimistic in your last letter. I've devised the habit of contenting myself with the happiness of the present day. You try to do the same, Dirk." He nodded, squeezing her arm, and after a silence, she murmured: "I have something to tell you—but later. On our way back, perhaps."

Mrs. Clarke received them with great joy. She was not, as a rule, an emotional woman, but her eyes grew moist when she hugged the children. They had dinner with her, and at about six o'clock, Rose suggested Dirk's taking her to pay a brief call on Jacob and his family. "We can leave the children with Mama, Dirk, and call back for them in an hour's time."

"You won't have to persuade me to keep them for you," said Mrs. Clarke, taking Ernestine on to her knee. "You can leave them overnight if you care."

Dirk laughed. "She couldn't do that, I'm afraid. Father and Mother would call out the garrison to have them fetched back to New Signal."

The Fricks lived in one of the few buildings in New Amsterdam that could be described as imposing. It was three-storeyed, and situated on the eastern side of what had once been known as the Water Path or Water Street, but which now had been made up into a good carriage road and called The Strand. It was the commercial section of the town, and the Fricks' house commanded an excellent view of the harbour. The lower story consisted of a dry-goods shop that bore a sign reading FRICK & GREEN, *Dry Goods Merchants*. Jacob and his family and his parents-in-law lived in the two upper stories. The shop was managed by Henry Cole, the young man who had married Joanna Green, Jacob's sister-in-law, and by old Benjamin Green himself. Jacob was still in charge of Dirk's sawmills and timber concern (as well as shipping manager, for Jacob had persuaded Dirk to secure a sloop and a schooner for intercolony trade; their ships plied between Surinam as well as Demerary and Barbados).

Jacob's home was furnished and decorated like that of any white planter's or merchant's, and his way of life was no different.

"See how Jacob is prospering?" said Dirk, as he and Rose were admitted into the long gallery by a black servant girl. "And his isn't the only coloured family, either, rising in the world. There are quite a number of them in this town. All battling to live up to planter standard, and succeeding. One Mr. Harper, an educated fellow from Georgetown, has started a small school—private school for the sons of coloured gentlemen. Negroes not admitted."

"We shall not see it," smiled Rose, "but the society of these colonies will be an interesting one in another fifty or sixty years. There'll be an intermediary class of ladies and gentlemen of my complexion and racial admixture."

"It's virtually there already, my love. Ah! Here's the devil's godson!"

Tough, burly, even with the suggestion of a paunch, Jacob appeared. The floor vibrated under his powerful tread. But his grin was no different.

"My dear Rose! I heard you'd come this morning. Trust this unpredictable monkey to bring you round unannounced!"

"Give him a cuff for me in that paunch of his, Rose," said Dirk. "He's envious of me because I've remained lean like a monkey."

"He's only changed in size," smiled Rose, "but otherwise he's the same."

And then Millicent joined them, voluptuous, but not yet ungainly, of a dark olive, with a round, good-natured face. Her smile was shy and hesitant, for she had not yet cultivated the ease and poise of a lady. Dirk could not help contrasting her with Rose, who was always so relaxed and sure of herself.

They spent a pleasant hour together, reminiscing about the old days at New Signal and at Millicent's old home on the edge of the Winkel district, in the northeastern part of the town.

"Remember how you wanted to marry me off to Rose, Dirk?"

"Thank heaven she was spared such a fate," growled Dirk, casting Millicent a look of heavy sympathy. "Speaks well for your constitution, Millicent, that you've survived to see this day. He had designs on you since you were ten, did you know?" Millicent smiled and blushed, and said: "I think that's an exaggeration, Dirk. He didn't know me when I was ten."

Rose laughed and said: "Dirk and Jacob are still boys at heart."

"I don't believe they'll ever grow up," Millicent said. "When they're seventy they'll still be taunting each other as they do now."

Jacob and Millicent took them upstairs to show them the children, who was settling down in their beds. There were five of them—"I've beaten him by one," said Jacob, with a glance at Dirk—and of the two girls, Cynthia, the four-year-old, was Dirk's favourite. Dirk lifted her out of her cot and said, "What a lovely little bundle, isn't she, Rose? Millicent deceived him on this occasion. Jacob couldn't possibly have fathered a child so pretty. Tch, tch!"

Of a dark olive, like Millicent, Cynthia had long, wavy dark hair like Rose's, large grey-brown eyes, and a captivating smile. There was little of the negroid in her features.

On their way back to Mrs. Clarke's cottage, Dirk said: "She's going to be a regular siren, that child." He touched her hand. "So much like you, my love; that's why I adore her as I do."

He watched her face in the dusk. She smiled faintly, staring ahead. Then she said, without looking at him: "Remember I said I had something to tell you?"

"Yes. You did say so. What is it?"

"Dr. Hepburn pronounced that as a result of what I went through with that last child it is virtually out of the question that I could prove pregnant again."

He felt the evening air suddenly chilly against his cheek. He murmured: "Did he say that?" And she nodded. "Yes. He explained in rather unintelligible medical terms—but I gathered it was something to do with a prolapsed uterus."

They fell silent, listening to the clack-clack of the horse's hoofs, smelling the sweetish scent of the leather upholstery.

"You know why I mention this, don't you, Dirk, love?"

He nodded. He took a deep breath and told her: "But it must not happen between us again, Rose. No. We played with fire last August —and look how badly *you* were burnt, my dear. We must be strong, Rose. Strong. Another conflagration may destroy us all. We must guard against such a disaster."

Outwardly, during the next few weeks of her stay, she gave the impression that she had accepted the situation for what it was. She made no attempt to inveigle him into any indiscretion. Inwardly, however, she had not surrendered, Dirk could sense; her eyes often betrayed her, especially when he happened to be alone with her—and Cornelia continued her policy of giving them many opportunities to be alone. So much so that Rose remarked to her, when she was alone with her one morning in the southeastern room: "You're brave, Cornelia, my dear—much braver than I would have been, in your place." And Cornelia nodded and replied: "Behind my bravery I tremble with cowardice, if you only knew!" They stared at each other, their cheeks slowly flushing, then Rose smiled and said: "Dirk has always told me how fond you are of me." And again Cornelia nodded. She said: "That is true, but you mustn't give me credit for it. I think if Dirk hadn't felt about you as he did I wouldn't have been fond of you. My feelings for you have been fashioned by his." She laughed and added: "Oddly enough, there are times when I identify myself with you. This happens when I'm in the depths of despair. I try to feel I am you, and try to imagine how devastating an experience it must be to see him take fire as he glances at me, to feel him tremble when he touches me. I'm a greater fool than you think, Rose dear."

Rose brushed quickly at her eyes, murmuring as she averted her face: "You are not a fool." They both sat in their chairs, staring out of the window at the grey, rainy morning. It was after coffee, and they were in négligé. Dirk had gone to town, and Storm and Elizabeth were downstairs in the sitting-room with their grandchildren and the nurses. The turpentine scent of mango blossoms was in the air, mingled with the reek of running water and sodden grass.

Abruptly Rose got up and said: "Cornelia, you know, I feel as desperate as you do sometimes. Of late—this past day or so—I have been considering something. I didn't mean to tell you, but now I know I must. You must decide for me. You deserve to." She hugged her morning gown closely around her body, as though the chill in the air had just penetrated to her skin. She seemed to steel herself, then said: "I'm thinking of ceasing to be Mrs. Greenfield, and going back to being a seamstress in New Amsterdam."

Cornelia paled a trifle, but said nothing.

Rose watched her face, tense. They both seemed to listen to the rain on the roof. Then Rose said quietly: "You're alarmed, aren't you?"

"Are you serious, Rose?"

"Yes. I would do it. I've spoken to Mama, and she would be pleased to have me live with her again. She has heard about Graham's effeminacy. Like yourself, she is fond of me, and she sympathises with my position."

Cornelia nodded. Her hands were clasped tight in her lap.

"You know what it would mean if I came back to live in New Amsterdam?"

Cornelia looked at her suddenly. "Have you spoken to Dirk about this yet?"

"No. And I'm glad I haven't." Rose dropped down before her and gripped her thighs hard. "Cornelia dear, tell me. You wouldn't want that, would you? You wouldn't be able to bear sharing him with me, would you? Tell me frankly."

Cornelia shook her head. "No. I wouldn't be able to bear it, Rose."

"Very well. That is enough. I'm fond of you, too, my dear."

A long silence came upon them after that, Cornelia squeezing her hands together in her lap and watching the erratic progress of a black ant on the floor, Rose standing in the middle of the room, hugging herself, her head slightly tilted upwards, her gaze on the ceiling, as though she were listening to the monotonous dribble of the long-wet-season rain on the shingled roof, and communing with it.

The day before she returned to Georgetown, she and Dirk went for a walk along the bank of the canal, aback, and the weather that day was hot and sunny, though the ground was very muddy from the heavy rain of the night before. They went barefooted, sloshing through the mud as they had often done in their childhood days. She had to keep her skirt and petticoats held halfway up her shins, and he had rolled his trousers up to his knees. There was no one to see them, for it was late afternoon, and the overseers and the slaves had all gone in from the fields. The punts lay idle, moored to the bank of the canal, empty and awaiting the next reaping of canes.

The tamarind tree was still there, thick-trunked and sturdy, showing no signs that it meant to yield to the years. They talked about it, reminiscing, and he told her about the one at Don Diego. "Lightning once struck it, but it's still there." They talked about the larks they had had under it, with Cornelia and Jacob—and the picnics. Then suddenly she gave him a look, a strange glitter in her eyes, mischievous and teasing and a little lascivious, and said: "And it was under there you first had Cornelia."

He flushed. "Did she tell you of that?"

She nodded. "Yes. That shows you how close in each other's confidence we have been, Dirk—and still are." Then she told him of the talk she and Cornelia had had in her room two or three weeks before.

He listened with a vaguely stunned air, and after she had finished, said: "You weren't serious, Rose? Would you really have gone back to your dressmaking with Miss Henson?"

She nodded. "Yes. I was serious, sweet. I would have done it—and I know I would have broken down your resistance one fine day. Not next week, perhaps, nor even the following week—but perhaps on the eighteenth of August—or of September—or October." She laughed, and patted his cheek with her fingers. "Yes, I'm conceited enough to feel I would have managed it."

He frowned and muttered: "There is no conceit involved in that."

She looked up into the fine-leafed foliage of the tamarind tree, and suddenly hugged herself as though a shiver had passed through her body. "No regrets, dearest. That is the way it must be. Back to Kaywana—and to my hammock in the old barn. Books and books and books and . . ."

"Well?"

She shook her head slightly, watching the black water in the canal. "Oh, I don't know. I shall try to be strong, but rum and gin do help sometimes."

"You promised me not to go back to that habit, Rose."

"Certainly, certainly. I shall try to be strong, I tell you. I've kept my promise up to now, haven't I, love?"

It was getting dark, and the crickets were shrieking around them, making so high and shrill a noise that it created a background pall of silence—a screen of vibration against which their own voices sounded clear and significant.

"I still cannot envisage what the future for you will be like," he said, and gripped her roughly, impulsively, and kissed her, his head in a tremble.

She rubbed her cheek against his, and murmured, with a chuckle: "I shall write a long letter to you, and you will write a long letter in reply, and I shall write again, and you will write again, and meanwhile our children will be getting older, and we shall be getting older ourselves." She stopped speaking abruptly, for the tears had come. She withdrew from his arms and said that it was time they went back to the house. "Let us not try to see into the future, my darling. Let us henceforth only keep looking into the past—and seeing nothing but hot August Mondays, with the sound of the sea in the distance, and a clock striking the hours beneath us. Three o'clock. Four o'clock. Five . . ."

36

SHE had hardly been back at Huis Kaywana a month when Pelham once more began to throw out ensnaring feelers. As on former occasions, they were very discreet, very unobtrusive, but they were unmistakable. She pretended to be unaware of them, but that did not discourage him. At Christmas, Clara and John Hartfield brought Harvey and his wife to dinner—it was the first time Harvey had dined at Huis Kaywana since Graham's marriage—and Harvey, too, began to cast hungry glances at her. One morning when she was driving through Georgetown, Harvey was standing at the entrance to a large mercantile house, and he actually smiled at her and lifted his hat, breaking off his conversation with a business acquaintance to do so. She glanced back and saw his gaze following the carriage—a distinct indiscretion, for the street was crowded, and Newtown was at its busiest. Within an hour gossip would be at work.

A week later, she told Dirk in a letter: "He certainly lacks Pelham's capacity for discretion. Elfrida says she has heard it rumoured that his wife is in a pique over the incident in Newtown, and this is probably true, for she did not accompany him to dinner at Clara's two nights ago. Graham, too, has begun to throw out sarcastic remarks. Not that these affect me in the slightest. The truth of the matter is that Harvey only amuses me. Not in my wildest flights of fancy could I see myself yielding to his advances. . . . You ask if I am happy. It would be an untruth to say that I am. I exist in a limbo, resigned and, sometimes, content and assuaged by the memories that mean so much to me. Moments there are, however, when I simmer within me, sweet, and then hysteria threatens to overtake me. I do my best to control these fits of unrest, but one day they may get the better of me. I am strong, as you have said, but my strength is human. . . ."

A new admirer appeared in the form of the children's tutor, a man of about forty called Sidney Heffer. He was an Englishman who had come over from Trinidad, where he had recently been attached to the Secretariat; he had resigned for reasons not revealed, and was now earning his living as a tutor. He was of medium height, like Dirk, and roughly of the same build, and very masculine, but there was something untrustworthy about his grey eyes. He could not meet her gaze for long. On the other hand, he was a brilliant conversationalist, and he was widely read. She sometimes sat with him on the bench near the honeysuckle arbour, after breakfast, and they would talk about books they had read and of the people he had met in Trinidad who had interested him. He was a good raconteur.

"Nevertheless," she told Dirk in a letter in June that year, 1825, "he is not the kind of man I should like to invite to accompany me into the old barn. My spirit does not take to him."

Dirk replied: "I note, my dear, that you express definite feelings in respect to both Harvey and Mr. Heffer, but you say nothing about Pelham. Must I assume that you have no aversion to my dear cousin, and that it is a mere matter of discretion that forbids you from being friendly with him?"

She replied: "As you would prefer me to be frank, Dirk, love, I may tell you this: I like Pelham, and have always done so. He attracts me as a man, and, indeed, but for your visit to Demerary two years ago I am fairly certain I should have yielded to him. There! I have brought the matter in the open, but I believe you already knew that I have never despised him nor felt that he would not have made me a satisfactory lover. . . ."

One Saturday in July—she was spending the weekend at Flagstaff— she was reclining in the hammock on the back veranda, after breakfast. The others had gone upstairs to their rooms. It was very hot and humid. Rain had fallen heavily all the morning, and now the sun shone from a sky patchy with grey-white clouds. She was swinging herself gently and beginning to feel sleepy when footsteps sounded in the dining-room, and Pelham suddenly appeared on the veranda.

She did not sit up, but she tensed. He held her arm, smiled down at her and said in a whisper that she was accustomed to now: "I'll never stop hoping, so you needn't try to avoid me as you've been doing these past few weeks."

She said nothing. She smiled faintly, staring up at the ceiling.

"Somehow," he whispered on, "I'm going to arrange it for us to be together at some time, in some spot." He was not smiling now; he was staring down at her, his eyes with the same light Dirk had seen in them at dinner one afternoon two years before. He turned his head and glanced inside, alert, but the house was silent with the silence of siesta time. He uttered a soft gasp, and bent and kissed her throat— and she did not say him nay, did not stir, and did not respond in any way. She remained very still.

Abruptly he turned off and went inside. Not another glance nor word nor gesture passed between them for the rest of that weekend that could have been construed as irregular by an onlooker.

Her room at Huis Kaywana was on the southern side of the house, and from its windows she could watch the old barn. During the afternoon hours, however, it was very hot in there, and she sometimes had her siesta in one of the northern rooms. On that side of the house the trade winds hummed continually in at the windows, and even in August and September it was pleasant.

A few weeks after the incident on the back veranda at Flagstaff, she was in her own room writing a letter to Dirk, defying the heat purposely, for it was a Monday, and thunder rumbled at frequent intervals in the south. "I am sitting near the window," she told Dirk, "and I can see the thunderclouds over the roof of the old barn, and I am simmering, for I am conscious that today is a Monday in August. I wish this month would pass quickly. I wish . . ." She had to break off and put down the quill. She pressed her hands to her face. The heat wound spectral sheets of silk about her, and she felt suffocated. She shrugged the gown off her shoulders, and sat staring out at the shimmering day. Her body was damp with perspiration. She took up the quill again, and crossed out the last two words she had written. "Unless something happens—I cannot say what—I shall go out of my mind," she wrote. "There is a point beyond which my endurance will break. . . ." She put down the quill, and this time she pressed her hands hard against her breasts and shut her eyes. There was a dizzy singing in her head, and the heat wove its way even into the brown gloom behind her eyelids. A dark-blue spectrum moved slowly to the right, turning green, then brown, then jerked back to the centre, and began moving back to the right. She opened her eyes and wagged her head, breathing in agonised gusts, rubbing her hands slowly down her stomach and hips. She rose, and looked down at the three sheets upon

which she had written. She took them up and tore them into pieces,
drew her gown about her, and left the room. She clapped her hands,
and in the corridor Lucie, her personal servant, appeared. She was a
sambo girl—three parts Negro, one part white: dark olive in complexion, like Jacob's wife, but thin and unattractive and a trifle flighty.
She was always giggling.

"I'm going into the room over there, Lucie—where the hammock
is. Bring me up a bottle of rum and a glass and a mug of water."

Lucie giggled. "You, missy? You want rum? I ent see you drink
rum long time now, missy."

"True, Lucie—but go and do as I say, will you?"

"Yes, missy. I will get it from the sideboard for you now, now,
now."

When Lucie returned, Rose was naked in the hammock in the northeastern room. Lucie giggled and said: "It hot today, missy. You right
to lie naked-skin in de hammock. I bring de rum, missy. Pour out
some for you?"

Her mistress heaved a deep breath, and without glancing at her,
said: "No, don't bother, Lucie. Take it away. I don't need it."

"Eh-eh! But you ask me to bring it for you, missy!"

"Take it away, I said. Put the bottle back in the sideboard."

"Eh-eh! Awright, missy. You funny, funny today. Never see you so
funny."

All the way down back into the dining-room Lucie kept giggling.

Early in November, Clara, at dinner one evening at Kingston, told
Rose and Graham that in the spring of the following year she and
John and Harvey and his wife were planning a trip to England.
Harvey's son, Timothy, was at preparatory school in England, and
they would spend the summer with him at John's cousin's place in
Sussex. Sir Ralph Hartfield, John's cousin, was a baronet.

Clara's lined but still handsome face beamed upon Rose and
Graham with all the old kindliness and affection as she said: "We
want you to come with us, my dears. The trip will do you both good,
and, in any event, those two children of yours must be sent to school.
Time flies so quickly. Before we realise it the day will be here when
Reginald must enter Eton. John's people will see that a good preparatory school is found for him in the meantime."

Graham said that it was a splendid idea, but would Clara give him
some weeks to think it over? Rose was definite. She would go. "I feel

cooped up," she said. "I'll go anywhere you suggest, Clara—even to India or the South Seas."

A vague look of pain and understanding passed over Clara's face as she glanced at her and murmured: "I understand, my child."

Graham was saying something to John, and neither saw the look nor heard her. He had got greyer at the temples during the past year or so, but his face was still young-looking. He had acquired the mannerism of smiling reflectively to himself during pauses in any conversation; sometimes the effect was one of good humour, sometimes of eccentricity. His gestures were finicky but much less affected than of yore. They had become an integral part of him now.

Dirk still corresponded with Elfrida, though much less frequently than of former years. In a letter in January of the following year, 1826, he asked Elfrida to give him news of Rose's attitude to life. "She writes me very irregularly now, and very sketchily," he said, "and I feel that something is wrong. Give me your views on the matter, as you know how much her welfare concerns me."

In reply, Elfrida told him: "It is difficult to put one's finger on anything definite, but she is not happy, I know for certain. She reveals this in a number of ways—in a certain detachment of manner, in long silences, and sometimes in false laughter and assumed bouts of gaiety. This trip to England in April should prove very beneficial in several ways, though, for some reason, Pelham feels that it may unsettle her. He is of the opinion that a long, quiet holiday at Machaica might be far more favourable to her well-being than a long sea voyage and the excitements that will assail her in a new and strange land. Pelham is a stay-at-home, and naturally would view the matter in this light. . . ."

"There are a number of delightful little cottages at Mahaica, Rose. Such an opportunity may never occur again," whispered Pelham. This time it was in the dining-room at Huis Kaywana, one morning in February when he had come to see Graham on plantation business. Graham had just left for the factory with his head overseer, and Rose was entertaining Pelham until Graham returned in about an hour's time. They had wandered round the sitting-room, and now had wandered into the dining-room. She listened to him, her face neutral, every now and then, however, a gleam coming into her eyes. Once when she paused near the sideboard he held her arms and kissed her hair, and she did not repulse him—but she did not respond in any way. She stood limp and relaxed.

"I often go to Mahaica," he whispered. There was no need to whisper, but it had become a confirmed habit with him; he always whispered when they were alone together like this. "It would be perfectly discreet. I know of just the cottage. I could visit you without anyone knowing. Don't go to England, Rose. Tell Clara you've changed your mind, and want to be quiet at Mahaica for a few months. She will understand. She knows what you have to endure in this house."

After a pause, she said quietly: "I'll think about it."

"You will? Please. Please, my dear. I have waited so long."

"I'm not promising, remember. Don't let me raise your hopes."

He gripped her arms again and turned her round to face him. "Why are you so cold towards me, Rose? Why? And yet I can sense you are not inwardly cold. Is it Dirk? Will you never be able to forget Dirk?"

She smiled, but her face was still noncommittal. She made no comment—but she let him hold her, let him kiss her hair again, and her lips, tensed and shivered slightly when he slipped his hand down her bosom—but still did not repulse him.

In April she sailed for England with Graham and the Hartfields. In a brief letter to Dirk she said: "I should enjoy this trip if I could know while I was away that at the end of it I would be seeing you. Yet I don't want to see you again unless we could be physically together. I am developing a hard shell, my dearest, but so hard is it that I fear it may crack suddenly. Excuse my hysterical rantings. I can say nothing sane or rational by mouth or letter these days. Think of me when I'm gone, as I shall think of you when the ship rolls. I may not write you any letters after this, my love. I shall try to forget you, impossible as this may seem. Good-bye."

During all the months she was away in England, Dirk received not a single letter from her, and in the background of his awareness he was worried. In the foreground, however, there were other matters to distract him from the subject of Rose. In June one of his ships—the schooner called *Millicent*—went aground on Crab Island and was nearly lost. In September a forest fire up the river destroyed more than forty acres of valuable greenheart trees. He had to make a trip to the timber grant to inspect the damage and decide and discuss various little points relating to the situation, and accompany Hartman, his manager, on a prospecting mission higher up to look for new sites where greenheart and mora might be worked. Encamped on Lake Mappa, they were nearly poisoned by their Indian cook, who, it turned out, bore a serious grudge against Hartman because Hartman had once interfered with his wife. Added to this, *kaburi* flies and mosquitoes made life distinctly unpleasant. Arrived back in New Amsterdam, Dirk was in low condition, and two days later, he developed a fever which kept him in bed for three weeks. Meanwhile, Elfrida's letters told of quarrels and unhappiness. Pelham was drinking heavily, and had become very difficult to live with.

"I cannot understand what could have brought about this change in him," wrote Elfrida. "It began since Easter or thereabouts. He is bitter and disgruntled for some reason that is not apparent, and will discuss nothing with me in his old genial manner. I am truly baffled, Dirk. Could it be a distemper peculiar to your family? His parents are as upset as I am, and as puzzled."

Dirk grunted and said to Cornelia: "Poor thing. She still hasn't guessed what is at the bottom of it all. We here haven't got to be puzzled."

"Perhaps it is as well that she does not know," Cornelia murmured. "The shock of hearing the truth might damage her health. Her heart is not good. She has told me that herself."

"I didn't know that. She has never mentioned it to me."

"Valvular trouble, I think Dr. Hepburn diagnosed it as. And her excessive fat does not help matters." She was sitting by his bed in the northeastern room, for he was still laid up, though the fever had abated. Outside the sun shone from a sky grey-blue with heat. Rain had not fallen for over five weeks, and everything was parched and dusty. The leaves of the mango trees had a shrivelled look, despite the green that still lurked in them. The compound was covered with a grey, thick layer of powdery dust, and the children were always complaining of chigoes in their feet. The sun had a perpetually brownish-reddish look, the result of smoke from forest fires that drifted in the higher strata of the air.

Three days later, however, a thunderstorm came roaring in from the east, and the rain poured in bucketfuls, turning the compound into a morass. The sun blazed down again on the three days following, then more rain came, and after that the weather turned cloudy and drizzly as November began, and it seemed apparent that the short rainy season had started prematurely, for November was, as a rule, a fairly dry month.

Graham and Rose and the Hartfields arrived in Georgetown on the seventeenth of November, all of them looking in exceptionally good health, especially Rose, whose cheeks had acquired a definite bloom.

On the day following their arrival Pelham called at Huis Kaywana. He went in an open gig, and arrived at siesta time. Ostensibly he was in town on plantation business. It was the gig that was kept at Edward House he had taken to drive out to Kaywana. The family carriage was in Water Street, near the American *stelling*, waiting for him, the coachman idling away his time with some stevedores and two other coachmen also waiting for their masters.

Rose, in *négligé*, but not resting—she was still engaged in the business of superintending her unpacking—frowned when she heard the gig coming along the driveway, wondering whether it could be Graham returning already from town. He had gone out since before breakfast, and had said that he would not be returning until late afternoon. Albert was in town.

When one of the girls brought up the message that it was Pelham, Rose clicked her tongue and said: "Tell him I'm resting, Celia. Offer him some refreshment, and tell him the master is out, and will not be in until very late."

The girl was not halfway down the stairs when Rose relented, and ran down after her, calling: "Celia! I'll see Mr. Pelham. Go back to the kitchen."

Pelham flushed, with embarrassment as well as with pleasure, as she entered the sitting-room. The gown she was wearing was a flimsy affair, and there was nothing under it. "You had no right to come at this time, Pelham," she said, unsmiling, "but I forgive you as it's the first time you've acted in a flagrantly indiscreet manner." She broke into a smile at this point, and held out her hand, adding: "I make no apologies for my attire. This is siesta time."

"I came at this time on purpose," he said, drawing her to him. "Rose, I'm out of my head. Oh, my dear! How lovely you look! Your cheeks are pink. The cold must have agreed with you."

"I can't say I liked it." She shrugged herself out of his embrace, stood away a pace or two and regarded him with a frown. "You don't look very well. What have you been doing with yourself during the past few months?"

"You're to be blamed. I've been miserable."

"Drinking hard again?"

He nodded, lowering his gaze. He looked up suddenly, his eyes wild. "Rose, Graham is in town. I saw him in Newtown—that's why I took the gig from Edward House and came here."

"Very precipitate of you—and not prudent, Pelham." Her voice was indulgent and a little mocking, but affectionate. She laughed and said: "You don't expect me to take you to the old barn, do you?"

He struck his clenched hands together and shook his head distractedly. "You're making fun of me, Rose. When will you realise I'm desperate from wanting you? I'm tired of being prudent. I'm beginning not to care who knows."

She was silent, staring past him reflectively, then she nodded slowly and said: "I appreciate how you feel, Pelham—and I sympathise. I like you. I've told you, haven't I? But you must wait. Be very patient. Very patient, my dear. I have my desperate moments, though you mightn't think so."

He made another attempt to take her in his arms, but she avoided him. "No, please don't touch me—not today. You must go now. Come to dinner—with Elfrida—on Saturday afternoon. And be your old prudent self." She smiled briefly, turned and left him, and ran upstairs, her eyes with as haunted a glitter as his own as he made his way outside to the gig.

A week later Dirk received a letter from her in which she said: "As I knew, it was impossible. I failed to forget you, despite my travels abroad. We spent a week or two in France and Belgium, and in Brussels I nearly fainted, for I saw your double. At first glance, that is, he looked like you. He was a perfect stranger in the foyer of the theatre, and after the shock had worn off I fell into a reflective mood for the rest of the evening, and I knew then that no matter how I tried, no matter where I went, I would never succeed in obliterating you from my memory, nor from my heart. . . . I miss the children, but I believe they will be happy at their school in England. I see myself now as a single woman again, and more lonely and purposeless than ever. . . . My dearest, it is more than two years since we have seen each other. Don't you think it is time we remedied this state of affairs? Won't you and your family come and spend a month or two in Demerary, and this time stay at Huis Kaywana? Couldn't you come for Christmas and stay until February?"

Dirk replied: "Plantation affairs and other business relating to timber compel me to be here for at least another three months, but couldn't you come and spend Christmas with us, Rose, my dear? We should all be delighted to see you, you may be sure. You could stay until Easter if you care. . . ."

Rose wrote back to say: "I think it would be preferable to wait until you are free of your business affairs and can come to Demerary. Perhaps you could come in August. Please say that you will Dirk, love. It is urgent that you tell me whether this is a request you can grant. . . ."

Dirk replied: "How mysterious you sound! Why is it urgent that I should tell you whether I can grant your request? However, may I hasten to say that it would be impossible for me to plan so far ahead as August—this is only December—but what I do think I ought to say with some definiteness, Rose, is that August is a dangerous month for us, for reasons that I need not state here. Moreover, Cornelia is pregnant, and in June or July there should be a happy event; thus you can see that, in any case, August would appear to be ruled out for our travelling. . . ."

She was attacked by a series of shivers when she read this letter. She was sitting in the hammock in the southwestern room, which she had occupied since her return from England—it was the one farthest from Graham's, which was at the extreme eastern end of the house—and she could see the river. It looked amber and depressing under the grey December sky. No rain was falling at the moment, but it had fallen steadily all the day before and during the night—in a light, monotonous patter on the roof, seeming as though it would go on for ever. The trees looked green and soaked, and the air was steamy-humid. Not the faintest puff of wind could be felt, though the river looked gently rippled.

She got out of the hammock slowly, and her breath left her in a laboured hiss. She stood at a window and looked down at the water tank in the compound. A kiskadee stood on the pipe connecting the tank with the house gutters. It kept crying "Kee-ee-ee!" very mournfully, as though depressed because of the weather. Or perhaps because its mate had strayed off somewhere too far away. . . . Distressed because it knew there was no hope of finding the lost one. . . .

37

ELFRIDA and her three children spent three weeks, at Easter, with Dirk and Cornelia. She was much happier now. In her letters during the past two or three months, she had said that Pelham had improved considerably; he still drank, but not so heavily, and he was far less moody and quarrelsome.

"He's not really his old self," she told them, on the first day of her stay. "He has changed towards me. He is colder, and inclined to be forgetful of my comforts. He tries to be attentive, but there is a difference. However, I suppose I must be thankful that his ugly moods have passed. I was getting terribly worried about these moods of his."

"When did they cease?" asked Cornelia, her voice casual and innocent: the voice of someone interested in Elfrida's happiness. Dirk sat, rather tense, but Elfrida did not seem to remark this. They were on the portico in the late afternoon, awaiting the dinner gong.

Elfrida frowned in an effort to remember, then said: "Some time in February, I think. A month or two ago. I must have mentioned it in my letters, Dirk. For one whole week we never had a single quarrel, and I mentioned this to him, and he laughed, and actually gave me a hug and said he was sorry he had behaved himself so boorishly. He said he had no idea what had come over him, but he must have been worried over plantation matters."

"And since then he hasn't suffered a relapse?" smiled Cornelia.

"No, I'm glad to say he hasn't, my dear," said Elfrida. "I thought I would have been able to persuade him to come with me to Berbice, but he said he's expecting some new machinery for the factory, and must be in Georgetown to receive it and see it safely transported to Flagstaff."

"I'm expecting some new parts myself," murmured Dirk, his gaze out on the mango trees. "Machine parts always require some super-vision when they arrive."

Neither he nor Cornelia betrayed what was really in their thoughts at that moment. They allowed Elfrida to prattle on. Elfrida gave them all the news from Demerary. Willem and Christina were speaking of sending their Lucy to school in England. How they did dote over that one child of theirs! Willem was always very cordial whenever she happened to meet him anywhere, but Christina studiously avoided speaking. "Not that it bothers me in the slightest," said Elfrida. "She has always been envious of me because of Francis. Willem used to taunt her that she couldn't give him a son like Francis—all in fun, of course, but she took it to heart. And Pelham once remarked—not for her to hear, but she did overhear—that with a physique like hers it was a marvel that she had even succeeded in having Lucy. She never forgave Pelham for that remark. That's why we had to live apart. Their excuse about Rose's visits to Flagstaff was only their way of circumventing the real issue. They left Flagstaff because they came to loathe Pelham and myself. Oh, but talking about Rose, I did men-tion about her drinking, didn't I? Poor thing. She's gone back to her old habit, I'm afraid—not so openly, but it's happening in secret, and frequently. Her breath gives her away. Don't you and she correspond any longer, Dirk?"

"The last letter I had from her was in December," said Dirk quietly. "I told her it was not possible for me to spend time with them at Huis Kaywana in August. She never wrote me since then, even though I wrote her twice enquiring what was the matter. I'm worried about Rose."

"I am myself," said Elfrida. "She's rather withdrawn these days. She seldom comes to Flagstaff. I believe she misses the children more than she will admit, and Graham is such a poor companion for her."

An awkward silence suddenly came upon them, for Elfrida seemed to realise that she had ventured on delicate ground. Fortunately, the dinner gong saved the situation. As they rose to go inside, Dirk remarked abruptly that he had promised to take Francis to New Am-sterdam on the following day to see the sawmill at work. "I believe he's interested in engines, Elfrida. Perhaps he'll take up engineering one day. How is he progressing with his lessons?"

"He's doing very well, his tutor says. He's quite bright."

Dirk kept his word to Francis, and took him to see the sawmill.

At twelve, Francis was nearly as tall as Dirk. Fair like Pelham, he had Elfrida's features and Elfrida's frank, forthright manner. He was very talkative, and in the carriage on the way to town, kept up a continual conversation with Dirk.

"Cousin Graham has a sawmill, too," he said at one point. "It's at Werk-en-Rust in Georgetown, and Father takes me to see it sometimes."

"Does he?"

"Yes, very often. And after we look at the engines for a while Father takes me to Kaywana to see the factory there. They have a much better factory than ours at Flagstaff. It's bigger, and they make more sugar, Father says."

"But why does Father take you on to Kaywana after leaving the sawmill at Werk-en-Rust?" asked Dirk, frowning. And Francis replied: "He says it's such a pity to be in Georgetown and not drop in at Kaywana, so we always go there. It's generally in the afternoon, and he leaves me at the factory while he stays at the house to talk to Cousin Rose."

"Ah. Yes, of course."

"Can you keep a secret, Cousin Dirk?"

"A secret? Why, certainly. What is it?"

"It's only for men. Father told me, and he says I must keep it a secret, because it's only for men. I must never tell Mother or Grandma or even Grandpa, because he's an old man. It's a secret for youngish men like Father and you, so I'm sure he wouldn't object if I told you. Well, it happened like this. One morning when Father and I were at Kaywana—yes, we went in the morning that day—well, that morning I returned from the factory by myself without waiting for Father to come and fetch me, and what do you think? I couldn't find Father, so I went searching for him. He sometimes takes walks with Cousin Rose in the grounds. Well, I walked round the side of the house, and I found them under that little honeysuckle arbour—do you know it? And he was kissing Cousin Rose. They were lying down together under the arbour in the shade, and Cousin Rose was naked, and Father only had on his shirt, and nothing else. I backed away quickly and went round to the portico and waited there, and when Father and Cousin Rose came after a while they asked me what I was doing there, and I said I had come from the factory and was waiting to go home. I didn't tell them what I'd seen them doing. But when I was in the carriage with Father I told him, and he was angry at first, then he told me that I must never say a word to anyone about it, especially to ladies, because it was a man's secret. Only men should know about it, and he trusted me as a man not to speak of it. He said men often kissed ladies like that and lay with them on the ground and in beds without any clothes on, but it was always a man's secret, and I must never tell anyone if I happened to witness it happening. That's why I've kept it to myself. Father said old men shouldn't hear about it, either, for they didn't do it, so I didn't tell Grandpa or anybody at home. But you're not old—you're like Father, so I don't think I've done wrong in telling you. But you'll keep it to yourself, won't you, Cousin Dirk?"

Dirk, white, tense, controlled himself sufficiently to nod and smile and say: "Yes, I shall keep it to myself, my boy, no fear. A man's secret."

"That's it. A man's secret." Francis nodded slowly, and said: "But I know why people do that, Cousin Dirk. It's to have children, isn't it? I've heard our nurse telling the cook about babies and how people have them. Father didn't tell me that, but I know that's how it happens. If Cousin Rose has a baby, it will be because she and Father kissed and lay together under the arbour naked. But I'll never speak of it. I am good at keeping secrets. Especially men's secrets."

Francis was not the only boy who watched the sawmill in operation that morning. Jacob's three elder children were there with two of their cousins—George and Marjorie Cole. Jimmy, Jacob's eldest, was nine— a quiet, unassuming boy, much as Jacob had been at his age, though he was slim and wiry, unlike his father at nine. Charles, a year younger, was a light olive, and freckled, with grey-green eyes and a mischievous smile. Cynthia, at seven, was living up to Dirk's prophecy. She was a lovely child. Her large grey-brown eyes were fearless in their gaze, and twinkled often with a lazy humour reminiscent of Jacob's.

George and Marjorie, their cousins, eight and six, repectively, were a sharp contrast in complexions. George was a dark olive like Cynthia, but Marjorie was sallow, and could have passed for white, though her hair was very kinky.

"You can always tell when it's not schooltime," sighed Jacob. "All through the holidays they're going to haunt me here."

"Oh well, that's the way with children," smiled Dirk mechanically —and Jacob frowned and asked: "What's the matter, Dirk? You look pale about the temples, boy." And Dirk laughed and returned: "Do I? Your imagination." Then added quickly, for he knew that he could not deceive Jacob: "One or two matters on my mind. Nothing very serious."

Jacob did not press him for an explanation.

Francis made friends with the other children in his usual easy way. He was a very friendly boy, and Pelham and Elfrida had not taught him to be stiff with coloured children. After they had all watched the mill at work for some minutes, Jimmy suggested going out on the rafts that lay on the mudbank to watch the fishes, and Francis endorsed this suggestion. "I didn't know you could see the fishes," he said. "The water is so muddy."

"Only the four-eyes," Jimmy explained. "They come right up to the edge of the water and swim around in the mud. They have large, bulging eyes."

About an hour later, when the carriage was on its way back to New Signal, Dirk asked Francis whether he had enjoyed himself looking at the fishes, and Francis said: "Yes, I liked to watch them squirming in the mud. They have such strange-looking eyes. As though they're about to drop out of their heads. Jimmy says they're called four-eyes." He prattled on, and Dirk did not try to stop him. Dirk listened with half an ear, for his mood was still abstracted. He was still hearing Francis say: "I found them under that little honeysuckle arbour—do you know it? And he was kissing Cousin Rose."

He began to drum with his fingers on the leather upholstery, grunting and smiling in acknowledgement every time Francis uttered some remark that could not be ignored. Only once did he stiffen and become fully attentive to the boy's pratings. It was when Francis said: "Oh, and Cynthia! Isn't she a lovely little girl, Cousin Dirk! Beautiful! She kept smiling at me all the time. I'm sure she's going to be pretty like Cousin Rose. Perhaps one day I'll lie naked with her under a honeysuckle arbour, and then I'll have my own man's secret to tell my son about. What do you say to that, Cousin Dirk?"

Dirk was aware of a shudder of premonition deep in his consciousness. It was a though a chilly finger had touched that old nerve of foresight. He gripped the boy's arm and snapped: "You must not indulge in such flights of fancy, Francis. Did you notice—did you——? Never mind! We'll say nothing more of it." He released the boy's arm, angry with himself, alarmed, confused, ashamed. He had been about to say: "Did you notice her complexion? You must never harbour the thought of being intimate with a coloured woman." But the words would not take shape on his tongue; his vocal cords balked at producing them, as though in protest at being party to such heresy, such base perfidy.

Francis, baffled and astounded, gave him a stare and asked: "Have I said something wrong, Cousin Dirk?"

Dirk patted his hand hastily, flushed and frowning. "No, no. It was foolish of me to rebuke you, my boy. My apologies. You are perfectly correct. Cynthia is a lovely little girl. Pretty, like Cousin Rose—and I have no doubt that she will be as fine a woman. Now, tell me more about the mill. Were you interested in the engines? Did you understand how the saws worked?"

Two or three times during the next few weeks, Francis asked to be taken again to New Amsterdam to see Jacob's children, but on every occasion Dirk made an excuse. . . . "Mr. Frick is a busy man, my boy. He can't always be expected to keep an eye on you young people at the mill." And another day: "Couldn't I go to Jimmy's house, Cousin Dirk? Jimmy said they live in a big house." . . . "Yes, but there is a shop beneath, Francis. Think of the noise you children will make romping around upstairs. It would be very disturbing for the customers." And again: "Will I never be allowed to go and see Jimmy and his brother and Cynthia, Cousin Dirk? Mother says we're going back to Demerary the day after tomorrow."

"Perhaps the next time you come to Berbice, my boy. We'll see. Jimmy and his brothers and sisters are always there."

38

AFTER Elfrida had gone, Cornelia suggested that Dirk should go to Demerary for a few days and try to reason with Rose. "You could make it appear you had business to transact in Geogetown, dearest. Elfrida would be none the wiser—nor anyone else, for that matter." But Dirk shook his head. "What right would I have to go and try to reason with Rose, my dear? Three years ago she was on the point of death, and I urged her to fight and live on. I raised in her the hope that she and I might be together again as we were that Monday in August, four years ago. I disappointed her in that respect, though she herself, through her consideration and affection for you, agreed that it would have been wrong to indulge in such an illicit relationship. Graham is a negative quantity, as husbands go. Her two children are in England at school. Only some of her relatives and one or two white families accept her as a social equal. Well, there! Can we blame her for yielding to the overtures of Pelham—and the consolation that rum and gin offer? What could I say to her if I went to Demerary? She once gave up her drinking habit, at my earnest request, but then the circumstances were such that she felt it would be worth her while. She was happy and full of hope. Now—well, she must see only pointlessness in the prospect before her. I can even understand why she has stopped writing to me."

"So we are simply to stand by and see her go to ruin?"

He gave her a cold stare. Graham would have called it his raccoon look. In a voice as cold, he asked her: "Can you suggest the remedy?"

She had nothing to say.

In September, Elfrida wrote: "I'm being made rather unhappy by some rumours that are going around concerning Pelham. No doubt, it is malicious gossip and nothing more, but it still is not pleasant for me to hear such things spoken. I shall not make a mystery of what it is, though I am very disinclined to mention it, especially in a letter. The substance of the matter is that Pelham's name is being linked with that of Rose, simply because Pelham has once or twice during the past few months had occasion to drop in at Huis Kaywana during the morning to transact some plantation business with Graham. It appears he was seen on these occasions walking in the grounds with Rose. Also, the rumour is that he takes her to Edward House, where they dine alone and spend long evenings. This, Pelham assures me, is a base lie. He does dine at Edward House occasionally, but only with planter acquaintances and an odd stranger from the West Indies who might happen to be in port. It is my firm belief that Christina is at the bottom of this slander. Pelham has never shown the slightest *penchant* for Rose in all the time I've known Rose since her marriage to Graham, nor has Rose herself ever lifted a finger to attract him. No, I'm convinced, Dirk, that this is the work of Christina. . . ."

"I've heard she thinks it's Willem's wife."

Pelham nodded, staring out of the window at the muddy ripples of the canal. It was dusk, and Newtown was quiet, except for the occasional clack-clop of horses's hoofs and the rumble of carriage wheels. "Are you afraid?" he asked.

Rose shook her head and laughed, her gaze on the painting above the sideboard—a nude study of Luise by Edward. Luise in her thirties, shapely and lovely. "I fear nothing or no one, Pelham dear. It's you who should speak of fear. Your relatives and your friends. They're talking about us, aren't they? And they aren't like Elfrida. They believe, and *know*, that we're indulging in scandalous and illicit relations. The servants in the house here talk, my sweet."

"I suppose they do, though Jackie is very discreet, and he discourages the two females from gossiping. Very little leaks out. Not that I care," he snarled of a sudden. He jabbed his fork into a piece of chicken with a kind of reckless spite. "Life at Flagstaff depresses me, Rose. Hardly anyone visits us these days, as you know——"

"Because of me, I know, my dear." There was more amusement than bitterness in her voice. "It's the price you have to pay for entertaining Graham's mulatto wife. Did you think your white friends would have overlooked such a serious breach of social etiquette?"

"All the more reason why I feel so little guilt about our friendship."

She chuckled. "As for me, I have nothing whatever to lose—but all to gain, I should say." She rang a little silver bell, and Jackie, the butler and caretaker, a thin, small Negro of forty, appeared immediately. "Some of the Jamaican rum, Jackie," she smiled at him, and he murmured: "Yes, mistress," and moved across to the sideboard.

Pelham chuckled and said to him: "Do you miss Barbados, Jackie?" And the man uttered a low respectful laugh and replied: "Sometimes, massa. But I like it in Georgetown better." He brought the bottle of Jamaican rum and filled their schnapps glasses, and Pelham twinkled mischievously. "Better young girls, eh?"

Jackie smiled, but made no comment. He knew when to be silent.

"Who am I dining with this evening, Jackie?" asked Pelham.

"Mr. Tom Haley of Jackson & Hailsham, massa," said Jackie, his face solemn. "Gentleman from Antigua who arrive this morning on de *Carricou*."

"Good man!"

"And who am I dining with, Jackie?" asked Rose. And unhesitatingly Jackie replied: "Mr. Barclay, Massa Greenfield's London factor, who arrive last week by de *Anna Christina*, missy."

"That'll be two silver dollars for your excellent memory, Jackie. Catch!"

Jackie caught one of the coins, but the other fell to the floor with a loud jingle. He retrieved it swiftly, and as he was going out of the dining-room Pelham told him: "Light the candles in the northwestern room, Jackie, and send Bella and Kate off home at once."

In February of the following year, 1828, without warning, Elfrida and her three children arrived at New Signal.

Storm and Elizabeth were in the portico with the youngest of their grandchildren, Peter Hubertus, born in July the year before. He was sitting in Elizabeth's lap, and every now and then Storm, smoking a cigar and reading, would glance up from his book and grimace at him.

It was Elizabeth who happened to glance along the driveway and notice the stout female figure and the three children with her approaching.

"Storm! We seem to have visitors."

"Have we invited anyone? I don't think I recall——"

"Good heavens! Am I seeing aright? It's Elfrida—Pelham's wife."

A few minutes later Elfrida was telling them: "I'm sorry I had to descend on you unannounced, Aunt Elizabeth, but I had to come.

Please tell me you don't object to my staying here a while." Her voice
was tearful, and her whole manner agitated. When Storm and Elizabeth assured her that she was welcome to stay as long as she liked, she
broke down and wept profusely. Francis turned away, frowning sensitively, embarrassed, and Matilde, fair and stout, began to bite her lip.
Harriet, dark and thin, with Pelham's pale blue eyes, cried in sympathy.

Eventually Elfrida, after Elizabeth had taken her upstairs and she
had controlled herself sufficiently, was able to tell in detail why she had
come to New Signal. She could not live any longer at Flagstaff, she
said. She had discovered that Pelham had been deceiving her in the
most despicable manner. "For more than five or six months, Aunt
Elizabeth, I've been hearing odd tales of his relations with Rose, but
I disbelieved them. He denied them all when I challenged him, swore
they were vile untruths, but last Saturday I caught them out—yes,
caught them in the very act, Aunt Elizabeth. Rose was staying with
us at Flagstaff, and during the night he went to her room. He thought
I was asleep, but I heard him go out of the room, and I got up quietly
and investigated. I caught them together in Rose's room. I nearly died
from the shock. Pelham, whom I have always trusted so implicitly.
Oh, heavenly Father! I can't believe it even now, Aunt Elizabeth. And
to think that Rose, to whom I've been so kind, should come into the
house there and betray me!"

"I never heard," murmured Elizabeth, "that Pelham and Rose have
been the cause of rumours. Neither Dirk nor Cornelia mentioned
anything to me."

"I wrote telling Dirk of the rumours I'd heard, but perhaps he
thought it might disturb you to mention it. Aunt Elizabeth, I've never
felt so utterly miserable in all my life."

"Pelham had a mulatto mistress before he married you, I was told."

"Yes. Frances. We named Francis after her. But he never touched
her after we became betrothed. I'm certain he didn't. Oh, God! Perhaps I should have remembered that he had always had a weakness for
mulattoes. What a fool I've been!"

She broke into sobs again, and Elizabeth tried to soothe her.

Outside, kiskadees and sackies were noisy in the branches of the
mango trees. It was a fine, cool, pleasant morning of the short dry
season, and the air still seemed to hold the scent of dew-wet leaves and
the early-morning dankness of clayey earth. In the distance, over the
cane fields, a thin, bluish mist like muslin kept hovering mysteriously
despite the bright nine-o'clock sunshine.

Elfrida, her fit of sobbing passed, asked after Dirk and Cornelia, and Elizabeth told her that they were both very well. Cornelia had left for Don Diego only an hour ago—just after morning coffee. She was spending the day there with her parents, and had taken Sybil and Hendrik. Dirk was at the factory. He had taken Amelia and Mary, and should be back at any moment.

For nearly a week, a little storm raged around Dirk. Elfrida was certain that if he went to Demerary and spoke to Rose and Pelham it would shame them into putting an end to their scandalous conduct. Dirk did not agree. Elfrida persisted, and Dirk was compelled to be brutal. "Do you imagine that this friendship between Rose and Pelham has only just begun? It has been in existence for years. It came to a head months and months ago. I can do nothing to stop it at this stage." Elfrida refused to believe that he was speaking the truth. For years? For months? She began to grow hysterical again. She appealed to Cornelia, and Cornelia reluctantly confirmed what Dirk had said. Then why had they not told her about it? demanded Elfrida. Did they call themselves devoted friends of hers? Was it an act of friendship to conceal such a thing from her?

Then Cornelia tried to persuade Dirk to go to Demerary. Dirk, she argued, had influence with Rose. If he wanted, she was certain, he could persuade Rose to come to New Signal. That, at least, would get her out of Pelham's reach, and eventually might remedy the situation. Dirk laughed and asked her if she were losing her sense of balance. "That doesn't sound like you, my dear," he said. "Can you seriously suggest that if I persuaded Rose to come here it would remedy the situation? More likely it may worsen matters, for then our own home here may be threatened with dissolution."

"I am willing to risk that, Dirk. I know you well enough to be fairly certain that you wouldn't let Rose ruin our home."

Again he laughed. "You know more about me than I do about myself, then." His eyes suddenly hardened. "It is no use. I shall not go to Demerary. Rose and Pelham must shape their lives as they wish. I'm as much upset about what has happened as you are, my love, but I don't feel it is my duty to interfere. Elfrida and her children are welcome to take up permanent residence here, and we must do everything we can to console her and make her comfortable, but that is as much as we must do in the matter. And that's my final word."

In Demerary, Edward said to Pelham: "As it is, my boy, Flagstaff has, for the past ten or eleven years, been under a social shadow because we decided to entertain Rose in this house. But what are we to expect now that you have thrown all discretion to the winds and taken up with her like this! And Elfrida and the children gone. We shall be looked upon as social outcasts."

"Your father and I," said Luise, "are the last people to be prudish in such matters. We weren't saints in our youth—but, at least, we did strive our best to avoid open scandal."

Pelham said he understood. "I think there is only one solution," he went on. "I shall go and live at Edward House. Willem can come back here and run the place, and I'll drop in occasionally to give what help I can."

At Kingston, Willem turned brick red with rage. "Now that you've made a mess of your life you come to me!" he bellowed at Pelham. "Why should I want to return to Flagstaff to be insulted by your wife and your mulatto visitors?"

Short and paunchy, with his pitted, leathery face, Willem, at forty-six, seemed to vibrate with frustration and disgruntlement. He kept stamping about like a restless bull that had been penned up too long.

Pelham, accustomed to him, was in no way intimidated. "Elfrida," he told him, "has decided to remain permanently in Berbice, so you'll not be bothered by her. And I can promise you that Rose will never set foot in Flagstaff again."

Willem snorted and bayed as a matter of habit for several more minutes, stamped around and bellowed reproach at Pelham, then finally agreed that there was nothing else for it; he would have to return to Flagstaff. "And if you'll take my advice," he shouted after Pelham as Pelham was going down the steps, "you'll keep that damned mulatto wench out of Edward House! Father should have that place shut up, besides! Whoever heard of a gentleman's residence in the middle of the stink and bustle of Georgetown! It's demeaning!"

Graham's attitude, as expected, was one of resigned cynicism. When he heard of Elfrida's departure for Berbice, and the reason for it, he chuckled and remarked to Clara, who brought him the news on Sunday: "I shall pray for them all, Clara dear. God is a just God, and He moveth in a mysterious fashion in adjusting the affairs of our lives. Poor Elfrida! It is sad that she should have had to suffer, but she will be happier in Berbice. She has been wise to go at once."

"I'm so disappointed in Rose," sighed Clara.

"Are you?" He patted her wrist, shaking his head. "But you should not be, Clara. Here is the guilty one. Blame it all upon me, my dear. I am the root cause of all the misery. Pray for me—miserable sinner." He sighed—but the expression on his face was not one of penitence, but of self-satisfaction. Clara gave him a pained, puzzled look, then smiled musingly and murmured: "Perhaps in a way, it is your fault, Graham. And who knows? I myself may not be blameless."

"You? No. You are all sweetness and goodness, and shall be so to the day of your death." Now there was sincerity in his voice and on his face. He gave a reminiscent grunt, and said: "What centuries seem to have elapsed since the night of that thunderstorm when I saw you in my room, standing near the wardrobe. Remember? With nothing on. What magic, Clara! It still seems like something I dreamed. In the northeastern room at New Signal, with dear Nibia in her hammock and the raccoons coughing in the night outside. A four-year-old fantasy!"

It was late afternoon, and the air was fresh and cool and dry, with the fragrance of dry-weather grass and earth strong around them.

"We never hear the goatsuckers now. Too much noise and bustle." He uttered a reflective grunt. "Only aback, near the bush, where it's quiet. . . ."

"Where is Rose this evening, Graham?"

"At Edward House. She is dining with Pelham."

March came and went, and then it was April, and the scandal began to pall. Other scandals came up for discussion. The long rain season set in. Willem and Christina were entertaining again at Flagstaff. Graham went up the river to Ubaree, and Albert came to town to buy the usual stores to take up, staying a few days, as he always did, at Huis Kaywana, he and Graham dining alone in the large dining-room while Rose dined at Edward House. Sometimes she would spend a weekend at Edward House. And in Berbice, Francis and Matilde and Harriet went three times a week to the home of the Hopkinsons' in New Amsterdam, where Dirk's Amelia and Sybil and Hendrik received their tutoring together with the Hopkinson children. Their tutor was a youngish, sad-faced lady—Mrs. Marjorie Clough—whose husband, a Yorkshireman, had died some years previously. He had been the manager of a cotton plantation on the Corentyne coast.

May and June passed, and during a thunderstorm lightning struck the portico of Doctor John's house in New Amsterdam, but caused no other damage. Elfrida suffered a heart attack in July, but recovered, though Doctor John advised that she should be kept very quiet in future. To keep her from pining Dirk and Cornelia had been taking her to see all their friends on the Creek as well as in New Amsterdam, and the strain of so much social activity, added to the fact that she still secretly pined, had told on her.

In August, Mr. Malcolm Rayner, Dirk's London factor, paid a visit to the colony, and was entertained for three weeks at New Signal. On the twentieth of August, Millicent Frick gave birth to a daughter, and Jacob swore that this was to be their last child. Six, he told Dirk, was the fitting number at which to stop. And then he told Dirk that Frick & Green were thinking of enlarging their premises to accommodate a grocery department.

In this same month, Willem's Lucy, a frail but rather pretty girl of fifteen, sailed for England in the company of the younger Hartfields and Jim and Beatrice Menzies. Jessie, Harvey Hartfield's twelve-year-old daughter, and Andrew and Priscilla Menzies were, like Lucy, on their way to school.

And so the long dry season set in, and the days grew hot and dusty, and thunder rumbled in the far south, and now and then a thunderstorm would come over from the east or northeast to relieve the burning days. And in September news was received from Jamaica that Hermine's husband, Jim Lafferty, had died after a brief illness earlier that year and that Hermine had married again five months later—in July—and was very happy with her new husband, who did not drink. He was a Boston merchant, and Hermine and her children would be accompanying him to America early in December.

September and October passed, and late in November rain began to fall in desultory showers, then more frequently, and the first week in December was grey every day and damp and dreary with the dribble of rain. And the new grocery department of Frick & Green was opened to the public. In this month—on the nineteenth—Claas Lieker, on the West Bank, died at the age of eighty-two, and Dirk said that he thought it would be the proper thing if he made a trip to Demerary for a few days in order to pay the Liekers a visit of condolence on behalf of the Berbice members of the family. He arrived at Flagstaff on Boxing Day, having travelled by mail phaeton from Rosignol. The roads, despite the rains, had not impeded the mail phaeton very much, and, as it happened, Christmas and the two days previous had been rainless. The journey took seven hours, and he was at Flag-staff in time for dinner at six.

Willem and Christina and Edward and Luise welcomed him warmly and no reference was made by any of them to Rose or Pelham. The following day Dirk crossed the river to the Liekers' plantation, where he was also very warmly welcomed. He did not return to Georgetown until Sunday, the twenty-eighth, and then he went straight to Huis Kaywana.

It was midafternoon, and Graham had just arrived home after a service at St. George's Church. He had breakfasted with the Hartfields in Kingston after the service, he said. It was such a great pleasure to see somebody from the dear old Canje! "I heard you had come for a few days to condole with the Liekers. Poor old Claas! But he did well. Oh, he did well. I'm sure I won't live to eighty-two. See my head, Dirk! The grey hairs are spreading—and I'm only thirty-eight."

"Where is Rose this afternoon, Graham?"

"At Edward House. She's spending the weekend there." Graham spoke with relish, his eyes agleam with a special kind of self-satisfaction. He tapped his hands together lightly, wagging his head, and murmuring silkily: "I pray for her every morning and evening. I keep praying for her, the sweet child."

Grimly, without the trace of a scowl, however, or even a frown, Dirk asked: "When is she likely to be home?"

"Ah well, now! This is the Christmas season, isn't it? It may be tomorrow evening, or perchance Tuesday or Wednesday. Everyone is in a festive mood, my dear Dirk. Rose and Pelham are probably being thoroughly festive at Edward House. I feel in my bones theirs will be a long weekend."

"Very well. I shall be here until Wednesday," said Dirk, "if it won't be trespassing too much on your hospitality."

"Oh dear, oh dear! Trespassing, Dirk! Come, brother, remember whose ghost haunts Huis Kaywana. Cousin Hubertus won't care to hear you use such a word—you, the most illustrious of the van Groen-wegel clan!"

At Edward House, Rose lay on her side on the big four-poster in the southwestern room, watching the buildings on the opposite side of the canal. All wooden, boxlike structures, painted white or pink or cream. Most of them warehouses or shops or offices where, on the morrow, Monday, the tradespeople of Georgetown would be busy with barrels and boxes and packages and ledgers, and the raucous voices of porters and stevedores would disturb the peace of the day. There would be the thump of packing cases, the grating of chains in punts and schooners and lighters, the clack-clack of horses' hoofs, and the rattle and rumble of carriage wheels in the street. And then the various stinks would rise from the canal—the stinks of sewage and rotten potatoes and vegetables of all kinds. Broken boxes and rotten boards, tree branches, bits of rope, and every kind of flotsam conceivable would drift past on the muddy water on their way to the river through the open *koker*. Then when the *koker* was shut the flotsam would grow stationary, and the stench of mud and refuse rise in leisurely whiffs.

Today all was quiet, so it must be Sunday, Rose assumed. She was not sure, for since Friday morning when she and Pelham had arrived at Edward House they had been drinking and sleeping and making love, with irregular breaks for the meals which were left on a table in the corridor just outside the door. For Jackie had had his orders. "Leave food on the table, but don't disturb us, night or day." They had not gone downstairs since Friday morning, and the hours had simply taken care of themselves. For all she knew, this was Saturday afternoon. But no. A little time ago there had been the sound of church bells, so it must be Sunday. Yes, she was certain it must be Sunday.

Pelham, in an easy chair, was dozing. The cigar he had been smoking lay in its tray on the floor, smoke twining upward from it in a thin blue coil. The windows were all open, so the room did not become fuggy. In tropical fashion, too, the walls were open at the top, with latticework for cross ventilation. And it was warm, even though the sun was blanketed by a dense mass of cloud that seemed in no hurry to break up and disperse. A humid, rather sticky day.

The sight of the buildings suddenly annoyed her, and she turned away from the window with a click of her tongue. The bed was in a very rumpled state. It had to be. She wondered how many times she and Pelham had made love since Friday morning. Not that it mattered, of course. Forget time. Forget numbers. Forget how to count. Forget . . . She shut her eyes, and felt the tears burning. . . .

"Pelham."

Pelham started awake. "Yes? You called? Yes, Rose?"

"A drink. Pour me a drink, love."

Pelham uttered a groaning sound. "Enough. Let'sh shleep."

She giggled. "Come into bed, then. Let's sleep together."

He rose uncertainly, stared around, blinking, mumbled: "What's today?"

"Sunday, I think, love."

He staggered towards the bed, and collapsed on it beside her. In less than a minute they were both asleep, sprawled flat on their backs, he in a shirt, she with nothing on. Rain began to drizzle, stopped, began to drizzle again, and then the sky cleared slowly as darkness fell.

Rose awoke first, stared up at the tester for several minutes, then sat up, got out of bed and lit two candles in a holder on a side table. The buildings of Newtown looked grey and ugly in the gathering dusk. The taste in her mouth was disgusting. She drank some water, and then, in a whim, poured a few drops on to Pelham's forehead. He awoke with a grunt, snarled, and then sat up, swearing. Then he began to laugh in bass guffaws, shaking his head, blinking, swaying as he sat there in his soiled shirt. He muttered: "Feel hungry. Want some food."

There was food on the table outside the door, and after they had steadied themselves with a drink, they ate some chicken and bread and yams. It was still warm, and Jackie must not long ago have put it on the table out there.

"Good fellow, Jackie—faithful servant," he mumbled. And she grunted agreement. They heard church bells ringing for evening service. A carriage went past in the street, and from the river came the sound of anchor chains.

"When do we leave here, love?" she asked. And he grinned: "We? I live here, love. You mean you." And she giggled and said: "Yes, me. When do you take me home." And he grinned and returned: "Afraid hubby may scold you, sweet?"

"Might beat me, who knows? Oh, forget time. I don't care when I go home."

"Forget time. Forget time. Let the hours bury themselves."

"Without funeral. So say I. Pour me a drink, love."

A few minutes later she put her hand over her left breast and pushed him off gently, murmuring: "I've told you. Never there. Never there, Pelham."

He gave a twisted smile and nodded. "Always never there. What's so sensitive about that beauty spot on your left breast?"

She shrugged, staring past him at the darkness outside the windows. He watched her face, then suddenly grunted. "Think I know now."

"Know what?"

"It's something to do with *him*."

She smiled weakly, mumbling to herself.

"Tears. You're very tearful this weekend, sweet. I wonder why."

"I wonder why myself."

"I don't wonder very much, because I know."

She giggled. "Do you? Tell me why."

"He was to have come on Boxing Day by mail phaeton. I wonder if he came."

"I've been wondering, too," she murmured—and the tears ran down one after the other. "Make love to me, sweet. Distract me—quickly, quickly."

The hours went, one after the other, lost in a haze of rum and love —and still more rum and love. Even the bustle of Newtown on Monday hardly penetrated the thick fog of stupor. . . . "He might be at Huis Kaywana now, Pelham." And a deep grunting. "Do you want me to take you there now?" A quick shaking of her head. "No, no, no. Never. Not there. I must never see him. Pour me a rum, love."

More rum and more love, mechanically, stupidly, in a stupor, in a fog. And the room began to grow foggy around them, but they were dozing and did not notice. Nor did they hear the shouts and footsteps in the street. The room grew more and more foggy. And then footsteps thumped in the corridor. It was Jackie. Rose heard a hammering on the door. Pelham opened his eyes.

"Someone's knocking, love. It must be Jackie."

"Told him not to disturb us, damn him," snarled Pelham. He sat up. Coughed.

Rose sat up, too, swaying from side to side as she sat. She coughed, too.

"Smoke, sweet. There's smoke in the room."

They heard Jackie shouting: "Fire, fire! Mr. Pelham! Miss Rose! Fire!"

They looked at each other dully. "Hear that? He said 'Fire!' " mumbled Pelham. And she nodded. "Yesh. He said 'Fire!' Smoke all about us, love."

They got out of bed, staggering wildly about the room. "Jackie!" Pelham called, while the hammering still continued on the door, and

Jackie still shouted "Fire, fire! Mr. Pelham! Miss Rose! Fire! De house on fire!"

Pelham lurched across to the door, turned the key, and opened it. "What's it, Jackie! What's it! Fire, you say?"

Jackie, in shirt sleeves, beckoned them out. "Quick, massa! Fire! Newtown on fire. De whole street burning! De house catch fire downstairs. Hurry down!"

Jackie turned and fled along the corridor. They heard his footsteps thumping down the stairs. Pelham staggered back towards the bed, then staggered over to a window. He looked out and saw flames and smoke. The room began to grow dense with smoke. Smoke billowed in from the corridor. There was a roaring and rumbling outside and a crackling downstairs. The whole house seemed to vibrate.

"Come, Rose—outside. Quick!" Pelham darted to the door. Rose, however, had collapsed on to the bed again. She was giggling and coughing.

"Rose! You fool! Come on!" He spluttered and lurched halfway across the room towards her. "The town is on fire, didn't you hear? The house here has caught. We've no time to lose. Come!"

"Leave me, sweet. I'm happy. Go, Pelham. Go. Quickly, sweet."

"My God! Are you mad? Get up! Get up!"

They heard Jackie's voice downstairs calling. "Mr. Pelham! Massa! Miss Rose! Hurry down. The stairs ketching fire! Quick, massa! Quick, missy!"

"Rose. Rose my dearest!" Pelham pleaded. He reached the bed, spluttering, and caught her arm, tried to drag her out of the bed. A dense cloud of smoke billowed into the room, and they both began to cough. Something rumbled and crashed downstairs. Jackie's voice came like a thin thread. "Massa! Massa! Miss Rose!" And then the thread broke. More smoke came billowing in upon them. Pelham, quavering, spluttering, gasping, dashed for the door. The corridor was dense with smoke. He could not see. He dashed blindly for the stairway.

He paused and called "Rose!" defying the urge to cough. Under him the floor felt hot. Remotely, from the bedroom, he heard a shrill laugh. Heard Rose reply: "I'm happy, darling! Hurry! Hurry!"

"Oh, my God!" He began to splutter. Rushed forward.

The instant his foot touched the first tread of the stairway, there was a rumble and the whole stairway collapsed amidst an uprush of flame and sparks.

39

THERE was a quiet moment on Wednesday afternoon—Harvey Hartfield and his wife had just left after their visit of condolence—when Graham shed all affectation and was truly penitent. He admitted that as a family man he had failed.

"I used to laugh at you over those letters in the canister, Dirk, but it might have done me good if I'd taken them as seriously as you did." They were in the portico, and the afternoon was bleak and damp, though the sky was blue in patches, and sunshine slanted through the foliage of the trees along the driveway.

Dirk kept drumming with his fingers on the arm of his chair and staring at the trees. Graham's head was bent. He stroked the greying hairs at his temple.

"The Old Blood. I shouldn't have scoffed at it as I did. I still don't think you were right to be so obsessed, but, in the main, your aims were good, and because of your aims, because of your ambitions for the family, you showed a much greater sense of responsibility than I have done." He began to fidget in his old way, crossing his legs and uncrossing them, running his fingers through his hair, wagging his head. "It is so difficult to decide sometimes—I mean, about one's duty. Should one's family come first, or people as a whole? I've always been so sorry for these poor slaves. Human, yet treated like beasts. Well cared for—but cared for as we care for our cattle. A valuable part of our assets. Only a few of us—and the missionaries—have recognised them as human beings with human feelings. I've tried to do all in my power to alleviate their lot, but it seems as though I should have been more comprehensive in my policy of kindness. I should have included my own family—but I didn't. I yielded to an infatuation and married a girl of colour. Now I know that was wrong." He heaved a great sigh, striving to control his fidgetings, but without avail. "I was sick in mind and spirit when I went to New Signal that time, Dirk, but it was a special kind of sickness, if I may so express it. A boyhood sickness of which I've seldom spoken. I've never been able to fathom it thoroughly myself, but I feel it has something to do with Nibia—that terrible fascination I found in fondling her breasts as a youngster of four. I remember it so vividly—and with so much excitement. The intense pleasure of those moments has always remained strong in my fancy. Often I have identified Clara with Nibia in my passionate moments during those early years in this house. And in Rose, too, I saw something of Nibia." He stirred painfully, sighed again and murmured: "Even in Albert. It is a sickness—but I might have conquered it if I had had the strength of your convictions about our blood." He wagged his head, and brushed at his eyes. "You were right. I'm of the Soft Streak, Dirk, lad. Weak. But for me, Rose and Pelham might not have—would not have—lost their lives in that fire in Newtown. Pelham would never have met her. She would have married some fine coloured merchant like Jacob or his brother-in-law in New Amsterdam. It's I who plucked her away from her humble little cottage and turned her into what she became—through my weakness and neglect and lack of a true family spirit. I even threw off our name. Think of it!"

Dirk still said nothing, his green eyes cold and blank.

"And now the burden is all on you. Willem without a son. Pelham dead. His children in your home, his widow in failing health. You're the sole binding force—the one driving spirit behind the family, when there should have been three of us. Four—if Willem had had a son. Willem is strong. Such a pity he did not have a son——" He broke off, for carriage wheels sounded in the driveway.

It was Raphael and Larsen.

Even at sixty-six, Raphael still retained his youthful charm. Larsen, at fifty, looked the elder, in manner if not in actual physical appearance—his dark hair, plastered to his large head, held not a streak of grey; he was the perfect mourner, the perfect condoler, for his was, perpetually, a funereal face. Raphael, on the other hand, had to make an effort to be solemn.

"I liked that girl," said Raphael, his blue eyes with a musing glint. "She had an incredible vitality, and an inimitable charm. One felt her presence."

Larsen nodded and grunted in confirmation.

"What did this fellow Jackie have to say? This servant fellow? Didn't he warn them in time?"

Dirk nodded. "He did, according to what he says—but the fire swept through the house so quickly that they probably had no time to get out. Jackie says he called again and again outside their door. They seemed to have been well in their cups—and it was a minute or two before the door was opened. He left them and went downstairs, calling on them to hurry. But there seemed to have been some delay. He told me privately, Uncle Raphael, that he believes Rose purposely would not leave the room. She wanted to remain and be destroyed."

"What! I won't credit such a tale! Tch, tch! Rose was too full of life, my dear boy. She wouldn't have succumbed without a fight. Committed suicide! No, no. Not that brave, vital, charming creature I knew."

"It is strictly between us, Uncle Raphael. That information must not be noised outside the family. Jackie says he overheard her calling to Pelham to go and leave her. She said she was happy. Pelham pleaded with her but without avail."

"Didn't he try to leave?" asked Larsen.

"The stairs collapsed under him. It was already on fire when Jackie ran downstairs."

"What a disaster for the colony, that fire!" sighed Raphael. "Practically every shop and warehouse and office in Newtown razed to the ground. That's the danger of these wooden buildings of ours."

After Raphael and Larsen had gone—they stayed to dinner, on Graham's invitation—Dirk and Graham sat in the drawing-room and smoked. They were silent for long intervals, their gazes roving round the candle-lit room.

Graham was still in his penitent mood, and once he said: "It was as well that I took the name of Greenfield. I have forfeited the right to be regarded as a van Groenwegel." Suddenly he tensed, and his gaze moved towards the portrait of Rose. He got up slowly. "Dirk, that picture." He walked across and stopped under the portrait. "Look, Dirk. Rose—Uncle Edward's portrait of Rose." He turned and looked at Dirk who had not stirred, though the green eyes were enquiring. "I gave you the one of Cousin Hubertus—and now I feel that this ought to be yours, too."

"I think you should keep it, Graham."

"No, no." Graham's voice quavered. "You—she would have liked you to have it. You deserve it. It—it may lighten for you the burden that's ahead. She was of your ilk, Dirk. Her portrait will inspire you —in the decades to come. Will you accept it? Say you will."

"Very well. Thank you."

40

THERE were occasions during the years that followed when, finding himself suddenly in an oasis of quietude, Dirk would recall that Wednesday afternoon and evening at Huis Kaywana, and, with unfailing monotony, his memory would bring into focus Graham's doleful, sententious voice—a voice that always seemed to carry a weight and significance it had not done that December day in 1828. An illusion, of course, for it was not really the voice but the words he had uttered that held the true weight and significance. . . . "And now the burden is all on you. . . . You're the sole binding force—the one driving spirit behind the family. . . ." Those were the words that recurred persistently, and they produced in him a sense of deep satisfaction—and of solace.

Another memory that remained strong was the memory of Newtown in blackened ruins, and himself standing near where Edward House had been, Graham and Willem and Harvey Hartfield with him, and, later, after Graham and Willem and Harvey had moved on up the street to interview two porters who had worked for the Newtown branch of Hartfield & Clackson, himself alone with Jackie, the caretaker of Edward House. . . . "Is there nothing else you have to tell me, Jackie? Nothing at all?" And then Jackie had told him what he had not cared to let the others hear. Tears on his cheeks, he had told about Rose calling out. . . . That memory would carry more solace than any other. His fancy had worked on it so much that it might have been he instead of Jackie who had heard her calling out to Pelham. . . . "Go on, Pelham! Leave me! I'm happy! I want to die here!" He was certain that those must have been her exact words. He had persuaded himself into believing that that was what she had called out to Pelham, and he would hold to this until he died. . . .

"I'm happy! I want to die here!" The flames had not hurt her, for she had given herself to them. He believed this—and was not ashamed of his heroics.

Smiling up at the portrait of her, which he had had hung in the southwestern room at New Signal—used as a guest-room and generally kept locked until required—he would nod and tell himself that she had earned her place of honour in the history of the van Groenwegels. Another Kaywana. Another heroine like those who had died by violence in the past. . . . In that letter from Laurens to his daughter, Grandma Hendri—Grandma Hendri a young woman on the Berbice, near Fort Nassau—there was an account of the happenings on the Essequibo in 1708. . . . "When the raiders began to plunder downriver, Rosa, arguing that she was a van Groenwegel and could not flee, refused to leave her home, and this in spite of a message brought in that her husband had been shot in the fields. . . . She fired upon the raiders from the kitchen, but was soon brought down by a shot. She and her five-year-old son perished in the flames that destroyed the house."

Yes, Rosa, Grandma Hendri's younger sister, had her place of honour in the Tales of Old—but Rose Greenfield—Cousin Hubertus' daughter—would go down as his own special heroine, Dirk decided. No tales must be told about Rose. She must remain, for the rest of the family, a background figure, sacred and profane: a legend of shame and glory. Only within the silence of his own memory would her tale ring out in clear and unconflicting tones. Only he would see her with glory and without shame, sacred and never profane.

Meantime, there was the burden to bear—the burden of keeping the family together—and it was not, he discovered, so difficult a burden to bear as to keep balanced on his back. He enjoyed bearing it, but relished less the tricky, awkward moments when all his ingenuity was called into play in order to sustain just the right balance. Sugar and timber created stresses and strains with which he was familiar; he was inured to these, and could handle them with confidence. But the presence of Elfrida and her family at New Signal, on a permanent basis, presented new and delicate problems in personal relations. Added to which was that other problem that, in the years past, he had been inclined to put behind him as something that would take care of itself but which, daily, he began to see looming up, tangible and uncomfortable, in the foreground of his view, and which, to himself, he called, dependent upon how fanciful his mood, by various names.

The Grave Imponderable. The Grim Imponderable. Tomorrow's Storm Signal. He would try to laugh off his fears, and laugh at his fancy's odd trick of fashioning names for the problem, but this did not dispel his uneasiness, for he knew that eventually he would have to face the feat of getting the balance right. Yes, eventually he would have to make up his mind just where the line must be drawn between the growing generation of van Groenwegels at New Signal and the growing generation of Fricks in New Amsterdam. A painful, precarious matter that would tax him to the hilt. If only he could have been spared *that* burden!

Only the bigger mercantile concerns of Georgetown had been insured against fire, and among these was Hartfield & Clackson. Even this circumstance, however, did not comfort John Hartfield, who had founded the business before his marriage to Clara, over forty years ago, and who had thrown his whole heart into it, putting it often before the most urgent social occasions. Fortunately, the main branch had been transferred to the southwestern section of the town—the Werk-en-Rust district—more than ten years previously, but the Newtown branch, not a hundred yards from Edward House, had been the original shop. Above it, John and Clara had lived in the old days. It was there that Edward and Clara had made love when Edward had painted Clara's portrait.

When John came to New Signal and discussed the question of whether Dirk would care to put some capital into the firm, Dirk did not hesitate to give him a favourable answer. John said that his intention was to enlarge the shipping department; the firm planned to acquire three new ships some time during the next five years. He was certain that, as a planter, Dirk would be the better off on this score alone if no other; it would facilitate the shipment to New Amsterdam of his plantation supplies, and occasionally one of the firm's ships would call at New Amsterdam to take cargoes of sugar and timber for England.

John also approached Graham, and when the newly organised firm emerged, both Dirk and Graham were named as shareholders, in addition to John and Graeme Clackson and Harvey and Jim Menzies, the former shareholders. Clara wrote Dirk a letter expressing her deep gratification. "It is like another precious link," she wrote, "in the chain that already binds our two families together."

Jacob said to Dirk: "It's a very good move you've made there—

and for a reason that you probably don't even suspect." They were standing on a raft of mora at the sawmill, and Jacob jerked his thumb north. "See that, Dirk? Crab Island? Serious problem, boy. You may think me a pessimist, but I believe that in another twenty or thirty years New Amsterdam will be a dead port."

"A dead port? What do you mean?"

"I mean not a big cargo ship will be able to cross the bar, either to come in or go out with anything. That island is growing, haven't you noticed? It's gathering all the silt that the river washes down, and the channels, on both sides, are narrowing. The bar, too, outside the estuary is building up."

"Which means what, then? That our cargoes would have to be sent in sloops and schooners to Georgetown for transshipment to ocean-going vessels?"

"That," agreed Jacob, "is what it will mean."

"Not a pleasant prospect for Berbice."

"No," said Jacob, "but with Hartfield & Clackson behind you, and their ships at your disposal, your own cargoes won't suffer very much."

"Nevertheless," murmured Dirk, "it will be a setback."

Jacob grinned and shrugged. "That's the way it is in this life of ours, boy. The big thing is to be able to foresee the setback and be prepared for it."

That conversation took place on a morning in March of 1831, and there were others they had, virtually on the same spot, on other rafts, during that year—other conversations that were fraught with solemn prognostications.

It was on the afternoon of the twenty-second of July that they stood on a raft of greenheart, watching Crab Island and discussing the proclamation that had been issued the day before. Governor D'Urban, in Georgetown, had announced that in future Berbice was no longer to be regarded as a separate colony. The Home Government had appointed him, D'Urban proclaimed, "Governor and Commander in Chief in and over all the settlements, territories, and jurisdictions hitherto comprised in our United Colony of Demerary and Essequibo and the colony of Berbice, and which shall henceforth collectively constitute to be one colony, to be called the colony of British Guiana."

"There goes," sighed Dirk, "our Council of Policy." And Jacob glanced towards Colony House, whose roof was visible from where they stood, and murmured: "Dear old Colony House—henceforth only a monument."

"And don't forget," said Dirk with a rueful grin, "we must no longer say we're making a trip to Demerary. There's no more Demerary."

"No—only Demerara."

"One thing, however," said Dirk, "that I'm pleased about is the College of Kiesheers. I'm glad they've restored it. We were only seventeen at the time, but I well remember how that ranting fool, Carmichael, with his love of everything British, wanted to suppress all our Dutch institutions, and the College of Kiesheers was one of the things he put down. In 1812 that was. This act of restoration should give us planters a louder voice in the Government. We'll be able to submit our two nominations as in the old days."

"One day," grinned Jacob, "I'm going to see you in the Court of Policy."

"Me? Never. I detest politics."

Only a few months later, in October, they were discussing the sensational experiment that D'Urban had ordered to be carried out in the Winkel Village, an area on the northeastern side of New Amsterdam. The Home Government had ordered D'Urban to free the two hundred and ninety-eight slaves in this village. They were the property of the British Government, having been retained as part of the spoils of war when the colony was captured in 1796. Mostly artisans —carpenters, masons, and tinsmiths—these slaves had been quite happy in their bondage, and were in no way desirous of being freed.

"Did you witness the commotion when the news reached them," said Dirk. He clenched his hands. "These damned fools of humanitarians! If only they could live in these colonies themselves to see at first hand what conditions obtain before spouting their specious nonsense! The irony of it, Jacob! Most of those slaves are upset about this innovation. They're raising a shindy about it. They say they don't want to be freed because under the Government they were being adequately supported. But no! They are not to be given any choice in the matter. They must be freed. Ah well! It's the beginning of the end, I suppose. I warned them all in Demerary in 1815."

The very next month another sensation broke upon the colony. D'Urban announced that by an Order in Council the Consolidated Slave Ordinance must now come into effect. Slaves could henceforth purchase their own freedom, whether their masters approved or not.

"Do you see why I could have nothing to do with politics, Jacob!" cried Dirk bitterly. "We have no real power to fashion our own destinies. That manumission bill was thrown out of the court in 1824 when D'Urban introduced it—but what difference does it make! Against our wishes, the Home Government proceeds to enact an Order in Council, and now it's law."

"That will always happen, Dirk, boy," said Jacob, unflustered, as usual, the old casual smile on his freckled olive face. "England is England. We're British Guiana—only a colony. And so long as we remain a colony we've got to resign ourselves to being handled in the way *they* want to handle us."

"Why do they bother with a local council, then?" raged Dirk. "Why don't they abolish the Court of Policy and simply rule us from London! It's a farce to ask us to elect our own representatives in a local body of government, and then flout our decisions. And there it is, you see! We planters are accused of being complacent in politics. What's the use of our being actively interested in the affairs of government when London can kick us around as they please!"

Jacob patted him on his shoulder, chuckling. "Cool down, boy. Cool down." He pointed at Crab Island. "See that? That's something we've got to worry about. Remember what I told you a couple months ago? We have enough on the spot to hurt our heads over. Forget the British Parliament. Now, listen. I want to send Jim to school in England, Dirk, and I want your help."

It was characteristic of Jacob to introduce a brand-new proposition in this abrupt fashion, and Dirk was not surprised. He simply frowned and said: "To England? But isn't he being educated at this little school run in the town here by Mr. Harper, the coloured schoolteacher from Georgetown? Why England?"

"Because," said Jacob, "he wants to be a doctor, and I, too, would like to see him become a doctor. I have the money, Dirk, and I can see no sense in keeping it to pass on to my children simply as money. My aim is to use it to better them in life. Educate them, give them professions. They can't all be timber managers and storekeepers, you know. Frick & Green might expand in time, but that doesn't mean that my children must go into the business as a matter of course. They must have the chance to choose for themselves what they want to make of themselves. See my point?"

Dirk nodded slowly. He grunted and said: "And to think I told Cornelia one evening long ago—an evening in July 1815—that you were indolent in mind and not ambitious! I misjudged you so badly, Jacob, lad. Oh well, but that's irrelevant, I suppose. About Jim—it's as good as done. I shall write to my London factor, and he'll arrange everything for you. Remember he paid us a visit at New Signal three years ago? Malcolm Rayner. A very reliable fellow."

"What about your own boys, Dirk? Aren't you thinking of sending them to England? Not to be doctors, of course—but just for the education?"

Dirk shook his head. "No, I don't think it would be wise, Jacob—not for mine. Planters are different, lad. All the education my sons need is the education they can acquire from experience on the plantation itself. Read and write and work sums—yes. They must know to do that well, so we tutor them. Even if they learn a little Greek and Latin as they go, no harm done. I know a little Greek and Latin myself. The van Groenwegels always had good tutors, but we're a planting family, and it's the running of a plantation that must come first in our educational scheme of life."

Jacob grinned. "I only wanted to hear you say it. I knew already."

The following year Jim Frick went to England, and Elfrida said: "I wish Francis were going, too, Dirk. I'd like to see Francis a doctor. I don't think planting is what he has been intended for by nature." And Dirk laughed and returned: "Not by nature, no—but by the grace of his Creator, who caused him to be born a van Groenwegel."

Elfrida, who had declined neither in health nor in spirits since the tragic event of December 1828, laughed, too, and gave Dirk a mocking glance. "Perhaps I'll persuade him to change his name, then. Papa would be delighted to have a grandson named McLeod. He's never forgiven Mama for not producing a son."

Though it was a bantering exchange, Dirk discovered that he was perturbed. He kept recalling Graham and his children. Reginald—Reginald Greenfield—was at Eton, and Ernestine at a very exclusive school for girls in Belgium. What Graham hoped to achieve by turning Reginald into an English gentleman Dirk was unable to understand. Surely Reginald would have to return to the colony to take over from Graham at Kaywana? Or was it that Graham did not plan matters this way? Would he, when he retired, leave Kaywana to be run by a manager? That was not in the van Groenwegel tradition, but then his name was Greenfield. His children were coloured. . . . Yet, and this was the disturbing part—yet, Greenfield or coloured, who could alter the fact that in their veins ran the blood of Adriansen and Kaywana, of Hendrickje and Hubertus—the Old Blood!

It had become customary, every Sunday afternoon, for him to sit by the window and reread some of the letters in the canister. As the years passed, the letters seemed to assume a greater value; the aura of veneration with which his fancy had surrounded them grew brighter rather than dimmer; the perusal of them never palled on him. Yet, once or twice, though these instances were rare, he would glance up and out of the window at the mango trees and find himself swept by a feeling of absurdity. A sense of the ephemerality of things would saturate his spirit. Once he thought: Suppose this canister had been kept at Edward House, wouldn't it have been, at this moment, a mass of twisted metal and the letters in it a pile of ashes . . . ? But the next instant, almost as though some shadow had swooped from a corner of the room and merged with his awareness, he heard a cold whisper in his spirit: "The metal and the parchment are as nothing, my boy! It is the words on the parchment and what they have conveyed to you that contain the element of indestructibility!" In that instant the feeling of absurdity vanished. The contents of the canister glowed afresh in his imagination. Pride made a throbbing like the roll of drums, or of August thunder, through his spirit, and all his old hopes and dreams for the family assumed a tremendous significance.

41

EARLY in the next year, 1833, Dirk had a new wing built on to the house at New Signal. The children were qrowing up and more space was needed. Elfrida, who was quite well off within her own rights—Willem, immediately on Pelham's death, had written to inform her that her share in Flagstaff would not be disputed—suggested building a house in New Amsterdam for herself and the children, and her father, Angus McLeod, one of the leading planters in Essequibo, offered her a home at the plantation there, but Dirk would not hear of either plan.

"What would we do without you here, Elfrida, my dear! You have become a vital part of New Signal—one of the main supporting crossbeams. To remove you now would cause a disaster, and I'm sure you wouldn't like to witness such an event." To which Elfrida returned: "You needn't try such flattery on me, you old rogue. I know why you are anxious for me to stay, and you know it, too."

Dirk put his arm around her ponderous bulk and grinned. "Very well. It's so that I can keep an eye on Francis and keep him instructed on plantation affairs, and see that he chooses the right girl to marry. It's so that I can have him and his sisters near me to instil in them a proper respect for the name of van Groenwegel. Tell it all to me in your waspish, forthright manner, and then say that you agree. You love me too much to disagree with me. Isn't it so?"

"I should be the last to want to deny what is true, Dirk dear. Go ahead and build your new wing. The crossbeam will remain."

By the middle of March the new wing had been completed. In April, Jan and Benjamin Lieker came to spend a week, at Dirk's invitation. Jan had written to say that the family was selling out and going to Surinam. "The old problem, Dirk," sighed Jan. "Not enough labour. And coffee prices are bad. We should have taken your advice in 1815 and switched over to sugar. You were right."

"Are you going to try sugar in Surinam?" asked Dirk. And Jan said yes, that was their intention. Benjamin put in: "We have already arranged to buy over a place a few miles from Paramaribo. The owner wants to go to Holland to retire."

"His name is Bakker," said Jan. "Cornelis Bakker. He was very friendly with Father when Father was alive. Father met him in Paramaribo when he was on a visit there some twenty or thirty years ago, and they've corresponded regularly—a letter arrived from him only two days before Father died. He claims to be related to the van Groenwegels."

"Related to us? In what way, pray? Did he ever explain?"

"From what Father says, the Bakkers originally were an Essequibo family. One of them married a van Groenwegel and went off with her to settle in Surinam. Sometime in the seventeenth century, I believe."

"That's interesting. When you're established there, perhaps you could make enquiries and try to trace which member of our family it was."

They were at dinner when this conversation took place, and Francis, who was listening, intervened to say: "Carry out a search in all the cellars in Paramaribo, Cousin Jan, and see if you can find a canister of letters."

The whole table exploded with laughter.

Dirk, flushed, but joining in the laughter, too, rebutted: "I may send you to do that, young man. It's an excellent suggestion." He turned to Jan and said: "Take him seriously, Jan. Keep an eye out for any old letters. I mean it. Send me anything you can find relating to our family."

Both Jan and Benjamin promised that they would do their best.

The Liekers left for Surinam in May, sailing only three days after Governor D'Urban, who had received a transfer to a new post in the Cape of Good Hope.

On the twenty-second of June the new Governor, Sir James Carmichael-Smyth, arrived in Georgetown, and the rumour immediately went around that he was a Negrophile. "No doubt, carefully handpicked by the Anti-Slavery Party," snarled Willem at Flagstaff. "Before we know it we'll be having another insurrection to deal with, you look out!"

"I'm not so sure," said Graeme Clackson, lighting a cigar. They were on the portico, after dinner. "Reports say that he is a strong character. He loves the niggers, but he knows better than to let them get out of hand."

"Really? We'll wait and see. The next few months will show him up."

As it turned out, the colony had to wait only a few weeks for Carmichael-Smyth to show what kind of man he was.

The rumours were not false, for the new Governor made it clear, almost from the first day of his arrival, that he regarded the Negroes as fellow creatures who deserved humane treatment at the hands of their master, but his first big administrative test came on the twentieth of July, barely a month after his arrival. For it was on this day that news of the passing of certain resolutions in the British Parliament reached Georgetown. Had Carmichael-Smyth been a man of Governor Murray's calibre, there might have been a repetition of the events of 1823. But immediately a proclamation was issued—a proclamation that gave the details of the resolutions passed by Parliament. And Carmichael-Smyth warned that any disturbances would be put down by force. This warning was blunt, and it hinted at action directed not only towards the Negroes, should trouble result from the issuing of the proclamation, but towards white disrupters of the peace as well. It was a warning that was very necessary, for the resolutions passed by Parliament were no ordinary ones.

It was Willem who read them out to his parents in the dining-room at Flagstaff, and his leathery face was a greyish purple, his eyes like dully shimmering granite pebbles unshifting in their sockets.

"One," said Willem, "That immediate and effective measures be taken for the abolition of slavery throughout the colonies. Two, That all children born after the passing of an Act, or under the age of six, shall be free. Three, That all slaves are to be registered as apprenticed labourers, and have all the rights of free men, subject only to their obligation to labour for their owners under conditions to be fixed by an Act. Four, That all owners be compensated for the freeing of their slaves. Five, That funds should be provided for an efficient Stipendiary Magistrate, and for the moral and religious education of the Negroes." Willem let the slip of paper fall to the floor. That's all," he added, his gaze moving towards the portrait of Pelham and Elfrida over the sideboard.

It was Luise who broke the silence eventually. She murmured: "We laughed at Dirk that afternoon at Huis Kaywana, Willem, remember?"

"I'm getting out of this colony," growled Willem, his hands clenched.

Luise sighed. "Never mind, Willem my boy! Never mind! We'll paddle our way through. The van Groenwegels never run!"

Edward wagged his head, twinkled at Luise, and said: "You can afford to indulge in heroics, my dear. You're eighty in October."

Luise tittered. "True, true! Ah well, that reminds me. We must celebrate the occasion, Edward, my love. Willem, my boy, if you're thinking of running away to Surinam after the Liekers, wait until after my birthday, at least. We must have a grand party, Edward—and I want every member of our family to be present."

But Willem was too frozen with fury to speak.

Other planters not only spoke of running away to Surinam, but actually made plans to smuggle their slaves across the Corentyne to Nickerie. When it came to the hearing of the Governor, Carmichael-Smyth issued another warning. Anyone caught attempting such a move would be hanged.

On the twenty-eighth of August the act giving freedom to the slaves in the empire was passed, and news of the details arrived in September.

Dirk and Jacob held their usual confabulation at the sawmill, standing on a raft and gazing across the estuary towards Crab Island, and in Demerara, Carmichael-Smyth addressed the slaves personally, explaining to them that though freedom had been granted to them, they would be still bound to their masters for a period of six years—but as apprentices, not slaves. He made it clear that, according to the act of Parliament, their freedom did not commence until the first of August of the following year, 1834. Their term of apprenticeship would, therefore, end on the first of August 1840—though house servants would be released two years earlier—and not until that date in that year would they be entirely free to do as they pleased.

In Berbice, Dirk uttered a contemptuous laugh when Jacob mentioned the twenty million pounds which Parliament had voted as payment to be made in compensation to the planters in British Guiana and the West Indian colonies. "That won't pay for the losses we're going to suffer, Jacob, boy. For my part, I'd say to them: 'Keep your twenty million pounds, and give us labour instead. Send us twenty thousand field labourers from England to take the place of the Negroes you're robbing us of.' That's what I'd tell them if I were in authority. Twenty million pounds! What good is the money to us when we can't buy slaves! Bah!"

Willem did not carry out his threat to leave the colony, and, in October, the family party in celebration of Luise's eightieth birthday came off as planned. Graham was invited, and attended, and Storm and Elizabeth, for the first time since their visit for Willem's wedding in 1812, saw Demerara again, though it took two weeks of earnest persuasion on the part of Dirk and Cornelia to get them to agree to make the trip. "Good heavens, sir!" Dirk exclaimed. "Do you mean you'd want to vegetate in this house and go to your grave without setting eyes on Demerara even once more in your lifetime!"

Dirk told Francis: "I'm leaving you in charge, my boy. You're nineteen—old enough to supervise the place in our absence."

"You can trust me, sir," said Francis, smiling. "I'll see that nothing goes wrong while you're away."

Dirk thought it must be his imagination, but, for some reason, Francis seemed inwardly excited. Not quite as tall as his father, Francis was, nevertheless, a giant in contrast to Dirk. He had Elfrida's features, but not Elfrida's frank gaze. His blue-green eyes were inclined to waver somewhat when you looked at him, as though he suffered from acute shyness, though Dirk knew that he was not a shy fellow; he was fond of the company of girls, and by no means bashful. In fact, he was already showing a decided partiality for one of the Hopkinson girls, and Dirk was encouraging the friendship, for the Hopkinsons were old friends; Harry Hopkinson was a cotton planter. He had two estates on the Corentyne, but lived with his family in New Amsterdam. A match between Francis and Laura Hopkinson would be highly satisfactory to both families.

Dirk gripped the boy's shoulder and said: "You keep them all in order in the house here, and make the usual tour of inspection every morning. Don't leave it to the overseers, Francis. It's an old van Groenwegel custom to ride around the plantation during the morning to see what's going on. I want it kept up."

"Trust me, sir," said Francis, avoiding Dirk's eyes, but trying to smile reassuringly. "I'll see that everything functions as required."

"Good." As Dirk turned away, he felt a twinge of uneasiness, however. In many ways—ways hard to define—Francis baffled him. There was a part of him that Dirk could never fathom. Unlike the days when he was twelve, Francis said very little to anyone; he had lost his garrulity entirely. Tractable and very willing to conform, he nevertheless possessed a certain reserve that made Dirk often suspicious of his sincerity. He was just a little too bland and suave for Dirk's liking—yet his manner towards the overseers and slaves was not weak; on the contrary, he commanded respect from them all and received it. Though—and this was another disturbing factor—the overseers did not like him. Dirk had never been able to discover why, but he had sensed it on more than one occasion.

The other children reacted towards him in a way that puzzled Dirk. They obviously respected him as the eldest among them, but in their manner there always seemed to lurk a vague fear whenever he was present. Cornelia had remarked on this more than once. Cornelia did not like Francis; she had said so openly to Dirk, but she, too, had never been able to define exactly why she disliked him. "It's a matter of instinct," she had said once. "I simply don't take to him. Something about him upsets me—and even repulses me."

Elizabeth responded towards him in much the same manner, though she had never expressed her feelings openly to anyone. Storm and Elfrida were unreservedly fond of him, though Elfrida seldom indulged in any demonstration of excessive maternal affection. Among her children she had no favourites, and, indeed, often scolded Dirk for his obvious weakness where his own daughter Mary was concerned. For Mary was still very much Father's Pet.

The evening before the Demerara trip it was Mary who, sitting in her father's lap after dinner, murmured: "You won't stay very long in Demerara, will you, Father?" And Dirk shook his head, stroking her red-gold tresses, and told her: "We'll be back in eight or nine days— no longer. Cousin Francis will take care of you all while we are away."

"Couldn't I go with you, Father?" she asked, looking past his head at the mango trees along the driveway. They were in the portico, and dusk was gathering. The scent of dry-weather grass and leaves was strong in the air, and the compound was very dusty. Now and then the squawk of a *hannaqua* came from the Creek bushes. It was a very pleasant evening, though overwarm with the overwarmth of October.

"There wouldn't be room for us all at Flagstaff, Mary. And if I took you the others would want to go, too, wouldn't they?"

Mary nodded, her twelve-year-old face very grave. Could there be something a trifle frightened about her blue-green eyes as they stared out at the dusk? Dirk frowned and asked: "Anything the matter, love?"

She shook her head, and said quickly: "No, no. Nothing at all."

"You're not frightened about anything, are you?"

"No, no." Then abruptly: "But I'd prefer you to be here with us. Father, I don't like Francis. Please never tell him. Will you promise? I hate him, hate him. But please don't tell him. Promise me you won't."

"I promise. But why? Why do you hate him?"

A slightly troubled look came to her face, and she stirred and said: "Oh, it's foolish of me, I'm sure. But I just hate him. He frightens me," she whispered, and grasped the lapels of his coat, her whole form tensing.

"Why does he frighten you? Come, tell me, pet. Has he ever done anything to frighten you—or any of the others?"

She hesitated, then shook her head and murmured: "Little things. Stupid, you'll call them, and I don't want to speak of them. But he's not good. I'm sure he's not. And sometimes he looks at us like a devil."

"Like a devil?" Dirk laughed. "You're being fanciful now, Mary dear."

Mary sighed. "Oh, I dare say I am being fanciful—but, all the same, I'll be so glad when you and Mother and the others come back."

Dirk said nothing to Cornelia of this conversation, but the memory of it nagged at him throughout the entire stay in Demerara. At one moment he tried to convince himself that Mary was simply being childishly fanciful and that there was nothing whatever to be concerned about; then the next moment his background uncertainty over Francis's odd disposition would overshadow his reflections, and a definite uneasiness would settle upon him. If there was one thing he found intolerable it was an intangible menace. Mysteries had never appealed to him, and never would. He resolved that when he returned to Berbice he would carry out a thorough investigation of the whole matter and get to the bottom of it.

In the meantime, Francis was in charge at New Signal.

The carriage with the elders had no sooner turned out of the driveway into the road when Francis looked round at the other children and said in a silky, half-teasing voice: "And now they are gone. Gone for more than a week. Know what that means? It means that for more than a week I shall be master here." He smiled at them in a way that Dirk and the other elders had never seen him do. It was more an evil

leer than a smile; only his lips partook in it. It was something with
which the children were very familiar.

"Tonight," said Francis, in a voice of portent, "there'll be evil
deeds, van Groenwegels—evil deeds done in the dark. The angels of
Satan will flit around this house. Better get into bed early, every one
of you!" He uttered the last sentence sharply. It was an order.

Mary muttered: "You're not my father. I haven't got to obey you."

"Oho! You! Father's Pet. You of all should be careful, my pretty
wench. The Powers of Darkness have a special eye on you."

Sybil and Amelia laughed. Sybil, tall and fair, was fifteen, and
Amelia sixteen. Amelia was dark like her mother, but short and slim
like her father. Amelia had something of her mother's mystery, but
Sybil was a frank, down-to-earth person, with a touch of irony in her
manner. She said: "One day your tricks will land you in serious trouble, Francis."

"Will they?" Francis turned a baleful look upon her. "What do
you know about my tricks that you can speak with such certainty?"

"Oh, you don't deceive me," chuckled Sybil. "I know what you do.
I won't shame you by speaking in front of the others, but I still
know."

"He's a devil," Mary muttered, glaring at him, though there was
fear in her eyes. Matilde and Harriet, Francis's sisters, seemed afraid,
too, as they gazed at their brother. Matilde was fair and plump; it was
evident that she would be a huge woman like her mother. She was
eighteen, and a very quiet girl; docile and unassuming—but men liked
her. There were two suitors on the scene already. Harriet, dark and
thin, with Pelham's pale blue eyes, was a quiet girl, too, though in her
manner there was a slyness that made her seem untrustworthy; in
some ways, she was not unlike Francis, though there was nothing in
her that could be recognised as positive evil. She was a hypocrite.

"Francis is no more a devil than Hendrik," said Harriet—and Hendrik, a solemn-faced boy of thirteen, sturdy and tough, not unlike
Jacob in general physique, but fair like Dirk and with Cornelia's dark-
blue eyes, gave a low growl and glared at Harriet, whom he disliked
intensely.

Peter, the youngest, who was six, a wiry little fellow with sandy
hair and grey-green eyes, was very attached to his elder brother, and
always alert to anything that was said against Hendrik. He glared at
Harriet automatically, though he held his peace. He lived in secret

terror of Francis, and, like the others, only very rarely showed his feelings.

Francis looked from one to the other of them, and each of them lowered their eyes under his stare. "You'd like to defy me, wouldn't you? Remember what I told you one day near the water tank? I have the power to kill any of you—to frighten you in your sleep, and prevent you from ever awakening. You had better be careful how you move."

They were silent, and at that instant the voice of the nurse was heard in the portico calling Peter. "Massa Peter! Come and eat! Time for your dinner!"

That broke the spell. Peter ran off, and the others began to move slowly after him. Francis detained Harriet. He gripped her arm and said: "You wait a moment, Harriet. I have something to say to you."

Harriet tensed, her pale blue eyes wide with surprise and nervous apprehension. Her thin body shuddered slightly. "What is it, Francis?"

Francis waited until the others had gone out of earshot and then said: "I want you to have an eye on them this evening and tonight, Harriet."

Harriet tried to smile. Her fifteen-year-old face always took on an older and sophisticated look when she smiled. "What are you up to tonight, Francis?"

"That's my affair," Francis told her gruffly. He gripped her arm again, and this time twisted it so that she cried out softly. "You do as I say and keep an eye on them. See that none of them leaves the house after dark and tries to follow me. Understand? If any spies get after me tonight I'll blame you, and I'll make you suffer most of all. I'll punish you in the worst way imaginable."

"You're hurting my arm."

"Am I?" Francis grinned. "You'd better look out I don't hurt somewhere else—and that will really hurt."

Harriet flushed deeply and tugged her arm free. Her head trembled in rage and shame, and she said quietly: "One day Cousin Dirk and Mother will discover about you, and then you'll be thrown out of this house."

"They'll never discover anything—unless one of you tells them. And none of you will tell them. You wouldn't, would you? Would you, Harriet?" He kept his eyes upon her, and she averted her gaze, flushing again. She tried to smile, and then murmured: "You needn't be afraid of me. But Mary or Amelia or Sybil may be your undoing. You had better watch your step with them."

He pinched her cheek. "You watch them for me, sister. You worship me, don't you? You'd eat out of my hand, Harriet—you know you would. You know my worst secrets, and you've kept them. And I know some of yours—a man's secrets. You can't afford to make an enemy of me, can you?"

Harriet gave him a swift glance in which there was hatred as well as fear.

"Remember the afternoon aback, near the jamoon tree? Remember what I caught you doing there with Hammond, our dear, innocent young overseer?"

Harriet paled, but still could say nothing. She breathed hard, and her hands kept clenching and unclenching.

"Last year that was, Harriet. You were only fourteen, my little sister."

"You spied on me or you'd never have discovered it."

"It's my business to know what happens. I didn't spy. The spirits told me."

"Go on. Go on," said Harriet, her manner breathless. "That Elvira is going to lead you into hell one of these nights with her obeah— and all her dark dealings with the Devil. The others—the other children—know you go to her logie during the night. Hendrik saw you on two nights, and Amelia woke up one night and smelt incense. You don't know what you're dabbling with, Francis!"

"No fear! I know all right, sister. A man's secret. Remember what I told you I once caught Father and Cousin Rose doing near the arbour at Huis Kaywana when I was a young fellow? A man's secret, Father called it." He laughed harshly. "What a jest! Elvira often laughs over it when I tell her. We both laugh over it. The things I've discovered about men and women since I was twelve! Do you know how Father and Cousin Rose met their deaths? They were burnt alive at Edward House in that big fire that swept through Georgetown in 'twenty-eight. And what have Mother and Cousin Dirk told us? They were dining together, and when they tried to escape the stairs inside the house collapsed with them. Haw, haw! What a tale! See how deceptive our elders are, Harriet? You and I know better about Father's death, don't we? Elvira cleared up the mystery for me through her little chats with the spirits. She discovered all, and I confided what I learnt in you. You've never told the others, I hope?"

"Of course not," murmured Harriet, still pale. The evening was getting on. The sunshine was red and weak, and slanted past them, throwing long shadows on the dusty compound, their own as well as the shadows of the mango trees.

"And see you don't whisper a word to them. Let them persist in their ignorance. Heed me, and help me, and you'll share in my power."

"What power is this you hope to gain, Francis? Aren't you being foolish to hope that Elvira and her evil dealings will help you in the world?" Harriet spoke in a panicked manner. She trembled slightly. "You make me afraid with the things you keep saying. You frighten us all. I wish you'd stop going to Elvira at night. She's a bad woman."

"You mean a wise woman. A woman with the power to control the spirits of the dark. Oh, you should see what we do together in her logie at midnight! I'm being initiated, you little fool! I'm learning to control the spirits, too. When the day comes that I am proficient, then we shall see what we shall see."

"What do you mean to do, then?"

"That is my affair. Don't question me too closely. You simply obey me when I speak to you. Watch the others and see they don't pry into my affairs—that's all I ask of you. Fail me, and I'll not only expose what you and Hammond did last year, but I'll frighten you out of your wits in bed at night. Already I have the power to haunt you people to death, if you only knew it. I can turn this house into a bedlam of noise at midnight if I willed it. So be careful."

They heard the gong sound for dinner.

"Come on. Inside we go, Harriet. Oh, what a week is ahead of me! There won't be a night Amelia won't wake up and smell incense!"

42

T H E events of that October week at New Signal probably altered quite considerably the future history of the family. In the years that followed Dirk never ceased to blame himself for having so badly assessed the character of Francis. "I should have taken warning from Jacob," he said to Cornelia. "Look how hopelessly I judged Jacob's character. And even you I've been wrong about. It's a blindness from which I suffer. There were clues I should have taken note of. I knew he was going to the logie of this woman, Elvira. I knew he had been intimate with her for the past year or more—but I winked at it. Granted that I myself never touched a slave woman, but that was no reason why he should be like me in that respect. Far better that he should have his fling in the logies than in respectable homes. And I knew that this woman practised obeah, but by God! I never dreamt that Francis would have made himself a party to such debased and ignorant practises. What a smooth, slimy hypocrite! I trusted him absolutely and had such hopes for him. He fooled me to the hilt. Never in my wildest flights of fancy would I have conceived of him indulging in such a disgusting display! I can hardly credit it even now."

He was not the only one who found it hard to credit the tale the other children had to tell of Francis's deeds that week. Storm and Elizabeth and Cornelia and Elfrida were equally as stunned.

On the first night it began.

Francis came into the large southwestern room in the new wing at about nine o'clock and told the girls: "Put out your candles and get undressed for bed, and I don't want to hear any gossiping in the dark. Understand?"

His eyes were bright and shifty as he regarded them. Sybil and Amelia were sitting on one of the two four-poster beds, reading together Sir Walter Scott's novel, *Ivanhoe*, which Sybil had received from Dirk as a birthday present the month before. Matilde's plump form was settled comfortably in a rocking chair by a window. She had been humming contentedly to herself before Francis appeared, her thoughts on Anthony Parrott, who, three evenings before, at a dance at the Hopkinsons' in New Amsterdam, had declared his heart.

Mary and Harriet were not present. They were skylarking with the boys in the next room, their thumps and laughter and scurrying footsteps mingled with the drawling, admonitory voice of Joanna, Peter's nurse.

Sybil glanced up from the novel and replied: "Why don't you go to bed yourself? You don't usually see us to bed, do you?"

Francis grunted ominously. "No, I don't—but remember who's master here tonight. I'm giving orders, and I order you to get undressed. Now!" He turned off and went into the next room where the boys slept. "Mary! Harriet!"

The noise ceased immediately. Peter and Mary, who had just turned a somersault on the four-poster, grew rigid, and sat staring at Francis. Hendrik and Harriet, wrestling for the possession of a pillow, desisted and froze where they were in the middle of the room. The pillow dropped from Hendrik's hands with a plop.

Joanna sat near a window, mending Peter's nightshirt. She, too, stopped what she was doing to look at Francis, but her face did not reveal fear. She exclaimed: "Eh-eh! What happen to you, Massa Francis? Why you look so cross?"

Francis ignored her and told Mary and Harriet to get out of the room. "Go into your room and get undressed for bed. At once."

"I'm not going now," said Mary belligerently. "It's only nine o'clock."

Francis broke into a grin. "I anticipated trouble from you, young miss. Good." His hand dived into his coat pocket, and when it emerged again it looked vaguely shiny and damp. The candle-light revealed something slippery grasped in it. Francis took two paces towards Mary, and his hand shot out.

Mary screamed, but too late. The slippery blue-grey coil had already slid down into her bosom, and Mary began to tear frantically at her bodice. Joanna rose with a startled gasp, and the girls from the next room came crowding in.

Francis stood there and smiled, his arms folded across his chest, while Mary tore her bodice down. With a slushy plop, the coil of chicken's entrails dropped to the floor, and the girls screamed. Joanna wailed: "Oh, God! Oh, God! Massa Francis, where you get dat piece o' guts? Dat is obeah t'ing, massa!"

"I know it is," rasped Francis. "Glad you recognise it, Joanna. I warned the idiots that they were in my power. They wouldn't heed."

Mary was clutching Joanna and whispering hysterically, but Sybil, furious, cried: "Francis, are you out of your wits? What filth is this you've brought into the house? Pick it up at once!"

Francis turned upon her with a growl. He grasped her wrist. "You pick it up! It's meant for you, too, you defiant vixen! Pick it up, or, by God! I'll turn Satan loose upon your naked body this night." He uttered obscenities that had never before been heard in the house, and Sybil flushed and struggled to free herself from his grip. "You're mad! You're a devil! Loose me, Francis!"

Joanna, wringing her hands, began to weep in fear, and Mary, as though sensing that Joanna could not protect her, rushed across the room and clutched at Matilde. Meanwhile Francis continued to struggle with Sybil. He held her wrist in such a way now that his nail kept sinking deeper into her flesh, and Sybil uttered cries of pain as she squirmed and struck at him with her free hand. Suddenly Francis pinioned both her arms behind her, and then forced her down to the floor, bringing her face closer and closer to the wet mass of entrails that lay sprawled across one corner of a small rug.

Matilde and Amelia shrieked. Amelia took a step forward as though to intervene, but Harriet caught her arm and dragged her back. "Leave them! Leave them!" Harriet gasped. "You'll bring the evil on yourself, too."

Peter uttered a frightened yell and ran out of the room, Joanna following him, wailing loudly. And just as Francis had pushed Sybil's face within an inch of the ugly filth Hendrik swung the pillow he and Harriet had been wrestling over and brought it down with a swishing plop on the back of Francis's head. Francis, thrown off balance momentarily, lurched into the back of a nearby armchair, and Sybil collapsed forward, her face missing the mess of entrails by a narrow margin.

"Beat him, Hendrik! Beat him!" sobbed Sybil. But Hendrik needed no urging. He kept on belabouring Francis's head with the pillow. Francis snarled at him to desist, uttered another string of obscenities, but Hendrik struck at him fiercely. Eventually Sybil wrenched free and dashed blindly into the bed, nearly smashing her face against the mahogany post. Francis turned to spring after her, then suddenly seemed to change his mind. He uttered a growling laugh and said: "Very well. Enough for tonight. I think that will teach you I'm serious when I say I mean you to obey me. I'm going outside, but I'm going to watch these windows, and if your candles haven't been put out in a quarter of an hour from this minute I'm coming up here again—and hell will be let loose amongst you. Real hell, I warn you! I'll stink you out of existence with the fumes of Satan. Chicken guts won't be the only filth I'll push down your bosoms, I swear!"

He went rushing out of the room, and they heard his footsteps descending the stairs. Sybil and Harriet uttered whimpering sounds. Mary sobbed, and Matilde and Amelia, pale and incredulous, squeezed their hands together and babbled at each other. "He's mad, he's mad, Matilde!" Matilde suggested that they leave the house and try to get to Don Diego, but Harriet advised them not to attempt it.

"He's a demon. You don't know him, I can tell you!" cried Harriet. "He told me to keep an eye on you all and advise you not to spy on him. He's gone now to Elvira's logie to work black magic with her."

"Look at that mess on the floor," wailed Mary. "And to think it was in my bosom, right against my skin. I feel filthy." A damp smear could be seen between the pink-nippled hillocks of her twelve-year-old breasts, and Matilde said that she had better go and have a bath. "You'll come with me to the bathroom?" asked Mary, and Matilde said she would. But Harriet cautioned: "We'd better get into bed quickly. He might do something worse, Matilde. He said we must put out our lights and go to bed." Hendrik cut in with: "He's a stupid fool! Let's burn our candles all night. I have fresh candles in the cupboard. He can't tell us what to do."

Amelia said that was a good plan. "Yes, let's burn our candles all night. I won't be able to sleep in the dark tonight." And Sybil said: "Hendrik, you and Peter had better come and sleep with us in the other room. The two beds in there are big enough to hold us all."

"Who's going to throw away this mess?" asked Harriet. "I won't touch it. Where's Joanna? Joanna should come and clean it up."

"Joanna is scared," said Matilde. "She must have taken Peter with her to her room downstairs. She'll never come upstairs here again to-night."

Hendrik settled the matter by picking up the coil of entrails gingerly between his thumb and forefinger and hurling it through the window.

"Good boy!" gasped Amelia. "Now, get the candles from the cupboard and come and sleep with us in the next room, Hendrik. Let's hurry."

The girls and Hendrik passed a restless night in the southwestern room. Despite Harriet's fearful entreaties, they left the candles burning, and Francis did not put in an appearance to carry out any of the vile things he had threatened. They slept fitfully, dozing and waking, every instant expecting to hear the footsteps of Francis in the corridor, every instant waiting to hear the handle of the door being rattled as he demanded that the door be unlocked.

When the grandfather clock downstairs struck midnight Harriet and Sybil happened to be awake. They were in different beds, Harriet between Hendrik and Matilde on one bed, and Mary between Sybil and Amelia on the other.

Both Harriet and Sybil raised their heads when the clock began to strike.

The candles, in their glass holders on the table in the middle of the room, burned steadily; there were four of them. Four fresh ones lay on the table in readiness to replace the ones burning when the necessity arose.

The night was very still and warm. When the clock stopped striking the stillness seemed to close in with denser and more pressing rigidity within the room, and the October warmth pullulated new silken threads to stifle them and lure the sweat from their pores in tiny salty strands.

Sybil and Harriet looked at each other in silence, and, after an instant, lay back again. Within a few seconds, however, they had raised their heads once more. Sybil hissed: "Do you smell it, Harriet?" And Harriet nodded and replied: "Yes. It's the incense." Beside her, Hendrik stirred and moaned in his sleep and Mary, on the other bed, shivered and opened her eyes and sat up abruptly.

And, at this same moment, in the logie fourth from the one near the tool shed, on the southern side of the house, Francis and Elvira, a short, flabby, unattractive Negress of about thirty, were lying entwined in one of a variety of unnatural sexual positions Elvira had taught Francis during the fourteen months of their intimacy.

On a small box beside the mattress on which they lay—the mattress was flat on the floor—a coal pot stood, and from out of it rose a steady column of incense smoke.

Two black candles burned on a shelf set in the wall space between the only two windows—they were of the louvred type—the logie possessed. The light they cast, however, served only to reveal the dense incense fog that swirled within the ten-foot-square interior of the logie.

Near the floor the fog was not so dense, and the half a calabash that had been placed beside the mattress was clearly visible to the two rhythmically moving humans whose bodies, the one milky white, the other dark brown, glistened with sweat. This calabash contained a reddish-brownish, gluey mess that gave off a stink too powerful to be overcome even by the incense. In the midst of it the bill and comb of a rooster could be seen like some evil growth rising out of the filth, and every now and then the two writhing people would pause and stare tensely at the calabash, as though in expectation of some startling occurrence.

Suddenly, Francis, in a voice of fear and anxiety, quavered: "When is it going to happen, Elvira? Why don't you call?" And Elvira uttered a shushing sound, scowling and hissing: "Keep your mouth quiet! You want scare dem away?"

They went on writhing together, casting quick glances at the calabash, until abruptly, when Elvira seemed at the point of her orgasm, she moaned and gasped: "Call! Call quick! De power coming! It coming!"

Francis, trembling, began to mutter an incantation Elvira had taught him. It was couched in a mixture of Dutch and English and some African dialect, and sounded like utter gibberish. He stared at the calabash as he muttered, but without warning, Elvira, in the violence of her orgasm, seized his head between her hands and pulled his face down to her neck, whining and whimpering, and gasping hoarsely: "It come, it come! De power come! Hide you' face or you dead, you dead!"

A few minutes later, as they lay on their backs staring up into the swirling incense, Elvira panted and slapped her stomach slowly with her hands, and Francis, trembling, asked her in a frightened voice: "Have we succeeded, at last? Have I got it now?" But the woman made no reply, seemingly in a state of exhaustion, though her eyes looked wide open and glazed in the candle-light, almost as though she had fallen into a trance. Francis raised himself slightly and gave her an anxious stare. "Are you all right, Elvira? Tell me what has happened."

The woman's eyes lost their unnatural look, and a shudder passed through her sweating body. She sighed and said quietly: "It happen. De power in you."

"Good! Oh, good! You're sure? I have it? I can have whatever I want from them? I can command them and have them obey me?" He babbled excitedly, his face flushed, his eyes bright. But Elvira shook her head and told him: "Not yet. De power in you, but you can't use it till you get de sign from de spirits."

"What!" Francis's face took on a scowl of disappointment. "Another delay? It's always the same. Every time we have a ceremony like this something is postponed to the next time. Why? Why? If I have the power why can't I use it?"

Elvira's face grew cold and baleful. "Shut your mouth! Shut your mouth!"

"I won't," panted Francis furiously. He drew away from her. "It's months and months now you've promised to give me full power over my family. Tonight we carried out one of the most elaborate of any of the ceremonies we've performed—and yet now you say I have the power but can't use it. I don't believe you! It's a trick you're playing on me. You're afraid of me because I've got the power."

"You think so, na?" snarled Elvira, sitting up. "Well, try to use you' power on me, and you will see where you end up." She uttered an obscenity, spitting into the calabash. "Go on! Try your power on me!"

Francis, frightened but still defiant, glared at her. "What more have I got to do now to get this sign from the spirits? I've put three silver dollars into that mess in the calabash there, as you asked me to do. Every time we hold a ceremony I have to put money into your calabash. Is it more money the spirits want? If I felt you were tricking me I'd murder you, Elvira. Remember I'm a van Groenwegel. I'm your master. I won't have you play around with me."

Elvira, as though realising that she had gone a little far in her campaign of threats, lay back, saying in a propitiatory voice: "Lie down and let we talk. You getting excited. It won't help you. You got de power now, and if you want to keep it and be able to use it, keep cool and listen to me."

As always, her voice and manner succeeded in calming him down. He lay back on the mattress beside her, and she began to tell him what the next ceremony would be like—what and what she would require of him. Even when she said: "Five silver dollars de spirits must get dis next time," he only frowned, but did not attempt to interrupt her.

When she had finished telling him everything he was convinced that he had been foolish to doubt her. He sat up and squeezed his hands together, and said: "You think that will do the final trick, Elvira? You really think that will make them give me the sign?"

"Dat will do it. I sure, sure," said Elvira. "But you got to get what I ask for. Don't mek no mistake about it."

He uttered a sound of doubt. "I'm going to try, but it will be hard."

"Missy Harriet can help you. She can get de hairs from dem when they in bed tomorrow night. We not holding our ceremony till Friday night."

"Yes, I'll get Harriet to do it." He clenched his hands. "She won't dare disobey me. She's too afraid I tell Cousin Dirk how I saw Hammond kissing her and touching up her nipples under the jamoon tree last year." He laughed. "The ignorant fools! They don't know what is in store for them when I gain the mastery. I have fooled the old people I'm a saint, and they'll get a shock, too, when I begin to issue my orders. Cousin Dirk will discover that he isn't the most powerful van Groenwegel, after all. All those letters he made me read about Grandma Hendri and her cruelties—and Uncle Pedro and Uncle David and the others. Wait until I begin to be cruel! I'm going to make them squirm. Within a year this plantation will be mine, and mine alone. I'll be the van Groenwegel this colony will remember in after years—not Grandma Hendri. I! I! I, Francis! I'll hold them all in my hands, and turn and twist them as I please, with the help of the spirits at my command. And that Mary! I mean to get her. I mean to strip her and lie naked with her on the grass, just as I saw Father and Cousin Rose doing near the arbour at Huis Kaywana. A man's secret, eh? I'm going to teach her all my man's secrets. She's the most defiant of all the girls. . . ."

Trembling, his eyes a-glitter unnaturally, his hands clenching and unclenching, he babbled on, and Elvira watched him—coldly, slyly, mockingly, recognising him for what he was, an unbalanced fool, a dupe to be exploited, the means of her obtaining the sum of money she required to purchase her freedom before the year was ended.

43

W H E N Dirk and the others arrived back from Demerara only Francis was at home, and he was not in the portico to greet them. They had to search for him. There were no servants in the house. It was Cornelia who found Francis. He was sitting in an easy chair in the guest-room, his feet resting on the canister that contained the family letters, his gaze on the portrait of Rose above the chest of drawers. He did not move as Cornelia entered the room. When Cornelia exclaimed: "Francis! What are you doing in here? Where are the others? Where are the servants?" Francis merely grunted and stirred a trifle. He looked pale and haunted, and there were livid marks down his cheeks, as though some wild animal might have clawed him savagely. His clothes were soiled and torn.

Then Dirk came in. "Have you found him, Cornelia?" He started at sight of the boy. "Good God! But look at him! Francis! What is the matter? What has been happening in this house?"

"I'm not well, sir," said Francis in a low muttering voice. He scowled and passed a hand across his forehead. "I'm ill unto death."

"But what has happened? Where are all the others?"

"They said they wanted to go to Don Diego. They must have gone. They haven't returned yet." Suddenly his eyes flashed with hatred. "I've failed. I've been tricked. I've been made a fool of. That's why I'm ill. I haven't any power. There are no evil spirits, as she tried to make me believe. I'm a fool, a fool!"

It was several hours before any of them were able to get a grasp of the situation. Lugarde, the head overseer, arrived and told Dirk he had a serious report to make, and Dirk and the man sat for nearly an hour talking in the portico. Then Cornelia and Elfrida, who had gone to

Don Diego in the carriage, returned, bringing with them the children and Joanna, Peter's nurse.

Then the whole story was told, each of the children contributing his and her bit. Mary told of the chicken entrails on the first night, and then Harriet related how Francis had forced her to collect hairs from between the legs of the others. Dirk, puzzled and astounded, exclaimed: "Hairs from between their legs! What hairs——?" Then he broke off, flushing—and Harriet, too, flushed and explained in a stammer exactly what she meant. She had had to do as Francis had asked, for she had been afraid of the spirits. "What spirits?" Dirk interrupted again—and Cornelia said: "Oh, Dirk, give her a fair chance to speak, dearest. All children are afraid of spirits. It's the tales their nurses tell them when they are young and impressionable. You should know that. Didn't it happen to us as children?"

Harriet continued with her story, telling them how she had clipped pubic hairs from her sister and from her cousins when they were asleep, and given the hairs to Francis. "He made me clip some of my own, too," sobbed Harriet, and Mary interrupted to tell them: "I woke up when she was trying to get mine, Father, and I asked her what she was doing, and she said Francis wanted the hairs to give to Elvira, because they wanted to work obeah with them. I asked Harriet to give me back the hairs she clipped from me, but she wouldn't."

Dirk looked at Cornelia, and Cornelia returned the stare. As Cornelia remarked afterwards, it was like listening to some Gothic tale. "We might have read it in a book, and then had it told to us again by the children that afternoon."

It was on the night before, Friday, that the situation had come to a head, Sybil told Dirk and Cornelia. Shortly after midnight Francis had come into the house and awakened them all in the southwestern room, and told them that they must get up and get dressed and come down into the sitting-room. He looked wild-eyed and dishevelled, and had a calabash in his hand. "There was blood in it. Yes, blood, Papa," said Sybil. "And when we told him to get out of the room, he just laughed and said: 'I alone must give orders now. I am master of this house. I am supreme!' And he dipped his hand into the calabash and began to sprinkle us with the blood. We screamed and jumped out of the beds, and he went on sprinkling us with the blood. He told us to take off our nightgowns because we were all his slaves and he could do with us what he pleased."

Here Mary cut in and took up the tale. "He rushed at me and

splashed me all over my face with the stinking blood, Father, and then he held on to me and ripped down my nightgown. I screamed, and Hendrik took up a candlestick and hit him on his head, and he loosed me and staggered away, and we all ran out of the room and went downstairs to Joanna. Joanna and Peter have been sleeping in Joanna's room since the first night when Francis threw the chicken's entrails on me. We knocked on her door, and she opened it and we all went in, and Joanna said we mustn't remain in the house any longer. She said we'd all better take the tent-boat and go to Don Diego until you and Mother came back."

"We were just getting ready to go," Amelia said, "when we heard a shriek, and Francis rushed through the dining-room shouting that he had been deceived. He shouted: 'I've been tricked! She has deceived me! I have no power. They have defied me and disobeyed me even though I sprinkled them with the evil blood of the spirits!' That's what he shouted, Mother—and then he ran out the house. We didn't wait to hear any more. We rushed upstairs and got our clothes and we left the house with Joanna, and got one of the boatmen to prepare the tent-boat for us. He woke up two others and we must have left for Don Diego about three o'clock."

"Luckily it was not rainy," Matilde said. "Oh, heavens! I can hardly believe it happened. Francis is mad, Cousin Dirk. Elvira has turned him mad with her obeah. We used to warn him not to go to her logie at night, but he wouldn't listen to us. You should have her flogged, Cousin Dirk. She's a bad woman."

Dirk shook his head, looking grave. "There would be no sense in doing that, I'm afraid, my girl." He hesitated a moment, then added: "She's dead."

"Dead?"

Dirk nodded. "Lugarde found her this morning. She didn't turn out to work, and he went to her logie to look for her. She had been strangled."

At this moment Elfrida appeared and said in a worried voice: "I've got him to bed, Dirk. I think he'll sleep. We'd better send for Doctor John."

"I've already sent off for him," said Dirk.

Elvira's death, through the presence of mind of Lugarde, who had guessed exactly what had taken place, and through Doctor John, who certified that the woman had died of a fit, was not made the subject of an enquiry by the authorities. Rumours flew around, as was only to be expected, but everyone conspired to be discreet and not inquire too closely into the matter.

Doctor John pronounced Francis as suffering from a nervous distemper, and advised complete rest for at least a fortnight. Francis, after nearly eighteen hours' sleep, seemed himself again. He apologised very humbly for everything that had happened, and cried for nearly an hour, pleading with Dirk to forgive him.

"It's those letters, Cousin Dirk," he moaned. "I kept remembering what Grandma Hendrickje said. The pinnacles—and power. I was determined that I would win for myself all the power I could, so that I could take the family to the pinnacles—that's why I fell in with Elvira. She said she could get in touch with evil spirits and win for me the power I needed, and I believed her. Nurse used to tell Matilde and me about jumbies and *baccoos* and Satan's black angels—when we were little, at Flagstaff—and I really believed there were such things, and I was sure Elvira could put me in touch with them. I used to give her money, and she said that soon I would be able to work magic on my own, and order people to do whatever I wanted them to do. I used to try ordering the other children around, to see if they would obey me—to see if I was gaining in power—and Friday night I was certain, after the ceremony Elvira and I performed in her logie, that I had got the power—supreme power—so I went upstairs and took the calabash with the consecrated blood—it was goat's blood, and the hairs Harriet got for me were mixed with it. I was sure it would give me absolute power over the girls and Hendrik when I sprinkled them with it—but it failed me. It didn't work. I—I wanted to kill. I was furious. I rushed out and went back to Elvira's logie, and I caught her by the throat and—and the next thing I knew she was drooping back with her tongue hanging out and her eyes bulging. She scratched my cheeks with her nails, but I was so furious I didn't care."

Dirk was firm in the matter. He said that Francis could not remain at New Signal. His decision precipitated a crisis. Elfrida could not see with Dirk. "I know he has behaved in a shocking manner," she said, "but Doctor John thinks it was only a temporary aberration, and is unlikely to occur again. And the boy is now quite his normal self, so I fail to understand your attitude, Dirk."

Dirk told her: "No one held out greater hopes for Francis than I have done, Elfrida. You know that yourself. I wouldn't have built the new wing and persuaded you and your family to remain here hadn't I felt the urge to see that Francis made something of himself as a van Groenwegel. I wanted to give him my personal guidance in planting and in acquiring a knowledge of our family traditions. I've sat with him on many a Sunday afternoon, as you know, and read the letters in the canister aloud to him. I feel more depressed than you probably realise over this decision of mine. It has been a hard decision for me to take. But I stand by it. I will not jeopardise the safety of my children by permitting Francis to remain in this house. He must go."

"Then I'm afraid I must go, too, Dirk."

"That is not necessary, Elfrida. I've written to Flagstaff, and Uncle Edward and Aunt Luise—and Willem, too—they are all willing to have Francis with them for a year or two. There are no young people at Flagstaff, and Willem will see to it that the boy is given adequate matters to occupy his mind on the plantation. He will meet a variety of acquaintances, and it should benefit him considerably. If after two or three years he proves that he is quite fit in mind, then I might even consider his coming back here—but not before, Elfrida. Meanwhile you and Matilde and Harriet can remain here——"

"That does not suit me, thank you, Dirk," said Elfrida quietly. "I shall take my family to Father on the Essequibo."

Dirk smiled sadly and said: "As you please, then, my dear. You must do as you think fit, of course. But it grieves me, Elfrida—grieves me deeply. I shall miss you. You are, apart from Jacob, the best friend I've ever made."

"I, too, shall miss you, Dirk—and I shall still be your friend. We are not parting enemies, my dear."

About two hours after the carriage with Elfrida and her children had left, Cornelia discovered the note pinned to a pillow on the bed in the northeastern room. It read: "Cousin Dirk—you are driving me out, but I shall be revenged on you, and I know what will hurt you most, and it is that I shall do. You'll hear of it in due course. My curses on you, Francis."

44

O N this occasion Dirk did not stand alone. Cornelia and Storm and Elizabeth agreed that he had been right in insisting that Francis should be sent away. Not that this softened very much the great sorrow and disappointment for Dirk. "It was a mistake to have shown him those letters," said Dirk. "They put ideas into his head." But Cornelia smiled and shook her head. "The letters," she said, "might have put ideas into his head, dearest, but it is something more than that that was responsible for his conduct. He was born with a bad streak."

In March, the following year, 1834, Elfrida wrote: "Francis is causing us great worry. He interferes with the women in their logies, and even in the fields during the day, and the overseers have taken a dislike to him. It is such a pity, because he can be so charming when he wants to be. He is friendly with a girl at Parika, and she is very much in love with him, and it would be a splendid match, but I'm almost afraid to encourage the friendship—for the girl's sake. Francis is cruel, Dirk, and now I'm beginning to feel that you were right in insisting that he should leave New Signal. I'm his mother, but I must be frank and truthful. Last week he flogged a slave girl aback near the canal, and would have killed her had not one of the overseers gone to her rescue. It is as though a demon enters him sometimes. I really cannot understand it. His father was not like that, nor were any of my own people. . . ."

In August, during the disturbances that resulted from the official freeing of the slaves on the first of the month, Francis disappeared for more than a week. It was at the time when there was a serious rising in the Essequibo, and this caused Elfrida and her parents even more worry.

Some of the apprenticed labourers, as they were now known, went on strike and occupied a church, announcing that the building did not belong to the planters, but to the King. That gave them the right to use it, because they were no longer slaves and had civil rights. The situation became so grave that it was necessary to call out the military. The captain in charge, a Captain Groves, showed an admirable restraint, and did not fire upon the mob, and eventually Governor Carmichael-Smyth arrived on the scene and handled the situation calmly but severely, again proving that, though he was humane in his attitude towards the Negroes, he had no intention of standing any nonsense from them.

The mob broke up, and several arrests were made. The men who had been responsible for the trouble were tried. Four were sent to prison, and given severe floggings, too. Two were transported, and one of them—a man called Damon, and the worst of the lot—hanged. Thirty others were sentenced to the treadmill, but Carmichael-Smyth pardoned these—and was promptly attacked for his Negrophile tendencies in the *Guiana Chronicle*.

On the West Coast, Demerara, the Negroes were also giving trouble, and every day there had to be a trial of some group of wrongdoers. The justices of the peace whose business it was to handle these cases were hard pressed, especially as the prisons were not large enough to cope with the great number of prisoners.

It was among a batch of arrested people on the West Coast of Demerara that a white man, blacked up to look like a Negro, was discovered. Investigations revealed that he was from Essequibo, and that his name was Francis van Groenwegel. He had been found in the logie of a woman called Jankie who was notorious as an obeah practitioner—a dissolute character and a general troublemaker on the West Coast.

Fortunately, the captain of the military was on very friendly terms with the McLeods of Essequibo, and the matter was hushed up. Francis was sent back to Harcourt, the McLeods' plantation, surly and unrepentant. He once again gave as excuse that he had been attempting to get in touch with evil spirits in order to win power over men. "A hopeless case," said Willem at Flagstaff. "That boy is determined to bring disgrace on our name." And Raphael sighed and clicked his tongue. "I'd intended to bequeath my share in our place to him, and Larsen was willing to do the same—but now we couldn't consider it. Could we, Larsen?"

"Most decidedly not, Uncle Raphael," Larsen confirmed, nodding gloomily.

In Berbice, Dirk said: "Perhaps this is how he hopes to get his revenge on me. By dragging our name in the dirt."

Dirk, however, as it proved, was wrong. The revenge Francis had planned was not accomplished until two years later.

Before then, one or two happy events occurred. There was a double wedding in March of the following year, 1835. Amelia, Dirk's eldest, and Sybil, the next after Amelia, were married, Amelia to Ronald Hopkinson, the second son of Harry Hopkinson, the cotton planter, and Sybil to Anthony Parrott, from the West Coast. He had once been fond of Matilde, Elfrida's daughter, but after the departure of Elfrida and her children Anthony had gradually become friendly with Sybil. He was the son of an old friend of the Rueffs, Cornelia's parents, and was half Dutch and half Irish. It was a big event at New Signal, though Storm, for days after, brooded sadly on the going of Amelia and Sybil, upon whom he had doted.

"They have promised to write to me regularly," he said, smiling a musing, old-man smile. At seventy-two, he was still an avid reader, though his sight was failing; he was compelled to use spectacles with thick lenses. He had acquired the mannerism of mumbling to himself, though he was by no means withdrawn. He liked company, and he and Elizabeth lived an even more social life than had been the case fifteen or twenty years before.

Elfrida wrote to say that Matilde was getting married in June to a Lieutenant Banfield of the Royal North British Fusiliers, and Willem announced proudly that Lucy, his daughter, had become betrothed to Sir Hobart Hartfield, Baronet. The marriage was planned to take place in August in Sussex, and Willem was going to England to give the bride away. Clara and John Hartfield and Graham accompanied Willem, for they had been invited to the wedding. The bridegroom was John's second cousin. Harvey Hartfield could not go. Business affairs compelled his presence in Georgetown.

A rumour went around that Ernestine, Graham's daughter, might soon be married to a member of the nobility. She moved in the best circles in England, and both she and Reginald, her brother, still at Eton, passed for white. She was a very attractive girl, by all reports, and extremely cultivated.

In February, the following year, 1836, a death occurred at New Signal, and it created for Dirk a rather tricky little problem.

Retired for several years and living in a little cottage on the outskirts of the plantation, Albertus Frick, onetime head overseer, died of a kidney complaint. He was sixty-nine, and without any relatives in Berbice.

"I'm afraid, Jacob, lad," Dirk said to Jacob, "you and your family will have to attend his funeral, if only for appearance's sake. He was supposed to have been your father, and Mama, at least, would think it odd if you ignored his funeral. I rather liked the old fellow, and I've decided to have him buried on the plantation, so bring along your whole crew tomorrow afternoon."

It was a very quiet affair, and after the interment, Jacob and his family were entertained, according to the custom, at the New Signal house. This, for Dirk, was the most awkward part of the proceeding, for it happened to be the very first occasion on which Jacob and his family had been received in the sitting-room of the New Signal house. The children had often met at the sawmill in New Amsterdam, and were well acquainted, but they had never been at ease with each other, for it was understood that they could not be on visiting terms.

Jacob was the only one who seemed quite at ease that evening, and the following day, at the sawmill, Dirk said to him: "I felt pretty bad yesterday, Jacob. It baffles me how you were able to retain such an easy air."

"Things like that never trouble me, boy," grinned Jacob.

Dirk frowned and said: "But they trouble me. It's such a difficult, awkward situation, damn it! It hurts me to my heart that I can't receive you and your family in my home as equals. Why the hell did you have to be coloured!"

"I don't worry," said Jacob, with a shrug. "If I were in your place I would have acted the same as you do. You're white. Why should you risk your children mixing with mine and perhaps getting attached in a sentimental way? In the same way, Dirk, that I won't let my children mix with black people because I wouldn't like to see any of them marry a black man or woman, in the same way you have to protect yours from mine. It's simple when you look at it like that, boy, so I don't know why you get upset about it."

Dirk scowled and said: "It's not so simple, Jacob. What you don't take into account is the blood between us. Yes, damn you! The blood. Never, never could I shut my mind against the knowledge that in the veins of you and your children runs van Groenwegel blood. The Old Blood, Jacob! The Old Blood! That's what makes it hurt, boy. By all rights, you and yours should have the freedom of my home."

"Not by *all* rights—only by the rights of blood, and that's a secret between you and me."

Dirk gave him a keen stare. "Jacob, tell me. Don't your children know? You've never told them that—that you and I are half brothers?"

Jacob shook his head. "I've never even told Millicent or Papa Green."

Dirk could say nothing. He just gripped Jacob's arm and squeezed it hard. They stood there on the raft, in silence, staring at the wilderness of Crab Island in the February sunshine. The tide was out, and they could see the roots of the jungle of *courida* showing above the mud. The river made a soft shushing roar a little way beyond the raft, and four-eye fishes disported themselves at the edge of the muddy waves, grey like the mud, grotesque with their bulging eyes.

That same year, Jacob's second boy, Charles, left for England to study law, accompanied by his parents. Dirk travelled to Georgetown to see them off, and Jacob said: "Are you going to die without seeing England, Dirk, boy?" To which Dirk replied: "It's probable I shall. I have no desire to go anywhere. The Canje and New Amsterdam are enough for me."

Dirk took the opportunity to call on Graham and the Flagstaff people, and to inspect the new buildings that had sprung up in the burnt-out area of the town. His Uncle Edward had designed the new building erected by Hartfield & Clackson in Water Street. It was a three-storeyed place, and the top storey was used as an office suite for the shipping department.

Huis Kaywana had been considerably renovated, and Dirk noticed that the arbour on the southern side was no longer there. For this he was thankful. The memories the sight of it would have awakened in him would have been unbearable. As it was, he could feel the spirit of Rose in the house. Sitting in the portico with Graham and watching the late-afternoon sunshine on the trees outside, he would not have been startled to hear quick, tapping footsteps and shrill, gay laughter, and turned his head to see Rose appear from inside. Graham seemed to sense his mood, for once he glanced round and said with a sigh: "Memories, memories, Dirk. Poor Rose. She would have been so proud of her children today. Ernestine is a lovely girl. So cultivated—

and English through and through. To hear her speak, you wouldn't believe she was born here."

"She's getting married next month, I hear."

"Yes. A very good match. He's an attorney and the son of a knight. An old county family. Mortimer Purfield. He's a Member of Parliament."

"Purfield and Greenfield, eh? And what of Reginald?"

"Still at Eton. He'll soon be off to Oxford. Very tall and distinguished-looking. Really fine fellow."

Dirk stirred in his chair, frowning. "But, Graham, what's going to happen to him? Isn't he going to come back here to take over from you?"

Graham shook his head. "No. I don't want him to, Dirk. Here he will be known. His mother was coloured, and he will be looked upon as a *mestee*—a quadroon. In England he is a white man—and an Etonian. He will move in the best of society, and will probably marry into a good family."

"I see. So he will live in England and join the ranks of the many English absentee proprietors. Is that it, Graham?"

"That is it, Dirk," smiled Graham affably. "And he will be in good company—the Mosses and the Gladstones, and the Hartfields. By the way, I met old Mr. John Gladstone when I was in England last year. His son, William, has entered Parliament, and I'm told he's very brilliant. The old man wants to send Eastern labourers to his plantations here. He has some scheme afoot to get them from Calcutta. I don't know whether anything will come of it."

"Eastern labourers! What nonsense! Can these Orientals work in the field? I thought they were only good for sitting on elephants and keeping seraglios."

Graham laughed. "It does seem a harebrained idea, but we never know. The colony is so badly in need of labourers that everything possible must be tried."

Dirk snorted. "Those Portuguese they brought a year or two ago have proved a miserable failure. Most of them went down with yellow fever, didn't they?"

"Yes, they are rather poor in physique, though I've heard they are hard workers. The Maltese, too, were no good. Fell ill in no time."

At Flagstaff, Luise was still as strong and active as ever, even though nearing her eighty-third birthday. She cackled gaily, and was full of sly jokes. "One doesn't change, Dirk, my boy," she said. "I'm just what I was at twenty, even though much, much less eager in bed. Oh, don't blush. The truth—remember what Grandma Hendri said in her letters! Face the truth, no matter how ugly, no matter how lascivious. You won't change, either, my boy. What are you? Forty-one next month, aren't you? A September baby—I remember well. You haven't changed. The same fierce-eyed fellow you were when I first saw you at two or three or whenever it was. The fanatic. Grandma Hendri, returned to take care of the family! Hoo, hoo! Ah, my dear little Dirk!"

It was Willem, paunchy and florid-faced at fifty-four, who told Dirk about Francis. "A thorough ne'er-do-well, my boy. He is always in town, hanging about these gambling establishments. Goes in for cockfighting and betting at the horse races. Flings around Elfrida's money, and mixes with the lowest of the lowest in the town. A terrible pity, a terrible pity!"

"Cornelia was right," said Dirk, nodding gravely. "He was born with a bad streak. Not only soft, but bad as well."

It was in November of that year, 1836, that a letter, very brief, was received by Dirk. It said: "Cousin Dirk, Yesterday I took my revenge on you. Remember I promised I would be revenged on you? I never forget. Yesterday I married a girl in Georgetown. She's a *sambo*. My sincere curses on you and the name of van Groenwegel. Francis."

45

DIRK did not try to dismiss the matter as something that could not have been avoided, nor did he try to pretend that he was not acutely disturbed. Somehow, Francis had succeeded; despite the armour of contempt that Dirk had built up against him during the past three years, despite the fact that Dirk had written him off as a van Groenwegel, he had succeeded in getting his mean little revenge. Little? No, it was not little; he had struck in a vital spot, and had justified the boast in his note, three years before, that he knew what would hurt most. Dirk realised that he had underestimated him. "It never struck me," he said to Cornelia, "that he would have sunk to anything like that. I underestimated his rottenness." Mary, who was present, sniffed and remarked: "I have never done, Papa. I knew him to be rotten through and through." Dirk flashed her a look and said: "Pity I wasn't blessed with your insight, my girl. I'd have shot him before he left this plantation." His voice vibrated, and Mary put an arm around him and said: "Don't let it upset you, dear. He isn't worth being upset over." But her father shook his head. "I mean it. I would have shot him had I thought he would have gone as far as this in his degradation. A *sambo* girl! You know what that means! The daughter of a pure-blooded Negro and a mulatto—three parts black, one part white. His children will be dark-skinned and probably frizzy-haired. And they will bear the name of van Groenwegel. Good God! At least, in Graham's case, Reginald and Ernestine can pass for white, and their name is Greenfield—but dark-skinned van Groenwegels! It's intolerable."

Mary continued to stroke his hair and make comforting sounds, and Cornelia, seated opposite them, smiled her imperturbable smile and said: "Dirk, dearest, the trouble with you is that you are waging a war against imponderables. Human beings are unreliable, Dirk, and your own family, as you should know from the letters in the canister, is emphatically so. Or perhaps I should say that, as a family, you can be relied upon to be unreliable. It's blood, dearest, can't you see? These traits are bound to come out. Look at the striking contrasts you've had! Cousin Hubertus, strong and pious—and Grandma Hendri, cruel and vicious—and your grandfather Jacques, a kindly, softhearted man who admitted that he was a physical coward. And we've read of your Great-aunt Juliana, who was reputed to be such a fine soul, and brave to boot. Didn't you yourself tell me how that slave, Cushy, described her bravery when she was captured by the rebels in 1763? In a family like yours, Dirk, you must be prepared for anything, my darling. Strength, nobility, bravery—and knavery, weakness, perversion. It simply happens that Francis has inherited something of the dark side. You can do nothing about it, I fear."

Elfrida wrote saying that her family had decided to cut off Francis, and she herself was in complete agreement. "I shall not survive this shock, Dirk, dear friend. I feel that the end is near. I've done my best for him, and so have you, and I do wish that you will not take this disappointment too much to heart. He is no longer a van Groenwegel. Think of him as never having been born. Oh, my dear, that I should have had cause to write in this vein of a child of mine. . . ."

A week later, a letter arrived from Angus McLeod announcing that Elfrida had died. The strain of recent events had been too much for her heart. "It was no shock to us," wrote her father. "Poor child, she knew it was the end. She said that she mentioned to you in her last letter to you that she would not survive. . . . If ever you should be in Georgetown, Dirk, my lad, go to Francis and try to impress on him the gravity of his deeds. It is too late, I know, but I still feel that that boy should be severely reprimanded. I am in no state of health to tackle the job, but it would give me great satisfaction to know that someone else had done it for me, and you are the fit person. . . ."

Dirk did not have cause to go to Georgetown until January in the following year, 1837. He had business to transact with Hartfield & Clackson in respect to some recent shipments of sugar, and there was another matter that needed attention. Early in the month, a letter had come from a firm of attorneys in Georgetown, and it had informed him that one Sarah Hubert had died and bequeathed to him her provision shop. (Her will, which was later shown to Dirk by the attorneys, contained this sentence: "He the said gentleman, Mr. Dirk van Groenwegel, showed great kindness to one for whom both he and my humble self had great love.")

Cornelia would have accompanied him, but she was not feeling very well—she had recently complained of dizziness and a certain lassitude—so Mary asked if she could go, and Dirk decided to indulge her, giving as an excuse that she would be able to assist him in sorting out his documents and refreshing his memory in respect to any details that might escape him. It was a plausible excuse, for, during the past year, Mary had been helping him with secretarial work at the saw-mill office. She was learning a great deal about ledgers and journals, and had already announced that she was not interested in getting married, though no one took her seriously.

Dirk always stayed at Flagstaff when in Demerara, and, as usual, he was very warmly welcomed. Edward, the instant he saw Mary, announced that he would do a portrait of her. "That red-gold hair of yours, my child! I can see it on canvas. Dirk my boy, you have a beautiful daughter here. I wonder if you realise it!" And Luise cackled sarcastically and shrieked: "Oh, Edward dear! What has happened to your memory! I'm eighty-three to your seventy-three and I can still recall that Mary is her father's dearest possession. How could he be unaware of her charms!" And Willem and Christina interposed here a few jests about Dirk's new status as a grandfather. "Can you see him as a grandfather, Mama?" asked Christina, her thin, shrunken form shaking with laughter; shaking and rattling, as Mary remarked to Dirk in privacy later. This led to a discussion of the infant grandchildren. In England, Lucy had already produced the future baronet; his name was Archibald. And Dirk told them of Amelia's Gertrude and Sybil's Desmond. Luise enthused over the news of Matilde's twins.

Soon, however, the thunder-heads of depression loomed up, for Edward remarked on Elfrida's death, and that led on to the subject of Francis.

"I don't like to think of it," growled Willem. "Her father is a coarse, crude nigger—one of those who managed to purchase their freedom in '32, soon after the Consolidated Slave Act came into operation. He carries on a provision shop in Charlestown, and believe it or not, but Francis lives with the family above the shop. Yes, he's become one of them, Dirk. After all his upbringing! It's incredible—really incredible."

"As human beings, they are not a bad lot, though," said Edward, his white head at a reflective angle. "I went to see them at Christmas. They're from the West Coast. The mother of the girl used to run a small shop there. She and her daughter were free people, and the man, Jason Clark, used to be a house servant of the Fields. A steady, honest fellow—and so is his wife. I was impressed by them both. The girl, Matilda, struck me as rather a weak character, but she is very pretty in a Negroid way. The truth of the matter is that Francis imposed his will on the girl and got her pregnant, and the parents are very religious, and only agreed to her marrying Francis to prevent her from living in a state of sin and giving birth to a bastard. These coloured folk are even more particular about these things than white people, as you should know. The impression I gained was that they are even less happy about the match than we are."

"But what is Francis doing?" asked Dirk. "Is he living on them?"

"Apparently," nodded Edward. "He gives them help in the shop, I understand, but I've heard reports that he still frequents gambling-dens and promotes cockfights. And some say he goes in for obeah and black magic. Oh, it's heart-rending."

Dirk asked for the address in Charlestown, and Edward told him where to find the shop-residence, but Willem advised Dirk to keep away from the place. "Don't see that you can serve any useful purpose going there, Dirk," frowned Willem. "You'll only be insulted and humiliated."

Dirk said he had not decided what he would do, but, within, he felt a compulsion in the matter, and knew that inevitably he would find himself seeking out the shop in Charlestown. Mary knew this, too, and two days later, when she was in the carriage with her father and they were ostensibly on their way to Kaywana, she expressed no surprise when her father told the coachman to go to the address in Charlestown. She chuckled and squeezed his hand and murmured: "The Old Blood."

He flushed and laughed, and returned: "Yes, yes. Suppose I can't help it, my girl. I'm doomed to make myself a fool over our blood."

Charlestown was a very poor district. Very few whites lived in this part of the town, and the houses were mostly one-storeyed, though here and there were shops combined with residences, the residential section always being the top storey. Many of the buildings, however, were new-looking, having been erected only within the past seven or eight years to replace those lost in the great fire which had swept

Charlestown in September 1828—only two months before the New-town fire.

The shop-residence to which Dirk had been directed was in a part of Charlestown which had not been affected by the fire, and it was a rather dilapidated-looking place, perhaps twenty or thirty years old and never once repaired. A crude sign announced that the proprietor was JASON CLARK—Best Provisions Sold Here. A wobbly wooden bridge spanned a narrow trench and led into the shop, and Dirk and Mary stepped on it as gingerly as they could, fearing it might give way at any instant under them.

Only two customers were in the shop, and the black man, shortish and thickset, with a curly moustache, behind the counter, immediately broke off his conversation with one of the customers to give his attention to Dirk. His manner was respectful without being blatantly subservient. "Good day to you, sir!" he said. "Can I be of some service?"

Dirk explained who he was, and asked him if Francis was at home, and the man, who admitted that he was Jason Clark, the father of Francis's wife, said that Francis was out, but that it would be an honour and a pleasure if Dirk and the young lady would step upstairs for a short while. "Mister Francis said he would be returning for breakfast, sir, so he may be back at any instant."

A few minutes later Dirk and Mary were climbing the outside stairs to the upper storey, escorted by Mr. Clark. His wife, who had evidently observed the advent of the carriage from an upstairs window and was expecting them to appear, opened the door and asked them to enter, her voice as respectful as her husband's. She was an olive-skinned woman of forty or so, with features more Negroid than European, and of some corpulence, but she was extremely clean-looking in person, as was the small sitting-room in appearance. There were only two chairs and a small bamboo table, and she asked them to be seated, but Dirk insisted that she should have one of the chairs. Jason Clark, meanwhile, asked to be excused as he had to go back down to the shop.

They were all three, Dirk, Mary and Mrs. Clark, still arguing about the seating arrangements when a light brown young woman, who could easily have been taken for a pure Negress, appeared from inside. She was in an advanced state of pregnancy, and had a shy, simpering air, though, Dirk had to admit, was not bad-looking. Mrs. Clark introduced her as "Matilda, my daughter, sir." And Dirk immediately

beckoned Matilda to a chair. "I think that settles the matter," he
smiled. "In your condition, my dear lady, you must have a chair. Mary,
you have the other, my girl. I'm sure Mrs. Clark and I won't mind
standing."

Matilda and Mary had hardly been seated when footsteps sounded
on the outer stairs, and Francis, shabby and unshaven, entered.
Matilda gave a soft gasp, and Mrs. Clark turned anxiously, but Francis
evidently did not react as his wife and mother-in-law seemed to have
expected he would have. He smiled and exclaimed: "Is it possible!
Cousin Dirk! And Mary! Now, then! And some people do say that
miracles ceased in biblical times."

Dirk flushed, and Mary frowned and paled a trifle, but both of
them took the hand Francis held out. Dirk said stiffly: "We thought
we would come and see you as we happened to be in Georgetown,
Francis. I trust it doesn't inconvenience you considerably?" And
Francis laughed harshly and returned: "Not one whit, Cousin Dirk.
I am glad you have come to see me and my family—my affianced
family, I mean, though, as you can observe, my own family is not far
away. Haw, haw, haw! Stop fidgeting, Matilda, my buxom wench!
It's the truth. Cousin Dirk will tell you that we must always face the
truth. Grandma Hendri said so in more than one of her letters to
Grandpa Jacques." Francis turned his gaze upon Mary, and a strange
glint came into his eyes. "Ah, but my sweet Mary! Lovelier than ever,
isn't she? I would have married you if I had remained at New Signal,
Mary, my sweet. Did you know that my heart was set on you?"

There was no smell of liquor in his breath. It was simply his way
of behaving, Dirk realised, and felt convinced that he could not be
sane. As though by mutual agreement, they all let him talk without
attempting to interrupt him.

"I have just won quite a large sum," he said, jingling the money in
his trousers pocket. "Cockfighting is a magnificent sport, Cousin Dirk.
I wish I could persuade you to come and watch with me sometimes.
But you're too much of a gentleman to venture in the places I do.
Haw, haw! Ah, well. Pity. And I can't lose, you know." He bent his
gaze on Mary again, and his eyes narrowed lasciviously. "I can't lose,
my sweet child," he said, his voice falling to a hoarse murmur. "I never
lose, Mary. I win all the time—at the races and at the cockfights. It's all
done by dreams. I have powers. The spirits speak to me in my dreams,
and I am guided what to do." He uttered a throaty laugh and turned
to his wife. "Eh, Matilda? You sleep with me, wench. Tell Mary how

the spirits come to me at night and speak to me. All night long they hover over me in blue mists. I keep incense burning by our bed until midnight has struck——"

"Come, Francis," Dirk suddenly interrupted, "tell us something of the practical side of your life. Do you feel you would like any help in obtaining a post in some good commercial house? I was thinking of discussing you with the Hartfields, but I must know what you feel on the matter first."

Francis turned pink with laughter. He tottered about, hugging himself and laughing. He made jabbing gestures with a forefinger at Dirk. "What a jest, oh, what a jest! Matilda! Did you hear that? Cousin Dirk is thinking of my welfare. He drove me out of New Signal, but now he has come to make amends."

Mary rose and said: "Papa, I think we'd better go."

Dirk, red and angry, flashed at Francis: "I think you're impossible, boy! It's hard to believe that you have not been drinking."

"Me? No, no, no. I never take strong drink, Cousin Dirk," said Francis. "The spirits don't like it. It would dull my powers, and the fumes of rum and gin are most inimical to those who dwell in the Darkness." His mood changed with an abruptness that seemed incredible. He scowled and snarled: "You leave me alone, Cousin Dirk. You must not come here again. I'm beneath you now—and I'm mad. You all think me mad. Well, keep away. I need no help from you— nor from the Hartfields. I wouldn't take a stiver from you if you went down on your knees and begged me to. Leave me alone. My wife is a nigger. That hurts you, eh? I knew it would—that was why I married her. To get my revenge on you——"

"I suppose," Dirk cut in savagely, "you wouldn't have the decency to change your name by deed poll to Clark if I offered to pay you a sum of money to do so? Would you do this, Francis? I'm asking you."

"Not for twenty million pounds sterling," rasped Francis, his eyes blazing malice. "No I wouldn't. My name is van Groenwegel, and it stays van Groenwegel. And my lawful children—hear that!—lawful children will bear the name of van Groenwegel. You see the power I have, Cousin Dirk? Yes, power. I, Francis. I told you the spirits would give me power. I—yes, I am going to shape the future of our family. Wait and you'll see what my darkie children will do. You'll be ashamed of them, but I'll put the power of the spirits into them. I'll train them up to use the power of the Dark for their benefit."

Matilda and her mother uttered not a word throughout it all. They looked like beings hypnotised, Matilda sitting erect in the chair, her hands clasped upon her bulging stomach, Mrs. Clark standing stiffly near a window, her eyes wide with both fear and embarrassment.

Francis followed Dirk and Mary down to the carriage, talking without cessation, his eyes, with their unnatural glint, sometimes wild and maniacal, sometimes frankly lascivious as they settled on Mary. Just before they got into the carriage, he said: "One day I'm going to send out the call for you, Mary. I'm going to tell them to bring you to me, wherever you may be, and what I shall do to you, my sweet!" He went on to babble obscene details, and the coachman gasped, and shouted at him before urging the horse to be off. His cackling laughter sounded behind them, and the coachman's dark brown face looked scandalised. The man glanced down at Dirk and Mary, and called: "Dat's a bad man, massa! No decency in him!"

46

BEFORE returning to Berbice, Dirk dropped in at the shop Sarah Hubert, Rose's mother, had left for him in her will. It was still being carried on by a free *sambo* young man named Tom Watson, who, Dirk learnt, was in no way related to Sarah Hubert, but merely the son of a good friend of old Sarah's.

Dirk had been greatly touched by the sentiments expressed in Sarah's will. After the Newtown fire he had gone round to see her, and recalled vividly the look of resigned grief on her face, and how she had nodded slowly and murmured: "It had to be, Mr. Dirk. It was the nature God gave her. She couldn't live and die like anybody else." And then after a pause, the smile as she glanced up and added: "You gave her some happiness, though, Mr. Dirk, and for that I shall be always grateful to you."

Tom Watson received a commission on the sales made in the shop. It seemed to be his sole livelihood, and Dirk told him that nothing would be changed for the time being. "The attorneys will handle my interests. You may see them whenever you need any advice."

Dirk delayed his return by a week in order to give his Uncle Edward time to finish the portrait of Mary he had commenced. Edward, in making a present of it to the girl, said: "I haven't lost my cunning, Mary child, but the moments of inspiration are not many these days. It's nearly a year since I painted anything."

It was an excellent portrait, and Mary was delighted with it. "I'm going to keep this always, Uncle Edward. I shall be proud to show it to my nieces and nephews," she added—and Edward raised his brows, and said: "Nieces and nephews! What of your grandchildren and your own children!" And Mary, as though anticipating this reaction, smiled and shook her head. "I won't have any, Uncle Edward. I've made up my mind not to marry."

Willem snorted. "Get away, girl! You couldn't escape marrying if you tried. I pity you, Dirk, when they begin to flock round her in a year or two."

"If I weren't seventy-three," sighed Edward, "and your great-uncle, my child, I myself would make certain you didn't go through life single."

Dirk laughed and said: "She's sixteen in April. I've wagered her that by April next year she'll be pleading with me to give some young blood permission to visit her." And Mary, pinkening, but otherwise unabashed, smiled and said: "You may as well pay over the hundred guilders now, then, Papa, for you've already lost the wager."

"But what have you got against marriage?" asked Luise.

"Nothing at all," Mary answered, and in this moment her face reminded Dirk of her mother's—and, for some reason that he could not explain, Dirk felt disturbed, even felt a vague shudder of premonition quiver through him.

"It's simply," said Mary, her manner very calm and confident now, "that I feel I'd be happier if I remained single. My nature, I suppose."

The next time when Dirk felt this premonitory shudder was in March when Cornelia announced to him that she was pregnant. "I thought there was something strange about that lassitude and dizziness I suffered from in January."

Mary was present when Cornelia broke the news to Dirk, and Dirk saw the girl's face pale, saw her lean forward, her hands clenching in her lap. They were in the sitting-room, before dinner, and the dry-weather late-afternoon sun was shining in at the southern windows, making a narrow parallelogram down the portrait of Hubertus. "At your age, Mother!" Mary exclaimed, after a pause. "I thought you'd long ago given up the idea of having any more children."

Cornelia raised her brows. "A surprising remark for you to make, isn't it, Mary?" And Dirk frowned and nodded in agreement, stirring in his seat. He growled: "Hardly proper of you, Mary."

Mary flushed and cried—a trifle hysterically, thought Dirk: "But isn't it the truth? I've heard you both say that years ago."

"Very well, very well," snapped her father. "We did say so, I suppose—but now and then accidents happen for which neither your mother nor I can be blamed. That's enough on the subject, I think."

"I'm sorry," Mary murmured—and rose and hurried away.

The dinner gong went shortly after, but she did not appear at table, and Cornelia told Hendrik to go upstairs and see what was the matter with her. Dirk, however, stopped Hendrik. "I'll go up myself, my boy. A child of moods, Mary."

Cornelia gazed after him as he left the room, and smiled—a slight, inscrutable smile. Peter, nearly ten, giggled and said: "Papa spoils her too much."

The child was born in September, a boy, and they called him Adrian Charles—and Mary, on seeing him for the first time, exclaimed: "Fancy! An uncle younger than his niece and nephew! But he's a dear little fellow!" Dirk and Cornelia saw her face suffused with affection. "I'm going to treasure him."

Doctor John warned Cornelia, however, that she would have to be careful in future; her kidneys were not functioning as they should. "I felt more anxious for you than I revealed, my girl," he said. "You have been lucky that everything went without trouble. Very, very lucky, I can assure you."

Dirk laughed and said: "She's a tough old war horse, Uncle John. Her kidneys won't give out in a hurry."

"We must take him to Flagstaff as soon as he is a year old," said Mary. "I'd like Uncle Edward to paint a portrait of him."

As it happened, however, this was never to be. The very next month, news came from Demerara that Edward had died. "Suddenly but undramatically," wrote Willem, "he leaned back in his chair, and sighed, and the next thing we knew he was dead. We could hardly believe it, for he was in perfectly good spirits all the morning, and never complained of any aches or pains. . . ."

As though Death had given a signal that the family had been too long neglected, Luise felt the dusty touch on her shoulder in January of the following year, and Willem wrote: "I felt she would not last longer than a few months, for she and Father were too close in spirit. I believe that if Father had lived she would have gone on to ninety. However, eighty-four is a ripe age. . . ."

The other death came in February—only a few days before the death of Governor Carmichael-Smyth on the fourth of March—and it was an untimely one. Timothy van Groenwegel, ten months old, suffered a fall; there was internal bleeding, and he died. Francis, on arriving home and being told what had happened, stared at the dead

infant, then, without a word, snatched up a letter-wood walking stick
and beat Matilda until she collapsed on the floor, pleading for mercy.
She was four months pregnant, but miraculously she did not suffer a
miscarriage.

The death of Carmichael-Smyth was mourned throughout the
colony, especially by the Negroes, who had looked up to him as their
champion and hero—the man who had brought them their freedom,
they felt; the man who had always taken pains to explain every new
law passed, and that affected their welfare, in detail, and in person;
the man who had listened to every little complaint they had taken to
him, and patiently attempted to help them out of their difficulties;
the man who had not feared the wrath of the planters, and who, before
his death, had become highly popular with the planters themselves.

The ghost of Carmichael-Smyth must have looked on with a smile
of approval when, a few months later, on the fourth of July of that
same year, 1838, the Court of Policy passed a motion that all slaves,
those in the field and those employed in the houses of their masters,
should be freed on the first of August, thus annulling the former plan
to release only house servants on that day and field slaves two years
hence.

Meantime, only two months before, the ships *Hesperus* and *Whitby*
had arrived, bringing more than four hundred immigrants from Calcutta—the first East Indian indentured labourers to enter the colony.
They were immediately put to work on Mr. John Gladstone's plantations on the West Coast of Demerara—sixty-four men, three women
and three children went to Plantation Vreed-en-Hoop, and thirty-one
men to the other plantation, Vriedestein. Others went to plantations
owned by the Moss brothers.

The first of August was greeted with a salute of nineteen guns at
Fort Willem Frederik, and the Negroes ran riot in rejoicing. Rain fell
heavily during the morning, but the rest of the day was fine, and the
streets of Georgetown could not contain the crowds of prancing,
shouting black people.

From a window in Hartfield & Clackson's, Willem watched them
and wagged his head, and his mouth twisted in contempt. "Savages
—only savages. They think they're free and happy now. They don't
realise that their loss is as great as ours. They'll soon see that it was
their massas who pampered them and the Anti-Slavery Society who
turned them loose to be paupers."

John Hartfield and Graeme Clackson, who were with him watching the crowds, nodded in agreement, but said nothing, their faces grave.

At Kaywana, Graham arranged a grand fete for all his own labourers, and himself went around among them, accompanied by two missionaries and their wives, congratulating them and uttering pious platitudes. Albert Laver was there, too, and in the evening, he and Graham played their violins, for Albert, too, was a good violinist. At the height of things, John and Clara, and Harvey and his wife and Timothy, recently returned from England, arrived. Clara, at seventy-eight, was very grey and rather shaky on her feet, though her spirit was still young. There were tears in her eyes as she embraced Graham and said: "You of all people, I know, my dear, must be sincerely pleased on this great day." The two of them sat for a long time on the portico alone, reminiscing: recalling the days of Mr. Wray and the services in the old barn.

In Berbice, Dirk's feelings were very similar to Willem's. "If they could see the ruin that's facing this colony," he said to Ronald Hopkinson, his son-in-law, "they wouldn't prance around as they're doing now." He and Cornelia and Mary and Hendrik dined with Ronald and Amelia that day, watching the usually quiet streets of New Amsterdam dense with milling black faces, and listening to the varied fragments of wild language that drifted up to them as they sat on the veranda, after dinner, with two-and-a-half-year-old Gertrude and the seven-month-old Storm. Ronald agreed with Dirk, saying: "Cotton is as good as finished, I'm afraid. What with the poor prices and now this new situation. Papa and I are discussing a project to buy some sugar interests in Barbados."

"So he told me," nodded Dirk. "The best thing you can do, my boy, though I don't suppose the labour situation will be any better in Barbados."

Mary intervened to say: "I would advise going in for commerce instead of planting. I believe it's the merchants who are going to prosper in the years ahead of us." Both Dirk and Ronald glanced at her, Dirk smiling and remarking: "What a young woman! At your age Amelia wasn't interested in such topics. Were you, Amelia, my girl?"

"Even now I'm not," said Amelia as she bent to fondle young Storm seated in the lap of his nurse squatting on the floor beside Amelia's chair. Ronald began to say something teasing, but Cornelia exclaimed: "Here's Harry, Dirk!" and all eyes turned to the street where a carriage had come to a stop at the gateway.

"Yes, Father said he would probably drop in," Ronald murmured. And then Mary frowned and said: "Mrs. Berton is with him, I see" —and Dirk glanced at her sharply—and Cornelia glanced from Dirk to Mary.

Harry Hopkinson, tall and thin and hearty, was Dirk's age, actually a trifle older—he was already forty-four—but almost as youthful-looking as his son Ronald. With him was his sister, a widow, who had recently come from Barbados, where her husband had died. Janet Berton was in her early thirties, and voluptuous not only in build but in voice, manner and languid brown eyes. Hers was a frankly animal charm, and since her arrival some five or six months before—she lived with her brother in New Amsterdam—had been the main topic of masculine conversation in the town and countryside. She had already received three proposals of marriage, but had turned them down —and no one was puzzled to understand why, for within the first week of her arrival she had made it only too clear where her preference lay. If there was one thing she lacked, it was a sense of discretion.

"Ah, Dirk!" she exclaimed, her eyes alight the instant she entered the portico. "I told Harry you would be here. Watching the grim rejoicing on the street." She held his hand, and kept on holding it, so that Dirk, flushing and frowning, and smiling all at once, was compelled to withdraw it.

Mary glared at her, but Cornelia's face was calm.

Dirk said: "Control yourself, please, Janet." And Janet chuckled— she never laughed out loud at any time—and returned: "I've told you that that is something I'm quite unable to do, Dirk, my dear—especially when you're present." She sighed and gave Mary a sly glance. "Your daughter is regarding me with the deepest disapproval. I can hear her saying to herself: 'What a shameless hussy!'" She turned to Cornelia. "Cornelia, you must forgive me, but I've told you, my dear. I can't help it if your husband has swept me off my feet, can I?"

"I'm not at all upset, Janet," said Cornelia, smiling. "If he has swept you off your feet, I'm certain he will be capable of keeping his balance as well as yours. Dirk is an excellent juggler."

"I don't know when you'll be serious, Janet." Her brother frowned and then laughed—though a trifle uncomfortably. And Janet uttered a crooning sound of mirth, her whole shapely form in a tremor of abandon. Turning, she looked at Dirk, and said: "Harry never takes me seriously, Dirk—but *you* know I am. Always."

Not only Dirk, but everyone else knew that her banter was a mere muslin cloak for her wanton intentions. It was Mary who had overheard her one late afternoon at New Signal, in the corridor, saying to Dirk: "I'll never rest until I lure you into bed with me, Dirk—and that's no banter."

That was why every time Janet appeared on the scene, Mary would frown, Dirk grow tense and uncomfortable, and Cornelia alert. It was a situation that Dirk deplored, yet secretly enjoyed, for he was not immune to Janet's sensual charms. The animal in him responded to her barefaced overtures even while the ascetic and the responsible family man glowered reproachfully. At no instant, however, did he ever feel unsure of himself. It was a situation that he could handle. As Cornelia said, he was capable of keeping his balance—as well as Janet's. What disturbed him more than he cared to admit was Mary's attitude. More and more he found himself pondering on Mary's outlook —not only towards Janet, but towards society as a whole, and life; it was not the outlook, he felt, a girl of her age should have. So far, she had shown little interest in young men, and every day she became more deeply immersed in the affairs of the plantation, and in the timber business, and even in the politics of the colony. Admirable as this might be in its way, it was not entirely wholesome, he was certain. His instinct warned him that something was wrong somewhere.

47

AS he told Jacob at the sawmill, one morning a few weeks later, it was not life itself he feared, but the complications life produced to baffle him.

"I can bear any burden, Jacob, provided that I know exactly what I am being asked to bear, but it's when there is doubt as to what the contents of the bundle may comprise that I get afraid and unsure of myself."

"The moral," Jacob replied, handing him back the letter, "is to refuse point-blank to handle any doubtful goods." Then he grinned and asked: "Wasn't it you yourself who asked his father-in-law to keep you informed?"

Dirk nodded. "I admit that. It's my own fault, of course. I chose to get myself involved, so I should not grumble. What do you advise, anyway? Should I go to Georgetown or shouldn't I?"

"I'd say don't go—but that won't stop you."

Dirk laughed. "What a cynic you are, Jacob, lad! But you're right. I'll go."

So Dirk went to Georgetown and arranged with Graeme Clackson to get Francis out of the colony. Jason Clark, who had written to Dirk to tell him of the dismal affair, was the only one who knew where Francis could be found, and when Dirk interviewed him in his shop the Negro said: "He's wicked, sir, but he's my son-in-law, and I feel I must protect him. I promised him I would not say where he is hiding —not even to you. But I will assuredly help you to get him on to the ship when the right moment comes. Simply tell me the hour and it will be done. And let me say how much I appreciate your great kindness, sir. After what happened here when you last came with your daughter to see us, you would have been well in your rights to have turned your back on Francis."

Dirk smiled, and replied: "It's not kindness, Mr. Clark. He's of my blood."

Two days later when the hue and cry was on—the body of the mulatto girl Francis had beaten to death in Werk-en-Rust was found in the two-roomed shack—Dirk visited the Clarks again, and was shown the two-month-old baby—a boy. The complexion was definitely olive, but the hair was straight, and the eyes grey-brown. It was unmistakably a coloured child. A coloured van Groenwegel.

"We christening him Jason, after Papa," said Matilda.

"Good," murmured Dirk, touching the infant's cheek with a finger. "Sturdy little fellow. You must take good care of him." He nearly added: "Better care than you did of the last one," but he was certain Matilda would have burst into tears, and checked himself in time. Instead he said: "And remember, keep in touch with me. If ever you're in difficulties, write and let me know."

Matilda, blinking quickly, her eyes moist, said: "Thanks, Mr. Dirk. You're very good." Her mother, more practical, asked: "Sir, you don't think Francis will come back to the colony to worry us again?"

"I don't think so, Mrs. Clark," Dirk told her. "By now he should be nearly in Trinidad, and from there he'll be taken to Jamaica. The captain will see to it that he is left in the right port. The ship is going to Panama."

As the carriage bore him away, a few minutes later, towards Kingston, where he was having breakfast with Harvey Hartfield, he had to smile to himself, wondering where it would all end. I keep on, he thought, fretting myself over the welfare of every human with a drop of van Groenwegel blood in his veins, but I can discern already that the task has got beyond me. The ramifications of blood are too widespread and intricate. Threads will persist in eluding me.

He reflected on Harvey. The son of John and Clara Hartfield, according to the law and the cognizance of society—but, by blood, the son of his Uncle Edward. Yes, there was van Groenwegel blood in Harvey, and in Harvey's children, Timothy and Jessie. And hadn't Willem whispered to him some years ago that many people felt that Graeme Clackson was actually a son of Cousin Hubertus—the result of an affair between Cousin Hubertus and Faustina, Cranley Clackson's wife. . . ? For all I know, Graeme Clackson, too, has van Groenwegel blood in him. Where and when would my duties as the family watchdog end?

That feeling, born within the past decade or so, swept over him—that feeling of absurdity and of ephemerality. Watching the wooden houses of Georgetown rush by, he wagged his head slightly, smiling and telling himself that it all had to fade away some day. The houses looked brave in their white paint, but the paint was flaking, the wood was rotting. Nothing lasted. Even he himself would one day be too old and worn to trouble about such matters as blood and family honour.

A few minutes later when Harvey greeted him with, "You look pensive, old fellah. What's up?" in his English accent, Dirk smiled and said: "I feel as I look. I have just been indulging in the tritest and dreariest of thoughts."

"Some gin will cure that, old man," said Harvey. "Oh, and by the by, here's a letter for you. It was sent in care of the firm."

Dirk frowned as he looked at it. The handwriting was Mary's. A few minutes after he had read it—he had had his drink and asked Harvey to excuse him while he read the letter—Harvey heard him murmuring to himself, and asked: "What's up, Dirk? More trite and dreary thoughts?"

"Cornelia is ill," Dirk answered. "Mary thinks I should return home at once."

By the time he got back to New Signal she was very much better. "When I wrote," said Mary, "she was very bad. Uncle John had virtually given up hope."

Dirk sat by her and murmured: "Those kidneys, eh?" And Cornelia nodded. Stout and ungainly, she lay there on the big four-poster in the northeastern room, so different from the tall, elegant, shapely creature who had walked with him to the canal aback of Don Diego in the moonlight, that July night in 1815. Only the dark blue eyes with their look of mystery and inscrutability seemed the same. Yes, they had not changed.

"Mary has been very good."

"Has she?" Dirk frowned and stirred slightly. Mary was right behind him, her hand on his shoulder. Why would he have preferred if she had not been so close, if she had not been in the room at all? Nevertheless, he turned and smiled at her, patted her arm, as he knew she expected of him.

Later, when he was alone on the portico, Mary came out to him and said: "Uncle John says there is no hope. She might last for weeks or months, but we must resign ourselves to losing her sooner or later."

"He said that, did he?"

"Yes." She seated herself on the arm of his chair, and stroked his hair. "But you mustn't let it worry you, Papa. Be strong. As you've always been," she added in a murmur. He felt a drop of moisture on his wrist.

They were silent, watching the early afternoon sunshine on the mango trees. Thunderclouds loomed over them in the southeast, and after a moment they heard a far-off rumble. Mary asked: "She's older than you, isn't she?"

He nodded. "A few months. She was forty-three in June last."

"And you're forty-three this month. A September baby."

"Mary."

"Yes?"

He fidgeted, and found that he was unable to say what he had intended to. Her hand had stopped stroking his hair. It rested on his shoulder now.

"What is it, Papa?"

"Nothing." He rose, trying not to appear abrupt in doing so. "You'll be dancing tomorrow evening at the Parrotts, won't you?"

He could feel her gaze on him, keen, probing. "You're upset, I suppose," she murmured—though her tone was unsure. Abruptly: "Yes, I suppose so—though I'm not certain yet. If you had been still in Georgetown I'd have gone, but now that you're back . . . You won't be going yourself, will you?"

He shook his head, parted his lips to say something, and again found that his courage failed him. "No, no. Of course not. With your mother ill? But you must go and enjoy yourself. I insist."

"I'm not particularly keen on going, Papa."

"You must go." He spoke almost angrily. "I insist. It is essential that you meet young people. You're too much at home. It isn't healthy."

She recoiled as though he had struck her. He did not look at her directly, but could feel her gaze on him, hurt, sensitive, resentful, vaguely suspicious. Her voice was barely audible as she said: "Very well. I'll go—as you wish."

At Christmas, Cornelia was well enough to participate in the festivities, but in January of the next year she was in bed again. Towards the end of February, she was up again. And so it went on throughout that year.

Meanwhile, Janet Berton was a regular visitor at New Signal. She came on the pretext of visiting the invalid, and she never came without flowers or fruit. Mary detested her, and made no attempt to disguise the fact, but Janet ignored her, or treated her with an airy indulgence. One day—it was in March—Mary accosted her in the sitting-room and said: "Aren't you ashamed of yourself?" And Janet raised her brows and shook her head. "No, Mary dear. Why?"

"Have you no modesty? No—no sensitivity?"

"Not much of either, I fear. Why do you ask?" Janet's air was one of bland innocence, and Mary flushed, furious, and snapped: "You're beyond hope." Her head trembled. "To come here taking advantage of my mother's illness! You know very well you don't care a stiver for her."

"Oh, but that isn't true, dear. I love Cornelia."

"You're a hypocrite."

"I'm not. I love your father, too, if that's what you mean." Janet chuckled—and her body trembled all over in that sensual earthquake that only she could produce, her breasts seeming on the point of overflowing out of her bodice.

Mary turned her back on her and left the room.

In April news came that Clara Hartfield had died on the second of the month, and been buried on the following day. Willem wrote, and Dirk immediately planned to go to Georgetown to pay a visit of condolence on John and Harvey.

Janet announced that she would travel by the same opportunity. "I know Harvey very well. We met in England some years ago."

Mary asked Dirk if he would let her go with him, but Dirk told her: "Most certainly not, Mary, my dear. You must remain to have an eye on your mother."

"Mother is quite well at the moment, Papa. We won't be away more than a week." There was a desperate note in her voice, and Dirk wavered for an instant.

"I indulge you too much. What necessity is there for you to accompany me! I can take care of myself, I hope. I'll think it over, but I don't feel you ought to go." Abruptly he tensed, and said: "No, definitely not, Mary. The Halls have invited you to their silver-wedding dinner on Tuesday. You must go to that. There'll be a number of young men there who, I'm sure, will want to meet you."

"But I don't want to meet them!" Mary flared. Her eyes grew moist with tears of rage. Her head trembled slightly. "Do you hear me, Papa! I'm not interested in any of them. Not one of them."

Dirk turned off, clasping his hands together hard, and Mary, contrite, said: "I'm sorry. Papa. I will lose my temper. Forgive me."

Without looking at her, he murmured: "Perhaps later in the year you can come with me. I'll have to pay a business visit, in any event."

Janet was seasick all the way to Georgetown, so did not prove a nuisance, and friends were there to meet her when they arrived. They swept her off, and Dirk breathed in relief as he and Willem entered the carriage and set out for the East Coast. Willem, as usual, was in a temper about the state of affairs in respect to labour. "There it is," he blazed, "we've been robbed of our slaves, they pay us a mere one third of their value as compensation, and now that we want to bring in immigrants to work as labourers, that damned Anti-Slavery Society in London is doing its best to balk us. That fool of a Scoble who they sent out here to report on how the apprentices have been treated has gone and upset everything. He has complained to London that the Hindustan people on Gladstone's plantations are being ill-treated, and —whoof! London goes up in the air. They have put a ban on further importations of people from India. And by God! That was the one thing we were putting our hopes on more than ever. How the deuce do they expect us to carry on if we don't get labour. Look what these niggers are doing! They work two or three days a week, and then for the rest of the week they wander off and laze. Or they come flocking into the town and set up as hucksters, content to sell a few ground provisions and fruits, squatting by the side of the street. Some of them want to work as porters, doing the lightest of jobs."

Dirk sympathised, for even on his own place on the Canje, and on other places, the tale was the same. "Many of them in Berbice," he told Willem, "won't work at all—yet they expect to have their old free lodgings, provision plots, and allowances—just as when they were free before. And there is Scoble inciting them to demand more, to demand their 'rights,' as he calls them. It's a sickening state of affairs, Willem. This colony is finished—unless a miracle happens, and happens quickly."

Later that day, when on his way to see John Hartfield, Dirk could not help admiring the lovely appearance of the town with its trees and wooden houses in their spacious gardens, and the canals with their floating lily plants. Such a handsome town, and spreading eastward and southward all the time. It had a Mayor and Town Council now; the corporation had come into being two years before—in 1837. And now a police force was being organised, and there was a scheme afoot to start building a railway along the East Coast.

How much further would progress go, he wondered, if the planters were not given more consideration than they were being given at present? Sugar was the only thing that could save the colony from retrogressing. Southern America had killed cotton, and even coffee was on the way out because of competition in other parts of the world. Sugar—only sugar could save the day.

John agreed with him, though he admitted that at the moment the merchants were doing an excellent trade. "I suppose what hurts one lot benefits another," smiled John. "Since last August when the Negroes began to flock into the town we have done more business than in the two years previous put together. The stupid fools buy anything —fling their money around recklessly. Clothes, cheap jewellery, shoes, trinkets of any or every kind—they buy anything at all their eyes alight on. I was hearing last week that some fellows at Sandbach's succeeded in selling even a gaudy show card advertising a new type of goods. What can you expect? Their freedom has gone to their heads."

At Huis Kaywana, Graham was worried about the drought. The short dry season, so far, showed no signs of coming to an end. Since January no rain had fallen, and the canes were beginning to suffer. Dirk agreed that it was unusual the weather they were having this year. "By now we should have had some rain. It would be pretty grim if the weather turned on us as well."

Graham, at forty-nine, was almost completely grey, though, in face, he looked younger than his years. Still finicky and inclined to fidget, he was much less affected, and his benevolence held more sincerity. He did not refer so often to God and prayer, and his general approach to life was more down to earth.

Even about Clara's death he did not sentimentalise as much as Dirk had anticipated. He said: "I'm sorry she did not get to see Reginald before she died—I mean as he is now, a tall, handsome fellow. He's coming on a visit next summer." He added quickly: "Summer next year, that is. We here so seldom speak of summer. Dry weather and wet weather are all we know of."

"He's at Oxford, isn't he?"

"Yes. And doing very well. He hopes to take his degree in Classics next year." Graham spoke with a quiet pride. "A brilliant fellow."

"I hear you're a grandfather, too," smiled Dirk. And Graham pinkened, and fidgeted. "Yes, yes. Ernestine has a daughter. I think I'll go and see them the year after the next. Good chance to get Reginald settled in, too. He's going to keep an eye on things for us in London."

"Excellent plan," Dirk nodded. "We need someone in London to supervise our affairs." To himself, he thought: I rather wonder, though, whether an English-bred gentleman of leisure is the right person to assign to such an undertaking.

As though Graham had read his thoughts, he said in a musing voice: "He's a serious youngster—and I believe he will take an interest in the plantations. That is why I'm having him pay us a visit, in fact. So as to take him round to see what conditions are like here. I want him to have a first-hand knowledge of our enterprises here. I'm even going to take him up to the timber grants."

"Good. Good," said Dirk. And then turned his head, for a carriage was coming up the driveway. Graham said: "Ah, here are the Bentleys! I've invited them to dinner. I think you've met them?"

"Yes, yes. I'm acquainted with them."

"Langley Bentley's father was a very good friend of Cousin Hubertus's."

Accompanying Langley Bentley and his wife, Jane, was Janet Berton.

Four hours later Janet said that she was spending the night with the Parnells. The Parnells' place was only a mile from Flagstaff, so Dirk had to offer to have her come with him in his carriage. The carriage had hardly turned out of the driveway into the road when she sidled down against him, and nestled her head against his shoulder, murmuring with her sensual chuckle: "You see how determined I am, Dirk, sweetheart?"

"And somewhat annoying, too," growled Dirk, but allowed her head to remain where it was for the rest of the journey to the Parnells'. It was dark, and the coachman was a discreet fellow.

48

APRIL advanced, but still no rains came. The sun glared down from skies blue-grey with heat, savannah fires broke out on the East Coast, and in Berbice, Dirk and Cornelia would sit by the window in the northeastern room and watch the smoke of distant forest fires. Dirk had to arrange all-night patrols to move about the plantation, in order to report if any sign of fire was seen approaching the fields aback.

May came, and June, and still the sun spewed down heat from cloudless skies. The canes were thin and straggly, and when the grinding season commenced early in September, the yield would be poor.

In October, Cornelia suffered another severe spell of illness, and they all gave up hope—but she recovered. "Tough old war horse," Dirk said with a grin, holding her hand and watching her smile. "I'm almost willing to wager you'll be ninety before those kidneys succeed in carrying you off."

She shook her head. "No, dearest. It will be much, much sooner than ninety." And abruptly: "Dirk, you must marry again."

"What! Marry again? What for?" He scowled. "Look here, stop that kind of talk. It's morbid. You behave as though you were on the point of death—and even if you were it would be in bad taste to tell me to marry again."

She regarded him for a moment in silence, with affection, and also with a certain appraisement. Then she said: "Still, I feel I should tell you, Dirk. I'd like you to marry again. It will keep you out of complications."

"Will it?" He grinned, and then frowned. "I wonder. Has being married to you kept me out of complications?" He gave her hair a playful tug. "If anything, I should say it's increased the complications.

What with you always scheming to hurl my canister of letters in the Creek, and I striving to preserve it and the family name from extinction." His banter, however, was forced, and he knew that she sensed it, and was not surprised when she said: "For you there will always be complications, because you are so earnest. Where you are now you're not as gay as your voice and words might indicate. Dirk, you're worried over Mary, aren't you? Her refusal to mix with young people?"

He nodded, instantly uncomfortable. It was a subject they had persistently avoided up to now—and even now he knew they would never dare touch on certain aspects of it. "Yes, I don't like her attitude towards her acquaintances," he murmured, frowning out at the blazing day. The sky was reddish with the smoke of forest fires. "Such a pity, such a pity. Only yesterday I received a letter from young Pendleton asking my permission to visit her. Of course, when I told her about it, she laughed and ridiculed the idea of his paying court to her. I know of at least three other young fellows who would give a gallon of their blood merely for the privilege of kissing her hand—yet she sniffs on them all."

The chug-a-chug of the factory came on the air, and a sudden whiff of cane juice and megass swirled through the room on a warm breeze from the southeast.

"And she's nineteen in April next."

Cornelia touched his hand and said: "It's not your fault, Dirk. I mean, you should not feel any guilt in the matter."

He started. "What do you mean? Guilt?"

"I mean, it's not due to your spoiling of her—making a pet of her."

"Oh." He breathed in relief, though his hands began to clench and unclench.

After a silence, she said: "I know what's on your mind—and your assessment is probably correct."

Again he started, and gave her a keen stare.

"I mean, it's blood, Dirk. Heredity."

He nodded—again with a feeling of relief. "Yes, I know. I remember what you said when we discussed Francis some years ago. In a family like ours we must be prepared for anything—strength, nobility, bravery—and knavery, weakness, perversion." He rose nervously. A carriage was approaching along the driveway. "That must be your dear friend, Janet. Tch! One day I shall go mad," he grinned, bending and fondling her under the chin. But she was serious when she gazed up at him and said: "No, you won't, dearest. And I like Janet, despite her brazen airs. I think you should marry her when I'm gone."

Before he could comment on this, she turned her head quickly. He, too, glanced round. Mary was standing in the doorway.

"What is it, Mary?" Dirk snapped.

Mary seemed to steel herself before saying, her voice strangely bated: "It's nothing important. I only came to tell Mama that Mrs. Berton is here."

That was the worst year in the memory of any of the planters alive then. The yield was so poor because of the drought that many a plantation was ruined, and had to be sold for less than a tenth of its value. In Berbice, Plantation Enfield, which ten years before had been worth nearly thirty thousand pounds, was sold at execution for two thousand, and on the Corentyne Coast, Plantation Port Mourant, valued before August 1834 at thirty-five thousand pounds, went for a mere seven thousand. Some coffee and cotton estates, formerly worth five or ten thousand pounds, could not find purchasers, even when offered for as low as fifty pounds. "Abolition," Dirk murmured one afternoon by Cornelia's bedside, "and now the drought." And she smiled and said: "Never mind. You'll overcome them. There's nothing you aren't big enough to overcome, Dirk dearest."

She died in January of the next year, 1840, and it was raining when they buried her in the private cemetery on the plantation. The cabbage palms were getting tall, and their dark green fronds looked mournful against the grey sky.

When Dirk and the Lutheran pastor and the crowd of mourners began to move back towards the house, Storm and Elizabeth lingered to watch the masons at work on the big brick vault, Storm wagging his head and uttering low, mumbling sounds. The rain dribbled drearily around them, as though determined to make up for the hot, blazing days of the previous year. Storm looked up at the cabbage palms, and said, with a sigh: "It was raining heavily that Sunday when old Wilfred fell from his mule. It was a Sunday, wasn't it?" And Elizabeth nodded. They listened to the click-clack of the mason's tools, and then Storm again broke the silence. "I should have been the next to go in there. Seventy-seven in March, my dear." And Elizabeth smiled faintly, sadly, and murmured: "Nothing happens in proper order in this life, Storm. You should be old enough to know that."

Storm turned his gaze to where other tombs stood. Not vaults—

merely tombs. One was Marta's. Another was Graff's—Graff had been a good man; the best carpenter-overseer New Signal had ever had; he had once been in charge of a gang of slaves in the Winkel. A mulatto —free mulatto. Faithful servant. Only faithful servants were buried here. . . . Nibia, who had died only three weeks before. . . . Albertus Frick—another good man. . . .

"Elizabeth."

"Yes, dear?"

"Something I must confess. We never can tell, my dear. I may soon be going into the vault there—and I feel you should know." He pointed to Frick's tomb. "Old Frick. Remember Jacob—and Nibia? Frick wasn't his father, Elizabeth." He found that his hands were trembling. "I lied to you all, my dear."

Elizabeth smiled again—this time not sadly but with amusement and affection. "Never mind, Storm dear. Don't upset yourself. It is years and years and years since I knew that you were Jacob's father."

"What! You knew!"

She nodded. "When Marta fell down with that stroke, I sat with her in her logie, and before she died she mumbled a few things to me. And Nibia also told me." She took his arm. "Vile old man. Come. Let us go back to the house."

On the way to the house he kept blinking rapidly and wagging his head, mumbling to himself. All the wetness on his cheeks was not rain, and he trembled so much that she had to keep a firm grip of his arm, fearful that, in his perturbation, he might stumble in the mud and fall. She had never yet seen him so upset.

There was crisis on every hand. In Georgetown, the Court of Policy refused to pass the Civil List unless the Governor agreed to sanction a loan for immigration. The Governor refused, and the annual estimate was not passed. After the thirtieth of June no taxes could be collected and no salaries paid to civil servants. The Court told the Governor to let the Home Government stand the burden of the forty thousand pounds needed for the Civil List. Governor Light rejected this suggestion as absurd. The colony must bear the burden of its own Civil List. How, the planters asked, was the colony to meet such heavy expenditure when the Home Government had wrecked the economy by destroying the supply of labour needed to work the plantations? An impasse had been reached, and there was a rumour afoot that the

Governor of Trinidad, Sir Henry McLeod, might have to be called to arbitrate in the matter.

Willem wrote in May to say that Flagstaff would have to be put up for sale unless he could find some capital to see him through for another year. Would Dirk come at once so that they could confer on the situation?

Dirk was off to Demerara at once. He told Willem: "It comes back to what I told you people at Huis Kaywana in 1815. We must combine—that's the only expedient, Willem. We must pool our resources."

"Very well, very well," said Willem irritably. "I grant that you were right and we were wrong—but how do we go about pooling our resources, as you express it? Explain in detail what you have in mind."

Dirk explained—and not only explained but himself consulted Graham and Raphael and Larsen and the Hartfields and planned with them the whole scheme for combining. With Graham he had no trouble, but Raphael and Larsen were reluctant to lose their independence, and took much convincing—though Dirk eventually succeeded. John and Harvey Hartfield and Graeme Clackson were also hesitant, but they, too, after a long discussion, agreed that there was wisdom in taking the step Dirk suggested.

And so Flagstaff was saved, the factory scrapped, and all canes conveyed to Harrow's Castle, Raphael's place, for grinding at the factory there; this alone constituted a tremendous saving in factory labour and in machinery maintenance. The new company was to be called the Demerara-Berbice Sugar Combine, and New Signal included as one of the holdings. Dirk would have thrown his timber business in as an asset, but was restrained by the fact that he and Jacob had gone into partnership some years previously. But Graham, a free agent, had no hesitation in putting the capital of his timber concern at the disposal of the new company, even though John Hartfield and Graeme Clackson told him that there was no urgent necessity to do so.

Graham shook his head and said: "I have come lately to see that Dirk's way is the way to survival, John. We must be unbreakable—absolutely rock-secure. I wish I had something else to throw into the pool, I assure you!"

Mary accompanied Dirk on his trip to Demerara, and on their way back, he had to admit to her that both as companion and amanuensis she had come off with full honours. She smiled and said: "And yet you keep fretting yourself because I don't do the conventional thing and get married." He grunted and replied: "I'm a conventional person, my girl. You should have discovered that by now—and apart from that, Mary, my instinct tells me that, as a woman, your greatest happiness lies in marriage. I shall never yield on that point."

They watched the muddy waves, standing side by side at the deck rail, as the steamer ploughed its way eastward. An inch taller than her father, Mary stood erect and stiff, her hands resting on the rail, and Dirk smiled to himself, recalling himself as he was at her age. There was about her the same stiff tenseness from which he had suffered so frequently at nineteen. Like himself, too, she did not relax easily, no matter how casual the occasion; whether disturbed or not, whether challenged on any issue or in concord with her audience, she had to be on the alert, nervously keen to all that went on about her.

After a silence, she suddenly asked, her gaze still on the waves: "Tell me, Papa, are you serious in your intention to marry Mrs. Berton?"

He had been waiting for the question, and was not put out. He replied: "I haven't made up my mind yet, Mary. Why do you ask?"

"I should never be happy again in my life if you did."

"You have shown that plainly enough, I should say." After a pause, he said: "Throw your mind back to last October. Did you overhear something your mother said to me just as you had come in—or just before you came in—the room?"

She nodded. "Yes, I heard. She advised you to marry Mrs. Berton."

"I thought you must have overheard. Well, that weighs quite a great deal with me, I may say."

Her head trembled, and her eyes seemed to grow a deeper blue-green as she said: "Are you in love with her, though, Papa—that is the point?"

He had the impression that she was holding her breath; his reply was of tremendous importance to her. He said: "No, I don't think I am—but she is a very attractive woman, and I'm sure she will make me a devoted wife."

"She will be a disrupting influence, Papa. I can foresee it—and you won't be happy. Remember your role. You're the backbone of the van Groenwegels. Yesterday I heard Uncle Graham call you the binding element—and how right he was! But for you Flagstaff would have been sold. Whenever there is trouble in our family it is you who run to the rescue. You ought to think well before contracting another marriage."

"I'll be forty-five in September, Mary—not sixty-five. Would you care to see me remain celibate for the rest of my life?" He grinned and patted her arm. "You are only nineteen, my girl. Very intelligent, but inexperienced."

"I know full well what you mean," she said, flushing. Her lips parted to say something, then she seemed to think better of it. She shrugged and clicked her tongue. After a pause, she said: "You're strong, Papa. You're no ordinary person. I'm sure you could live that way if you willed it."

This both flattered and irritated him, and he said: "I think we had better shelve the subject, my girl. Let us discuss something else."

"Very well. But it will come up again."

It came up again—at least twice during the next few months— but on each occasion it was again shelved.

One evening in November, on the veranda of the Laffertys' house —it was a musical concert, with amateur theatricals; the Laffertys were very talented—Janet said something that gave Dirk a severe jolt. "Do you know what is being said of Mary and yourself, Dirk dearest?"

"What do you mean?"

She told him, and his hands clenched. His eyes hardened. "Let them say what they will! By God! It's untrue—but I don't care. It won't be the first time the van Groenwegels have been accused of something grossly vicious."

Unwittingly Janet had hurt her own cause.

49

EVEN the tranquil, easygoing Jacob began to discover that he could be thoroughly upset and exasperated over the doings of some member of the family.

James was doing well in the hospital in England, where he was studying medicine. Both Cynthia and Olga had made very satisfactory marriages—Cynthia to a young bookkeeper employed with a firm of old standing in The Strand; he was very fair-complexioned—a *mestee* who might go far with his employers, who were white, but not against advancing a man who was highly competent and whose complexion was fair enough for him to pass as white. Olga had married the son of a Werk-en-Rust merchant, and was living in Georgetown. Lawrence, eighteen, was very keen on going into Frick & Green, and Jasmine, twelve, was doing well at school.

Charles, twenty-two, returned from England with an English wife. "Think of it!" stormed Jacob. "A barmaid! No manners whatever, no deportment—and she drops her aitches. She can barely read and write. And what do you think she wanted to do! Go into the kitchen and cook—scrub the floor! And you should hear her ideas of us! She says she thought all coloured people in the colonies went about half clad, and she had expected to see us living in huts. Oh, I'm disappointed in Charles, Dirk, boy. To go and pick up a creature like that! Only a white skin and nothing else. I could have found him dozens of local coloured girls to make his choice from—every one of them superior in breeding to this piece of English trash he's brought out here."

"I agree, I agree," said Dirk—and laughed. "By God! But I must say it's a treat and a revelation to see you flustered for a change, Jacob, lad."

"Flustered? I'm fighting furious. He's let me down heavily."

Dirk wagged a finger at him. "Take it from me, boy, his children won't feel so. They'll be damned grateful, and you know it. The woman may be a dragged-up nobody, but she's going to give your grandchildren very light complexions and straight hair. Socially they'll go up in the world, Jacob. And Charles is a qualified barrister-at-law, isn't he? You have no worries at all, old man!"

"I hope I'll come to feel that way—but I don't at the moment."

"I wish I could exchange worries with you." Dirk told him about Peter, who had announced recently that he was not interested in planting. He wanted to go to England to study to be a doctor. "What do we want with a doctor in the family, Jacob, boy! Uncle John is a doctor, but that's as it should be, I suppose. He's a Maybury, and a very quiet and retiring man. But a van Groenwegel a doctor! We're planters. I was hoping that Peter would be able to take over from Willem when Willem retires. Willem is getting on in years. He's fifty-eight. Peter is fourteen this year. By the time he is twenty Willem should be just ready to retire. There's Hendrik, of course, and I must say he's very keen on planting. A good fellow. But he wants to remain at New Signal. He's already familiarised himself with the place, and I can safely trust him to do well in the future."

They were in Jacob's sanctum in the sawmill office, which had, five years previously, been completely renovated and greatly enlarged. Jacob sat in his leather-lined chair, and Dirk leaned against a corner of the desk. They stared thoughtfully out of the window at the bush on the west bank of the river, two and a quarter miles across, and after a silence Dirk shrugged and sighed.

"Nevertheless, I'm arranging for Peter to go to England," he said. "I see no point in forcing him to do what he has no will for."

"I think you're wise," murmured Jacob. And in the silence that came between them again they heard Mary's voice in the adjoining room, taking some junior bookkeeper to task about something. Suddenly Jacob's face lost its gloom. He smiled his old lazy smile, and said: "Remarkable girl you've got there, Dirk. I've never seen anyone with such a memory for figures. She forgets nothing."

Dirk nodded and grunted, a slight frown coming to his face.

Jacob grunted, too. "I understand," he said.

"What do you understand?"

"You'd prefer her to be like her sisters."

Dirk nodded—then suddenly: "Jacob, you see a lot of her in the office here. She thinks a mighty lot of you. What impression have you gained of her so far? Does she confide anything in you?"

"She has moods. Sometimes she's very reticent—and sometimes very confiding. And I think I know what regulates her moods."

Dirk said nothing, waiting for him to go on. And Jacob said: "You know without my telling you, Dirk. That Berton woman you go about with sometimes. When you don't see her Mary is happy and talkative; when you do see her Mary is silent and moody. Mary doesn't like her, boy. And, of course, she worships you."

Dirk clenched his hands, and glancing at Jacob, said: "You think you have problems, eh? You don't know what I have to handle." He bent close to Jacob, and said in a whisper: "Remember when I went to Georgetown last week to attend that meeting Hartfield & Clackson held? I got married again, Jacob."

"You what?"

Dirk nodded. "Very secretly done, boy. Only Harvey Hartfield and his wife know of it. They were the witnesses. The Presbyterian minister performed the ceremony in Uncle Raphael's house in Kingston, and I spent a three-day honeymoon there before returning here. That's what I've come to, Jacob, lad. A man of clandestine deeds."

"Good God! And the bride? Not Janet Berton?"

Dirk nodded. "Who else could it have been?" He gripped Jacob's arm. "For God's sake, I'll shoot you if you breathe a word to a mortal."

"But why the secrecy?" whispered Jacob. He glanced towards the next room. "You mean Mary?" And Dirk nodded. "Yes, yes. I mean that. I believe it would kill her if she knew. She mustn't know, Jacob."

Dirk explained what had precipitated things. The Hopkinsons had sold their cotton plantations on the Corentyne, and bought a small sugar plantation in Barbados. They had left for that island only a few days before, Amelia and her children with them—and, naturally, Janet Berton would have had to go, too, for she was a dependent of her brother, Harry, Amelia's father-in-law. "That would have been the end of everything between us, Jacob, and I'm fond of her—and by God! I'm not impotent yet. Cornelia liked her—even advised me to marry her. So—well, that's how I was forced to act in the matter. She's going to live in Georgetown for the time being, and I'll be with her when I go there. An odd and not very satisfactory arrangement, I admit, but it must be so for the present."

"Why must it be so? I don't see that. You have a right to live with your wife, haven't you?"

Dirk nodded, a haunted, distracted light coming into his eyes. "My family, Jacob, lad. My family. I don't know how they'll react to my having Janet home there. Apart from Mary, who, we know, would be desolated, there is Hendrik—I don't think he likes Janet, either." He shook his head. "My attitude is cowardly, I'm well aware—but there it is. I can't help what I am, can I?"

When, in August, Peter was going to Georgetown to take ship for England, Mary wanted to accompany her father and brother. "The last two occasions you went to Georgetown," she said, "you went alone, and now you want to prevent me again."

"It's your own fault," Dirk laughed. "You've made yourself so indispensable to your Uncle Jacob"—the children had always called Jacob "uncle"—"that he can't spare you in the office there now. And apart from that, my girl, you know I always like to have you at home here in my absence—especially since your mother's death. You're the virtual mistress of the house now, you know."

That always did it. He had long discovered her weakest point. Remind her of her responsibilities and the battle was won.

In Georgetown, after he had seen Peter aboard and he and Willem and Harvey Hartfield and Janet were on their way to Kingston, where Janet lived in a cottage under her former name of Berton, Willem asked Dirk why he had not brought Mary, and Dirk said: "Has her hands full with the family in Berbice," trying to make his voice sound as casual as possible. "She's like a mother to young Adrian—and as you know, she keeps all the books for me, both at the sawmill and the plantation. Not all those at the sawmill, of course," he added quickly, getting confused. "We have clerks—but she supervises the bookkeepers there." He began to fidget, and Janet, on his right, gave his hand a surreptitious squeeze.

It was the Flagstaff carriage, so after dropping Dirk and Harvey and Janet at Harvey's house in Kingston, Willem continued on towards the East Coast. After dinner with Harvey and his wife, Dirk and Janet strolled across to the cottage—it was dark by then—where Janet lived.

Dirk, whenever in Georgetown, spent all his nights with her, though it was only through the collusion of Harvey and his wife that this was possible; so far as anyone else knew, he slept at Harvey's house, where, officially, he now always put up when in Demerara. Willem had accepted his excuse that Flagstaff was a little inconvenient in view of the fact that most of his business was in the town itself.

Janet's attitude towards the situation was that she would have preferred being together with him in the conventional way, but she was not unhappy living as she did at present, for Harvey and Catherine were most kind to her and took her everywhere—besides which, of course, there were her other friends, in the town and on the East Coast, who invited her frequently to dinner parties and dances and to the race meetings at Kitty and Turkeyen.

"Oh, I have a gay time, Dirk, sweetheart," she laughed. "I'm not going to seed, you may be sure—and, in any case, I don't think I could live at New Signal with Mary in the same house. I'm afraid of her, Dirk. Truly I am. She hates me terribly. I believe she would try to poison me if I lived there."

"And you're sure this clandestine sort of life doesn't irk you? Don't be afraid to tell me, Janet. I want to know the truth."

She rubbed her cheek against his, and uttered her sensual, crooning sound of mirth. "Nothing upsets me, my darling. I take everything as it comes. If I hadn't assumed that policy I wouldn't have won you. I kept after you for more than two years, didn't I—and consider the opposition. Rebuffs from you yourself, rebuffs from Mary, sniggers from all your friends, sneers and sniffs, and reproachful glances. But did I worry? Did I give up? No."

Dirk smiled, thinking what a contrast she was with Cornelia—the complete antithesis. No mystery about Janet. On the contrary, she hid nothing whatever. An overt sybarite. A frank, gay female animal. Flimsy, on the whole, and far inferior to Cornelia, but diverting, and, physically, extremely satisfying. She would never move him deeply; of that he was certain.

Driving with her and Catherine Hartfield to Huis Kaywana the following afternoon—they were dining with Graham; Dirk had decided to take Graham into the secret—a disturbing incident occurred. As they were passing through a busy street in Werk-en-Rust, Dirk broke off abruptly in what he was saying to Catherine and froze. When the two women asked him what was wrong, he replied: "Unless I'm greatly mistaken, I saw Francis go into that little shop we've just passed." He pointed at a tiny one-storey place that seemed to be an eating house or shop of some sort. "This district was his old haunt."

"You got him out of the colony three years ago, didn't you?" said Catherine. And Dirk nodded. "We gave the captain orders to put him

off at a port in Panama, and leave him there. I gave him enough money
to keep him going for at least six months. It would be disastrous for his
wife and that little fellow, Jason, if he went back there—and he might
be arrested for the murder of that mulatto girl and drag our name in
the dirt."

"Poor Dirk," sighed Janet. "Perpetually concerned over the family
name. Don't think of Francis, dearest. You might even have been
mistaken. It might have been someone else resembling him."

The next morning he went round to see the Clarks in Charlestown,
and they confirmed his fears. "Yes, he has been seen," said Mr. Clark,
"but, thank God, he has not come here to worry us yet, and I trust he
won't, sir. I'm praying that he will keep away and leave us in peace."

"What is he doing, do you know? Who saw him?"

"My wife saw him one morning in the market near the *stelling*—
but he didn't see her. He was talking to two Portuguese hucksters."

"Portuguese hucksters? I didn't know the Portuguese immigrants
were turning hucksters. That must be very recent."

"Yes, sir. Of late one or two of them have been leaving the plantations to come into town. Mean people, Mr. Dirk. Mean and dirty.
They don't wash themselves from one week to another, and they only
eat salt fish and rice. No wonder yellow fever carry off so many of
them. And they are all Papists."

"H'm. I hope they won't make it a habit of deserting the plantations
to come to town, or all our immigration schemes will be in vain."

Another pebble added to the general burden of worry, thought Dirk
when he left the Clarks. For the planters had begun to put much hope
in the Portuguese. Dirty they might be, but they were hard and conscientious workers. Willem had secured a number of them for Flagstaff.

Since the Civil List crisis of the year before had been settled by Sir
Henry McLeod, the Trinidad Governor, an immigration ordinance had
been passed, and it had been agreed that a loan of four hundred
thousand pounds should be used to inaugurate a new immigration
drive. Several shiploads of Portuguese had already arrived, as well as
other immigrants from the West Indies, but if they were going to turn
from the plantations and become hucksters and pedlars, like the Negro
and coloured folk, the same old problems of labour shortage on the
plantations would recur. Old John Gladstone had been compelled to
sell Vreed-en-Hoop and Vriedestein because of the ban put on East

Indian immigrants. Again that damned Scoble and his Anti-Slavery Society in England had been causing trouble for everyone in the colony. Whole pack of them should be shot!

As it turned out, his anxiety was not without justification, for during the next year the flow of immigrants came to a virtual standstill. Yellow fever so decimated the Portuguese that the Government was compelled to stop the Madeira authorities from sending them, and the survivors steadily deserted the plantations and began to set themselves up as shopkeepers in competition with the small coloured and Negro traders, who were by no means pleased at this intrusion. There were grumbles everywhere among them.

"They're cutting prices," Jacob told Dirk. "They don't care how they live. You should see the food they eat! Even the black people have more pride than they've got. They're only concerned with hoarding their money."

"They'll probably be richer than you and me in no time," sighed Dirk.

Mary was more sanguine. "The yellow fever will drive them all out before long," she said. "Our local people are immune to it, but they are not."

"Those who have escaped it appear to be thriving all right," said Jacob. He grinned and added: "And they have their saints to pray to, don't forget."

It was in November, when Dirk was in Georgetown on a business-cum-marital visit that a porter came up to the office and told Mary that a Portuguese man was downstairs to see her. "He won't give no name, missy, but he say it urgent."

"I don't know any Portuguese," frowned Mary. "What is he like, Barrow?"

Barrow grinned. "A thin, half-starved looking-man, missy. In ragged, dirty clothes. Same as all dem Pottagee does look like."

Mary hesitated, then said: "Very well. Show him up and let me hear what he wants. It may be some message he has for me."

In less than a minute Barrow was back with the Portuguese. In addition to being dirty and ragged and half-starved-looking, Francis was unshaven. When he smiled he showed broken, blackened teeth, but Mary recognised him quite easily.

"My God!"

Francis chuckled. "Surprised, eh?"

Barrow lingered, as though to make sure that everything was all right. Mary told him to go. "I'll ring the bell if I want you, Barrow."

"You can't trust dese Pottagees, missy. You better careful."

"It's all right, Barrow. This is no Portuguese, I can assure you."

Puzzled, the man left the room and went downstairs, and Francis kicked the door shut after him. "Damned impudent nigger! If he only knew who I am!"

"What do you want here, Francis? Papa is not here."

"No, he's not, Mary, love—that's why I am here. I've come to see you, my sweet." He uttered an obscenity, his eyes glittering in their old mad way in their sunken sockets. "You look good, believe me. I can take you to bed here and now. I've seen some edible morsels along the Main, but none to equal you, Mary."

Mary flushed angrily, though for an instant a vaguely flattered look flit across her face. "I shall ring the bell for Barrow if you don't explain the meaning of this visit, Francis. I'm busy."

"I've heard how you work over journals and ledgers. No use for men—only Papa." He guffawed hoarsely. "I've heard hundreds of rumours about you and Papa in Georgetown." He made sensual, clucking sounds, ogling her obscenely.

"Is that what you have come here to tell me?"

"They aren't true, are they? You wouldn't do that, eh, Mary? Been waiting for me to turn up some day, weren't you? Remember the chicken entrails? I did that purposely because I wanted to see you rip down your bodice."

Her hand reached out towards the handle of the bell, but he stayed her with a gesture. "No, no! Don't ring the bell yet. Wait. I have a message for you, Mary, love. Important news. Something you'd give one of your arms to hear."

"Well?"

He held out a grimy hand. "First I want some money. Give me a few dollars, and then we'll talk. I won't trust to tell you before you hand over the dollars."

She sniffed. "I'm not surprised. I suspected it was that you wanted. Why bother to concoct a tale about a message and important news!" She pulled out a drawer, and took out a bag of silver. "There! I think you'll find about fifty dollars in that. Take it and go."

He snatched the bag from her and pocketed it. "Fifty, eh? Good. That's more than I'd expected." Suddenly he began to tremble as though attacked by an ague. A tear ran down his grimy cheek and glistened amidst the stubble on his chin. He gave her a mad stare, and shook his head a little, blankly, idiotically. "Look what I've come to, Mary, girl. Can you believe it? Me, Francis—your cousin."

She averted her gaze, wincing, biting her lip. "You'd better go."

"A beggar, Mary. Can you believe it? Oh, my dear! And I wanted you. You never knew it, but I used to dream of marrying you. What went wrong with me? That bitch, Elvira! It was she who began it— but that was no excuse. And Father and Cousin Rose—what a pair! Fornicating in the middle of the day near the honeysuckle arbour at Huis Kaywana. I've never forgotten that day I surprised the two of them. Cousin Rose was quite naked—but I didn't let them see me. I waited in the portico until they were finished. A man's secret. Mary, suppose I made something of myself, after all, you wouldn't consider marrying me?"

Mary sighed—but a flush came to her face, and she said in some confusion: "Francis, I'm busy, I think I told you. I—no, what you suggest is too absurd even to be considered. Please go at once."

He stood there staring at her, as though sensing something about her that had eluded him before. He smiled and said: "Perhaps one day. We never know."

She thought he was about to turn to go out, but he suddenly smiled and said: "Mary, I do have news for you. It's about Cousin Dirk. Did you know that he has a mistress in Georgetown?"

"What? What's that?"

"Ah. I knew that would interest you." He tittered, the obscene glitter returning to his eyes. "Yes, I've been doing some spy work, and I've discovered where he sleeps with her. It's a little cottage in Kingston. He stays with Harvey Hartfield by day, but by night he and his mistress go across to their cottage and spend the whole night there."

"What lies are these you've concocted, Francis?"

"They aren't lies. It's true, Mary. I've kept watch myself on more than one night, and I've seen them myself. I don't know her name, but she's a lady by the look of her. No cheap fly-by-night. Cousin Dirk has good taste."

Mary had gone pale. She moistened her lips and said: "You say the cottage is near to Harvey Hartfield's place in Kingston?"

"Yes. Just across the road—obliquely opposite."

She stood still, her hands clenched hard, her eyes shifty with agitation. Her lips parted to speak, but no sound came.

Francis regarded her with a dull fascination, his hands pressed together tight. "I can see the rumours about you are partly true, Mary. He made you his pet since you were a tiny child. He must regret it now—now that he sees what it has done to you. He forgot that the van Groenwegels have devil blood in them. We're no ordinary family, Mary, sweet. Eh? Oh, but it's good to see you again. I came on purpose to get a glimpse of you while he was away in Georgetown—and to get some money. Yes, I won't fool you. I'd hoped that you'd pay for what I had to tell you about him."

Mary shook herself; a shiver seemed to go through her as she looked at Francis and said: "Do you want some more money?"

"Eh? More money? I can always do with money, Mary. What have you in mind for your poor cousin?"

"Go back to Georgetown and try to find out who it is he meets in this cottage, Francis. Gather as much information as you can, and then come back here and get in touch with me—but be discreet, please." She spoke in a panicked voice. "Don't let Papa or Uncle Jacob know. Get a note to me by some means, and I'll arrange to meet you alone in some quiet spot where we can talk in privacy. Go now. Go at once." She rang the bell.

50

D I R K was so worried over the steadily worsening state of the general planting economy that when he returned to New Signal he failed to take note of the change in Mary's attitude towards him, though, in actuality, the change was not an obvious one. It was a background thing, subtle and indefinable. Her brisk, practical manner became a trifle more brisk and practical, her keen, alert eyes glittered more keenly and alertly, her customary gaiety seemed in some way over-charged and studied, she fussed over his comforts with a greater nervous concern, her maternal attachment to her youngest brother, the five-year-old Adrian, intensified. All this, to Dirk, in his preoccupied state, seemed normal for her, and nothing to remark on or inquire into. She was Mary the moody, and he must expect anything from her.

Not many months ago, there had been labour disputes and disturbances in Demerara; the labourers had gone on strike for weeks, and, eventually, many of them had had to be put out of their logies as a disciplinary measure, and in order to force them to come to terms. Meantime, however, the plantations had suffered great losses, and once again several places on the East Coast went into liquidation and had to be put up for sale. Now Willem wrote to tell Dirk that the Negroes had clubbed together and were themselves buying these ruined estates. "That is the latest development," Willem wrote. "Along here, Victoria was sold to the niggers for 25,000 guilders—can you credit such a thing, Dirk? One of the most flourishing places on the Coast. And Buxton, too, has gone; it fetched 125,000 guilders. Friendship did a little better; that went under the hammer for 200,000. Yes, that is what Demerara has come to. Our estates being taken over by these black savages, who, no doubt, will turn them into stinking villages, undrained and uncared for. . . . But for you, my dear cousin, Flagstaff would be in their hands, too, today. I shall never cease to be grateful to you for your efforts, Dirk. . . ."

"There you have it, Father," said Dirk at dinner that day when Willem's letter was received. "One by one they keep falling by the wayside. I hear that big place on the West Bank of the Berbice is soon to fall into the hands of the niggers, too. Ithaca. And I doubt whether it will fetch a big price."

Storm nodded and made soft, clucking sounds. "Nothing lasts, my boy. Nothing lasts. We must be thankful that we ourselves can still struggle along."

A twinkle, ironic and sly, came into Elizabeth's old-lady eyes. She murmured: "And what are we to thank, Storm dear? A canister of letters and our son Dirk, or merely a kind Providence?"

Mary laughed. "There should be no question at issue there, Grandma! The canister and my dear father, of course! Providence, indeed! Papa is Providence!"

"You needn't be blasphemous, Mary, my girl," growled Storm, frowning.

"But it's true, Grandpa! It's true!" shrilled Mary. "He did it, didn't he? Papa is the genius who has fashioned our prosperity. Who can deny it?"

Hendrik, seated between his grandparents, sturdy and thickset, quiet and rather solemn in mien, frowned at his sister and said: "Why must you shriek like that, Mary? Who is trying to deny anything?"

"Sometimes one must shriek," laughed Mary, "to make one's point felt. No one gives Papa enough praise for all he has done for us."

Dirk, uncomfortable, scowled and growled: "That will do, Mary." And Mary, who sat at his right, laughed again, seemingly unabashed, and patted his head. Only she was aware that her finger tips were cold, and that her hands trembled.

Elizabeth switched attention from Dirk and the family fortunes by mentioning that she had received a letter from Amelia in Barbados. "Another great-grand for us, Storm. She says the event may take place in March or April."

"Good. Good for Amelia," mumbled Storm. "How is Ronald doing? And Harry?"

"They're all well," said Elizabeth. "And evidently prospering, too."

"What of Janet Berton?" asked Storm. "We don't seem to hear much of her."

Dirk, now well trained in controlling his emotions when Janet's name was mentioned, continued to eat without the flicker of an eyelid.

"She didn't go to Barbados with them, Grandpa," Mary answered for her grandmother. "Are you forgetting that she was asked to go to Jamaica by some old aunt of hers there? That was the plan, according to what Amelia said before they left the colony here a year or two ago."

"Ah yes, I think I recall hearing something of the sort," said Storm. And Elizabeth asked Dirk: "Has she never written to you, Dirk?"

"Not a line, Mother," said Dirk, assuring himself that this, at least, was no lie. And Mary laughed brittly and remarked: "A woman scorned hath no heart to write letters, Grandma!" At which Dirk gave her a cold glance and snapped: "An improper remark, Mary! I shall ask you not to repeat it."

"My apologies, Papa dear. Oh, I'm so sorry. Of course, it is an improper remark." She stroked his neck and added in a pleading voice: "Do forgive me."

Hendrik gave her a lowering glance, clicking his tongue in irritation.

After dinner, locked in her room—she occupied a room in what was still known as the new wing—Mary spent an hour going through the sawmill books, two of which she had had brought home that afternoon; she was accustomed to spending her evenings in this manner, though perhaps twice a month, on an average, Hendrik would persuade her to accompany him to a dance or some other social function.

She worked with great concentration, then put away the books, undressed, and unlocking the door, went into the next room—the room in which young Adrian slept. Every night there was the ritual of tucking him in.

He was awake, awaiting her arrival, an oval-faced, rather frail boy with red-gold hair like her own, and the green eyes of Dirk. He sat up in his bed and smiled and asked her if she had finished writing in her books.

"Yes, dear. At last. Are you very sleepy? Have I kept you waiting too long?" She sat on the bed and hugged him to her, and he said: "No, I'm not very sleepy, but I'll sleep after you've gone. Will you read a letter for me?"

"Would you like me to? Are you sure?"

"Yes, please, Mary. I like hearing you read about Grandma Hendri."

She laughed and tousled his hair. "How Papa would open his eyes if I told him of your morbid tastes! Very well. I'll go and get one or two." She returned into her room, and pulled out the canister from under her bed; it was kept in her room now, by her special request. With a bundle of the renowned letters in her hand, each letter with its English translation attached, she returned to her brother, and sat for a while on the bed, reading aloud for him. He listened intently, now and then smiling in an impish manner, now and then dreamily as his gaze wandered round the room. He always waited until she paused after reading any particular letter before commenting or asking questions . . . "Who was Juliana?" . . . "Why does she advise Grandma Hendri to get rid of Atta? Who was Atta?" . . . And Mary would be very careful to answer all his questions to the best of her ability. . . . "Aunt Juliana was a sister of Uncle Pedro and Uncle David and our great-grandfather, Jacques. . . . I don't know who Atta was myself, but it seems as though he might have been some troublesome slave, for Aunt Juliana speaks of him as a troublemaker. Yes, Atta must have been a slave. I must ask Papa. He may know."

"Grandma Hendri was very cruel to her slaves, wasn't she?"

"Yes, very cruel—but she was a great old lady in other ways. She was one of the Hard Ones, Adrian—strong like Papa, dear. You must love her."

"Even though she was so cruel?"

"Don't think of her cruelty. Think of her strength. Love her as you love Papa, and think of her as a great van Groenwegel."

"I've heard Papa say she is. I'll try to love her, then. Do you love her?"

"Yes, of course."

"As much as you love Papa?"

She flushed slightly and pinched his cheek playfully. "Not as much, no."

"You love Papa very much, don't you?"

"Yes, yes. The same as you do." She shifted nervously, and began to tie the letters together again, her hands shaking slightly. "And the same as I love you, you pestering little boy." She put aside the letters and, with a squealing gasp, caught him to her and hugged him close. "I want you to grow up into a fine, strong man like Papa, do you hear me, Adrian? Strong, strong. You must never yield to weak, fleshly temptations, my darling brother. Oh, God! Oh, God!" She released him as abruptly as she had gripped him, and began to pace about the room, and he watched her curiously, not surprised, for she often behaved in this way. After a while, his eyes narrowed in admiration, and he smiled, and said: "I'll be strong when I grow up, Mary—strong like Papa—and you."

She seemed not to have heard him. She stared before her in an unblinking, bright-eyed manner, and he heard her muttering to herself . . . "How will it all end, I wonder! I shall go mad, mad, if what Francis said is true. . . ."

"Why will you go mad, Mary? Who is Francis?"

Mary started, glanced at him and said: "You heard what I said, did you? Never mind. I was speaking to myself, Adrian dear." She uttered a distracted laugh. "We're all mad. Mad and bad. A mad, bad family." She darted towards the bed and pulled him to her, hugged him, kissed his hair, moaning and laughing by turn, trembling.

At Christmas, Dirk received a letter from Jan Lieker in Surinam. The family was doing well in sugar, according to what he said; there was no labour problem there, for slavery was still in existence. "We certainly don't regret having made the move, and, indeed, feel sorry that it had not occurred to us before to come here." Towards the end of his letter, Jan said: "The Bakkers here are definite in their assertions that they are related to us distantly. Old Jacob Bakker says he remembers hearing, as a boy, of an old lady who was called Suzette or Susannah—he is not certain—but she lived to a great age, and he believes that she was the daughter of a van Groenwegel, and came from the Essequibo. I enquired about old letters and documents, but he is doubtful whether any survive—though he remembers that an uncle of his went to Holland late in the last century, taking with him a box of old letters and papers concerning the plantation. Among them there may be something of interest to us, but Holland is a long way off, and the letters may well have been destroyed by now. . . ."

"Let us trust they have been," chuckled Elizabeth after reading the letter. "Those in the canister upstairs are quite enough for us."

"Not for me," said Dirk. "I mean to pursue the matter later on."

It was early in the new year, 1843, that Francis turned up again.

A black boy came to the sawmill with a note addressed to Mary. Barrow, the porter, brought it up to the office and handed it to her, saying: "A lil' boy bring dis, missy. He say a white man give it to him on Perot's *stelling*, and say he must come right away and give it to you here."

Mary flushed, then paled, and took the note eagerly, stammering:

"Oh, thank you, Barrow. Is he waiting? Did he say whether an answer was needed?"

"No, missy. He didn't wait. You want me to run after him and call him back? I know de boy. I can find him if you want."

"No, no, Barrow. Please don't trouble. It's all right, I'm sure."

She waited until Barrow had returned downstairs before opening the note. It was sealed at the back with blue sealing wax. It was very brief.

"At Gertie's sandbox tree this afternoon late, after dusk. F."

As children, they had heard many tales of superstition from their nurses, and one of them was that the big sandbox tree near the old sugar barn, about two hundred yards from the house, had been planted on the grave of a slave called Gertie. Gertie's jumbie was said to haunt the spot, though none of the children had ever seen it, despite secret nocturnal expeditions led by Francis on many an occasion during the dry weather.

Francis could not have chosen a better place as a rendezvous, for, apart from being secluded, it was a spot Mary sometimes sought out of an afternoon when she wanted to be alone. No one would think it odd if she were seen going towards the big sandbox tree, especially at six o'clock after dinner.

It was a damp afternoon, for rain had fallen heavily during the morning. But the sky now was flecked with small grey-white clouds, and as Mary set out after dinner for the sandbox tree, the moon, large and red, was rising beside the tall, dark chimney of the sugar factory showing over the trees in the east. Tree frogs chirruped in a frenzied chorus, as they always did in the rain season, and the air smelt of wet mud and wild-plant leaves, rank but familiar, recalling childhood adventures in the open air.

Big frogs kept hopping out of her path, and fireflies made an occasional arc of light amidst the bushes. The track led through blacksage shrubs and guava and jamoon trees, whose shadows were growing dark on the ground in the ever brightening moonlight and as the sunset glow in the west rapidly faded.

She looked anxiously round the cleared space under the sandbox tree, but there was no sign of Francis. He would almost certainly come from the direction of the public road, and she had just decided to continue along the track, which led eventually to the road, when a crackling sound came to her ears, and she saw a slim male figure appear round the huge trunk of the sandbox tree.

In the moonlight he did not appear to be as dirty as on the previous occasion. He had shaved, and his hair was neatly brushed. He came to a halt and tittered in his old evil way, squeezed his hands together and said: "You wouldn't fail to turn up, eh? Tch, tch! What a vision you make in the moonlight!"

"Say what you have to say, please, Francis," she snapped. "I don't want to linger here longer than necessary."

"Don't you? But I do. I could stay here the whole night long with you, my love." He rubbed his hands together and told her in obscene detail what and what he would do with her if they remained here all night. She interrupted with an impatient click of her tongue and an angry exclamation. "Is it impossible for you to be clean in your speech, Francis!"

"Am I being dirty? I'm only telling you what I'd do with you. Would it be dirty to make love, with a moon like this shining on us?"

"Have you brought the information I asked you to get?"

"Yes, I've brought it—but you won't like it, Mary, my sweet. Poor, pestilent Francis. He can bring only bad tidings to his beloved. Hee, hee!"

"What is it? Who is the woman he meets in this cottage in Kingston?"

"Her name was Janet Berton—but now it's Janet van Groenwegel."

"Janet Bert—what nonsense is this? What are you saying?"

He sighed. "I wondered how it was that Cousin Dirk could keep a mistress. He's not the kind of fellow for that sort of thing. And it was as I'd thought. He married her. She's his wife, Mary."

She stared at him, speechless and rigid, then almost shrieked: "But Janet Berton is in Jamaica. She went there nearly two years ago."

"You don't go to Georgetown very often, then, Mary, sweet, do you?"

"I—well, no. I haven't been for a long time. I'm kept so busy here—but—but—oh, Francis, please explain what you mean."

"I've kept watch on her cottage for some time. She's a gay one. Friends are always arriving to take her out in their carriage. That's how I had my opportunity to search her bedroom. I tried her back door —the kitchen door—one day—it was last Sunday—and I found that she'd left it open, so I went in, and searched her bedroom. I found what I wanted in one of the drawers of her writing table. Not a single drawer was locked in any of her furniture. A careless woman. I could have stolen her jewels if I'd been so disposed——"

"What were you looking for? Oh, please explain! Please explain!"

He fumbled in a breast pocket and produced a folded slip of paper. He held it out to her, and she took it automatically. "The moonlight is bright enough, I think. Read it and see what that is, Mary, love. I knew she would have it. Oh, I can be clever sometimes. I'm not always a fool."

"My God! My God!"

"Ha! See! Pestilent Francis! Bearer of bad tidings. No good for anything else. Never mind. You'll never see me again, love. I'm sailing early in the morning for Brazil. I've signed on on a ship. She's in port now. We're only here for a few hours. I'll never again plague my sweet Mary."

Mary was staring at the document in her hand and muttering to herself. "A marriage certificate. The Presbyterian minister. Oh, my God! Oh, my God!"

"See! A sly one, that father of yours, my girl. Hee, hee! But what baffles me is why should he have been afraid to bring her here to New Signal? Was it you he was considering, Mary? Mary, tell me something. Those rumours—they are not true, are they? You've never denied them——"

"Don't be a fool! Of course, they are untrue! I'm not so degraded —nor is he. You have a dirty mind—dirty, dirty!"

"True. Filthy. Pestilent Francis. Diseased in soul. Never mind, my sweet. Be comforted. What a vision you look in the moonlight!"

She put her hand in her bosom, and brought out a small bag of money. She thrust it at him. "Here! There's a hundred dollars in that. Take it and go."

He chuckled, but made no attempt to take it from her. He shook his head. "No, Mary dear! I don't want money from you. It's you I want— only you. You know it. I haven't done what I did for money—only for love, my precious."

She gave him a wild, distracted stare and stammered: "I—I fail to understand you. I—I told you I'd pay you if you brought me the information I wanted. Well, you've done so—and brought more than I even bargained you would. You have earned your money. Take it and go."

Again, however, he shook his head. "Only for love," he chuckled, his voice low, tender. He uttered a quavering sound, hysterical, feeble, hurt—the sound an animal in pain might have made. "I'm going, Mary, love. To Brazil. I've been there before. I can even speak Portuguese. Yes, I can, believe me. I've been passing myself off as Portuguese in Georgetown. Very convenient. But I mustn't stay any longer there. Those nigger people—my wife's family—they know about me. They can put me into the hands of the police if they wish—and I won't be at the mercy of niggers. No. I must go. To Brazil. Good-bye, Mary."

She turned away, sobbing wildly. He hesitated, then strode forward and held her arm. She turned quickly and pressed herself against him. "I feel like dying. Dying, Francis. Oh, my God! Francis, what am I going to do?"

He patted her head, stroked her hair. "Never mind. You'll live that down. You'll put that behind you. Get back to the house now before they miss you and come searching. There'd be hell let loose if they found me here."

"Don't go yet. Please! Where are you going to? The ship? When are you sailing? Francis, let me go with you. Let me go. I can't live here any more."

He laughed softly, stroking her head, as though she might have been a child of eight or nine who needed his affection and protection. "Never mind. It will pass. You're upset. Go back to the house now——"

"I won't go. I won't. Take me with you."

"How gladly I'd do that, my dear! But me? Dirty me? I shouldn't even hold you like this, Mary." He tried to push her away, but she clung to him.

"Take me with you. I'll go. I mean it. I'm in earnest."

He threw his head back and laughed. "Mad! Mad! You're mad, Mary. Like me. We're both mad alike." He held her off from him at arm's length and regarded her anguished face, glistening with tears in the moonlight, wild-eyed, wisps of her hair dangling over her forehead. He wagged his head. "My lovely, lovely Mary. If only things had been different!"

She shut her eyes and moaned.

"Remember the chicken entrails? Hee, hee! I did it on purpose. . . ."

She opened her eyes. "Do you want me? Have me. I don't care now. You can do with me all the filthy things you mentioned you wanted to do."

She uttered a frantic, whining sound, flung the bag of money to the ground, and ripped the front of her bodice down. "There! You don't need chicken entrails to make me do it this time. Take me,

Francis! Take me and soil me. Do everything ugly and dirty with me that you have a mind to."

He stood absolutely still and stared at her, a look of unbelief on his face. After a moment his lips began to move, but without sound.

"I'm serious. Do as you will. Take my body as your reward if you won't have the money. Make me as foul as yourself. I won't care! I won't care!"

He trembled slightly, took a step towards her, and brushed the palm of his hand lightly against the tips of her breasts.

"Enough reward," he murmured, his voice in a quaver. "Only to do this. So often I have wanted to touch your breasts, Mary."

He turned away—turned away and darted off out of sight behind the trunk of the sandbox, and trembling, she looked down at her breasts, streaked with the glistening rivulets made by her tears, and listened to his footsteps receding in a hurry along the track. She waited until the sound of them had died away before raising her head. She stared at the moon, now well above the trees—still large but not so red.

The crickets shrieked around her, and the tree frogs chirruped their frenzied chorus, liquid and confused, like a vast jumble of spectral leaves of noise threatening to pervade the universe and smother for ever all other sounds.

"A man's secret."

Dirk, in his room, writing a letter to Willem, started round.

"Mary! In the name of heaven!" He sprang up from his chair. "What has happened? Your condition! Have you been attacked?"

She smiled and shook her head. "A man's secret." She held out the marriage certificate to him. "Your secret, and how well you kept it, Papa."

"What is this!" He took the paper, and paled. "How did you come by this?"

She told him.

"Francis! What was Francis doing here? Is he in Berbice? Was it he who tore your bodice down like this? Explain, Mary. Explain."

The hysteria in her manner disappeared, as though expired out of her system with the great sigh she heaved as she smiled. In a voice steady and unhurried, she explained in detail what had happened. He listened with clenched hands, but made no attempt to interrupt her.

"Poor Papa. To think that you had to practise such a deception— that you had to deny yourself—and treat your own wife as though she were a common harlot. And all for my sake." She looked up at him. "It was for my sake?"

He nodded, glancing about him, confused, embarrassed. "Yes, yes, I suppose it was." He wagged his head distractedly. "Francis. My God! What a strange boy! Why did he spy on me? What could possibly have prompted him, in the first instance, to keep an eye on my movements? To trace my whereabouts in Kingston, and to—to watch me. He's mad—mad."

"I, too. Not only he, Papa. I'm mad, too." She laughed, and the hysteria threatened her again. She looked down at her breasts. "He said he always wanted to touch my breasts. The chicken entrails, remember? I tore my clothes like this. I offered myself to him—but he— he only touched my breasts, and then went. He could have taken me, befouled me—but he didn't. He spared me. He can't be all bad, can he, Papa? Poor Francis." The tears began to make rivulets down her cheeks, but she did not sob. The hysteria did not return.

"Go and get changed, my girl. Get dressed. You mustn't walk around the house like this. It's—it's immodest."

She nodded. "Yes, I'll go and get changed—but I don't care. I don't feel immodest. It must be the madness in me. The Old Blood, Papa. Francis and me. I wonder what became of Harriet." She looked at him again. "Papa, you must let Janet come and live here. I won't mind. I'll try to be nice to her."

"Truly? You won't mind? Do you mean that, Mary?"

She nodded. "She's your wife. Her place is here with you. Poor Papa. For your sake, I shall be very nice to her. Only . . ."

"Well?"

"She must not interfere with Adrian. She must never try to be a mother to him. I shouldn't like that. You will speak to her about that, Papa?"

"Very well. I don't think she will be interested in Adrian, in any case. She has never had any children of her own—and from what she has told me, she is not fond of children."

"I want to train him in my way. He must be fine and strong—like you."

He flushed slightly, and frowned. "Go, Mary. You should go to bed at once. You're upset. You need some rest."

She nodded. Stood for a moment regarding him, smiling and blinking, her eyes moist. Suddenly snatched his hand and pressed it to her cheek, moaned and wagged her head, shut her eyes and kept murmuring over and over: "The van Groenwegels never run. The van Groenwegels never run. . . ."

"Mary, my child, you're overwrought. Go and rest."

"No. I'm not overwrought—not now." She smiled at him, and her eyes were alight with an intense happiness. "Not even mad. I feel very calm and sane. I see the future so clearly now. I shall never be hysterical again. It's doubt and anxiety that make one hysterical. I shall never be in doubt again—nor anxious. I feel stronger than ever now. And sure of myself." She uttered an affectionate sound, kissed his hand, pressed it to her cheek, rubbed it gently against her breasts, then released it, and turned and left the room, her movements unhurried and easy, completely relaxed.

51

WITHIN a week Janet was settled at New Signal and the marriage revealed. Mary went out of her way to give her a pleasant welcome, and even made a great fuss over seeing that everything was to her comfort in the northeastern room. So much so that Janet was considerably embarrassed as well as astonished. "It's a miracle," she said to Dirk. "She's not the same person I knew a few years ago, Dirk. You must tell me what you have done to her, sweetheart, to accomplish such a change. I'm overwhelmed— really I am."

Nothing more was heard of Francis. If he had gone to Brazil, then he must have settled there permanently, or died, for he never again appeared in the colony in all the years that followed.

Life at New Signal was once again tranquil and happy. Storm and Elizabeth had always been fond of Janet, and gave her a warm welcome, though Storm, in his old-man tactlessness, committed one or two *faux pas* at first. He remarked on the day of her arrival: "Poor Mary has felt she must be a mother to little Adrian. Now she can be free to marry and make a home of her own."

Janet blushed, making no response, for Dirk had already spoken to her on this subject, making clear Mary's wishes.

Again, however, Storm blundered by saying: "Well, now I shall be looking out for my new crop of grandchildren, my dear."

This time Janet replied: "Poor Papa. You may be disappointed. I've never been able to have a child. Gerald, my first husband, would have given a fortune if I could have presented him with a son." She spoke with much sorrow and embarrassment, and Dirk, coming to her rescue, said: "Just as well. I can't contemplate what it would be like having another brood running round the house. I should go mad."

In March, Dirk asked his parents whether they would object to entertaining to dinner Dr. James Frick and his English wife, just arrived from England.

"Most certainly not," said Storm. "They're respectable people, aren't they? Not all carpenters and masons nowadays, these coloured folk. Ladies and gentlemen in their own rights. Yes, yes. Invite them by all means."

Elizabeth, too, said she had no objections, though she asked with a sly smile: "Is she a barmaid, too, like Charles's wife?"

"Far from it," said Dirk. "She's been academy taught. Very well bred."

And so, for the first time in his life, Jacob sat down to dinner at the dining table at New Signal, for Dirk had asked him and Millicent to come with Jim and Eva, the English wife. Jacob behaved as though he had always been accustomed to dining at New Signal—and even Millicent, who nowadays had lost a great deal of her original awkwardness, was quite at home.

Jim, much slimmer in build than his father, had an English accent, and with his little waxed moustache, presented a very distinguished appearance. His wife, Eva, was taller by at least two inches, a fair, pretty girl of nineteen, who seemed extremely intelligent, and whose speech was cultivated. It was obvious that she, unlike Charles's barmaid wife, was accustomed to servants.

Hendrik was very much taken with Eva, and gave her such long and fascinated looks that Mary, who sat next to him, once frowned and murmured: "Hendrik, why are you staring like that? It's rude, don't you know that?" At which Hendrik started and frowned, continuing to eat with an air of guilt.

That year, 1843, was another year of deaths. In April, Cynthia Clackson, Graeme's wife, died, and in the very week following, John Hartfield contracted pneumonia, after a fall, and died; he was eighty-three. Then in June another octogenarian felt the bony touch on the shoulder—this time, Raphael.

Dirk and Janet and Mary travelled to Demerara for the funeral, which was delayed twelve hours longer than the customary twenty-four in order that the Berbice relatives might be able to attend. They went in a carriage lent by Sybil's husband on the West Coast, Anthony Parrott. Anthony's overseer, Michael O'Brien, accompanied them; he was being sent to Georgetown on urgent business connected with the

Parrotts' two cotton plantations. He was a pleasant man of about forty-two or forty-three, and knew his place, speaking only when spoken to. Mary and Janet both went out of their way to make him at ease, but, for some reason, Dirk did not like the look in his brown Irish eyes. An untrustworthy type, he decided. His Irish brogue irritated Dirk.

When they got out at Harrow's Castle and watched the carriage continue on its way to town, Dirk sniffed and said: "Can't say I enjoyed the company of our travelling fellow—though I noticed that you two ladies seemed quite taken with him," he added, with a grin. And Mary laughed and replied: "I liked him, in a way. A bit shifty-eyed, perhaps, but very cordial and friendly."

"I thought him fascinating," said Janet, and spoke fervently—so fervently that Mary gave her a sharp glance. "He's so gay," smiled Janet. "I like gay people. Berbice is such a quiet place that it is certainly refreshing to meet someone as jovial as O'Brien. And he wasn't at all disrespectful."

"Yes, I must say that for him," Mary admitted. "He knew how far to go with his jokes and sallies."

Dirk sniffed again and said: "A mere overseer to create so much comment! Tch, tch! He must certainly have a masculine charm to which I am quite blind."

"Naturally," laughed Mary. "You're a man. You must be blind to it."

The following day when Raphael's will was read out, they learnt that he had bequeathed his share in the estate to Hendrik, "the son of my gallant and serious-minded nephew, Dirk, whose interest in and loyalty to our family has impressed me more than I have cared to express in my various conversations with relations and friends, and whose great speech at Huis Kaywana in 1815 still lingers in my memory."

"In mine, too," Larsen murmured lugubriously. "A great speech, without doubt." At sixty-five, Larsen looked seventy in face—yet his hair was only sparsely streaked with grey. It was still difficult to guess at his real emotions. His mournful mask was as impenetrable as ever.

"I believe you'll go on to eighty-one yourself," Dirk said to him—and Larsen grunted deeply and nodded. "Perchance. Perchance," he rumbled. "All in the hands of Providence. I'm glad for Hendrik. You must send him to see me."

Willem took them in his carriage to Flagstaff, and on the way he asked after Hendrik. "How is he shaping up as a planter? Still taking a lively interest in the place as you told me he was some time ago?"

"Very keen interest," Dirk nodded. "A good boy, Hendrik. He was suggesting we buy some of those ruined cotton plantations on the Corentyne and turn them into sugar when the labour situation takes on a brighter aspect."

"Not a bad plan—but I wonder *when* the labour situation will take on a brighter aspect. Now that the Government has halted immigration again, I can't imagine what is to happen in the near future. It's so disheartening."

Mary laughed and put in: "The number of times I've heard that word 'disheartening' used by some one of you planters! Anthony must have uttered it at least twenty times when we were at his place yesterday morning."

"They're in a bad way, too, aren't they?" said Willem.

"Yes. Things are getting pretty low, I fear," sighed Dirk. "Another year at the most—and then crash! Cotton and coffee are finished, Willem. Finished."

"O'Brien seemed quite cheerful," Janet remarked. "Cheerful and hopeful."

"Oh, he!" snorted Dirk. "Irish blarney!"

After they explained to Willem who O'Brien was, Willem asked again after Hendrik. "Isn't he thinking of getting married? I'm eager to have him come and get settled at Flagstaff, as you suggested some time ago."

"He's very fond of the ladies," said Dirk, "but he doesn't seem to have found one yet to suit him. And he was twenty-three last March."

"Better hurry him up," frowned Willem. "I'm getting on. Sixty-one last January. I don't feel I'm good for eighty."

"The van Groenwegels are long-livers, Cousin Willem," Mary laughed. "I'm sure you'll reach ninety—like Grandma Hendri."

Willem's leathery, purple face turned more purple with pleasure. "Hope you're right, my girl, but we never know."

The next death that year occurred in September, and this time it was John Maybury—known as Doctor John by relatives and friends alike. His wife, Mary, was too prostrate with grief to attend the funeral, for she and John had been a devoted couple; they had lived a very quiet life, seldom attending social functions of any kind. Both of them shy and retiring, they had been a perfectly matched couple, and even their childless state had never caused any breach between them.

"Only sixty-eight," moaned Storm when the mason was at work on the big family vault at New Signal. "And I am eighty. I should have been the next to be put in there, shouldn't I?" To which Elizabeth, holding his arm, replied: "You are a dreary old man. You said the same thing at Cornelia's funeral."

"Mm. Did I? It was raining that afternoon. I remember that." He looked up at the cloudless, dry-weather sky. "Poor John has been luckier with the weather."

"He has been a good brother to me," sighed Elizabeth. "Do you think we should ask Mary to come and live with us, Storm?"

"By all means, my dear. If she will come. She's such a retiring soul."

Mary Maybury, however, declined the invitation. She preferred, she said, to live on in the big house in the High Street in New Amsterdam. "His presence will always be here with me," she said, her eyes still mesmerised with grief.

Many times during the visit Dirk and Janet paid her she kept mumbling to herself, as though forgetful of their presence in her room. She was still in bed. Just before they left she smiled weakly and said: "You didn't like me when you were a boy, Dirk. Do you remember how you treated me when I first arrived? You refused to let me take you for a walk one morning when I offered to. And when I asked you if you liked me you said: 'You're not a van Groenwegel. Why should I like you?' Your exact words. I've always remembered them. Do you remember?"

"I'm afraid I don't, Aunt Mary. I must have been very small, I suppose?"

"Eight or nine, I think. Yes, very small—but very aggressive."

"What a depressing woman!" exclaimed Janet when they were in the carriage on their way back home. "As depressing as New Amsterdam."

Dirk gave her a swift glance. "Do you find it depressing in Berbice here?"

"A little, I'm afraid, dear. I do miss my friends in Georgetown. We had such gay times, going to dances and dinners and musical evenings, and the races at D'Urban Park—and sometimes at the old racecourse at Kitty." She tucked her arm through his and said: "Never mind. I'm happy with you, all the same. And I'm thirty-seven. Only three years to forty. Time I sobered down, isn't it?"

Reassuringly as she spoke, Dirk was troubled deep down. He found himself attacked by one of his old premonitory shudders. "How are you getting on with Mary, by the way—I mean when my back is turned?"

"Oh, very well, darling. She's the same to me behind your back as before your face. Most charming and pleasant—though I can sense that secretly she still loathes me. I think she is going to harm that little boy with her pampering. It isn't good for a boy to be so pampered, Dirk."

"Leave her alone. Adrian loves her. They get on very harmoniously."

She shrugged. "As you say, dearest. I wouldn't dream of interfering. I promised you I wouldn't, and I shall keep my word to my dying day."

He put his arm around her. "You have your faults, I suppose, but you're a wonderful diplomat, Janet, love."

"Is that all you like about me?" She uttered her crooning sound, her hand beginning to stray, so that he had to take hold of it firmly and reply: "I'll give you the answer to that in about three hours' time."

"Oh, I love being in bed," she sighed.

Once again that premonitory shudder moved like a trail of tiny grey feathers through his spirit.

In January of the next year, 1844, Reginald and his wife, Rowena, came to the colony on a visit. When Reginald had come in 1840, Dirk had not met him, for Reginald had barely stayed a fortnight. This time he and his wife proposed to stay until April, and so there was ample time to invite them to spend a week at New Signal.

Not quite as tall as his father, Reginald was, nevertheless, of a fairly good height—five feet nine—and build, and a handsome fellow, though he had none of Rose's intensity, nor, for that matter, was he in any way like Graham. He was very ordinary in manner—and extremely English. There was nothing Guianese about him whatever, in fact. He was an old Etonian from top to toe—or as Mary put it, in an attempt at wit: "From tie to toe." Though, unlike Timothy Hartfield, he was not affected. His English upper-class air was natural, for it was a part of him. Only to discerning Guianese eyes did he appear coloured. His sallow complexion and crispish wavy brown hair gave him away— but it was easily conceivable that, in England, no one would suspect his black blood.

His wife, Rowena, was an insipid young woman with a horsy face and a gasping, giggly manner. Graham told Dirk that she was the daughter of a baronet, and Dirk said: "I wouldn't doubt it for a moment." Graham gave him a sharp glance, then smiled, and murmured: "I think I know what you mean. That nose! Ah, well! But think of the good connections attached to it, Dirk. Very useful."

One day, before Reginald returned to Georgetown, Dirk took him into the old guest-room and showed him Rose's portrait. "Your mother," said Dirk.

"Oh," said Reginald softly. "Wasn't she lovely!"

"Understatement," mumbled Dirk, scowling.

"I beg your pardon!"

"Nothing, nothing, my boy. Merely talking to myself. Bad habit of mine these days. A sign of old age, I suppose."

Dirk had to admit to Graham that Reginald showed a keen interest in plantation affairs; he was well informed in respect to the situation in the colony, and could discuss all the current problems like a local planter. "I'm trying to do a bit of lobbying at home," Reginald said one evening. "I'm acquainted with William Gladstone—an Eton man, too. Very, very brilliant chap. He's going to get far. He has often given me a sympathetic ear, especially because of his own father's connections with this colony."

"Yes, the old man had to sell Vreed-en-Hoop and Vriedestein," said Dirk. "Because of the fuss that nasty Scoble made over the East Indian coolies whom Gladstone brought out here. We're trying hard to get the Government to lift the ban. I believe if those Indians could be brought here in large numbers our labour problems would cease to exist. The trouble with the Portuguese is that they're all ambitious to leave the fields and set up in commerce, but these coolies from India would be content with field work."

"Why are you so sure they would be?" asked Reginald.

"Well, they're not Europeans, for one thing," said Dirk. "Naturally, when the Portuguese come here and find that they have to work alongside all these niggers in the fields, they must resent their lot and do their best to rise to something better, but the Indians shouldn't feel that way. They have dark skins themselves, and, if anything, they're even more ignorant than the niggers."

Graham laughed and said: "When it comes to the Portuguese and the black people, I can assure you, my dear fellow, it's the blacks who look down upon the Portuguese and resent having to work with them."

"Yes, but that's because the Portuguese are so mean and dirty in their habits—and they are Papists. The niggers are all Protestants, remember. Racially, the niggers feel inferior, and that's another reason why they hate the Pottagees, as they call them. Anyway, the point is, we must have more labourers. That is our crying need at the moment, Reginald my boy. You do your lobbying in London and see if you can persuade them to help us in that respect, and we won't have much else to grumble at."

Shortly after Reginald and Rowena had returned to Georgetown, Janet asked Dirk to allow her to spend a few days with Sybil on the West Coast. "I'm in love with those delightful little grandchildren of yours, Dirk, and Sybil says she and Anthony may soon be leaving for Trinidad."

"Yes, the Parrotts are selling out. They want to go into commerce in Port of Spain. Go by all means, my dear. I'm sorry I can't accompany you, but I'm very busy here."

Janet went across to the West Coast to the Parrotts' place. On the third day after her departure from New Signal, Mary received a letter from Sybil which told her: "I don't like to say it, Mary, but I'm not at all pleased with the way Janet is behaving. Please don't tell Papa, but do you know that she and O'Brien went off yesterday morning in the carriage to Georgetown? She said she wanted to attend the races there, and as O'Brien happened to be going on business for us, it was a good opportunity for her to go. To my mind, she seems a little too familiar with O'Brien. . . ."

Mary laughed softly as she read the letter again. She was in her room, seated on the edge of her bed, and staring at her reflection in the large looking glass set in the door of the wardrobe, she smiled and told it: "See! Only a matter of time. I knew it. I can be patient. Poor Papa." In her voice there was more compassion than exultation. She sat there for a long while, pensive, sad-faced, toying with the letter, the late afternoon sunshine on her head. These days she combed her hair in severe fashion, parted in the centre, braided down flat, and with two buns on the top. "You look like an old spinster already," Hendrik often told her. "And not even twenty-three!" And she would retort: "I may as well be at once what I intend to be."

In taking down her hair at night before bed, however, and regarding herself in the looking glass, she would experience vague regret. A tiny red spot in her fancy would seem to glow brighter, turning white, and there would be a breathless hunger in her which compelled her to shut her eyes and clench her teeth. In such moments she told herself that she was cursed; a terrible isolation would possess her so that she felt an inclination to scream for help. The old hysteria would enfold her like the wings of an angel of Satan, and she would remember Francis and his mad obsession with obeah and necromancy. She would find herself muttering: "Why didn't you take me away, Francis? Why didn't you befoul me, humiliate me? I have no right to be pure in body when my mind is like a dung heap!"

Adrian was a great solace. Many times her fancy saw him as her son, and she was almost tempted to tell him to call her Mama, but immediately her sense of humour would intervene; she would smile and feel herself swept by the absurdity of the notion, and a cool resigned peace would flood her spirit. What did it matter? Her son or her younger brother, he was still under her wing. Their mother was dead, and her stepmother did not count. He was all her own.

Footsteps sounded in the corridor, and she started up, slipping the letter under a pillow. It was her father. He came in, and in his hand was a sheet of paper. He, too, seemed to have been reading his post.

"Mary, my girl," he said, "I have some news for you."

She flushed slightly, as she always did when he entered her room for some reason. "Good or bad, Papa?" She spoke with a loud cheeriness.

"Oh, good, I should say. Graeme Clackson died on Monday night, and he's bequeathed his entire estate to you."

"To me!"

"Yes, to you. I've just received a letter from his attorneys."

"But why to me? I have never been close to him. I barely met him twice."

He grunted, nodding slowly, his green eyes musing. He stared out of the window, and smiled, sighed softly and said: "There was another letter—from him personally. He wrote it years ago, and gave instructions that it was not to be forwarded to me until the day of his death." He drew two sheets of paper from his pocket, and seated himself on the edge of the bed. "I'll read you bits of it, my girl. It will tell you something about our family and the unpredictable blood that runs in our veins."

Tensely, tiny feathers trembling inside her, she seated herself beside him, and waited until he had put on his spectacles, for these days his sight was not what it had been four or five years before. She watched the lean, narrow head, observing the grey hairs at the temples; there were one or two grey strands on top, too, and he was thinning at the back. The tiny red spot glowed brighter and brighter, and she had to take a firm grip of herself.

"Yes, here we are. I won't read you everything—only the parts I feel you ought to hear. He says: 'As you are aware, Dirk, I am childless, and my sister Mathilde died many years ago in Antigua. Like Susan, she married a military fellow, after her first husband died, and went to Antigua to reside. The position, then, is that I have no heirs, or one would believe so, at any rate. However, may I say that I do not feel that I am without blood relations. Indeed, evidence has come to light within the past few years which leaves me in no doubt whatever that I am, by paternity as well as maternity, a van Groenwegel. Before he died, Dirk, I asked Cousin Hubertus to confirm or deny a certain rumour then in circulation to the effect that I was his son through an illicit affair of his with my mother (your worthy grandmother, Faustina). Cousin Hubertus, as I will call him for convenience, denied that I was his son, but I felt that he was lying—and lying, of course, to save me pain. I have forgiven him for that lie, but the doubt in me has always been a source of much perturbation and heartburning. It is not pleasant to feel that one may be a bastard, Dirk. However, that was the situation until, as I say, I obtained information through an impeccable party that I am, indeed, what I suspected. Such information came to me from a woman whom you know well, I think. Her name is Sarah Hubert.'"

Dirk paused and turned towards Mary with a look of inquiry. "You do know who Sarah Hubert is, don't you, my girl? She bequeathed her shop to me——"

"Yes, yes, Papa," Mary interrupted, frowning and nodding in nervous impatience. She sat erect, her hands clasped tight in her lap. "My memory is good—you should know that," she added with a laugh to cover up her impatience.

"Rose's mother," murmured Dirk, then adjusted his spectacles and went on: "I'll continue reading what follows. He says: 'It was soon after Rose's death that it occurred to me that Sarah might know something, and might be prepared to divulge what she knew. Clara, in her customary benevolence, had suggested that Cynthia and I should call at the shop and condole with the old woman. Cynthia, I fear, did not approve of this notion, being, as you must know, never kindly disposed to the Negroes. Nonetheless, I resolved to call myself on Sarah, which I did. She lives in a very neat and clean little room at the back of the shop, and it is in here that she entertained me. I condoled with her on Rose's death, and later in our converse together, made bold to allude to the subject of my birth. In brief, she was not unwilling to discuss the matter, and admitted that she remembered the evening when I called at Huis Kaywana to see Cousin Hubertus. It was an evening in September 1803, and very shortly after the English ships of war had forced upon us a surrender. News had just come from upriver that my father had died, and it was this chiefly that prompted me to visit Cousin Hubertus. Sarah says that he wept bitterly that night after I had left him, and confessed that the reason for his grief was that he had been compelled to lie to me. Indeed, she is of the opinion that it was the remorse he felt succeeding his interview with me that hastened his death. . . .' "

Dirk paused again, and turned to another part of the letter. "Yes, here we are. 'I had intended to die intestate, Dirk, but on learning that I was, indisputably, of your old—*our* old, I should say now— and venerated family, I took it upon myself to review my former policy, and resolved to make my will, and the thought of bequeathing my estate to you was foremost in my mind, but, on reflection, I formulated the notion that perchance it might cause you, the most loyal and devoted member of the family, the most active in keeping the honour of our name alive, greater pleasure if I should bequeath my estate to one who from birth was dearest to your heart, and I allude to your daughter, Mary. . . .' "

Dirk lowered the letter and turned to soothe her. She was sobbing uncontrollably. He chuckled and said: "It's the truth, my dear. Father's Pet. It was probably very wrong of me to single you out in the way I did for special affection. Your mother used to chide me for it, but how can one help such predilections! If only I could see you safely and happily married——"

He broke off. There had been a knock on the door.

Dirk rose, calling: "Come in! Come in! Who is that?"

It was old Benji. "Massa, Missy Sybil and Massa Anthony downstairs. They come to see you on big matters, they say." He turned away with an exclamation. "Oh, look! They come upstairs. They here now, Massa."

"But I wasn't expecting Sybil and Anthony——"

"My God, I wonder," Mary gasped—but before her father could ask her what she wondered Sybil and Anthony had appeared at the door, Sybil the tall and fair, the frank and down to earth, Anthony the soft and charming, red-haired and densely freckled, always with a smile on his moon face.

There was no smile on Anthony's face now. Nor on Sybil's. Sybil looked fierce—a warrior woman. "Didn't you get my letter, Mary?" she asked without a word of greeting to her father or Mary. Anthony had mumbled a "Good evening, sir!"

Mary began to stammer out a reply, indeterminate, confused. Dirk intervened with: "What is this, Sybil? What has happened? I don't understand——"

"Don't you, Papa? Then Mary hasn't said anything. I asked her not to, but I still thought she would have had the sense to give you a hint. Our overseer—Michael O'Brien—has absconded with more than eight hundred dollars—the wages of the labourers included with other moneys entrusted to him. And your wife has gone with him."

"My wife—what the deuce—you mean Janet——?"

"Yes, Janet. She went off with him, and when we made enquiries on discovering the loss, we learnt that they sailed for Trinidad last night."

52

T H E effect of the shock on Dirk was superficial, for he had never cared deeply about Janet. One afternoon about a week later he went into the old guest-room, gazed with a smile at Rose's portrait, and murmured: "You were right, my dear. You knew me better than I knew myself. Not another has ever moved me to the marrow as you did. And Cornelia will not think me disloyal for saying this, rest her dear soul!"

Like Francis, nothing was ever heard again of Janet. She vanished completely. A rumour did trickle back to the colony that she and O'Brien had crossed over to Venezuela, but this was very vague and could not be substantiated.

Dirk refunded the sum embezzled by O'Brien, and a few months later, after the sale of the two plantations, the Parrotts left for Trinidad. Dirk felt more sorrow at the departure of Sybil and her children than he had felt at Janet's going. He was extremely fond of his grandchildren.

Much of Mary's artificial gaiety and inward tension disappeared, for now there was no need for her to pretend a cordiality she had never felt, as she had had to do when Janet was in the house. The basic tensions, however, remained, but there was the double solace now of knowing that she could be close to both her father and Adrian without fear of competition. Now she had two people to fuss over instead of one. Life for her was as full as it could possibly be.

News of Peter was always good; he was progressing with his studies in medicine, and, from what they could gather, he seemed to be leading a fairly steady life. Willem and Christina confirmed this on their return from England in October, after a visit to their daughter,

Lady Hartfield, in Sussex. They paid Peter a surprise visit at his quarters in London.

Hendrik, too, seemed in no danger of indulging in van Groenwegel aberrations of any kind, though Dirk was beginning to worry about his marital intentions. Hendrik, solemn-faced and imperturbable—not unlike Larsen Hubner in looks and manner—always shrugged when his father broached the subject. "I can't force myself to fall in love, Papa," he said. "I haven't seen one girl I'd like to marry, and that's the truth."

Mary had her own views of the matter, and confided them in Dirk one day. "He has a weakness for bookish women, Papa," she said. "He looks down on the girls around here because of their silly airs and lack of interest in serious subjects. I know that—and I know the woman who attracts him above all others."

"Well?"

"Eva Frick—Jimmy's wife. Didn't you notice how he stared at her that evening when they dined here? I had to rebuke him about it."

"Perhaps I'd better send him to London, then, and let Peter find him some suitable blue-stocking."

"I think that would be a very good idea—and I mean it seriously."

Hendrik, however, would not hear of a trip to England. "I hear they freeze there even in the summer. I can't see myself putting on a lot of heavy clothes."

No argument would move him, and the situation remained as it was. Though when, in March, the following year, 1845, Willem wrote suggesting that Hendrik should come and spend a few months at Flagstaff to get himself familiarised with the running of the place, Hendrik agreed at once, and was off to Demerara the next week. And a month later, Willem wrote saying that he was very pleased with Hendrik. "A boy after my own heart. Born planter, there is no doubt whatever about that. I could dispense with my manager tomorrow and be sure that Hendrik would be capable of carrying on in his stead. I'm taking him about in town so that he can meet one or two young women, and who knows that he may not find what he wants. . . ."

In August of that year, 1845, to the relief of the planters, an ordinance was passed permitting the importation of immigrants from India on the basis of a five-year period of indenture, and in the months that followed a steady flow of labourers began to pour into the colony. More Portuguese came, in addition to the Indians, and the prospect suddenly looked rosy. Hopes soared on all sides, the grumblings died away, and the hogsheads of sugar steadily piled up. Work was begun on a railway along the East Coast in Demerara.

Eighteen forty-six was not far advanced, however, when the Home Government, yet again, and in their usual fashion, casually shattered the colony's economy.

A policy of free trade came into operation. . . . "a policy of freedom from integrity," Willem called it. By this policy Britain could import sugar from anywhere in the world. Despite the fact that the Anti-Slavery Party had ruined the colonies by abolishing slavery and thus compelling the planters to pay wages to their labourers, the Government could now find it in no way unethical to buy sugar from countries which still adhered to the old barbarous system.

"You see what damned hypocrites these English are, Jacob!" Dirk blazed, at the sawmill one morning. "So humane, so passionately abhorrent of seeing the poor niggers ill-treated, that they'd sweep us planters all into the sea just to satisfy themselves that they have put a wrong right! And by God! Look what has happened now! They discover how cheaply sugar can be bought in the countries that still uphold slavery, and what do they do? Turn their back upon them with indignation and horror? No. Oh no! They conveniently forget the hullabaloo they kicked up only a few years ago, the invective they showered upon us because of our supposed brutality to the poor niggers —and quite calmly, quite innocently, they arrange to buy sugar from the slave countries. There! That's the English! And then you keep asking me why I'm not eager to go and visit England! I spit on them! I never want to set foot on their damned island!"

At the end of 1846 the price of sugar had dropped from eighteen pounds sterling to ten, and once again plantations began to be put up for sale. When some planters tried to cope with the situation by lowering the wages of their labourers a strike resulted—a strike that lasted all through the first six months of 1847. Angry meetings were held in both Georgetown and New Amsterdam, and petitions worded and sent off to the Home Government. Some of the planters demanded that the constitution should be changed, though the older ones frowned on the idea of actual political innovations. To add to the unhappy state of things, the Negroes and the Portuguese began to quarrel. In New Amsterdam there was a riot in which the Negroes raided the shops and homes of the Portuguese and created havoc. All over the town went up the cry: "Kill the cheap Pottagees!" For the men from Madeira were still leaving the fields and setting themselves up in commerce. Many of them were already firmly established; they were content with low profits and a low standard of living; they were thrifty, and did not fling around their earnings as the black people did, so the black people became envious of them, and took every opportunity that offered to harass them.

In February of 1848 Hendrik fell in love, and announced that he intended to marry. He had proposed and been accepted. His beloved was an English niece of Alpheda's. Alpheda, Willem's youngest sister, had married into an Essequibo family in 1814, and with her husband had gone to live in England. In January she returned to the colony for the first time since her departure nearly thirty years before, accompanied by one of her sons and his wife and her niece-in-law, Dora Hammers—a spinster of thirty-three, tall, rather shapely, but not particularly pretty. Her blue eyes bulged too much, and her face was long and narrow. She had an extremely pleasant personality, however, and could sing and play the piano and paint in water colours. She was an avid novel reader.

Hendrik met her at Flagstaff, for he had not returned to the Canje, but had remained on to help Willem run the place. He was immediately attracted to Dora Hammers, and within a month had asked her to marry him. The attraction had been mutual, and Dora had accepted.

Dirk was a little doubtful. He said to Hendrik: "She's five years older than you, my boy, if you say she's thirty-three. Do you think she'll bear you sons to carry on the name?"

Hendrik sighed softly, and said, his face as solemn as ever: "Sir, believe me, it is a matter of indifference to me whether we have children or not. I'm not enthused over the prospect of having a brood of children annoying me every moment of the day—and, no matter how many nurses you put in charge of them, children always make their presence felt in a house. I'm marrying Dora because she's the first really intelligent and cultivated woman I've met—at least, in an unattached state—in this colony." The slightest of smiles crossed his face. "I'll leave it to Peter and Adrian to carry on the family name, if you don't mind."

It was only a fortnight before the wedding took place—it was a June wedding—that Dirk discovered that Dora Hammers was a relative of Cynthia Clackson's, and that, on Cynthia's death five years before, had come in to Cynthia's estate. For Cynthia had been wealthy in her own right. She had owned three plantations on the Essequibo as well as shares in plantations in Barbados and Antigua. Dirk learnt this through Hendrik.

"She was a bitter woman, that Cynthia Clackson," said Hendrik. "Dora says she has letters written to her uncle by Cynthia in which Cynthia spoke very disparagingly of Graeme. She always referred to him as a bastard, and said that if she had been aware at the time of his proposing to her that he had been illegitimate she would never have accepted him. It appears she didn't hear the rumour of his doubtful origin until after they were married. Another thing that rankled was the fact that Cousin Hubertus was a quarter Indian. Imagine her being married to a man who had Indian blood in his veins!"

"Cynthia was a narrow-minded person," frowned Dirk. "I understand now why Graeme ignored her entirely in his will. Poor fellow. He must have suffered at her hands behind the scenes."

Hendrik and Dora were married at New Signal, but they settled at Flagstaff, and Hendrik immediately acquired a piano. Within less than a year Flagstaff had become renowned for the musical evenings which Dora arranged and directed. Willem enjoyed them, but his wife, Christina, found them irritating. Hendrik approved of, and enjoyed, whatever at all Dora did. In his eyes, she was the fulfilment of everything he had ever wished for.

In Berbice, meanwhile, music was playing an important part in the conflict coming into being between Mary and Adrian. For the past three or four years, Adrian had been showing a distinct love for the violin and the piano; at the Laffertys' place, where he was tutored with Jim Lafferty's grandchildren, he would often be inattentive to his lessons when the elder children, Patrick and Maureen, were practising a duet on the piano in the next room, and one day he had asked to be allowed to play the piano. Dirk and Mary both agreed that it would be a good thing for him, and so arrangements went forward, and soon the report had reached New Signal that Adrian was progressing apace with both piano and violin; old Jim Lafferty had insisted that the boy must learn to play the violin as well.

Mary was not musical, and within the past year or so had begun to chide Adrian for neglecting his regular curriculum for his music. "Music is all very well, Adrian, but first things must be put first. You are very weak at your arithmetic, Mr. Henty tells me, and you neglect your English composition shamefully." There was something else she could have added, but did not. To her father, however, she said it, in privacy. "I want him to be strong and virile, Papa. Music is an effeminate pastime for a boy of his age. He's in the formative stage, and this passion for the piano and violin won't help to make a man of him. And I can't prevent myself remembering that Uncle Graham has always been a keen musician—and you know very well what happened at a certain stage of his life."

Dirk nodded slowly; he always took seriously anything she discussed with him. "Yes, we'll have to watch him—but I don't think he will go the way of Graham. How old is he? Ten last September, wasn't he?" A twinkle came into his eyes. "He's definitely devoted to the ladies, I can assure you. I've already caught him out in one or two little escapades that leave no doubt in my mind which way he is inclined."

Mary flushed. "I know what you mean," she said, stiffening. "He interferes with the maids. But that is no guarantee."

"Isn't it? Hendrik used to do the same at fifteen." He shook his head. "My dear Mary, I'm coming to realise that it is no use trying to shape human beings the way we wish. Each will go his and her own way, despite all the training and rigid schooling we may attempt. At your age I used to think I could fashion the destiny of our family by merely exerting my will, by merely drumming into all my relatives the notions of greatness and glory, by bullying them into states of mind wherein only the idea of the family would seem of urgent importance. Now, at fifty-two, I know only too well the utter futility of my obsession. I still work for the family—I still put the welfare of the van Groenwegels before everything else—I still hope to see us prosper as a planting family—and I still want our name to be carried on throughout the decades ahead with credit and honour—but my illusion of power has long been crushed out. I know that I myself can never decide the issues. In the final reckoning each member of our family will achieve only that which his inborn nature dictates that he is capable of achieving. The strong will prove strong. The weak will prove weak."

53

T H E parting of the ways was so slight as to be unnoticeable, but there was a parting, and it dated from that afternoon. In bed that very night, recalling her father's speech, Mary thought: Could it be that he is weakening? I may be mistaken, but I had the feeling there was something of defeat in his voice. I wonder if it isn't that the time has come for me to do more than merely support him in his dreams and ambitions for the family. . . . "My illusion of power has long been crushed out. I know that I myself can never decide the issues." No, that did not sound like the old Papa—the strong, determined, invincible Papa who refused to admit that any situation was beyond his power to handle, who always felt that he and he alone could shape and influence the destinies of the members of our family. Could it be that I must now take over from him and be myself the binding force, the driving spirit? For I don't admit that it is beyond my power to mould the lives of other people, especially the people within one's own family circle. It can be done. I'm certain it can be done. And I shall try. As much for his sake as for the sake of the family. He is getting on in years, poor dear! I must take some of the weight off his shoulders. This is August 1848. He will be fifty-three next month. I was twenty-seven in April—just a trifle more than half his age. My illusions—though I don't believe they are illusions—are still intact. . . . And Adrian—ah! Adrian is eleven next month. Green, green terrain. Think what I can do with *him!* Yes, I shall certainly try.

Adrian began his music lessons seriously in October, and by January the reports had begun to come in from the Laffertys about his remarkable progress. "A little genius, Dirk," old Jim Lafferty told Dirk one day when they met on the ferry *stelling*. "Takes to music like a frog to a shower of rain. It's a gift. We've got to encourage it, my boy. Too good to be lost."

Every morning, before the household got out of bed—at half past five—Adrian was up and practising on his violin. He went downstairs and locked himself into a small room adjoining the pantry—a room that had once been his nurse's, and the same one to which Joanna, Peter's nurse, and Peter had had to flee in such a hurry the night when Francis opened his reign of terror with the chicken entrails. In here Adrian's violin did not prove a nuisance to the rest of the house. The sound of his playing came thin and faint upstairs.

One morning in February, Mary got up at half past five, went into the boy's room, and stopped him as he was on the point of going downstairs. She said: "No practising this morning, Adrian dear. I want you to come walking with me."

"Walking where?" asked Adrian, in dismay. "At this time? Why, Mary?"

She smiled. "We'll go as far as the canal—near the tamarind tree."

"But why? I have several exercises I want to practise."

"Tomorrow, dear. Every other morning, in future, I want you to come out with me for a walk. You'll see why."

"Then I can't practise every morning?"

"No. Every other morning will be sufficient. I'll tell you all about it as we walk. Just wait one moment until I get changed into a few light things."

A few minutes later, as they set out along the path that led towards the canal aback, she took deep breaths of the cool, dew-fresh dawn air. The sky in the east was barely pink and dull orange; the sun would not be up for at least twenty or twenty-five minutes. Blue sackies had begun a twittering and cheeping in the mango trees, and at the top of a sombre-leafed star-apple tree a *creketteh* hawk kept screeching irritably at intervals, as though it might have spent a sleepless night and was annoyed that dawn should have broken already.

"The reason for this, Adrian," she said, "is that you have been leading too sheltered and pampered a life these past few years. Only a month ago I was speaking to you about your music. It is very pleasant to be able to play the violin and the piano, dear, but first things must come first, remember——"

"I'm doing much better at my arithmetic, Mary—and my English, too. Mr. Henty told me that himself only last week."

"He told me, too. Very good. I'm pleased. But there is something else now. Exercise, fresh air, Adrian, make you strong and manly—and you've not been having much of that recently. When Papa and Uncle Jacob were your age they went running everywhere—swimming, playing at soldiers and hunting in the bush. They spent hours in the open air. They got wet in the rain, they dried themselves in the sun. That's why today they are strong and manly. Didn't you say you wanted to be strong and manly like Papa?"

"Yes, I did—and I mean to be, but I can still play the violin and the piano, can't I? Why should that prevent me from being strong and manly?"

"It can, if you let it—because it's a pastime that keeps you indoors. Everything done in moderation is good. I'm not trying to discourage you at your music, but I want you to be healthy and sturdy as well in body. A keen, fine mind, and artistic accomplishments, are to be admired—but you must have a fine body to go along with them. Do you see what I mean?"

He nodded. "Yes, perfectly. You're right. I like walking—especially when it's cool like this early in the morning. Kathleen goes for walks, too, in the morning. I've heard her telling Patrick."

"Very sensible of her, I'm sure."

"She's very pretty, isn't she?"

"Very."

"She doesn't look at me, though. She's nearly nineteen. I'm only eleven." His oval-faced, frowning frailty seemed to quiver beside her with a kind of grey lightning—some gloomy emanation of the dying night. She caught his hand and squeezed it, and said: "That's as it should be, I think. Are you upset?"

"I like Kathleen. I often play pieces for her—when I'm in our own house. She would think me stupid if she knew. She laughs at me because she knows I like her. Jasmine is so different. Jasmine smiles at me when I meet her in the street, and she stops and talks to me. I like her, too. She's almost as pretty as Kathleen. I could marry her when I grow up—if Kathleen won't have me."

Mary frowned. "Jasmine is coloured, Adrian."

"Oh. Yes, I know. She's Uncle Jacob's daughter, though, and she's a lady. She dresses like a lady and speaks like a lady."

"That is so—and I like her, too. But you must remember that you are white—and a van Groenwegel. *Only* a white girl will do for you as a wife."

"If you say so," he sighed. He gave her a teasing glance and said: "When are you going to get married, Mary? You're so pretty."

She chuckled, her face seeming to absorb some of the pink from the east.

"Mr. Henty likes you. Loves you, I should say. He would marry you if you only lifted your finger to him. Do you ever answer the notes he gives me to bring for you? You never give me any to take back."

"I don't think it necessary to answer them."

"Do you hate him?"

She smiled. "I don't. I am rather fond of him, in fact."

"Then why don't you let him visit you as he wants to do?"

"Because I don't intend to marry, Adrian. That's why." She uttered a soft, gasping sound, then added quickly: "I have work to do at the sawmill."

"Ladies don't work. You're the only one I know of who goes to an office."

"Exactly. That's because I'm what I am. I have chosen to be different."

He squeezed her wrist. "You're good and sweet, though, even though you do things differently. I like your hair hanging down in a plait. You should always wear it like this, Mary. The other way makes you seem older."

They emerged on to the bank of the canal, near the old tamarind tree. The trunk was knotty and thick, and the branches tangled with vines and parasites, but it was the same tamarind tree under which Jacob and Dirk and Rose and their friends had disported themselves. It was even bearing at the moment. The fingerlike pods hung amber-green in the brightening morning; they were not ripe for picking, but Adrian reached up and broke one off.

"Want a piece of green tamarind?"

"No, I don't. Come. We have no time to lose. Undress. We're going to take a swim in the canal." She was already undressing. He had grown up accustomed to seeing her unclad, hence neither of them experienced any embarrassment.

"I'm not a very good swimmer, Mary. I can't swim very far."

"All the more reason why you must learn. At eleven, you ought to be ashamed to admit that you can't swim at least from here to the factory."

He grinned. "I don't want to be a swimmer when I grow up. I want to be a pianist and a violinist."

She gave him a sharp look as she discarded her last garment, and said: "I want to remind you, Adrian, that this plantation will one day be your responsibility. Your music *must* take second place to planting."

He sighed. "I suppose you're right. You always are, Mary. I think you're very wise—like Papa. But I'm never going to give up my music."

"No one asks you to. Come on. Let us go in."

He hugged himself. "Oooh! It's cold, Mary. The water must be like ice."

"Nonsense. In this country water is never really cold. Remember what Cousin Willem and Uncle Jacob said? What we call cold water here would be deemed lukewarm in England." She clenched her hands, for her skin had just acquired vast areas of goose flesh, and she wanted desperately to shiver. "You must try not to be soft. You must try to tell yourself that discomforts are there to be endured and over-come. Tell yourself that you can overcome anything, anything whatever, so long as you will it so. And you can't fail."

He nodded, but grinned and said: "Where you are there now you're as cold as I am, and I know you want to shiver. Ugh! Don't let's go in, Mary."

She smiled, her sense of humour tickled—and this time she let herself shiver. "Yes, it is chilly—but we're van Groenwegels, Adrian. Let's face up to it and go in. Come on."

"I wish Mr. Henty could see you like this! He'd write you an epistle, instead of a note, today. You look like that woman we were reading about."

"Who was that?"

"Boadicea. The British warrior woman. When she was naked she must have looked like you. With her golden hair flowing behind her as you have yours now, and her breasts sticking out in front like weapons to gore the Roman legions."

She flushed deeply, but laughed and said: "Your imagination is far too vivid for your age. Come on! In we go now! The van Groen-wegels never run!"

They plunged in.

Every other morning they went swimming in the canal, and Adrian soon came to like it immensely. His thin arms and legs began to grow tough and developed, and his chest, which formerly had been rather sunken, filled out.

He was an extremely tractable fellow, and Mary felt very satisfied with his physical progress. His mental attitudes seemed quite normal, and he was without any strange moods; always cheerful and easy to get on with. Yet he disturbed her deep down. His very easy, cheerful, tractable qualities struck her sometimes as being ominous. Were these the qualities, she would ask herself, that ought to go with a strong character? Again, his way of poking fun at her, naïve and yet sly, left the impression that he saw through the whole mechanism of her system of discipline, and was secretly, though affectionately, mocking her.

Dirk now and then congratulated her. "That swimming of yours is working wonders on his physique, my girl. Carry on!" But his manner was casual and matter-of-fact, and always made her feel that he took it for granted that she should make a success of her brother's training, physical and otherwise. He did not behave as though he realised the energy she had to put into everything, her sawmill work, the plantation business, the affairs of Hartfield & Clackson, and Adrian. It was as though he had written her off as a marriageable person, and resigned himself to her spinsterhood, accepted her as an efficient machine upon whom he could depend on all occasions. She would not have minded this had he shown towards her an awareness of the sacrifices involved for her. A grain of resentment would come alive in her on each occasion when, on looking at herself in the mirror, the tiny red spot in her fancy glowed brighter, whiter, and the breathlessness overtook her, when she looked down on her dressing table and saw the box in which she collected all the notes that had been written to her, not only by John Henty, the tutor, but by others throughout the past nine or ten years. A dizziness would attack her when she thought of the sons that might have been her own to mother and train into manly men. . . . She would shut her eyes and bite her lip and think: If only he would show that he understood fully the bitterness of my accursed state, but he treats me as if my aberration is of the past, an ugly misfortune now fortunately left behind, something I've already successfully lived down and suppressed. That hurts, because nothing is past; the red spot burns as bright and white and hot as ever it did.

In October of that year, 1849, Peter came back from England, a qualified medical man, a shortish, wiry, sandy-haired fellow, not unlike his father in appearance; though his grey-green eyes held no fanatic light; they were lamb's eyes rather than raccoon's. He brought with him a wife, whom he had married a few weeks before sailing from England —her name was Gwendolyn, and she was Welsh, dark, quiet, always with a pleasant, humorous twinkle in her grey eyes, and somewhat voluptuous in build, putting them all in mind of Janet.

Peter and Gwendolyn settled down in the house in New Amsterdam where Ronald and Amelia had lived, and within a matter of weeks Peter had become established in his profession. Doctors were few.

Mary Maybury gave him a hysterical welcome. "You have come to take my John's place!" she wept. "Oh, how pleased he would have been, Peter!"

In mid-December a servant found her dead in her room. On the table beside the bed was a vial of laudanum and a note addressed to Elizabeth which read simply: "Elizabeth, my child, you will all forgive me, please, but Peter is now with us, and last night John came for me. He wants me with him. Mary."

In her will, she bequeathed her entire estate (which included a share in New Signal) to Peter.

Dirk was very pleased that Mary Maybury had seen it fit to indulge in this gesture, for he had been fearing that she might have bequeathed her estate to the Methodist Church, of which she had always been a staunch member. Indeed, Dirk would have been jubilant over Peter's good fortune had not his mood been so heavily dampened by the general state of things at that time in the colony. It was a period of great strain and depression, and hardly a planter was not on the very brink of utter despair.

Hitches had occurred in the immigration schemes and the flow of East Indians had slowed down, and the free-trade policy of Britain was working havoc with the sugar industry and, as a consequence, with the prosperity of the merchants. Only the fittest saw any hope of survival. In Demerara, between the Mahaicony and Mahaica Creeks the only plantation still in cultivation was Plantation Farm; the others had either been completely abandoned or turned into pasture land for a few head of cattle, or planted with ground provisions. In Berbice, of the six sugar plantations on the Corentyne Coast only four were operating now. Virtually all the onetime flourishing cotton plantations were now reverting to bush and swampy savannah, the buildings on them crumbling to bits, and only a few squatters remaining to plant provisions and rear cattle. The roads were neglected and, in many places, had become hopeless bogs. All communication with New

Amsterdam was cut off, and lawlessness increased. A smuggling trade was started between the British settlements and Nickerie on the Dutch side of the Corentyne River. Between Devil's Creek, a little tributary of the Corentyne, and the Canje Creek there had once been over twenty prosperous cotton plantations; now the whole area was jungle. And in the Berbice River estuary Crab Island continued to grow in size; the bar of silt across the mouth of the river daily became more and more difficult to negotiate, and ships had to wait for the high tide before attempting to cross it, for fear of going aground. Jacob's prediction was coming true.

The next year, 1850, was just five months old when Storm, in rising from his chair on the portico, suddenly stiffened and sank down again. Elizabeth glanced up and was on the point of uttering a teasing remark when she noticed that his mouth was gaping slightly and his head lolling sideways. He was quite still.

While the others were moving back towards the house, she alone stood watching the mason at work on the big brick vault. It was a bleak afternoon, the ground sodden from a morning of rain, and the frogs chirruped and croaked in a cacophonous chorus around her.

Moving back with the crowd of friends and relations towards the house, Dirk murmured to Mary: "There goes the last of the Old Ones. Did you know that he was born on a ship called the *Standvastigheid* in March 1763—at Fort St. Andries, Mary. Only a few miles from here—and at the height of the slave insurrection. Old Faustina was a brave soul. One of the strong ones."

"Papa, shouldn't you go back and wait with Grandma? I'll take charge of everyone until you get to the house."

He started and murmured: "Yes, yes. Mama is still at the vault, is she? Yes, I must go back and wait there with her." He squeezed her arm. "I value you more than you may imagine, my child. In you, I believe, is the greatness of Hendrickje—without the inhumanity."

He turned away quickly, but she had already seen the glisten of moisture in his eyes.

54

THAT one remark of Dirk's destroyed within Mary the accumulated bitterness of months—a bitterness to which she had so inured herself, enclosing it in an isolated pocket and thus preventing it from poisoning her whole outlook, that she had almost come to forget its existence.

On the night of the funeral, cool shudders of relaxation made a rippling through her spirit as she lay in bed listening to the rain on the roof. Now and then it was almost as though the rain projected itself through the roof in soft invisible drops of peace that she could hear pattering deliciously on the network of her solaced and sagging nerves.

Before falling asleep, she began to mutter aloud to herself.

"Wrong. . . . I was quite wrong. . . ." The tiny red spot remained red—sunset mild. Tonight it would not trouble her; it would not turn white tonight. . . . "Quite wrong. He doesn't take me for granted in the way I'd imagined. . . ." The rain ran in rivulets of harmony along her limbs, as though Adrian might have distilled them on his violin through some mysterious but delightful conspiracy. . . . "Entirely wrong. Dear Papa. How I misjudged him. He knows—he knows of the great sacrifice I've made. . . ."

And in the weeks and months that passed after this night, her happiness seemed to consolidate within her. A new freshness and bloom came into her face, and her twenty-nine years seemed to dwindle to nineteen or eighteen.

Both Dirk and Adrian commented on her youthful air when they were on their way to Demerara, on the very last day of that same year, for another funeral. Willem died after a stroke. The message from Hendrik had said that if they hurried they might be in time to witness him breathe his last, but as it turned out, Willem died an hour before they arrived at Flagstaff. Peter and his wife travelled with them. They went overland and, despite the muddy state of the roads, reached Flagstaff at four o'clock, an hour before the funeral.

It was when they had just passed through Harrow's Castle, Larsen's place, three miles to the east of Flagstaff along the coast, that Adrian smiled at his sister, who sat opposite him in the carriage—it was a fresh one lent to them by a family at Mahaica—and said: "Mary hasn't got a funeral face. You look as if you're on your way to a wedding, Mary." And Mary laughed and flushed. "Yes, I believe Mr. Grant at Mahaica must have thought the same thing, too—only he was too polite to say so. When we stopped to change carriages he addressed me in a distinctly frivolous manner." Then Dirk, beside her, patted her hand and said: "You have grown younger within these past six or seven months, my girl. I've observed it. You look seventeen." And Adrian added: "That's right, Papa—and she behaves like seventeen, too. Yesterday she beat me in a race from the tamarind tree to the factory when we went on our early-morning swim in the canal."

"She has probably been working on some secret formula Francis gave her unknown to us," said Peter. "Some necromantic elixir she's at last succeeded in concocting has begun to do its work in her system."

"Take no notice of them, Mary," smiled Gwendolyn. "When they hear you sing in the cantata at Easter they'll probably say you're thirteen." Gwendolyn was an active member of the Methodist Church, and had taken complete charge of the choir. She was musical, and had a good voice; she was planning a cantata for Easter, and had persuaded Mary to sing in the choir (though Mary was a member of the Lutheran Church). Adrian had promised to play his violin in the string orchestra Gwendolyn was trying to muster for the occasion.

Graham, in a quiet chat with Dirk, the day after the funeral, at Kaywana, also referred to Mary. "She seems quite remarkable, that girl of yours. It isn't often one finds such beauty combined with high intelligence."

Dirk nodded. "Yes, she is remarkable. A high type, Graham. Hendrickje, as I've told her, without the cruel strain. A refined Hendrickje. But I'm still sad about Mary. I want to see her married and settled and happy with her children. I've stopped telling her that recently, because it upsets her, but that is my earnest wish still. I feel she is being wasted—shamefully wasted. A loss to herself and to some deserving fellow who, as her husband, would have valued her at her true worth and given her a fulsome happiness—as well as himself." He clicked his tongue and stirred in his chair, frowning out upon the pale sunshine on the fruit trees. "Words, words! So useless uttering these sentiments. What power have I to help her in affairs of that sort! So you're off to England for this great performance, I hear."

"What perform—oh, the Exhibition! Yes, that's right. I thought I'd as well combine it all, you know. I haven't yet seen Reginald's children. Why don't you come with me? This exhibition at Hyde Park promises to be something very special—and you've never yet been to England, Dirk."

Dirk shook his head. "I don't want to go to England," he murmured —angry with himself for appearing obstinate and sour, but unable to counteract this impression. There were too many matters bothering him at the moment.

He felt Graham's gaze on him, not mocking in the old way, but, if anything, gentle and sympathetic. These days Graham's company was welcome, for Graham had won for himself a peace that Dirk envied. At sixty Graham was grey, and there were crow's feet around his eyes, but his face was that of a man at accord with life and his inner self. Since the death of his timber manager and intimate friend, Albert Laver, some three or four years before, this look of peace in Graham had intensified, almost as though sorrow had done the work of some beneficent chemical of the spirit.

"Of course, you haven't a manager," said Graham. (Twenty years earlier, he would have added with a sneer: "Naturally, it would be against van Groenwegel tradition to hire a manager to run your plantation. Ah well!") He lit a cigar, and murmured: "You should consider getting a manager. You'd be able to relax more than you do. It's a terrible strain, especially in these days of depression."

Dirk nodded, conscious of the lines on his own face, of the strain of the times that must show in his eyes. Perhaps he looked as old as Graham, who knew?

"Give Reginald my regards. And his wife. He must bring his children to see us some time soon." He spoke automatically, dutifully, in a tired voice.

It was not until he was back at New Signal that he revealed to anyone the burden of his immediate reflections. On the way back,

Mary had tried to probe his silence, but he had evaded her with banter. In any event, he could not speak of what was on his mind in the presence of Adrian and Peter and his wife.

It was to Jacob, at the sawmill, that he first spoke. There was a special sympathy between them nowadays, apart from the old and consolidated brotherly camaraderie. Like himself, Jacob was a worried and tired man who refused to give in, who refused to take the easy path and relinquish his responsibilities, delegating them to an assistant or manager. Indeed, Jacob's case was worse, for he was not in good health; within recent years he had developed dyspeptic troubles, and Jim kept advising him to retire, kept warning him that his heart was being affected by the strain of work imposed upon it. And Jasmine, his youngest girl, from eighteen had been giving cause for concern; she had formed an attachment for a young man much beneath her in social status—the son of a small shopkeeper in the extreme southern part of the town, the poor section; she had become pregnant by him, and her brother Jim, much against his will, for he was strict about his medical ethics, had had to perform the necessary operation to prevent her from having the child. Somehow it had leaked out, however, and now young men, though attracted to her, for she was very pretty, seemed not eager to contemplate marriage with her. She continued to be a flirt, carefree and unconventional, and Jacob was fearing that there would soon be another scandal.

Dirk and Jacob, as they might have done twenty years ago, stood on a raft and talked, staring across at Crab Island and the ferry *stelling* at Rosignol on the western bank of the river.

"It's Willem's death that's thrown me off balance a bit, Jacob," said Dirk. "He was just nearing sixty-nine. I didn't expect him to go off like that. Thought he would have attained to our family average of eighty, at least. Now there is the problem of Hendrik in charge alone at Flagstaff, and with Christina, a soured old shrew, to contend with. Naturally, Willem has bequeathed his share in Flagstaff to Christina—and Christina is a difficult person to get on with. She tried to make Elfrida's life a misery, remember. Now she'll turn her attention on Dora, Hendrik's wife. It was only Willem who had been keeping the peace so far between them, Hendrik has told me. And she's sixty-four, and seems likely to live on to seventy or eighty. Thin, shrivelled, but as hard as iron."

"I know the kind," said Jacob, essaying a smile. "Lawrence's mother-in-law is like that to the last detail. She's stopped speaking to Milly and me."

"Of course," said Dirk, "that's only one aspect of the situation. There are other worries that you'll probably tell me are unnecessary, but, I see them as annoying obstacles to my hopes and dreams. Hendrik's wife shows no sign yet of giving him a child. And Peter's Gwendolyn suffered a miscarriage a month or so ago—or is abortion the right term? It's all this church activity of hers. Choirs and cantatas and soirees. That's the worst with these educated women. At Flagstaff, Dora devotes her whole life to musical evenings. She's even arranging amateur dramatics now, I've been told. Why can't they forget their cultural accomplishments until they have done their duty and produced some children? These French and Belgian schools for young ladies are more a menace to society, if you ask me."

"I agree," Jacob nodded. "Though I've been lucky with my boy's Eva, so far. She confines herself to reading. Not so keen on music and the church. She's pregnant now with her fourth."

"Mm. Two sons and a girl up to the moment are not to be sneezed at, eh? And Charles's barmaid has also produced three so far, hasn't she?"

"All girls—but she expects a happy event next month, I understand, and Charles is hoping it will be a boy." Jacob sighed, the lines and bags on his face smoothing out a trifle as a smile followed the sigh. "No use worrying about it, Dirk, lad. You yourself have come to agree with me on that of late."

Dirk grinned, and gave him a gentle shove. "Agree with you, yes— but do I stop worrying? Why, even Mary I was telling the other day about the family—the futility of trying to shape the members of our family the way I think they should be shaped. But I still secretly hatch my little schemes, Jacob. I still want to see the van Groenwegels go on to glorious heights. I still want to see our name honoured in this colony, and the family firmly established, with enough sons alive to ensure that our name never dies out." He tapped his shoe nervously against one of the logs of the raft on which they were standing. "Sons, Jacob—sons! I'm worried about the sons. Mine are still in the running, so to speak, but look what happened to Pelham's. If Hendrik and Peter and Adrian fail me, then we're lost. The family name will be on the way to extinction."

Jacob chuckled and said slyly: "You haven't mentioned Jason, Dirk."

Dirk flushed, but he had been half prepared for this challenge. He smiled and said: "I hadn't forgotten him, Jacob—but he isn't white, is he?" After a pause: "I went to look up his mother and grandparents when I was in Georgetown some weeks ago. I saw the boy, too. Getting quite tall, and has a slight look of his grandfather. Pelham's forehead and shape of head." They stared at the four-eye fishes in silence, and then Dirk said: "Have a little scheme in mind for him, too—but it must wait until he is older."

Jacob chuckled again. "I can guess, Dirk. Greenfield or Benfield?"

Dirk gave him another shove. "You're too clever at guessing, damn you!"

Many of Dirk's worries vanished during the months of that same mid-century year, 1851, for Christina, contrary to what Dirk had feared, became like a lamb after Willem's death, and gave Dora a free hand to run the Flagstaff household, neither interfering nor even commenting. She even became an enthusiastic member of the audience at every musical concert given. Moreover, news came to Dirk that Dora was pregnant. Dirk, in a letter to Hendrik, asked for confirmation of this in as delicate a manner as he could, and Hendrik replied that it was so; Hendrik expressed neither pleasure nor annoyance at the coming event.

The colony situation, too, was improving rapidly. A new immigration drive commenced. The Home Government had made a grant of two hundred and fifty thousand pounds, and the greater part of this sum was being used to bring in more East Indian coolies. The surviving sugar plantations in the colony—a hundred and seventy-three out of two hundred and fourteen—found themselves in a position to double, and, in some cases, even treble their former output. Graham, on his return from England, reported that everyone over there was extremely sanguine of great prosperity for the colony in the immediate years ahead. He had met a number of absentee proprietors at a gathering convened by Reginald in London, and the whole planting situation had been fully discussed.

Mary, who, like her great-grandfather, old Wilfred Maybury, had a mania for collecting statistics and old records, told Dirk in January 1853 that in the year before, 1852, the colony had exported slightly over fifty-six thousand hogsheads of sugar. "That's double what we exported in 1850," she said. "We here at New Signal contributed eight hundred and twenty hogsheads of this amount. And Kaywana,

Flagstaff, and Harrow's Castle produced two thousand three hundred between them. You won't say the prospects are disheartening now, would you?"

She sat on the edge of her writing desk in her room as she said this, shuffling her papers together and regarding her father with a teasing smile. It was a cool, dry afternoon, more like February than January, and the smell of cane juice was strong in the air, for the factory was grinding.

Dirk grunted and rubbed his hands together slowly, returning her smile in a reluctant, grudging manner. "Yes, I admit we have done well this past year or two, my girl. As long as the flow of labour can continue as it's doing at present there is nothing to trouble ourselves about. But don't lose sight of what's happening, Mary. The coolies are beginning to do just what the Portuguese did, and are still doing. They're trickling into the towns and setting themselves up as hucksters and pedlars. Not a good sign, that. Soon they'll be competing with the Portuguese and the coloured folk as shopkeepers, and there you are! We'll have a fine mess of a confusion in the commercial circles of the colony."

"What an arch-pessimist you are!" she cried, and, approaching, stoked his thin, silver-grey hair; the sandy strands were all gone. She had lost her shyness now, and had returned to the days when she could be free in caressing him. His tired, fifty-seven-year-old face no longer awed her as it had done two or three years before. The strength and masculinity were still there—the raccoon eyes could still flare in green fury—but the weariness gave it a vulnerable look and this provided her with the excuse to be bold in her demonstrations of fondness; he needed to be comforted, needed to be fawned upon, to stimulate his courage and bolster up his natural strength and male drive. She felt no guilt in being overtly affectionate. Moreover, she had acquired more self-confidence. The menace of the tiny red spot, still alive, did not unnerve her so much, for she had devised ways of keeping it just beyond the perimeter of her defences.

"The Chinese are coming now," she said, pacing back to the writing table. "A shipload of them is due this very month." She began to search through her papers. "There was something in the *Gazette* about it. I think they're consigned to Booker Brothers through Hyde, Hodge's."

"I did hear some talk of it." He snorted. "What sort of colony we'll be having at this rate! Portuguese, Indian coolies. And now Chinese!

The irony of it! Every language of the world will soon be heard here—
save Dutch!" He began to pace about in his old agitated manner,
abruptly halted and asked: "Where is Adrian this afternoon, by the
way?"

"At the Methodist Church. Choir practice."

"I don't know why Gwendolyn will persist in luring him to the
Methodist Church. I'm sure the Lutheran pastor cannot be pleased
about it."

"It isn't simply Gwendolyn who lures him there, Papa," she smiled,
putting away her papers. "He's infatuated with a certain member of
the choir, poor boy."

"Who is that?" asked her father sharply. And she replied: "Jasmine."

"Jasmine? Not—surely not Jacob's Jasmine?" And when she nodded,
he frowned and said: "That flirtatious young woman! She's his senior
by nearly ten years. What absurdity is this? A boy of fifteen and a
young woman of twenty-four!"

"It's nothing to trouble about, Papa. He'll soon get over it. She
doesn't take him seriously, I'm certain." Though she spoke carelessly,
Dirk could detect a background note of uneasiness in her voice. He
grunted and moving over to the bed, bent and pulled out the canister
containing the letters. He asked for the key, and she unbuttoned the
top of her bodice and pulled out a thin silver chain. The key for the
canister was attached to it.

He laughed. "Such odd habits you have. Keeping the key in your
bosom on that chain." He took it from her and opened the canister,
began to fumble about for a moment, then exclaimed and brought up a
notebook. He turned a page or two, then paused and told her to have
a look. "See that? Uncle Edward was born in March 1763, and Aunt
Luise in October 1753. He was only eleven when she fell in love
with him and began to pursue him. She twenty-one and he eleven."
He gave her a stare. "Strange blood, ours, Mary, my girl. You must
speak to Adrian."

"Nothing will happen, Papa. She's coloured, and he understands."
Again, however, there was a note of uneasiness in her manner.

55

IT was on a Sunday in October of that same year, 1853, that
the first notes were sounded—the first notes in what Adrian
afterwards called the crescendo air of doom. ("An air for orchestra, though," he had added, "not for a solo instrument.")

It was one of the hottest Octobers ever experienced in the colony.
The heat continued even into the night, and hardly any wind blew.
Though there was no real drought, for twice during the month rain
poured, and thunder and lightning made a dramatic display. But these
were mere breaks in a period of scorchingly fiery days. At night the
grass smelt dry and haylike, though still green, and the crickets
wheezed like a thousand infinitesimal violins amidst the leaves of the
fruit trees and the clumps of black-sage bushes near the water's edge.
The frogs, however, were silent, hushed by the heat. And one night,
in bed, Dirk heard a goatsucker crying "Hoo-yoo!" far away. It was
years since he had heard one. They were birds that liked the quiet of
the bush; the ever increasing bustle and activity of New Signal had
driven them away—driven them south, beyond the canal aback, into
the outer cane fields and the bushes and savannah terrain beyond the
outer cane fields.

At two o'clock on that particular Sunday, Mary was in her room,
which was on the southern side of the house—in the new wing—
and therefore far hotter than Dirk's and Elizabeth's rooms on the
northern side. Downstairs Adrian was practising on his violin. The
sound came up in clear thin threads, and, if anything, made her drowsy
as she sat by the window going through some correspondence relating
to the affairs of Hartfield & Clackson. The heat trailed through the
room in sticky, stifling filaments that threatened to strangle her. Even
though, on her coming home from church an hour or two before,

she had undressed and wrapped herself only in a light gown, she could feel the perspiration trickling down her arms and down her back and bosom.

Adrian's violin grew silent after a while, and he came upstairs. His room was still the one next to hers. She called out to him when she heard him enter it.

"Some work for you, young man," she told him. "Come in at once!"

He came in, scowling, and said: "It's siesta time, Mary. I'm sleepy." He was in trousers and nothing else. His chest and arms were shiny with perspiration. The muscles showed up to advantage—his swimming muscles, as he called them, for it was the early-morning swimming in the canal that had developed them.

She laughed. "You won't fool me. I know what you want to do now. It's that composition of yours you want to get back to, isn't it?"

He grinned—and it was Dirk's grin, swift and humorous.

"Only sixteen last month, and trying to compose music. Whoever heard of such idiocy? Come on. Sit down at the desk there. I have at least three letters I want you to reply to for me."

He sat down at the desk, sighing. "Well, I must do them, I suppose— but you can write much faster than I, Mary, and yours is a much better calligraphy. Why don't you do them yourself. I'll watch you so as to understand what they're about."

"A splendid way of getting out of it, I must say. It's useless trying to flatter me, Adrian. And remember, it's because I want you to practise your handwriting that I insist on your writing these letters, so resign yourself to the task." She got up and crossed to the writing desk and arranged the stationery before him. He admired her blotting pad and said: "I must get one like this myself. I think they stock them at Frick & Green's."

She settled herself in a chair beside him, a severe figure with her hair piled up on her head in spinster fashion, erect of back, the stack of letters in her lap, only the revealing gown destroying the effect of austerity, for here and there it stuck to her skin, wet with perspiration.

Adrian tried to delay matters by indulging in trivial conversation, but she hushed him and began to dictate the first letter. Obediently he set himself to write, and after he had done three letters, she said: "Very good. And do you understand what they are about?" He nodded, and replied: "Perfectly." But she smiled and said: "Explain. I'm waiting." So he went into details about the shipments of sugar and the timber which had been the subjects dealt with in the letters. "The bills of lading were not enclosed in their last letter, so we can do nothing yet here. And Mr. Daly of Vlissingen is still to advise us. . . ." His voice droned on until suddenly she stopped him, chuckled, and said: "Very well. That will do. You seem to have grasped the matter."

He made to rise, but she checked him. He scowled. "Can't I go now?"

"Just a moment. Tell me. All this bores you intensely, doesn't it? Be truthful, please, dear. Don't be afraid to tell me."

He grinned, put out his hand, and patted her cheek lightly. "I'm never afraid of you, Mary. You're too good—and pretty. Yes, it does bore me."

She was silent a moment, staring past him at the candlestick on a shelf near the writing table, then she fixed her gaze on him and said: "It may be boring, dear, but you will have to go on with it. Remember what I've told you, Adrian. We're depending upon you to carry on New Signal."

He nodded. "Don't go over it all again, please. You and Papa are so tiresome over this family notion. What's he doing in Georgetown now, by the way?"

"He's gone to see the Clarks," she told him, frowning slightly, as though he had reminded her of something disturbing. "It's the shop— old Sarah's shop. We got a letter from the man who was running it. He wants to branch out on his own in one of the East Coast villages, so Papa has gone to Georgetown to ask Jason Clark to take the shop under his management. Papa wants the boy to be put to work in the shop—Cousin Francis's son, Jason. He's fifteen—old enough to start working." She began to drum with her fingers on the arm of the chair, her face musing. He regarded her keenly, and said: "I suppose Papa has some little scheme up his sleeve for our coloured relative. Do you know what it is?"

"I know of no scheme," she murmured coldly. Stirred in her chair, whistled at the heat, and said: "How did you get on in the choir today?"

"Fairly well. How was the choir at the Lutheran Church?"

She ignored his inquiry and asked: "Was Jasmine at church?" And he grunted assent, avoiding her gaze and beginning to pick at his thumbnail.

She watched him, waiting for him to make some comment, but he said nothing. He began to whistle a Bach air, engrossed with his thumbnail.

"Adrian."

"Yes?"

"Hendrik's Dora had twin girls a year or two ago."

"Why are you telling me? Do you think I'd forgotten?"

"And Gwendolyn," his sister said, as though he had not spoken, "had a girl last month. And she may never have another child. As it is, she had suffered several miscarriages before she eventually—well, I needn't go into improper details. But the point I'm trying to make, Adrian, is that the chances are that Hendrik and Peter may never produce any sons."

"Ah, now I see it!" he exclaimed, laughing. "You mean me. The old subject. Don't bother to say it, Mary, sweetheart. I know. Everything may depend upon me. If I don't marry and have sons the name of van Groenwegel may die out." He grimaced at her, and uttered weird boyish catcalls. "Forget all that. It's so hot today." He sprang up. "What about going for a swim, Mary?"

"It's no light matter, Adrian. You're only sixteen, I admit, but you are very intelligent for your age, and you know full well how much is on your shoulders."

"Sssh! Don't bother, Mary dear. I'm not going to marry Jasmine. She's coloured—and she's twenty-five. When I'm ready to marry she'll be over thirty. Come and let's have a swim. It's Sunday, and no one will see us."

She agreed that it was an excellent idea, and they set out for the canal. It was when they were undressing under the tamarind tree that she mentioned about Captain Brandon. "He's having dinner with us this afternoon."

"Who is he now? Oh, you mean that old sea captain who has bought over Don Diego? But Papa isn't here. Are you and I alone going to entertain him?"

"Papa had invited him before he knew he would have had to go to Georgetown. It'll be no trouble. He's probably a quiet, undemanding fellow. And Grandma said she would try to be down for dinner, so that should help us out."

"Dear old Grandma. Eighty-five—even though she is of Maybury stock."

She laughed. "Don't be sarcastic. Oh, what a relief to contemplate taking a swim—let alone actually to dive in! Aren't you ready yet?" She gave him a frowning glance, for though he had already stripped, he had made no move to dive in. He was staring up into the foliage of the tamarind tree, smiling one of his secretive smiles. Of late she had caught him frequently doing this.

He started, and muttered: "I was thinking of something."

"Your composition, I suppose."

"How did you guess? Yes. Mr. Randolph thinks it good so far. I've showed him the first five bars. He's teaching me a lot of valuable things about harmony."

It was she now who suddenly grew reflective, staring into the black water with a secretive air as she idly cupped her breasts. A cricket uttered a lonely shriek somewhere in the bushes behind them, and it was as though it were mocking her. It seemed to keep deriding her in its high, shrill voice—and the memory of an occasion five years before seeped like a hot ghost through her body. . . . "At your age, I used to think I could fashion the destiny of our family by merely exerting my will . . . by bullying them into states of mind. . . ."

" 'Like two young roes that are twins. . . .' You have lovely breasts, Mary. So firm and upright—and you're thirty-two. You're going to be like Grandma Hendri and Cousin Rose. You'll never lose your figure, no matter how old you get. 'Like two young roes——' "

"What on earth are you babbling about?" she asked, starting and glancing at him. "What two young roes are these? I don't——"

"That's the name of my composition. It's from the Bible."

"The Bible? I didn't know you were in the habit of reading the Bible."

"Not often. Sometimes—in the Methodist Church."

She tilted her head in perplexity. "When do you do this reading, pray?"

He shrugged, avoiding her gaze, picking at his thumbnail, chuckled and said casually: "Sometimes after choir practice. You know the big lectern near the harmonium? There's a big Bible on it."

"Do you remain alone in the church to read the Bible?"

"What questions! Forget all about it," he said, reddening. "Come on! In we go! Plunge!" He turned off and plunged in, and after a slight hesitation she went in after him. They swam in the direction of the koker that opened into the Canje, for had they gone, as they usually did in the early morning, towards the factory, there would have been the chance of some odd coolie or overseer seeing them. The canal, as far as the koker, ran between cane fields.

They emerged and sat on a hump of grass near the koker, the gates of which were closed. They could see the Creek, with clumps of Missouri grass going past slowly on the ebbing tide. The heat shimmered around them even in the shade of the *cookerit* palm under which they squatted. They both uttered ecstatic sounds as they slapped their bodies, now cooled and refreshed by the water.

They reclined there for a while, chatting idly about nothing in particular. Once during a silence they heard a rustling and tinkle of water splashing, and both turned their heads quickly to glance towards the Creek, from which direction the sound had come. There was no craft in sight, however.

He grinned. "I'd have given anything to see your face if a boat had just suddenly appeared and surprised us." He grunted and went on: "Why is it we are never ashamed to see each other naked, Mary? It never bothers us at all, and yet if I only dare imagine . . ." He broke off, reddening.

"Well? Imagine what? What were you going to say?" she asked, staring at him in keen suspicion, noting his confusion. And even when he laughed and said: "Oh, it's nothing," she still stared at him, a cold fear within her. In a slow, portentous voice, she said: "I think I know what you mean, Adrian. Keep your thoughts off Jasmine Frick, do you hear me? It will do you little good. She's a young lady—and an experienced and rather wanton one, too."

"Oh, I know what you mean," he growled, scowling. "I heard about that fellow Lambkin, the grocer's son. Doctor Jim had to operate on her."

"Indeed! You seem to have been well informed by someone on the matter!"

He gave an awkward grin. "These things are rumoured around."

"Who told you that?" she demanded. But he refused to say. He adopted a teasing manner, and said: "That's a good mystery for you to solve. Solve the riddle! Who could have told me such immoral things! Never you mind!"

"Remember, you're a boy! You're only sixteen, Adrian. Only sixteen."

"And what of that? I can still do manly things. Look at that! What do you think of *that*?"

"Stop being obscene," she snapped, averting her face and flushing. He laughed a loud, cackling laugh. "Your own fault! Every time you go calling me a boy I'm going to shock your modesty by bringing him to attention to show you. See him? He's a dangerous fellow."

Unsmiling, she rose and plunged in, the while he continued to

cackle. He had just risen, too, to plunge after her when on glancing
to his left, he saw one of the branches of a *courida* tree that over-
hung the water in the Creek move a trifle. He stared hard, and then
could have sworn to himself that some dark object glided off out of
view, round the clump of trees, in an upstream direction. Possibly
an alligator, he told himself, and plunged in and struck out after Mary.
In a few minutes he had forgotten the incident.

As she had predicted, Mary found no difficulty about the dinner
that afternoon. Captain Brandon arrived at half past four, and she
and Adrian sat with him in the portico until dinner was announced
at shortly after five. Elizabeth came down and joined them, and endorsed Mary's apologies for Dirk's absence. "He's so busy these days,
Captain Brandon. I'm sure you must be relieved that your own era of
activity has now come to a close."

"Yes," smiled Captain Brandon, "very relieved, indeed. I never
want to see a ship again—drat the things! Give me a little skiff, though,
to row myself quietly on the Creek of an afternoon, and I'm as happy
as a lark."

Mary was certain that it must be her imagination, but as he said
this he gave her a stare, and his grey eyes seemed to gleam with more
than mere conversational joviality. He was a man of about forty-eight,
with a red-brown, weathered face, very thin lips, and black, tobacco-
stained teeth that often showed in a brief smile—but a smile,
thought Mary, that was callous rather than mirthful. In build, he
was of medium height—a trifle taller than Dirk—and lean and tough,
with long-fingered hands that always seemed to be itching to clutch
and crush something soft and weak. He had a head of shaggy, greying
black hair.

Before he got into his little gig, he squeezed the hand Mary held
out, and Mary winced and nearly gasped. He had not clasped her
hand like this when he had arrived for dinner two hours ago, and
she was taken by complete surprise. He seemed aware of the pain
he caused her, too, for he showed his black teeth briefly as he released
her hand, remarking: "I've got a bear's handclasp, I've been told.
Well, so long! I'm only at Don Diego. You must come and see me,
Miss van Groenwegel—and Master Adrian! Me alone in the big old
house—and bush all round! I can do with company sometimes. No
wife nor chick! Mouldy old bachelor!"

As they were returning to the house, Mary kept massaging her hand,

and Adrian asked: "What's the matter? Did he hurt your hand when he shook it?"

She started, and flushed, and replied hastily: "Why do you think so? No, no. At least—no, of course not. What makes you think so?"

"The way you keep squeezing your hand. I think he's a crude man."

"Well, he's a sea captain, isn't he? Most seamen are rough in manner."

"I suppose so. I only remarked on it. Well, I must be off. I'm playing my violin at the service this evening, and I promised Jas—I promised Gwendolyn I'd be there early to run over a few passages before we go into the choir space."

"The choir space?"

"Yes—the part where the choir sits—near the harmonium—I—I mean——"

"Adrian, you're stammering."

It was too dark for her to see the flush that came to his face, but she could sense it. And she had not missed the slip of the tongue he had perpetrated a moment before. A dark dust of fear seemed to sift through her spirit, as though the warm October twilight were conspiring against her amidst the drooping leaves of the mango trees between which they strolled. The crickets shrieked—a chorus of them now—not a lonely one deriding her, but dozens of them, hidden and crouched in the grass, under dead leaves, on grey twigs. . . . "At your age, I used to think I could fashion . . ." Her hand ached, and she massaged it—and more dust moved in swift clouds through her body. Not through her spirit this time—but her body. Warm dust that created a hollow in her stomach, and put an itching ache into the tips of her breasts.

"You—you make me want to stammer," Adrian stammered on, his voice petulant. "It's your way of asking me anything as if you think—— Look here, I'd better be off at once." He ran ahead of her, and she saw him vanish in the gloom of the portico.

56

WHEN Dirk returned from Georgetown nothing seemed changed. Mary was still the efficient secretary and manager of New Signal and of the timber business. Adrian still went to the Laffertys' for lessons, and for his tuition in music. Mr. Henty gave good reports of his progress, and Mr. Randolph, the music teacher, pronounced him a genius. Adrian continued with his composition, and two mornings every week Mary and he went for their dawn swim in the canal. On Sundays and Wednesdays he attended service at the Methodist Church, where he played his violin in accompaniment to the singing of the choir and the squeaky harmonium.

Dirk and Mary, one afternoon in November, went to dine at Don Diego with Captain Brandon—but Dirk noticed nothing unusual in Mary's manner; he did not suspect that throughout the meal she was in a state of tension, nor did he observe the swift glances she threw at their host and the slow blushes that would come to her cheeks whenever the grey eyes happened to rest upon her.

Eighteen fifty-four came, and still nothing appeared to have altered —though in March one of the maids entered Mary's room in a state of hysteria to announce that something was the matter with the old missy. "Come quick, Miss Mary! She lie in bed quiet, quiet. She won't wake when I talk to her, miss."

This time Dirk alone stood and watched the mason sealing up the vault. It was a cool, cloudless afternoon, and blue sackies kept chattering in a star-apple tree on the eastern side of the tiny cemetery. Before following the others to the house, he grunted, and murmured: "Eighty-six last month. I don't think I shall do as well as that, Mama." He clicked his tongue, annoyed with himself, scowled at the trunk of the cabbage palm on which Adrian had scored his initials three years before, and began to move off along the path towards the house.

That year there was much patriotic talk—all through some remote war in the Crimea. Dirk snorted impatiently whenever the subject came up in conversation—but he was among the first to contribute to the fund organised in Georgetown for the relief of the widows and orphans of the soldiers who were being slaughtered five or six thousand miles away.

Graham told Dirk that Reginald had made a donation of sugar and medical supplies to the Government of Britain for the war effort. Graham imparted the information in a casual spirit, during a casual conversation in which he was merely giving him news about Reginald and his two sons and daughter. Rowena was expecting a happy event some time in May, said Graham. Neither he nor Dirk had, on that occasion, in the least anticipated any sensational news in the near future.

Graham was as much surprised as Dirk when, early in the new year, 1855, the announcement was made that the Queen had been pleased to confer a knighthood on Mr. Reginald Greenfield of Paxley Hall, Sussex.

The society of the colony was shaken to the core. A *mestee*—a coloured man whose mother, a mulatto, had died in scandalous circumstances—to be awarded a knighthood! What were things coming to?

Nevertheless, Graham was congratulated and feted everywhere. Reginald's coloured blood became a matter of trivial account; Rose was dead, and so was the scandal. And Reginald could pass for white; he was an old Etonian, had graduated at Oxford, and was the squire of Paxley in Sussex. That was good enough for most people. Forget the seamy side and think only of the honour he had brought to the colony. It was not every day a colonial-born subject was knighted.

And Dirk—Dirk took nearly a week to absorb the significance of the news, then, at last, his feelings coalesced. . . . Sir Reginald Greenfield. No doubt about it. It sounded well—distinguished. There was glory there. And to think that it might have been Sir Reginald van Groenwegel. That hurt. That made him breathless with pain. . . . Sir Reginald van Groenwegel . . .

In the old guest-room he stood before the portrait of Rose and talked to it, as the late-afternoon sunshine daubed a mild red stain on the lower part of the frame. He wagged his head and talked.

"Did you hear that, my dear? Your son, Rose love. Sir Reginald. Do you see how I'm being punished? But for me, his name would have been van Groenwegel. Through me—supreme irony, Rose!—our family has been cheated of glory. You must be laughing at me. He might even have been my son—yours and mine—if I hadn't scorned your black blood. Forgive me, Rose."

He began to look round the room, smiling, and certain that he could sense her presence. He began to squeeze his hands together, and chuckle.

"Old age. I'm getting old, Rose. Drooling, my dear. You're not laughing at me, though. I can feel you're not. Thank you for your sympathy. Always loyal . . . Sir Reginald Greenfield. Congratulations, my love! The Old Blood!"

The portrait blurred. He left the room in a stumbling hurry.

It was in February—a few weeks after the news of Reginald—that something happened to shock Dirk into the realisation that, unknown to him, certain changes in the spiritual climate of New Signal had taken place during the past year or two. He was startled that he could have been so blind, so obtuse.

He entered the sitting-room one afternoon at about four o'clock, and settled himself in the old easy chair that had been his father's favourite. Under Hubertus' portrait Adrian had set up his music stand and was playing on his violin. Half amused, half entertained—music did not appeal to him particularly—Dirk listened. A dull, rather mournful piece. Dry.

Footsteps sounded, and Mary appeared, dressed for going out. Captain Brandon had asked them to dinner. What a lovely creature! No doubt about it. The Hendrickje strain was there. Even physically, the child had inherited the old harridan's perennial youth. What a figure! And as pretty as any nineteen-year-old!

He smiled, and indicated the chair nearby, and she sank into it, and for the next few minutes they listened in silence to Adrian's playing.

Suddenly the boy put aside his music stand, and began to play something from memory, and Mary murmured: "That's his own. He's finished it at last."

"Is it? What is it supposed to be?"

She put her finger to her lips for silence, leant near and whispered very softly: "It's a rhapsody, he says. It's called 'Two Young Roes That Are Twins.'"

Dirk frowned, but desisted from asking the reason for such a title. Like Mary, he tried to be indulgent where Adrian's music was concerned. Adrian hated conversation in the same room where he was playing; it upset him, he said.

The composition meant nothing to Dirk. It seemed as dry and meaningless as any of the other pieces Adrian was in the habit of playing. Bach, Paganini, Mozart, they all seemed the same. Tuneless, pointless, hysterical.

There were animated moments that were not bad. Moments when the music rose to a kind of intense frenzy, shrieking higher and higher through the room, and with a melody that was distinguishable. Then would come the dull moments when a parallel theme would take over, wheezing and whining and moaning lugubriously. It all sounded like complete madness, and, glancing at Mary's face, Dirk could sense that she reacted as he did. She did not appear in any way moved.

Adrian, as though unaware of other presence in the room, played on. His eyes had a glazed, faraway look—they were not the eyes of a planting van Groenwegel, thought Dirk, with a sigh—and his body swayed gently in time with the music. . . . The piece seemed to be coming to an end now. From another frenzy of shrieking the tone fell and fell, and gradually the whole thing melted away on thin threads of sound.

Mary applauded, and Adrian lowered his violin and grinned. "You don't understand it, so why applaud?" he said. "Isn't the carriage here yet?"

"No," said his father. "I told Harper we won't be leaving until a quarter to five. It's only five or six minutes to Don Diego, remember."

"Tell us about the piece, Adrian," said Mary. "Describe it so that Papa can understand what you intend to portray."

Adrian seemed reluctant to accede to this request, but eventually he told them about the piece; Dirk had to support Mary in a show of interest to convince him that they wanted to know something about the music.

"It's loose in form," said Adrian, "but there are two twin themes, the one sad, the other gay. One is symbolic of the strong and the other of the weak, and they keep intermingling and—and warring with each other, if you see what I mean"—he flushed a trifle and gave his father an uncertain glance, as though expecting some comment from him; but Dirk's face was impassive—"and eventually the strong one takes command near the middle of the piece, and the other one seems as if it's going to die away, but suddenly it comes back into its own, and another warring takes place. Then towards the end you hear them both interlaced, and both are being resolved in a *perdendosi*."

"A what?" asked Dirk.

"A *perdendosi*," Adrian repeated. "It's Italian. All musical terms are expressed in Italian. It means a gradual fading out."

All the way to Don Diego, for some reason, the word kept recurring in Dirk's mind. *Perdendosi*. It sounded as mad as the music the boy had composed. . . . *Perdendosi* . . . And why had the two themes to fade out gradually? The sad and the gay; the strong and the weak . . . Something occurred to him, and his heartbeats quickened. The strong and the weak. Surely, it couldn't be that the boy intended to portray in symbolic form the struggle that had always been a feature of the story of the family. The Hard Ones. And the Soft Streak . . . Mary had made him read the letters in the canister since he was a small fellow. He must be quite familiar with the Tales of Old. . . . A *perdendosi* . . . A feeling of panic swept through Dirk, causing him to clasp and unclasp his hands in his lap.

Mary noticed his agitation, and wondered what could have caused it. Had he, she wondered, begun to suspect what had been happening within her this past year or two? She had taken pains to conceal the struggle, and, to the best of her belief, she had been successful, but one could never be sure. . . .

And Adrian was thinking: That was a ticklish moment when Mary asked me to tell Papa what my composition was about. I think I've fooled him. I had to use my wits to invent that description. If only he and Mary could know what really inspired me to compose that piece. . . . *Two Young Roes That Are Twins*. I hope they don't inquire too closely into the origin of the title, or it might be awkward. As it is, that Sunday when Mary and I went swimming I nearly betrayed myself. I was so nervous I mentioned about my reading the phrase in the Bible when I hadn't intended to. . . . "Thy two breasts are like two young roes that are twins, which feed among the lilies." I remember the first time I quoted it to Jasmine. That evening after choir practice, behind the harmonium. . . . What lovely breasts! Even better than Mary's. . . . I love Jasmine. I shall never love anyone else. We won't marry, but she has promised to be my mistress forever. I shall never forget Christmas Eve last. For the first time she let me love her as a man should. And again after service on the Wednesday evening following. Now she knows I am not a boy. Like Mary, she kept teasing me because of my age. But now she knows. . . .

At dinner Dirk was more alert to the presence of his children than he had let himself be for a long time. He kept observing them surreptitiously—and this time he noted the odd byplay between Mary and the captain. It shocked him when he saw the glitter that came into their eyes when their gazes met. A nerve in his memory quivered. He found himself jerked back in time to an afternoon in August 1823, the occasion of another dinner—on the northern veranda of Huis Kaywana. The shock he had felt then had been the same as the shock he felt now. Rose and Pelham angling to become lovers. . . . But surely this was out of the question. Mary and this crude old sea salt? He was nearly fifty, and not what one could call a real gentleman. It was only because of his long service with Hartfield & Clackson that Dirk had decided to be on terms of social intimacy with him. . . . I'm sure I'm mistaken. It simply could not be. I am misinterpreting their looks. Some trick of the candlelight. This is a gloomy dining-room. Remember mentioning that to Cornelia's father when the Rueffs used to live here. . . . Mary and Brandon! Too absurd for words.

Nevertheless, it stuck in his awareness. He must be certain.

After dinner, he said casually: "My wife and I, before we were married, often walked along that path near the Creek there, Brandon. I think I'll take a stroll, if you don't mind. This moonlight brings back memories."

"Papa!" Mary laughed. "Are you still as sentimental as all that?"

"Haw, haw!" guffawed the captain, settling himself into the most comfortable chair on the portico. "You don't know much about men, young lady. I've told you that before, haven't I? Sentimental to the bloody grave, I tell ye!"

Even in the uncertain light of the portico—there was only one large candle in a holder in a corner—the blush on Mary's face was obvious to Dirk.

"I agree," said Dirk. "I myself am exceptionally sentimental about the past, as you should know, my girl." He went down the steps, sighing softly and saying: "I won't be long. The air is delightful. Unmistakably February."

Dirk had no sooner vanished round the first clump of bushes bordering the Creek path when Adrian said: "I think I'll go and see if Harper is dozing," and left Mary and Brandon alone on the portico—for Adrian, unlike Dirk, knew what had been happening during the past year. And Mary knew that he knew. It had been impossible to disguise the reason for her boating trips on certain afternoons. . . . She made no attempt to stay him. She merely said: "Very well. An excellent idea, I think. But don't get into any mischief yourself."

Sly creature, thought Adrian, but I don't think she's right this time, even though I'd like to see her married. She's losing her wisdom. An old hardback of a man like that would be no suitable husband for her. She'll only be thirty-three in April, and still so lovely. She ought to look for a man of thirty-five. The captain must be at least sixty. What can she see in him, I wonder?

Adrian had no sooner vanished in the direction of the kitchen when Matthew Brandon rose and crossed over to Mary's chair. He seated himself on the arm and gripped her wrist. There was nothing soft or sentimental about his manner. He growled: "Keeping me still on a rope end, huh? I'm going to kill you, you nasty little bitch!" He gave her wrist a twist as he spoke, and she gasped and said: "There's no need to be savage, Matthew. I've told you before that it will take me some time to make up my mind. You must give me an opportunity to weigh the matter carefully."

"That papa of yours, I know. Must consider him first. But what about me? Think I'm not burning to . . ." He went on to describe in filthy language what he was burning to do to her, obviously revelling in the obscene images he conjured up. Mary sat very still and made no attempt to interrupt him, nor to reproach him. She shut her eyes and bit her lower lip hard—that was all. Nor did she utter any denial when he guffawed and said: "You love to hear what and what I'd do with you, huh? You only look pure-minded, but you're like a cesspool inside. Not true, wench? Open your eyes and tell me something."

She opened her eyes, and stared at him, her head trembling. He was still clutching her wrist. He bent his head down and kissed her, and she responded fiercely, gasping as her lips parted to receive his mouth.

When he raised his head she tried to rise, murmuring in a strangled voice: "You're upsetting me. I think we'd better stroll for a while," but he pushed her down roughly, and said: "Stay just where ye are till I tell ye to get up." She gasped again—but obeyed, her attitude one of complete surrender.

"Something's got to be fixed up soon, young lady, d'ye hear me? You'll speak to that papa of yours tomorrow and tell him you and me want to get together." He caught her by the throat, and broke out into more obscenity. "You've kept me dangling on a rope end this eight, nine, ten months, whatever it is. It won't do, d'ye hear me? What's a cussed kiss and a rub on your front works? I want all the rest, d'ye hear me? Since that Sunday afternoon I saw you and your brother near the *koker* I've been afire for you, wench. If only you'd known I was spying on you from my lil' skiff round the *courida* bush. Haw, haw! She's blushing! Wait till I get you in a four-poster. . . ." He proceeded to go into details—but Dirk, listening behind the screen of vines that covered the latticework on the northern side of the portico, did not wait to hear these fresh obscenities. As stealthily and silently as he had returned and posted himself where he was, he crept away and moved back towards the Creek path.

About an hour later, in her room, he stroked her head in an attempt to soothe her. "I understand much better than you think I do, my girl," he told her. "Nothing startling, Mary. Indeed, I'm surprised that more of you aren't on the odd side. I've been lucky, comparatively, I feel. Amelia and Sybil, Peter and Hendrik, they all escaped. It's only you and Adrian who have inherited the strange streak—and it could have taken a much more virulent form. I'm one of them, my dear child. The warped ones. Aunt Luise noted my oddity since I was three years old. She told me herself. A precocity—and a strangeness of some sort: that's the heritage of the van Groenwegels, Mary. It runs in us, so we must never be surprised at anything that turns up. Why, look at Francis——"

"I'm not any better than Francis, Papa," she sobbed. "I'm just as vile. Worse—because I'm a woman. Oh, my God! To think that you overheard what passed between us this evening! I shall never be able to look in your eyes again."

"Don't be a little fool. You were able to face me after that astounding scene with Francis when you tore your bodice, weren't you? Come, my girl. I don't speak vainly when I say I understand your aberration. This is nothing new in you. Why were you ready to run off with Francis that evening? Because he was a brute who used the same filthy language this fellow did this evening. Because he was the same kind of crude rascal." He tried to chuckle. "That's your oddity, my child. The Old Blood in one of its peculiar forms. Ugly and unfortunate, but you must face it bravely. Remember what old Hendrickje used to tell them? The truth. Always face the truth, no matter how ugly."

"I am facing it, Papa—and it frightens me. I don't feel I can live without him—and yet—yet I despise him from the bottom of my heart. That's the truth—but what am I to do about the truth? What decision must I take? I've been at my wits' end for months and months trying to make up my mind. I've been deceitful to you, Papa. I've taken trips in the small boat up to Don Diego and met him without your knowing it. I've behaved like a common trollop. Oh, this is too much for me. I wish I could die."

"We all wish that at odd times in our lives, Mary. Never mind. In a way, it is my blindness, my obtuseness, that brought this about. I'm not as alert as I used to be." He put a finger under her chin and raised her tear-wet face, but she shut her eyes tight and resisted, wailing miserably that she could not look at him. "I'm too ashamed, Papa, don't you understand?" Then abruptly she opened her eyes, and there was a wild, defiant gleam in them. "Well, don't you want to advise me? Aren't you going to tell me how to behave in future? You and your Old Blood and your family obsessions! I hate the Old Blood! I hate the family! I wish you'd burnt those pestiferous letters with all their tales of cruelty and misery and ugliness. They've had as baneful an influence on me as they've had on you—and Adrian—yes, Adrian! I was wrong to let him read them. . . ."

He let her rave on, unperturbed, a look of tired resignation on his face as he stared across the bed out of the window at the fireflies in the dark. In the air was the strong smell of megass. A land breeze must be blowing, bringing the smell from the factory yard. That sourish odour of cane trash and refuse had assailed him, he remembered, when he and Rose were sitting on the bench near the honeysuckle arbour at Huis Kaywana. The factory had been grinding that morning. . . .

He gave a start, and said: "Come, come. Stop being hysterical, Mary." He gripped her shoulders and shook her, and the raccoon's gleam came into his eyes. "Where will this tirade lead you? Be strong. You're a full-grown woman, aren't you? If you want to marry the man, make up your mind and do so. I wouldn't dream of putting any hindrance in your way, so if that's what is worrying you cease to let it do so."

She gave a gasp, her hands clutching at her bosom, stared up at him in a tense, wild-eyed silence, then said: "You mean you wouldn't be grieved, Papa? You would let me become the wife of that filthy, loathsome—that foul-mouthed cur of a man at Don Diego? Do you really mean that?"

He smiled coldly, and said: "All your melodrama, Mary, will not cancel the simple truth that his filthy, loathsome manner gives you intense physical pleasure. He is the kind of man you need. Face up to it. Resign yourself to that fact, and accept the situation as it is. You have my full consent to marry him."

He turned abruptly and strode out of the room, lean, rigid, his lips in a tight line. A hard van Groenwegel.

His footsteps had hardly faded along the corridor when Adrian came in from his room adjoining hers. Only a thin wooden wall separated the two rooms, and the top of the wall was open in tropical fashion for ventilation.

She gave him a dazed stare and said: "You heard what he told me, Adrian?"

He nodded. "Yes, every word." His face was very serious. "But you mustn't do it, Mary. You mustn't marry that beast. I hate him. He's dirty, crude, no gentleman. I should be sickened to have him for a brother-in-law."

She pressed her hands to her eyes and moaned. "But Papa was right, Adrian. He spoke the truth, dear. I need him, loathsome as he is, filthy and foul-mouthed and depraved. That's the kind of sister you have, Adrian. Oh, my God!"

She could feel his wondering, incredulous gaze upon her. After a pause, he said: "Truly? You need him, Mary? You would let him—let him love you?"

"Yes. Truly. Truly, dear. I'm like him—filthy, loathsome."

Another pause, then: "You've been meeting him for some time—on the Creek—when you go on those trips in the small boat, Mary. Have you ever let him—let him love you in the way—— I mean, you know how? To have a baby?"

She shook her head, moaning. "No. No, no—not yet—not in actuality, dear. But in my fancy a thousand times." In the gloom behind her eyelids the red spot burned—not a tiny spot now. Now it seemed a blob. A blob of blood, perhaps. It kept whirling—on the verge of getting brighter, whiter, but not doing so. Only whirling, whirling. "I'm going mad, Adrian. Mad, mad."

He sank down beside her on the bed and put his arm around her. "I feel like that myself sometimes, Mary dear. It will pass. You'll be steady again soon." To himself he said: "If she only knew about Jasmine and me—about what happened on Christmas Eve in the church—and on three Wednesday nights behind the harmonium—and if she knew what's on my mind now—what Jasmine told me yesterday! I feel a little mad myself, but I'm trying to hide it. Hell, hell!"

"Adrian, you're trembling, dear. What's the matter?"

"Nothing." He released her and rose. Clenched his hands and said in a musing voice: "It started on that Sunday in October, the year before last. The Sunday we went swimming, remember, Mary. It was on that day that the first notes sounded in the crescendo air of doom. Yes, it's like a piece of music—and not a slight thing. It's symphonic—an air for orchestra. Not an air for a solo instrument. I am the strings, Papa and that brute Brandon are the percussion, and you and Jasmine are the woodwinds and the brasses." He uttered a mirthless chuckle. "It's a horrible piece, Mary. Composed by a fiend of Fate. I almost feel that when the finale is reached only the drums will be heard. The strings and the woodwinds and the brasses will have been silenced. It will end on a loud prattling devil's tattoo."

"Adrian! Adrian dear! What are you saying? I don't understand a word you have uttered."

He gave a gasping, half-muffled sob, and turned away his face quickly. She heard him gulp, then chuckle. He looked at her again and said: "It's the madness, Mary. Didn't I tell you? I feel mad, too, sometimes."

"Are you worried? Is anything preying on your mind, Adrian?"

He stared at her in silence for a moment, then suddenly lunged forward and gripped her arms and put his mouth close to her ear, began to whisper something in a fierce panic. She stiffened, and her eyes widened.

"Adrian, no! No! I don't believe—but you're only seventeen, Adrian. And she was twenty-six in August last."

"Mary, please. You won't tell, will you? Not a single soul? Promise."

"I promise—but I won't believe it. Seventeen—and she—she—oh, it couldn't be true!" She drew his head against her with a sob.

57

THREE days later Jacob told Dirk that there was something he wanted to ask him to do for him. They went out on to a raft to talk. It was always the safest place for privacy. Only the four-eye fishes could hear them.

Jacob said: "It's Jasmine again, Dirk—she's pregnant."

"Good God! Who's the fellow this time?"

"She won't say, Dirk," groaned Jacob. His complexion looked muddy grey and unhealthy. His eyes had a bleary glaze. He was ill and old. "She simply refuses to tell us. Milly and I have reasoned with her, threatened her, pleaded with her—but she won't say. But worse still, Dirk, boy—oh, God! Why should I have to be worried like this? I'm not well—worse still, Dirk, Jim won't do anything to help. It happened once before, remember, and Jim, against his will, performed an operation and saved her from the disgrace of having the child. But this time he won't budge. Can't blame him, I suppose. He's a church warden, and very upright—he takes his profession seriously—says medicine is an honourable and solemn trust—you know what I mean? Sentiment and ethics and so on. Anyway, he won't do it, Dirk, and Jasmine won't say who the man is. Milly and I thought we could fix up a marriage between them, whether he was suitable or not—just to avoid the scandal of her having an illegitimate child—but she refuses to the last to give away his name. What am I to do, Dirk? What can you advise?"

Dirk gave him a keen stare. "It's you who generally have to advise me, Jacob. I have always asked your advice."

Jacob gave a sickly smile, the old sly, humorous light coming into his eyes for an instant. He nodded. "I suspected you'd see through me, boy. Yes, I've only put it that way. What I'm angling after, Dirk, is to ask you to do me a favour—but it's not the kind of favour I like asking."

"Go ahead."

"Could you speak to your Peter and ask him if he'd do the operation?"

Dirk froze. "Oh. Oh, I see what you mean now. Yes, that's awkward, Jacob. I shouldn't like to do that—and I'm fairly certain Peter wouldn't agree."

Jacob nodded faintly, clasping his hands together. A resigned, almost relieved, expression settled over his olive-grey face. "I understand, Dirk. You're right, too. In your place, I think I would have said the same. But I had to make the attempt. I had to ask you—just to satisfy myself that I did everything I possibly could in the matter."

Dirk rested a hand on his shoulder. "I'm sorry, old fellow. Truly sorry. Couldn't you arrange to send her to one of the West Indian islands until after the child was born?"

"I thought of that, and we've discussed it with her, but she wouldn't hear of it—and we didn't press the matter, Dirk, how could we? She's our child, after all. To send her away to be among strangers at such a time. No, no. I'm resigned to it now. She must remain here and have the child. We'll have to face the scandal out." He chuckled drily. "Dirk, you're a fool where this family business goes, and I've scoffed at your ideas about the van Groenwegels and their supposed strangeness. Every family has its ne'er-do-wells and freaks. But somehow, with Jasmine, I've come to believe that she really has inherited some queer, queer, devilish twist—something really out of the ordinary."

Dirk wagged his head, sighed softly and murmured: "The Old Blood, Jacob. The Old Blood."

After a silence, Jacob asked: "How is Mary's fever? We miss her at the office." And Dirk smiled and replied: "I lied, Jacob. She has no fever, boy. She is not indisposed physically. It's her mind." After a pause, he told Jacob about Sunday evening. "She, too, Jacob, was born with a queer, queer, devilish twist. She hasn't left her room since Sunday night. I'm worried—worried to my heart."

That same day, at about three o'clock, a messenger from Don Diego brought a note for Mary which read: "Why haven't I seen you since Sunday? See you come to me this afternoon. I shall be at the landing place to look out for you. M."

"Any answer, Miss Mary?"

"No, Beatrice. No answer. Give the boy a bit for bringing it."

"Two stivers enough, miss. He's a rude boy."

For several minutes, Mary sat very still, the note crushed tight in her hand. Then she began to smile. Then the smile gave way to a soft, fluttering laugh. She rose, crossed to the writing desk, and scribbled a few words on a slip of paper. She opened the front of her bodice and drew out the chain with the key for the canister. She moved over to the bed and pulled out the canister, lay the slip of paper on it, and put the key and the chain on the paper, then pushed the canister back under the bed.

Ten minutes or so later, she left the house, and walked to the little *stelling* where the tent-boat and three small boats were moored. She got into one of the small boats, and rowed off into the stream. The tide was flowing strongly, and her progress upstream was swift. In less than a quarter of an hour she was at the Don Diego *stelling*.

Matthew Brandon was on the back veranda, reclining in a hammock in shirt sleeves when she suddenly appeared and said: "Well, here I am!"

He uttered a cry of astonishment, nearly dropping the blackened clay pipe he was smoking. He was unshaven, and unkempt in his person as a whole; the shirt was soiled with dried food and perhaps nicotine-stained saliva which had dribbled down on to it when he was asleep. A faint, frowsy smell came to her nostrils.

"You! What's this mean? I wasn't expecting you at this time—and here!"

"I know you weren't—but I've come. Don't you want me, Matthew?"

He got slowly out of the hammock, the look of incredulity still on his face. "I don't understand. You keep away for days, and now—now you turn up like this. In broad daylight, too. What about your good name?"

She laughed—a dry, harsh, hacking laugh. Her eyes glittered in an unnatural way, but he put this down to excitement; it did not occur to him that it might be a sign of mental derangement; he knew nothing about the red spot that even now was slowly brightening in her fancy. "You smell, Matthew. I've surprised you in a careless moment, haven't I?"

He flushed, then scowled. "What if you have! I wasn't expecting you, I tell you. You're out of your mind to come at this time. Your good name——"

She interrupted him with an impatient exclamation, darted forward and gripped his arms. "Stop prating about my good name, and take me." She buried her face in his shaggy hair. "Take me upstairs, you fool! Do all the filthy things you've been threatening to do to me. Now, now. What are you waiting for?"

That roused him, and he flushed and trembled. He gripped her wrists and said: "You're out of your wits, drat ye! Suppose I take you at your word!"

"I mean you to. Why do you think I've come here at this time of the afternoon?" Her voice sounded cracked, wild. "I want you, I tell you. Soil me. Humiliate me. Why don't you spring at the chance now I've given it to you? Have you lost your manhood? Have you been boasting in vain?"

"But we aren't married, confound ye! Look here, you'll be sorry afterwards, I'm warning you. You're trifling with me, wench."

"Take me upstairs, take me upstairs. Stop talking, Matthew." She clutched at his hair and tugged it savagely. "Why must you talk so much?"

He took a pace towards her, trembling, his face aflame. "Very well," he growled. "You've asked for it." He glanced round, as though fearful that he might have been overheard by a servant. "Your good name will be in the mud, but if you don't care, why should I? Eh? Why should I?" He broke forth into his usual string of obscenities, and she laughed and said: "That's more like you. I love to hear you belching out your filth. Oh, God! How sweet it will be to be smeared by you! I can die in peace after——"

She broke off with a cry, for he had slapped her across her face. He was grinning lasciviously. He slapped her again, caught her arm and twisted it. "See what you're in for? Ready for more? Eh?" He struck her again. "Ready?"

She laughed, even as the tears began to trickle down her cheeks, nodded violently, and sobbed: "Yes, yes. Ready. I'm quite ready, Matthew."

He grasped her by the arm and dragged her into the dining-room. Dragged her upstairs to a room on the northern side of the house. It had once been Cornelia's room. It was in an incredible condition, frowsy and in such an utter state of confusion that it was barely possible to discern one piece of furniture from another. Discarded garments, odd pieces of burlap or oilcloth or canvas overflowed from tables or the chest of drawers onto the large bed which itself was piled up with oddments ranging from clothes to carpenters' tools and mariners' instruments. When he flung her on to it, she found herself lying across a chessboard and what looked like a ship's logbook. It was open, and she glimpsed a phrase—"took soundings outside river mouth"—which she had seen in other logbooks at the sawmill when the schooner captains came to report. For an instant sanity returned, and she experienced terror. She gasped and trembled at the immensity of what she had done. In this filthy room with this filthy monster. She, Mary van Groenwegel of New Signal, known, even in Demerara, as a steady, correct, austere young woman. Yes, even in Georgetown, people spoke about her unusually strong and severe character. "Remarkable," everyone called her. The whole society of the colony had heard about her office work and of how capably she managed her father's affairs. . . . And now this.

But the instant passed, and the red spot whirled in her fancy. The frowsy chaos around her seemed as something normal—something she had always known and desired. She felt a warm shudder rush through her as the unshaven face came closer, and the blackened teeth grinned at her. As the grimy hand crashed across her face and the red spot spattered into stars like splintered rubies, as her bodice was ripped down with a swish, she heard herself chuckling and mumbling: "I'm the woodwinds, the woodwinds—and you're the drums, Papa dear."

At shortly before six Adrian arrived home in a state of panic. He rushed upstairs to his sister's room, calling: "Mary! Mary!" And when he saw that the room was empty, he turned and ran back downstairs, calling Beatrice, the bedroom maid. "Beatrice! Where is Miss Mary? Beatrice!"

Beatrice appeared from her room near the pantry. "What's it, Master Adrian? Something happen? Miss Mary not at home."

"Where is she, Beatrice? I must find her. Did she say where she was going? I didn't know she was going anywhere." He was panting, and his eyes glinted wildly. He trembled uncontrollably.

"What happen to you, Master Adrian? Eh-eh! Hold yourself in, massa. You trembling. Miss Mary not at home. Nobody at home. De master dining at the manse. He not coming home till late."

"I know that. He mentioned it this morning. But Miss Mary, Beatrice. Where is Miss Mary?" He was sobbing now. "I must find her. I must, I must!"

"She gone out, Master Adrian. Since three o'clock time. I don't know where she gone, but she tek de small boat and she go upstream. So Jim, de boatman at de *stelling*, say. She must be taking a lil' outing as she sometimes do."

"And she hasn't come back yet? Are you sure, Beatrice?"

"No, she ent come back yet, massa. Massa, what happen?"

Adrian, however, left her without answering, dashed downstairs and ran all the way to the *stelling*. He got into one of the small boats and rowed off upstream. The tide was on the point of turning, and the water was wrinkled with little whirlpools. Leaves kept moving in circles here and there, and Missouri grass had grown stationary in midstream, like little islands awaiting orders from some unseen geographer. Dusk was falling rapidly, and along the banks fireflies winked palely amidst the *mucca-mucca* stalks, and, to Adrian, they seemed evil eyes signalling at him panicked messages—messages of death and the crumbling of the world. Every now and then he uttered a little whimper and sob.

He had hardly rounded two bends when—he had just got past the *koker* that controlled the canal where he and Mary swam in the morning—his gaze alighted on a figure crouched up on the bank at a point where there was a small clearing; an old Indian path had once ended at this spot. Even in the dusk he recognised Mary.

She stared casually at him as he sprang ashore, as though she might have been expecting him. He clutched her arm and gasped: "Where have you been to, Mary dear? I was looking for you." Then he noticed the state of her clothes. They were torn in places. And the twilight was not deep enough to conceal the weals on her wrist. "What have you been doing, Mary? Your wrist. Look. It's bleeding."

She nodded. "I'm happy, dear. Very, very happy." She shrugged off her bodice as she spoke, and he saw that her back and shoulders above her petticoat were raw and bleeding. "Not only my wrist. Everywhere over my body, Adrian. I'm happy. I've been befouled, humiliated, degraded. Papa was very good."

"Papa!"

"Yes. Matthew, I mean, dear. Matthew did it for me. He was savage—just as I felt he would be. And filthy. He is terribly virile, Adrian. The red spot is gone. It turned white, and got whiter and whiter and then it was gone. Oh, I've never been so happy in all my life, Adrian dear. Papa was very good."

"Mary, I don't understand what you're saying. You're—you're not telling me Matthew Brandon—no, no, I won't believe it. You let him——"

"I went to him. Yes, I let him, dear. I wanted him to have me. I'm no longer your sweet, pure sister. I'm vile—like him—and Francis. Do you see how evil I look? I was always so at heart. Francis knew. That's why he threw the chicken entrails down my bosom. But he was not so bad, poor Francis. He could have soiled me that evening under Gertie's sandbox tree, but he spared me. But Matthew didn't spare me. He beat me and ravished me in the vilest way——"

"Mary! Please! I—I was looking for you to tell you of something dreadful. Mary, Jasmine is dying."

"Papa was very good to me. He gave me what I wanted, what I asked for."

He gripped her arm and shook it. "Mary, did you hear me? I said Jasmine is dying. She jumped out of a bedroom window—about an hour ago."

"Dying? Jasmine?" She smiled. "She is like me, then. Happy. How happy to be dying, Adrian. I'm dying, too, so I can speak with truth."

He sank down beside her and pressed his hands to his face, sobbing.

"Why are you crying, Adrian? Aren't you happy like me?"

"I don't want to live. I don't want to live."

"Like me, then. We're both happy. We must die together, then."

"Mary, why are you here? Why didn't you go home? I don't understand."

"I'm waiting for darkness, dear. It's nearly time." She looked round at the bush behind them. "The dusk is getting deeper and deeper. The twilight of death is gathering, Adrian. The twilight of the van Groenwegels. It was here Matthew had his boat moored that Sunday afternoon, Adrian—the Sunday we went swimming in the canal. He spied on us from this very spot. He saw us naked sitting by the *koker*, and he grew mad with desire for me. Remember when he came to dinner the same evening? From then it was he wanted to befoul me —and now, at last, he has had his wish. Oh, I'm so happy. Papa has always been good to me. He has always spoiled me in everything— and now he has given me the final happiness. Death will be sweet for me, Adrian."

"Mary, Jasmine—did you hear? She's dying. She jumped out of a bedroom window and hurt herself. Uncle Peter and her brother Jim are at the house now—but there's no hope, they say. She wrote me a note and sent it to the Laffertys where Mr. Randolph was giving me a music lesson. She said—look, here it is—I'll read it." He fumbled in his trousers pocket and brought out a slip of paper. He put his face close to it and read the message on it. "She said: 'Good-bye, my sweetheart. I can bear it no longer. I have sinned, and I must pay for my sins.' That's all, Mary. As soon as I read it I left the Laffertys and ran all the way to Uncle Jacob's house—but it had happened already. The servant told me she had thrown herself out of a window—an upstairs window. When they picked her up she was bleeding from her head and—and her thighs. She was so lovely, Mary. I loved her with all my soul. I shall never love anybody else as I loved her. And now she's dying—dying with my child in her."

"Look, Adrian. The tide. The tide is ebbing. So dark and ugly, the water, isn't it? Creek water." She was undressing. "Look, Adrian. The water. Like blood—dark and mysterious, unpredictable. Like our blood. The Old Blood. And it's ebbing. Ebbing fast. We must go with it, dear."

"Why are you undressing, Mary? What are you going to do?"

"Swim, Adrian. Swim and never look back. Swim until the water swallows me down. It's blood—dark old blood. I was waiting for twilight to come—and now it's deep enough. No one will see me. Are you coming with me?"

He stiffened. His hands clenched. "I see. I see now what you mean. You want to swim out into the river and drown, don't you? You don't want to live. I'll come with you, Mary. I don't want to live, either. Jasmine is dying. She's dying because of me—and the child I put in her. I should die, too, shouldn't I? Yes, I'll come with you." He rose and began to undress.

The crickets wheezed behind them in the bush, and a firefly made a swift arc past their heads, blue-white in the deep dusk. Missouri grass, in clumps, was moving slowly downstream as the tide ebbed. The water gurgled softly along the edge of the bank, and there were many little whirlpools.

PERDENDOSI

Book Three

58

T H E sun had already gone down, and the bleak June air seemed to grow bleaker as the three of them remained behind, at the foot of the tall cabbage palm, to watch the mason at work on the tomb. Millicent's hand rested lightly on Peter's arm, but Dirk stood alone and apart. None of them spoke, and the only sounds were the click-clack of the mason's tools and the shuffle of footsteps as Gwendolyn and the other mourners moved back towards the house.

The dusk gathered, and, at last, Millicent murmured that they had better be going back to the house. Peter murmured assent. Dirk did not move. He said: "Go, Peter. Take Millicent to the house. I shall remain until it's dark."

Peter hesitated, then, holding Millicent's arm, led her away. When they were out of earshot, Peter murmured: "I wasn't certain what to say to him. Do you know if Uncle Jacob told him anything final about Jasmine before he died?"

Millicent nodded. "Yes. I overheard. I was at the door. He repeated that it was a boy from the country. He mentioned the same false name."

Peter nodded. "I see. I understand."

"It was to spare his feelings, Peter. Jacob knew it would have doubled the burden of his grief if he hadn't confirmed that. Jacob wanted him to believe that he didn't know it was Adrian who—who was responsible for what happened to Jasmine in February. Poor Dirk. We must never let him know that Jacob knew, Peter."

"He'll never learn through me," said Peter, fingering his little trimmed moustache. "Uncle Jacob asked both Jim and me not to tell him—and I know Jim won't. He suspected, though—and he tackled

Jim, but Jim denied that it was Adrian. I did, too, when he asked me—but I wasn't certain what Uncle Jacob had told him finally on his deathbed."

"It was so good of him to allow Jacob to be buried at New Signal."

"Papa has always looked upon Uncle Jacob as a brother—it's no surprise. That's why we children have always called him Uncle Jacob."

Later Dirk asked Millicent to remain. "I'd like to talk to you, Milly."

They stood under Hubertus' portrait in the bright lamplight.

He asked her to sit, indicating the easy chair that had been Storm's favourite. "I'll stand, if you don't mind. I'm in that kind of mood this evening."

She smiled and seated herself, without comment, and he took a handkerchief from his coat pocket and dabbed at his chin, then at his forehead. They chatted about trivial matters; the fittings of the coffin, the wreaths, the large number of mourners. He paced about now and then, toying with his handkerchief. Then casually he said: "Poor fellow. I believed that tragic business in February had a lot to do with his quick decline." He halted and regarded Hubertus. "That little chat we had, Milly—we couldn't say much—but he mentioned about Jasmine. The fellow who got her into that trouble, I mean. Jacob repeated his name."

"Did he?"

"Mm. Name of Lashley—Charles Lashley. Couldn't trace the name, though I tried to investigate. I—when Jasmine spoke before she died —you were there, weren't you, Milly? With Jacob and Peter and Jim? In February—at her death?"

"Yes, Dirk." He could see the tension that had come into her manner. Out of the corner of his eye he could note the way she sat forward.

"And you heard that name, Milly? Charles Lashley? You're sure?"

A hesitation—then: "Yes, Dirk. Why do you ask?"

He flicked the handkerchief about. "Nothing, nothing. Only wondered." He turned his gaze to the portrait of Mary. Mary at fifteen. Uncle Edward's last portrait. "Milly, has Jacob ever told you anything about his mother?"

Out of the corner of his eye he saw the opposite happen now. She relaxed. "About his mother? You mean Nibia, who used to be a slave here? No. Why?"

Dirk grunted. He paced again, then halted. "What about his father?"

Millicent looked puzzled—and he knew she was not acting. "Nothing out of the ordinary that I can recall, Dirk, unless you mean the fact that he never lifted a hand to help Jacob in any way. I always wondered why he treated Jacob so badly—but Jacob said you and your father had practically adopted him, and that's why old Frick never troubled in the matter."

Dirk sighed. Wagged his head. He began to laugh softly, musingly —a trifle madly, Millicent thought. But he had been behaving oddly for months. And who could blame him—after that terrible affair with Mary and Adrian! Poor fellow.

He paced about, muttering: "Jacob, Jacob, Jacob, Jacob . . ." And this time he used the handkerchief to dab at his eyes. Again he halted —looked at Mary's portrait, and said: "Far to the south of the town they found her body, remember, Milly? And Adrian's was found near the sawmill—near one of the very rafts Jacob and I had stood on the day before, talking. It should have been hers. Or perhaps she was afraid to be too near the scene of her secretarial activities. I'm talking such utter nonsense. Excuse me, Milly." He began to pace again, and mutter: "Jacob, Jacob, Jacob, Jacob . . ."

Suddenly he sank down beside her in Elizabeth's chair. "Milly, one day I may tell you something—about Jacob and me. But not this evening, girl." He was silent, staring past her at the tall bookcase filled with Storm's books. Then he began to chuckle—he shook and chuckled, the tears trickling down his cheeks. "The old vagabond. Jacob, Jacob . . . Not even to Milly, his wife."

"What's it, Dirk?"

He sighed, patted her arm. "Never mind, my dear." He touched his temple. "Not too right up here of late, you know. Upset, upset, upset. Distracted."

"Was there some secret, Dirk? Something Jacob kept from me?"

"Mm. We had many secrets between us, Jacob and me, Milly. Young fools—that's what we were." He rose, began to pace again. "I'm putting a manager in charge here. Breaking with the old tradition, girl. Can't live here any longer."

"Yes. I heard you're building a house in the town."

"Mm. That's right—quite right. I'll live there in future—with these pictures. Rose's is in the old guest-room upstairs. That will go over my bed."

She watched him standing under Hubertus, staring over her head, his green eyes bright and unnatural, not too sane, but watery with grief.

"What was this secret, Dirk?"

He shook his head, went on shaking his head, still staring over her. After a pause, he murmured: "I shall never reveal it. For reasons . . . My family." He began to shake with chuckles again. Sank down into the chair beside hers. Patted her wrist, and said: "I'm more contempt-ible than you think, Milly, girl."

59

T H E new house was in the extreme northern part of the town, near Ferry Street, and not too far from the place where Jacob and his family had been living for the past fourteen years. In the distance, he could see the buildings of the fort across the Canje—Fort St. Andries. From the western windows the river and Crab Island could be viewed without any hindrance, for he had had the wild trees cut down, and had planted sapodillas and mangoes, which would take years to form a screen between the downstairs windows and the river.

His housekeeper was a pleasant, retiring old creature—a *mestee* distantly related to Millicent's mother. Mrs. Chalmerson never intruded on his privacy. He could talk to Rose without fear of interruption.

He began to gain the reputation of an eccentric hermit, but he did not care. Even in the old days ridicule had seldom bothered him, and now he had developed a thicker skin—though he had to admit that the thickness was pitted with pores that were vulnerable. The chill of criticism, of reproach, sometimes struck through, and caused him to shiver in desperate misery.

He shivered when Peter admonished him one day near Christmas. "I've told you it would be unsafe, Papa. I must consider Gwendolyn's health, mustn't I? It's all well and good for you to talk of my having a son to carry on the name, but these things can't be conveniently arranged if Nature is against it. Try to understand that."

And shivered again when, at Larsen's funeral in January the following year, he tackled Hendrik, and Hendrik said with a sigh: "This strange obsession of yours, Papa! Dora and I have no desire to have any more children. I've told you that before, I think. We're delighted with the twins—but they're enough. Child-bearing isn't an occupation every woman enjoys, and Dora emphatically doesn't enjoy it, I can assure you."

"Never mind, never mind, my boy! I mean no harm." He made nervous gestures with his hands. "But all the same, it would have been good to know that there was still some hope of saving our name for the future. A son, Hendrik. A son. It's so important that there should be a son. Peter's wife is incapable through ill-health. But Dora is a robust woman. No excuse, my boy—no excuse for you two."

Undaunted, he tackled Dora the following day, at Flagstaff, and this time there was comfort, for she was sympathetic. Tall, fair, massive, and with her bulging blue eyes, Dora might have been some heroine of German folklore. At forty, she exuded good health. She towered over Dirk as she smiled and pinkened and said: "I know how worried you are, Papa—but think of my age. At forty, do you think I should contemplate having another child?"

He patted her arm agitatedly, coaxingly. "For my sake, my dear. Getting old and foolish. Sixty last September. You must indulge me, Dora."

Her eyes suddenly grew moist, and he knew that she was pitying him. He must seem a freak in her eyes—or a doting fool. He lowered his gaze, mumbling: "Think it over. Consider it carefully, my girl."

"Very well," she smiled. "I shall, Papa." He gave her a swift glance of gratitude and caught her hand. "You mean to consider it, Dora? You will?"

"Yes." She uttered an uncertain laugh. "But, Papa, don't raise your hopes too high. It may be another girl. I can't control that, can I?"

"Yes, yes. That is so." He tried to laugh, too. "But the chance, my dear—the chance. We never know. We must hope for a boy. Pray and hope."

He felt so cheered that he went wandering vaguely about the streets of the town on the following day. Kingston was now virtually a suburb of Georgetown, and so were Werk-en-Rust and Albert Town. The old parade ground had been turned into a promenade garden. The streets were narrow, and muddy in the rain season, but the canals solved the problem of drainage—and they looked so pretty with their floating plants; at least, those that ran north-south did. The ones that ran east-west and that drained directly into the river were still rather foul and cluttered with refuse. There were no floating plants in these.

Dirk told the coachman to wait by MacInroy Sandbach's building in Werk-en-Rust. "I shall be back very shortly, my man," he said—

but as it turned out, he forgot time and kept on walking until the sun had disappeared behind the warehouses in Water Street. Eventually, when he did come to himself he was in Cumingsburg in the northern part of the town. And then he was at Sarah Hubert's old shop. He chuckled, telling himself that unconsciously this must have been his intended destination.

The shop had recently been painted, and was looking prosperous, though the buildings on either side dwarfed it considerably. It was, in actuality, a mere shack of a place with a shingled roof. Two rooms had been added on at the back, and Jason and his grandfather lived in these. Mrs. Clark had died some years ago, and her husband had sold his Charlestown shop which had fallen on bad days since the Portuguese had come on the scene.

"Those Pottagees, Mr. Dirk," the old fellow sighed as he admitted Dirk in behind the counter. "No honest man can do business nowadays, sir. They stoop to every mean trick you can think of to kill trade for other people. Even this shop here would be closed if it wasn't that you have the money to keep it going."

Dirk nodded, his eyes glinting. "Be sure they won't kill this, Mr. Clark. I'd like to see a Portuguese who could compete with a van Groenwegel!"

Customers were in the shop, and young Jason was busy attending to their wants. At seventeen, he was not an impressive youth, thought Dirk. No personality. Simply a coloured youngster like any other you saw about the town. He is nothing I can lash myself into any enthusiasm about, he told himself. No character in that face, I fear. Shy, cringing manner. No spirit.

When the shop was empty, a few minutes later, Dirk spoke to young Jason. "How do you like working in the shop, my boy?" And Jason smiled sheepishly and returned: "I like it, sir." He seemed tongue-tied after that, and Dirk had to press on: "You can read and write, I presume?"

"A little, sir." Jason began to dig with a thumbnail at the edge of the counter, his gaze on the door.

His grandfather said: "I try to teach him what I can, Mr. Dirk, but he never seemed to like lessons, sir."

"Oh well, oh well! As long as he's happy behind the counter here, I suppose that's all that matters. Don't let the customers cheat you, though, my boy," Dirk added, trying to chuckle pleasantly. He felt only contempt for the boy. . . . I must keep in mind that project.

Mustn't change my mind about it. In addition to his damned Negro blood, he's a piddling specimen of a human. Depressing.

On his way back to Werk-en-Rust, he paused by the Stabroek Market to frown at a Negro who was shouting at a mob gathered in the open space before the market building. A fanatical-looking fellow. He was saying something about the Portuguese.

" . . . they robbers and cheaters—everyone of dem! They come to dis colony special to ride on your back. And who send dem? De Pope in Rome! De Pope hate all black people. He want to keep you down, and he send de Pottagees here so dat they can bleed you, and cut your throat, and stamp 'pon your children. Dat Roman Catholic Church! Satan is its god. You listen what I tell you! Almighty God in Heaven ent got nutting to do with the Roman Church. It's Satan who rule it, and tell de Pope what to do. . . ."

Later, the coachman told Dirk that the man's name was Orr—John Orr. He was known as the Angel Gabriel, and had left the colony some years previously. He had returned only a week or two ago, and was holding meetings every day in the town. "He's a bad man, sir. Ah hear he mek plenty trouble in New York and Glasgow. He rouse up de people and mek dem burn down Roman Catholic churches. And now he come back home he trying to rouse up de people here. Every day you hear him blowing a horn to call a crowd together."

Less than a month later, Orr had been so successful in rousing the Negroes that a full-scale riot started in the town against the Portuguese. On the fifteenth of February the Government had to forbid all public meetings on the streets, and this began the trouble, for Orr defied the edict and held a meeting outside his mother's house in Albert Town. He was arrested, and the Negroes ran amok, bawling out curses against the Portuguese and brandishing sticks, breaking into the homes and shops of the Portuguese. The police were unable to handle the situation, and the Second West Indian Regiment had to be called into action. But the rioting spread to the country districts and even to New Amsterdam. Peter and Millicent each were obliged to take in two Portuguese families for a night in order to protect them from the rampaging mobs of negroes. The High Street, as in 1847, was littered with the goods of the Portuguese—and with broken furniture from their homes.

"Savages, that's what they are," snarled Dirk when order had been finally restored and he was over at Peter's house. "At least the Portuguese have the guts to make something of themselves in commerce, mean as they may be—but these black brutes haven't got the self-respect to do an honest day's work. Pure envy, that's what it is! Lazy savages! Soon the Chinese and coolies will be outstripping them. Then the damned missionaries whined and whimpered when we kept them slaves. Bah! That was what they were intended to be. Serfs! Nothing will change my views on that score. Stinking serfs!"

He got so red in the face that Peter had to warn him to be careful. "You will have a stroke, Papa, if you aren't careful. You get worked up too easily. Can't afford to do that at sixty."

That scared him, for he was not ready to die. His job was not yet done. There was still Hendrik's Dora. He must live on and hope. Never would he admit defeat until—until what? He was not certain himself, but the fire was still alive in him. He must fight on. The van Groenwegels never run. . . .

"Did you hear that, my love?"

She was smiling back at him. He gripped the bedpost, and nodded.

"They never run, Rose. They fight to the last, don't they, my dear? You did. Went down in the flames. Refused to give in. Refused to submit tamely. By God! By God! We'll see. We'll keep after Dora, eh? Yes, we'll nag her into it, my love. It will be a son. A son to carry on the glorious name."

60

T H E grandchildren were fond of him and did not mind his odd mannerisms, nor his sudden soliloquies. Peter's Hyacinth, a brown-eyed creature with Gwendolyn's dark tresses, would sometimes, after a scolding from her nurse because of inattention to her food, wail for her grandfather. "Grandpa won't scold," she would assert. To which her nurse would rebutt: "He spoil you too much. You'll grow up bad girl."

Mavis and Margaret, Hendrik's children, looked forward to his visits, and he visited Flagstaff at least twice every six weeks. Hendrik called him secretly the Haunter—though Dora scolded him whenever he gave voice to the nickname.

"I don't mind his haunting us," she said. "I like him—and I admire his family spirit. I think it's a fine thing."

"He's always thought it a fine thing," Hendrik scowled. "What do you think he comes here for? Simply to discover what *you* are doing about the family spirit."

"Poor old dear. I did promise him, you know, Hendrik."

"More the fool you. At forty-one! Put the idea behind you."

Reginald's children liked him, too. Reginald and Rowena and their four children—three boys and one girl—came on a holiday in August of 1857, and Dirk invited them to spend a week at his home in New Amsterdam.

Two of the boys—the eldest, Hilary, and the last child, Christopher —were blonds; there was not the faintest trace of coloured blood in them. And the other boy, Gerald, and the girl, Evangeline, were dark-haired, but of clear, pink complexions and blue-eyed.

Dirk took them for walks along the plantation dams in the late afternoon—and raised no objections to the two elder boys swimming in the canal that bordered Vrymen's Erven. "We'll treat it as a secret between us, eh?" said Dirk, winking. "Say nothing to them when we get back." He told them the names of birds, took them to spots aback of New Signal where they were able to see mongooses and salempenters. One afternoon, returning at dusk, they saw a goatsucker flutter down and lie flat on its breast on the dam, and heard it cry "Hoo-yoo!" before it flew off again.

Every evening before bed—it was a ritual—he took them into his room to show them Rose's portrait. "See her there! Your grandmother! Admire her!" And while they admired, he would pace about, muttering to himself, gesticulating, chuckling. One evening Evangeline challenged him on something he muttered.

"What did you say, Uncle Dirk? Black blood? You scorned her black blood?"

He flushed. "Didn't intend you to hear that, miss. Yes, I did—and I've regretted it, my child. Regretted it bitterly. Poor Rose. My dearly beloved."

"Did she have black blood in her, Uncle Dirk?"

"Eh? Yes, yes. Of course she had." He winked, and put a finger to his lips. "We'll keep that a secret, too, shall we? Mustn't mention it."

"Then we have black blood in us, too?" asked Hilary.

"Sssh! Of course, you have, my boy. But never mention it. Put it behind you, do you hear me? You're English—son of Sir Reginald Greenfield. Put the rest behind you. See her there? A true van Groenwegel, black blood or no black blood. She was a fighter. Iron in her soul. Fire in her blood."

Some minutes later, he stood rigid, hands clasped together, alone in the room, and thought: What have I said? Have I been indiscreet? Have I set something in motion by what I've told them? I have spoiled so many lives by the words I've uttered. Between myself and that canister, I wonder which has brought more unhappiness to the van Groenwegels this past half century?

He pulled out the canister from under the bed. The key, still attached to a thin silver chain, lay on top. He opened the canister and gazed down at the black notebook in which he had recorded birth dates and death dates of as many members of the family as he had been able to. On it rested a slip of paper. He took it up and held it under the lamp. Though he did not need to read the words written on it, for they had been burnt on his memory for eternity, he read them; read them for the hundredth time, or was it the thousandth?

"Dear Papa—the crescendo air of doom has reached its unbearable peak. May the *perdendosi* be not too sad for you. Good-bye from your loving Mary."

It was a long time before he could fall asleep. He kept listening to the drums in the distance. Hindu drums. Those coolies from India were flowing into the colony in their hundreds and thousands, and bringing with them their oriental customs. Drum beating and tuneless, wailing songs. *Dhotis* and *urnis*. Curry and rice. And Hindustani . . . And the Chinese, too—hundreds of them pouring in. In their black silk trousers and pigtails. They didn't beat drums, but they smoked opium. A lot of filthy dens were springing up in Georgetown —in the Werk-en-Rust district. Lombard Street and that neighbourhood . . . Oh well, it couldn't be helped, he supposed. The colony needed their labour. No grumbles these days. Everybody was prospering in earnest. . . .

I shouldn't have mentioned about Rose's black blood. It might have upset them—especially the girl, Evangeline. She seems a sensitive type. . . .

The crescendo air of doom. . . .

Heavy-eyed, his head aching, he stood at the window at six o'clock and stared east towards New Signal. He could make out the factory chimney, a thin prong on the horizon, a black pin of omen amidst the early-morning haze. . . .

This was the time of the day Adrian and Mary would take their swim in the canal. . . . "May the *perdendosi* be not too sad. . . ."

There was a letter for him that morning. It was from Dora, and in the course of it she said: "I think I have kept my promise to you, and the doctor who came yesterday said that my slight indisposition can mean only one thing. There will be a happy event before long, dear Papa."

61

I T turned out to be a girl. She was born in February of the following year, 1858, and when Dirk received the news—he spent a month at Flagstaff in anticipation of the event—he sank back into his chair on the portico and murmured: "The *perdendosi* it must be, then." The midwife stared at him curiously. "The what did you say, Mr. van Groenwegel?" she asked. But he only shook his head and waved her off.

Later that day he kissed Dora as she lay in bed beside the child. "You did your best, my child, and I'm grateful. What are you going to call her?"

"A name beginning with D," she smiled. "Something as near Dirk as possible."

He smiled and said: "Call her Diana, then. We can't have two Doras."

He put such a good face on it that none of them guessed the bitter dust of disillusionment that kept sifting through him for days after, for weeks after.

In July he visited the shop in Georgetown and put his proposition to Jason Clark. The old man was bedridden, but the room was very tidy and clean, and the interview, from that point of view, was not unpleasant.

Before entering the shop, Dirk noticed that the roof needed re-shingling, and that one or two facings were rotting. Even the paint could not disguise the poor condition of the little building. The sign board could hardly be read, for the letters had faded into the greyish background tint of flaked paint. Only old customers could discern the legend, SARAH HUBERT—PROVISION DEALER, at a glance because they had known it when the paint was fresh.

"This is what I'd like to do, Mr. Clark," said Dirk. "The boy is twenty-one next year, isn't he? Born in July 1838, I think. Oh yes, oh yes. I have a habit of making a note of these things. It's not simply good memory. But as I was saying. He'll be of age in July next year —and I want to make a settlement of this shop on him."

Jason, at the door of the room, keeping an eye out for customers, smiled shyly in pleasure, and Dirk saw a look in his dark eyes that annoyed him. Greed. Sheer greed. He was a bad type. Not malevolent like his father, perhaps, but still bad. Mean, chicken hawk look about him. However . . .

"However, there is a condition," Dirk went on. "I want him to change his name by deed poll to anything you care to suggest. Clark, let us say?"

"I'm sure Jason wouldn't object, sir," said the old man. "Jason, you hear that, boy? Mr. Dirk wants to give you the shop, but you must agree to change your name to Clark."

"Oh," said Jason, and Dirk saw the dismay on his face.

"Is that all the comment you have to make?" snapped Dirk.

Jason flushed under his olive-brown, and began to screw his hands together. He gave a simpering grin and said: "Why must I change my name, sir?"

"Why? Because that's the condition I'm laying down. I prefer it so," said Dirk coldly. "Have you any objections in the matter?"

Jason wriggled, shifted his feet about, and with lowered gaze, said: "No, sir, but—well, you see, the people who owe—you think they would want to pay me for old debts if I change my name? They might say if my name different they don't owe me nothing no more."

"That's nonsense." What an utter fool! Of all the absurd arguments to adduce! "What difference could it make to the debts they owe the shop! Of course they will have to pay up—no matter what your name is."

Jason was silent, cowed by Dirk's tone. Suddenly the old man chuckled and said: "Sir, I think I know what's bothering the boy. He very careful with how he spends his money, and he went recently to a painter and had a new sign done to hang outside the shop. It only came a few days ago, and he had to pay nearly five guilders to the painter for doing it. He was going to write you to ask your permission to put it up, because he had the painter paint on his own name on it instead of the old Sarah Hubert name what on the old sign out there now. He thinking to himself how he will have to lose his five guilders if he has to get a new sign painted."

"Oh, I see! And where is this sign, pray? Let me see it."

Jason brought the wooden sign. It was crudely painted. On a background of pale green Dirk read the legend, JASON VANGREEN—PROVISION DEALER. ONLY CASH, in scarlet letters.

Dirk was on the point of snapping "But you can't even spell your name!" when something checked him. Why enlighten him? Since in his ignorance he imagined this was the correct way to spell van Groenwegel, very well, let it stand at that. Vangreen. Excellent! No intelligent person would think of that as a corruption of van Groenwegel. The coloured children would be known as Vangreen. Splendid!

"You have my permission to hang it," said Dirk. "And I won't bother to insist you change your name. Keep it just what it is on the sign. Agreed?"

"Yes, sir," said Jason in a voice of relief—and Dirk suddenly realised what it was about him that was contemptible. He was a miser. Only a miser could show such relief at the thought of not having to spend another five guilders even though he was being left a whole shop and its stock.

"By the way, may I see any documents you have signed? You must have signed one or two papers from my attorneys. Have you anything at all here showing your signature? I want to see it."

The old man it was who produced from an old box under his bed some documents which Jason had signed within the past year. On every one of them Dirk saw the laboured, barely legible signature: Jason Vangreen.

Early in the next year, 1859, the settlement was effected, and Dirk saw to it that his attorneys arranged for the name Vangreen to be put on a legal basis. When Jason was tackled about it, he raised no obstacles. He admitted that he was indifferent what name he bore. It was merely the cost of having a new signboard done that had worried him the July before!

It became one of Dirk's stock jokes. For years after, he was fond of relating the story. It came to be known as the five-guilder signboard joke. Any instance of meanness that was mentioned in the course of a conversation when Dirk happened to be present provided the excuse for Dirk to drag out the hackneyed anecdote.

He even told it to Mr. Anthony Trollope when that gentleman

dined with him in New Amsterdam one afternoon a few months later. Mr. Trollope had remarked that he had never suspected that such hospitality could exist. "A total stranger in the colony, and I was invited to so many dinners and social occasions in Georgetown that I might truly have been a long-lost relation of one of you planters. And now I come to New Amsterdam and the same performance is being repeated. It is incredible, sir—really incredible. Whatever may be the drawbacks of living in your land, it would be a knave and a liar who could leave here and take away any tales of inhospitality or parsimony."

"Ho! Parsimony, eh?" chuckled Dirk. "There's parsimony here, sir, make no mistake." And while Peter and Gwendolyn sighed silently, exchanging desperate glances, Dirk proceeded to tell the story of Jason and the signboard.

Later in the evening, on learning that his guest, apart from being a civil servant, was also something of a novelist, Dirk took him upstairs to show him Rose's portrait. "There she is, sir! One of the finest women that ever lived. She was an enthusiastic reader of novels. Very fond of Miss Austen's works."

This, too, began to be numbered among Dirk's eccentricities—this eagerness to take people upstairs to show them Rose's portrait. To himself, however, he chuckled at the comments he overheard. And once he told Rose: "They see it as an eccentricity, my dear—the foolish quirk of an ageing dolt. Only you and I know that beneath the surface lies the true reason—the guilt in my poor heart that must be assuaged. It solaces me to make a fuss over you now, Rose—now that the gall of defeat is thickening in my soul. But *they* won't know that!"

It was a day early in 1862 that he took no less than nine people up to see Rose, for it was on this day that Graham arrived to spend a week, and to be feted on the news received a few days before that Her Majesty the Queen had been pleased to confer on Reginald a baronetcy.

Before going to bed that night Dirk told her; "That's glory, my love. Your son and grandson and great-grandson to carry an honoured title. The victory is yours, Rose. All the way! Laugh at me, my dear —but comfort me in my sleep!"

62

EVENTUALLY he developed delusions about Rose. Once he was certain he saw her reclining in a hammock on the back veranda of Peter's house. "She was reading a novel of Miss Austen's," he averred. "There *are* spirits, Peter, my boy. I'm convinced of it now." Peter did not argue. He and Gwendolyn merely exchanged glances.

It was not always spectres that he saw, however. One Sunday, in St. George's Church, when he and Graham were at midday service—Jim Menzies's funeral had taken place the day before—Dirk nudged Graham, and told him that the young woman in the second row was the very image of Rose. "Look," he whispered fiercely. "See her there! It could be Rose herself, Graham." Graham smiled indulgently, affectionately, sympathetically, and nodded. Whispered back: "Yes; there is a striking resemblance, I agree."

Dirk's gaze never left the young woman throughout the rest of the service. On the way out of the building he kept jostling people in his efforts not to lose sight of the girl. At the church door he watched her get into a carriage with an elderly woman who might have been her mother or an aunt. The carriage had just driven off and Dirk was sighing sentimentally and strolling with Graham towards Graham's carriage when the cry seared through the noonday peace of Sunday.

"Fire!"

Dirk came to a halt. His head jerked round, and he was staring towards Newtown. As the shout crashed into his hearing for the second time—"Fire!"—a quavering whimper escaped Dirk's lips. He clutched Graham's arm. "Quick! Quick! We must warn them, Graham! The stairs!"

"What is the matter?" asked Graham, in astonishment. "Warn whom? What stairs?"

Sanity returned in a shuddering flood. Dirk sighed. "My apologies, Graham. Oh dear!" He gave a sheepish smile. "My mind suffers these lapses occasionally. I—I—you know what I mean. Newtown. I was thinking of Pelham and Rose at Edward House. But that's long, long ago, isn't it?"

Graham chuckled. "Oh well, never mind. We're both getting old, Dirk, boy. Seventy next year September, aren't you?"

"No excuse," frowned Dirk as they got into the carriage. "I should pull myself together, confound it. Getting embarrassing——"

"Good heavens! Look!" his brother interrupted, pointing. "It's a fire all right, Dirk! Over there! Do you see?"

Dirk saw. Over the housetops in the southwest a black cloud of smoke billowed into the hot noon sky.

"Tch, tch," clicked Graham. "And I was certain it must be some trivial case of a lamp overturned in one of these shacks somewhere. You hear so many fire alarms these days all over nothing at all."

"Anyway, they've got fire engines these days. Shouldn't be as bad as the Newtown business in '28."

"Shall we drive up the High Street and watch it for a while?"

"By all means," said Dirk. "Seems somewhere near Water Street. And I won't say it's very far from Newtown."

In the High Street they heard somebody among the hurrying crowds say that it was in South Street, near Klien's shop premises.

"Heard that?" said Dirk. "Near Klien's. Bad area. Very crowded. And there's something of a breeze on today."

A horse-drawn fire engine went clattering past them, on its way south along High Street, and almost immediately after hurried a fire reel.

By the time the carriage had got to South Street the roar and crackle of the flames could be clearly heard farther west along the street. At least three buildings were involved, and the flames leapt up like brassy tongues out of the billowing black smoke. A panicked cry ran through the crowds. "No water! They can't get water!" And somebody said that one of the fire engines had broken down.

On that day, the third of April 1864, virtually the whole of Robb's Town was wiped out in a matter of two or three hours. The Reading Rooms of the Royal Agricultural and Commercial Society and the

British Guiana Bank and all the stores and shops on either side of Water Street were reduced to blackened ruins.

When the fire was at its height Dirk asked Graham to take him to Cumingsburg. "Never can tell. It might reach as far. I'm anxious for that poor old fellow Clark in the shop there. He's bedridden."

"An excellent idea," said Graham, though his benevolent, old-man face showed surprise, and Dirk could hear him saying to himself: "Fancy Dirk being concerned over the welfare of an old Negro bedridden in a tiny room!" Graham told him to take the carriage. "I'll wait here and watch the progress of things. The fire seems to be heading north, but we never know."

Hartfield & Clackson's office was in Newtown, south of the burning area.

Dirk did not have any difficulty in finding his way round to the back of the little shop in Cumingsburg, for the ground was dry and hard; rain had not fallen for weeks; the short dry season had overlapped into April. Every back yard in Georgetown was noted for its slushy, muddy condition.

Jason Clark was overjoyed to see him. "Come in, Mr. Dirk, come in! The door is not locked!" he called out, after Dirk had knocked. "How good of you to call! I'm in such a state, sir. Jason hasn't come home from church service, and this terrible fire raging yonder. It seems to be getting nearer every minute."

"Has he left you alone here? At least I had expected to find him somewhere in the yard. At a time like this he should be at home."

"I know, sir—but I haven't seen him since he left for church at ten."

Dirk sat down for nearly two hours with the old fellow. He did not find it irksome, for he was rather fond of Jason Clark. He was the only Negro man for whom he had been able to cultivate a genuine respect, just as Sarah Hubert had been the only Negro woman he had not felt like spurning or shouting at.

They discussed young Jason, and the old man told him that the boy was all right, very hard-working and upright, but so close with money still. He had begun to lend out money on interest, and people were calling him Miser Van. Marriage? No, not so far as he could see. Jason did not seem interested in women particularly, though he smiled and talked to one or two young persons of the opposite sex, and even went to church with two sisters every Sunday—but he was not a warm fellow, if Dirk understood. No, he thought only of money, money. The old man had asked him if he did not contemplate marrying any girl, but Jason had spoken of the expense. And where would he put a wife to live? It would mean a cottage.

Every now and then they would pause in their conversation to look through the door at the towering mass of black smoke above the house-tops. Once the old man expressed concern for Graham—wouldn't he be wondering what had happened to Dirk and be wanting the carriage? But Dirk told him that Graham would get a lift in any of a dozen carriages in the High Street if he wanted to go home. "There are crowds of other gentlemen watching the fire, too, Mr. Clark. This is a bad day for the merchants, I fear. The loss is going to be heavy. Nobody will want to go home until the fire has been brought under control."

Suddenly the sound of explosions vibrated on the air, and Dirk said: "Aha! They're probably blowing up some houses to stop the fire from spreading. They had to do that in '28 too."

Not long after, Jason arrived and confirmed this. Yes, they were blowing up buildings, Jason told them. He was dressed in black, like a respectable gentleman—with high collar and tie and top hat; though the suit and the hat were obviously second hand. He must have bought them cheap in some Lombard Street shop. The trousers were too short for him, and the jacket too tight. He looked like a caricature but did not seem aware of it. He simpered at Dirk and said how good of him to come and stay with his grandfather. "God will bless you, sir! I was so anxious, but I had to remain in Water Street to see how the fire was going. I think we're out of danger now." He squirmed and uttered more pious platitudes about God and God's goodness in sparing Cumingsburg. Dirk felt like kicking him.

Above the housetops the smoke was now a mere wispy haze. The fire had been beaten at last.

The loss to Georgetown was assessed at over five hundred thousand pounds sterling, but it was agreed that many of the buildings in Water Street had been a disgrace, and that the fire had done the town some good by wiping them out.

Casually, one day, some months later Dirk heard through Timothy Hartfield that Jason Vangreen had foreclosed on two ruined small shopkeepers and taken possession of their cottages in Albert Town. "He lent them money," said Timothy, "and the fire cleaned them out. Then Jason pounced on them, poor fellows. And they're fellow churchmen of his."

63

J A S O N had hardly brought off his coup, and the débris of the April disaster had not yet been cleared away, when fire again swept through Water Street, and this time in Cumingsburg. It started at one in the morning of the fifth of July and devoured building after building.

Dirk heard afterwards—he was not in Georgetown on this occasion—that Jason, at one time, was seen kneeling before the shop praying in fervent tones. Tom Menzies, a nephew of Jim Menzies, told him about it: "There he was in his nightshirt, right before the shop in view of the crowd, praying in a loud voice. Beating his chest and shedding tears. No exaggeration, sir. And the crowd jeered at him, but it had no effect. They kept calling out at him: 'Miser Van! Look. Miser Van on 'e knees praying to God! He forget money is 'e god! Now 'e praying to God in heaven!' Oh, you missed a sight, I can tell you!"

The fire, however, approached no nearer than a hundred yards of the shop—and two weeks later Jason had brought the law into operation to foreclose on another unlucky small shopkeeper. Another little cottage in the town—this one in Werk-en-Rust—fell into Jason's maw.

In August, Dirk went to Georgetown and dropped in at the shop. "So you're becoming quite a money hawk, I hear, young man," he said to Jason—and Jason looked hurt. "Me, Mr. Dirk? Oh, sir, you shouldn't listen to what people say about me." He seemed on the point of tears. "I only want to live, Mr. Dirk. These are hard times for us all. I got to be careful about my investments. No man can say I'm dishonest. It would be a lie. How would I be able to answer at the Judgment Seat when my time comes if I robbed my fellow men, sir!"

"There's no question of robbing involved," said Dirk coldly. "But perhaps you don't know what it is to be compassionate, so we'd better drop the subject."

Dirk left in disgust. That evening he took a walk towards Werken-Rust, and in Lombard Street, just when dark was gathering, came to a halt outside one of the notorious Chinese gambling dens. A fire in June of the year before had wiped out a number of them, but more had sprung up since, and the Chinese continued to weave their oriental spells of vice and opium throughout the length of Lombard Street. It was an exciting street, and Dirk liked to roam through it of an afternoon or early evening, despite many warnings from acquaintances in the town.

It was no different this evening. Pigtailed Chinese strolled in couples, or singly, pushing barrows of sweetmeats or vegetables, and here and there a Portuguese face mingled with the slant-eyed ones, for there were rumshops in Lombard Street, and the Portuguese had the monopoly in the rumshop business. Rumshops and pawnshops had not to be entered in order to discover the race of their proprietors.

Here and there, sitting by the side of the street, were mulatto or Negro hucksters with their trays of vegetables or sweetmeats, and now that dusk was gathering torches were being lighted—torches stuck into bottles. All along the street these flickering blobs of light came into being, adding colour to the variety of smells, the jabber of English and Portuguese and Chinese, and here and there even Hindustani, for occasionally a coolie in his *dhoti* could be seen outside a shop entrance, squatting on the pavement with hand outstretched, begging alms in a groaning voice. "Ow, *sahib! Pisa! Lil' pisa!* Baboo poor, *sahib!*"

It was another delusion that brought Dirk to a halt outside the Chinese den. In the darkened doorway a slim, shapely mulatto girl was standing, arm akimbo, watching the passers-by. It was Rose.

She smiled at him as he halted, and he felt the breath in him fading. Before it could vanish completely he heard himself gasp: "Rose! It's you, my dear!"

She chuckled and took a step towards him, asked him if he wanted to come home with her. He nodded mechanically and began to follow her along the street. She turned into an alleyway, slushy and smelly, and he followed. In a daze, he went up the long stairway and entered a dimly lit gallery.

Then an elderly woman—she might have been anything between

forty-five and sixty—appeared from a room, and said: "All right,
Kate. You wait. I'll talk to him and arrange matters for you." She was
a white woman, and in the dim lamplight had the kind of face he
would have expected of a bawdyhouse keeper. Thin, vulturine, with
cold, pale blue eyes, and straggly dark hair.

"Good evening," she said in a soft, ingratiating voice in which there
seemed to lurk a venomous threat.

"Good evening," murmured Dirk, glancing aside quickly to see
what had happened to the girl he had taken for Rose. She was standing at the twilight end of the gallery, a ghost beyond the range of
the lamp.

"You want to go in the room with Kate?" asked the white woman.
And, without waiting for an answer, told him: "Ten guilders, if you
please."

Perhaps it must be another delusion, thought Dirk, but suddenly he
found himself staring hard at the woman. That forehead, those pale
blue eyes, the eyebrows—wasn't there something somehow familiar
about them?

"Ten guilders, I said, sir."

"Look here, tell me. Who are you, woman? I'll be damned if your
face isn't one I've seen somewhere before."

For several seconds they stared at each other, she puzzled, impatient, baleful, he frowningly curious, suspicious, desperately reflective.

Then it came to him. His heart contracted, turned to steel.

"Woman, tell me. Aren't you Pelham's daughter? Isn't your name
Harriet?"

He heard the hiss of her breath. Her hands clenched.

"You?" She stepped back. "I know now. Your eyes. Yes, your eyes.
It's Cousin Dirk. Oh, God!"

There was a long silence. Dirk could only nod slowly. At length
he groaned and said: "I'd always wondered what had happened to
you, Harriet."

She said nothing, her eyes shifty but in no way shamed.

"Did you ever marry? What is your name now?"

She shook her head, "No, I never married," she said. "My name is
still what it was. I think you'd better go—and don't come back in this
district. It isn't safe here—for your kind."

He chuckled. "For my kind. I see. For *my* kind. You damned slut!

But I'm *your* kind. I'm a van Groenwegel—and so are you. We're of one blood."

"Please leave at once."

"Of course. My God, my God! To think of it! A van Groenwegel carrying on a bawdyhouse. And this is the glory I'd dreamt of! These are the pinnacles!"

He left in a hurry.

64

FR O M the shock of that incident he never fully recovered. It deepened the lines down his cheeks, thickened the sediment of defeat in his spirit.

"Not much longer to last down here, my love," he told Rose. "I won't reach the traditional eighty of the van Groenwegels. The dark is overtaking me, Rose."

In November he received a letter, written in an abominable hand, from Jason saying that his grandfather was very low and not expected to live out the rest of the week. So Dirk went to Georgetown and sat beside the old man, and the old man was very happy. He could only mumble out an occasional sentence, but every word was distinguishable and lucid; he was a clear-thinking old man: a Negro with both character and brain. Had he been given the opportunity, he might have risen to heights in the world . . . Sir Jason Clark, Bart.

Dirk was the only white man at his funeral.

"Black blood, Rose. Black blood. I might have been richer in spirit had I taught myself not to scorn it. Ah yes. You smile. I know, my dear. You yourself secretly scorned it, didn't you, Rose? You never behaved as if you had it in you."

Many an evening he would stand in silence for long spells and stare east out of the window, brooding on the past and on the present, remembering the old New Signal and the New Signal as it was to-day. Every Monday he took the carriage and went there. His ritual weekly visit. And while the carriage waited and the coachman wandered off towards the servants' quarters of the old house—now the residence of the manager and his family—Dirk took the path that led to the canal. The manager and the overseers knew well not to offer him any conveyance or to approach anywhere near his person. They knew his whims and quirks, knew that the big master must be left severely alone to wander where he wished, to think his own thoughts and mutter to himself.

They shiver every Monday when they see me appear. They think me a snob and an autocrat. They feel their jobs are in jeopardy when I am on the premises. They might change their attitude if they could see into me.

New Signal . . . Stable in its prosperity, but no van Groenwegel in the big house. No van Groenwegel rode around in the morning on his tour of inspection. A manager . . . ! And a deputy manager . . . ! And look over there! Coolies in charge of the oxen team pulling the punts along the canal towards the factory. Indian coolies—Hindus and Moslems. And look yonder. Chinese cutting canes. Chinese and Hindus . . . What had things come to! Was this New Signal? Where were all the shiny black faces . . . ? In the town—and in the villages they had set up for themselves on the ruins of so many good old plantations. Freed men, lazing away their time in shacks instead of doing a solid day's work in the fields. Aiming at being gentlemen like the successful coloured men and the white planters, but too indolent to work their way up. . . .

Though I wonder . . . As he swished at the black-sage bushes with his letter-wood stick, something occurred to him. Poor devils—perhaps it was the memory of their bondage that scared them away from the fields. Yes, it could be that. Field work held, for them, too many painful associations. The overseer's shout and the sting of the whip on their backs. It would be a long time before that memory was left behind. And in the meantime they would continue to be underdogs, idling in their villages, living on their provision plots, or coming to town to sell their vegetables and fruits, or to work as porters or menials, those of them who felt they should do some work. In the meantime the Portuguese would continue to oust them in trade, outsell them as hucksters and small shopkeepers, because the Portuguese did not aim to be idle gentlemen of leisure in shacks. The Portuguese were thrifty people who were determined to get rich through hard work and much starving and self-denial. And the Chinese were beginning to follow their example. The Chinese were turning shopkeepers, pedlars, and hucksters. Even the coolies—the Indians from India—were trying to break away when they could from the fields to come into town and turn tradesmen. Damn their impudence! As meagre and dirty as the Portuguese had been when they first arrived in the colony. A

fine state of affairs it would be in the town if they, too, set themselves up in cottages and established shops around the place!

So strange and inexplicable these racial urges. Why was it that the
jungle Indians—the aborigines—had never wanted to better their lot
by becoming hucksters and shopkeepers? Why was it they had always
been content to remain a quiet and retiring jungle people, hunting
and fishing and planting and cutting timber? One saw so little of them
these days. More and more they kept retreating upriver into the
shelter of the bush. To them, it meant nothing that Demerara sugar
was world famous, or that the railway on the East Coast of Demerara
was the first to be laid down in the whole continent of South America.
Progress meant nothing to them. They were not out to win glory, to
reach the pinnacles.

Who knows if they aren't sensible! Look where the hope of glory
has got *me* today! Mooning along the canal path, a disillusioned fool.

He halted suddenly and stared up into the foliage of the tamarind
tree, sighing heavily. What a hoary old devil! Simply refuses to die.
Must be well over a hundred years old. Think of all the pranks we
used to play under this tree . . . ! Rose, Hermine, Graham, Jacob,
the Lafferty children. . . . And where have those days gone to? They
might never have happened. All vanished like early-morning mist
over the cane fields. Rose a mere portrait in my bedroom. Hermine
died last year in Boston. Jacob is a marble slab over there near the
cabbage palms. . . . Old Jacob. But he did see some glory. He left
a doctor and a barrister in fine houses—and a son managing the old
firm of Frick & Green. The cream of the coloured middle class. Yes,
he has enriched the olive-skinned stratum in the colony's society.
Cultivated people. In Georgetown they were even going in for
theatricals and musical societies and competing with the whites. Jacob's
Olga, who had married that Werk-en-Rust merchant in Georgetown, was active in some newly formed dramatic club. The Histrionic
Club. They put on plays and musical evenings in public halls, and
were said to be as good as the Amateur Dramatic Club, which was
the one run by the whites in the town. They were doing everything
the whites did, these coloured people. Turning themselves into lawyers
and doctors and surveyors and engineers, and living in style. They
turned up their noses at the Portuguese, even though the Portuguese
were Europeans. Understandable, though, when you considered the
low living standards of the Portuguese, and their ignorance and un-
couthness. The Portuguese might be amassing money but they cer-

tainly were not showing any eagerness to cultivate their minds—or their manners.

Yes, Jacob, boy, you've done well, in your way. Much better than I, when all things are compared. Your name will go down the generations to the twentieth century. You have enough male grandsons bearing the name Frick to be sure of survival. . . . But me and mine . . . Ah well! It's the *perdendosi* Adrian spoke of. Yes, the gradual fading out. I wanted too much, I aimed too high—and I ignored the imponderables when making my plans. Nature, heredity. Nothing you can do about those things. . . . Some English scholar wrote a book not too long ago. Something to do with the species. *Origin of the Species*, or some such title. Harvey showed me a copy of the book. Interesting. Traces us back to the monkey. There may be something in that. A tricky business, heredity. . . . Old Hendrickje. Cousin Hubertus. Uncle Edward. Aunt Luise. Me. Pelham. Rose. Francis. Mary. Adrian. . . . The unstable, unpredictable ones. Strange fires have possessed us few, and led us into the twisted by-paths of human behaviour. Who could have planned for any of us? Who could have foretold our ends?

Papa. Willem. Peter. Hendrik. Pelham's Matilde. Jacob. And Jacob's Jim and Charles and Lawrence. The stable, predictable people. No unholy flame had touched them. But even you had to see your youngest in the throes, Jacob, lad. Yes, your Jasmine did not escape. She was the only one, though. . . . Twisted twig.

Ah well, let me get back home. "Take care of yourself, tamarind tree. You may outlive me. Yes, I'm sure you will. Not much longer to last down here. The dark is overtaking me."

65

H E kept telling everyone that. "The dark is overtaking me."
But the dark was tardy, for he lived on, thriving on defeat, robust in disillusionment, fed by dismal reflections,
but never satiated; perpetually whetting his appetite for more; nour-
ished by might-have-beens, comforted by fantasies and delusions. Some
days he talked to Rose and some days to Mary. He had had Mary's portrait brought up into his room, too.

"Happier where you are, my child, I feel certain. You were never
meant to be a conventional wife and mother. Nor Adrian a planter.
Our genius with the fiddle. Old Jacob thought he fooled me, Mary—
but I knew. It was Adrian, wasn't it? Adrian and Jasmine. I guessed,
my girl. Those choir practices in the Methodist Church. He used to
meet her after services. . . . And you and your boating trips up the
Creek to Don Diego. That nasty old rake! Perhaps your spirit watched
him when he blew his brains out two nights after they found your
body. Can't imagine why he did that. Did you jilt him that afternoon you went off to see him at three o'clock? Suppose we'll never
know. Your secret, eh? A woman's secret . . . Wonder what became
of Francis. Simply vanished like smoke in the treetops. And Janet
and that overseer fellow . . . another mystery we'll never solve. . . ."

Life was never boring. He was in and out of Peter's house—and
always on the move. One week he was at Flagstaff, the other week
at Huis Kaywana, then back to New Amsterdam. Once Sybil asked
him to go to Trinidad to see her and the children, but he refused.
"I have no desire to leave these shores," he wrote back. "Come and
see me and I shall be overjoyed." In Barbados, Amelia had grown
tired of inviting him over, and suddenly she and Ronald and their
children appeared, and the house took on the atmosphere of a lived-

in place. For the month they spent with him in New Amsterdam, it was as though the old days had returned and he was back at New Signal with Elfrida and her children and his own swarming upstairs and downstairs.

Then there was the gay occasion at Flagstaff when the double wedding of Hendrik's Mavis and Margaret, the twins, came off. Two short chubby misses, but passably pretty, and both with tall bridegrooms, the one a highly placed civil servant, public-school English, who had just received his marching orders to Africa, where he was to be the governor of a small colony there; the other Harry Menzies, a nephew of Jim Menzies, Beatrice's husband, who had died just before the big fire in April 1864. Harry was a director of Hartfield & Clackson's.

To each bride, before she departed, Dirk whispered: "Remember your blood, my girl. You've lost your grand old name, but *live* like a van Groenwegel. Aim for the top! Get to the top!"

He told Peter's Hyacinth the same thing when she was married two years later, a voluptuous young woman of twenty with Peter's features and Gwendolyn's body, his favourite grandchild, though he had always tried to disguise this fact, remembering Mary. Like Mary, however, she had always been inordinately fond of him. She replied: "Of course I shall *aim* for the top, Grandpa, but as to whether I'll get to the top is another matter." In a lowered voice: "Remember what I've been telling you since I was six or seven. It's so hard for me to get to the top when I have such a big *bottom*." And shrieks of laughter—like Rose's.

Yes, no doubt about it. There was a touch of the fire in the girl. A twig with a twist. Only hope her husband would be able to appreciate her to the full. Had a peculiar name—Flynn Baxter-Hough. English and Irish. A sugar chemist brought to the colony recently by Hartfield & Clackson. He had taken up permanent residence on Harrow's Castle in Demerara. Hendrik would be able to keep an eye on him.

Dark or no dark in the offing, life was full of interest. He was never bored. And there were no worries nowadays. Wealth flowed in. Labour was plentiful. Sugar prices high. Travel was easier. The railway had passed Mahaica and was heading steadily for the Berbice River. Everything was on the up trend. A few years before—in 1870—the museum of the Royal Agricultural and Commercial Society had been opened to the public in Georgetown. The streets of the city were decorated with trees along the grass borders. And at night there was the pale blue glow of gaslight. The military band played in the Promenade Gardens, and you could watch cricket matches on the parade ground or attend the race meetings at D'Urban Park.

The van Groenwegels were on the way out, but the colony of British Guiana was blooming fairer with the passing of every year—and he could console himself with the thought that the van Groenwegels had contributed to the burgeoning sap that fed the widespread blossoming. As planters, we've won all the way. No one can deny that. Through the blackest days we fought with might and kept our pennant high.

One Monday morning in March of 1875 he had just returned from his visit to New Signal when he heard a carriage approach and stop at the gate. It was Peter. He had brought a message.

"Mr. Parrott has just arrived from Georgetown, Papa. It's Uncle Graham. He died yesterday afternoon."

In November he would have been eighty-five. He had requested that he should be buried at the family cemetery at New Signal.

The house of every planter and merchant of standing in New Amsterdam and the surrounding district was taxed to capacity to provide accommodation for the mourners who arrived from Demerara for the funeral. There were over a hundred carriages in the cortège that set out from Dirk's house in the town.

For Dirk it was an occasion of glory. For though it was the corpse of Mr. Graham Greenfield that was being interred, everyone knew that it was the funeral of a van Groenwegel—and a distinguished van Groenwegel; the father of Sir Reginald Greenfield, Baronet, of Paxley Hall, Sussex. My brother, by God! And damn the name of Greenfield! A van Groenwegel, the son of Storm van Groenwegel, the great-grandson of Hendrickje van Groenwegel! Damn Greenfield!

Sitting between Peter and Hendrik in the carriage, he began to tremble, and Peter asked him in a murmur if he was feeling unwell.

"No, my boy. No, no. Only proud—and angry." And he sat back, trying to control the shaking in his limbs.

Graham . . . One of the select who had been touched by the unhallowed flame of strangeness that was a heritage of the Old Blood, and yet had not been consumed. Unique, when you came to think of it. Singular fellow. He had conquered the warp in his nature, and had come through to peace of mind in the final decades of his life. All the way up from fondling his nanny's breasts to Clara Hartfield and Rose and Albert Laver—and then peace of mind. No itching obsessions had disturbed his sleep. No canister of letters had plagued his Sundays. . . .

And yet, ah well—yet I would still not have wanted to be different from what I have been. I would not have been he if given the choice. He admired me, respected me, in the long run—even though he must have pitied me in the last two decades. . . .

He rested his hand on Hendrik's knee. "In September I shall be eighty, Hendrik." He turned his head and glanced at Peter. "Eighty, Peter. September."

Peter smiled and murmured: "You'll see ninety, Papa."

"A hundred is my estimate," murmured Hendrik.

Dirk shook his head. "Perhaps not even eighty, my boys. This is March, is it? I may not see September. The dark. The dark is overtaking me."

It was in August that the letter and the package arrived from Surinam. The letter was from Paulus Lieker, a son of Jan Lieker—and the package contained letters written by Laurens van Groenwegel to his sister, Susannah Bakker.

Laurens, the father of Grandma Hendrickje.

66

IT was a long time since he had spoken Dutch, but he had kept up his reading, and the letter from Paulus Lieker gave him no trouble. After explaining that he was the son of Jan Lieker, Paulus went on to say: "Before he died some years ago, Father told us of your interest in letters relating to the van Groenwegel side of our family. My brother, Cornelis, recently paid a visit to Holland, and on his return brought a collection of documents which had been taken to Holland many years ago by a relative of the Bakkers, and from a perusal of these I was able to confirm that the Bakkers are related to us, as they have always claimed. Indeed, I am sending you by this same post a package of letters which, as you will see, were undoubtedly written by one Laurens van Groenwegel of Essequibo to his sister Susannah, who married a Bakker and came to Surinam some time about 1671 or 1672. If they are of any interest to you, you may retain them. . . ."

Some of them began "My dearest sister," others "My dearest Susannah," and the handwriting was strong and clear. They were all signed "Laurens."

They were of absorbing interest, but contained nothing of a startling nature—all except one. And it was this one that caused Dirk to grow pale and rise from his chair. He discarded the whole lot, flung them under his writing desk with a nervous, indeterminate flick of his hand that was not intentional—the whole lot save the one in his grasp. He gave the portrait of Rose a blank stare, then uttered a quavering chuckle, and muttered: "It couldn't be true, my dear. I'm mistaken. My sight is playing me false."

He sank back down into the chair, adjusted his spectacles and began to read over the sentences that had startled him:

". . . it was very sad, my dear sister, and I would not have had it happen in this fashion if I could have arranged it otherwise, but so it is, and what can we do but accept it? Hannah drowned herself during the night, but her body was found some days later and buried not far from where Grandma Kaywana was laid to rest after her tragic death. Father swears that he will never forgive me for having married Katrina, for having brought a taint of black blood into the family, as he expresses it. There was a painful interview at which Hendrik Rol was present, and Hendrik supported me, saying to Father that in the colony as it is at present there are so few eligible wives for respectable men. Not more than a dozen or two—if so many. Katrina may be a slave, said Hendrik, but she's three quarters white, and is as fair in complexion as any white woman. Who is to question the pedigree of our family in the years ahead of us? said Hendrik. When Father had left I thanked Hendrik for his support and told him that both as a man and as the Commandeur of the colony, I respected and admired him. I told him that he had been a true friend to me, and he said in jest that he would ask me for reward in the matter, the reward to be that if my firstborn should prove a son I should name him Hendrik, or if a daughter, Hendrickje. . . ."

Dirk rose again, and this time slowly paced across the room and paused near the bed. For nearly two minutes he stared in silence at Rose. Then he began to nod and chuckle. "Did you read that, Rose? Did you stand beside me in spirit and read it? The final irony, my love. Grandma Hendrickje's mother was a quadroon—a *mestee*. Like Sir Reginald Greenfield. She had black blood in her, Rose. That cruel, arrogant, beautiful, magnificent harridan—the queen of the van Groenwegels. After Kaywana, our greatest heroine. An octoroon, Rose. One eighth Negro. Like your grandchildren—the future second baronet and his brothers and sister. . . . That makes even me not pure. What am I? One one hundred and thirty-second part black. Ridiculous, I know—but, still, something to ponder on. Had you known, you could have thrown it up at me that afternoon in July 1815 when I rejected you and made you put on your clothes. . . . Oh, but this is something we must laugh over, Rose. Tell Mary about it for me, my love. Tell Graham. Tell Cornelia—and Papa and Mama. Grandma Hendri's mother was a *mestee* slave. . . ."

67

HE destroyed the letter, but in December, when he was at Harrow's Castle—he spent Christmas with Hyacinth and her husband—he told Hyacinth. He could always confide in Hyacinth. She had inherited nothing of Peter's proper Victorian outlook, nor of Gwendolyn's, for that matter. No church choirs for Hyacinth. Like himself, she was not in harmony with the spirit of the times; she thumbed her nose at the prudery and propriety of her peers. The Old Blood ran strong in her veins. No other way of accounting for that ribald streak. She was always shocking some dinner party or drawing-room gathering with an outrageously indecent remark. The number of times she succeeded in accidentally revealing her ankles to the gaze of gentlemen had become too numerous to be deemed fortuitous. In the upper-class white circles of the colony, she was rapidly earning the reputation of a woman with loose morals, but neither she nor her husband, Flynn, cared, it seemed, for they were well matched and perpetually in the gayest of spirits. They had named their son Dirk Patrick.

Flynn was at the factory on the day after Boxing Day, and Hyacinth was on the back veranda, with young Dirk at her breast, when Dirk told her.

"Keep that to yourself, my girl. I haven't confided it to any one else. I don't want it to be noised around, Hyacinth. Not that it matters, really. A *mestee* in the seventeenth century hardly counts, but, still, I must do or say nothing that might cast the remotest racial slur on us as a family. It is for the same reason that I have never told Millicent Frick or her children the truth about Jacob."

"Oh yes, I remember you mentioned that some years ago. Great-grandpa Storm was really his father, you said."

"Sssh! That's right. But not a word, my girl! Not a word to anyone. When I'm dead, perhaps, it won't matter. But while I live keep it a secret. Humour the old man." He drummed with his fingers on the arm of the chair, chuckling. "Odd creatures, human beings, eh? So fond of deluding themselves. That's why I appreciate you so much, my girl. You're no hypocrite. You're no simpering Victorian. Pah! When I look around me at all these stiff-necked idiots with their pompous airs and graces, and their pretended morals! So much damned pretence! So much muffling and covering up of the stern elements of life, the harsh, heated facts of existence, under a polite heap of sniggering gentility! People have lost their guts these days. Laurens and Katrina—a *mestee* slave girl. See that, Hyacinth? The sexual urge. *That* is the driving force, my child, behind all our actions and all our destinies. It colours our lives from birth to grave. Only blinkered fools like the fools we see about us these days are unaware of it. The sexual urge. Yes. It can make or break a family. Mary. Adrian. They would have been alive today but for the madness of the urge that drove them to what they did. Francis. Pelham. Uncle Edward and Aunt Luise. Cousin Hubertus. It was the sexual urge that fashioned their destinies."

"The mainspring, Flynn calls it."

"Eh? What's that? Mainspring?"

"Yes," smiled Hyacinth. "That's what Flynn calls the sexual urge. He reads very widely. He says the sexual urge is the mainspring of our physical existence."

"True, true. I agree. A scientist—he would think along those lines. I think you have been lucky, my dear. He's the right man for you."

"Oh, I'm sure of that, Grandpa. We agree on everything. I even enjoy reading the books he reads. I'm as much an enthusiast on the works of Professor Huxley as Flynn."

"Good. Good. And this young tadpole at your breast—see you bring him up sensibly. No damned hypocrisy! No polite sugar-coated half-truths. Tell him the facts. Drum into him Grandma Hendri's adage. 'Face the truth, no matter how ugly.' Put some iron into his soul. Teach him to fight. Teach him that only the fighters of this world can survive. The cringing toads get crushed underfoot. The drooling pussyfoot weaklings with their turn-the-cheek policy get washed down the drain."

68

NOW that he had passed his eightieth birthday he discovered that, instead of a resigned and brooding quiescence, there came upon his spirit a new urge to be active and alert, almost a militancy. He visited New Signal twice a week, pottered around in the factory, questioned the manager and the overseers on the running of the place, criticised and censured, praised when he thought praise due.

He was at every social function of note in both Georgetown and New Amsterdam, attended concerts and theatrical performances in the Assembly Rooms, entertained lavishly in his own home, with Gwendolyn as hostess—and sometimes Hyacinth when Hyacinth and Flynn happened to come and spend a week with him.

He wrote letters to the newspapers, criticising the Government on this or that project. Once he annoyed the engineers in charge of the building of the sea wall along the East Coast in Demerara because, in a letter, he accused them of tardiness and the Government of lack of drive. "A scheme begun since the '50s not yet completed! Perhaps it would not have been begun at all if Kingston had not been flooded by the sea in 1855! A colony as prosperous as this should be able to do much better, surely. . . ." He criticised the railway, too. "Another flagrant instance of tardiness," he wrote. "What is the projected distance of this railway? A mere sixty-odd miles between Georgetown and Rosignol on the west bank of the Berbice River, yet in this year 1877 barely more than half the distance has been covered. It is a disgrace. What is the use of boasting that this was the first railway to have been laid down in the continent of South America when progress on it continues at this snail's pace! Started in 1848, it should have been a hundred miles or more in length instead of a mere forty. This colony will soon be the laughing-stock of the outside world. . . ."

Both Peter and Hendrik disapproved of this literary activity. "It's highly undignified," said Hendrik. "It's most unbecoming for your age."

"My age?" Dirk guffawed. "What has my age got to do with it? Pah! Be silent, boy! You're a dull fish. A man is as old as he chooses to conduct himself—and these days I feel eighteen rather than eighty-two."

Hyacinth and Flynn were his loyal champions, and never failed to congratulate him every time one of his letters appeared in the *Daily Argosy*.

Another of his admirers was Michael Hartfield, Timothy's son and Harvey's eldest grandson, who had now taken over from his father as managing director of the combined van Groenwegel sugar-estates company—the sister company of Hartfield & Clackson, which Dirk had engineered into being during the 1840 crisis. Michael looked upon him as a hero, and he and his wife often took Dirk for carriage drives round the city when Dirk happened to be in Georgetown.

One afternoon, when Michael was delayed at a directors' meeting, Laura went driving alone with Dirk, and she told him as they were going past St. Andrew's Kirk: "Have I ever told you what happened when we were christening our son at the church here, Uncle Dirk? Michael and I were alone in a pew at the right of the christening party, and when Angela—she was the godmother—handed our baby to the minister, Michael whispered to me: 'There goes another van Groenwegel masquerading as a Hartfield.' "

Dirk gave her an astonished stare. "Did he really say that, Laura?"

"He did. Is it true, Uncle Dirk, that something scandalous happened long ago between Michael's great-grandmother and your Uncle Edward?"

Dirk turned red and shook with laughter. Eventually he grew composed and told her: "Some things must not be discussed, young woman. How old are you? A mere twenty-six, eh? And Michael only thirty-two. Clever boy. Clever boy. The managing director of our sugar-estates company at thirty-two. That doesn't happen every day, does it? Shows he must possess some special genius for executive work, eh? Where could he have got that genius from, I wonder? Ah well, ah well! Between you and me, my child—strictly between you and me, I repeat—he knew what he was talking about when he said what he did at the christening of your son. Now let us change the subject and cast our gaze around upon the beauty of the city. What building is that going up there, do you know?"

"That? It's to be a match factory, I think Michael said. Another of the projects of that dreadful man in Cumingsburg."

"What dreadful man?"

"You've heard of him, I'm sure, Uncle Dirk. Miser Van. The man who owns nearly a whole street of small cottages in Albert Town, and about a hundred different shops over the city."

"Good heavens! Of course. Jason Vangreen."

Laura frowned. "Didn't I hear that he, too, is supposed to be remotely connected with the van Groenwegels, Uncle Dirk?"

"What!" Dirk shook his head. "Nothing of the sort! You heard quite wrong, my child. Years and years ago I did happen to give him a helping hand with a little shop he was managing for me—a shop bequeathed to me by an old servant of Cousin Hubertus's—and no doubt that must have started some rumour to the effect that he was related to us. But that is not so. Why, he is coloured, isn't he? You don't think he was an indiscretion of mine, do you?"

It amazed him how easily his wits came to his aid in disposing of the matter. He felt no guilt for the lie he had told. It was a necessary lie.

Laura believed him. "That probably explains it," she said. "He's a terrible man. I don't know how he sleeps at night. Michael says he's brought misery to dozens of families. Even the Portuguese aren't clever enough to cope with him. He's foreclosed on two Portuguese shops within the past five years."

Dirk shook. "By God! He must certainly be a business genius to be able to get the better of the Portuguese. Give him his due there, eh? Tch, tch, tch!" Then casually he asked: "Is he married, do you know?"

"Not so far as I know. But I've heard he—well, must I say it?"

"Please do, my girl. I'm not easily shocked. I've told you before."

Very pink, she held her fan to her face and said: "He sows his wild oats rather freely, I've heard. Michael says—oh, it's dreadful!—Michael says he has unlawful children with women of every race—Portuguese and Chinese and even East Indian—and yet he goes to church every Sunday without fail, wearing the shabbiest black suit you ever saw."

"Tch, tch, tch! Certainly an odd character, eh? Bad blood somewhere."

69

H E never disagreed now when anyone told him he would live to ninety. "It's possible—quite possible," he said to Flynn one afternoon in March 1880 when he and Flynn and Hyacinth were on their way home from Harvey Hartfield's funeral. "Grandma Hendri was over ninety when she died. And according to what the Bakkers in Surinam said, Susannah, who was old Laurens' sister, lived to ninety-five or some such astounding age. I feel fit enough for ninety."

Hyacinth laughed and said: "Well, old Mr. Harvey Hartfield was ninety-one and two months when he died yesterday, so I don't see why you shouldn't do as well, Grandpa."

Hardly a month later, news came that Sir Reginald Greenfield had died while on holiday in Switzerland. He was sixty-one.

That summer Sir Hilary Greenfield, fair-haired and blue-eyed, a tallish, pleasant fellow of thirty-five, and Lady Greenfield came to the colony on a visit. Dirk had them stay at his home in New Amsterdam, and pulled Hilary's leg about his exploits in the canal at Vrymen's Erven as a boy of twelve.

"I suppose you've forgotten those walks I used to take with you and your sister and brothers along the dam out there. Eh?"

"Not in the slightest, sir," smiled Hilary. "I remember them only too vividly, I can assure you. And this house as well. Wasn't there some picture of my grandmother you were fond of showing us every night before we retired?"

"Quite right, quite right! It's still there in my room. Come and see it."

Lucille, his wife, accompanied them up to the room, and it was she who, as they were regarding the portrait, squinted critically and remarked: "But I say, is she—she doesn't seem pure European. Or am I mistaken?"

Dirk was silent. Hilary flushed, glanced sharply at his wife and said: "She was born here in South America, my dear. Probably Spanish blood somewhere."

"Oh. Yes, yes. That could account for it, I dare say. I hadn't thought of that," said Lucille, laughing. "How romantic to think our son has Spanish blood in him, Hilary! I must tell him when we get back home."

A guileless, ingenuous creature, Lucille. Dirk was certain she would go back to England and tell her children that they had Spanish blood in them.

Ah well, he sighed when he was alone in the room. Spanish or Negro, what did it matter, anyway? Time . . . Time erased all—even the memory of a dusky past. And what did they have to worry about? Wealth and titled glory weighed heavily in their favour. A rumour of black blood would do them little harm.

Time . . . Time, Rose, my love. Time turns us all into shadows. Soon I'll be one myself wandering with yours in whatever misty vales lie beyond this life.

He stood at the window and looked at the steeple of the Presbyterian church, towering high above a sandbox tree, hardly a hundred yards away. . . . You and I were never very pious, Rose, were we? The predicants never succeeded in scaring us with their talk of hellfire. Nowadays even the niggers are admitted in church, my dear. Times have changed. The heathen niggers are now more Christian than the white men who brought them Christianity. Yes, times have changed, my love. You would wonder, when you looked on our streets now, to see the mixture of faces. . . . Coolies in *dhotis*—Indians from India. And Chinese from China. Men with pigtails. They're setting themselves up now as shopkeepers, competing with the men from Madeira. It's becoming very hotchpotch, Rose. Portuguese mulattoes and Dutch and English mulattoes—and *samboes* and *mestees* and quadroons and octoroons in every shade of brown and olive imaginable. The poor coloured and the rich and educated coloured. You wouldn't know the Fricks and the Coles and their friends and relatives these days, my dear. They are lawyers and doctors and engineers and solicitors and surveyors and civil servants and—yes, and parsons, too. Jimmy Frick's son is a Wesleyan parson, and Charles's second boy is a barrister like his father. Hear he is going in for politics, too. It's a civilised little colony we have here, Rose. They've found gold in the interior, and who knows if they won't soon be tearing down the jungle and building towns up there, too. We can't always remain on the coast. We must go back inland, mustn't we? We came from there. Fort Nassau was fifty miles up the Berbice. Kyk-over-all and Fort Island were well up the Essequibo. We had plantations a hundred miles up-river. We must defeat the jungle again, Rose. I'm writing to the Press about it. This very evening I must write a letter about it. . . . Back inland!

70

IT was wealth all the way. The '70s had been fulsome enough, and now the '80s seemed determined to outdo the '70s. The market price of sugar stood at well over £20 per ton, and it was rising all the time. Everyone was a speculator now. They were bringing to life old plantations, and some that had been long abandoned and gone to jungle. Immigrants flowed in at an ever increasing rate; labour was plentiful.

Dirk was not really surprised when Michael Hartfield arrived one day in September 1883 and outlined his scheme for expansion.

"This is our big opportunity, Uncle Dirk. We have the money, and we can do things on a scale far beyond that of any of these petty speculators. If you agree to what I've planned, it would mean the realisation of your great dream. Remember what you've always talked about? Power. Yes, Uncle Dirk. We'd have more than three fifths of the whole sugar industry in our hands before five years had elapsed."

"But the outlay, Michael, my boy. The outlay. To purchase all these abandoned places and the machinery you mention would mean sinking a tremendous sum—more than two thirds of our capital assets. Can we take that risk?"

"But where's the risk? Did you see the latest quotations for Demerara Ordinary Crystals? And the price is rising, sir. Rising."

Dirk frowned, rubbing his hands together slowly. "I know, my boy. I know. I can see your point—but all the same, we seem to be in such an unassailable position, so well established and firmly entrenched in our prosperity that it strikes me as tempting Fate to try to go any further."

Dirk could see the disappointment on his face. "Uncle Dirk, I didn't expect that of *you*. I've always looked up to you as our most dynamic and daring hero. You're no stick-in-the-mud. You've always got things done. You're noted for defying convention, and for your enterprise. Haven't you stressed that the family should strive to be the most powerful in this colony——"

"Yes, yes. Oh well." Dirk laughed and patted him on the wrist. He rose and sighed. "You've cornered me there, Michael. I have no defence. Well, look here, my boy, give me a few days to think it over, will you? In a way I was half expecting you to come to me with some such scheme—but still, I'm inclined to be prudent, you know. Put it down to old age. Eighty-eight this month, my boy. You must make concessions for me."

"You don't look or speak more than fifty, Uncle Dirk. Well, shall I come back say next Tuesday? We can't delay much longer. Places are being snapped up right and left every day."

"Have you taken options on any places?"

"Yes—seven so far, but the owners say they won't wait more than three weeks at the longest. They're being besieged by too many prospective buyers."

"Very well. I'll give you my decision definitely next Tuesday."

Once again he felt as though a burden of great responsibility were poised precariously on his back. Twice, during the following day, he paused before the portrait of Hubertus in the sitting-room and asked for guidance. . . . "It is a momentous decision, Cousin Hubertus. If something went wrong it would be stark ruin. The whole edifice of our wealth, built up throughout the past four decades, would topple and disintegrate. What would you have done, old fellow? Would you have shaken your head and given the boy a lecture on greed? We have enough. Why should we scheme to win more? Is that what you would have told him?"

His gaze moved to the big black Bible on a small corner table.

"Perhaps you would have looked in the Book for guidance, sir." He began to shake. "You pious old hypocrite! You never believed in God. You revered yourself. You worshipped the god Hubertus. Ah well! It's the cowardice in me. I'll tell the boy it's all right. We'll go forward with the scheme."

On Monday night he slept badly. He had disturbed dreams that made him toss and moan. Near dawn something frightened him. He awoke and was sure that he had felt a touch on his forehead. He sat up and gazed at Rose, visible through the mosquito net in the light from a floating wick in a glass on his bedside table. He always slept with a night light these days. He shivered. Something was in the room with him—some evil presence. . . . "What is it, Rose? What is afoot? Something touched my forehead. Was it your hand, my dear?"

He lay back again, telling himself not to be foolish. Mustn't permit himself these delusions again. It was a long time he had not suffered from them.

But he had hardly fallen asleep when again he felt that touch on his forehead. This time he was not sure that he awoke, though he could see someone hovering by the window. Francis—with an evil leer on his face. Laughing at me, that boy. . . . Wishing me ill. . . . Then he turned his head and saw that beside the bed Rose was standing. She stretched through the net and touched his forehead, and he knew that there was nothing to be afraid of. She would never let Francis harm him. He smiled up at her—but she would not smile back. Her face seemed very sad. "Rose, what is it, my love? What's troubling you?" She stood there, unmoving, then abruptly bent over him, and this time her face was frightened. She shook her head violently, and he heard her murmur: "Don't. Don't, Dirk, my sweet. Please don't." He tried to raise himself to ask her what she meant, but she withdrew, murmuring: "Don't. Don't, Dirk. It will be ruin. Ruin." She uttered the last two words with a sob, and then vanished.

He opened his eyes to see the room grey with dawn. He was trembling.

When Michael arrived at three o'clock he told him: "I'm sorry, my boy. I've decided against. I don't think it will be a wise venture."

Michael seemed stunned. It was obvious that he had been expecting a favourable answer. "What are your reasons for deciding against, Uncle Dirk?"

Dirk was silent a moment, then sighed softly. "It's a feeling I have, Michael. A feeling."

"Sir, surely you don't mean to throw away an opportunity like this merely because you have a *feeling*, as you put it. It's not like you, Uncle Dirk. I refuse to believe that old age has changed you to that extent."

Dirk sighed again, and said: "Shall I be frank, then, Michael? Well, I'll tell you. I'm not afraid to say it. I have been warned against it."

"Warned against it? By whom?"

"Rose. I had a dream, Michael. Rose came to me and warned me."

"What! A dream! Uncle Dirk! You're not serious!"

"I am. Her spirit came to me, boy. It was no delusion this time. It happened. I know it happened."

"Good heavens! But this is incredible. You of all people. Why, with Flynn and Hyacinth you've been a staunch defender of the theories of that man Darwin and Professor Huxley. How do you reconcile dreams and spirits with biology, Uncle Dirk?"

"Each in its own sphere, my boy. Biology is of this life—spirits and dreams concern the other life."

"Is that final? You won't agree to the scheme, then?"

"No. No, my boy. It will mean ruin. Rose would not have warned me if she had not foreseen ruin."

After Michael had left, he paced for a long time on the back veranda, his spirits low, a dull cloud of regret settling upon him. . . . An itch of uncertainty stirred far within him, and he began to tell himself that he had wrecked the high opinion Michael had held of him. He had valued the boy's esteem. And who was to tell that he had not yet again suffered a delusion! . . . It seemed so real, though. She spoke to me. She touched my forehead. . . .

He went nowhere during the next two months. A lassitude had come upon him. The final lassitude, he dramatised it to himself. The wages of defeat.

"I'm going soon," he told Mrs. Benjamin, his housekeeper. Mrs. Chalmerson, his first housekeeper, had died seven years before. "I can feel it in my bones."

It was not far from Christmas when Peter called one morning. He looked worried, and he had with him a batch of papers—the *Argosy* and one or two other newspapers and some sheets of writing paper. He looked more like a Government official than a doctor.

"Papa, there is bad news," he said. "The sugar market is collapsing."

71

IT'S the dumping of beet sugar on the market by European countries that's behind it!"

"The Home Government has let us down again!"

"We'll have to appeal to America!"

Once again, the babble of panic spread—and the sugar prices fell and fell.

". . . and no matter what you say, Michael, the truth remains. Uncle Dirk saved us," said Laura. "By now you'd probably have put a bullet in your head."

Michael did not deny it. "His delusions didn't delude him this time, I agree. My God! To think of it! A narrow shave, if ever there was one!"

"I think we ought to go to New Amsterdam and apologise. You have ignored him studiously since he turned down the scheme in September."

He nodded. "Yes, it's an excellent idea. We'll give him a surprise and drop in on him the day after Boxing Day."

"And let's pick up Flynn and Hyacinth on the way. I'm sure they'll be glad to go and see him."

It was an afternoon of pale sunshine. Rain had fallen heavily during the morning, but the sun had triumphed, at last, over the sheet of cumulo-stratus, which was breaking up slowly and drifting towards the southwest. No wind blew, and the air was sticky and humid. The carriage wheels swished in and out of the pools of water on the street. Flynn said that the house could do with a painting. Hyacinth thought that the vines on the portico latticework needed trimming. "Grandpa has no eye for that kind of thing, I'm afraid." Laura disagreed. "I think he's far more poetic than you imagine. He's a dreamer." Michael grinned and said: "God be thanked for that! Hope he'll continue the habit. Should prove useful again."

Mrs. Benjamin admitted them with her usual ingratiating smile, obviously awed at seeing all four of them at once like this. "I'll go up and tell him you are here, Mrs. Baxter-Hough. Will you please be seated?"

"No, we'll go up ourselves, Mrs. Benjamin," said Hyacinth. "It's a surprise visit. It would spoil things if you announced us."

"He isn't resting, is he?" asked Laura anxiously.

"No, no," said Mrs. Benjamin. "He's in his room sitting by the window, looking at the picture over the bed—just as always. I took him up a glass of milk only a few minutes ago. He was talking to the picture."

When they entered the room he was still staring at Rose. Attired in a shabby purple dressing gown, he reclined in the leather-lined easy chair by the northern window, the glass of milk on the floor beside him.

On his face there was a slight smile—musing, a trifle fatuous, tender. It did not alter as they came crowding round him. Nor did he even remove his gaze from the picture to glance at them.

Hyacinth spoke first, but he made no reply.

"Uncle Dirk, we've come to see you. It's a surprise," said Laura. Still there was no reply.

72

A S directed by his will, the letters in the canister were handed over to the Reading Rooms of the Royal Agricultural and Commercial Society in Georgetown. To Hendrik went the portrait of Hubertus, and to Hyacinth the portraits of Rose and Mary. For each of Hendrik's daughters there was a letter, and one for Hyacinth, also, and each letter ended the same: "My spirit shall be watching over you all. See that you and yours defend our name whenever the occasion should arise."

Only Hyacinth's Dirk—they called him Young Dirk—took this adjuration to heart. Unlike his great-grandfather, he was a tallish, well-built boy with the Irish dark hair and dark eyes of his father. He was very bookish, and even took an interest in politics. He attended the meetings held in Georgetown in 1884 over the sugar crisis, for he was lodging with Michael and Laura Hartfield in Georgetown so that he could attend a small private school there.

When Hendrik heard about this he took Hyacinth to task about it. "A boy of nine to be allowed to attend political meetings in the evening! It's improper."

"I don't think so, Uncle Hendrik," laughed Hyacinth. "Remember his blood!"

At one of these meetings, Young Dirk overheard two coloured young men in the row in front of him discussing Miser Van. "He's de only body who profiting by dis bad time we going through. Every day he raking in some shop or house."

"Yes. Ah hear so meself," said the other one. "He got a devil in 'e, boy. He born wid greed and wickedness. It just show you, you see.

Big family don't make you a saint. He fadder was a rich sugar planter
—van Groenwegel—and look how he turn out!"

Young Dirk leaned forward and tapped the young man on the
shoulder. "Mr. Vangreen," he told him quietly, "is not related to the
van Groenwegels. You're quite mistaken in that."

When he was twelve he asked his parents to address him as Patrick,
his second name. "I don't want to be called Dirk any more," he told
them. "It's bad enough that people are saying that I'm trying to imi-
tate Great-grandfather—and one day I want to write a short account of
his life for the *Argosy*, and it wouldn't very well sound correct for me
to entitle it 'Dirk van Groenwegel,' by Dirk Baxter-Hough."

Flynn and Hyacinth acceded to his wishes, but Flynn shook his
head, and said one day to Hyacinth: "He's one of them, you know. A
twisted twig, as the old man used to express it."

In the two years—1889 and 1890—preceding the granting of a new
constitution for the colony, Patrick was an interested listener at every
political discussion of the new Reform Party, which was composed
mostly of men of the coloured middle class. He attended several of
their meetings, and it was said that it was through hobnobbing with
so many coloured people at this time that he became attached to the
Fabers, an olive-skinned family, the father of whom was a civil servant. He married the second girl, Daphne, despite the furore of protests
from his friends and cousins. Flynn and Hyacinth did not oppose the
match. They liked the girl; she was an accomplished pianist and
singer, and knew dozens of recipes for rum punches and swizzles; it
was this last circumstance that made her seem, in Flynn's eyes, to
possess the quality of divinity, for he himself was a connoisseur of rum
punches.

Patrick studied surveying, and amused himself by taking trips into
the interior to explore and chart unknown areas of the colony. This
was his hobby. His other pastime—he grew annoyed if it was called a
hobby—was historical research. He spent hours every day, for weeks
sometimes, in the Reading Rooms of the Royal Agricultural and Commercial Society, poring over old books and documents—and the van
Groenwegel letters. He had a regular column in the Sunday issue of
the *Daily Argosy* headed "Peregrinations in the Past."

During the boundary crisis, when Venezuela tried to rope in a size-
able area of the western part of Essequibo, Patrick became pontifical,

and traced the quarrel right back to 1850, pronouncing Venezuela to be emphatically in the wrong. And when the matter was settled finally by the Paris Tribunal in 1899, he implied in one of his articles that but for his findings published in the *Argosy* a year before, the quarrel might still have been continuing. "Who knows," he wound up, "if your humble scribe did not avert a war between the United States of America and Great Britain!"

Through the Hartfields, he was able to send his son, Leonard, to Eton.

In 1908 he attended a reception in London at the Brook Street residence of Sir Hilary Greenfield, and in the course of the evening overheard a young man with a babyish voice—he was Ronald, the youngest son of Sir Hilary—say to a middle-aged duchess: "I don't know what Eton is coming to nowadays. All these coloured colonials twying to get their sons sent there. It's a weal shame if you ask me. Don't you agwee, Duchess?"

The duchess wagged her fan and nodded in assent, and then gasped as a hand shot out and tapped Ronald sharply on the shoulder.

"You shouldn't have gone there, then, my boy, to add to the shame," Patrick told him. "Don't you know there is coloured blood in your veins?"

"I beg your pardon, sir! What absurdity is this?"

It might have created an ugly scene had not a thin, elderly lady nearby—she was Lady Evangeline Cranshaw, Ronald's aunt—intervened and rasped in Ronald's ear: "Of course it's true, you young fool. Your great-grandmother was a mulatto. I saw her portrait myself when I was a girl—and I've told your father a hundred times that he ought to have instructed you children to hold your tongues about the colour question." She turned with a titter to the duchess. "What a charming gown, Duchess! Tch, tch, tch! Leave this tiresome fledgling and come and meet Sir Henry Brack. I hear he's sighing —positively sighing—with eagerness to make your acquaintance."

Lady Evangeline was renowned as an eccentric. In her younger days she had been the centre of innumerable scandals. "The centre, but never the central object," as some wit had expressed it. She had never been ostracised by polite society. Society was too fond of her. She was known as the Beloved Lunatic.

73

IN December 1913 Patrick was being driven to Kaywana in the new Ford car he had purchased in place of the family carriage —the car had just turned into High Street from Brickdam, where Patrick lived—when a dull, booming sound from the southern part of the city caused him to lean forward and ask the East Indian chauffeur: "Are they dynamiting something in the harbour, Seenarine?"

"I don't know, chief," said Seenarine. "I ain' hear anybody talk say so."

By the time they had got to Lombard Street, Patrick did not need to make further enquiries. There was a huge fire raging, and a dozen different voices were discussing the explosion that had occurred in the cellar of a Chinese shop where fireworks had been stored.

This fire did three quarters of a million dollars' damage in Werk-en-Rust, and several lives were lost, among them that of the seventy-five-year-old Miser Van, who, an invalid for the past six years, had been living in a house above a shop in Lombard Street with Yen-Moo, his Chinese common law wife. The story went that Yen-Moo tried to get him out of the house, but the stairway had already caught fire. It collapsed under them before they were halfway down.

The lawsuit contesting the old man's will dragged on for more than three years. It was contested by Alma and Charles Boodoo, illegitimate children of an East Indian woman in La Pénitence. The defendants were John and Edward Yen-Moo, also illegitimate, but children of Yen-Moo, the common-law wife to whom Miser Van had bequeathed his whole estate. Alma and Charles Boodoo claimed that they had as much right as John and Edward Yen-Moo to share in the estate. They were all illegitimate together, weren't they? As usual, the lawyers got the biggest share in the end. Two Portuguese-mothered children, Vincent and Teresa Vangreen—they had taken their father's name—never put in a claim, though their younger brother, Carlos, still at school, said that if he had been old enough he would have tried for something. He was a spirited boy.

In September 1915 the Union Jack was flown at half-mast at the head office of Hartfield & Clackson in Water Street, and also at all the various shops scattered about the city—drugstores, dry-goods stores, provision stores—owned and run by the firm, for news had reached the colony that Second Lieutenant John Greenfield, a grandson of the firm's Chairman, Sir Hilary Greenfield, had been killed in action in France.

A month or two later, the announcement was made that Second Lieutenant Greenfield had been awarded the Victoria Cross posthumously.

In 1919, when Patrick Baxter-Hough was in London, he heard a detailed account, over the lunch table at his club, of what had happened in a little wood near a village in the vicinity of Douai . . . "I got it at first hand," said the army major, "from one of the sergeants in his platoon. Miserable business, Baxter-Hough. Only nineteen of them lived to tell the tale out of that whole platoon. This sergeant chap said it was suicide, plain and simple. He said young Greenfield went off his pins. The order was received to retreat, and there was ample time to slip out of the wood and rejoin the main unit, but Greenfield refused to move. He began to babble some nonsense that it would take more than a pack of dirty Huns to frighten a Greenfield. The sergeant said he kept bawling at them all through the business like a raving madman. Even after more than half the platoon had been mown down by the most punishing fire any bunch of men ever stood up to, there was Greenfield screaming at them wildly: 'No retreat, damn you! We fight to the last man! The Greenfields never run!' Mad as a hatter. Those were his last words, the sergeant said, before a bullet got him. 'The Greenfields never run!' "

During the next ten years, Patrick wrote, and had published locally, a number of books and booklets on the early history of the colony, always with a stress on plantation life.

At directors' meetings he was generally absent-minded and inattentive, and in the Hartfield & Clackson board room only one thing interested him—the large oil portrait of the founder of the firm, John Hartfield, by Edward van Groenwegel. It had become a stock joke with the other directors, and at swizzle parties they were fond of relating how Patrick could never leave the board room without manufacturing an excuse for mentioning that the painter of the portrait had been a blood relation of his.

His mania for attending political meetings had not abated, though he never took sides in politics. One evening, Alfred Webber, one of the most vociferous of the 1920s' Popular Party politicians, challenged him on his complacency, accusing him of possessing the old planter mentality, and Patrick replied: "It's a sound mentality. I'm not ashamed of it. It puts the economy of the colony first, and leaves fools like you to batter your heads to death against the walls of Whitehall."

Murder trials attracted him, too, and he was often in court as a spectator.

In 1938 he even took notes on the trial of Paul Vangreen, accused of murdering his Portuguese mistress and their seven-year-old daughter.

Mr. James Ramsammy, the well-known criminal lawyer—he was an East Indian originally from the Corentyne Coast—tried to get the charge reduced to one of manslaughter, but without success. Nevertheless, in the end, Vangreen was acquitted, Mr. Justice Frick pointing out to the jury in his summing up that there could be no doubt, from the evidence led, that obeah was involved in the matter, and that there were several other persons who could have been responsible for placing the mess of chicken entrails where it was found on the dead child's chest. The jury, in coming to their verdict, took into account this "reasonable doubt."

A Friday afternoon in February 1945 Patrick was in the Carnegie Free Library poring over Rodway's three-volume *History of British Guiana*—he was working on a series of articles for the *Daily Chronicle* on outstanding personalities among the governors of the colony during the past hundred years—when the sound of voices outside caused him to click his tongue in annoyance. He glanced out of a window and saw people hurrying past the War Memorial towards Church Street corner, and had just decided to resign himself to the situation when a voice in the sacred silence of the library itself cried: "Fire!"

He rose and went to the window and, looking out, saw clouds of black smoke billowing out of the upper windows of Bookers' Drugstore, just next door to the *Daily Chronicle* building across the way in Main Street

By the time he had left the library the whole of the upper storey was a mass of roaring flames. He made his way south up High Street, and stood watching the sight for a moment, then had just decided to move on into Hincks Street when he heard a voice cry: "The Assembly Rooms! Look!"—and, to his horror, he saw that the fire had crossed the street and that the Assembly Rooms was ablaze.

A cold panic stirred in Patrick, and he hurried off down Hincks Street—but a policeman stopped him. "No further, sir! You'll get in the way of the fire brigade." Patrick, furious, shouted: "But I must get by, man! I want to get to the Reading Room—the museum Reading Room."

"Sorry, sir! Sorry! You can't pass here now."

"I must, you fool! It's important. There are some valuable letters in there I want to see after. They concern my family——"

He broke off, for the crowd had wailed a new cry. "The Museum on fire!"

Yes, it was too late, in any case, he saw. The building of the Royal Agricultural and Commercial Society was beginning to issue black smoke. The tall white tower, with its flagstaff on which the signal pennants of ships approaching the port were flown, was hazed in a sepia pall of smoke that grew denser with the passing of every second. He could hear the roar and crackle of the flames as the main body of the building began to be devoured.

To Patrick, it was not the wood he could hear splitting and twisting in an agony of heat, but paper—yellowed sheets of paper with century-brown handwriting: the writing of two, three centuries ago. Letters dated 1763, 1738, 1712, 1708. . . . Letters signed Jacques, Jabez, Adrian, Juliana, Hubertus, each with its attached English translation in the handwriting of Dirk van Groenwegel. . . .

74

EVEN at seventy-eight Patrick still found it amusing to listen to political speeches. One evening in April 1953 he paused while taking his after-dinner stroll to entertain himself at a street corner by giving his attention to what a youngish, coffee-complexioned man was saying to a small crowd:

". . . Think back! Think back! When did the British first take over? In 1803. And this is 1953. And what have they done for us in that century and a half that's past? See for yourselves! Eighty-six thousand square miles of territory—the size of the whole of Britain—that's the area of British Guiana—and how much of it is cultivated and populated today? A mere strip along the coast two to three miles deep. Who had to put their capital in this colony to develop the bauxite that was discovered here about 1915 time? The Canadians and Americans—not the British! The British don't give two damns about their colonials! They only want to exploit us. That's why we in the People's Progressive Party want to break away from Britain. Yes, that's what our leader, Dr. Jagan, agitating for—and that's what we going to get in the weeks ahead of us. This new General Election this month is going to surprise the whole world—yes, the whole world! We're going to put our foot down hard on all these capitalist imperialists! You see how they're oppressing the sugar-estate workers! All these big sugar-estate companies like Hartfield & Clackson don't care what happens to the poor estate labourers, so long as they can live on the fat of the land. But all that will be changed when the People's Progressive Party get into power this month——"

He was interrupted by a loud cheer.

"Who is that young man?" asked Patrick of a short black man who might have been a carpenter or a stevedore. A rather old fellow. His head was quite grey.

"That's Georgie Boodoo, sir," the man replied. "I knew his grandfather. They used to call him Miser Van."

"Confounded fool," muttered Patrick as he moved on. "Thank God he's no relative of mine!"

MILL HILL, London, N. W. 7
August 12, 1956–February 16, 1957

GLOSSARY OF CHARACTERS

*(Major characters and characters frequently or prominently
featured are listed in capitals)*

ADRIAN van Groenwegel—youngest son of Dirk van G.
Albert Laver—Graham van G.'s timber manager and intimate friend.
Alpheda van G.—daughter of Edward van G.
AMELIA—daughter of Dirk van G. (married Ronald Hopkinson).
Anthony Parrott (*see* Parrott).

Baxter-Hough, Flynn—sugar chemist; married Hyacinth, Dirk's granddaughter.
BAXTER-HOUGH, Patrick (*see* PATRICK).
Beatrice—daughter of Edward van G. (married James Menzies).
BENJI—a slave at New Signal plantation.
Bentinck, Governor of Demerary-Essequibo.
BERTON, Janet (*see* JANET).
BRANDON, Matthew—retired sea captain; settled at Don Diego plantation, Canje.

Carmichael, Hugh Lyle—Governor of Demerary-Essequibo.
Carmichael-Smyth, Sir James—Governor of Demerary-Essequibo.
Charles Frick—barrister; son of Jacob Frick.
CHRISTINA van G. (born van Banff)—wife of Willem van G.
CLACKSON, Graeme (*see* GRAEME).
CLACKSON, Cynthia (*see* CYNTHIA).
CLARA Hartfield—wife of John Hartfield, founder of Hartfield & Clackson; stepsister of Storm and Edward van G.
CLARK, JASON—Negro shopkeeper in Georgetown; Francis van G.'s father-in-law.

CLARKE, Mrs. Kathleen—midwife in New Amsterdam; foster mother of Rose C.

CLARKE, Rose (*see* ROSE).

CORNELIA—(born Rueff)—Dirk's first wife.

CUSHY—a slave at New Signal plantation; Nibia's father.

CYNTHIA Clackson—wife of Graeme Clackson.

DIRK van G.—younger son of Storm van G.

DOCTOR JOHN (*see* JOHN Maybury).

D'Urban, Major General Sir Benjamin—Governor of Demerary-Essequibo.

EDWARD van G.—planter; portrait painter, and architect; owner of Plantation Flagstaff, East Coast, Demerary; twin brother of Storm van G.

ELFRIDA van G. (born McLeod)—wife of Pelham van G.; mother of Francis.

ELIZABETH van G. (born Maybury)—wife of Storm van G., New Signal Plantation, Canje Creek, Berbice; mother of Dirk and Graham.

Elvira—Negress slave on New Signal plantation; an obeah woman.

Ernestine Greenfield—daughter of Graham van G. (Greenfield); educated in England and married there.

Evangeline Greenfield—daughter of Sir Reginald G.; granddaughter of Graham van G. (Greenfield) and Rose. Afterwards Lady Evangeline Cranshaw; nicknamed the Beloved Lunatic.

Fletcher, Roger—English naturalist who found the canister of letters.

Flynn Baxter-Hough (*see* Baxter-Hough).

FRANCIS van G.—son of Pelham van G. and Elfrida.

Frick, Albertus—overseer on Pln. New Signal; gave his name to Jacob Frick.

Frick, Charles (*see* Charles).

Frick, Cynthia—daughter of Jacob Frick.

FRICK, Jacob (*see* JACOB).

Frick, James (*see* Jimmy).

Frick, Jasmine (*see* JASMINE).

Frick, Lawrence—youngest son of Jacob Frick.

FRICK, Millicent (*see* MILLICENT).

Frick, Olga—daughter of Jacob Frick.

GRAEME Clackson—illegitimate son of Hubertus van G. (with Faustina van G., mother of Storm and Edward van G.); director of Hartfield & Clackson.

GRAHAM van G.—elder son of Storm van G.; later changed his name to Greenfield; owner of Pln. Kaywana, East Bank, Demerary; brother of Dirk; father of Sir Reginald Greenfield.

Greaves, Lizzie (see Lizzie).

Green, Benjamin—a carpenter in New Amsterdam; father of Jacob Frick's wife.

Green, Joanna—daughter of Benjamin Green; Jacob's sister-in-law.

GREEN, Millicent (see MILLICENT).

Greenfield, Christopher—son of Sir Reginald G.

Greenfield, Ernestine (see Ernestine).

Greenfield, Evangeline (see Evangeline).

Greenfield, Gerald—son of Sir Reginald G.

Greenfield, Graham (see GRAHAM).

Greenfield, Sir Hilary—second baronet; son of Sir Reginald G.; grandson of Graham van G. (Greenfield).

Greenfield, John—second lieutenant; grandson of Sir Hilary; killed in action in France, 1915; awarded V.C. posthumously.

Greenfield, Lucille—wife of Sir Hilary G.

GREENFIELD, Sir Reginald—knight, then baronet; son of Graham van G. (Greenfield) and Rose (Clarke) Greenfield.

Greenfield, Ronald—youngest son of Sir Hilary G.

Greenfield, Rowena—wife of Sir Reginald G.

GWENDOLYN van G.—Welsh wife of Peter van G., Dirk's son.

HARRIET van G.—daughter of Pelham van G. and Elfrida.

Hart, Paul—a boatman on the Canje Creek.

Hartfield, Catherine—wife of Harvey H.

HARTFIELD, Clara (see CLARA).

HARTFIELD, Harvey (see HARVEY).

HARTFIELD, John (see JOHN).

Hartfield, Jessie—daughter of Harvey H.

HARTFIELD, Laura (see LAURA).

HARTFIELD, Michael (see MICHAEL).

HARTFIELD, Timothy (see TIMOTHY).

Hartman, Benjamin—Dirk's timber manager, Berbice River.

HARVEY, legally Hartfield—unacknowledged illegitimate son of Edward van G. (with Clara H.); Eton-educated; legally the son of

John H.; director of Hartfield & Clackson.

Heffer, Cornelis—a Berbice planter; friend of Storm van G.'s.

HENDRICK van G.—son of Dirk van G.; became owner and manager of Pln. Flagstaff.

Henson, Miss—a seamstress in New Amsterdam.

Henty, Mr.—tutor to the Lafferty children and Adrian van G.

HERMINE van G.—daughter of Storm van G. (married Jim Lafferty and went to Jamaica); eventually married an American; went to Boston.

Hiemens, Mynheer—tutor to Storm van G.'s children and Rose Clarke.

Hooper—an overseer.

Hopkinson, Amelia (see AMELIA).

Hopkinson, Harry—a cotton planter on the Corentyne Coast; brother of Janet, Dirk van G.'s second wife; father-in-law of Amelia.

Hopkinson, Ronald—son of Harry H. (married Amelia, Dirk's daughter).

HUBERT, Sarah (see SARAH).

HUBNER, Larsen (see LARSEN).

HYACINTH van G.—daughter of Peter van G.; Dirk's granddaughter (married Flynn Baxter-Hough, a sugar chemist).

Jackie—male servant at Edward House, Georgetown.

JACOB Frick—illegitimate son of Storm van G. with Nibia, a slave girl; Dirk's unacknowledged half brother and lifelong friend; a director of Frick & Green; Dirk's business manager.

JANET Berton—sister of Harry Hopkinson; a widow; Dirk's second wife.

JASMINE Frick—youngest daughter of Jacob Frick.

JASON Vangreen—legal son of Francis van G. Also known as Miser Van; never openly acknowledged as a van Groenwegel.

Jimmy Frick—eldest son of Jacob Frick; a doctor.

Jim Lafferty, senior and junior (see Lafferty).

Jim Menzies (see MENZIES).

Joanna—children's nanny at New Signal plantation.

Joanna Green—Jacob's sister-in-law.

JOHN Hartfield—founder of Hartfield & Clackson; husband of Clara H.; "father," in the eyes of the law, of Harvey H.; "grandfather" of Timothy H.

JOHN Maybury—brother of Elizabeth van G.; a doctor resident in

New Amsterdam; popularly known as Doctor John.

Lafferty, Jim, senior—a planter on the Canje Creek; good friend of Storm van G. and family.

Lafferty, Jim, junior—son of Jim L.; married Hermine, Storm's daughter; an engineer who went to Jamaica with his family.

LARSEN Hubner—son of Mary Hubner, a daughter of Hubertus van G.; part owner (with Raphael van G.) of Pln. Degries, West Coast, Demerara, then of Pln. Harrow's Castle, East Coast, Demerara.

Lashley—an overseer at Pln. Kaywana.

LAURA Hartfield—wife of Michael H.

Laver, Albert (*see* Albert).

Leahy, Colonel—officer in charge of military operations against rebel slaves in Demerara insurrection, 1823.

Lieker, Benjamin—son of Claas Lieker.

Lieker, Claas—husband of Jacqueline Lieker, eldest daughter of Hubertus van G.; a coffee-planter on West Bank, Demerara.

Lieker, Dahlia—wife of Hendrik L.

Lieker, Jacqueline—eldest daughter of Hubertus van G.; wife of Claas L.

Lieker, Jan—son of Claas L.

Lieker, Hendrik—son of Claas L.

Lizzie Greaves—mistress of John Hartfield; a mulatto girl who once a huckster, became a provision shopkeeper in Cumingsburg, Georgetown.

LUISE van G.—a daughter of Hubertus van G.; married her cousin Edward van G., ten years her junior.

McLeod, Angus—an Essequibo planter; father of Elfrida (Pelham's wife).

McLeod, Elfrida (*see* ELFRIDA).

Margaret van G.—one of twins; daughter of Hendrik van G. Married Harry Menzies, a nephew of Jim Menzies.

Marie—a servant girl in the home of Mrs. Clarke, the midwife, New Amsterdam.

MARTA—an old slave at New Signal plantation, Canje Creek.

Mary Maybury—wife of Doctor John M.; English; sister-in-law of Elizabeth van G.

MARY van G.—youngest daughter of Dirk van G.; Dirk's business secretary.

Matilda van G.—*sambo* daughter of Jason Clark, Negro shopkeeper in Georgetown; wife of Francis van G.

MATILDE van G.—daughter of Pelham van G.; married Lieutenant Banfield of Royal North British Fusiliers.

Mavis van G.—one of twins; daughter of Hendrik van G.; married a colonial civil servant and went to Africa with him.

Maybury, Mary (*see* Mary Maybury).

Maybury, Primrose (*see* PRIMROSE).

MAYBURY, Wilfred (*see* WILFRED).

Menzies, Beatrice (*see* Beatrice).

MENZIES, Jim (James)—Scotsman; attached to MacInroy Sanddach, then to Hartfield & Clackson as a director; married Beatrice van G., daughter of Edward van G.

MICHAEL Hartfield—son of Timothy H., and grandson of Harvey H.; managing director of the van G. estates allied to Hartfield & C. in the latter years of the nineteenth century.

MILLICENT Frick—daughter of Benjamin Green, carpenter; married Jacob Frick.

MISER VAN (*see* JASON).

Murray, Brigadier General John—Governor of Demerary-Essequibo.

NIBIA—Negress slave on Pln. New Signal; Graham van G.'s nanny; mother of Jacob Frick (with Storm van G.).

O'Brien, Michael—an overseer on the West Coast, Berbice.

Parrott, Anthony—son of a cotton planter, West Coast, Berbice; married Sybil van G., Dirk's daughter; eventually went to Trinidad when cotton failed, taking his family.

Parrott, Sybil (*see* SYBIL).

PATRICK Baxter-Hough—son of Flynn Baxter-H. and Hyacinth; Dirk's great-grandson.

PELHAM van G.—second son of Edward van G.; managed Pln. Flagstaff, and married Elfrida McLeod.

PETER van G.—son of Dirk van G.; a doctor; married a Welsh girl, Gwendolyn.

PRIMROSE Maybury—wife of Wilfred Maybury; mother of Elizabeth van G. and Doctor John.

Randolph, Mr.—music teacher to Adrian van G.

RAPHAEL van G.—elder brother of Storm and Edward van G.; part owner and manager of Pln. Degries, West Coast, Demerara, then of Plantation Harrow's Castle, East Coast, Demerara; a homosexual and dandy.

Rattray, Harvey—manager of Pln. Kaywana before Graham's advent and for short while after Graham arrived.

Rayner, Malcolm—Dirk's London factor.

ROSE Clarke—illegitimate daughter of Hubertus van G. with a Negress slave, Sarah (afterwards Sarah Hubert); married Graham van G., who changed his name to Greenfield—hence Rose Greenfield; mother of Sir Reginald Greenfield.

Rueff, Karl—a planter, owner of Pln. Don Diego on Canje Creek; Dirk's father-in-law.

Rueff, Cornelia (see CORNELIA).

Sarabelle—a slave, Pln. New Signal.

SARAH Hubert—a Negress slave at Pln. Kaywana in the time of Hubertus van G.; freed by Hubertus; the mother of Rose Clarke; owned and ran a provision shop in Cumingsburg district of Georgetown.

Smith, Jane—wife of John Smith, the missionary.

Smith, John—a missionary, accused of not warning the government of plot by slaves to revolt, in Demerary, 1823; tried and condemned to death, but died in prison of tuberculosis before reprieve.

Swiffermann, Janet—daughter of Rachel Swiffermann.

Swiffermann, Rachel—widow-owner of Pln. Lambden, West Bank, Berbice; a friend of Storm and Elizabeth van G.

STORM van G.—twin brother of Edward van G.; part owner of Pln. New Signal, Canje Creek, Berbice colony; father of Dirk and Graham and of Jacob Frick.

SYBIL van G.—Dirk's daughter; married Anthony Parrott of West Coast, Berbice.

Teuffel, Dirk—Lieutenant from Fort St. Andries. Dirk van G. named after him.

TIMOTHY Hartfield—son of Harvey H.; father of Michael H.

Van Batenburg, Abraham van Imbyze—Governor of Berbice, end of eighteenth and beginning of nineteenth century; gay, cultivated man; as popular at first as he was unpopular later; rumoured to have had over eighty illegitimate children.

Van Batenburg, Mme.—wife of Abraham van B., also a cultivated person; a charming hostess at Colony House, Berbice.

VANGREEN, Jason (*see* JASON).

VAN GROENWEGEL family (*see under* individual Christian names).

WILFRED Maybury—father of Elizabeth van G.; part owner of Pln. New Signal, Canje Creek, Berbice; originally came from Pln. Signal, upper Demerara River; father of Doctor John; maternal grandfather of Dirk and Graham.

WILLEM van G.—eldest son of Edward van G.; part owner and manager of Pln. Flagstaff, East Coast, Demerara.

Wray, John—missionary.

Wray, Colonel—officer in local militia, Demerary, at the time of the insurrection, 1823.

9472

Due 28 Days From Latest Date

FEB 2 8 1975

WITHDRAWN

Mittelhölzer, Edgar.   Fiction
  The old blood.

          ⅮⱲ

Redwood

Library and Athenaeum

NEWPORT, R. I.

LIBRARY BUREAU CAT. NO. 1166.3